The Shore

Jonathan Grant is the real name of Jonathan Gash, the bestselling crime author of the following LOVEJOY novels all published by Arrow:

Firefly Gadroon
Gold From Gemini
The Gondola Scam
The Grail Tree
The Great California Game
Jade Woman
The Judas Pair
Moonspender
Pearlhanger
The Sleepers of Erin
Spend Game
The Tartan Ringers
The Vatican Rip
The Very Last Gambado
Lovejoy at Large: Omnibus

THE SHORES OF SEALANDINGS

Jonathan Grant

ARROW

Published by Arrow Books in 1992

3 5 7 9 0 8 6 4 2

First published in the United Kingdom in 1991 by Jonathan Cape

Arrow Books
The Random House Group Limited
20 Vauxhall Bridge Road, London, SW1V 2SA

Random House Australia (Pty) Limited
20 Alfred Street, Milsons Point, Sydney,
New South Wales 2061, Australia

Random House New Zealand Limited
18 Poland Road, Glenfield
Auckland 10, New Zealand

Random House (Pty) Limited
Endulini, 5a Jubilee Road, Parktown 2193, South Africa

The Random House Group Limited Reg. No. 954009

www.randomhouse.co.uk

A CIP catalogue record for this book
is available from the British Library

Papers used by Random House are natural, recyclable products made from
wood grown in sustainable forests. The manufacturing processes conform to
the environmental regulations of the country of origin

ISBN 0 09 978710 5

Printed and bound in Great Britain by
Bookmarque Ltd, Croydon, Surrey

For Matthew John, Sarah Kate, Jack, and for Brian.

Acknowledgement

Thanks to Susan.

Author's Note

As tribute to the admirable Sabine Baring-Gould, I have incorporated his own description of the lonely East Coast sea marshes he so loved to hate.

It was almost as though she heard her name being called. By a man's voice, deep and joyous, and that joy mad.

Her hair was somehow twined around her face, and she knew she was dying. Drowning? The sensation was the result, perhaps even the gift, of others. She knew this instinctively but was far from understanding. The name she was being called wasn't her own. That too had been the gift of another, and him the man she had hated then perversely loved.

She knew it was the sea. Everything in her life was the living sea, her one constancy. But soon life would be no more, except in the Great Beyond where life came full circle and her old mother would be waiting, still smoking her terrible pipe and spitting on the same fallen hearth floor by the fire of wood beachcombed from saltings and the low sea marshes.

The voice called again. That name. Not her own, yet it was the one by which he called her and loved her with his crazed furious love. It was the name he'd finally chosen as he set out to drown them both, taking her into his great broad hands as they'd sunk beneath the waters in the fog. The image was stiflingly close, of him crying out her name and his face almost radiant with ecstasy at the knowledge that they were both forever to remain as one in death, in the eternal living sea.

The slow breeze had been backing all day from its early point towards the north-east, but had stubbornly refused warmth to the men in the Yorkshire lugger.

The fish too had remained obstinate. Old Jervin whose boat it was finally had to relent and give orders to make home for Sealandings.

'There's nothing for us this day, lads,' he decided.

'Happen we should try outside the line of the Bantings, Masther,' young Baines called reluctantly from the prow, as he responded to Jervin's command to prepare to go about. Master Jervin gave out a share of the catch. In coin of the realm.

'We'll not clear the Bantlings afore nightfall. No, we'll make for harbour and bid the day farewell.'

'God be thanked,' the third man responded.

'Amen,' Jervin said piously. He was calling about when the youngster gave a shout and pointed.

'Masther! Masther Jervin! There's a corpse in the water!'

'Where away?'

'Larboard, no more than two cables!'

'I don't see nuthin', Master.'

Jervin ignored the older man's grumpy comment. Old Lack was thinking of the responsibility of testifying to the authorities on land, and the susperstition he harboured about the sea. Indeed, Jervin thought, it was fortunate for the poor drowned sailor that it was *The Jaunty* that had stayed out until last, when all the other boats of the fleet had turned for shore, for many a skipper would sail past the Queen herself if she was floating drowned in this cold North Sea. Half the tavern talk among the people of these low foggy coasts was of sea creatures which effected amazing transformations. They lured poor fishermen into traps, and doom.

'I'm taking way off her,' Jervin shouted, swinging the wheel to bring *The Jaunty* round into the wind. 'How far now?'

'Half, Masther!'

'The wind's cuttin' to a veer, Master Jervin,' from Old Lack as Jervin shouted for the youngster to take a boat hook to the side.

'That'll do from you, Lack,' Jervin shouted angrily. 'Go with the boy this instant. Help to haul the poor soul aboard.'

'It might be a sea man,' Old Lack whimpered. 'And be our ruination. We should be levanting home – '

Jervin was outraged. 'Slip away? From our Christian duty? We must give the poor corpse a proper burial. Why else would we be guided to come this way?'

'Easy, Masther Jervin!'

'Are you within reach, Hal?'

'Aye, sir. I've caught hold . . .'

'God preserve us!' Old Lack muttered, leaning away from the weighty mass of sodden clothing the boy had hooked.

The Jaunty lost way altogether and swayed sluggishly in the waves. It had not been bad weather, not for this part of the East Anglian coast. At this time of year when Michaelmas was near and the autumn storms were skulking low on the horizon, weather could be notoriously fickle. Fortunately a backing wind was a lessening wind, they said locally, as long as you stayed north of the Blackwater estuary and held to the north-east line of the treacherous sandbanks.

The Yorkshire lugger was a heavy craft of three masts, but with her beamy shape, simplified rig and lack of jib sail she was good enough to do the job with a small crew. She coped easily with quiet seas. Jervin felt her shoulder the additional burden of a heavy weight being pulled aboard.

'I'll need a hand here, Masther Jervin!'

'Hold on, Hal Baines. Lack, give a sharp hand, else it'll be land sailing for you in the future, as God's my judge!'

'Aye, aye, Master.' The old man left the sheet he was clinging to and went to help the lad.

'It's a woman, Masther!'

'A mermaid!' cried Old Lack, staggering away at the shock.

'Lack, that does for you, man!' Jervin knew he couldn't leave the wheel, for Old Lack wasn't beyond heeling *The Jaunty* over and gaining wind to pull the vessel away from the drowned creature.

'I'm helping, Master! I am, I swear!'

The bundle was dragged unceremoniously inboard, the lad anxiously checking to see that his hook hadn't penetrated the woman's body. The coastguards and the watch could be very sceptical about injuries, especially along North Sea coasts like this where centuries-old wars had been waged between smugglers, wreckers and Excise men. No. He had been fortunate.

He bent to wipe the hair from her face, and started back with a yelp.

'What is it, Hal, booy?'

'Masther Jervin,' the boy breathed in awe, staring at the heap on the deck. 'I think she's alive!'

'How can that be?' Jervin made a resolve. 'Here, Lack. Come and hold this. Bring her round tardy, catch this wind slow, like. Don't have us all off our pins. Y'hear, man?'

'Aye, aye, Master.'

Jervin went forward, stood beside the boy looking down at the body. Only this wasn't a body any longer. Now she was alive, things weren't so simple.

'You certain, Hal?'

'Aye, Masther. Her's warm, not cold like dead. And her sickened up water as I lifted her from the –'

'You're right, booy.' Jervin crouched, checking by touching though he did it gingerly, mindful of old fables and superstitions. You never could tell, even if you were a true god-fearing Christian. 'Her's living, as ever was.'

'We must lift her bent, Masther. Freshen the waters from her lungs. That's what they say.'

'Then let's get doing it. Lack?'

'Aye, Master?'

3

'Give a hand with Baines. You'll have to hold her and Baines can put air back into her lights.'

Jervin hurried to reclaim the wheel, desperately worried. Should one interfere with a drowning woman? After all, God had seen fit to put her into the sea. To interfere was to risk the wrath of the Almighty, acting against His divine will. But if drownded dead properly, she would be no problem. Worse still, who was to pay her way if they managed to get her back on shore alive?

'Cover her with that weather cloth, Baines,' he shouted, fetching *The Jaunty* round to take the wind. 'Lack, that foresail, if you please.'

'Aye, aye, sir,' they called, obeying. But all in all they were dispirited. It had been a wasted, troublesome voyage this day. No catch except an unknown creature from the sea who didn't have the courtesy or politeness to come aboard dead like a decent drowned corpse should. No prices ashore either, for want of fish to sell. Only expense. Jervin was a decent man, much given to religion and going churchwise to listen to Reverend Baring every Sunday twice, but unwarranted spending of good hard-earned money, to no gain, was the one thing inclined to send him into a towering rage. Yes, altogether the arrival of this woman, now having the audacity to cough and splutter and not having the decency to cover herself when she vomited sea water all over the pristine deck, was a thoroughly bad omen. Jervin glanced at the woman whom young Baines was trying to make sick by thumping and shaking her against the bulwark. The state she was in! But from where had she come? Well, thanks to God, it was none of his problem. He'd done his duty, bringing her from the sea. Now it'd be young Doctor Carmichael's responsibility to get her better, and then for Squire Hunterfield to dispose of.

As ever, *The Jaunty* shuddered rounding the northern point of the Hopeness Sands, so shallow in the water yet so treacherous, and stood in towards land with a quickening. Jervin almost smiled in spite of all this bad luck. The old *Jaunty* knew she was going home, to Sealandings.

There seemed to be light, a weirdly glowing light which diffused into her mind and left her wondering.

Had he gone? The voice wasn't his. And that must prove his absence, that man who had rejoiced in their drowning as he'd deliberately sunk the small craft miles out from shore . . . Yet what shore? And if she had loved him even as they were dying, ending their life together, so enwrapped with hatred, why did she feel such release?

For relief it was. Death, nothing but indistinct voices and that all-pervading shine. Was that light God? If so it was remarkably resemblant of an ordinary lanthorn, though that thought surely must be sinful, for the Almighty cannot be criticized. Especially in this place which, when she came to see it full clear, must certainly be His own domain of Heaven itself.

Worse, she would now be examined in her Last Judgement, questioned terribly by the saints themselves about every single detail of her past earthly life. That would be hard. And what if she couldn't remember, as indeed she was unable to remember anything this very instant? Surely provision must be made for such hopeless ones as I, she thought. The saints would help, actually show her the scenes of her life as they had happened. Yet she fought against memory, of that frightening house filled with the oppressive presence of the man. He had loved her murderously, brooked no competition or other existence. And he might be here, chuckling, ahead of her, waiting to reach out and take hold of her hand . . .

She felt someone strong, purposeful, grasp her hand, and she screamed.

Doctor Ven Carmichael was reading the latest edition of Macaulay's *Dictionary of Medicine* and thinking of his life as the doctor of Sealandings.

The difficulty was that, here in the small coastal town, there was no one else with whom to hold a conversation about the problems of medicine, surgery, the diseases afflicting his patients. The hazards of surgery were formidable, as with everything in East Anglia. Roads were treacherous at the best of times and impassable in wet and snowy seasons. Sending for assistance was therefore out of the question. As if he had the money anyway! As for transferring a sick woman or man to another place – like the large city of Norwich, say – that was a fantasy dream which he knew would never be realized. No world could ever be that organized, so sophisticated, so compassionate. Or even so brilliantly understanding of a doctor's work that allowance would ever be made for the simple human desire called kindness.

He sighed. That was the wish of every physician in practice. To achieve results, to defy superstition, to gain logic, to use common sense. And to advance treatment.

Hungrily he tackled Macaulay's latest wisdoms. Elaterium, now. This drug would represent a serious expenditure, were he to buy a quantity. He turned up the oil lamp, tilting his book to read easier. Mrs Trenchard wished to light a fire in his study in the late afternoon, and pointedly laid the fire each day in good time – when there was money enough to afford one. Recently he had to forbid the practice, on account of the cost. Sea coals were not for everyone, and the very fact of being a doctor seemed to invite every scoundrel on the coast to charge higher than they should. He decided to keep his outdoor boots on after returning from his rounds in Sealandings, and hang what folk thought.

Elaterium, from the fruit of the wild cucumber, *Momordica elaterium*. It surrounded the very seeds, and Macaulay extolled the substance as being remarkable for its powers as a cathartic, and producing copious watery stools. Might it succeed when other cathartics and diuretics failed? But there was the risk of overdosage in the susceptible. And some sick folk here on the weathered coasts declined swiftly, especially those with debilitating diseases such as the phthisis – not uncommon hereabouts. He knew only too well that patients could die of the doctor as well as of their disease. Doctor Paris, now, advised a dose of one grain for the average adult, but here was the famed Macaulay preaching that a half grain, and even a quarter, was sufficient! Repeat the dose half-hourly until it begins to operate. Indeed, Macaulay claimed it to be the best that doctors possessed with the present state of knowledge. Remarkable! It would be worth it, then. He made a pencilled note in the margin of page 228: seek the price from the apothecary when that wretched drunken oaf came visiting. Or should he pen a letter to him and invite some local farmer to convey it on market day? But it was all expense, and he was already living on short commons. So many of his patients defaulted from payment of his fees, some blamelessly, others not.

He sighed and laid the book on the table. Somebody was calling,

6

hammering on the door, and here was Mrs Trenchard running with her hands mangling in her apron for dryness.

'Doctor! A woman's been brought out of the sea! Come quickly!'

'Where is she, Mrs Trenchard?'

He was already moving, clutching his bag and stamping his heels on the bare flagged floor to sit the boots round his heels. He knew only too well the problems of stumbling on the dark unmade roads all about Sealandings.

'Taken into the Donkey and Buskin inn, Doctor!'

'From a ship, or from land?'

' 'Tis not known, Doctor.' She followed him, flinging his threadbare cloak over his shoulders as he made the front door.

'Who's out there?' he called, latching his cape.

'Please, Doctor, Hal Baines.' The lad held a lantern.

'He's got a tax cart beyond the gate, Doctor.' Mrs Trenchard came with them down the path, in spite of the drizzle. 'Now you drive with care, Hal Baines,' she cautioned, 'and see the doctor gets there apiece, y'hear?'

'Yes, m'm.'

Hal Baines ran round, climbed in and, checking the doctor was in his seat, clicked his tongue to set the horse in motion. It was one of Hal's cousin's two-wheeled carts, Doctor Carmichael saw. The beast was probably known to the lad, thank heaven. The way some of these lads drove farm waggons along the roads! As if they disbelieved in tomorrows.

'Who brought her in, Hal?'

'We did, Doctor.' Hal was bashfully proud. 'I seed her, roight from the prow of *The Jaunty*. It was just as Masther Jervin was going to fetch us about and run for home.'

'Good lad. That's a sharp pair of eyes you've got there. If the woman survives, it'll be you she has to thank for it, then.'

'Thank 'ee, Doctor. Masther Jervin were well pleased.'

'Was he indeed?' Doctor Carmichael settled back in the bucking seat. The lad's enthusiasm for speed was getting the better of his caution. The tax cart was a small conveyance only, and driven quietly made good progress even on the wretched East Anglian tracks. But driven hectically it had lost many a man his life or livelihood.

'Best take it calm, Hal, eh?' he tried, but the lad only agreed and kept up his speed, the horse's haunches gathering and easing as it bounded through the night towards the lights of Sealandings. Half a mile didn't sound much; indeed, it was but a small walk in a fine summer. In

7

treacherous weathers, though, those four furlongs stretched almost into an infinity of risk and time, for the track actually vanished in pools or slid down some shallow hillside, making an abyss where a road should have been.

No use. The lad was almost thrilled to be the bringer, not only of a woman drawn from the perilous sea, but also of the doctor who would miraculously restore her to instantaneous health. It was possibly the greatest moment of Hal Baines's life, now or ever after.

Doctor Carmichael clung to his bag and seat and life as Hal clicked and encouraged the lunging animal to greater efforts.

'Her's a fair piece of a woman.'

'Now, Jason Prothero,' the publican's wife cut in sharply. 'I'll say again what I said when the poor woman's body was brought in: there'll be no talk like that in the Donkey and Buskin while I'm here, or Mr Weaver will set about me, true as life.'

Just then the unconscious woman cried out fitfully, threshing her limbs. They had placed her on the first of the tables in the taproom.

'*She's* no corpse,' an old sailor said with disgust. He was slipping ale into his own tankard from the vessels of others while they were distracted from their drink by all the excitement. 'She's alive. Set her outside a glass of that Frenchie, Sarah Ann. She'll be up and singing your praises in no time.'

'That'll do from you too, Gunner.' she answered. 'Mr Weaver'll be along within the hour, and I shall tell him who's behaved and who not.'

'I'm pleased to hear you say that, Mrs Weaver,' a voice said. Miss Baring was standing in the doorway of the taproom, tall and elegant in the tavern lantern light. 'May I enter, please?'

'Oh, Miss Baring! Do come, if you please. I'm worrying what to assay, with this poor creature picked drowning from the sea.'

'We've done the best we could, ma'am,' Jervin explained.

'I think you did very well. Has anyone sent for Doctor Carmichael?'

'Yes, indeed, ma'am.' Jervin was delighted to be praised by the sister of the village rector. He'd have a great deal to tell the wife when he got home. It was a wasted voyage, but even so he did not arrive with nothing. Honour from Miss Euterpe Baring was honour indeed! Some Sealandings folk said she hadn't a kindly word in her head.

'How long ago, pray?'

'Ten minutes, young Baines was sent.'

'He ought to be back,' Gunner said with a growl and a spit. 'That doctor's giving him a glass of some brandy wine, that's why he's not returned.'

'Her's groaning,' Jason Prothero observed, unable to stop eyeing the woman's form.

'As indeed I shall be, very soon, if I find too many unnecessary people around this tavern room when there ought to be none save the physician!'

'But we can't be ousted!' Gunner wailed as Sarah Ann Weaver shooed the men towards the door. Miss Baring was right, of course. There were sights to be seen soon which weren't seemly in the presence of men.

As soon as the door was closed on the sullen men, deprived of their ale, Euterpe Baring gave a great smile to Sarah Ann.

'Well done, Mrs Weaver! I can see that this lady was very fortunate to be brought here.'

'You are very kind, Miss Baring.'

'It is true, Mrs Weaver. She'll have cause to express fervent thanks, should she be restored.'

'Will we remove her clothes, Miss Baring?' Sarah Ann naturally let the superior woman take charge, thinking admiringly that not all higher-born people were so appreciative of ordinary folk. Such condescension! She admired the set and carriage of Miss Baring, and always had, in fact, since the lady had arrived from London to keep the rectory for her brother.

'As much as we can, remembering always that Doctor Carmichael will shortly be arriving.'

As she spoke, her colour heightened a little. Sarah Weaver noticed, but was too busy covering the poor wretch with a blanket to give the occurrence much thought, filing it away until later. She sent Alice from the taproom scullery to fetch a second rough blanket from upstairs, and busied herself removing the woman's leather shoes.

'She is quite well attired, Miss Baring, d'you see?'

The survivor wore a rough guernsey above a loose skirt of coarse woollens, as if she had been working in some part of an estate before the calamity struck. This was decidedly odd. Her hands were quite delicate. As they cleaned her with a piece of Bolton fustian it became apparent to them both that they were dealing with a woman of quite possibly some standing.

'Does this mean that she's from some passing ship, then, Miss Baring?' Sarah Ann asked.

'I'm not at all sure, Mrs Weaver. Her hands are clean underneath this corrugated skin, and her nails aren't chipped. In fact . . .'

9

Euterpe brushed away the wretch's hair from her face and marvelled at the smooth skin, browned slightly from the sun, and the hair which, given half a chance, would be something to see. Even in its salt-soaked state it showed natural waves and a shine deep in its raven blackness.

They had prepared her for the doctor when he finally came, breathless and swaying from the careering gallop. He smiled to see Euterpe already there, and nodded a greeting to Mrs Weaver as he cast off his old cloak before moving to the table where the woman lay.

'It's but a girl, Miss Euterpe!' he exclaimed, raising the girl's eyelids to examine the eyes. Brown, young, without the arcus senilis showing around the margins of the cornea. The conjunctiva was a clear white, the brown irises startling in their russet intensity. He glanced at the two women, beckoned Alice who was standing by the staircase.

'We must attempt to regain the sea here, ladies,' he said. 'Please assist. I'll need the lady lifted on to her side before ejecting the last water from her lights.'

They managed between them to get the girl on her side, hanging down over the edge of the table. Doctor Carmichael squeezed her chest, lifting her suddenly and then giving her a shake. It was novel, but it had worked in numerous situations and was being tried in all cases of drowning. The girl breathed, choked, but was still blue from cold. There was no telling how long she had been in the water.

Within minutes the girl was choking and wailing as the doctor repeated the manoeuvre, Alice and the publican's wife helping in the turning.

The movements intruded on the girl's consciousness. She shook her head, and made a few muttered sounds, to Miss Baring's delight.

'She's trying to speak, Doctor!'

'We mustn't put our trust in a few sounds, Miss Euterpe. It mayn't be for some hours before I can pronounce on the state of her brain.' Carmichael was concerned. Some rescued souls never recovered their wits again, and spent the rest of their sorry lives as imbeciles in abysmal poverty. 'It's well known that prolonged immersion in the seas may leave a person devoid of memory and even sanity, unable to work properly ever again. We'll have to be patient.'

'I shall try to find her a bed, Doctor,' Mrs Weaver said, signalling to Alice to see where a pallet could be laid.

The Donkey and Buskin was filled, with so many people travelling the coast for the election hustings for Parliament. Alice hurried off, mystified. There was hardly a corner of the second floor not already promised. It would be best to give the poor woman a place by the

10

scullery fire, somewhere warm and dry, rather than trying to impress Miss Baring like this. Perhaps Mrs Weaver had no intention of giving up one of the paying guests' spaces, and as soon as the doctor and the rector's sister left would return to her normal brisk voice and settle things more predictably.

'This is very charitable of you, Mrs Weaver!'

Doctor Carmichael stood looking down at his charge. Life was returning to the face. Instead of a waxen shape there were features, a sense of animation. It was returning to a balance, life against the forces which strove to extinguish that vital spark from a creature. The soul was here, returned to the very body to which it belonged. He felt a sense of triumph, but was too experienced to show it. He simply nodded to Miss Baring.

'Nothing here remains for me except to express deep appreciation to you two ladies, for your charity and kindness in attending on this creature. An example of devotion to the very best cause on earth. Miss Baring. Mrs Weaver.'

'There's no call for that, Doctor Carmichael.'

Miss Baring's colour changed, though she strove to show only a casual manner. Sarah Ann bobbed a curtsey and wiped her hands on her apron. She felt she had come out of this encounter very well. Reverend Baring would be less inclined to rant on about the terrible perils of drink – especially that taken at the Donkey and Buskin – now that she had acquitted herself so favourably before his sister and Doctor Carmichael.

As she acknowledged Alice's signal, delivered from the shadows by the stairs, to the effect that there was nowhere to lay the poor survivor's head this night, Sarah Weaver was struck by the appearance of the two visitors. Doctor Carmichael, in his worn cloak, its broad collar rolled so high at the nape, the old cravat so loosely tied testifying to the haste with which the gentleman had left his house out there on the Essex inland road. And Miss Euterpe Baring, quite daringly attired in a pelisse, which was sometimes still favoured even among the gentry, though in Miss Baring's case its choice was determined with an eye to the economy of her brother's parish living. She wore a feathered bonnet, and a boa around her neck, loose-hanging and long and thin, of fur. These were said to be of diminishing interest to the carriage trade and London ladies, but on Miss Baring, standing there with defined grace in the light cast by the fire and the oblique golden brilliance of the candles set about the room, the effect was quite startling and worthy of anyone's attention. The pelisse was practically a second dress, though

11

it was naturally proper to have it partly open at the front. The rector's sister had not been too surprised, however, Sarah Ann candidly observed, to forget that her pelerine would look quite fetching, even though the material of which this shoulder cape was fashioned lacked a proper fur edging. Very creditable, she was still thinking, when the girl on the table was retchingly sick and broke the spell for them all.

3

They brought news to Squire Hunterfield in the middle of supper, which was the wrongest time possible. He became aware of the principal servant hovering and making inadequate coughing noises behind his gloved hand and nodded resignedly to his sister Lydia.

'What is it, Crane?'

'Begging your pardon, Mrs Vallance,' Crane said, with relief at being finally noticed. 'There's an urgent matter brought to the door for the squire.'

'I shall attend to it.' Mrs Vallance rose to make her excuses to the company. Mercifully there were only two guests to the Hunterfields this evening, so the interruption would not prove of signal consequence.

'Don't let it keep you too long, Lydia,' Henry Hunterfield called down the long table to his sister. 'I need you to keep the strictest control over these guests of mine!'

'Very well, my dear,' his sister said, smiling apology. Crane held open the door for her to proceed into the hall.

Ven Carmichael was standing there, his cloak dripping on to the carpet.

'Why, it's Doctor Carmichael, isn't it?' Lydia exclaimed.

'Indeed it is, ma'am,' he said awkwardly, 'and very sad to be the occasion of disturbing Lorne House. But an urgent concern for Squire Hunterfield has arisen – almost literally arisen, in fact.'

'You mystify me, Doctor. Could you explain? Nothing too tragic, I trust!'

'Rather a moment for rejoicing, Mrs Vallance.' Doctor Carmichael explained the bringing of the unidentified girl ashore.

'And is she our countrywoman, Doctor?'

'I trust so, Mrs Vallance, but none has as yet heard her speak.'

'When will you be able to set her talking? My brother needs a full account of the lady's travails. It will be almost as difficult for him to act upon no information as it will upon very little.'

Carmichael flushed at her tone. She had no hint of jocularity in her voice, which might have lessened the implied criticism.

'As a doctor I can guarantee only effort and a little skill, Mrs

Vallance. I cannot work miracles. That privilege the Almighty reserves to Himself.'

'Then perhaps a little more skill, Doctor? And a little extra effort?'

He swallowed the insult. 'I shall endeavour to provide those, Mrs Vallance. In the meantime, please allow me to consider my duty to the magistracy discharged by my attendance at Lorne House with the information I was able to bring.'

'And very ably done, Doctor, if I may say so.'

She smiled distantly. Lydia Vallance was well aware of the effect she had on the young doctor, how little used he was to entering the grand houses of the neighbourhood. Medical problems at Lorne House were always the province of great London physicians lured north from the Royal College of Physicians. There was no question of entrusting Quality's health to mere local quacks, however promising their skills seemed to be and whatever their reputation. She was glad to have selected her drop earrings and the long gold chain looped round her throat, and twice she had seen his eyes struggling to keep away from the cameo which caught her bodice tighter than it otherwise would have been.

'Thank you, ma'am.' Doctor Carmichael bowed slightly and withdrew.

Lydia re-entered the dining room feeling she had scored a small triumph. Her brother would be quite proud of her when she recounted the details after the guests had left.

'It was nothing, Henry dear. Just some woman brought in on one of the fishing luggers.'

'Indeed.' Henry grimaced, feigning exhaustion to the amusement of his guests. 'Into where, precisely?'

'The hard at Sealandings.'

'Has she survived?'

'It was Doctor Carmichael, to advise that with luck, God's assistance, and the wind in the right quarter, she might well see the break of day!'

There was general laughter, Mrs Thalia De Foe laughing more than the rest.

'Did Doctor Carmichael manage to explain how this woman had come to be floating without the assistance of some sort of ship?'

'He was unable to say, Mrs De Foe.' Lydia Vallance made the answer as light as she was able, but Thalia De Foe interrogated her pointedly.

'I confess myself disappointed, Mrs Vallance. I should have hoped

14

that you would have been able, if anyone, to worm some details from the young doctor!'

'Unfortunately, he is of a profession which believes that ignorance is truly bliss – as long as it resides in the breast of the undeserving!' Lydia Vallance gave Mrs De Foe one of her famously brilliant smiles.

The company laughed, but quietened as the squire spoke.

'I could well do without this,' Hunterfield sighed. 'What with the hustings causing problems, the magistracy in three of the Hundreds having to rely upon the militia to control political arguments among people who should have no political effronteries whatsoever . . .'

'That's the consequence of being trusted, Henry.'

'How would an old friend like you know whether I could be trusted or not?'

The company shared the laugh at Sir Trev Bunyan's expense. It was a safe jibe, since he and Hunterfield had been at Cambridge together and now had mercantile interests in common.

'That's a perfectly terrible thing to say!' Tabitha Hunterfield chided. She considered herself Henry Hunterfield's favourite younger sister, and could take liberties others dared not. 'Trev was conferring a compliment, Henry. As your sister I have a right to defend Sir Trev – even if he *is* a rogue!'

'Have you no defence for him too, Letitia?' Henry asked mildly.

'I beg pardon, Henry?'

Henry smiled the length of the table, but his feelings were suddenly harder. His sisters were something of a trial to him, since the death of his father overseas. Lydia, the eldest, was well provided for. She was able, businesslike, far-seeing and very capable of managing her husband's affairs during his enforced absences in the new empire of the Indian subcontinent. Her rumoured indiscretions were possibly substantiated, of course, but as long as the details remained the close secret they should be, then for the sake of the Hunterfield reputation – and that of Captain Vallance, naturally – he too would wink at them.

The other sisters were not so easily classed. He would to heaven that they were.

Tabitha, with her smart appearance, her slightly self-indulgent attitude to life, and her willingness to provoke responses in the most taciturn individuals who came to talk politics and county responsibilities, was already something of a legend. She was in a way a true copy of Lydia.

Letitia, on the other hand, was an utter amazement. How could the same parents, the same seed, the same family, produce such a disparity

15

in siblings? Tabitha might be a true copy of her older sister, able and indeed formidable, eager to shoulder the responsibility of managing the household when occasion allowed, vivaciously coping with visitors who were, for heaven's sake, vitally important to Squire Hunterfield's family. But Letitia . . .

The quieter sister was a serious problem. Pale of mien, blonde and milk-white, she seemed almost ephemeral, quite unlike the Hunterfields in colouring. And as for her manner . . . Recessive, almost, a silent sister who would look owlishly at anyone who spoke, without even trying to coin a reply which contained any meaning. As for spontaneity. . . ! Well, the girl was almost an imbecile. He could think that dangerous thought, but it would be a duelling matter were anyone else even to hint it. She was pretty enough, yes, with her bodice fashioned and the puff shoulder sleeves showing so little bare arm. But was it any surprise that his good friend Trev was ignoring one young sister and taking exceedingly notable interest in the other?

No, Hunterfield thought in some concern. Before long he would have to compel Lydia to take Letitia in hand. It was a source of mystification to him how women managed to acquire their knowledge and household skills. But surely to God Letitia could stir herself, couldn't she? Was it too much to expect her for once to pull her nose from those wretched books and enter the world like the rest of humanity? He smiled at the girl's almost blank expression, but sighed inwardly.

'I asked if you have no defence to bring to Sir Trev.' He paused helpfully. 'In the way your sister did.'

'Hardly, Henry.' Letitia smiled a little. 'Sir Trev cannot require my poor aid when such formidable assistance is already granted him.'

Henry stirred, smiling in an attempt to raise the riposte's reception, but he felt slightly uncomfortable. The girl sometimes managed, through no fault of her own, to put her foot in it. She somehow used words which were descriptive of herself, yet which had remained unspoken in his mind. She couldn't know him so well that she instantly understood his thoughts, of course; she was far too elementary-minded for that. But it was truly extraordinary how often it happened.

'This woman, Henry. What will become of her?' Thalia De Foe asked, as Tabitha blushed winningly at her sister's compliment and Lydia smiled with approval at the best sally Letitia had ever brought forth.

'I suppose I shall feel responsible for the old crone,' Henry said.

'But surely she must not be an expense carried on Lorne House's estate, Henry!' Lydia exclaimed. As mistress of the Hunterfield household she was responsible for costs. 'Are there no others with duties in Sealandings?'

'Lydia, my dear. You know how it is. As the news spreads, every tenant farmer in the neighbourhood with more than half an acre will suddenly discover outrageous responsibilities all over the entire kingdom. All will plead poverty. The Church, with that incompetent fool Reverend Baring bleating about his plight, will deny the affair and send her to me for assistance. Doctor Carmichael will shelve any recollection of this evening the instant she can totter upright on crutches. And the parish trustees will scream about the Poor Law and the rates and the need for Christian charity in this noble country of ours . . .'

'And then?' Mrs De Foe prompted mischievously.

'Then I shall be left to admit her to the workhouse and maintain her out of my own pocket – until such time as I can hunt down a stray member of her family and get her back to the parish from which she embarked.'

'The poor woman!' Letitia exclaimed. There was a sudden silence. Sir Trev glanced uncomfortably across the table and toyed with his wine glass.

'What was that, sister dear?' Tabitha purred. She deliberately leant over the table, to pretty effect with the candlelight shining on her jewellery and casting freckles of illumination into her face.

'Yes, Letitia. What was your meaning exactly?' Thalia De Foe asked.

Letitia paled slightly, but spoke quite firmly into the quiet. 'I think it piteous in the extreme, Henry, that we as a country are unable to cater properly for such poor defenceless people as this old lady surely must be.'

'Cater?' Sir Trev said, surprised at the use of the term.

'Properly?' Henry's face grew serious.

'I didn't mean that, quite,' Letitia explained, starting to stutter in her anxiety. Henry's spirits sank as he recognized the symptoms. Again Letitia was going to call attention to her deficiencies, and in company, where a family could only provide so much protection against critical appraisal.

'Then what did you *quite* mean?' Tabitha pressed unkindly.

'Surely you can't impugn your brother's attitudes towards provision for unfortunates, Letitia?' Mrs De Foe asked, sweetly cruel. 'He has the most enviable reputation among all of East Anglia's notables. Not only for his charity, my dear, but for the proper disposition of public moneys among the idlers you seem to feel such compassion for!'

17

'I know that, Mrs De Foe. But I feel that – '

'Oh, it's all right, everyone!' Lydia said brightly, coming to the rescue as she knew Henry would wish. 'It's only one of Letitia's *feelings*! We may all sleep soundly in our beds this evening!'

'And my little sister means her remarks in the kindliest way, I'm sure,' Henry said to close the subject, giving Lydia a glance of approval. 'Sentiment was after all my dear mother's favourite subject for songs.'

'Perhaps we should try to sing one, Henry,' Lydia suggested.

'A perfect idea, Lydia! Into the withdrawing room, everyone! Trev, lay aside those smoker's requisites until you have warbled a favourite melody for the ladies!'

'Oh, must I?' Sir Trev groaned.

'For certain you must! The ladies demand it!'

'Once word gets out I shall never hear the last of this!'

Joking amiably, the company retired for Sir Trev Bunyan to sing his favourite songs. He would have been furious had nobody insisted. Henry Hunterfield was relieved that Lydia had been so quick, perceiving the brief discomfiture over Letitia's remarks. Yes, he thought, following the ladies in, it certainly was high time he took some action in the matter of Letitia's training. Lydia would have to take more of a hand. He had done all he could. And now, just as he was trying to find time to devote to the Parliament business in the Eastern Hundreds, here came bodies drifting in from the sea practically on every tide. A senior magistrate was required to solve a world of problems.

As if the country expected him to have a magic wand to hand, when he had only a few coins and a whip. He put on his best smile, and tried not to look too hungrily at Thalia De Foe as he offered her his arm. Soon, thank God, his hunger for her would be assuaged.

He led the applause as Trev Bunyan took his stand and Letitia placed herself at the keyboard.

4

The voices had gone.

She felt freed, lifted, but that was all. Where was the singing there was supposed to be? No heavenly voices? How could that be? Perhaps they would soon come. Nor had she yet been examined by saints. And her mother, her ancestors, were not to be heard either. She must be patient, quiet, and wait upon God to call her name, in the words of those strange Quakers.

Name. That was a difficulty. You had to have a name. She knew she had one. It was an old name, her mother always said, one not given to many. There were no names in her head. She could remember a man, young, who went off for a . . . soldier? Sailor? In uniform, then returning no longer in uniform. Something to do with his wound, limping slightly, returning discharged and smiling. Where had she seen him last, this handsome young man with his old stained uniform and his limp? It had been somewhere on the sea marshes, with the wind a- blowing and him embracing her, saying how he'd been pressed aboard a ship for the Royal Navy, a King's ship, and then . . .

She wanted to see him again, but now knew it would be impossible for . . . for . . . No, his name would not come. He was not dead, and she definitely was. Yet he wasn't her husband, no. For her husband was the man who had drowned with her, as she was clutched in his great hands, and him crying in exultation at the enormous death-defying power of his love. It was to transcend death, even that . . .

Her eyes opened.

Reverend Josiah Baring's anxieties were all on account of his youth. Or rather, he thought, lighting a spill at the fire, his *comparative* youth. A necessary qualification. This was no time to be young, what with the country in the grip of dissenting forces among the working poor, the classes in upheaval everywhere. And, ghastly even to think, religion itself in pandemonium. It would have been better if he were ten years older, even thirty-five, forty years of age. Or, pushing existence to the limits of credulity, fifty or even more. Then his active days would be behind him, and he would be able to spend his time simply writing letters, reading the classics he loved, and have done with his efforts at pleading the Lord's cause to the bovinely inactive.

Then, his ministry done, he would be able in all conscience to leave this benighted east coast, shake the dust of Sealandings and its rural district from his feet and go to the west country, somewhere down in Frome, say, or Stowford, the sort of places where he felt he naturally belonged. The Devon people were blessed with open faces, were bright and talkative, taking a man as he tried to be, not simply as they or others saw him. This remote and sombre part of East Anglia was indeed a wretched location for a poorish vicar, one not blessed with important sponsors or kindly benefactors. He smiled as his pipe started to draw. The expression he had used in his mind a few moments ago: shake the dust off his feet! How absurdly inappropriate! Scrape the thick clay mud from the soles, ankles, lace-holes, more like! The place was sodden – 'daggly', as the locals would have it in their barbarous dialect.

And they were surly, displeased with him because he happened to have been born elsewhere. They came and listened to his sermons, yes, but only to grumble that he was never likely to prove as powerful a preacher as his predecessor. Not only that, but there were Church problems locally. These miserable Methodists, with their incantatory reasons and jocular hymns, their riding about the countryside in endless pursuit of converts, their hatred of the Established Church, their sheer intolerance . . . Well, it was all too much. No, age would prove the antidote for the plight he was in.

There was one bright light, however. Since Euterpe had come to keep house for him the rectory was a deal improved. She had brought living expenses into bounds. Heaven alone knows how, he thought, but was pleased. She proved, calm, wise, gradually winning with those of Sealandings with whom she came into contact. It was most delightful to see her extract conversation, showing sympathy and kindness, even though she was in no position to dispense material largesse, and gain in return smiles and pleasant rejoinders. An astonishing phenomenon, because he last remembered her, several years ago, as a shy retiring miss: small, dependent on everybody around for a mite of praise. Without great tact and understanding she'd invariably dissolved in tears. In fact, to put it bluntly, Euterpe had been rather tiresome.

Then had come the day when, still tiny, she had been sent to board at St Mary's Lodge in Bloxham, Oxfordshire. There she had stayed some years, with several other little maids similarly placed. She had returned capable, quite spirited, and even became quite good company. As was proper for the son of the family, he then had had to go away to be educated, while she stayed behind looking after Mother and Father. She had done quite well by all accounts, helping out in the parish where Father was the rector. But they had grown apart. In spite of occasional meetings when he returned from Trinity, she became a mere incidental Someone always only standing in the background. After he became the rector of Sealandings, however, he found himself in dire need of a housekeeper and approached Euterpe by letter asking her to make a recommendation. Her response had come as a complete surprise: she herself might be able to acquit herself adequately, and accordingly was preparing herself to come.

He had agonized for days over that letter before writing to accept her offer. By then Father and Mother had passed away, leaving just the two of them. Father had written a year previously hinting that Euterpe ought perhaps to stay with her brother, but Josiah had been far too pressed at the time to agree. He had failed to reply, so Euterpe actually arrived many months after the proposal was first mooted. She proved an immediate success in every way. Even he, a distrusted rector from the outlands, was in better standing with the parish than before. He supposed much must be due to her.

She returned just as he was beginning to be anxious, for the nights were particularly black hereabouts, unrelieved and forbidding. The friendly velvety dark of the Devon countryside was never seen in these parts.

'Good evening, dear.' She entered, flinging her cover aside and coming to stand by the fire. She had divested herself of her bonnet in the hall. 'Such excitement! A young woman has been rescued from the waters . . .' She told him of the survivor, the doctor, the gathering at the Donkey and Buskin.

'And I was not called, Euterpe?'

'There was no need, brother. She will be well, it seems. Doctor Carmichael was soon on hand.'

'And where is she now?' Josiah Baring was slightly put out. He should have been called in any event, for what if she had died, her soul unshriven? Though she too might be one of these pernicious Dissenters, Knoxians, Quakers, Nonconformists, so many groups. Everybody on earth seemed to be forming his own sect.

'She is staying at the tavern. Mrs Weaver proved most capable, and has offered a place for the night.'

'What accident led to her being nigh drowned?'

'That is not known. The lady is hardly able to speak yet, though Doctor Carmichael is hopeful.'

21

'It seems most unsatisfactory, Euterpe. I should have been summoned.'

'There was no time, Josiah, I'm afraid. The call came with such urgency that I had to hurry. You were reading your office in the church, and I know how devoted you are to your private prayer. My intention was to examine the circumstances and send a message back, should your presence prove necessary. As it was . . .'

'Thank you.' Perhaps it was all to the good that Euterpe had coped. And Ven Carmichael, with whom he was on fairly cordial terms, was by all accounts reasonable and very active.

'The squire has been told, I think. Doctor Carmichael said he would visit Lorne House on his way home.'

'There's a supper party there this evening. I only hope his interruption is greeted without acrimony.'

'Why should it be otherwise?' Her hand went to her throat in anxiety.

'Hunterfield does not take kindly to interruption at board, Euterpe. Especially when he has as guest Mrs De Foe from Milton Hall.'

'What are you suggesting, Josiah?'

He was uncomfortable, reaping the harvest of his careless words. But he had seen the swift concern in her eyes when he mentioned that Doctor Carmichael might meet with a warmer reception than he anticipated. Her agitation warned him. It would not do for his sister to become emotionally attached to a small country doctor. For one thing, she could do a deal better for herself, in his judgement. Once, he might have rejoiced to see her settled with somebody of Ven Carmichael's stamp, even though he was a poor quack. But now Euterpe had shown herself capable at housekeeping. She was astonishingly well tutored in music, adept at needlework, strong and capable. And intelligent, as women went. She was a voracious reader, a writer of amusement, and corresponded with gentry whom he had never met, but with whom she had found an agreeable acquaintanceship in Father's parish in the west country.

Not only that, it would seriously inconvenience him, were Euterpe to become too close to Carmichael. She could hardly run two separate households, no matter how strongly she was attached to her brother. No, this would have to be nipped in the bud.

'I wish I had not spoken, Euterpe. But it is said that Henry Hunterfield has a particular . . . fondness for the company of Mrs De Foe.'

She was puzzled. 'I know she has been a friend of the Hunterfields, and tutored Miss Tabitha and Miss Letitia in certain social . . .'

'I do not refer merely to the kindess Thalia De Foe has shown to Squire Hunterfield's two youngest sisters, Euterpe. I mean Mrs De Foe herself.'

'Mrs De Foe?' Euterpe was still surprised. 'But naturally he shows gentlemanly concern for her, seeing that her husband is forever into London at his investments and merchanting, and on matters of government. It behoves him to . . .' Her eyes rounded suddenly.

'There, Euterpe,' he said gently. 'I see you realize.'

'Josiah! You can't mean that there is a . . . a . . . Between Sir Henry Hunterfield and Mrs De Foe?'

He saw his sister sink on to the fireside stool, appalled at the news.

'A relationship based on over-familiarity, Euterpe. Yes. I'm afraid that is what is said. Perhaps I am wrong to bring this to your attention, but you have to learn some unpleasing facts of life here in Sealandings.'

'But that is impossible! It . . .' She searched for the right words. 'It . . . doesn't happen, not among people one . . . one *knows*, Josiah!'

'Sad to relate it does, Euterpe.'

'Here? In Sealandings?'

'Indeed.'

'How long has this . . . this terrible thing been going on?'

'For quite some time, it is said. I tell you this now, because the occasion has arisen, and because it is essen-tial for you to realize that good and bad coexist. Yes, Euterpe. Disgraceful events can occur in the most unlikely places.'

'How on earth . . . What do those poor sisters of his *do*? How can they bear to tolerate that woman's visits? How can they show towards her that civility which they must, at church on Sunday, in their very home. . . ?'

'Don't distress yourself, Euterpe. It does no good. As for the ladies of the Hunterfield household, they have to accept what their brother decrees. His is the authority, his the administration of the estates.'

'And his is the state of the unmarried,' Euterpe said slowly.

'Indeed. This calamity would not occur, nor would it be an occasion for idle gossip and speculation if he would only marry some kindly and efficient wife. In my church, of course! He needs one, who could assist him in his duties and take up the household.'

'It seems, brother, that the unmarried condition for both man and woman bears a great responsibility until it is ended.' She was looking into the fire as she spoke. He was not at all sure he approved of the direction the conversation was taking.

'When the time is ripe, Euterpe,' he said evenly, 'marriage is a step which we must all contemplate.'

23

'Even you and I?'

'Yes, Euterpe,' he said comfortably, 'even you and I.'

There, she thought to herself. He's said it, given his approval in a way. She felt authorized to start taking steps. She was careful to warn herself: I must remember this conversation, for when I need to refer to it later. Josiah was a great one for keeping his word, and she would need to confront him with proof that he had spoken about the step in terms of approval. She thought of Doctor Ven Carmichael in his threadbare cape, and smiled inwardly.

The Reverend Josiah Baring had given his blessing, in a kind of way.

Jason Prothero was lyrical about the woman brought from the sea.

'Grand woman, she were,' he told Ben Fowler, publican and confidant at the Goat and Compass. 'She'll make somebody a fine bed, soon as she wakens.'

'Aye, and I'll bet I know who he wishes that company'd be,' Old Lack cackled to his cronies on a nearby bench.

'Watch your tongue to your betters, Lack!'

The publican was eager to please, for it wasn't often that such farmer's wealth flowed into his small wharfside tavern. Ben Fowler knew that the crowd this night was swollen only because of the goings-on up at the Donkey and Buskin. Still, charity was the biggest fool of all, as folk said. Even the silly Samaritan learned that, though the hard way.

'She were a sight when I fished her from the sea, God's truth.'

'It were young Baines did it, Lack,' a longshoreman claimed. 'I heard him tell it.'

'Were you there, Codgie?' Lack cried. 'Well, were you?'

'No. And I'll lay you weren't, either!'

A roar of laughter and catcalls greeted the sally, to Old Lack's disgust.

'Whoever pays her commons for the night will be out a pretty penny,' Lack said sulkily.

'Why so, Lack?' Ben Fowler was never loth to discover events as they happened, and preferably before. The rivalry with the Weavers up at the Donkey was a sore contest.

'Because she's lost. No mind, no money, that's why. A corpse is best.'

'Especially if their wallets and purses are loaded with coin, eh?' Prothero said aside to Fowler.

Jason Prothero prided himself on his knowledge of seafaring ways. He had never set foot from the shore. Ben Fowler chuckled as if the farmer had made a profound witticism.

24

'That's true, Mr Prothero. These shores was never made for charity. Fish or farm, it has to be fought for, worked from seas and soil.'

'True, Fowler. I wonder who will take charge of her?'

'Mistress Weaver has promised Doctor Carmichael to take care of the woman until she rouses.' Old Lack swore this was the case, for he had listened at the door.

He narrated the conversation, all to Ben Fowler's satisfaction. It looked as if the Donkey and Buskin would lose almost all of its evening trade, and to the Goat and Compass at that. He went through to tell his Martha to make provision for extra victuals. Four boats were in today, and even though the catches were not great cullings, there'd still be money spent and ale drunk over and above his usual expectation.

Prothero had gauged Ben Fowler's state of mind by the time the publican returned. 'I think it'd be charitable were somebody local, perhaps the folk of Sealandings, to make a gesture. What do you think, Fowler?'

The publican was at a loss. 'Ah, well, there you have me, Mr Prothero. Who could afford to want the cost come his way?'

'You, perhaps?'

'Me, Mr Prothero? Oh, I doubt if my Martha has room for any more in the scullery. And out here . . .'

'It might be an arrangement which could operate to your advantage, Fowler.'

The publican stared implacably at Jason Prothero. They had drawn apart as by mutual consent and now talked quietly. 'How so, sir?'

'Let me talk a moment, while you draw another round.'

The big farmer strolled casually to the counter where Fowler stood to draw ale from the cask.

'I don't take your meaning, sir,' the publican said. Money was always a considerable problem. He had no inclination to worsen it.

'Suppose that someone in a slightly more advantageous position than your good self made the offer, Fowler?'

'What sort of an offer, Mr Prothero?' Ben Fowler pulled two pints in pewter, one for himself and the other for Prothero. He was beginning to catch the drift, but wanted it spelled out in full lest he got himself caught.

'A paying offer, Fowler.'

'To do what, exactly?'

Prothero checked the company with a sharp glance. 'To reimburse you for any expenses you might incur in taking this sea waif into the Goat and Compass.'

'Ah, that's the problem, Mr Prothero.' Ben Fowler shook his head regretfully. 'Wouldn't be good enough. I could no more take that woman under my roof than fly. There's the cost, you see. Of her meals, clothes, lodging. And it would be quite some time before she was able to pull her weight. All's expense, y'see.'

'But if a little sum found its way to you regular, now?'

'A little sum, you say?'

'A shilling, perhaps?'

'How often would that be, Mr Prothero?'

'Let's say, weekly, until such time as the woman's . . . well, outlasted her stay?'

'I think five shillings would be more of a likely sum, Mr Prothero.'

'Sixty pence?' The farmer glowered at the publican's bland innocence. He drank from the pewter, holding Fowler's eyes with his own. The publican was aware of his intentions. It was no more than blackmail, an implied threat of revelation to Mrs Prothero and to the community. It would finish him here at Sealandings, with its starched public morality. Private morality was different, though. Clandestine relationships were what the place thrived on, as everyone well knew but didn't dare say openly. 'That's a powerful sum for an unknown woman taken from the sea.'

'Aye, sir, but who'd take the risk? It'd be me, sir, with the wife wondering who she was and why it was I decided to take her in. Having to make explanations to my Martha. Then there's the matter of persuading the woman to show proper gratitude to the benefactor, sir.'

'Proper gratitude,' Prothero said, musing on the words. It was a felicitous phrase, one which struck him as promising. Most promising. It would put him in the very position of which he dreamed, guardian of a good well-shapen woman, one vulnerable to his wishes. And one moreover willing to express her gratitude. In time, if she turned out to be anything like, why, the woman might actually prove a better catch than could be imagined.

'Especially as we don't know the woman, sir.' Fowler was a good judge of a man. He knew Prothero's reputation. It was well deserved.

'So?'

'So she might be of a good family, have possessions. She could have fallen from the rail of some packet bound for the Hook of Holland, or a coaster. Heaven knows it happens not uncommonly.'

'True, Fowler. Five shillings, then.'

'Thank you, sir. Most generous.'

26

The big farmer finished the last of the ale. 'And mind you keep your counsel over this.'

'Never spoke out of turn yet, sir. That's my reputation, and that's as is the case. Oh, sir.'

Prothero halted, turning to go. 'Yes?'

'Haven't you forgotten something, sir?' Fowler gazed calmly back at the big farmer. 'There's a small matter of the two half crowns you owe, sir. First week's commons and bed for the sea girl.'

He watched impassively while the farmer counted it out.

5

The room was small, dark-beamed. A babble of noise came from somewhere close. Outside she could hear as chickens clucked; one fluttered of a sudden. The pale light slanted across the confined space, showing a rough blanket partly covering her legs. She drew it up reflexly, shivering. Nearby there came a man's laugh, simple merriment at a remark of a friend. He made a jocular reply, gravel-voicing his doubts about the sanity of a rival. More laughter. Some man shouting for some mulled ale. It was a bland, shiny day.

She was alive.

All was strange, yet all familiar. This was no Heaven. This was earth, living earth. From the aromas it was some sort of alehouse, the sort she knew so well. Knew so well. . . ? She was remembering. Some kind god must have fished her from the water, brought her back. The thought made her shiver. Was he here too? Had they found them both, him still clasping her body? Or had they simply been seen from the shore at Red Hall. . . ?

The pressure behind her eyes was intense. Maybe she was simply about to die, on the way and the process not yet completed. If so, though, how long did these things take? She felt able to move. A little dizzy still, but quite herself. A cautious look around. The pallet on which she lay was on the floor. A bundle of rags formed her pillow, and the blanket had been flung over her. A truckle bed, its wheels making the maid's task of sweeping out the slut's fluff from underneath all the easier, was against the wall by the window. That, she knew, was a landlord's trick, so the wife could easily keep check on arrivals who might require service, any time of the day or night; and of course to keep an eagle eye on the pub servants, who all too often used their rascally reputation to the good effect of lining their own pockets, supplying intimate private services to gentlemen which the tavern was sometimes too moral to offer openly . . .

Had she too been a servant at some tavern, then? She tried hard to remember, and found the calls of the serving girls outside in the tavern yard blending with her memories so effectively that she became confused. Which was past, and which the present? She decided to risk rising, and had extended her hand to the bell rope to summon morning tea and possibly breakfast before realizing there was no bell rope, no morning tea, no . . . what was the name of her servant? An elderly, bustling, large woman who was not above admonishing the lady of Red Hall in spite of her position. . . ?

She cast the covering, crouched all ungainly while steadying herself, and rose, wobbling. The room swam. She took a step, found herself too giddy and slumped again, pressing her knuckles to the wooden flooring to keep some balance. It was awful, truly the most terrible experience. She stayed there a minute, breathing regularly, trying to be strict with herself. She was in some sort of old shift. It had been darned in a dozen places, and rasped coarse against her skin. A large patch was in the back, crudely imposed over the edge of the shift's once-elegant smocked catch-stitching. That needlework would have to be rectified, she decided. Hasty mending meant hasty unmending, her mother used to say before she died . . . Ready. She rose more carefully, padded to the roof window and looked out.

The sea! There it was, glistening in the pale East Anglian sunshine. And it *was* East Anglia. A coast in the distance showed its small headland curving from the North Sea, with a strand of sand, a hulk drawn up ashore with a chimney crudely fashioned from the roof of its cabin, almost exactly like . . . Baker? Was the name Baker? That man who'd throw a bucket of water over the side of his boat to deluge his wife as yet again she returned drunken and bellicose from the tavern on the small offshore island. And his wife, butt of the tavern wags, would shiver and scream on the strand beside the dark derelict hulk until her man, warm in the snug cabin of his grounded ship that would never again sail, judged her sufficiently sober to lower the ladder for her to climb aboard. She found herself smiling wistfully at the memories, then forced herself to look for clues through the glass.

The tavern seemed to be set on the south limit of the hard, in a small coastal township. She was unable to see from her position how big the place was, but to her right a church tower stood, squat and square to guard against the coastal gales of these parts. She could just make out the start of a series of rooftops, aligned in a way suggesting a harbour of substantial size. Smoke was rising from several places, domestic smoke of recently lit fires. Gulls were sailing, gliding, calling their usual insolences. Immediately below, the tavern yard was cobbled but without a well. That implied a brook, or some loan arrangement for water with a neighbouring household. Not for East Anglian taverners the luxuries of waterbringers, who would fetch from as far away as St Edmundsbury on great ungainly watercarts, at great expense and, as she bitterly knew to her cost, greater inefficiency . . . More facts, coming through faintly.

A mile offshore, a small fishing smack was standing away, drawing wind easily and without haste. Its two masts were barely dressed, and its ketch rig, very like the Lowestoft fishing smacks at their trawling business off the sandbanks of the North Sea, was being used hardly to its best advantage. The wind was south-westernly, so unless there was good reason to avoid the manoeuvre, she should have cast her first foremast's largest sail by now. Lazy, or headachy crewmen making their sally into the seas after a mite too much drink. That sloth wouldn't do for old . . . What was his name, that old salt, old friend of a few words and much wisdom? An old man, who spoke with her on a remote shore. No. Not yet.

As she watched, a couple of servants came hurrying out – a good sign of a house well run, this. She smiled, recognizing the familiar. Quick servants give cause to pause; more scurry, less hurry, as her mother would have said. They were girls of slightly less than her own age, coming up perhaps to marrying time, and were having a laugh as they bent to their task of carrying buckets of water. She rose on tiptoe to see. They pulled a wooden bung, as large as a human head, from a projection in the flintstone wall bordering the yard, and water gushed into a trough. They laughed, struggling to restore the pledget against the force of the water as soon as the trough had filled. They were a fraction too slow.

'You two shall have that water taken from your moneys!' a woman's voice called sharply, and they struggled all the harder, eventually managing to stem the flow.

'Please, Mrs Weaver,' one called back towards the house. 'The force be terrible strong this morning!'

'And some be terrible wasteful this morning!' the same voice chided. 'In future gauge ahead, stem the water a moment before the trough is filled. Don't dawdle like slatterns, the pair of you!'

'Yes, Mrs Weaver.'

The girls started filling their buckets. One glanced at the house surreptitiously, said something under her breath to the other. They both started a concealed giggling.

She withdrew from the window, reassured. A well-run house, this tavern, with contented girls and a wise tavern-keeper's wife. And one not so comfortably off she could afford to be prodigal with such vital considerations as water supplies, either. Or was this Mrs Weaver a widow lady? She knew of at least two taverns in Col . . . Well, in some

30

big town, not far away from Red Hall, where widow women kept taverns. And managed them very well too, in spite of their lacking a man to take on the burden of running the rougher element of the tavern trade, such as the redcoated soldiers piling in from the garrison at Abbey Fields on paydays. Heavens, but how they would rant and roar! She smiled, remembering how . . .

No. Gone again. She stood looking down at the truckle bed. No widow, this Mrs Weaver, if indeed it was she whose voice was so authoritative. For the bedclothes, as yet unmade, had held a man this night past. The indentations proved it, and the scent of the room reinforced her image of the taverner and his wife lying there still and huddled close, perhaps watching the girl taken from the sea sleeping on the floor pallet throughout the night. Her mother called it the Man Smell, that pervading gentle thickness of air. No widow had slept here, or a busy one.

The door opened behind her. She spun, drawing her shift about her. A young man stood there, with a woman in early middle age. He held a bag, leather and heavy. An apothecary? The woman wore an apron, her overskirt kirtled up on latches to allow freer movement while busy. The tavern, from this and the other clues, was already about its trade, and here was probably the formidable Mrs Weaver as proof.

'Good morning,' the man greeted her.

'You're better!' The woman was more relieved than pleased.

'Good morning, sir, ma'am.'

The girl didn't bob, Mrs Weaver noted, nor was she inclined to shrink away from them as they advanced into the small bedroom. And her voice, though local East Anglian cadence came through, was that of a woman who had held some position. No wedding ring, so presumably unmarried, though they did say that a person cast up from the North Sea was never the same again, was always short of something. Seafarers called it the sea tax. Perhaps the wild North Sea had taken its sea tax by sliding away her gold band.

'How do you feel, ma'am?'

'Very well, sir, thank you.'

'Then let me have a look at you, and . . .'

'Sir?'

'I do not wish to trespass against your modesty, ma'am, but I am the doctor who examined you last night, when you were brought in. Doctor Carmichael, at your service.'

'Last night?'

'Yes. You were brought ashore by *The Jaunty*, drawn from the sea. Do you remember anything of this?'

31

'No, sir. Only . . .' She passed a hand in front of her forehead, thinking of the voices, the faint glare of her brain's fever-light.

'This is Mrs Weaver, lady of the tavern here.'

'Ma'am. I must thank you, I can see, for your kindness in giving me a place to recover.'

'The least we could do, pet,' Mrs Weaver said. Her spirits were lifting with every passing moment. The young woman seemed to be of that class which people called 'local quality' – meaning not quite gentry, but solvent and significant in some district. That class was the backbone of commerce, land, farming, and besides was usually quite respectable. She was likely to prove no further expense to the Donkey and Buskin. And, who could tell? Perhaps she would be in a position to reimburse the tavern for the expenses already incurred.

'And to you, Doctor Carmichael, for your skill.'

'It was just a matter of clearing the ocean from your lights, ma'am, and returning that excess of sea to its proper place!'

'Might I inquire your name?' Mrs Weaver asked eagerly. 'We sought a means of identifying your family, but could find no purse or script.'

'I am . . . I am . . .'

'Please. Might she sit on the edge of your bed, Mrs Weaver? I can perform an examination without loss of the lady's dignity, if she will only sit with her back turned to me. It will take but a moment.'

'For sure, Doctor.'

They arranged the woman in a seated position, facing the door. Mrs Weaver moved away the candlestick and its flint lighter and wadding so she could be better placed to support the patient's body should she turn dizzy. Doctor Carmichael bent his ear, pressing it hard against her shift, then drew the clothing away from the skin with a murmured apology. He applied his ear to the skin of the young woman's back, listening.

'Breathe in as long as you can, please.'

He repeated the manoeuvre several times, alarming the woman somewhat when encroaching near her breasts, but finally he was satisfied and stood erect, nodding and signing to Mrs Weaver that the shift could be adjusted.

'Your lungs are not clear, ma'am, I'm afraid. They will take some five or six days to become restored to normality. However, they are less afflicted than I feared. I am relieved, and can give you a good prognostication. You should be fully recovered in a week's time.'

'A week's time?' Mrs Weaver said, trying to sound delighted.

'Not less, I'm afraid. But that is a cheap price to pay for a life recovered from drowning.'

'Drowning.' The young woman repeated the word, her eyes fixed on something distant through the wall. 'Drowning. Doctor, was any other soul brought in?'

'With you, you mean?' Doctor Carmichael turned to Mrs Weaver, shaking his head. 'No. We have not heard of any others being recovered – not in any state.'

'Was it a ship, dear?' Mrs Weaver urged her memory. 'Or were you on a mole, a wharf, a sea bank perhaps, and got taken by a wave?'

'I . . . I . . .'

'Don't try to recall everything, not at once. Things will come to you during the day.'

Carmichael took his bag to the bed and poured a tincture of ipecacuanha, estimating a dose of one and a half grains only. He made the woman take it, judging that the usual vehicle of white wine might set Mrs Weaver fretting at the further expense. It was swallowed, the patient's face grimacing at the taste. 'I have no lozenges, I regret to say. For protection of your lungs it might be expedient to give you some, in a three-grain dosage, but we shall have to manage without.'

He coloured slightly at the admission, and caught the young woman's assessing glance. He was not a fashionable doctor, not even in these parts on the coast. That much was obvious, for a more esteemed doctor would have apprentice physicians at his beck and call, carrying all types of drugs he might need and in virtually any quantity. Also, the tavern was not a rich establishment, for the Weavers would then be in possession of an apothecary chest, containing tinctures and powders in squared glass bottles, with the local apothecary calling to check every month or so on its stocks of drugs.

'A week, then, Doctor?' Mrs Weaver echoed.

'Not less. Then you will be able to return to your family . . .'

'Mehala,' the young woman completed for him, smiling in spite of the bitterness in her mouth.

Carmichael halted. 'Mehala?'

'Yes. Mehala.' The woman's expression was one of astonishment. It was her name, of a sudden, spoken by the doctor, and remembered by herself. It truly was her name. She was Mehala.

'Mehala. . . ?' Mrs Weaver encouraged eagerly. 'Your last name, my dear?'

'I don't remember,' Mehala said.

'Can't you just try?'

'I am trying, Mrs Weaver.'

Carmichael was watching Mehala's expression. There was a hint of stubbornness in her inflexion. She could remember far more than she wished, and immediately, if she wished. She was deliberately closing her mind to memories. There must be a great deal in her accident, her past, that she did not seek to bring to consciousness. Or to discuss with others.

'Your husband, Mehala?' Mrs Weaver pressed. 'Was he with you on the ship perhaps when. . . ?'

'I apologize, Mrs Weaver. I can remember nothing more.'

'Not even where you come from? Your father? Any members of your family? If you are married, in fact?'

'Nothing.'

Doctor Carmichael eased the slight tension in the bedroom by smiling, putting away his medicine and closing the worn leather bag.

'Very well. That should do for the moment.' He nodded. 'Let it be simply that, then, for the whilst. Just Mehala.'

'And thank you again, Doctor.'

'Not at all.' He gave her a smile. 'Good day, Mehala.'

The squire was noted for his heavy seat on a horse. He knew well that the grooms talked about his inability to ride well, but bore their side looks with great affability. His friend was less tolerant.

'I'd not tolerate their insolence, Henry,' Sir Trev Bunyan told him as they set out to ride the sea walls that same morning. 'If any man of mine gave me that, I should whip him from the stables and into penury.'

'It's their game, Trev. Don't fash yourself, please.'

'Game? *Game*, Henry? Is it a game when folk of that class up themselves to criticize their betters? That, sir, is the gravest insolence. And not only that, it is insolence against the law of God. We are placed in our social positions by God's will. He has seen fit to establish Quality in one status, and commoners in another.'

'Wasn't that decided quite oppositely once long ago, Trev?'

'When, sir?'

'Why, when the rebels executed King Charlie.'

'That's uncomfortable talk, Henry, and well you know it. That England invented the modern republic goes well forgot, even in the Americas and France where they perpetuate our wicked social innovation!' As distraction from the uncomfortable topic, Sir Trev pointed to the seashore which they were approaching along the cart track. 'Should we take that first dyke, perhaps make our way southwards, and take in the oyster beds?'

'You are a devil for those, Trev, and no mistake!' Hunterfield was laughing openly as he urged his horse along the track his friend indicated. 'But it might not be safe to carry away a bag of them, not yet.'

Sir Trev snorted. 'There are more superstitions over oyster eating than over wedding and bedding, Henry! I never stop eating pearly fish, and never a day's trouble have I had.'

'You've the constitution of an ox, Trev.' The squire gave his friend a glance. 'But is it your love of oysters which makes you suggest we take this route?'

'Why else? One sea wall is as good or as bad as another, Henry. Remember I am a townee born and bred. Once I step away from London I am lost.'

'I was thinking of Widow Maderley. You made quite an impression when last we rode this way. Or *she* did! Do you not remember? We called in to take a dish of tea with her.'

'I can't say I do.' Sir Trev hauled at his horse's mouth to prevent it shying as an otter splashed in a ditch beside the track. He cursed. 'This countryside of yours, Henry. I'm dashed if it isn't filled with surprises every single yard!'

Hunterfield laughed. 'No less than London, Trev. What with your gaming clubs, society, things they show on the stage nowadays. London strowed with rarities, eh, Trev?' It was one of Dean Swift's titles, in which he had ridiculed London's fashion for the spectacular.

Trev Bunyan got the allusion and laughed. 'Touché, Henry. But this widow. She wasn't that handsome lady who keeps the water millock? A place with some ornamental trees, near the wood?'

'Ah! You've remembered after all! Yes, beyond the sloping wood. Whitehanger, folk hereabouts call the wood. Some ivory figurine was excavated there in the past. It stands now in the museum at Norwich, I believe. And a hanger is, to us East Anglian residents, a wood. Some old language they still speak amongst themselves, in a sort of dialect.'

'See the smoke, Trev?' Hunterfield stood in his stirrups, halting his mare to see. 'The charcoal burners are at it already, so early! They usually wait until they are well into the day, for ease of lighting their fires.'

'So?' Trev asked. 'That's what they do, Henry.'

'Yes, but not often, Trev. They have the most amazing skill in keeping fires alight, for years at a time sometimes. My father used to tell of one old charcoal burner who kept his fire lit from his sixteenth birthday until he was sixty-five.'

Sir Trev laughed and shook his head, baffled by his friend's interest in such mundane matters. Over the sea marshes smoke was drifting,

35

the trees of the sloping wood in the distance clinging to the thin blue clouds in strands. 'For heaven's sake, Henry. I do swear you are turning yourself into a poet of some kind, with all this country living! It's time you came back to London, my friend. It might save your soul from this rurality!'

'Back to London? I wouldn't be tempted, Trev, and that's a truth. You manage our mercantilism there well enough for my interest, thank you.' He clicked his tongue.

The two horses started along the summit of the sea dyke, which was broad enough for most of its length to accommodate the pair. Sir Trev looked about.

'These must take every penny you possess, Henry.'

'The sea walls, you mean?' Hunterfield sighed. 'Yes. It isn't all rural gentility, Trev. Five times – five! – I've had to hire labourers from anywhere I could find, mending the damned things. They should be a government concern, if anything should!'

'And are they your responsibility, Henry?'

'Not mine proper, Trev. But what can you do? The rates can hardly bear the Poor Law costs, no matter what revisions the Acts lay down. And that ocean out there is a blight on the land, strange to say.'

'Isn't that a paradox, Henry?' Sir Trev caught at his hat, which was tugged by a quick gust. The wind was rising. 'As I see it, your Sealandings gains its money from the sea, mostly, and only a small part from the land.'

'True. But the sea costs lives, Trev. It takes them no matter what. Fine weather can be as treacherous along this coast as foul, and claim as many lives if it so desires. Also, there are good and bad sea harvests. Some days – weeks, even – there are no fish to be had, for reasons nobody is able to give.'

'But that is the Almighty's doing, Henry. We all must accept it.'

'Yes, Trev. But it comes harder each year, it seems to me. The sea walls broken down by a succession of gales. The land suffering sea floods in mighty spates, inrushes we haven't seen for generations.' He pulled his cloak round him as the dyke curved so that they were heading into the wind rather than riding broadside on.

'And you bear the expense?'

'Mostly, yes. I've appealed to the County itself to accept part of the burden, but it's a question of the land being spoiled for a succession of years, or setting to mending the dykes.'

'You need one of those Hollanders, Henry.'

'So I do, Trev, so I do.' Hunterfield sighed. 'The cost of those fellows is inordinate. They have such great skills, derived from their low flat lands. If my ship comes in, I might be speaking Dutch afore long!'

They laughed. They were coming in sight of the water mill now. The tide was incoming, with its silent approach slowly filling the great basin in the bay. Two men were checking the level, preparing the wide sea gates for closure once the peak of the tide was reached.

'There's Widow Maderley's mill, Trev,' Hunterfield said evenly. 'You remember, the one you don't remember!'

'Fortyish, brown hair done in a bun, pale face, talked of Doctor Johnson and London fashions, with a sound·knowledge of the French language? No, I don't remember a thing about calling there!'

They laughed at that. The dyke ran seaward from the apex of the water mill's catchment, and formed one wall of the basin. Inland, the dark rise of Whitehanger swelled the horizon and made the sky above it seem brighter, even a little bluish. They had a choice, to turn and pass the water mill, or to follow the common track round and so avoid it. Hunterfield reined in.

'Well, Trev? What's it to be? This way a feast of oysters, or that way a morning greeting of Widow Maderley?'

'Don't you mean her daughter?' Sir Trev asked innocently.

'Her daughter?' Henry shrugged, wryly realizing he had been taken by his friend. Perhaps Sir Trev Bunyan also was more interested in the widow's daughter Olivia than the lady herself? Perhaps to call on Olivia had been his purpose all along. Henry felt a little piqued.

'Yes. What's the name, now. . . ? Olivia, isn't it?'

'That's it, Trev,' Hunterfield replied evenly, and caught up his mount, guiding her down towards Widow Maderley's domain of Watermillock.

6

Letitia was walking, reading, by the summerhouse at Lorne, hoping to catch her brother and Sir Trev Bunyan on their return from riding the sea dykes, when she heard the argument between her sisters. Lydia was about to enter the carriage she had summoned when Tabitha came out of the portico. It was most unfortunate, because three of the Hunterfield servants were also well within earshot.

'Lydia?' Tabitha was able to make any name sound like an imperious question. 'Might I inquire where it is you are away?'

'Oh, just a short distance, Tabby.'

'To Mrs De Foe's, I take it?'

'As it happens, Tabby.' Lydia's acknowledgement was almost a rebuke.

'Without doing me the courtesy of extending the invitation?'

'Invitation, Tabby?' Lydia laughed, using her placatory laugh, Letitia noted. She could sense the coming battle, as surely as Lydia. 'It was a mere suggestion on Thalia De Foe's part as she took her leave last evening. Nothing so formal as an invitation.'

Tabitha flared. 'Yet you exclude me as a matter of course, Lydia Vallance!'

'Nothing of the kind!'

'Yes, you do. By taking the carriage while Henry is out, you make it a deliberate avoidance!'

'Goodness gracious, Tabby! Such a tantrum, and all on account of my taking the air to make a quick call on a neighbour!'

'You know very well I expressed my intentions of seeking Mrs De Foe's company at the earliest opportunity, Lydia! Yet you slyly make preparations to leave Lorne House without as much as informing me that you will be absent! I shall tell Henry the moment he returns!'

Letitia was upset. She moved away, quietening her feet on the gravel path so as to conceal her presence as eavesdropper. The tension between Tabitha and Lydia had grown all the more since Lydia's return to take over Lorne House, instead of easing into the warm sisterly relationship which she had hoped for. Of course, Lydia was a married woman and conscious of a whole new world of sight, sense, sound, human behaviour. Such was the broader, more experienced world of the married lady. But it was laid upon a younger sister, as a real familial duty, to show respect, acceptance of position, just as it was laid upon an older married sister to exhibit toleration and, occasionally, a little more charity than Lydia seemed to have. It was all very distressing.

Miserably she sat in the summerhouse, looking at its relatively poor state of repair. It was her favourite place, one with so many associations of childhood. The games they used to play here! She began to smile, remembering the days when Mummy would come and try to catch them, scurrying round among the seats while they squealed and shrieked! And then, sometimes, Papa would abruptly appear from the bushes, pretending the children were escaped animals, that he had been sent from London to catch them and put them in some menagerie! She bent her head to read, smiling. Escape into literature was the only sure means of making all the terrible new thoughts and challenges go away.

Josiah Baring went to the door himself before the sound of the bell had died away. He was barely into his house slippers after returning from conducting Morning Service. He was extremely displeased. Two crones at church, and some straying dog seeking its master from some neighbouring farm, and that was all the enthusiasm which Sealandings could summon in the interests of the Lord. Congregation? Not worthy of the name. Outrageous! What on earth did people think gave such ammunition to the Dissenters? What else but apathy drained life from the one true Church? And what else allowed the evil Catholics, Dissenters, Methodists, those cunning carping Puritans – who, by all accounts, were growing faster than any sect, being unhampered by wealthy bestial popes and established procedures – to increase their own hideous sects, but the unwillingness of the laity to even come to church and pray? It was all very dispiriting.

It was the doctor.

'Good morning, Doctor Carmichael.'

'Good morning, Rector.' Carmichael smiled a greeting, but the rector stood his ground and declined to offer him admission to the vestibule.

'Is there any way I could help you, Doctor?'

'Ah, indeed, Rector. If I may, could I request a moment's audience with Miss Baring?'

'A moment's audience, Doctor? It seems hardly worth putting you out of your way, this mere "moment". I trust it is of some importance, in spite of its brevity?'

'Indeed it is. At least, I think so. But it can be quickly communicated.' Carmichael waited, still smiling, but feeling his face taut. The rector of Sealandings was taking no pains to conceal his reservations about the medical profession.

'Might I speed your release by taking the message for you?'

'Very well, Rector. It is simply to say that – '

'Good morning, Doctor!'

Euterpe bustled along the hall and entered the vestibule to stand beside her brother. She had heard Carmichael arrive, but had waited as was proper in the withdrawing room until his presence should be announced. It was only by listening hard that she caught the change in his tone, and realized what was happening.

'I was fortunate to catch sight of you! I was just about to see to the upstairs rooms when I glanced – '

'Good morning, Miss Baring. I am rather in haste, I'm afraid.' Carmichael now felt the worst thing would be an invitation from Euterpe to enter and have coffee. Josiah Baring would show an even greater antagonism. He couldn't bear that.

'Oh, I am sorry. You could have come in.' Euterpe recognized the reasons for his reluctance and decided to give aid. 'Did you see the young lady this morning, if I may ask?'

'Yes. That was my reason for calling unannounced.'

'Is she recovered?'

'Yes. She is speaking. Her name is Mehala, but the circumstances of her being swept into the sea still escape her. I'm sure she would welcome a call from your good self, if you were able to give the time. There will be very little I can do from now on. It is simply a matter of time and her own adjustment to the ordeal.'

'Oh, I shall go this instant! Has she no recollection of her family, her location?'

'Not as yet. Mrs Weaver is still caring for her, thank heavens, though I don't know how long that arrangement can go on.'

'I thank you for having called, Doctor,' Reverend Baring cut in. This was becoming too habituated for his liking. Extended conversations between the two of them, in as many days! There was a risk of impropriety here, something which could not be tolerated. 'Come along, Euterpe. There are duties to perform before your jaunt to the village.'

'Very well, Josiah. Good morning, Doctor.'

'Good morning, Miss Baring. Rector.'

Euterpe stepped back as her brother closed the rectory door. She was

40

angry with herself rather than Josiah. She should have expected, as well as hoped, that Ven Carmichael would have called with news of the girl's progress, and kept watch for him somehow. It would not have been too difficult, for the bay window looked down towards the road which led to Shalamar, the doctor's house. The pity was it could not be seen from her position in the withdrawing room, for it stood at the crest of the slope where the London coach always struggled on leaving Sealandings.

Miserably she faced the prospect of the morning.

'I wish we could have offered Doctor Carmichael a seat for a few moments, Josiah,' she said lightly, trying to seem casual.

'How much time do we have to waste during a day, sister? I for one have very little.'

'It would have been a small gesture, Josiah.'

'Doubtless he too has work to do. I wish he would attend to it a mite more assiduously.'

'He works too hard, Josiah!' She corrected herself instantly: 'I mean *so* hard, of course. He is indefatigable. Everyone says so. In fact, I wish he wouldn't exercise himself so unrelentingly in his calling.'

'Calling? Euterpe, doctors are mere servants of the sick, the indigent, the poor, the ailing. That is hardly a calling, as you express it. A churchman has a calling. A grocer, a taverner, a ship chandler has a job, mere employment. As does a doctor.'

'That is hardly fair to . . . to the man, Josiah.' She was finding it increasingly difficult to keep control in the face of his obduracy. 'I'm sure almost everyone in Sealandings thinks highly of him.'

'Everyone in Sealandings is emotionally swayed, Euterpe. They should think with the brains God gave them, instead of letting emotional enthusiasms sway their minds.' He paused in the doorway of his study. 'I have letters to write, letters which, but for the doctor's pointless and time-wasteful visit, I would have practically finished by now. And, note, he has shifted to your shoulders the burden of looking after this old woman taken from the sea, instead of accepting that burden himself!'

'Josiah, that is unfair! I asked him to keep me apprized of her progress – '

'An invitation he accepted with unbecoming alacrity, Euterpe!' He saw her flush at the rebuke, which confirmed his suspicions. Was she being tempted perhaps to seek out that troublesome physician on her journey to the Donkey and Buskin? Women were always at risk, and had to be protected against themselves. In Euterpe's case, giving that

41

protection was his stern duty. 'Perhaps it would be wise if you were not to journey to the tavern this morning, Euterpe.'

'Oh, Josiah! I have promised. You heard me agree to – '

'No, I think it would be wiser for you to conform to our usual propriety, Euterpe. One visit to a tavern for the purpose of attending to this woman is quite enough.'

'I shall feel so bad about this, Josiah!'

'Then feel your regrets here in the rectory, Euterpe. Doctor Carmichael was able to reassure us that this Mehala woman is recovered. And Mrs Weaver is as capable as ever.'

'Yes, Josiah.'

'Now, let us speak no more of this. You have other duties, Euterpe, sufficient for the day.'

Euterpe thought of the old saying. Yes, brother, like evil. She went towards the kitchen where the maid-of-all was preparing drop cakes. This was simply not good enough. She ached from the confinement of the rectory, where a moment ago it seemed so free and filled with prospects.

Something had to be done now, with Josiah's approval or without. Of course, the clever thing would be to make him think he was the decider, when in reality she would do all the arranging. With a little thought it could be achieved, but it would have to be speedily. If not, she would explode.

Mehala savoured her new-old name. Then turned her attention to the clothes she had been given.

The kindness of Mrs Weaver! She had sent along one of the servant girls with a broadcloth skirt, oversize, and two moth-eaten petticoats. The new fashion of knickers had not yet reached the coast, though there was talk of it among ladies in London and the major cities, Mehala had heard. How uncomfortable it must be, to wear those short pantaloons underneath one's skirts! Even if, as was being murmured in East Anglia, it was true that the material of which these knickers were made was silk, or fine cottons. And of course they would inevitably be quite an expense.

Mrs Weaver had provided a pair of old flat calfskin slip-ons, another kindness, since at least two of the servant girls coming through the yard had been bareshod. There was no mirror in the small bedroom. Mehala tried combing her hair with her fingers, finally tying her tresses into a loose knot, giving it a single turn on her nape. No ribbon of course. She opened the door and descended, anxious and worried by the reception she might receive. The taverner might not be as accommodating as his kindly wife. She would ask of the dispositions to be made for her. Suddenly she wished Doctor Carmichael would return, simply be here while her fate was considered.

There was chatter coming from an open door as she came down into the wide hallway. She saw an ostler carrying horse tackle past the far door, which opened into the yard. Servants were preparing vegetables, clattering dishes, one calling breathlessly for help in carrying the copper to the fire. To the left was a closed door, heavy with a huge Suffolk latch, from which came the booming laughter of men at their victuals. She turned under the staircase and made for the rear of the ground floor. There might lie the taverner's place. How she knew this might be so she did not consider. She paused before a door which stood half ajar, and heard voices. Mrs Weaver, talking with her man.

'The girl – she's not much more than that, I'd say, husband – is better. Doctor Carmichael said so this very morning.'

'What is she, though?' A pleasant enough voice, slow and warm.

'She's a good enough looking creature, speaking well and deporting herself properly.'

'But she's recovered her name?'

'Mehala, she says. The poor thing cannot recollect her folks, her family, or her station in life.'

'Nor the ship she was lost from? Nor the ship she was brought on, either?'

'That's not the main difficulty, John. For us, we have her under our roof.'

'What then, Sarah Ann?'

'We must find a place for her, John. It isn't right for her to remain here. She's neither guest nor servant, nor is she any longer in need of our charity.'

'You mean we should turn her out?'

Mehala listened, stricken.

'Not in so many words, John. But we must try to speak with people, tell Squire Hunterfield of our plight, perhaps. Maybe send word for Reverend Baring to come and . . . well, give advice.'

'Or other magistrates?'

'Possibly that too, though I'd be reluctant to spread suspicion that Mehala was some sort of miscreant, John. She seems well brought-up, quite a lady in her way.'

'Miss Baring was here last evening, you said?'

'Indeed, and most solicitous.'

43

'Then we should see if Miss Baring comes. If not, call and ask her advice to find the girl a place. It can't be long before she remembers details of her family. Then we can send letters on her behalf.'

'Very well, John. I'll go by noon if Miss Baring fails to call.'

'And don't put too fine a point on it. Make it quite plain that you are seeking guidance from the Christian lady. We must not seem overhasty to get rid.'

'Yes, John.'

Mehala pressed herself against the plaster wall, aghast. This was truly dreadful. She was being spoken of as a liability, a burden – something she had never been – and she only lately plucked from the sea! The shame of it made her eyes fill. It wouldn't have happened to a dog, back in Red Hall, on the coast where the small island rose from the sea marshes glistening all about . . .

'Come in, Mehala!'

Mrs Weaver had opened the door, carrying some linen, and seen her. Behind, John Weaver was seated at a long oaken table, finishing a plate of cold meat and bread. He was a large, broad man with a stocky frame. He wore a thick canvas apron and looped around his waist was a thick coil of rope, the typical trick of the taverner. It would be used should any of the regulars became so drunk that they became rabbish and started damaging the wattle-and-daub walls of the tavern or smashing the drinking vessels in argument.

'John, here's our rescued Mehala.'

'Good morning, sir. And I thank you for your kindness in giving me protection and a place to rest.'

John Weaver looked up at the woman in the doorway, framed against the gloom of the passageway.

She was beautiful, in spite of her dishevelled appearance and the ungentle clothing. Black hair, brown eyes, a startled look about her which was possibly the result of finding herself in a strange place, not really knowing who she was. Even motionless she had a smooth, gracious quality. She seemed a centre of stillness, yet within there seemed to exist a core of reserved warmth.

'Yes, well.' He cleared his throat. 'Good morning to you, ah, Mehala. It was the least we could do. Our Christian duty. Anyone along these coasts would have done at least that.'

'That's not true, Mr Weaver, saving your presence. There's many along these shores would have left a soul in the sea, and not given shelter even if she was washed in by the tide and her life depended on help.'

44

'That's true, Mehala.' His eyes wrinkled in question. 'You know the coast, then?'

'I . . . I only surmise, Mr Weaver.'

'But your surmise is correct, Mehala. It sounds to me as if you can't have come very far from your wetting.'

'I can't say, Mr Weaver.'

'We shall send along the coast to ask of any ship foundered, Mehala, or ask after some young lady being washed out to sea.'

'It's quite possible that you come from quite near here,' Mrs Weaver said eagerly, displeased inwardly by the light Mehala's appearance had created in her husband's eyes. 'Wasn't there that terrible case not too long ago of that young girl who was taken by the sea at Blakeney in Norfolk? And she only gone walking, barely two hundred yards from her father's house!'

'Yes, Sarah Ann, and no storm.'

'As the night that Mehala was recovered, John.'

'Mr Weaver. I repeat my thanks to you for your charity. I shall be mindful of it ever. Yet I do not wish to be a burden, either of expense or industry. I shall make an attempt to discharge any obligations towards you. May I perform some duties at your home, until such time as I may recover my mind and be in a position to repay your kindness more substantially?'

'There's no need to speak like this, Mehala,' John Weaver said. His wife jumped in quickly.

'It *would* perhaps be better for you to start some sort of work, Mehala,' she said as if thinking deeply about the matter. 'It might act as a restorative, help your recovery all the more.'

'That's exactly my meaning, Mrs Weaver. Now, how may I assist?'

Thalia De Foe welcomed Lydia Vallance with ostentatious pleasure, accompanying her into the great parlour of Milton Hall and speaking extravagantly of the reception at Lorne House she had enjoyed the previous night.

The ladies settled beside a small table on which silverware was laid in preparation for tea. Ratafias and sweetmeats were brought as they made small talk. The housekeeper, an elderly lady with a London accent, ceremoniously unlocked the tea caddy on the heavy side table, and used the decorative silver spoon to dispense the exact amount.

'You must come more often, Mrs De Foe,' Lydia said. 'I regret that it was such a small gathering, but Sir Trev Bunyan does tend to arrive at short notice!'

45

'I enjoyed it all the more,' Thalia said. The housekeeper and the maids having withdrawn, she risked her invitation. She had been planning it for days. 'Might I be so bold as to ask if you would grace me by using my given name, Mrs Vallance?' She made a gesture of familiarity, to link her guest with herself. 'I feel that we have become more than simple acquaintances, and we never were merely neighbours.'

'How very kind and condescending, Mrs De Foe!' Lydia felt a fleeting twinge of annoyance at the expression Mrs De Foe had used. Certainly, from her own knowledge this woman had become far closer to one in her family than any mere neighbour had right to be. 'I shall be delighted.'

'You are very gracious.'

'And may I in return invite you to a like expression of friendship?'

'I am thrilled, Lydia.'

'Thank you, Thalia.'

The hostess had told the maids that she herself would pour, which meant that something more was coming, Lydia thought. This woman did nothing without an ulterior motive. She herself was here for a specific reason, and would see that she received a fair hearing.

'In fact, I was wondering if I might have your assistance in a personal matter,' Thalia De Foe began, as if making a grim announcement.

'Of course. Anything I can do . . .'

'It's that I feel it incumbent upon me to organize some small entertainment, perhaps a ball. On a very meagre scale of course, but definitely one in which celebration will be the theme.'

'How marvellous! I shall be thrilled to assist in any way I can.'

This meant the most extravagant ball the neighbourhood was ever likely to experience, Lydia recognized with despair. She smiled, as if enthralled at the idea, but felt sickened. The De Foe woman would be on her home ground, as Henry would have expressed it vulgarly. Which meant her machinations would be difficult to counteract, and brother Henry would be more vulnerable than ever. She knew immediately that she had stupidly fallen into the trap of agreeing to support the function before knowing quite what was in Thalia's mind.

'I shall hold you to it, Lydia,' Thalia warned, smiling.

'I shall be extremely sad if you don't!'

'Will your sisters be able to come?' Thalia queried.

'I shall certainly enlist their help, with your permission, and would be very cross with both of them were they to demur.'

Which means only perhaps, Thalia registered. Oh, well, so far she had gained without loss.

46

'Will your function be soon, Thalia?'

'In a fortnight, or three weeks, Lydia. I shall have to see. What with the political hustings taking place soon, I shall have to take care they don't provide a distraction.'

'Very wise. I do hope Henry will be free.'

'Oh, but he must be, Lydia! Can't you persuade him that attendance is absolutely essential?' Thalia spoke brightly.

You have more influence with Henry than I ever shall, my lady, Lydia said inwardly. She nodded and returned the smile.

'I shall do my utmost, Thalia. Meanwhile, I shall enlist your assistance in a similar matter, if you are able to give it.'

'Able?' Thalia De Foe cried, in mock outrage. 'Why, Lydia! I insist on helping in every possible manner!'

'I knew you would, Thalia,' Lydia said sweetly. 'And I am so relieved to have your assurance.'

'Relieved, Lydia?' For the first time Thalia felt a vague unease, wondering if overconfidence had caused her to make a mistake.

'Yes, very definitely relieved, for I know that you view Letitia as somewhat too reticent for her own good, and – '

'Letitia?' Thalia echoed, startled.

'Yes. I had lately wondered how you would view helping to arrange a meeting between Letitia and your cousin at Bures House. Now that I know, I must confess I am delighted to know I can rely on your assistance.'

'My cousin Charles Golding?'

'Indeed. Not for any unworthy purpose, of course, but merely to effect an introduction on a more formal plane than hitherto. I believe Mr Golding shares Letitia's liking for poetics, prose works, the written word.' Lydia smiled, sipping at her cup. 'Henry says that Mr Charles Golding made such an excellent scholar up at Cambridge that he has never recovered from the experience!'

They laughed merrily at the wit. Thalia however was recording with annoyance the mention of Henry Hunterfield in the same breath as her cousin Charles, and realized that she had for once been out-manoeuvred. If she was now to default in carrying out Lydia's wish, and fail to arrange a meeting between Charles and that wretched mouse of a girl Letitia – hopeless in every way, and obviously quite unsuitable for Charles whichever way you saw it – then clearly Lydia would somehow prevent her brother Henry from attending the ball. And she had personal as well as political reasons which made Squire Hunterfield's attendance nothing short of compelling.

'Then I am only too glad that we have become even closer friends than hitherto,' Thalia said gushingly. 'This has been a most fortunate and auspicious meeting, Lydia.'

'Hasn't it, Thalia?' Lydia said sweetly. 'This is simply the best tea I have ever tasted.'

'You're so kind, Lydia.'

They exchanged fond smiles over the rims of their teacups.

7

Katherine Maderley saw the two horsemen approach. She smiled, having heard the night previously that Sir Trev Bunyan was to Lorne House for supper. She knew they would ride out this way. For one brief moment she wished she were out in her small millock garden, wearing her pelisse and her leghorn hat showing how graceful she could seem in the correct circumstances, among the roses with her coloured straw trug half-filled, but put the arrogant thought aside. She was a widow, for heaven's sake! And so much older than either of the gentlemen, who would probably hardly pause. In spite of that caution, she was near the door with her maid Harriet as Squire Hunterfield and Sir Trev rode up. They were taking in the operation of the watermill gates, Squire Hunterfield as ever standing high in his stirrups to check the progress of the incoming flood.

'Good day to you, Mrs Maderley,' he called. Sir Trev smiled and half bowed his salutation from the saddle.

'And to you both, sirs.'

They reined to. Widow Maderley noticed that Sir Trev was glancing round at the mill house itself rather than showing interest in the tide gates. Her Olivia was on his mind, she guessed.

'The operation of your tide mill never ceases to interest, Widow Maderley,' the squire said. 'How ingenious of its builders to gauge the inrush with such precision! And how very skilled you are to control household and workmen together!'

'You are kind, sir. Would you be pleased to grace us with your presence, take some refreshment? I should be honoured.'

'No, thank you, Mrs Maderley. We are about to ride beyond Whitehanger to observe the shipping in the sea lanes towards the Blackwater and the south.'

Sir Trev bit back a comment of surprise. This had been no part of their plan. And the mill mistress had clearly used the plural 'us', which meant that for absolute certain Olivia Maderley would be indoors still, rather than out sitting beside her lunatic brother while he painted those blessed irritating pictures of nothing but countryside and trees. Sir Trev resolved to express his annoyance to Henry as soon as they rode from the mill grounds. What on earth was the man thinking of?

'Yes, Squire. I too heard the news. Was it a ship which foundered off the Forestall Sands? Or merely some boat? Wreckage shows most quickly by the speight, near Whitehanger's promontory, if that was the case.'

'We do not yet know. But the woman is recovered, I learned today. At the Donkey and Buskin with the Weavers.'

'Praise be to God!'

'Amen, ma'am.'

She bobbed a curtsey as Hunterfield touched his hat and pulled the mare's nose round. Sir Trev did likewise, glancing at the mill house.

Olivia was at the window, seemingly sewing. Her gaze was interrupted by the passage of the two riders out of the mill house gate. Sir Trev raised his hat to her. Correctly she made no sign in return, but quickly bent to her needlework, more to show he was observed than to make progress. She had seen him smile in recognition, which was something.

She watched them break into a canter on the upward slope from the gates, following them finally by rising to see which road they took. Left, following the coast. They would miss William, therefore, for he was at the canal lock gate, painting the horses which today would be used for dragging the timbers into the turning-pool above the small weir. She knew William would be disappointed too, for he was aching to ask Squire Hunterfield about Letitia.

'Our fortune, and sometimes our wishes, Olivia!'

Her mother came into the room. Olivia sat abruptly and quickly resumed her work.

'Fortunes and wishes, Mother?'

'Both seem bound up with the Hunterfields more and more. This is my meaning.'

'I'm sure I do not understand. Squire Hunterfield's call here was a perfectly natural incidental of the day. It is his road to Whitehanger, after all.'

'You heard the gentlemen, then, Olivia,' her mother said dryly.

Olivia flushed. 'It was unavoidable, Mother.'

'I mean his frequent riding by, whenever Sir Trev Bunyan is down for the week from London. That and William's frequent painting at the canal not far from Lorne House. All of this is a little too coincidental for my preference.'

'Wishes may be misconstrued, Mother. And as for fortune – '

'Make no mistake, daughter. Fortune is a fickle goddess.' Mrs Maderley sat beside her daughter to gaze out at the tidal flood. Soon the men would have to start the gates' slow closure, to take up the heavy burden of catching the flood in the great basin, to use its slow release for powering the mill.

'Fortune? In the context of the Hunterfields. . . ?'

'Squire Hunterfield is a good man, child. A very able and good man. *Naturally* good, not coined on Sunday. Think who we could have had for chief magistrate. Not all gentry in the Eastern Hundreds are as condescending as Hunterfield. He speaks with a widow. He understands the locals. Why, even the workmen he greets of a morning! He considers the sea dykes. The canals are blessed by his attention. He gave relief in the Storm Winter, not long ago.'

'He is the fortune of which you speak?'

'Indeed.' Mrs Maderley gazed steadily at Olivia, who avoided her mother's eyes and frowned, attending to a troublesome detail of her stitching. 'And I should hate to see the squire disturbed in some way. In any way.'

'Why do you tell me this, Mother?'

'I am reluctant to say it to William directly, as he is head of the family since your father went. I noticed that Squire Hunterfield praised my abilities to control the household and the mill in one. He knows very well that William is too enwrapt in his paints and canvases to concern himself with any duties here. It is his way of warning that the day must come soon when William must attend to more manly pursuits.'

'You me wish to convey this to William?'

'Yes, if you will. But there is no immediate haste.' Widow Maderley gazed out of the window, thinking. 'They took the sea road, so should not encounter William. For today at least.'

She paused, looking closely at Olivia's embroidery, and tutted irritably. 'Olivia. An embroidered border in Chinese single face must be *entirely* in unshaded flat stitch. Have you taken leave of your senses, my girl?'

'But it is . . .' Olivia held it up to the light. Mrs Maderley tapped her daughter's head in reproof.

'Directions of the stitches, girl! Directions of the stitches! Haven't you the sense you were born with?'

'I can conceal it in reversing the next section, Mother.'

'You most certainly can *not*! Olivia Maderley, you will do it properly! You will unpick that part this instant! That's the trouble with your generation, always hasting and never thinking.'

Olivia sighed. 'Yes, Mother.'

She woke in torment. Moisture clung to her body. Her face was bathed in heat and sweat. Her heart thumped, pounded, tore almost at her chest as if striving to burst through her body. She felt stifled, disoriented in utter panic. She stared about in terror.

The firelight. The kitchen. The shadows, flung gentle as silence round the walls of the long room. The reflections from the skillets, the pans, the copper instruments, the flat matt shapes of the treen, the irregularities of the wattle-and-daub walling, the faint hiss from the fire as one log caught up the fire's flame in its resin.

She recognized the tavern, and felt a sense of peace. From upstairs, a faint thumping, doubtless one of the travellers at heavy night business with one of Nellie's serving maids. That was inevitable. The tavern's normality signalled to her that all was well. Tranquillity. The Donkey and Buskin was a place of peace. Turmoil, yes, and busy, what with the comings and goings and the coaches and the carters and waggoners and the fish barrels and the laden carts being whipped along the toll roads from Sealandings, but essentially peace.

The thought calmed her, made her wonder at the sort of place she must have come from, if this household's maelstrom seemed the height of tranquillity. The dream. She had been having a dream.

Of what?

She heard Nellie, the head servant for the taprooms, snoring faintly. Little Jane slept hard by. The oldest servant in the place, Alice, usually occupied the inglenook. Mrs Nelson the cook was given a pallet in an upstairs alcove by a landing, when the tavern was crowded and all the bedrooms were needed for travellers. Otherwise she slept in an upstairs cot, in a room adjoining that of John and Sarah Ann Weaver. Peace.

But the dream.

It had been of a flat expanse of sea marsh, where the wind blew with erring constancy, tugging and pushing its spray into the face and clothes. An island, and, most strangely, between it and the mainland a causeway that was overflowed at high tide. And a hard, very like that of Sealandings, but much more remote and unpopulated, a mere gravelly stretch where boats could be drawn up from the sea.

And, her memory hazing fast as the dream receded, a copious spring of water on the very hard itself, but which was also overflowed at high tide. And row boats plying between the hard and an estuary, to . . . to . . . to a village, of seafaring people who kept themselves as taciturn and mistrustful as the Lord had made them.

So why did she wake in fear?

There was no answer, for the fading nightmare had shown her

glimpses, pictures as fleeting as the sea wind itself. They were dull in simple appearance, but overlay a menace which had been the cause of her distress.

The island — how did she know it was an island? The island ran seawards for a mile, in the form of mere mud flats. Nearer the actual land itself, the clay — heavy, thick, glutinous clay which clung to the soles and made walking a fatiguing labour — had been dug out so as to form a sea wall on the landward side. This had left a great ditch between the dyke and the sea flats. The channel so caused was filled with decaying marine matter, vegetable and animal, and its intolerable stench was almost stifling. She could almost smell it now, as she lay on her pallet looking at the ceiling shadows. The mosquitoes humming in the ear, clouding the air in a long line following the course of the stinking channel . . .

Between the island and the mainland she remembered a low remote and lonely tract of marsh, with dykes to hold back the sea, channels and runs of mud and water, where the wildfowl and the ague could both be caught together. There, gentlemen and people of the locality shot their flintlocks and harvested great numbers of birds.

But where?

She remembered seeing punts, long low boats with a prow gun, the whole vessel painted grey for concealment, where hunters lay in wait for the wildfowl to alight in numbers on the open stretches of water. When the east wind blew on to the sea marshes, wild duck and geese came in flocks and skittered on to the surface, to their doom. Flock upon flock . . .

Another image flashed before her.

The women and children, skirts kirtled up at the waist, crossing the desolate mud flats, collecting . . . collecting what? Grubbing from the dark sea sands along the line where the sand became mud, collecting . . . winkles! She almost chuckled aloud at the memory as the pictures found words. She felt restored.

And in order to walk on the wet glutinous clay they wore flat boards cut into ovals under their soles, braced tightly with latchings of leather strip or rope over the instep and about the ankles. Walking or gliding on them, they stooped to collect the molluscs into a basket held in the left hand. The times she had smiled with sympathy, when another girl nearby had slipped and fallen! As, truth to tell, she herself had done so many times . . . For then the adhesive clay held you fast by the arms! She found herself smiling. Mud boards, they called them. Then her memory faded, as mind took over.

So she was of a local place, perhaps somewhere not too far? She too had searched for winkles along the sea lands, worn mud boards, and been a part of the local people, working with them.

Inaccessible, almost, her island had been. The roads were intolerable, for she knew somehow that she was familiar with the great rutted tracks which passed for roads in the area . . .

She found herself dozing fitfully. Here in the warm kitchen, the girls breathing around her, the air was pure if thick with the engendered heat.

There, though, there on the island, there were still more stenches, for great barges were brought up carrying 'London muck', as they called it locally, for the purpose of manuring the fields both on the island and across in Peldon beyond the sea marshes where the land rose towards the woods . . . London muck, horrid in its foul offensiveness, the street sweepings and the night soil, wafting stink across the entire place . . .

Seaward of the church, in the east village of the island's two, a sort of landing stage had been built, though only of wood on account of the dearth of local stone. Coal barges thus came to the island, and the muck.

She smiled in returning slumber's peace. Another dressing to manure the fields was that of sprats. Then the seagulls would come in great flocks, and the village boys were hired to scare them away with rattles, horns and drums, a pandemonium which, with the shouting and noise, was always a great spectacle and one which small girls greatly enjoyed as they cajoled their little friends and relatives to greater din . . .

The barges took away hay and straw for London, that Great Wen which lay south along the coast . . .

. . . And the mosquitoes, swarming about the trees in autumn so the very branches seemed to be on fire and smoking in the low slanting sun's haze . . .

The kitchen. This place with its clean air. That had set her reminiscing, her mind falling free in its unguarded moment . . . The rooms would have been laurel-scented, for laurel leaves were always placed thickly on the fire's red-hot coals to drive insect pests from each bedroom . . .

And the summer evenings when she had bathed in the fresh-water channels . . . And the harmonium in the moated church, where the sea wind, ever present, added its constant moaning in the iron stove's flue pipe. And the stove cowl squeaked and groaned to the amusement of the children of the island of Mersea, by the Blackwater and the Colne where she had lived and married . . .

She slept the sleep of oblivion.

8

Market day at Sealandings was a competition. The sea folk on the one hand, the land people on the other, and all vying for the small excess of circulating coin. Not only that, but people came from as far as ten, twelve miles on foot, bringing their wares in hopes of sales. Geese were walked from the fen country further north-west, tinkers and haberdashers brought goods, and wandering knitters would fashion a pair of socks while you waited and chatted.

Mehala was quite excited to be summoned to accompany Mrs Weaver, now more as a servant than in any other guise.

As they walked from the Donkey and Buskin, Mrs Weaver's curiosity about Mehala was roused even more. She found herself watching the girl for clues as to her origin. Was she a married woman? Was she single? Was she a lady, or someone strayed from some august home, someone she herself would be proud to have under her roof? There were times when the girl seemed too physical, too capable in too many ways, displaying skills that only servants knew. At other times she seemed so brisk, capable of even appreciating the coarser elements of life. Mrs Weaver believed she had the measure of Mehala. Almost.

Then, inexplicably, there would be times when her whole assumption was wrong, the girl utterly confounding her by some easy grace, a hint of knowledge of finer ways, grander living, a trace of authority that suggested Mehala had lived in some relatively exalted state.

And John Weaver had got word from the coastal shippers, north and south respectively as far as Maldon and the Wash, that no ship had lately foundered, no local ships had left for the Antipodes, and no poor woman had flung herself over the gunwales in despair at being parted from her homeland. Not that day, nor the preceding night. And the packet ships from Harwich to the Hook of Holland, John Weaver had further learned, had miraculously not lost a single soul this week.

'We must buy well, for the travellers will come a- plenty to the coming fair, Mehala,' Mrs Weaver said as they made their way among the hurrying Sealanders, along the wharfside to cut across the hard towards the gathering market. 'In Sealandings it's necessary to be early, for the market folk know their livestock and produce intimately. It gives the best choice, you see.'

'Yes, Mrs Weaver. Very wise. However, is it not sensible on market days to delay purchasing until the pace at which goods are being sold can be carefully gauged?'

So! She had bought for quite a large household, Mrs Weaver thought. But has had to watch the farthings. And she is not afraid to speak her mind, even when partially contradicting one such as I. Another clue to status?

'It is, Mehala. But sometimes delay means that prime meats, the best geese, the most solid root vegetables, are gone when you are finally prepared to buy. It's a matter of fine judgement, and one to which you should always attend.'

'Yes, Mrs Weaver.'

'Here is Reverend Baring, Mehala! It is to his sister, Miss Baring, that you are indebted for kindness in coming to help when you were brought in.'

Reverend Baring was standing at the corner of the gateway into St Edmund's Church, having seen Mrs Weaver approach. He raised his hat and bade the ladies a good morning.

'May I introduce Mehala to you, Rector?' Mrs Weaver made to edge the girl forward with a touch on the elbow, but was surprised to find that Mehala had withdrawn rather than advance to be introduced.

'Mehala?' she prompted.

'Good day, Rector. How do you do?'

Mrs Weaver coloured slightly. She had never seen Mehala so reticent, in the brief sojourn at the Donkey and Buskin. 'Mehala is not quite herself as yet, Rector,' she quickly interposed.

'I quite understand,' the rector intoned, scrutinizing the girl. 'It is not easy for anyone to recover from such an ordeal. You are very welcome in Sealandings, Mehala. I hope and pray that you will soon recover all your faculties and be reunited with your family.'

'Thank you, Rector.' Mehala still shrank slightly.

'We are just out to buy provisions against the fair, Rector.'

'Quite a task, Mrs Weaver.'

Josiah Baring kept his eyes on Mehala as he spoke. The girl was beautiful, even though her dress was old and patched, and her borrowed shoes worn to the welts. Her hair was raven, but occasionally trapped a deep russet light from the sunlight as she moved. Her eyes were brown, flecked with a darker umber speck to point the brilliant white in which the irises were set. He came to, aware that the publican's wife was waiting for him to continue. 'Yes, my sister Miss Baring is already assaying her fortunes among the market stalls. I'll let you get on, Mrs Weaver.' He raised his hat, more to Mehala now than the publican's wife. As they made to walk on, he ahemmed to call their attention. 'May I inquire what dispositions have been made for Mehala, ma'am?'

'That is being considered presently, Rector. I spoke with my husband and he was of a mind to tell me to seek advice from Miss Baring, should that be permissible.'

'I should be very pleased to allow that, Mrs Weaver.'

'Thank you, Rector.' They bobbed a curtsey and moved towards the market ground.

Sarah Ann was pleased with herself. She had accomplished almost before the start of the day what John Weaver had asked. The quicker the girl was found a place somewhere, the better things would be. She had not missed noticing the effect that Mehala had had upon the staid and bookish clergyman. In fact, that same effect seemed to be the common lot of all men in Sealandings, for drovers, complete strangers from as far as Wheatfen thirty miles away, were staring impudently at Mehala as they were arriving with their livestock.

Now to look out for Miss Baring, and raise the matter instantly.

'Isn't our rector a fine upstanding gentleman, Mehala?' she asked.

'Indeed he is, Mrs Weaver.'

'There's some as think him a little High Church for these parts, but that's only to be expected, for Low Church predominates sore around East Anglia. But he is known for his kindly condescension. And he is very well connected, educational like. He is from Cambridge, you know. He has degrees in religion.'

'Indeed, ma'am,' Mehala said in a small voice. 'That is the way the clergy get to heaven, I have heard – by degrees!'

Mrs Weaver was quite some time working out Mehala's rejoinder. But the time she had, they were in the thick of the market and she had no time for mild amusement based on mere words.

The market square was nothing as grand as its local name suggested. It was a muddy space, set at a junction of roads in the centre of the small town. On one side stood the Corn Market, an enclosed rectangle of ancient wood with a heavy beamed roof. It had served Sealandings as a refuge, a prison, a fever hospital and as a storm shelter. Now, it was the mundane area where the folk of Sealandings stood out of the rain when the weather was inclement on market days. There was often talk of some benefactor raising a second storey on its superstructure, perhaps to house an improved counting house, but no progress in this was ever made, for want of money.

On the west, inland, side stood the small school where Miss Matilda Gould ticked off her middle years and saw the generations round in the little faces attending in their smocked garments. Houses, mostly of seafaring folk and occasional land workers, stood on the south side facing the slightly larger houses on the north side of the square. On the west the churchyard sloped up to St Edmund's Church, the rectory alongside beyond a small yew hedge. Mehala could see that the township was a straggle, rather than a compact coherency, not at all like *Colchester*! Colchester, with its ruins of a castle, a tree growing with great eccentricity from its despoiled single tower.

She paused as Sarah Ann hesitated at the first stalls. Yes, she knew Colchester, high on its ancient hill with spires set all around the jagged castle outline, the river . . . the River *Colne*! Curling round the foot of St Peter's Hill – no, *North* Hill, with the mill at the bottom on the road to . . . to Bures, Sudbury, St Edmundsbury.

'It's a good market place, Mehala, I think you'll agree?'

'So it is, Mrs Weaver. I am very impressed.'

'You see over there, on the far side? The market barrows and stalls are allowed in front of the school on market days. The waggons must wait against the lychgate along the churchyard hedge. The trouble there's been about those in the past! I can tell you that incomers with their heedless ways can cause a spate of argument!'

'That is always the case, Mrs Weaver.'

'Have you experienced similar arguments, Mehala?'

'I cannot remember, ma'am.'

'Pity. Never mind. The way you are beginning to speak, total recollection should not be far away.'

'I shall remember your kindnesses and courtesy always, ma'am, whatever the condition of my memory, now or hereafter.'

Mrs Weaver felt that the girl seemed abstracted, almost distant in her behaviour. Then out she would come with some remark like that, which made the emotions well in the breast. And it was entirely without artifice, born of a natural innate quality which made this girl something special, over and above the rest of the people she herself knew round Sealandings. It was that indefinable yet lovely simplicity which made men stare, brought the heads of the women warily round as if to inspect some new challenge.

Occasional cattle were lowing in the cattle pens along the northern exit from the square. Mrs Weaver saw Mehala looking, smiling a partly concealed smile. Were the herds rousing some vague memory trying to gain release?

'The squire got agreement to permit the enclosure of a piece of common land along that there Norwich road – a grand name for a narrow cart track with many a league full of deep ruts before it winds into Norwich!'

'For a cattle market?'

'Yes. It is a very blessing. Before, the creatures would even run amok, here in the square! Now they are at least decently penned up before they can do their marauding. And anyone interested in a sheep – as we, Mehala, later – can go and make their talk with the farmers. They do nothing but smoke round their waggons and drink mulled ale sent over by the Goat and Compass.'

'Perhaps they can afford the tavern's prices, Mrs Weaver?'

'They? Not to listen to them, Mehala. Market days, that Ben Fowler and his wife at the Goat puts up his prices by as much as a penny a pint! And him supposed to be a god-fearer!'

'Perhaps we should supply those farmers, Mrs Weaver!'

'*We?*' Mrs Weaver paused, looking at the waggons trundling down into Sealandings from the Norwich road. There was lively custom to be had over there, right enough, but the Goat and Compass traditionally was the tavern which supplied that part of the market. Her John had been despondent about this when the cattle market had been established.

'Yes, ma'am. I'm sure that Mr Weaver would be pleased to set the Goat and Compass by its ears.'

'You're a sharp young lady, and no mistake!' Mrs Weaver nodded to Mehala, indicating that she should sit with her on the low wall along one side of the Corn Market. 'But it cannot be. The Goat is the nearer, and Martha Fowler guards her prerogative so jealously, that she's said never to sleep on market eve! She drives her maids and servants without mercy, that they'll all be in good time for the first drovers and carts. We should have to get up earlier than the stars above to take a leap on the Fowlers!'

Mehala sat, observing the growing bustle as townsfolk emerged and mingled with the stallholders. It was a fresh, rather windy, day with the sea scudding up its small white horses out near the horizon, but causing little more than a choppiness nearer to the shore. It was the usual sea in this kind of wind, here in East Anglia. Heavens above, but she had seen the pattern often enough, at this hour in the morning, off Mersea . . .

Island!

Mersea Island. That was home. That must be the place where Red Hall stood, louring and grim against the low sedge marshes and the stark wet saltings. That must be the place where he had taken her first, where her origins lay. Whence she had been taken in the boat to drown with him, the madman laughing as the boat sank in the sea drift.

Its name *felt* home. Not homely, but home. She bit her tongue in an effort to prevent herself speaking aloud of her new-found memory. And succeeded. She forced herself into a semblance of composure, and said, 'Perhaps, ma'am, with respects to the master and your good self, it might be worth while to examine what power these Goat and Compass Fowlers have over the waggoners there today? And make observations which might determine what hour might be auspicious for rising *next* market day?'

'You cunning madam!' Mrs Weaver laughed in spite of herself. 'Are you suggesting we should set to war with the Fowlers?'

'Far be that unworthy thought from me, ma'am,' Mehala said, smiling meekly in return. 'I express willingness to take over that duty, were you to think that I could thus repay your kindness.'

Mrs Weaver was still laughing when three servants started making their way down Blakeney Road towards the market. They accompanied a small cart, the three maids walking after. The cart was driven by a large aggressive lady in a mobcap, her kissing ribbon end caught up into her mouth, there to be chewed.

'Here they come, Mehala! Now you shall see why the course you propose is out of the question!'

The three girls were buxom and businesslike. They came chattering, eyes everywhere, calling pert rejoinders to such of the drovers as made a comment to them. The driver flicked her whip at the beast, hauling at the reins. The two wheels sank into the ruts, making it difficult for the animal to haul the cart along. The woman's gaze lit upon Mrs Weaver and Mehala on the wall, and she gave a cadaverous grin, rather than a smile. Mehala felt chilled.

'You see, child?' Mrs Weaver said quietly, steadfastly looking elsewhere. 'That is the woman of the Goat and Compass. Those are her three harridans, two of them her own daughters. She rules that tavern with a rod of iron, and her husband's as bad. They gain their brews from inland, they say, but the oceans out there know better.'

'Smuggling is an honest trade, if you know the right Excise men,' Mehala said. She was aware of Mrs Weaver's stir of astonishment, and quickly added, 'I've heard people say that, I am certain. Though it is a terrible risk, and most dangerous and immoral.'

'I am glad to hear your qualification, Mehala,' Mrs Weaver said tartly. 'There's too many folk on this earth think they can earn an honest penny from a dishonest farthing! And look you at those girls of hers. They have *fought* other women – and men on occasions – and not come out the worse! The Fowlers are an inbred lot, and best avoided.'

'They should be challenged, Mrs Weaver, in spite of their reputation.' Mehala turned innocent eyes on the taverner's lady. 'Isn't that what the Duke of Wellington always considered his prerogative when he faced a similar threat?'

'Well, I never did!' Mrs Weaver laughed, then checked herself when she saw the tax cart roll toward the livestock pens. Mrs Fowler was looking back, staring hard at Mehala. Her three servants were also looking their way, talking softly among themselves and nudging one another. 'No, Mehala. I appreciate your thought, but keep your hair and your teeth in your head, and what clothes I have been able to find for you on your back. Those witches would have every stitch off and you thrown in the ocean a second time. Better you don't risk it. That will be one less battle to fight. There'll be plenty of others.'

'I'd be willing, Mrs Weaver.'

The publican's wife turned and stared at the girl next to her. Mehala was calm, her countenance level as she gazed without fear at the three servants following the tax cart.

Dear God, she thought in astonishment. I do believe the girl means it! She is quite unafraid.

'Thank you, Mehala, but I forbid it. And John Weaver has already considered the matter and decided against it. That is an end.'

'Yes, Mrs Weaver.'

But it was said with a little-maid innocence that caused Mrs Weaver to glance again at Mehala, and be startled further to observe a half smile on the girl's countenance. What ever sort of creature was this to whom she had given shelter? Best not to think of that problem until the girl recovered her memory, then she could be offered any of the roads out of Sealandings, and her blessing to go with the journey.

The square was filling now apace. Awnings were being erected, more to indicate possession of an area than to serve as protection from the weak sun. The breeze tugged and flapped the canvas. One haberdasher had been so bold as to cast up a purple canvas, to the thrill of all who saw this astonishment, boasting as he did so of his many friends and influential customers who had insisted that he dye his canvas a particularly new shade, as an indication of the excellence of his products. 'Mostly from France and the Court at Versailles!' he kept calling, irrespective of the fact that all around limped many who had been maimed in the French wars. Goosegirls were congregating around the lychgate, reflexly flicking their long thin willow wands as they chattered. All were young and healthy looking. Mehala envied them their freedom, suddenly wishing she was away on the road with so simple a task to perform as they had.

'And here's our artist!' Mrs Weaver exclaimed, rather proudly. For some reason she felt herself anxious to portray Sealandings in its most favourable light to this girl, though why she did not know.

'Artist?' Mehala looked for the musicians. She had noticed a couple of flautists by the Corn Market, their wooden flutes under arm, talking with their grey-haired old leader who was smoking his pipe, all sitting on the paving. 'As everyone in East Anglia can play the English bagpipe, ma'am, I doubt that elderly gentleman is entitled to be called such, or be the object of special attention.'

'Not him, silly. Artist. Painter.' Yet more proof, Mrs Weaver thought. Mehala was from somewhere on this east coast, and not too far off. How else did she know that the old man's instrument, the underarm bagpipe of English pattern without any mouthpiece, was a common sight in the locality?

A young man was setting up his easel in the churchyard, the breeze ruffling his hair and making his smock huther with the sound of a pram's lug sail turning against the wind in mid harbour. Mehala glanced without seeming to, eyes lowered, earning Mrs Weaver's approval for modesty.

'Is he famous, Mrs Weaver?'

'Hardly, my dear. He only paints local things. The canals, the Stour, the horses by the Suffolk canals, suchlike. Of course, with his ability – and they say he is a gentleman of marvellous skills at depiction – he really should be painting Greek motifs, vases, lovely scenes of the ancient world, figures in significant poses full of classic artistic meaning. Pictures for betterment. Instead, he'll waste days, weeks even, painting a child drinking at a pool, or men building some old barge by the sluice gates. He is the despair of his mother, the Widow Maderley.'

'He is a local gentleman?' Mehala wanted to give him more than one glance now, but obvious interest would risk Mrs Weaver's censure. She desisted, though he seemed more interesting than any person she had yet seen here, with the exception of Doctor Carmichael.

'Yes. The sea mill, Watermillock, is his. Mrs Maderley runs it, by default of her son's interest. A great pity, for the mill is a valuable addition to local operations and economies. Otherwise there would only be the windmill out there to the north. The Bettanys live there and, they being Quakers and therefore not conforming to the real Church, choice would be all the more difficult.'

Indeed, Mehala thought with suppressed anger. There's altogether too much talk and argument of religion. Like that pompous ass of a Reverend Baring, so inwardly constrained by his beliefs that he risked all sense and compassion in its service. She hated the sound and sight of such bigotry. She had suffered so much from it in the past . . . But let the past be no more. Let her future begin now, here, at Sealandings.

'Poor man, though, Mrs Weaver. Imagine the suffering he must have undergone since a child, to love painting beauty that other folk think piteous and simple-minded.'

'Indeed, Mehala? Your kindly thought does not exonerate him. His duty is clear: to assist his mother in managing the tide mill. If he does not stir to it soon, he must stand condemned by all people's judgement.'

'I understand, Mrs Weaver,' Mehala said.

Mrs Weaver observed that she spoke meekly enough, but again there was that faint hint of withdrawal, reservation, as if the girl meant something totally different. She was driven somehow to make a vigorous defence of her position. 'Since 1827, the Excise and Custom law has been that even the mere frames of paintings from oversea have been charged at twenty pounds in the hundred for import, young lady. Coin of the realm! Were he to ply himself as assiduously to his skills even irrespective of the tide mill, he should be doing his mother a grand service, as that fact will inform you.

'Why, Squire Hunterfield only last year paid some wretched Italian artist forty guineas for a painting, only to have its admission to the kingdom priced by the Customs at no less than ten pounds and four shillings! And that by reason of its being above four feet square! Did you ever hear such? And William Maderley, hale and hearty as he is, paints common fields and hedgerows and the sky, all for nought! If that isn't waste, then Sarah Ann Weaver doesn't know what is! And no drawback allowed!'

Mehala knew that drawback was the sum of money returned by Customs and Excise when goods were sent for sale overseas after they had been charged tax on admission to the Kingdom. Mehala's swift understanding did not escape Mrs Weaver.

'Yes, Mrs Weaver.'

Mehala was thinking that this William Maderley was possibly worth more than two side-edged glances, when a carriage drew up and a coachman in heavy boots threw himself down. An imperious-looking lady, only slightly older than Mehala, descended and made her way to the church gate.

Mrs Weaver was instantly off the wall and curtseying.

'Good morning, Mrs De Foe!'

Mehala copied Mrs Weaver, curtseying, but not raising her eyes until she felt that the distinguished lady had passed into the gate. She was mistaken, for when she finally raised her face to glance after her, she found the lady paused in the lychgate. She was staring at Mehala.

'Is that the woman?' she asked, of nobody in particular.

The coachman seemed relieved that someone made to answer as Mrs Weaver bashfully stepped forward.

'If it please you, Mrs De Foe, yes, this is the girl. She was pulled from the sea last evening by *The Jaunty* and fetched ashore half-drowned.'

'And where is she from?'

'My regrets, ma'am. She does not remember.'

'Can she do anything? Work? Anything of use to you?'

'Please, ma'am, she is not yet recovered sufficient for me to discover. I am taking her into the market for her familiarity with Sealandings, that the expedition might start her mind back into itself. Doctor Carmichael suggested this promenade, this morning.'

'Indeed.' Mrs De Foe's gaze raked Mehala. 'I do hope that she will not become a burden of cost to the parish, Weaver.'

'Indeed I too hope not, ma'am.'

'Or that she will be the first of many who swim ashore and expect bounty, where they provide little reason for its provision.'

'Just so, Mrs De Foe.'

'Let me be informed as to her final disposal, Weaver.'

'Certainly, ma'am.'

Mrs Weaver smiled after the retreating figure as the lady moved up the path towards the church.

Mrs De Foe kept an even pace, as was proper. She had never opted for the Grecian bend, thinking it absurd and ridiculously painful to the lower back. Of course she had had to defend her resistance, and had a score of small bon mots ready prepared to strike back at sweet ladies who criticized her unconformity . . . The artist was there, William Maderley. He was observing her movements. An insignificant man, naturally, though nominally the mill owner at Watermillock and therefore of some commercial importance in the community. But without drive, except for his pathetic daubs. A man without ambition was no real man.

However, even one such as he was clearly being impressed by her beauty, doubtless recognizing in her natural grace a brilliant evocation of the ancient beauties of Art innate in a woman's form. If opportunity presented itself, she might detour across the grass path and assay a glimpse of his artistry, see how exactly he had caught her inherent charm. Though the attempt of a meagre country artist could not equal the impressive works of the mighty London salons.

'That is Mrs De Foe,' Mrs Weaver was saying, deeply impressed. 'She's the lady at Milton Hall. Her husband is a London gentleman, and not often home except for periods of rest. He is set to become a great figure in the Parliament before long.'

Mehala felt her face flaming from the degradation of the incident. The lady had deliberately spoken ill of her, for no cause. And there had been a hidden core of malice in her tone, also entirely without reason. For the whilst there was no way to counteract this hostility. But one day, Mrs De Foe, one fine day, Mehala of Red Hall . . .

Of Red Hall? *Of?* Not merely a servant *at* Red Hall? She had felt, in a brief instant, the mistress of that Red Hall, on that blurred image she was calling Mersea Island, so remote and ill-populated, yet so familiar.

'Look, Mehala! The market is starting now.' Mrs Weaver drew out a list from a small grey lace and silk reticule which hung from her wrist into the basket she carried. 'First, the spices. And we shall *not* pay what the scoundrels ask for nutmeg! I do not know if you are informed about these goods, Mehala. If you are, you may tell me. If not, be informed that import is charged at two shillings and sixpence the pound weight, a vast cost. The male nutmeg is the longer and more cylindric, and tends to be wormed. Hence, we must *never* purchase those. We always should seek the shorter, rounder female nutmeg, as being sounder and more aromatically flavoured.'

'I did not know that, Mrs Weaver. I thank you for your generosity yet again. Most ladies in authority of establishments and households are parsimonious with their knowledge.'

Mrs Weaver flushed at the praise, wondering again why this poor girl's approval meant so much.

'Yes, well. This way, Mehala.' She led the girl into the alleyway between two rows of stalls, inspecting the goods on display. 'You see this ginger? It is fetched from the Americas mostly – notice its colour? And at a Customs duty of eleven shillings and sixpence the hundred-weight, it cannot be priced very highly anywhere along the coast. You must always learn the Excise costs of import, for they alone prove a guide to the changes in market prices.'

'Yes, Mrs Weaver.'

Mehala followed dutifully. She glanced back. The artist William Maderley was staring after her. She felt pleased, almost warmed by his attention. He would not paint much this morning, if she understood his glance right. She intended to try to keep Mrs Weaver in the market as long as possible before they were obliged to return to the Donkey and Buskin. For one thing, she wanted to see that De Foe creature emerge from the church, and perhaps learn why she was there in the first place. And for another she hoped for a chance of seeing what that artist was painting.

'Come along, Mehala!' Mrs Weaver called. 'No dawdling!'

'Yes, Mrs Weaver.'

'I shall give you a treat later on, Mehala. If you are very attentive to my information, I shall let you buy the livestock from the market and the geese from the goosegirls across the way. Let's see how well you do!'

'Thank you, Mrs Weaver.'

9

William Maderley could not keep his eyes from the girl. She must be the one he had heard about yesternight at Watermillock from his mother, who had it from one of the tide-gate men, whose brother worked down on the hard where the boats brought in their fishing catch of an afternoon. And she accompanied Mrs Weaver, which confirmed it. A stranger, she 'moved through the fayre', as the ancient Irish lyric sang.

And he too had watched the grand lady Mrs De Foe sweeping along the churchyard path towards the church porch, where Reverend Baring waited, dry-washing his hands and bowing ceaselessly at her approach. The lady was undoubtedly beautiful and her attire was always compelling to the eye. Today, she carried herself in beaverteen with an applebloom hem, which he thought very risky with dark blue the predominant colour. Round her shoulders for warmth she wore a soprano cape, made of anglo-merino which, coming fine as any muslin, yet showed her London connections, for that wool was first available only from the sheep of his late Majesty, George III. Her gloves were ostentatiously the Limerick fashionables, short into the wrist, for only such as tradespeople and the Mrs Weavers of the world wore the common cotton Berlins or the costlier York tans. Indeed, very grand. She had grace and style.

He loved textures. He took black from his palette, and began artlessly to sketch with his hair brush, using the wine distillate he was now trying. Around, children scampered, delightedly squealing among the gravestones, making him smile at their antics. A small dog chased them, barking. He always began painting this way, never concentrating, always allowing the images and sights, sounds, impressions, to flow into him from the surrounding circumstance. Could that be why so few of his paintings found buyers among the gentry? They had also suffered consistent rejection from the London salons of weight. 'Where is your history, sir?' one critic had written him from the grand Academy there, making him too ashamed to recall that incident by submitting any more works. He had not even dared to call further attention to himself by sending for that painting's return. A rumour was circulating now, he'd heard, of some clever American gentleman who had made a collapsible thing called a tube, wherein paints could be sold in their usable state, in linseed oil – would you believe it? How on earth was that possible? Though, these days, with tales of iron horses, no more than engined mechanicals, pulling loads around the north of England on metal rails actually laid in the very ground, anything seemed possible. It was a world of wonderment. And in his opinion quite mad.

Was it wrong, as people said, for him to be concerned with more ephemeral things? For example, he loved the cambrics, the rep bluet with its silky feel when worn or witnessed, the sight of grass; even the blue plonket woollen cloth, still made at Norwich and worn by locals even this far south. In truth, all that was natural. Once, he had gone to paint one of his favourite places, the mill on the Stour, many miles inland, and, in early afternoon, had been about to start when he noticed a hawthorn leaf which had fallen upon his hand. He admired it – until realizing with sudden alarm that night was falling, that he must have sat there gazing at nothing more than a leaf for the entire half day, and so lost all his light. It was acts of forgetfulness like that that made him ashamed of being an artist. The shame was reinforced by his mother's reproaches and his sister Olivia's concern . . .

The girl Mehala was moving among the stalls and vendors with Mrs Weaver. The herbalist, with his herbs suspended on strings stretched between carrying poles; the haberdashers, the knife-sellers from Yorkshire, the farmers' wives with cheeses, the sellers of cloves, garlics, figs, oranges, best-quality prunes from Tours in France – 'best' because they were packed in six-pound hampers made of white osiers – and a score of other marketeers, were all receiving her attention.

He found himself staring. The creature was a wondrous colour. Could she be a local girl, as folk were whispering? But hair so very dark, jet, yet shining . . .

Quickly he caught up a trace of Payne's Grey on his brush. He could not afford sable, or even the commoner badger-hair brushes, so had to make do with whatever he could make or find. He used spirits of turpentine to meld the powders, with walnut oil or the linseed pressed oil, which was mercifully coming into common supply now. But the cries of the crowds surging in the market square distracted him, no matter how hard he tried to concentrate, and that occasional glimpse of her lovely head, without even a bonnet, proved too much. He left his oil brush in a pot of water, where it would not dry hard for quite several days, and hurried into the throng to catch better sight of her beauty.

'This church has always been dear to my heart, Rector.'

Thalia De Foe walked with indolence up the aisle, gazing at the stained-glass windows. Each carried saints, coats of arms, invocations drawn from the scriptures.

'I'm so pleased to hear it, Mrs De Foe.'

'There always has been a link between the Established Church and my family.'

'A famous link indeed, Mrs De Foe! And I for one am proud and conscious of it.'

'The links are becoming strained, in these modern days. It is so all around us. Do you not find that, Reverend Baring?'

'Oh, how true, ma'am! How very true that is!' He followed, hands clasped behind his back in an attempt to control his endless habit of fondling his own hands, quite as if he were a moneylender at a transaction in some alleyway. Euterpe had drawn his attention to it only recently, though probably unjustifiably.

Thalia paused at a window. A woman saint was depicted in it; she thought her stance too posed, too disingenuous. Some artist's bitch had stood for the original drawing, probably. 'I find, Reverend, that the world is altering so fast these days that I am at a sore loss trying to keep pace.'

'As is the Church itself, ma'am. Too many sects are abroad in the country today, ma'am. That was the very essence of a letter I wrote to the bishop's office, stressing the enormity of the problem – '

'Indeed.'

Mrs De Foe strolled along the altar rail, examining the reredos. Reverend Baring had the unpleasing feeling that she was weighing its value rather than appreciating the beauty of the carving, but it was doubtless only the lady's manner which gave rise to such an unthinkable notion. After all, she had summoned him here, and sinners were averse to consecrated ground.

'You know, Rector. I think this church must be one of the unspoilt beauties of this part of the country.'

'You do, ma'am?' He was pleased now. His prideful thought deserved penance, in some quiet moment before reading his evening office perhaps, in the quiet of his study with his breviary.

'I most certainly do. Not grand, I grant you, but a treasure of religious certainty and conviction.'

'How very marvellous to hear you speak so, Mrs De Foe! I have several plans for its improvement, if that is not presumptuous. One such concerns the side chancel – '

'That reredos, for instance, Rector. What carving! What religious thought has gone into its making! By brute woodcarvers no higher than animals!'

'Well, ah, ma'am . . .' He was tempted to say that Christ himself was no more than a carver of wood, judged in one manner, but the risk of giving offence to this great lady was too high.

'How many of our churches were despoiled, I wonder, by the Puritans? In the Great Civil War, for example?'

'Scores, ma'am, I shouldn't wonder.'

'Hundreds. Reverend Baring. Thousands!'

'Indeed. ma'am. A terrible time, when God's own buildings were – '

'Your church is very privileged to have survived without injury, Mr Baring.'

'Exactly, ma'am! Never a day passes but what I give thanks – '

'How truly awful it would be were any depredation to occur now, at this late stage!'

'Any. . . ?' Suddenly he was uncomfortable at the turn the conversation was taking. He began to wonder why the lady had sent word that he was to attend on her at the church this morning. His hope of an improvement in his benefice quickly receded. She was here for a definite purpose connected with herself, not his church.

'Yes, Rector.' She was studying the pulpit, gazing up at the stonework. 'Imported from Yorkshire, I think?'

'Yes, ma'am.'

'Oh, the happy hours I have spent as a child sitting in the pews of the various churches I supported! Listening to the wise instruction of the parson! It brings tears to my eyes!'

She looked singularly unaffected.

'I'm pleased that your memory of Divine Service is so salutary, Mrs De Foe.'

She smiled inwardly at his guarded tone. The idiot cleric had realized at last, and not before time.

'I am of a mind to consider ways in which I could . . . assist your church, Mr Baring.'

'How very kind, ma'am!' No longer God's nor even hers, but unequivocally *his* church. He took the point. 'I am sure that your reward in Heaven will – '

' – be adequate, Rector, once I am there.' She turned, elegant, perfumed, compelling. And dangerously single-minded. 'Until then we poor mortals must remain content with whatever rewards we can obtain here upon earth. Is that not correct, Reverend Baring?'

'Indeed, Mrs De Foe,' he said happily, still desperately trying to maintain the fiction that her visit was one of ordinary purpose. And trying to evade her steely eyes. He felt transfixed. 'That is the common lot of Man.'

She tucked a small piece of tiffany under her cuff. Ladies affected this common gauze these days as a vehicle for perfume. He felt almost giddy with her proximity, quite the wrongest emotion to be experiencing in the House of the Lord.

'So, Rector. Let us to business. You are well thought of at the office of the See, are you not?'

'Well, ma'am, it would be immodest of me to agree.'

'Nonetheless it is true.' She was instantly brisk, all pretence done. 'Therefore you may grant me a wish – quite like the fairies in the children's stories, Rector!' She dazzled him with a smile. 'My cousin Mr Charles Golding is offering himself to the electorate soon, here in East Anglia. I shall be very happy to learn that you have written to the bishop in terms of great precision and certainty, offering your support in his cause.'

He stuttered trying to reply to such astounding bluntness. 'Ma'am, I am uncertain about the – '

'Uncertain, Rector?' Mrs De Foe removed the tiffany, dabbed her lip with it, drawing his eyes along the line of her movements, and replaced it in the wrist of her Limerick. 'Uncertain? How can that be, when you and I have agreed about all essentials?'

'Agreed, ma'am?' he said nervously. This was politics, not a Church matter.

'Yes, Rector.' Her eyes hardened. She held his gaze, her eyes almost palpably stabbing warning into his mind. '*All* essentials, Rector. I bid you good morning.'

Without an acknowledgement towards the altar, she turned on her heel and moved from the church. He stared after her, his throat dry, almost in a sweat of anxiety about the task she had forced upon him.

Mrs De Foe emerged, pleased with herself. That could not have gone better. Reverend Baring could have proved difficult, especially now his sister had arrived to housekeep. She was confident that she had caught him exactly at the right time, and gained a perfect result. Her own ambitions deserved probably more attention than she had given them of late. How wise to make a start with Reverend Baring! Small hurdles first, before greater leaps.

The next task was to convince Henry Hunterfield that his own interests were inextricably bound up with those of her own – no hard task, in view of the stupid fool's infatuation. In any case, she had well and truly hooked *him*, as she had been instructed by someone far more vital. The difficulty lay in his sisters, but of those only Lydia was worth considering as a significant opponent. Letitia was too obsessed with her poetry and listless daydreaming. Tabitha had all the venom of a viper, yes, but was so afflicted with the passions of her exceeding and banal youth that she would be no threat for many a season. But Lydia was different: a married woman, with unspoken ambitions of her own. And the scheming bitch was now firmly established at Lorne House as her brother's housekeeper. Yes, Lydia was no simpleton. It had been a bad day indeed when she had travelled to Lorne House to take tea with Tabitha and Letitia one afternoon, and been greeted with the sight of Lydia, newly returned from London, wearing the chatelaine of the mistress of the house.

But for the moment everything was going splendidly.

She paused in her serene progress down the churchyard path. The children had stopped playing at the sight of the approach of so grand a lady, but she paid them no mind. Instead, she was interested in William Maderley. The artist's canvas was beside the path with his materials – cloths, a spare canvas, papers, a box of powders, brushes and a pot or two, as well as those revolting little animal bladders in which these strange people stored mixed pigments in oil. It was quite an industry, this painting!

That artist must have moved his position to one nearer her place of exit, so as to glimpse her the more closely without seeming too obtrusive. The silly man had gone off somewhere, and so would miss the glimpse of her! She paused, adjusting her glove, and then as if idling stepped closer to the canvas. Now to see what sort of attempt on her form that artist had made! She moved gracefully round, pausing and smiling at the swiftly outlined sketch on the canvas.

And her smile froze. It was not her face at all. It was some other woman's.

The background was a previously prepared 'sauced' brown, flat and matt, the weave of the heavy canvas showing through the underpainting in a minute speckling. On the brown, in a muted grey colour, there was depicted a face, at once sharp yet captivating, made in rapid, almost savagely crude cuts of the brush. The scent of turpentine caught her attention, its pungency making her nose wrinkle. The thing was hardly done more than a few minutes, but was executed with such skill that her breath almost failed her. And that face. She had never seen it before . . . Or had she? Had there not been some girl, dark of hair and dressed in lumpish clothes borrowed for the occasion of the market. . . ?

She looked up, her eyes hunting the market throng. And saw her immediately, that black-haired wretched servant, following the publican's wife slavishly around from stall to stall. Maderley had left

72

spaces against the brown in his underpainting, spaces where the girl's raven hair would show a deep illuminating russet, as it did even as she moved among the press. The bitch went like a lady, smiling at the tailor, shaking her head with stupid gestures, the horrid presuming little cow, at the purveyors of buttons, velveteens, fustians, treen and pottery. What right had she, a servant, to act so? A ragamuffinous sow aping her betters! And unless she was mistaken there was that simpleton artist, mooning around in the noisy throng, unable to keep his oafish orbs off the brazen little bitch.

Mrs De Foe moved through the artist's equipment, accidentally knocking over his canvas so it fell face down on to the grass, and stepped on his brushes so they spilled from their pot.

In her barouche Thalia De Foe avoided glancing at That Girl again. She was outraged to find a smudge of grey paint on her dress from the canvas she had despoiled. It was an insult, a presumption. She made herself lean back against the upholstered seat as the carriage pulled away. She would make a point of finding out who the little bitch was. One had to admit, there was a certain pleasure in revenge against a member of the serving classes who dared to pretend to quality. Discipline. Savage discipline. It was a necessary act of restoration of the Divine Law. In fact, exercising her rights to that correction had given her some of the sweetest moments of her life.

'Home,' she snapped to the coachman. 'And don't dawdle.'

10

At Lorne House, Lydia had been cheerful for several hours. The consequences for the household were significant, for Lydia's moods caused her to be severe and inflexible when she was crossed. She spoke affably to Tabitha, conversed with Letitia about the earliest of Byron's Romantic poetry, and accompanied the girl on her walk round the estate to see the autumn blooms. Letitia felt herself warmed by the eldest sister's good humour, and thought herself ungrateful for the sad thoughts she had been harbouring lately.

'I noticed that you were particularly downcast last evening, Letitia,' Lydia said, when she felt she had recovered enough of Letitia's confidence. That unfortunate supper party had apparently rankled in Letitia's breast for some reason, or the timing of her despondency and the supper had been an unfortunate coincidence.

'I am sorry, Lydia. Yes, I was.'

'The supper party? I guessed it.'

'No,' Letitia replied, to her sister's surprise. 'I quite enjoyed that evening. The conversation was almost all of it to my liking. And Sir Trev's company is usually quite an entertainment. I have reservations about Mrs De Foe's contribution, sometimes, but I recognize that as a possible flaw in my abilities to cope, rather than that lady's intentions to harm.'

Lydia's brow cleared. 'Then why so sad last evening?'

'Oh, it was nothing important, Lydia.'

'It was the sudden loss of Sir Trev to the brighter lights of a certain inland town, wasn't it?' Lydia was smiling with sudden understanding.

Letitia again surprised her by showing mild astonishment. 'Sir Trev? Well, naturally, sister, I am averse to losing our brother's friends to mere cousins, but only for Henry's sake and not mine, I assure you.'

Lydia was irritated at having jumped to conclusions, and letting her folly show. For Letitia to have an interest in Sir Trev would have been no bad thing, seeing Charles Golding was to become a possible contender for that same interest. Why were her sisters not more compliant? 'I see,' she said brightly. 'Something you had read in those books of yours?'

'Not at all. I was anxious to speak with Henry, that was all. I waited particularly to greet him from his ride, but he was too busy to incline an ear on his return, then too preoccupied with the business which had arisen with Sir Trev and himself out riding. Probably some mercantile problems.'

'Then you should have come to me, Letitia.' Lydia had to get to the bottom of this. 'I am after all your sister. I have responsibilities towards you which I can't properly discharge if I am kept in ignorance of circumstances which might benefit you.'

Letitia faced her. 'May I speak, Lydia?'

'Certainly, Letitia.' Lydia was ostensibly pausing to admire a small hedge rose, of the sort which were now becoming so common. Gardeners were even growing them as garden plants in their own right, instead of mere accessories. She knew that Letitia had had several long and earnest disagreements with the head gardener on the subject, though why the girl should so trouble herself about mundanities was beyond anyone's guess. 'How well these roses look, placed so in their own bed!'

'Oh, Lydia! Do you really think so?' Letitia was beside herself with delight. 'I am so pleased to hear you say that! I have talked with the gardeners, who refuse to admit that the practice will ever become fashionable, but I have insisted.'

'Is this the subject you wish to discuss with Henry, Letitia?' Lydia asked artlessly.

'No, Lydia.' Letitia led the way to the summerhouse and there sat, staring out at the lawns as her sister joined her. 'I . . . I have mind to agree to the company of a local gentleman. If Henry will allow, and of course if you and Tabitha, as my older sisters, concede.'

'What a splendid idea, Letitia!'

Lydia congratulated herself with relief on her perspicacity. She was thrilled. Not every woman was equipped with the foresight and brain to see her duties ahead of time. How marvellously accurate she had been! Going to meet that difficult De Foe woman and insisting on her agreement with her plan to join Charles Golding and Letitia! That it had been against Thalia's wishes was an irrelevance. The contest could be played out quite well, once the game was afoot. The important thing was to get it started at any cost. After that, she trusted to her own good instincts. She could outwit Thalia De Foe any day of the week, in so important a matter as the forthcoming courtship of Letitia and the exalted Mr Charles Golding of Bures House.

'Do you really, really think so, Lydia?' Letitia asked eagerly.

'Indeed, Letitia. In fact, I have been thinking so for some

considerable time now. Might I ask if you have any gentleman in mind?' She awaited the reply with knowing confidence.

'Yes, Lydia. But I do not know if you will approve.'

'*Not* approve?' Lydia cried gaily, laughing. 'Good heavens, sister! Why on earth should I have any say in the matter? Your choice is simply your choice! Of *course* I concur! Does the gentleman concerned have any notion? Or is it early days yet, and a problem towards which we should turn our attention?'

'I think he is overly anxious to meet with me, Lydia.'

'He is?' This was a miracle! All her work was being done for her! And by her clever little sister herself! And there were those who thought Letitia too still a water, running too deep, to be brought on to the marriage market. How foolish people could be!

'Yes. Though I am a little unsure of his family, Lydia.'

'His family? Faugh! Poof!' Lydia made a small sound as if blowing away mere chaff. Had she not already solved the family problem? 'We shall handle them with consummate ease, sister – and great skill, of course! We Hunterfield women come from a good stock, accomplished in all the necessary arts.'

Letitia was smiling at her sister's enthusiasm. This was far, far better than she had hoped.

'So you will allow me to speak with Henry, Lydia?'

'Letitia, my dear, I shall accompany you myself!'

'You will?' Letitia kissed her sister's cheek in blissful relief, all her fears groundless. 'And I thought his approaches would lead to nought!'

'His approaches?' Now this was truly astonishing. Lydia never dreamt that Charles Golding had it in him to instigate a courtship without the prompting of his numerous cousins, chief among whom was the redoubtable Thalia De Foe. 'You mean . . . he has actually intimated his desire to make . . . well, to seek Henry's permission to visit?'

'Not in so many words, Lydia.' Letitia felt colour come to her face. She lowered her head. 'But it is there. I know it. He has shown his admiration in several small ways, too minor to be of note to anyone but myself. And I reciprocate.'

Lydia felt a little giddy. What on earth had been going on here at Lorne House, a great ancient family seat of which she was the mistress, and her brother the head?

She managed to say, her voice faint, 'Since when?'

'Since Easter, practically. Twice I have come upon him, at his painting.'

'Painting?' Charles Golding a *painter*? Was there no end to the intrigues that. . . ? A horrid thought struck. 'Might I ask the name of this gentleman, Letitia? Or are you too modest to communicate that information to your sister?' She made a light joke of the question, and received a brilliant smile in return. The mouse had a sudden loveliness.

'Certainly you may, sister. William Maderley, of course!'

'William Maderley!' Lydia managed to exclaim, keeping her fixed smile with ghastly difficulty. 'Why did I never suspect?'

'Are you pleased, Lydia?'

'Of course I am, Letitia! I am ecstatic!'

'Oh, bless you, Lydia! I knew you would be understanding. You are such a stay and support for us!'

'It is my privilege, my dear Letitia.'

Lydia, in her sister's embrace, stared over the new rosebeds at the lawns and the distant house. Everything was suddenly wrong. Just as she had gained an agreement with Thalia De Foe not to interfere between Charles Golding and Letitia, her sister revealed her intentions to accept courtship from that weak son of a widow who ran a watermill. Henry would explode when he knew the facts. He would be especially angered when he heard of her negotiations with Mrs De Foe, on an utterly false premise. She herself was now deeply in trouble.

There was only one thing to do. She had to prevent Letitia's interview with Henry until she'd had time to think, work a way out of this awful mess. There was so little time. Thalia De Foe would already be excavating a pathway to inform Henry of the approach she had made concerning Charles Golding. Worse still, that pathway was a well-trodden thoroughfare; the secret assignations between Henry and Mrs De Foe made sure of that.

'I shall do everything in my power, Letitia,' Lydia said, holding her sister close. What, God alone knew. She would try to do her best, but do what? She now had no idea.

For one taverner to call on another was almost unheard of, except in times of great calamity. People who saw Ben Fowler stop at the Donkey and Buskin and ask for John Weaver were astonished. He had chosen his time well, having seen Mrs Weaver and Mehala walking to the market squre.

The two publicans of Sealandings sat at opposite ends of the kitchen table. Weaver had offered Fowler a mug of ale, as courtesy. As equal courtesy, Fowler had declined with a muttered thanks. Neither trusted the other.

'I'll not steal your time, John Weaver,' Fowler began, trying hard not to look around and take note of all the Donkey and Buskin's dispositions for market day. 'So I'll come straight to the point. It's about this new woman you have in the place, what is her name. . . ?'

'Yes, Ben Fowler?' Weaver said nothing other, simply waited for the visitor to come to it. Besides mistrust he did not like the man, and suspected that he in turn was cordially hated by the man from the Goat and Compass.

'In short, I have a place for a new helper in Mrs Fowler's kitchen.'

'And?'

'Well, I am willing to take her off your hands.'

'Meaning what, Fowler?'

'Meaning exactly that. Nothing more, I swear.' Fowler waited, but John Weaver did not take him up. 'I shall allow her bedding, a place to lay her head. I shall provide food and lodging both until such time as her family comes to reclaim her, or until she takes a-wandering off again. It's a fair offer, John Weaver, and one which will do you a deal of good, as well as assist Mrs Fowler.'

'Do me a deal of good, will it?'

'Indeed it will, Weaver. You have the keeping of the girl. You lose her food and even payments of the doctor's fees. A woman's a mortal expense when she does little. And even if they do much, they can be a heavy cost.'

Weaver appraised his man. 'She has not proved an undue burden, as yet.'

Fowler shook his head emphatically. 'No, John Weaver. You know very different from that. Taverners like you and me, we live by victuals and thatch. A space in a hostelry can be sold by the night to a thankful traveller. Provinder can be sold for money too, instead of given for no recompense to a hungry idler.'

'When would this arrangement begin?'

'As soon as you like, Weaver.'

'And will you pay the girl?'

'Pay?' Fowler looked stricken. 'Pay? For doing my Christian duty? Charity, which will cost me? That I should also pay out money, as well as incur costs for the girl?' He was almost speechless for a moment in the face of John Weaver's silence, then burst out, 'God, man! Are you mad?'

'What duties will she have?'

'That's my business, Weaver, not yours.'

'An unpaid servant at the Goat and Compass, then. Is that your arrangement, which will benefit me so much?'

78

'It'll take the girl off your hands, Weaver. I know you don't have the extra income which other folks along the shores have.' His voice turned to a wheedle. 'Think of it, man. She'll be off your hands tonight. That quick! You'll be able to sleep sound in your bed again, without lying awake there half the night wondering if she's a cutpurse, or a latchlifter. You don't know where she's been, who with, what she's done. She bears watching. All strangers do. I've learnt that on this coast, Weaver. She'll be worse afore she gets any better, too. Mark my word.'

'The doctor says she's not to work for a week.'

'A week?' Fowler was astonished. 'But God's sake, Weaver!' He was exasperated, almost beside himself. John Weaver watched his reaction with interest as Fowler went on agitatedly, 'I've just seen her with my own eyes going spritely as you please in the market! Jaunty as the boat as brought her in! She's fitter than two fleas, well able to work every hour God sends!'

'Is she, now?' Weaver thought a while, then nodded. The interview was over as far as he was concerned. 'Very well, Ben Fowler. I shall consider it.'

'Consider?' Fowler rose with him, puzzled. 'What sort of an answer's that, Weaver? Yes or no?'

'Who's to say?' Weaver walked Fowler to the kitchen door, taking his arm firmly so there could be no pause. 'This young woman is of her own mind. She'll do what she will do.'

'But she's sea-brought, Weaver! And so of no account!'

'Sea-brought or not, she is not chaff. For one thing, the doctor has virtually placed her under his protection. As has Miss Baring. I cannot say for the gentry, but Squire Hunterfield has been informed of her presence. There's nought I can do.'

'But, Weaver, think! You must *tell* her that coming to me's the thing she ought to do, and that immediately!'

'Yes. But she might just smile, and say a quick no, Fowler. Then how shall I look?'

'It's *your* tavern, man! Are you saying that you're not master of your own dwelling, for God's sake?'

'I am master here, Fowler,' John Weaver said mildly. 'But not of this young woman. I think she's a mind to be her own mistress. At least, until she chooses for it not to be so.'

'I never heard of the like, Weaver!'

Fowler walked off, in fury at the way things had turned out. Now he would have to think of something different, and probably finish up disappointing Prothero into the bargain. Unless he could entice

Mehala away from the Donkey and Buskin by some other means, which might cost a fortune. Wages, indeed. For a sea waif! As if a girl plucked from the sea could consider herself entitled to any money at all! Rescue, then pay the rescued? He'd never heard the like.

The world was a mad place, and getting madder by the hour. Mrs Fowler would go deranged when he told her of that lost five shillings a week from Mr Prothero.

She had married him. She remembered now.

Mehala sat on the low wall which bordered the hard, the late sun a red-gold ball hanging in the sky directly behind her shoulders. It was a scene so familiar to her, the same sun over that same sea. She had waited for the fisher luggers to land their catch just like this, but at a place many miles southward along the coast. This same coast.

And she *had* married him. At Virley Church, with its one clonking bell to toll or rejoice. Never a pure chime, since it was badly cracked almost the whole of its length.

The parish was always in dispute. Its curate in charge was maintained at the expense of the two vicars, for both were non-resident. Salcott and Virley, twin villages and twin churches, with hardly a churchgoer betwixt the pair, as people joked thereabouts. The church that day was crowded. All she could recall of that terrible, stupid wedding was fixing her eyes on the massive chancel-arch during the nuptial service. It seemed to her to be in the attitude of the sullen, lounging Virley men, leaning as its pillars did against the wall in a slouch, with its gaping space indicating that even this, the church's best feature, was also heading for ruination. A clear omen, had she but seen it.

Even for a run-down rural church, Virley was on the point of wretchedness. The altar was a worm-eaten deal table, the altar rails rotted at the base, and part of the floor had fallen in on one of the graves below. Rats were said to have gnawed their way through.

And he stood beside her. The ring he brought out was of iron, not gold. 'Our bond,' he had said, 'is not of gold, but of iron.'

His symbolism. It would have to be something grim, ominous, unyielding.

Children along the hard were playing Adam and Eve. How many times in her girlhood had she played that game, so silly and yet so cruel? Wanton injury, to any creature, seemed to her intolerable now after her drowning, though the antics of the children of Sealandings were transparently innocent. The coast folk said there was an Adam and Eve

80

in every brown shrimp – pull out the front paddles of the brown shrimp, and two quaint little humanoidal figures could be imagined in them, the Adam and Eve. Whichever is the greatest tells of the future, with imaginations running riot. The shrimp of course lost its life in the cause of providing such amusement.

Mehala looked along the hard, towards the north side of the harbour. *The Jaunty* was about to dock. People were gathering there slowly. Already they were calling out, wanting the crew to judge the catch as an indication of price. A hard life, as was so at Mersea Island, where too many folk depended on smelt, shrimps, dabs and eels, or what could be culled from the fishing boats. Women were passing her at a smart walk towards the jetty, some with mere scarves over their heads, or red neckerchiefs, occasionally a shawl. They were the walking people, the women who would carry those shore-side edibles, basket over one arm, with a half-pint measure held in that hand, and a stick in the other from which dangled the slimy eels. With fresh fish, bought fresh but cheap and small in number and size added to their load, they would set out to trudge the surrounding countryside, crying out their 'Fresh fish for sale!' and hoping to sell all to outlying cottages and hamlets.

Few of these stalwart women had much of a home, though her own mother had been one and somehow had accumulated the occasional treasure. Mehala heard the women laughing and joking as they progressed along the hard. Brave, in a way, the attitude of womenfolk. And they could smile and chatter! Hard lives, hard days and nights, and little expectation of better times, yet they cherished the merriment found in their own blessed company. What did it matter if they behaved less saintly than they were supposed to? And they fought among themselves, too, to the discredit of the towns and Hundreds of the east coast. But, so? Who could forbear under such circumstances? The actions of knights in battle were extolled. The conflicts of these women, over their small degrees of status, over their minuscule selling privileges, were regarded as discreditable squabbles – yet they too fought for their families and hearths. The difference between the warrior knights and the walking fishwives was only this: nobody sang *their* praises. Poets extolled the Crusades, the Agincourts, Ramillies, Boynes, Trafalgars, and paid no attention to the courage and indomitable nature of the fisher-women. Yet whole realms depended upon their stoicism.

There were almost tears in Mehala's eyes. Mother had died, not long ago. She had passed away in Red Hall, where Mehala had gone after that travesty of a marriage. Love had compelled acceptance of the man

– his love, not hers. She had succumbed to that fearsome pressure. Recollecting her utter subjugation, her terrible sense of loss, she vowed silently: Never again. She would choose. She had the courage, borrowed perhaps from examples all about Sealandings. She had lacked determination once. But no longer. Not now, after what she had been through. Her new strength was flowing into her from somewhere, and it was here at Sealandings. Here, she would fight to stay somehow, and feed on it.

She waved. Young Hal Baines had caught sight of her on the low wall and was waving, pointing her out to the master, Jervin. Old Lack was looking across, nodding his own surly pleasure at her seeming so well. She stood up on the wall to see and be seen all the more. Then she jumped down and set off along the hard, smiling with delight to hear the slithery sea-coast speech, where every v was pronounced a w: seas ran wery warious, among the fisher-women. They made room for her and chattered with her all the way to the fish wharf, rivals but companionably so for all that.

11

Mehala remembered pieces of her life with increasing clarity throughout the rest of market day. She said nothing.

At the tavern she occupied herself at the minor tasks set her by Mrs Weaver, helping in the kitchen preparing vegetables, out at the scullery washing linen, sewing. The other servants – so she classed herself now – were pleasant and not a little sympathetic, but they had their work to do, and on market day it couldn't all be strolling grandly round the market picking ribbons for shoe latches. The head maid Nellie pointedly said so, until the cook Mrs Nelson took a hand and scolded that the tavern master had given orders for Mehala's easy employment, and that if anyone wished a row they only had to go airing their views to John Weaver himself. After that rumpus they left her alone, except to give Mehala news of the locality when time allowed.

Little Jane served as the under scullion, and proved a chatterbox. She lived up to her name, a pert busy little creature. Mehala took to her at once. She was pleased when Mrs Nelson sent her to help Mehala at the vegetable table.

'See these beans?' Jane showed how she stripped the bean-pod strings after cutting the end by making it one movement. 'Hold it in your left hand, and tilt it so the string pulls right off in one go. See?'

'How very skilled, Jane!' Mehala smiled and expressed thanks.

'My grandmother showed me that. It makes it all the quicker.' Jane made sure that Nellie was busy at the copper where Mrs Nelson had set her to supervising the stock, then whispered, 'I hear things upstairs, Mehala.'

'Upstairs? Where the travellers stay?'

'Yes. Shall I tell ye?'

'Only if it isn't unpleasant, Jane.'

'It concerns you, Mehala.'

Mehala paused, then worked on. 'Someone spoke of me?'

'Yes. It was Mr Fowler, the taverner from the Goat and Compass.'

'And what would he want with me, this Mr Fowler?'

'He wanted you hired out to him. For a serving maid.'

'And what did Mr Weaver say?'

Mehala could imagine only too easily. It was a familiar story.

However, she was now armed with growing recollections and not all were pleasant. There were men who, in truth, were less than men with their machinations and their cravings on open display. They could be handled, though, as long as one was in control of oneself. It was the quieter, the more vulnerable man who sometimes proved a woman's downfall. What sort was this Fowler? Of the first kind, presumably.

Little Jane glanced over to Nellie and Mrs Nelson, making sure she would avoid censure for idle talk. 'Mr Weaver stood out against him. Said you were your own woman, and that it was not his place to go hiring you out or sending you to work while Doctor Carmichael said you were not yet recovered from a-drowning.'

'And Fowler accepted it?'

'He were mortal angered, Mehala. Face like thunder when he left. I saw him. He went to see Mr Prothero, 'tis said.'

'Prothero? Another tavener?'

'Heavens, no!' Little Jane laughed so much her mob-cap came askew and earned her a scolding from Mrs Nelson, who sharply bade the pair of them to attend to their work. 'He's a grand farmer,' Little Jane continued when the kitchen's bustle resumed. 'He owns all the land at Calling Farm. It's a beautiful place, though he be a hard taskmaster. He is sore disliked by his men.'

'What would so grand a farmer want with such as I?'

'He was here when you were fetched in from the sea, Mehala. He admired you mortally when he saw you. Old Alice was the one who told me, after. 'Tis said it'd be his pence which paid Mr Fowler, if you were took to work at the Goat and Compass, Mehala.'

'Was that to be my fate?'

'Not now,' Little Jane whispered. 'Our master said Fowler would have to contend with Doctor Carmichael, first, then Miss Baring.'

'Thank heavens for the pair of them!'

'Amen,' Little Jane said piously, and would have said a great deal more except that Mrs Nelson came charging over and admonished her for slow progress. She was quite pleased with the work Mehala had done, however, and expressed surprise at the toppings and tailings carefully preserved in a mound on the oak table.

'We throw those away into the swill, Mehala,' the cook said. 'The pigs can have those, as they are very little use.'

'I was not sure whether your kitchen observed the practice of steeping them in a muslin bag, as an aid to the stock pot.'

Mrs Nelson gave Mehala a look. 'I've heard that is done elsewhere,

Mehala, but here we do not. It takes too many hands to use up all these leftovers in a busy kitchen.'

'Thank you for the information, Mrs Nelson. I hope I have not given offence.'

'Not at all, Mehala. I am pleased you had the sense to act carefully in the absence of definite knowledge.'

'If there's a hand free over there,' Nellie called angrily across the kitchen, 'might I have a finger or two as a lend?'

'Coming.'

Mehala quickly went and was given the duty of tending to the stock pot over the huge kitchen range. It was always one of the most regular duties, this preparation and rendering of the stock. She wanted to seem willing as well as capable; after all these people had helped her. Little Jane was set to weighing ingredients. Mehala listened to the kitchen talk without seeming to, for cooks all over England were extremely jealous of their recipes. This newfangled method of letting everyone and anyone read of their secrets in printed cookbooks was thought of as a terrible iniquitous French habit, ostentatious and damaging to reputations of honest cooks. They each had had their own special recipes passed down to them by their mothers and were jealous guardians.

Nellie complained that Mehala was too meek at her stirring, shoving her against the inglenook angrily.

'See here, Mrs Nelson! What sort of a helper is this you've given us?' She shoved Mehala again. 'Too fine a lady to bend her elbow into the task?'

Of a sudden Mrs Nelson innocently was busy elsewhere, and Little Jane looked away. Mehala reddened, realizing that this was to be her fight. Sooner or later she would have to come out from under the protection of her weakness after an ordeal.

'Touch me like that again, Nellie, and I shall lay you out.' Mehala was astonished to hear the light easy voice in which she spoke.

'You'll what?' Nellie glared back, then laughed, slapping her apron and shaking with merriment at the image of Mehala taking her on. 'You? Have you any army, then, lady? Or are you risking me yourself?'

'You heard, Nellie,' Mehala said, her tone conversational. 'I am here on sufferance. That I know. But I will not take groundless abuse.'

'Oh, ye will not, eh?' Nellie shoved back her sleeves and adjusted her mobcap firmly.

Mehala knew that serving maids and kitchen scullions were as tough and fearless as the men they served, and often as strong. She could remember, in some town centre once, seeing two serving girls go at it like prize fighters, rolling and kicking each other for almost half an hour with the townsfolk yelling encouragement and taking bets on the outcome. But a fight it would have to be, if Nellie persisted.

'No, Nellie. Be warned. I shall not tell you again.'

'You'll. . . ! Why, the effrontery of the bitch!'

She flung herself at Mehala, who dropped the spoon and stepped away from the fireplace, quickly moving into the space between the long kitchen table and the door. She had not had time to kirtle up her skirt adequately, whereas Nellie was freer, having ribbon latchets round her hem to free movements. The head servant must have intended to force a fight before starting the argument. It crossed Mehala's mind that somebody had put Nellie up to this. Well, it wasn't the first time Mehala had fought another, and she was prepared mentally, if still physically weak.

Nellie rushed, depending on terror and speed. Mehala backed quickly before Nellie's outraged onslaught. The girl was screaming abuse, reaching with fingers held like claws and kicking out her feet as she came. Mehala grasped Nellie's outflung hand and pulled, stepping aside as the girl overbalanced and hurtled towards her. Mehala knew that she would have little reserve of strength, and struck with her closed fist under Nellie's rib cage, lifting the girl with the very force of the blow. Nellie dropped, whining, slithering along the flagged floor as far as the door. There she knelt, wheezing and whimpering at the pain of the blow. It was not a woman's way of fighting. She had never been struck with a man-shaped buffet before. She retched and hung her head, gasping for air as the pain flooded into her body in waves.

'What is this?' Mrs Weaver stood there, taking in the scene. She had just arrived back from a second visit to market, to bring the poultry she and Mehala had set aside for the afternoon journey.

'Alas, ma'am. I am at fault.' Mehala went over to Nellie, and helped her slowly to her feet. 'I am utterly to blame.'

'You, Mehala?' Mrs Weaver's eyes narrowed. She knew there were often disputes among the serving girls, that sometimes they erupted into frank battles. This had every appearance of such an affray.

'Yes, Mrs Weaver. Nellie was hurrying to answer a call from the taproom, and I unwittingly moved into her path, tripping her as she passed. It was very careless of me, ma'am, and I apologize.'

'Mrs Nelson?'

'Yes, ma'am?' Mrs Nelson came round the corner from the pantry, her eyes rounding with mock surprise. 'Goodness gracious! What on earth's been going on here, then?'

'Very well, Mrs Nelson. Attend to it.' Mrs Weaver slowly withdrew, looking at Nellie and Mehala.

'I can't turn my back for half an instant without you girls getting into all sorts of trouble . . .' Mrs Nelson gave a routine scolding until the intervening door had closed behind the mistress, then she quietened and looked knowingly at Mehala and Nellie. 'Very well, the pair of you. Perhaps you have both learned a lesson today. You, Nellie. You know you're on your last warning for behaviour. But for Mehala you'd be tramping the road to London now in search of a position. And you, Mehala. You have learned that Mrs Weaver understands, but will not tolerate too much of this.'

'Yes, Mrs Nelson.'

Mrs Nelson nodded. 'I want no more fighting or arguing, you understand? The Donkey and Buskin is hard enough put to survive without its servants fighting amongst themselves. Settle your differences, and let's get on with it.'

'Yes, Mrs Nelson.'

Mehala helped Nellie on to the bench and set to straining the stock. 'Do I clarify this with white of egg, Mrs Nelson? Or is it too soon?'

The cook glanced over. 'It is too soon, Mehala. And I don't want the whites to be used for it, unless it is absolutely necessary.'

'If we have sweet dishes, Mrs Nelson . . ?' Mehala did not continue, at the ominous glint in Mrs Nelson's eye. As the whole egg was not absolutely necessary when making sweet dishes, wise households usually kept back the separated egg whites for other purposes, such as clearing stock, and used only the yolks for the sweets.

'Thank you, Mehala,' Mrs Nelson said pointedly. 'Just keep on with your business there, if you please. Leave to me the decidings for this kitchen.'

'My apologies, Mrs Nelson.'

Little Jane looked pleased. She found time later to close up to Mehala and whisper that she was relieved that Nellie had not beaten her, for she was a terrible fighter.

'Thank you, Little Jane. I hope I shall have no more trouble in that quarter.' Mehala felt she had surmounted the first obstacles at Sealandings. Others loomed larger up ahead for her, she knew, and Time was not on her side. But for now, she was in a safe niche. It could not last. Her task was to identify the people of Sealandings, find out who could be trusted to let her make her own way – and who were the dangers to that hope.

Thalia De Foe had always entertained very firm ideas about her position in life. Her status was not merely to be defined in relationship to men, as an appendage of her husband Fellows, forever at his grand London clubs, avidly attending prize fights and similar worthless entertainments. For, she had reasoned at an early age, if she were merely a hanger-on of somebody little more than worthless, what did that make her? Why, a camp follower, a kept woman to be used as a spitoon, and with as little consideration. No, she knew from girlhood that she was made for better things, a greater position. There were after all women in history who had made signal achievements, and by dint of their own artifices, rather than riding on the back of another. And she would be one of them.

The difficulty was, she told herself with some asperity as she rode out in her coach to see her cousin Charles Golding that same afternoon, that an unexpected number of impediments to progress had occurred. And Carradine – her one true Carradine – would soon be on his way to Sealandings. She almost went weak at the thought.

The road to Bures House, her cousin's home, was not direct, but mercifully spared her from having to journey through Sealandings itself. The drive curved down through her ornamental gardens, laid out in the London fashion and much admired. Thence there was a little of the South Toll road, which the coach followed before turning right into the drive of Bures House. The scenery was quite pleasant, for a vulgar rurality, but ahead the smoke of the cottage chimneys and the distant bellowing of cattle in the market as the gathering started to disperse reminded her how far she was from London and real life, its promise to ambitions. London was the place she really belonged, the capital where power and influence bred.

A shabby man striding up from the town raised his hat to the coach. She did not acknowledge him, and was pleased at the slight. That was Doctor Carmichael, returning from Miss Matilda Gould's school where he conducted a free clinic every market day for the suffering poor. As if it did any good at all to fly in the face of religious authority! For it was written that the poor would always be with us, was it not? So wasn't it at best idiocy, and at worst blasphemy, to treat everyone as equally deserving of attention? The stupid misguided man would be far better employed looking after those of the area who could actually afford his ministrations, and leave alone those who couldn't. It was simply beyond comprehension. Which farmer treated animals all the same? A valuable hunter was scarcely to be handled with the lack of care one reserved for a donkey, after all. Such stupidity!

Sighing at the foolishness of mankind, she looked out from the jolting coach as it made the difficult turn into her cousin's estate. It had all the appearances of being really rather run-down, dilapidated even. She would have to speak with Charles about it. Their mothers had been sisters, and great friends until death had separated them. From then on, Charles had changed. Previously he had seemed to her the epitome of an active and vigorous young man. He was a couple of years her elder and someone she looked up to. After, he had degenerated, become listless and difficult. Not too wealthy, but sufficiently rich to run his own estate without problem and to enter politics should he so wish. She had often heard the criticism, from ladies as well as gentlemen, that constitutionally a woman was a creature of much ambition but little drive. It seemed that Charles Golding, left solitary, had suddenly reverted to the feminine pattern. He had no drive, his ambition boundless but without direction.

The house seemed well enough, with a maid servant at the porch and a manservant running down to set the steps for her to alight.

'The master is coming down to greet you, m'm.'

'Is he?' Thalia murmured bleakly. She waited sitting still in her carriage and making no attempt to descend. The coachman, also down to attend her on to the steps, hesitated, recognizing another of her sudden moods.

'Yes, m'm.' The manservant glanced anxiously from the coachman to the lady. The coachman shook his head minimally in warning. They waited.

And waited. The maid rushed inside, in panic, called in a stage whisper. At last Charles Golding emerged, buttoning his coat and trying to stop his cravat from unravelling down the steps before him.

'I am so sorry, Thalia my dear!' He was out of breath. 'That dreadful series of accounts I had to finish before . . .'

'Good afternoon, Charles.' Furious, Thalia alighted and swept by him without offering him her hand. She entered the house, casting her cloak at the maid and gliding ahead along the marbled flooring into the drawing room. She cruised to the fireplace and stood there, frozen and white with rage. Her cousin followed, guilty and apprehensive.

'I'm so pleased to welcome you to Bures House, Cousin Thalia.'

'Welcome? Hardly the most auspicious welcome, is it, Charles? When lackeys are sent ahead of the master? Leaving your guest – your *cousin!* – sitting outside for half an hour before you can be bothered to show your face? Welcome, was it?'

'Let me send for a hot drink, Thalia. A posset – '

'Tea, if you please.'

'But I have some excellent French brandy, and a sound port – '

'*Tea!*'

'Yes, my dear. Tea.'

Quickly he rang and passed on the order. Thalia refused to sit until, in silence, she had reduced him to docility by her glares. The tea was brought and the sofa table set. Icily she allowed herself to be persuaded to reply to his anxious attempts to converse. Golding spoke apprehensively, wheedling responses from her on estate matters, the weather, friends in the area, family, anything. Eventually, Thalia unbent enough but only when she had taught him a lesson. She stayed him with a gesture when he crossed to pour a glass of brandy for himself.

'No, Charles. I shall thank you to partake of tea only. I have come on a purpose. If you are ready to learn of it, and capable of understanding.'

He hesitated, glancing at the drinks on the bureau. 'I haven't had a great deal today, Thalia.'

She stared him down with contempt. To think that she had once liked, even admired, this weak drunkard. Her aunt and uncle would be turning in their graves at the spectacle.

'You are drunk, Charles. You stink of brandy. You are unsteady on your feet. You are too merry to reach your own front door in time to welcome your cousin indoors, and your state of dress is almost dishevelled.'

'Please, Thalia. Don't go on so. I'll go upstairs and – '

'You shall sit and hear me out, sir!'

'Yes, Thalia. I'm listening.'

'Tea, Charles.'

She made him pour, her lips set in a thin rigid line of disapproval. The man was a moron, a feeble copy of the men in her family. They were the way men always *ought* to be. They numbered among them great generals, and at least one admiral, who had framed laws for mighty empires and great nations over the seas. And for this very Kingdom too. Shamefully she was now reduced to pinning her hopes on this frail creature. He could be the greatest political talent in London. Look at him! He even slopped the tea over the side of the cups. For that performance the great Mr Wedgwood had created those small masterpieces, now so universally admired.

'Thank you, Charles,' she said, frostily accepting the cup. 'I am here for a specific purpose, needless to say.'

Golding racked his sotted memory. What had Cousin Thalia complained of, at her last visit? 'I've attended to the drainage of the fields down near the River Affon, Thalia. Honestly. I told my chief steward to – '

'You *told*? You mean you passed on the message and did not check that the man had executed your orders?'

'Well, Thalia, I've been very preoccupied lately . . .'

She snorted angrily. 'With drinking and taking your preoccupations to a certain house out on the Norwich road!'

'Thalia!' He was shaken, but more shocked than worried. 'That you should know about such dens of . . . of . . .'

'Vice is the word you seek, Cousin,' Thalia said coldly. 'I am not as ignorant as you suppose, Charles. Nor as blind. I'm quite well aware that a man such as your intemperate self would be unable to survive more than a single day without carousing and wasting whatever attributes or moneys circumstances had provided.'

'Thalia. Please. I honestly do try to . . .'

'No, Charles! You simply do *not* try! That is the matter with you, your life, the ruin of your ambitions and those of our family.'

'Now, Thalia,' he said mournfully. He couldn't withstand Thalia when she was in this vindictive mood. It was happening more and more frequently these days. What on earth had he done wrong?

'Well, sir, I am here to inform you that *your* indolence shall not be the ruin of *mine*.'

'Your what?' the dullard said.

'Ambitions, dolt. My ambitions. For you.'

'For me?'

'Stop echoing everything I say, for God's sake, Charles! And pull yourself together! Stop staring at me as if I were a stoat before a rabbit! I am here to help, to guide, to impel you to a better future!'

'But at what, Thalia?' He was lost before her tirade. Couldn't she simply leave him alone?

'At life as it should be lived, Charles!' She rose and paced to the window, unable to contain her impatience. 'You come from a great line! A sound lineage that was once the making of this country. And just *look* at you! You are dissipating your life, throwing your time and circumstance back in the face of the entire family.'

'I do try, Thalia,' he complained weakly. 'It's just that there seem to be so many obligations. Everywhere I look. It's as if some days are so

91

filled with problems that I just can't think. Honestly, Thalia. The drainage of the fields, the roads, the arguments over the tollgate. Then there's the tied cottages and the guilds – they seem to come to me for the least thing.' He fixed his cousin with his injured stare, hopeful she would make the problems go away. 'It's very difficult, Thalia. I can't cope sometimes.'

'You should pull yourself together, Charles! Other men in the family did!'

'But, Thal. They had good strong women to help. I haven't.' He tried to smile placatingly. 'Even when we were small, you used to . . .'

Fight all your battles for you, Thalia completed silently for him, close to despair. She came and sat beside him, exercising the greatest self-control. She modulated her voice, her anger, her words.

'I understand, Charles. The responsibilities of the gentry are numerous and very exacting. I do understand that.'

'Thank you, Thalia.'

'But my understanding *does* not mean that, though I donate it to you freely and with compassion, Charles, you have licence to do exactly as you wish for the rest of your life. You must stop frittering away days, months – years, even – in doing nothing except drink. And wassailing with the ladies along the houses of the Norwich road.'

'I promise, Thalia,' he said quickly, with hope that her anger was now expended. 'I'll turn over a new leaf and – '

'No, Charles. Your promises will no longer do.'

'But you want me to start out better, Thalia. Tomorrow I promise I shall – '

'*Stop it!*'

Her quiet words made him withdraw from her. Ranting and raving he could understand, for that was her usual method of assault. But this firm, still person with the quiet voice was something new. He watched her with trepidation.

'What do I have to do, Thalia?'

'I'm here to tell you, Charles. Now, I shall say this once and once only. You shall listen. I expect you to comprehend and be able to repeat everything – *every single thing* – that I say. Even in ten years' time I will need to be certain, absolutely certain, that what I am about to pronounce is engraved on your mind. It is that important. And furthermore I want your solemn oath that not one word of this will ever pass your lips to another.'

'Good heavens, Thalia!' he exclaimed, trying to seem bright in an attempt to lessen the tension. 'This is mortal serious talk for a fine afternoon!'

She waited, not tapping her fingers, but conveying to him the same feeling he used to have when their governess was about to administer punishment for some transgression in the nursery.

'Well, Charles?'

'Yes, Thalia. I promise.'

'On your parents' graves, please.'

'Thalia! As if I would ever betray a promise of any kind – '

'Yes or no, Charles?'

For one instant he was tempted. What would be the consequences of denying Thalia? But the steel in her eyes made him succumb.

'Yes, Thalia. I promise. On my parents' graves.'

'Thank you.' She sipped the tea, wrinkled her nose. 'Charles. This tea. Who administers the care of your household since Mrs Ventris departed for Sir George Haslam's household?'

'Oh, that's Judith . . . I mean, Miss Blaker. She's dashed good at it, too.'

She took a moment to open the tea caddies, nodded to herself. 'Well, another time I shall call and discuss the preparation of your afternoon tea, Charles.' And have out the small matter of fraud with Mistress Judith Blaker, housekeeper at Bures House, she promised herself with relish, returning to the matter in hand. 'For now, we have serious issues to discuss. Politics, Charles.'

'Politics, Thalia? Like . . . Uncle Gervaise?'

'Exactly, Charles. You are to stand for Parliament at the next hustings. I shall throw a ball of considerable scale, and use it – with a great deal of exertion – to further your cause.'

'But, Thalia . . .' He was gasping. He was already practically choking on this venomous tea drink. And now this. It was more than a man could take. He felt his head begin to balloon with ache. He needed a drink.

'But nothing, Charles. Now, before I go on. Have you any objections?'

'It's not my game, Thalia, and that's the truth. I couldn't stomach going to Westminster every damned day, listening to those bloody fools bleating about the Navy, national interests, moneybags in the City of London. It's too much damned responsibility, for God's sake.'

'None. I knew it. You have no objections, Charles, as ever. All you have is whimpers.' She nodded, replaced the cup and clasped her hands. She had no doubt he could be manipulated successfully once he got moving. 'Very well. Now let me ask you, have you any objections which you can foresee will be brought by others? Who for instance will protest at your acceptance in Parliament?'

'Practically everybody I can think of, Thalia.' He had done nothing of any political significance, so who could possibly take political offence? He brightened. It might offend Thalia for a day or two, but these, if he could invent some objections, would prove a great impediment at the hustings. Dangerous places, those. If he played his cards right he could even lose! Every time there was an election the militia was called out, rioting mobs burned some or other buildings down and careered around the streets of various country towns and the larger cities. Irish policing had even become necessary in one town, Bolton in Lancashire, as well as three huge cities of the nation – London, Manchester and Birmingham. Yes, hustings were events which wrecked the best-laid plans.

'Give me instances, not whimpers.'

He winced at her sharp tongue. 'Well, the clergy for one. Reverend Baring's a stickler for honesty and reputations. Too much, if you ask me . . .'

'Reverend Baring will prove no obstacle, Charles. He has already withdrawn any criticism of your new venture.'

He gaped. 'Is he in on this, Thalia?'

'No, dolt! I have seen to it that he will write to the bishop in support of your candidacy. Rest assured, Charles. The Church's pulpits will speak of you as a faithful and holy son.'

'Good God! In spite of my . . . my . . . ?' He couldn't bring himself to say the word.

'Your whoring, Charles? Yes, in spite of that. Any more?'

'There'll be opponents, of course.'

'That happens to everyone. Next?'

'Money, my dear. It costs a fortune. There are some thousands of pounds to be spent in bribes. Nobody gets into the House without becoming the poorer by a fortune.'

'That is quite true, Charles. But let's be perfectly frank. The family fortunes will be immeasurably recompensed by your advancement. And, once in the House, your way to a peerage is all the smoother.'

'So they say, Thalia.' He was becoming miserable. The wretched woman had thought this out.

'The work is not onerous. Very few politicians attend more than once or twice a week. And have paid agents of their parties, or use those of their friends, to do the bulk of the work for them. It is easy. But power resides there, Charles.'

'What about those northern johnnies, though? They're mortally convinced of their rights and causes. And these stirrings about what's right and fair. Politics aren't all that simple any more.'

94

'You are speaking of the job, Charles, not of opportunities there for the taking. Opportunities for you. For me. For the family's advancement. Wealth, Charles! Not a few acres, and such improvements as can be made in this hole called Sealandings.'

'You make it sound uncomfortably attractive, Thalia.'

'I take it you have no further anxieties, Charles?'

'About the hustings?' He smiled, waiting for the catch, half hoping that Thalia was still only jesting, not serious in her intentions about this madness. She gave him her most level stare. His hopes quickly receded. 'No, Thalia. I shall do as you say.'

'I'm glad to hear it, Charles.'

She rose to signal her wish to leave. He accompanied her to the door and into the hallway. Miss Blaker the housekeeper stood waiting there.

'Thank you for coming, Thalia. Bures House is all the better graced for your presence.'

Thalia smiled, recognizing one of the phrases laboriously drilled into him by their old governess. He wasn't altogether devoid of a sense of humour, this cousin of hers, inept and intemperate though he was.

'Thank you for tea, Charles.' She turned to go, Miss Blaker coming respectfully as far as the porch and giving a modest curtsey. 'Look after Mr Golding, Blaker.'

'Yes, ma'am. Thank you, ma'am!' Judith Blaker flushed with pleasure at being noticed by the lady, and gave a glance of triumph at Charles, who smiled but looked away, mindful of Thalia's eagle eyes.

Thalia descended the steps slowly, accompanied by her cousin, speaking mildly of the weather and the grounds. She made a few innocent suggestions about the upkeep of the landscaped gardens, then entered her coach and signalled for her coachman to proceed.

There was no need to stare, in order to see with what glee that Blaker woman would greet her departure. The slattern clearly thought she had pulled the wool over everyone's eyes. Until my next visit, Judith Blaker, so-say housekeeper at Bures House, Thalia promised with mute fervour. Then we shall see how well you stand up to scrutiny by Thalia De Foe. When that day dawns, you fraudulent, penny-stealing whore, you'll wish you had never been born.

She smiled as her carriage took the curve along the drive between the tall limes and the mulberry trees. Inflicting chastisement of that sort was something to look forward to.

12

That evening, Prothero took the news about Mehala calmly. He had glimpsed the woman at the market square that morning, and now marvelled that he had been so blind. To procure a woman-girl of such outstanding allure would cost a deal more than five shillings slipped to a taverner. He saw that now.

It would take thought, and active intervention. Well, he had bided his time before, and emerged in possession of the desired object. Like the land he now owned. Calling Farm, with its vast acreage, had once been tilled, dug, laboured by a young farmer's lad called Jason Prothero. Now, he was master here. And a voter, qualified before the Reform Bills started giving the vote to every pennypurse in the shires. And Mary, once a proud young beauty and sought by squires, masters and even knights of the Eastern Hundreds, was now his wife. She had been the pretty daughter and heiress of the Calling estates. He had sought her as avidly as a hawk seeks its nest once sure of its prey. Trophies. All life was but trophies. People, estates, titles. Mehala was but one more trophy. Desirable beyond most – indeed, beyond any that he could think of – but still nothing more than one more trophy.

He needed an instance of uncertainty. That was his principle, to find some unsettling event. Something to set Sealandings stirring. Then would be the time to strike, to capture that Mehala woman and make her as subservient as Mary. It would come. If it showed no signs of appearing soon, though, he would have to manufacture one to bring her to heel at speed.

It was in the Donkey and Buskin that evening, hoping to catch a glimpse of Mehala, that he heard of the impending return of Rad Carradine. And he was glad. He almost uttered a prayer of thanks, for that was the instance he required. When Mr Howard Carradine returned to Carradine Manor, lying so snug opposite the small eminence along the Norwich road, nothing was orderly in Sealandings. No two days came alike. And Prothero had performed a great favour for him once.

A visitor to Carradine Manor had embroiled himself with one of the whores at the infamous bawdy house of Two Cotts. The scandal would have been damaging to the gentry concerned, especially as the distinguished personage involved had somehow managed to get his wife to condone the entanglement. It had taken clever Jason Prothero to remove the bawd quietly, and have her lodged temporarily at Calling Farm, ostensibly a visitor. That had cloaked the misdemeanours long enough to let matters cool. Her bribe of course had been paid by Howard Carradine. The whore was hastened to London, where she was now the proprietress of an establishment near the Prospect of Whitby down on the Thames, hard by the swiftly growing docks.

Though Prothero tried all evening, he was unable to see Mehala. It was sore with him, listening to the fools all around argue and drink their swill in the crowded taproom, when he could feel the very air thickening by Mehala's presence. He drank sullenly and merely snapped replies to those who greeted him. He did not even show interest when the coach from Lowestoft arrived, one of the high times of evening. He went home in sour humour, staring back frequently over his shoulder at the tavern lanthorns.

By seven o'clock, after the supper things had been cleared by Mrs Goslett, Euterpe decided to take her case in her own hands and write to Doctor Carmichael.

She had been to the market square this morning, of course, but Mrs Goslett was getting on in years and quite unable to make the early start Euterpe required on market days. As going early and unaccompanied was out of the question, she had missed the chance of encountering the doctor with the right degree of accident permitted by the vigilant observers of Sealandings. She was still smarting over her brother's opinion – very well, to put it bluntly, *decision* – to disallow Doctor Carmichael's visits and conversation.

That evening she was in the parlour as soon as was respectable, with the firelight set high and the shadows plunging about the walls. That would give a good background glim and, with a candle nearby and an oil lamp burning against the far wall, ample illumination was available for letter writing. As a further precaution, she brought nearer her pole screen. Its beaded surface was set in glorious patterns, and was a source of pleasure by day and a reflection by eve. It caught the firelight most cunningly, scattering a milliard points of light around the room, aiding reader and writer alike. It was the work of Mother, and the more desirable for that.

Mother would have approved of her decision to write a letter directly to Ven Carmichael. It was outrageous, Euterpe knew, by all standards, for an unmarried lady to take it upon herself to write to a single man,

97

without the express permission of the man of the house. Yet was there not sufficient reason for such a letter? Or, Euterpe asked herself with determination, could she coin enough apparent cause to justify a message? She had put her mind to it all afternoon. She was now certain she could convince a jury of it.

Josiah came across her when the letter was half completed. He was pleased to see his sister actively engaged, and said so. He ranged his frame near the fireplace – six feet tall, and handsomely proportioned, slim and vigorous. And quite possibly wasted, Euterpe thought a little unkindly, readying herself for battle.

'Is the missive to your friend Mrs Coke at Wheatfen, Euterpe, if I may ask? I should like to make an enclosure if you will.'

'No, Josiah.'

'Then the Haslams, in Lancashire?' He wrinkled his brow. 'That seems an inordinate expense, Euterpe, since you wrote to our cousins there only a week ago, without benefit of reply. Should you not wait until – ?'

'It is to Doctor Carmichael, Josiah.'

A pause. Then, 'I see.'

There was silence. Euterpe for the first time felt genuine exasperation with her brother. These were his High Church pulpit tactics, the tricks of the trade – as he called them himself; the pauses, the hanging silences with the congregation holding their breath for fear of what scorching words would come next, the abusive anger of the Just God spoken through the mouth of the devout parson. How many times had she heard and seen these same ploys!

'You are not at a loss for words, Josiah?' She asked the question in a sudden impatience, wanting to get on with the letter. It was proving difficult enough without having to bear an interrogation to boot.

'No, Euterpe.' He assumed his gravest voice. 'I am frankly taken aback.'

'Had you intended to write to Doctor Carmichael yourself, brother?' she asked innocently.

'That is not my meaning, Euterpe. I am saddened by your assumption that it is seemly for you to communicate with a tradesman, without first approaching me for permission to do so.'

'Doctor Carmichael is not a tradesman, Josiah.' Euterope suppressed her anger. She had always been unable to avoid falling into his verbal traps. He was too adept at rhetorical trickery.

'Oh, forgive me, Euterpe. Sir Ven Carmichael, is he? From some great county family, perhaps? And so inexpressibly moved by the great fund of compassion he feels for the poor that he has given up great fortunes and position in order to clean up the cess of the common classes here in Sealandings, this metropolis of empire?'

'Please, Josiah.' Euterpe laid aside her quill, keeping the paper held down at the lower corner against its being stained by the fine sprayed ink which always arose from quilling, even with the finest sharp point. 'Please. I intend to correspond with Doctor Carmichael on a most important and Christian matter, that being my plain duty and one which you would not wish me to avoid, were you to give the issue precise clear thought.'

'So, Euterpe! Now I am thoughtless and imprecise? And unmindful of my duty?'

'No, Josiah. It is to avoid those sins of omission that I am applying myself. So must I risk the appearance of impropriety. I simply follow the example of our Saviour, who chose the same path, however humbly I do so.'

'You argue well, Euterpe.' Reverend Baring felt his irritation harden into anger. His sister was deliberately twisting words. A typical feminine device, and one which could not go uncorrected, in this house if in no other. 'But the fact remains that you intend to breach the confidence which has hitherto existed between us.'

She felt herself pale with anger at her brother's oratorial devices. He was using all the tactics she knew so well. She gained control before replying, gently shaking the inkwell so the oakgall colouring would not settle during the delay. Her argument was not going well.

'Were I to wish that, brother, I should have resorted to subterfuge, and been condemned by that very secrecy which you assume. In fact, it is evidentially plain that I am writing in our parlour, in open view, in the place we share of an evening. And furthermore, Josiah, when you asked to whom I write, I told you frankly. And I shall leave the letter once finished, again in open view, so that any suspicions you entertain might be allayed.'

'Very commendable, Euterpe. But that you persist at all in this is evidence that you are flying in the face of my expressed wish. Which is, not to communicate with this tradesman.'

'Higher authority than yours impels me, Josiah. I am only sorry that I have to say it in so many words.'

'Very well, Euterpe. Your position here at the rectory is in question.'

'That is your wish, brother. Let it be so.'

He went from the parlour, incredulous at his sister's wilfulness, furious at her arguments. The world was going mad.

How could any man, conscious of his responsibilities to society in general, ignore such a flagrant breach of etiquette? Or fail to be enraged by her words, at once so disloyal and so self-indulgent? She would have to be protected, from herself as much as from Carmichael. She did not, could not, know the forces of evil which lay outside the rectory. Indeed, it might be that her behaviour was nothing other than an outright plea for his own fraternal protection.

Pacing his study, he considered the problem as logically as his mind permitted. Euterpe Baring was putting herself at risk. There was now no question about it. Immediate action was needed. It was altogether too irritating for words, he thought in distress. Here he was, expecting a calm ease-giving evening with his own sister beside his own fireside. Inwardly he'd felt the need of tranquillity, for he was suffering the anxiety of having to concoct a letter to the bishop, no less, which was sorely against his inclinations. And what did he find? A rebellious sister! It was almost too much to bear. He had not yet decided how to word this impossible letter of support for Charles Golding, or what exactly to say. This was the lot of a clergyman these days, when the entire living was vulnerable to the wishes of gentry!

He flung himself into his leather chair and stared at the wall, feeling for the first time that things were going out of control.

Word spread quickly, that evening of market day, about the impending return of the Honourable Howard Carradine to Carradine Manor. Rumours flew about Sealandings. They told of a new prize fight being arranged somewhere near the boundaries of Suffolk, that the wild Carradine had gambled a veritable fortune on the outcome, that he was in deepest debt to White's in London, that he was having to emigrate to France or even the Americas for troubles involving some highborn lady, that he had killed another gentleman officer of the line regiments in a duel over some insult.

'They call him Rad, Mehala,' Little Jane said in her most awed voice. 'He's the Devil, some say. He's always flaunting the law.'

'Flouting, I think you said?'

'That's it, Mehala. He . . .' Little Jane was pounding oysters for oyster sandwiches, but so carelessly that Mehala had twice felt compelled to take charge and flavour with the cayenne pepper to a proper degree. The small servant had even forgotten the lemon juice in her eagerness to deliver her exciting news. Mehala twisted the mortar, pounding vigorously with the pestle as Little Jane watched and swung her foot. 'He got a girl into trouble last visit. And the parties he throws up at Carradine! The . . .' Little Jane glanced guiltily about the kitchen. 'The . . .depravity, Mehala! There's nothing like it even in French Paris, I shouldn't wonder.'

'Where does this paragon of virtue reside?'

'Carradine Manor lies out along the Norwich road. It stands near . . .' Little Jane giggled at the incongruity ' . . . near Bettany's Mill, which is north of the limits of Sealandings.'

'Why the amusement? Please pass the slices.'

'Why, Mehala!' Little Jane moved the wooden platter of sliced bread within Mehala's reach. 'They are famous Quakers, those Bettanys! They don't even speak to the Good Lord of a Sunday. Can you imagine? Going to the Lord's House, and never a word do they utter to Him! I call it a scandal. I think they should be suppressed for lack of proper humbleness.'

'But isn't it apt that this Carradine lives that way on, Jane? For didn't you say that there are ladies of easy virtue on that same road?'

'Oooh, Mehala!' Little Jane's eyes went round with awe. 'How you do *speak*! Yes, at Two Cotts, not far from where the cattle and livestock market stands in the fields adjoining. Facing on the east of the Norwich road, backing nigh towards the Goat and Compass. There are several of them live there. They dress very fine, and have a barouche all of their very own!'

'Such a scandal!' Mehala said, shaking her head dolefully, hearing Mrs Nelson's heavy tread.

'It is that!' Little Jane had also heard, and scampered to where the ingredients were weighed out for the Indian pudding.

'Mince the lemon peel, quickly!' Mehala advised in a low voice. 'Then the suet crust to be ready for rolling, Jane!'

'Thank you, Mehala!'

The kitchen was busy when Mrs Nelson entered. Nellie followed, carrying a prile of partridges.

'The oyster sandwiches are prepared, Mrs Nelson. Little Jane has just finished them. Do they be taken upstairs to the sick gentleman now, or later?'

'Very dainty,' Mrs Nelson sniffed, seeing the crusts cut off and the bread triangulated as was proper. 'Little Jane's skilled beyond her years today, I see! Now, if you please. Call Alice's girl.'

'Yes, Mrs Nelson.'

'You stay, Mehala. I'm about to prepare hashed partridges for those four guests arriving this evening. I shall tell you how, and once only. Nellie? You shall be responsible, and I shall work the rest of the kitchen, for this is a received order.'

101

Nellie listened Mrs Nelson out with anxiety, for the responsibility was more threat than reward.

Mehala gave Nellie a reassuring nod as the cook began to explain the procedure for hashed partridge, to sign that she would help as soon as the tasks were appointed. Nellie's brow cleared, and Mehala felt mild relief. They were not going to be enemies, which for women in a kitchen was a major achievement.

'Now, Nellie. This is my method. Pluck and draw the birds properly, then roast them underdone. *Never* let them brown, and *never* let them get overcooked, d'y'hear my girl?'

'Yes, Mrs Nelson.'

'What with the mistress at Reverend Baring's this evening, we shall look sore fools if this dish isn't prepared right in her absence. Now! Take six whole peppers, and two or three shallots . . .'

Mrs Weaver at Reverend Baring's, Mehala thought with quickening interest. To discuss my disposal? What else? They are debating my future. Perhaps tonight I shall learn the result, if I keep my ears open.

'Six peppers,' she repeated, and obediently reached for the shallots. One too few in her opinion, she thought but did not say.

Reverend Baring was in despair. Euterpe's letter was in his hand. He had certainly not shown subterfuge in returning to the parlour as soon as Euterpe had gone upstairs. That would have been beneath any man's dignity. No, he was merely acceding to his sister's natural invitation – nay, *request*! – to consult her letter before its dispatch. It was her express wish that he read the letter. So be it. He would.

It was about the girl Mehala. His sister wrote a goodly hand, soundly conveyed her anxiety for the girl's virtue and wellbeing, and expressed the hope that Doctor Carmichael could assist in advising Mehala as to her conduct and choice of activities during her sojourn in Sealandings. Euterpe also asked that Doctor Carmichael send the bill for his attendance upon Mehala to the rectory, where it would be honoured within the day. Any medicines would of course be an additional bill upon the rectory once their number and costs were finally known. Not only that, he fumed as he read on. This troublesome sister of his had the effrontery to extend an invitation to Carmichael, that he should reply to her at his earliest convenience. *His* convenience, note – nobody else's!

Baring lowered the letter, aghast. An outrage! This was unconscionable rebellion. It was departure from every moral standard that he knew of. How could. . . !

Mrs Goslett knocked and entered.

'Rector? If you please, Mrs Weaver from the tavern seeks to speak with Miss Euterpe. She is without, and anxious to ask advice concerning the drowned woman.'

'Please inform Miss Euterpe, Mrs Goslett.'

He heard the summons, his sister's descent of the stairs in great haste, a murmured conversation in the hall. He was desperate to hear what was being said, but listening any closer would have been as improper as . . . as this wretched letter.

The woman Mehala was proving a discordant note in Sealandings, that was sure. Yet since seeing her this morning on the approach to the market square he had hardly been able to get her face out of his mind. She was not pretty, not by most standards. And her hair had been most carelessly arranged. Her clothes were modest enough, but obviously cast-offs obtained from Sarah Ann Weaver. Also, she was pale and clearly not yet fully recovered. So what was it about her that fetched her continually to the inner eye? She was hardly of an age yet, so it could not be her wealth of experience which suggested to a man the secret store of knowledge that mature women habitually used to call attention without overt display. And it was not the charm of the purely innocent maid. No. It was something intangible, yet something so disturbing that he was unable to concentrate on his office, his breviary, his preparations for the next sermon, without seeing her move with that detached grace across his vision.

He shook his head as if to clear it. Euterpe would be in any moment now, for the Weaver woman was leaving. Then he would learn what was proposed. Perhaps there was no longer any need for this letter to be sent to Carmichael after all? And all would be as before between himself and an obedient, docile Euterpe.

To his astonishment he heard Euterpe ascend the stairs as the door closed on Mrs Weaver. Mrs Goslett's slow shuffling steps receded. The very impudence! She was simply out of control. And it was all that woman Mehala to blame.

He saw Mehala's face in the firelight, saw her moving into the square, her head tilted as she spoke to Mrs Weaver, saw her smiling at something the publican's wife gave back, nodding, her hair catching the light with a glow of russet in the deepest black.

Out of control. Serious measures were needed. He would have to bring his own authority to bear upon this Mehala, and so pull Euterpe from the burning.

13

Tom the groom was known as Simple Tom round Sealandings, for he was dumb.

The folk of East Anglia were thought worse than Venetians, in their hatred and suspicion of the lame and the deformed. Sailors putting into the ports of the region often remarked on that mislike. They had good cause, being among the most injured of races. So it was counted as something of a marvel when Squire Hunterfield, against opposition from two ladies of his family, took on Simple Tom and made him an undergroom in the stables at Lorne House. Tom was a mute, but had a way with horses that was nothing short of remarkable. And he was bright, intelligent quite. Also, he did not know the locality, being from elsewhere.

At eight of the clock, Tom came round as instructed with his master's mare Betsy. The night was making for a storm, blowing up from the sea into the front drive at Lorne. Tom had drawn a plodding old hack from the stables for himself, not knowing if he was to accompany his master far or not. He wore an old French cloak Hunterfield had said he should have, and a cloth country cap he had made himself. Hunterfield came to the porch, bidding good evening to Lydia.

'I shall stay overnight probably, with old Sir Philip, so do not trouble about me, sister.'

'Very well, Henry. But I do not see the necessity of your travelling at this late hour, especially as you have received letters from the Banks only this week.'

'A matter of the coming hustings, my dear. I'll wager old Banks will go on and on. I shall start back in the early hours.'

'Do take care, Henry.'

'I promise, Lydia. And tomorrow you shall talk with me about the concerns you wish to share.'

'Please if you would, Henry. It is rather important, and of some moment to the family.'

'Your wishes are my commands, Lydia, as always.'

'On with you, Henry Hunterfield! Count yourself lucky the issue can hold until the morning!'

Lydia dealt him a mock blow, grimacing ferociously. He caught her up, laughing, pretending to be sorely wounded and bellowing. It was their game from childhood. He swung her until she cried out, becoming dizzy. Letitia was hanging back in the grand hall, shy of addressing her brother in such intimate terms but smiling and laughing to see them both so happy. Lydia had evidently spoken with Henry, to claim his time concerning William Maderley. Tomorrow she would have Henry's answer. With Lydia so well favoured, how could she fail?

'Let me be, you troublesome sister! Or I shall be on the road all night.' He let Lydia down and went to buss Letitia, saying good evening to her. 'Where's that tetchy Tabitha?'

'She is somewhat out of humour, Henry,' Lydia said easily. 'She sends her best wishes for your safety.'

'Tell her my thanks, if she can be found,' Henry said dryly. 'And do not worry yourselves. I have Tom along of me, and we carry Mantons.' He always took along his pair of Joseph Manton flintlock holster pistols, ready primed, on any journey.

'And a lanthorn, Henry?'

'I leave all prepared, Lydia.'

'Go with God, Henry.' The two sisters came to wave as he descended the steps and took the mare, Tom holding the stirrup for him. The mounting stone was placed to the left-hand side of the balustrade for ease of use.

'It is only ten miles, my dears. See you in the morning.'

'Good night, good night.'

Hunterfield nudged Betsy into a canter down the drive, followed by Tom.

'That still silent man makes my flesh creep,' Lydia told Letitia, waving from the lanterned porch.

'I am pleased Henry was so kind as to employ him, Lydia.' Letitia was waving, but standing a little back from her sister so as not to usurp her seniority. 'The poor thing was starving, driven out by his people.'

'Then he should have applied for Poor Law Relief.'

'How could he, being dumb? And too unlearned to write? And he is faithful to Henry, come what may.'

Yes, dear Letitia, Lydia thought cryptically. And, many do hint, a great deal too faithful. For one thing is certain, and it is that this night we shall never know where our brother lays his head. And if he fails to reach the house of Sir Philip Banks this night, yet returns cheerful and smiling in the morning, what may we deduce from that? Henry will tell only the tale he wishes us to hear. One thing was sure, Simple Tom never told a different story.

'That's a great blessing, with the roads so dangerous.'

'And Tom carries a Manton too. I see him load it, and providing good Suffolk flints for it from Grime's Graves. He checks the priming pans in Henry's saddle holsters a full hour before every journey.'

'What things you do observe, Letitia!' The horsemen rounded the end of the drive and turned towards Sealandings on the South Toll road, out of the drive's last lanthorn light. 'I swear you know more of this household than I do myself!'

'I like to watch folk at their businesses, Lydia, though I am always careful not to demean myself. They have such wondrous skills, perform actions suited to the tasks with marvellous dexterity.'

They turned indoors, a maid shutting the main door behind them. The outside lanthorns would be left burning all night, as was required when the master of Lorne House was absent. An extra groom would sleep in the stables against marauders, and two gamekeepers would come to occupy the lodge house for further protection.

'I do hope you observe proper proprieties, Letitia.'

Letitia recognized the blunt interrogation in the bland comment, and hurried to reassure her sister. 'Oh, yes, Lydia! I only see when Tom comes into the kitchens here to check the priming, on account of the damp outside. He has a wondrous way of blowing the gunpowder along a paper kept for the purpose. When it moves as he wishes, he knows it is fine and dry sufficient to prevent a hanging fire in the Manton pistols! Our Henry is well served by him, that's for sure!'

How true, Lydia thought. How very true.

The two horsemen rode as far as the small bridge over the River Affon, then in single file decreased their speed to a trot. They rode into Sealandings, passing within a hundred yards of the Donkey and Buskin, and through the empty market square. No public lights were to be seen, but Miss Gould had conformed to her usual practice of hanging a lanthorn outside the schoolhouse. No lights showed at St Edmund's rectory, Hunterfield saw. He continued on, entering the Norwich road and leaving Sealandings between the space set aside for the livestock market – one of his better ideas, that, and very useful to the folk of the small town – and the whores' Two Cotts, where noise and shouts and laughter seemed to be the order of the evening. Then it was uphill with Bettany's Mill to the right and Carradine Manor on the left. He was mildly surprised to see lights and movement around the large mansion, almost as if Carradine himself were expected back. Was that troublesome gentleman due to return? Must be a prize fight due, or something sufficiently out of the ordinary to draw that scoundrel away from London.

They rode a further hour, taking small empty tracks where none roamed save nightwalkers as anxious to avoid detection as he himself. He saw nothing, nobody, and led Tom along the usual path, curving round to the west, inland away from the sea coast. A fine nuisance of a journey this deception made, but Thalia De Foe had her reputation to think of – and her husband's, of course. She insisted, so he would conform.

They came to the track which led down to Prothero's Calling Farm, and took the right fork, Betsy's hooves thudding quietly on the soft earth.

Milton Hall was the largest house in the locality, save his own. It stood back from the South Toll road, less than two miles from his own Lorne House as the crow flies. The distant lights were of the right pattern, two lanthorns showing beside each other on the side doorway. All would be well tonight. He breathed a sigh of relief. He could not have gone another night, nay hour, without seeing Thalia this way.

He rode to within a mile of the great house, then stopped and dismounted. He handed the reins to Tom, who took it with a touch to his hat.

'I shall stay for perhaps five or six hours, Tom.'

The mute man nodded, but gestured to the sky with a circular motion, lifting his head to gaze up.

'You mean the dawn will come a mite earlier tomorrow?'

Tom nodded, swinging his hand to and fro. A pendulum.

'Yes, Tom. I shall beware the hours. Be here.'

Tom touched his hat, and Hunterfield walked through the darkness down the grassy slope towards the twin lanthorns over the side porch of Milton Hall.

14

Two knocks, and he was admitted by Thalia herself. Her maid Meg accompanied her, for security, but as soon as the visitor's identity was revealed she curtseyed quickly and left. She took the lantern, leaving her mistress with a slender Norfolk lantern, which was no more than a lowly candle burning inside a decoratively fenestrated porcelain cup.

'Can that Meg be trusted, my dear?' He always had doubts about Meg.

'Oh, Henry! Your first greeting of any evening *does* irritate!'

She drew up her skirts and made her way along the corridor and up the main stairs. Hunterfield followed, conscious of his boots sounding loud on the flooring, and relieved when they made the carpeted staircase.

'It is clear,' Thalia whispered. 'I have given permission for the pale cider to be brought out, pretending that news has come about the master's impending return.'

'Very wise, my dear.' The shrewdness of Thalia De Foe never ceased to amaze. Here she was, alone in this great house but for her thirteen servants, administering her husband's large estates single-handed, and she yet had the cunning to consider all the small deceits necessary to receive a man at the side stairs. And into the bargain plan for every possible eventuality. He sometimes wondered about women –

'Shhhh, Henry! You're like a herd of elephants.'

'Sorry, Thalia.' He had stumbled against the banister, and the thud of his boot as he had recovered his balance seemed to reverberate throughout the house. They froze, halfway up the staircase. Meg's voice came from below, calling to the understairs gathering of distant voices.

'Here, Mr Ennis. This hall table is out of place again!'

'Is that you, Meg?' A man called. His footsteps sounded on the wooden stairs from below.

'It is. Who else would it be at this time of night? I've just seen to the mistress, and come along the hallway in the dark to find the furniture all awry. Second time this week! It's none of my doing, you can be assured . . .'

'Good girl, Meg,' Thalia whispered as Meg went with Ennis, leading him off the scent. 'You see, Henry? I choose my servants well.'

'You do *that*, my dear!'

They resumed their upward progress and emerged on to the large landing. In the gloom, shadows leapt and spread as Henry followed the lovely shape of Thalia De Foe along to her bedroom. The place was now in silence. They entered, Henry shedding his cloak and sighing with relief as he saw the familiar room.

'This is becoming more fraught each time,' he admitted.

'It is therefore more exciting, Henry!'

'And she laughs!'

Hunterfield wondered again at the skills of this woman, admiring her dress. She wore the red plush velvet, full in the skirt, with her medici collar of Dresden lace standing high and proud over her nape, falling away from the shoulders to nothing, revealing her breast glowing and smooth above the scoop of the bodice.

'I like that neat shape of yours, Thalia.'

'I had noticed!' She crossed to the sofa table and poured a sherry for him. This was his favourite. He swore by its anti-ague properties, as did many in this marshy countryside.

They talked as she sat with him on the bar-back settee. He was averse to overly comfortable seats, and approved of the sparse lines of the four-seater piece. In fact, she had prevailed upon her husband Fellows to bring this very piece for the bedroom, from Long Acre, basing her preference on Mr Hepplewhite's *Guide* published in the previous century. She had a flummery prepared for herself and spooned it, speaking softly.

'No real news of your Fellows's return?' Henry asked.

'No. Thank heavens. I couldn't bear it, not for a full month at least.'

'A month? Why so specific a duration, Thalia? Are you planning something?'

'Me? Plan?' She made a little-girl face, pouting false innocence and pushing him to laughter. He tasted the sherry, shaking his head.

'Incorrigible, Thalia. My word, but this sherry has a strawy face! And it still tastes a little of leather, just as I like it, truly raw and newish!'

'You are the only man I've ever heard of who likes his sherry so pale and new, Henry. Don't you know it is new London fashion to drink it well preserved, when that leathern Spanish-butt taste has entirely gone?'

'That is for London, Thalia. You are now in the mighty metropolis of Sealandings.'

She was watching him as he spoke, observing his laughter, the enjoyment which shone in his face when she amused him with her banter. His hair was neat, well tended. His garments were just so, conforming to the ideas of the period. Henry Hunterfield was friendly and considerate, but dull. And there was another ever in her mind, increasingly so of late, whose image gave her a kind of frantic despair which came to her in the owl hours.

That one was he who wore his hair carelessly, in a crude dishevelled attempt at a Cadogan, drawn back into a tied tail, dark and unkempt with sometimes even ugly patches of the dandriff showing on his M-cut collar. It was he who stood over her, in her passionate memory, readying himself to take her without question. He was the one who was not above thrashing her when she annoyed him, and who ever refused to speak words of endearment to her no matter how she tried to elicit them. It was in his service that she kept her assignations with Squire Henry Hunterfield, and submitted herself to these screamingly dull pursuits. It was all the more distressing to her that each of these receptions needed as much care as if she were meeting her one true lover. As such, they were simply so much waste, considered for her part. But if they served him whom she craved, why then her work was worth all the effort of pretence.

'I have a favour to ask, Henry. I want advice from you.'

'Ask away, Thalia.'

'It is this most tiresome cousin of mine, Charles Golding. I am at a loss to know what to do with him. He is such a burden to my worries, him whom I so admired when we were raised together as children. It seems such a terrible profligacy of a man. If given the right opportunities he would, I am sure, be a credit to me and mine.'

'What do you have in mind, Thalia?'

'I simply do not know.' She sighed, turning so he could begin unlatching her bodice. She caught his hands against her breast as he reached round her, sighing and making as if preoccupied. 'I met him only recently, and asked him this. He went on, rather, about the great increase in voters for the parliamentary elections. Something about the Reform Act.'

'The voters?' Henry could not keep his hands still. Soon he would be panting, begging, unheeding anything spoken. She hurried on, maintaining the pretence of concern for her cousin.

'Yes. I didn't understand all his arguments, but he spoke at length of the fact that the borough householders of ten pounds sterling were entitled to the franchise. And in the counties, outside the great centres of population like Yarmouth, Ipswich, Norwich and Lynn, there were the old forty-shilling freeholders. And he told me of the new introductions of the great classes of voters – the copyholders of ten pounds sterling a year or more, the leaseholders of that sum for sixty years' possession, and the tenants at will who occupy land at ten pounds sterling per annum. I confess, Henry, my head swam!'

'Why concern yourself with such matters, Thalia?'

The man was now desperate, she noted with detachment. He was breathing heavily and practically clawing at her dress, fondling her breasts as they became exposed, lifting her skirt and pulling her towards the dome bed with its decorative spiral posts, using a grip of one post to steady them both as they moved.

'It is simply on my mind, dearest,' she said.

'I shall think of something for you, Thalia.'

'Oh, Henry! *Please* don't spoil this evening by talking of such matters!'

'I promise, Thalia.'

He placed his mouth on her naked breast, breathless, struggling to free them both of their clothing. She stood inert as he rummaged.

'I won't have you preoccupied with that wretched cousin of mine, just to help me, Henry. I forbid it.'

'Darling,' he mouthed, lifting her on to the bed.

'*Promise* me you will not think of anything but ourselves.'

'I promise, Thalia. Honest to God.'

'And only afterwards will you think of Cousin Charles's furtherance?'

'I promise! Promise! Promise!'

'Then you may join me.'

She was smiling with delight as he came upon her and the threshings and movements began. No true enjoyment, though relief and sureness were together in her mind. She could tell Carradine when he came, that all had been arranged as he had wanted. It was his command, and she was sure that, before Henry Hunterfield rode away in the early hours, she would have earned his promise to assist Charles towards Parliament. And obedience to Carradine was everything for her, in marriage and out of it, in bed and out of it, in Sealandings and everywhere else.

'Darling Henry,' she murmured, feigning her climax beneath him. 'You are so *marvellous* to me.'

15

The Donkey and Buskin was hectic, thronged, smoky, crowded with a diversity of people satisfying themselves that the market day was a huge success yet again. Nellie called Mehala in to help the serving girls, and even Little Jane was commandeered by Nellie to assist, leaving Mrs Nelson thoroughly enjoying herself complaining in the kitchen and producing wonders.

Mehala, dashing with mugs and plates, reluctantly admired Nellie's expertise. The girl had undoubtedly a kind of genius at serving. Not only was she dexterous to a degree, balancing four plates along her extended arm while carrying three jugs and two tankards of small beer, but she continued a banter and coarse repartee with the menfolk, kicking and battering her way through gangs of drovers and fending off hands, joking with the gaggles of old women by the inglenooks and yet finding time to shout fresh instructions to her girls about requirements in upstairs rooms.

It was during one of these sorties that Mehala found herself yelled at to carry three new bottles of Portugal wine to three gentlemen in the upstairs recess and be sharp about it. She found herself running, not daring to pause and exchange jokes with the menfolk, even though one was that same young Hal Baines who had taken her from the sea, though she managed a bright smile of affection as she returned, shoving her way among the fisher folk and ruffling his hair.

'My hero, this!' she called, battling through, which set everybody jesting to make the young fisherman redden up and look down into his ale, grinning with embarrassment.

She managed the stairs in spite of a young goosegirl being heavily courted in the stair nook, which had been deliberately constructed for servants to rest and re- adjust their burdens on the way upstairs, the better to present the food and drink for the guests. She was carrying also a Westmorland-cured ham which Mrs Nelson had thrust on her for the same gentry, and a tray of collared eels. She was breathless, making her way up the curved staircase on to the landing. The gentlemen in question were at the far end, and she got nearby before the collared eels threatened to slip.

Amused if slightly irritated by the passionate preoccupation of the lovers in the stair nook, she paused, raised her knee against the wattle wall and tried to restore her balance. The din from below was almost deafening, even on the upper storey, but in spite of this, proximity to the dining recess made the men's speech audible.

'When Rad gets his hooks into somebody, that's the time to watch out. The fur flies then, and it seems that he's of a mind to do damage.'

'But he'll need help, Quilter. Carradine has no voice in the Parliament, and after his gambling episode down at the Pavilion he'll have precious little elswhere. And,' the speaker said with ponderous significance, 'you know of the circles of which I'm speaking.'

Mehala listened, uncomfortably aware she was accidentally eavesdropping.

'Rad Carradine won't stop. I tell you, Jeremy,' this Quilter voice remarked. 'Why else do you think he's coming back to this godforsaken hole, out in the wilds of the Kingdom?'

'Some woman, I expect, Quilter.'

'But what can he do?' The third voice sounded a younger man, affected and puzzled.

'The Honourable Rad Carradine can do what he damned well pleases, it seems to me sometimes,' Quilter answered gloomily. 'I'm owed a fortune, but nary a farthing moves either way between Carradine Manor and me in payment. It's all notes of hand.'

'I heard you was inclining to sell them to the note brokers,' the younger voice put in, interested. 'Them as will forever hang about outside the gaming clubs and buy at six shillings and eightpence in the pound.'

'For some, it's less than that, Alex. We're not dealing with a Prince Regent when we speak of Carradine. We're speaking of somebody who has fewer scruples still.'

'No disloyalty talk here, Quilter.'

Mehala was worried at the position she found herself in. This was serious talk, and about the dangerous Rad Carradine she'd already heard so much of. Below on the stairs the goosegirl was drawing up her skirts, pantingly oblivious to circumstance as her farmboy lover strove ever closer. Soon their noises would attract the gentlemen's amused attention, and Mehala would be discovered. She wondered whether to retreat.

'Sorry, Sir Jeremy,' this Quilter responded. 'Not disloyalty, but rather concern as to how long I can go on giving credit to the Honourable Howard Carradine without calling in my notes. Or, like you just suggest, Alex, selling his notes off to the Strand jews against part payment.'

'The Prince Regent's gambling notes of hand went for eighteen shillings and ninepence, I once heard, Quilter. That's not too bad a discount for a sovereign, is it?' The men chuckled at the pun.

'Excellent discount. But that's for a prince's scribble. For Rad Carradine, I'll be lucky to receive thirteen shillings on a good day, six and eightpence on a bad.'

There was laughter. 'Take my advice, Peter Quilter – go for honesty!'

'Honesty breeds losses even greater than my usual style!'

Amid laughter, Mehala seized her chance and arrived with great sounds and bustle, making herself more breathless and disorderly than she actually was.

'Sir, an y'please, your three Portugal wines, collared eels, and a Westmoreland-cured. Thank you, sirs.'

'Good God!' the youngest of the three men exclaimed. He reached for Mehala, who evaded him and moved round the loaded table collecting the used dishes. 'Do they always have girls of this stamp here at Sealandings?' That must be the one called Alex. He had a slight brogue in his speech, probably from somewhere in North Britain.

'Sir Jeremy Pacton, at your service, m'lady!' one said, rising a little tipsily and grinning at Mehala.

The third man, older and looking sour, was hunched into his thick bottle-green frock coat and said nothing, simply eyed Mehala with protuberant eyes. That was Quilter, she knew immediately. A money man, without a single thought but was translated into profit and loss.

'And I at yours, sir,' Mehala gave back. 'What orders, sirs?'

'For vittles, none, m'lady,' the youngest said. 'For you, a dozen.'

Sir Jeremy spoke in mock anger. 'I saw her first, Alexander Waite! Just you remember that. I shall send for you tonight, girl. Bring your best Portugal when I do, y'hear me?'

'Indeed, sir. Thank you, sirs.'

Mehala withdrew amid their shouts to hurry back. She rushed down to the taproom, managing to reach the bar counter for the next mission. Her mind was as active as it had ever been. She must seek out Nellie and Little Jane, in some quiet time – if ever there was a quiet time in this ceaseless uproar that was the Donkey and Buskin. It was suddenly important to discover as much as possible, as fast as possible, about the hierarchies in Sealandings, before she was disposed of in some fashion she might find displeasing and dangerous. From what she had just overheard, it seemed the great families of the district were all at loggerheads, or in difficulties.

She did not attend to the three men upstairs again. Nellie

instinctively recognized Mehala's avoidance of taking the supplies up after that, and kindly saw she was busily employed elsewhere. The substitute girl seemed well used to such summons, and whispered to Mehala that she would be a full two crowns richer by the morning. She was welcome, Mehala thought with relief.

16

Jason Prothero seemed singularly considerate that evening to his wife. He was even pleasant. Mary was worried by this sudden concern for her wellbeing, but was too experienced now to say so or make as if she doubted his sincerity.

'You need more help here, Mary,' Prothero told here after he had finished supper. 'You need another maid, some sort of maid-of-all-work who can take the load off your shoulders.'

'Do I, dear?'

He controlled himself. He had just told her so, hadn't he? The spineless bitch was too stupid even to listen properly.

'Yes, Mary,' he said evenly. 'Is there not somebody around one of the taverns suitable for you? Why not send a messenger to both, maybe to one of the farms also? See what they can find for you. It would give you some free time to yourself.'

'Which should I send to first, dear?'

'Can't you even make up your mind on such a simple matter? Try the Donkey and Buskin, then. At least make a start.'

'Very well, dear. Should I send a letter, or ask one of the girls to go over?'

'Anything you like.' To her dismay he was thoroughly exasperated by now and showed his displeasure. 'But do it soon.'

'Very well, my dear.'

Calling Farm was large in acreage. Its main house stood alone in a wooded copse, with its own drive and streams running into the bay at Sealandings. Mary, the only offspring of the Calling family, had inherited the house and farm on the death of her parents, and was taken under the wing of Prothero, by then the estate manager. They were married within six months, which everybody thought a proper interval after mourning had ceased. The property was now in Jason Prothero's name. They had not been blessed as yet with children of their own, and Mary had almost given up hope of ever conceiving. Prothero seemed to take less interest in her with every day that passed. This particular evening might signal a return to his former concern for her, a renewal of his interest. She dearly hoped so.

Hopefully she wrote a message, and sent to the kitchen for one of the girls to carry the word.

That same evening she sat late, using her mother's knitting needles, producing a small shawl for one of her father's old pensioners whose granddaughter was having a baby in three months' time. She used her mother's silver wool slave on her wrist, more from sentiment than necessity, reflecting on the changes which circumstances make in a man. Or woman. Jason, for instance, had been so kindly, so full of concern, and now the weight of the estate and the farming seemed always to take his mind elsewhere. Yet he had great ambitions. He often spoke of having the timbered Tudor frontage of the house made into good red brick partially faced with imported York stone. She had seen his scrawled designs, grand pillars like the ones at Carradine Manor or up at Squire Hunterfield's place at Lorne. They had even come to words about it. She deemed it a wasteful expenditure, seeing the timbered house had stood for centuries, being of flintstone construction beneath the Tudor façade. Jason had become quite irritated, not uncommon these days, and had blamed her for wanting no improvements to the house.

'How else can we expect to impress the nobility, Mary?' he had demanded angrily. 'Not by selling them vegetables. Nor by furnishing them with waggons and horses whenever they need. Any farm can do that for them. No. It's appearance that does it, gains acceptance into the world of Quality. To speak with Carradine, game with Charles Golding, and ride with the hunts! Speak on equal terms with the great people of the area!'

'Will it be a costly business, Jason?' she had had the temerity to ask.

'It will be an investment, Mary.'

He had stood facing Calling House, hands on hips, belligerently grinning up at the building in that attitude she knew so well. There would be no backing down from this venture now. She scented trouble, for Jason was wilful, given to making grand gestures which somehow never quite produced results. He had speculated – *invested*, he told her – in a venture to bring over from southern France a great quantity of wine. It had been so full of promise, and would make the fortunes of the Protheros. Only, the government had placed inordinate customs duties upon all French wines, and they had remained at that high costly level from that time on. It had been a grave disappointment to Jason, but he managed eventually to offsell part of the cargo in London, at a fifth of the cost. She had known all along that the English system was to rely upon the Portugal and Spanish wines, so avoiding the duties chargeable upon French imports. Jason had rounded on her when she had timidly asked if his speculation was really wise. His scheme of course

117

had been certain to succeed. To Jason, every scheme was an investment.

She knitted on, watching him snore before the fire. Her friends, one by one, had deserted her company since she had wed. Not for any definite reason, at least none she could identify. Only probably because she was now a married lady, and so obliged to comport herself more restrictedly. But the pleasantry of Miss Gould's company down at the schoolhouse of an evening, the chatter of the discussion circle which the Bettanys held on religious and other matters at their windmill's great room, with cakes and a posset afterwards . . . all those were now lost to her. Through no fault of anyone's, but simply the need to be always at Jason's beck and call. To be here when he came home from Sealandings, at any time he chose.

Thinking it all over this way, perhaps more alone than she had ever been, was enough to set her wondering wistfully how things would be, if she had had a different man beside the fire in Jason's place. Like Ven Carmichael, whom she had once known when little. The Carmichaels had come to the local coast on naturalist expeditions, and twice had stayed at Calling Farm, Mr Carmichael and her father being rather distant acquaintances. Perhaps he would not be snoring to quite the same degree. . . ?

Firmly, she put such disloyal thoughts out of her mind. Her duty was towards Jason, and plain to see. Clearly it had to be done, come what may.

Mehala scarcely slept that night, hearing as if for the first time the fading of Sealandings into the dark hours.

The edge of light had long since slid from sight. Outside the sea shone like a flat black pearl, washing and shushing as the tavern's raucous sounds receded to nothing. Here in the kitchen Little Jane snored, instantly asleep. Nellie was in front of the fire with a rug wrapping her against draughts. Other maids, who either were waiters-on or drawn from the township, had long since gone home to their fathers' cottages. Two ostlers slept in the stables, Mehala knew, and Bone the cellarman, a crinkled ancient with a deformed shoulder from some battle at sea once upon a time, slept in the entrance to the cellars beside the candle boxes, with his dog Ranter in a small hamper made of French wicker beside him.

She lay awake, listening. The sea. It was there, peaceful now, whispering its secret low songs to itself. Quite like a mother waiting for its child to awaken . . . or to come and be snatched from life? Mehala

118

shivered, seeing the firelight dance on the ceiling, watching the shapes come and go, and then occasionally seeing them synchronize with the shushings of the sea. It was eerie, yet somehow reassuring. It was the sea's truce with her: You and me had a high old time of it out there, Mehala, it seemed to be saying, but I judged you a-wrong, and gave you back to those who live on the shores. But one day, mark my words, I might deem myself changed short and come for you. So be ever watchful, Mehala Sharland, or there may come a time when –

Sharland! Her surname!

George, George De Witt, the young man she loved, who had been stolen from her by that madman husband Elijah Rebow, whom she had been forced to marry. Rebow, of Red Hall. Who had somehow sent George away. She almost retched at the intensity of her returning memory.

The force of love was as evil and treacherous as that of hatred, she had learned in the sea saltings and marshes of East Mersea. Truly horrid, fearsome, almost ghoulish. She waited, breathing steadily as her mind filled. At last, maybe an hour later, lying still on the pallet, she calmed enough. And allowed herself to remember, clearly and without restraint, the terrible moment when her husband Elijah Rebow had drawn her into his boat, steered out to sea and, violent as ever, set the frail craft sinking with the fog thickening God's clear air and the seas rising and spray lashing at her face as his hands drew her . . .

'Mehala! Mehala!'

'No! No!' Mehala struggled.

'Mehala! Come to, come to, girl, for pity's sake!'

It was Nellie, shaking her and trying to stifle her cries. Mehala found herself bathed in sweat, her skirt clinging to her body and her upper shift sticking as if painted on her skin. She tore away her skirt, which she had wrapped around herself against draughts, and sat panting, staring, until the familiar sights of the kitchen reasserted themselves. The fire was down to embers. She must have slipped into a prolonged nightmare.

'What is it, for God's sake? Mehala?' Nellie was pale as a sheet even in the gloaming. Mehala recovered her breathing slowly, shaking her head and brushing back her hair from her damp face.

'Nothing, Nellie. Nothing.'

'Nothing? Dear God, Mehala, but you was thrashing fit to reap a harvest! And whimpering and crying out in your sleep, all uncomprehending, so much I was afeared the mistress would waken and come to give you marching orders from here!'

'Thank you, Nellie. Thank you.'

'Here. Drink this.'

Nellie brought her a small pewter mug of milk, after warming it by the embers of the fire.

'You are very kind, Nellie.' Mehala made to drink, but Nellie held her hands cupped around the vessel.

'Calm, Mehala. Take it slow, girl. Clasp it round for an instant to bless the cow – that's what we says round here in Sealandings.' Nellie laughed quietly, shyly almost. 'It has the merit of letting your hands warm, so as not to drink warm on top of cold. That's bad for you. Even Doctor Carmichael'd tell you that.'

'You're being marvellous kind, Nellie.' Mehala obeyed, smiling up at the kneeling girl mischievously, and said, 'I promise I shall not clout you as I did earlier, in return.'

'And I promise you, Mehala, that I shall not let you deceive me that quick ever again. So there!'

They smiled together. Nellie allowed Mehala to drink slowly, her expression in the fireglow becoming serious.

'Mehala? That was a mortal bad dream you was dreaming, weren't it?'

'Yes, Nellie. It was truly . . . terrible.'

'Was it to do with your . . . well, your drowning, Mehala? From the ship which sank?'

'It wasn't a ship, Nellie. It was a small boat. A madman made it sink. As far as I am clear in my mind enough to tell.'

'And did he drown too?'

'I don't know, Nellie. I never recall seeing him after the waters closed . . .' Mehala could not go on. Nellie embraced her, nodding and clucking.

'Then it were a terrible thing, Mehala. You've seen all your life flash afore ye, and maybe seen God. Did you, drowning as you did?'

'No. And Nellie. Please could you stop talking of me as though I actually *was* drowned? You all do it. I am here, whole, safe in the kitchen . . .'

She was shivering as she spoke, and Nellie hummed her warning. 'You'll always be like that, Mehala. That's what we say here in Sealandings. You'll always be afeared, unable to rest a single night or even to look direct at the sea on any hour, day or night, less'n you make your trust again.'

'Trust? Trust the sea?' Mehala looked up at Nellie's grave face. 'Who on earth would ever trust the sea?'

'No one, silly. That's the point. It's a woman, like, we say here. She's mortal sly and jealous. You've got to tell her you still trusts her. That way she leaves you alone.'

'Tell her. . . ? Tell the sea? How can I do that?'

'Not speak to her, not in so many words. But you'm go out alone, to trust her. Show the sea you aren't afeared of her still. Then you'll sleep sound. It's what everybody does, everywhere.'

'They don't have that custom at . . . at . . .' Something made Mehala keep back from the revelation that her memory was almost completely restored.

'Well, we do here,' Nellie said firmly. 'And it's the only course you have. Take my word for it. Assay the sea again, alone. It don't matter exactly how you do it. Nor will she care if you feel a mite scared.'

'Do what, Nellie? Go sailing? Find someone to take me out in the harbour?'

'Not that, Mehala. Alone. She can tell, y'see. She knows what you're doing, being able to see more than a human can. But she can't truly *think* much, see? So you go a short journey.'

'Was ever anyone recovered from the sea before I, Nellie?' Mehala asked with some trepidation.

'Yes. Old Lack himself, as brought you in along of Master Jervin and young Hal Baines in *The Jaunty*. He was swept out to sea in a great storm one night, but was cast on the headlands over by Whitehanger. The charcoal burners found him the next morning, and milked his lights free of the sea. As Doctor Carmichael did yours.'

'And he went out again?'

'Course he did. He had to, or she'd never have let him rest. Same as she's troubling you, Mehala.' Nellie nodded emphatically. 'You know what he did?'

'No. Tell me.' Mehala felt blood drain from her face at the thought of leaping from the shore into the water, in payment of some mad penalty like Old Lack's.

'He rowed out next morning, soon as the storm and winds abated. He rowed from the harbour, out across the bay towards Whitehanger. And he cast a shilling in it there. Course, it should have been a gold coin, or a ring, same as sailors from deepsea wear in their ears, like. But Old Lack's a heavy drinking man, and wasn't going to waste a gold piece on any silly old bay. He said he'd drunk enough of the sea water while drowning, and it tasted mortal bad, too bad to pay that much for!' Nellie rocked with silent laughter, making Mehala smile in spite of herself.

'To Whitehanger?'

'That's what he did.'

'Then, God forgive me, Nellie, that's what I shall do.'

'Can you swim, Mehala?'

'I thought I could, once, but it seems that when I am called to perform that rude task I am unable.'

'Very good. That is all to the better. More trusting to go out on the bay when you can't swim. Sailors hate to learn, for that reason. They tell of dolphins coming to buoy you up if you're a-sinking, but they leave you alone to drown if you look capable in the waters.'

'Is there a boat out there, Nellie?' Mehala looked towards the door. It was barred against predators and thieves from the toll roads going south to London.

'One belongs to the tavern, yes. It's but a small pram, yet serves well enough. You can cross to the mussel beds and do some fetching. Mrs Nelson spoke of making mussel pies in the morning, and doing bowls of buttered mussels for travellers' arrival. She swears by that as a greeting taste, with koumiss for the palate. So somebody will have to go.'

'It might as well be me, Nellie,' Mehala said, glancing at the door. 'Sink or swim, what say?'

'Sink or swim, Mehala. Trust. You just remember trust, girl. And you shall be all right, and back here safe and sound in a trice!'

'Please God, Nellie.'

'Amen, Mehala.'

The two bade each other good night, and sank to their positions of rest. Mehala saw a small glint from the darkness, red in the blackness, and realized that Little Jane had been awake and listening. Well, if it was the local custom, there was nothing else for it but to make the mad journey across the bay to Whitehanger no matter what the weather, for she would never be allowed to rest by sea or Sealanders until she had conformed.

That was true for anywhere on earth.

122

17

The little boy died before dawn.

Doctor Carmichael sat with the child, despairing as the croup took hold and the dreadful paroxysms and stridor gripped the little one's chest. It was agony to watch, desperate to assist, knowing that no amount of medications would ever help.

The Darling family was small, as local families went, consisting merely of Jake Darling, his wife Emiline, and two children. The little boy's older sibling, Clare, sat fearfully by the firegrate staring in terror at the scene, her tiny neat face cast in bronze by the firelight.

The croup was of the sudden variety, with Harry's distress and sense of suffocation worsening over two days. The curious wheezing, sneezing and high-pitched coughing, dry and stertorous, had begun in all its hideous familiarity. Ven Carmichael had been called early, the Darlings having already lost one child two years before to the same disease.

Then had started the gruesome shrill speech, as if the little boy was trying to sing falsetto every word he uttered. Doctor Carmichael had seen the throat effusion with dread, knowing that this was going to become the typical and murderous form of the croup, with the sickening membrane forming across the throat and leaving the child gasping and struggling for air.

From there the child had worsened, becoming gravely ill over the next long day. Towards nightfall the thick white-patched membrane had assumed its dulled purple colour, and the lad had seemed to fight the heat generated in him. Racked by fever, wrestling for breath in his small lungs, pallor alternating with the lividity, and finally the grotesque abruptness with which his end had come, the picture was the most distressing ever experienced. Doctor Carmichael strove to help the lad breathe, even to the extent of madly wondering if it were somehow to possible open a channel through the throat and so enable air to whistle into the bronchi, but it was hopeless. There was no sane treatment.

He stood back exhausted, letting Emiline Darling cover the child's face with the sheet. Useless. His life at times like these seemed devoid of all purpose. What was the good of a doctor who was unable to save a child, one who moreover was innocent, a mere babe, just on his fifth year? He could not speak for anguish. Jake Darling took his elbow and moved him outside the room.

'Doctor.'

'I am sorry, Jake. I truly am.'

'Thank you, Doctor.'

The man was holding something out. Carmichael stood in the small passageway of the cottage, uncomprehending.

'Yes, Jake?'

'Your face, Doctor.'

'I . . . I . . .' A piece of clean linen cloth. He took it. Darling made a gentle gesture, his eyes. Carmichael understood at last. Tears were pouring down his face.

'Thank you. I'm sorry. I must apologize, Jake. It is not seemly.' He blotted his eyes, wiped his cheeks vigorously and cleared his throat. 'I have no right to weep. When I have so singularly failed. I should leave my occupation to others who are better, who can bring something more learned than I to the tasks Nature sets me.'

'Such talk has no purpose, Doctor,' Jake Darling said. His eyes too were red-rimmed and moist. 'You did everything that could humanly be done. I thank you for it.'

Carmichael swallowed. 'I have a dream of freedom, Jake. One day we shall rid ourselves of this disease. Perhaps by means of a potion, something in the air to insufflate, a mechanical contrivance which takes away the iniquitous membrane that chokes a poor mite so.'

'Please God that comes to pass, for the sake of others.' Jake Darling hesitated. The passageway was almost in darkness, save for the firelight leaking beneath the parlour door. 'Doctor. Your fee?'

'If I failed to save your little boy, Jake, how can there be a fee?'

'I shall pay one, in God's time, though.' The waggoner paused. 'About little Clare.'

'Yes? She too is not ill, is she?'

'Not so far. But is it possible that she too might be taken?'

'I do not know, Jake. There are instances of which I have read, where whole townships and villages have suffered epidemics of croup, with many children succumbing in a short time. But it is a disease of the young growing age. Strangely, no child unweaned ever seems to suffer it. Children over the age of twelve years usually do not show any tendency towards the illness. It is remarkably constant for all its cruelty and abrupt qualities. I only wish . . .'

'So she *may*, Doctor?'

'I fear so, Jake. We simply do not know if it is infectious from one to another. Or passable. Or is it contagious, by means of touch? Or is there something about an actual place in which a person lives with his children? We are woefully ignorant, Jake, strive though we may to lessen our ignorance day to day.'

'But thank you, Doctor. For trying.'

'Thank you, Jake.'

Thank you, Doctor. Once again, thank you, Doctor, as we bury our dead and you return home to your house alive and well. Thank you, as you sit in your chair while we scrape for pennies to slip through your door so you may stay well sated. Parasite, that was the proper medical term nowadays for such a one, who lives at the expense of others and manages to survive in a state of plenty while the parasitized host suffers, fails and eventually is no more.

Carmichael wearily collected his few instruments, most of them home made, and the three bottles: opiate, calomel purgative, and antimonial emetic. Perhaps all rubbish, waste of effort and waste of time, only perhaps increasing little Harry's suffering as he had struggled to breathe, and died. And *died*, may God forgive.

What was the use? What was his use?

Doctor Carmichael nodded to Jake Darling, and made for the door. He stood for a moment, his hand on the Suffolk latch.

'Please express my condolences to Mrs Darling, Jake. And to little Clare. Say I am very, very sorry.'

'Thank you, Doctor.'

Carmichael almost screamed *Don't say that! Don't ever say that to me again, not for anything!* He simply nodded, and stepped outside.

The air was chill. A low thick mist without drizzle was forming upon the shores of Whitehanger, the trees barely visible through the low-lying white. A moon showed faintly, providing some hint of direction and shapes about the cottage. Nearby, a narrow track led past the copse by which Darling's thatched cottage stood, towards the coastal path which eventually passed between the tide mill at Watermillock and the estate of the Hunterfields at Lorne House. He hesitated for a moment, wondering if he should risk the inland route, which would be shorter but would take him across the wooded slopes of Whitehanger. The charcoal burners there had a reputation of being rough and grim, and he as yet lacked sufficient confidence to trust himself among country people who might see in him a vulnerable prey rather than a mere homewarding pedestrian. No. It would have to be the seaward path, though an extra two miles was a labour he could well do without.

He set off, keeping the moon in the same quarter, feeling his way for the first hundred yards until the sea's reflection brought a sense of direction more firmly to his mind. Then he strode out more purposefully, wishing he had some lanthorn light. He began to wonder how they would manage in a hundred years' time, those doctors of the future. Might they have conquered this terrible disease? Was there some way, some clear and simple way which was staring him in the face, that they would perceive and instantly perform? How they will scorn us! he thought with growing dismay. They will laugh with derision at our puny efforts to heal these sick children, and shake their heads over the records we leave. For now, though, all was daydreaming and sorrow. And failure, as little Harry Darling was yet one more failure in the collective experience of thousands of doctors, all as baffled and as useless as he.

Mehala waited for the sun to show through. But as the Donkey and Buskin roused into the dark dawn bustle, nothing came of her expectations.

Old Alice came to chide her for idling and staring out towards the sea. Mrs Weaver had already given permission for Mehala to take the pram out, so whatever the weather there would be no turning back.

The moon had begun to fade, and daylight seeped through the low thick mist. No breeze could be felt on the chill.

Little Jane accompanied Mehala down to the hard where the small dinghy was moored. It had once been fitted with some sort of sail, she saw, but there was none now. It had two oars, with rowlocks of a crude hempen bond.

'Mehala. Nellie says you should take some water, and a crust.'

'For why, Jane?'

'Against the chance of drifting, Mehala.' The little maid carried a muslin twisted about a small loaf, and an earthenware flask stoppered by a leather bung.

Mehala remembered the caution, of trust in the knowing, suspicious sea. She shook her head. It was tempting the gods.

'No, thank you, Little Jane. I shall go without.'

'You mustn't mind those silly stories, Mehala! They're but tales told on these shores for the foolish! Why,' Little Jane said earnestly, trotting alongside as Mehala started down the hythe, 'there are sailors even in Sealandings who will pay all they earn in a year, in gold coin, for a baby's caul cased in pottery! It's a sovereign remedy against drowning, see? But everybody knows it's nothing more than a tall tale!'

'Yes. I too have seen those little caskets, carried on sailors' belts, some in silver, and worn by high captains of the Royal Navy too. But this is no charm I offer this morning, Little Jane. It is myself. And offer it I shall.'

'Then go with God, Mehala.'

'Back soon, Little Jane.'

'Have you the money, Mehala? Keep it safe. Mrs Weaver be mortal angered at servants who lose a farthing.'

'I shall lose none, and shall pay well for as much as I shall get!'

Little Jane stood above the hythe paving's edge, watching Mehala descend the steps.

'It's the fat one, Mehala,' she warned. 'That pram do drift to starboard a little, and is heavy on the incoming tide. She's bereft of her mast and sail, see?'

'Thank you, Jane. I shall manage.'

Mehala stepped aboard and inspected the minute vessel. It felt strange, but solid. The dinghy was not foreshortened in the prow, as was these days becoming a mark of some of the inland and estuary prams. This was curved, of a length, and heart-shaped at the transom. Mercifully, Providence had decreed that there be a stern notch for the oar if one wished to stern scull. The oars were heavy and ill-kempt. Nobody up at the Donkey and Buskin had bothered for many a season to tend to the small craft. It was time they looked to it, for boats were costly and deserved care, being the only thing that lay between the ocean and breath.

'Bye, Jane.'

'Steer close under the shore of Whitehanger, Mehala. And ask for the Dowsett boys by the hard there. They give good measure.'

'Very well. One hour, pray God.'

'One hour, Mehala. And amen.'

The tide was hanging, as Sealanding folk had it, neither waxing or waning, but lolling offshore for some signal of earth and moon to start its long inward pull. Mehala stood at the stern and thrust one oar over the notch, lying the wood in it, and giving it an expert twist to propel the boat into the low sea mist.

'You know how, Mehala!' Little Jane's voice floated after.

'Only good fortune, Jane!'

Mehala was reluctant to look back, another silly superstition. Though superstitions were patently absurd, it somehow seemed foolhardy to risk flouting them. So she conformed to the seafarers' habit and stared steadfastly towards the indistinct harbour mouth.

A ketch, old-fashioned and without a foremast, swung idly at its mooring on the north curve of the harbour. Mehala could hear the activity on board with astonishing clarity through the mist, though the small coastal vessel's outline was vague and its mass almost lost in the subtle minute swirls of the opacity. It made her shiver. It was as if the ship were hollow, a periphery of substance and a ghost for an interior, yet with the voices of men and the sound of their movements busy within.

She shook herself and bent to her task of propelling the dinghy out towards the open sea. Such thoughts were fanciful, nothing more than mere imagination. And stupid imaginings at that. For she had seen the very men of that ketch come ashore, laughing and drinking. Why, she herself had served two or three of them! There was no doubt they were as real as she herself.

A cat schooner, she knew, was warped to the south mole. She would have to pass to within a few cables' lengths of her to make the sea without coming too close to the point where the harbour lanthorns shone at night. She effected the slow move, finding herself easing into the work and settling down to a steady thrust. The small boat responded sluggishly but quite well.

Curious to find herself recovering the quicker in work rather than in rest. Strange. She wondered if that Doctor Carmichael would have some explanation for this, or if it were stupid fancy, like her sudden fear of that ketch against the northern mole. Offshore, a sudden clear patch allowed her a glimpse of horizon for an instant before the mist closed down again, hiding everything save the prow of her boat.

A large vessel was standing off from the harbour, about a mile or so, but evidently heading for shore. There was so little wind. The poor thing had possibly been hauling towards Sealandings for the whole night, though Mehala could recall looking out to sea, her habit these many years, and checking to see if any lights were showing out on the water . . .

For many years? She recalled the East Mersea village, its dark waters beyond, the sea sedge and the saltings, the winds moaning in the chimneys – of which so many visitors always complained, for the winds were constant and unrelenting on this eastern coast. Yes, that had been her practice, with her old mother staring out and looking from the windows of Red Hall, where they had gone after that Elijah Rebow had fired their cottage and forced them to concede his authority over them.

There was still no movement in the tide, still hanging. That large vessel, some sort of Navy frigate perhaps, with its one line of guns and the black and white chequered appearance along its length, might well put into Sealandings for some reason. Victualling, perhaps, as was usual? Or taking a few more seamen on after a particularly diminishing voyage where the crews were reduced by those strange sea fevers sailors spoke of.

Steadily, she thrust on. The day was almost about to break, seep rather, from the thickened sky. How weird it was, to see almost clear air above, when down here on the surface of the water good visibility could be no more than twenty yards! But if Sealandings were as Mersea Island, she would be enabled to see twice that distance in a few minutes. And with the coming of frank daylight and the recession of all shadows, the grey translucency which was East Anglia's habitual daylight would set in and she would be at home.

Fear had left her. She rounded the south mole and put it behind her, sculling with that wrist motion she had learned ... had learned ... from whom? From George De Witt? The one she'd remembered with such clarity last evening, only to fail even to call his face to mind this dawn? Or that same terrible madman Elijah Rebow, who had...? No. From someone kind, gentle, who had taken her little hands in his large old ones and, smiling and puffing that stinking tobacco in his old horn pipe which he always somehow managed to light without setting his old white whiskers afire, had showed her how to set the oars and move them together. 'It's what folk call synchrony, child,' he had told her, laughing and shaking his head as if at the stupidity of the word. 'Imagine! A special word, just to mean together!'

'Together, Abby,' Mehala said aloud. 'Abby.'

Old Abraham. Who used to catch fish in the Ray Channel, and watched for us to guard us on the Ray Island in the Blackwater estuary.

A man's voice suddenly called across the water. 'Hello, there! Who's there?'

'Mehala,' she called back. She must have spoken aloud, not realizing.

'What craft then?'

'Mehala. From the Donkey and Buskin tavern, of Sealandings.'

There was a burst of laughter from her right, perhaps from the schooner she had seen last night. 'Pass then, Mehala of Sealandings!'

'And call here on your return, lassie!' another voice called, amid laughter.

' 'Tis the pretty one,' a third offered, but then a stern voice called the men to get on with their work, and there was no more.

Mehala smiled. It was the schooner, victualling and receiving cordage by local purchase.

Now she could see nothing, here outside the harbour proper.

The sea was lifting slightly under her, feeling the boat, but still not drifting her from her course as far as she could judge. She was at home, easy within herself and thinking of all sorts of events so as not to dwell too much on her position, alone on the North Sea's shallows where she had lately nearly drowned.

The mark would be a looming of a dark shoreline, wooded and quite steep for these low-lying parts. That would be Whitehanger. She was to detect the smoke of the charcoal burners there, if the wind allowed. That would confirm her direction had held true. Then she was to continue a mile or so, until she felt the tide pulling her landwards, and let the boat follow. She would hear the sounds from Whitehanger soon afterwards, and there would land on the hard. She was to find someone, ask for the mussel fishers, and buy from the Dowsett brothers and start her return journey. There would be no difficulties then. In the estuaries hereabouts, she had been assured by Nellie less than an hour ago, the mists never lasted more than two hours after sunrise, and generally evaporated a deal earlier than that. She could row her fastest on the home leg, and be able to see all the way from Whitehanger.

The tide mill at Watermillock could be the mark by which she was to check progress on the way back, but would be no help on the outward as its flat basin always lay in the grip of the mist until broad day. A pity, this, Nellie had explained, since the lady there, Mrs Maderley, kept a light in her corner window for sails to go by, though it was really in the use of her strange son William, a dreamer whose strangeness lay in his staring at trees and rivers and the sea to gauge Nature's moods. He often painted at night by lanthorn. Still Mehala kept glancing to her right, straining to see if a faint glim showed, but to no avail. The mist had closed around her again. She strained on, looping the wrist round one way, pulling her arm in at the elbow, then scooping the blade the other way by a dexterous shift of the force of her hand. It was simple but laborious, considering the poor forward motion accomplished, yet it saved strength in the long run. And, if she needed to produce a sudden burst of her full power, perhaps to evade some careless large ship or cut out from a tide race on the edge of a sandbank, she would have a reserve of energy to achieve it.

And she could look the way she was going. She could stand, looking to right and left and ahead in turn, then again. And again, and again, and all the time. 'No job is ever done, little Mehala,' old Abby had insisted. 'On land or on the water. Never, ever done.'

'Never done.' She echoed her memory aloud.

She was beginning to think of cutting landward when she first heard it. A faint splash, so feeble that she wondered if she was imagining it.

The splash was a singular one, a regular thrash-thrash-thrash, then none. Silence.

She listened, even pausing in her sculling, standing motionless as the boat lost way. She glanced over the stern at her wake. Fatal to lose sight of that, for if she did there would be nothing left of direction. People, even experienced fishermen who lived all their days afloat, lost their lives by making that elementary mistake, failing to keep a check on direction in a mist or, worse, a closing sea fog. Let the boat spin once and you were lost, crying for help and hearing only the fog throw back your own voice at you as you drifted, drifted, drifted . . .

A whistle. A faint, singular whistle. No tune, nothing you could hear melody in, but only a whistle, as a man might make whittling or mending tackle in some stable. Then a gasp, again so unheard that she wondered about herself. Some sea creature? There were tales along these shores of the most sinister animals, some of them half men and half . . .

Then splash-splash-splash, then the whistle. It was odd. She felt fright, checked the wake, saw it had almost disappeared from view, and made three strokes of her stern scull. Paused, drifting, keeping the wake in view.

Whistle. Whistle. Silence.

'Who is there? Are you in need?' She heard the mist absorb her call, damply muffling the words as if the air were made of linsey-woolsey of a sudden.

The whistle sounded, fainter now, but in spurts of thin piping sound, whee-whee-whee-wheeeeey, as if the whistler's breath had failed. One splash more, then silence. She clapped her hands, holding the oar's end under her armpit so as not to lose it – another fatal mistake, should that happen in these mists.

Clap-clap-clap-clap.

Splashes, two, as if of a struggle, then whee-whee-whee-wheey, then nothing.

'Are you in danger, then?'

Her heart was thudding as if it would leap from her breast. She could hear her own gasping more than any other sound in the awful silence which settled around. Was it the mist, creating these sounds, she thought for a frantic moment, to tempt her from her proper course? It was the sea, that dark wild thing which had once nearly taken her and

131

which now was forming phantoms of sight and sound finally to capture her and drag her down . . .

But what if it were somebody in distress, drowning as she had once almost drowned? Was this the sea's obscure test for trust?

'I'm coming,' she called, sculling again but with all her force, dragging the boat's prow round to starboard. 'Make whatever sounds you can. I'm coming!'

Foolishly she thought of her stupidity. What if those sailors from the schooner, hearing her sculling past, had decided upon some small innocent trickery, to set her red-faced and embarrassed in the taproom this evening when they came off duty? But there had been something urgent, frightened, almost doomed in that whistle, and those repetitive splashes . . . Might some child be caught in the sandbanks? The tide was moving now, all of a sudden pushing her landwards faster than she wanted to go. She used it to assist, in her anxiety to make faster headway towards the direction of the whistling.

She heard it again in a quick pause. She listened, now gasping for breath, turning her head to gauge direction. Port a few points. Near? Far? How to tell?

'Sound what you can!' she called, desperately sculling, whipping the oar faster and catching the water up from the surface in a manner wasteful of effort and time, but she was frightened for the whistler. It might well be some stray woman out collecting mussels or something for her family when a sudden swirl of a tide turned her from a mere sandwalker to a creature marooned on a sinking foothold with the water rising –

She screamed. A figure was ahead, in the water. She found she had driven the prow straight at him, hitting his shoulder and driving him over into the water. He was half standing, with his head and shoulders barely out of the sea. He was gasping and sinking in the sands. She had seen it before, in the Ray Channel.

She called to him, stupidly. 'I'm here. Catch a hold!'

But the creature was too far gone, and she flung the oar down in the thwarts and leant out, grasping the man's hair with all her strength, yanking the boat to a slewed turn on the pivot of the drowning man's head. He gasped as water filled his mouth, and vomited into the sea. She lifted one of his arms inboard, placing the cold fingers over the gunwale and pressing them down against the wood. They curved, held. The man understood that here was something solid in his world of drowning and sinking and wetness and fluidity . . .

'Pull, man!' she shouted. 'Pull yourself in, can't you?'

The man was too far gone. She dragged his other arm inboard, laid it on the bulwark with his other and pressed the fingers so they too held. Then she tore a sleeve from her dress, and the other, and tied them together. She tried to loop the length round him, but he gave a sudden spasm, perhaps thinking that she was about to leave him or detach his hold from the boat. She lost her grip on the sleeves, which drifted off slowly while her boat swung and spun. She almost sobbed to see the cloth go, from fright as much as anything, for she knew that she too was lost, and no longer could know where the shore lay in this mist. But the man should be saved first, that was clear.

The painter! She kept hold of one of his wrists, for fear of his fainting and drifting off, and groped for the small painter rope in the prow. It came, and she managed to lean out, fearful of capsizing, and pass it around him under his arms. She almost recoiled when his eyes opened a fraction, and she looked into his from a distance of inches. He was almost unconscious. She had nothing to fear, save now from the sea.

There was little left of the painter with which to fashion a knot of sufficient strength, so she tied the free end round her ankle, keeping the line taut, and settled herself in the mid thwarts, catching up both oars.

She would have to row Dutch fashion, facing the prow and with her back to the stern, but drawing the man along as a ketch drew its pram, at the trail. A slow stroke showed her the feasibility of this, and she strengthened her actions, going with the tide after a moment's indecision. The tide was quickening now. It was bound to be. Surely she had been out here on the sea long enough for it to cease its hanging and start flooding in towards the estuaries? Surely?

After a few strokes she paused, listening for the sounds that Nellie and Little Jane had promised would come from Whitehanger. She sniffed desperately at the air for a scent of the charcoal burners' smoke, but gained no clues. She was alone, with the drowned man spinning slowly at the end of the painter as she tugged him along through the sea. His head was above water, thank God, so her painter, looped under his arms, was proving effective, but her ankle was numb now with the effort of pulling the painter tight, using the position of her foot. It was white and bloodless, but she had no way of getting the rope more securely fastened without help.

How long she rowed she could not tell. Her only guide for direction now was the tide, and she was unsure whether that was helping or hindering. Once an incoming tide made the shore line, it tended to run along the coast in sometimes dangerous and eccentric swirls. A boatsman was a fool to follow blindly, unless circumstances gave him no other choice. She felt weary, and knew her strength was failing. It had not been very long since she herself had been in the same terrible circumstance as the drowning man, and she had already expended more of her strength than she dared think of.

It was in one of her pauses that she decided she must conserve her powers. She did one more small stint of rowing in this horrid mist blanket, then stopped to rest for a full minute, tried to restore feeling to her tethered foot, and started shouting. She bent to the oars again, made three long strokes, and tumbled over with a cry as the boat crashed into something slithery and soft, halting with a judder that grated and lifted. She cried out again in alarm and fear, clawed herself erect, then stared round.

The boat was still, held fast, upon a shore. Sand and a fine gravelly surface. She could see trees vaguely rising from the shore line. Waves sounded on both sides, crashing softly with a familiar regular sound. And light was seeping through the mist. It was lifting. She could see ten, a dozen yards. She felt her head gingerly. Blood. There was a cut from the bulwark where she had fallen.

Her drowned man! She scrambled towards the prow, which stood out into the oncoming tide, and pulled on the painter. The man slid through the waves. She clawed for him, pulled him into the shallows with the last of her strength. It was total exertion, but she could not move him further. She was afraid to step out of the boat, though the sea's edge was shallow and only ankle deep where the prow lay. The tides could deepen with a terrible speed, she well knew. Never leave your boat when the tide is racing, Abby had told her. But the man was drowning, possibly had already died.

She kept his head in her hand, chin upward, and untied the painter from her ankle, yelping as the blood tingled pins and needles through the flesh. She drew the painter free, keeping hold of the man. He lay sprawled in the sea, supine, his legs lifting with each wave. The boat was beginning to stir ominously, signifying that the tide was quickening still more now, starting its headlong rush among the low sands and mud flats of the estuary.

There was not much rope to use, but enough to circle her waist. She made a belt of it round her, tying it on her left side, then against all reason kirtled up her skirt and stepped out of the boat. This way she was certain never to lose the boat in the sea mist. Even if it did start to drift, it now could not go without her. And she had hold of the man. She dragged him, sitting waist-deep in the water, cradling his head between her legs and thrusting her feet into the muddy sand beneath each wave

134

as it arrived. This way she inched up the beach, dragging the boat and the man a fraction at a time.

'Tom? Is that you, man?'

She screamed at the nearness of the voice. She turned in fright and saw the vast figure.

Silhouetted against the glowing early light rose an enormous shape, a great horse surmounted by a giant cloaked figure. It was petrifyingly motionless, looming above her.

'Sir?' she said faintly, wondering for an instant if she too was drowned and this some terrible emissary.

'What in God's name. . . ?'

The figure clicked and urged the beast down the slope. 'Care, Betsy, care now.'

'I found this man sinking in the sands . . .'

'A girl, is it?' The man dismounted, coming down the mud with a tut of irritation. 'And you hauling my man from the water like a sea goddess!' He stood over her. 'Well, stand up, girl!'

'I cannot, sir. My foot fails.' She lifted her foot. The ankle was bleeding, the skin scraped off by the rope's action as she had rowed ashore.

'How is he? Tom? You still with us, are you?'

'He showed some life, sir. I saw his eyes. And he whistled. But he has not spoken – '

'He's dumb, girl. A mute.' The gentleman bent, lifted her with ease and set her upright. She wobbled, but kept her balance. He stepped into the waves and pulled Tom on to the strand. 'Naturally he'd have nought to say, here or anywhere.'

'I've had to tie the painter round him, sir. I fear I might have injured him.'

'Little cost, that, girl, if you brought him out of the sand flats. There's many drowned for want of a girl with your endeavour happening by.'

'Thank you, sir.'

'Stay there.' The gentleman dragged the recumbent form of his servant further up the slope until he was able to lay him on the first line of the sea grass, near to where the trees began. He returned, taking her hand roughly and pulling her unceremoniously along.

'If you please, sir. I am tied to the boat.'

'What the hell for?'

'For fear of the boat's drifting and leaving us both stranded on the mud flats. The tide is coming in, sir, and I was afeared of being lost also.'

135

'Hmmph. Very sensible.' The gentleman stood looking down at her. The brow of the beach emphasized his natural height over her. 'Girl, you have done mortally good work this morning.'

'Thank you, sir.'

'Tell me the truth, now. Were you with Tom this night through?'

'Sir?'

'Was you lying with Tom on some nice remote spot where the Whitehanger folk would be unlikely to stray, while you and he. . . ?'

'No, sir! Indeed not!'

'Then how came you by him while he drowned?'

'I was out for the mussels, sir. I'm bound for Whitehanger, to fetch mussels for the tavern. John Weaver's. I have money, sir.' She fumbled anxiously to find the coins given her by Mrs Weaver, as if showing them would prove her story.

'And you were from. . . ?'

'Sealandings, sir. I was let out with the tavern pram, and given directions, sir.'

'And heard Tom whistle, you said?'

'The poor man was whistling, sir. I didn't realize he was dumb. And he made regular splashings, doubtless having heard my sculling as I passed.'

'Sounds a true tale. Which tavern?'

'The Donkey and Buskin, sir.'

'I don't know you.' The gentleman was gazing at her. 'I thought I knew all the people of Sealandings, and hereabouts. Where are you from? Some ship put in for victualling, or one of the market folk?'

'No, sir. I'm taken from the sea myself, less than a week ago. I'm lodged at the Donkey and Buskin. John Weaver and his mistress in charity gave me board, against work, until I am recovered.'

'So you are she?' The gentleman stared down in silence, thinking. 'Mehala, is it?'

'Yes. sir.'

'And your last name?'

She hesitated, then deliberately lied. 'I am not fully minded yet, sir. Doctor Carmichael said as how it might take a week or even more to recover.'

'I remember. He came to Lorne House the night you were taken up by *The Jaunty*.'

So this was Squire Hunterfield, the district's chief magistrate. 'Sir. Begging your pardon, but the man Tom . . . Should we not be aiding him, sir?'

'They either drown or they breathe, Mehala. But let's try to assist Nature.'

They tended to the man. He was still breathing, but cold and blue to his lips. They had barely lifted him to a sitting position when someone approached along the beach, leading a horse.

'Squire Hunterfield?'

'Carmichael! It's you.' The squire sounded relieved, and straightened to greet the doctor. 'This is becoming quite a gathering, but a fortunate one. Can you restore my man Tom? He was taken from the estuary by this girl in her boat. I fear he seems . . .'

'Your horse, Squire? Or your man's, perhaps?' The doctor bent to examine the recumbent groom.

'So it is. She must have wandered off, and Tom asleep on some firm sand.'

'And Mehala,' Doctor Carmichael said, smiling up at her. 'In no fit state to help, it seems.'

'I shall help if you wish, Doctor.'

'Then help me to get him upright. I shall then squeeze him and droop him over your back, and so rid his lights of the sea, with God's good agency.'

They managed to get the servant upright, while Squire Hunterfield went to collect his own horse and tether the two beasts to a shrubby tree. Carmichael nodded to Mehala, telling her to stoop over, and tumbled the groom on to her back. She grunted at the effort of keeping from being crushed beneath the weight, but held on to her own knees to take the strain as the doctor compressed the man's chest in sudden great squeezes. The sea water, expressed from the man, ran down Mehala's garments in frothy spurts.

She knew that she was more dishevelled than she had ever been. There would be a terrible time explaining this away to Mrs Nelson and Nellie and Mrs Weaver.

How absurd, this position, this circumstance. Always the sea, dangerous and malicious, that spoiled her life.

'Come out, girl.'

'Sir?' She was on the ground, her face against the grass.

'Come up, Mehala. You have passed out.' Doctor Carmichael was raising her feet immodestly, examining the skinned ankle and looking down at her. The man Tom was groaning and coughing, his back against the bole of a small tree. The gentleman was standing nearby. It was pale of day now, and the sea mist was wisping away, losing its strength as bits of the foreshore appeared, all innocent and easy, within reach. Sea birds were gliding in from the shoreline, and small dunnocks were already experimenting with beaks, eyes, ground, grasses.

'I am so sorry, Doctor.'

'Why the apology? This man owes you his life, Mehala. You have returned the sea's favour, with a great percentage to boot. He must have sunk in the mud flats. His horse ran, the scamp.'

'You did very well, girl,' Hunterfield said. He glanced from the doctor to the girl, then to the groom, who was coming round sufficiently to stir himself, trying to stand. 'I want a word with you both.'

'A word, Squire Hunterfield?'

Doctor Carmichael's voice was dry and uninflected as he said slowly, 'I called at Lorne House to inform you that this girl Mehala was fetched from the sea and asking your advice about her disposal, only to be sent away as an intruder by your sister, the Mrs Vallance.'

'I knew nothing of that until afterwards, Carmichael. Nothing. And Lydia had her heart set upon an uninterrupted evening that particular time.'

For a moment the two men were silent, as if assessing each other's intentions. Then Carmichael gave a nod of silent agreement. 'You wanted a word, Squire?'

'It's this. Tom, naturally, won't speak. I want your word, as a gentleman, that you also will observe discretion about this incident.'

'You have it, sir.' Carmichael turned to Mehala. 'It is important for Squire Hunterfield's name not to be mentioned in casual conversation, Mehala. Especially about this incident tonight, neither of Tom, nor me, nor the squire's presence here on the coast of Whitehanger. Will you promise to say nothing?'

'I promise, Doctor.'

'Can she be trusted, Carmichael?' Hunterfield asked gruffly.

'Indeed I can, Squire,' Mehala said. She was aware that she must look distressingly dishevelled and stained by mud, her sleeves gone, soaked by the sea water and grimed by the horrid struggle in the shallows. But she was determined to answer for herself, and speak with the authority she felt she possessed naturally, without the aid of an intermediary, even one like Doctor Carmichael to whom she owed a great deal. 'I can give my word as well as anyone in the Kingdom. And I do give it, sir.'

Hunterfield barked a short laugh, gauging her, then nodded. 'Very well . . . Mehala. I am indebted to you, and to you, Carmichael.' He swung himself up on to his mare, reining gently. 'Have you a position to go to, Mehala?'

'No, sir. As I said, I am at the tavern of John Weaver.'

'Very well.' He turned the beast round. 'Carmichael. Her disposition; see me in a day or two. I bid you g'day, Doctor. And Mehala.' He was smiling as he left, the mare clopping quietly on the grass. Tom was stirring, coming to well enough, looking around and no longer coughing.

'It . . . it is rather a delicate matter, Mehala.' Doctor Carmichael said with some hesitation and embarrassment. 'He is, you understand, naturally reluctant for this to come to public knowledge.'

'I understand, Doctor.'

'And he is naturally somewhat concerned lest his family learn of his absence during the night, you see. That requires our urgent attention to our promises. You understand?'

'Fully, Doctor.'

He suddenly smiled, openly and widely, as if for the first time. 'I really believe you do, Mehala,' he said, and they turned their attentions to Tom.

18

Carradine had his own way of returning home, as a man must. After all, Carradine Manor had been in his family's possession for over three centuries. It had grown over the years, but in such a way that his ancestors seemed to retain some sort of lien on the gables, the weird buttresses, the landscaped grounds. There was an unusual proximity between the manor and its stables and outhouses. The entire place lived somehow in Carradine, wherever he went. As did his ancestors. Their absence was unavoidable, as they had long ago left for their eternal reward, but they remained in Carradine Manor in spirit.

He dropped from his mount in the drive, bouncing on to the lowest step. The servants were breathlessly trying to present themselves in some sort of decent array as he landed, smoothing and patting and bowing. Carradine ran up the steps, grinning.

'Welcome home, sir! Welcome!'

'Morning, Mrs Tyll. Is the house well?'

The woman was thirtyish, handsome though plain of figure and manner, and even as she spoke was checking along the line of maids for aberrancy and inappropriate dress. They were in a ferment, since there had been no notice of the master's arrival for this hour.

'Well indeed, sir. Say a welcome,' she ordered.

The line chorused a faint greeting. 'Welcome, sir,' with wobbling curtsies.

'Welcome back to Carradine, sir.' Hobbes was the senior man in the house. Grey and quiet, he was a deeply religious soul who kept his own counsel, and most importantly could not be bribed or threatened into breaching his master's. 'You are a day early. I trust there is no urgency in your precipitate return?'

'Hobbes,' Carradine said, already exasperated by the man's gravity. 'How often must I tell you? There's *always* urgency. In everything, in every hour God sends – and in some which he doesn't!'

'Quite so, sir.' Hobbes bowed stiffly, retreating into his servitude.

Carradine grinned, shaking his cloak from his shoulders. The nearest maid gave a squeak and made a dive but failed to gather it before it fell to the stone verandah. Mrs Tyll glared at the unfortunate girl, which amused Carradine further. Hobbes would be huffy for two days now, thinking all references to God blasphemous save those made by some lunatic parson or other. It was a game Carradine played. This was his own house. He felt he had the right to say and do as he wished, even though it meant startling this formal little assembly under his portico.

'And Lennon. No news for me?'

'Sir. The counting table is prepared, and documents are available for you any time you send.'

Lennon was a smiley, seemingly untroubled man. With Hobbes and Lennon looking after his interests, Carradine felt he had a right pair. For as stuffy and reticent as Hobbes was, so Lennon was the natural smiler, brisk and ebullient, capable of laughing at a joke, pleased with life. As well he might be, Carradine thought, for he himself had not the time to pry into every nook and cranny, and perforce had to leave Lennon to manage the manor's estate as best he could without interference. It was not an exacting arrangement, of course. There were friends in London's gaming houses who whispered – or even advised openly – that Carradine should take over his own estate for a good four months of the year, and so ensure that Lennon's fingers did not leak overmuch. But time was of the essence in life. Carradine was a man in a hurry and told people so. He wanted wings, not chains.

'How many of the tenants are in arrears, Lennon?'

'I have the details. Only six so far, sir. There's a mortgage and an investment bond I shall advise you to see, if it is not too presumptuous. Whenever you wish.'

'Very well. After I have breakfasted. Mrs Tyll?'

'Sir?'

'Who've we taken on, in, up, of this lot?'

'Three maids, sir. All new.' She beckoned for the new girls to step from line as she gave their names. 'Becky, Sealandings, of the fisher families down the hythe. Joan, likewise. And Dee, an orphan girl sent by Miss Matilda Gould three months back, from the schoolhouse.'

Carradine eyed them swiftly, dismissed them with a nod. They were nothing out of the ordinary. And, dressed in the subdued style which Mrs Tyll insisted on, with hardly a waist or shape to be seen and their hair slammed back under the mobcap fringe, they could have been any sort of creature. The tall girl, Joan, might have possibilities, but there was no way of telling until later.

'The rest are all the same, then?'

'Yes, sir, if you please.'

'Cheap at the price,' he said, laughing.

Lennon laughed along with him. Hobbes showed only his sternest

141

face, and the servants followed Carradine in. Mrs Chandler the cook was only then bustling up the hall, and greeted the master with a glad cry. She was picked up, and carried bodily down to the kitchen, Carradine laughing and yelling for his breakfast every inch of the way and Mrs Chandler screaming to be put down, that he was a dreadful boy and what would the old master have said at this display, not to mention . . .

'The Honourable Mr Carradine will require his usual tour of the house immediately, girls,' Mrs Tyll informed the maids soberly as the noise receded. 'He returns in a particular manner, and will wish to inspect every single room. Do not be alarmed at his speech. If there is anything you do not follow, appeal to me and I shall interpret for you. If he wishes for any assistance, or drinks, or victuals, provide it instantly, or delay will incur his displeasure. He is extremely impatient, being a very busy and important person, and will brook no indolence whatever.'

As the maids curtseyed and scattered, Hobbes sighed and went with Mrs Tyll towards the library to lay a table of side fare for the consultations with Lennon regarding the estate.

'I keep steadfast the hope that one day the master will return from London a quieter and more sober man, Mrs Tyll, but on each occasion I am sorely disappointed. He is no better.'

'He is his own man, Mr Hobbes.'

The old man sighed. 'Indeed, Mrs Tyll. But I wish a little spark of religious quietude would enter in. His grandfather was such a deep-thinking man, a holy and god-fearing gentleman whose advice was sought by monarchs, in his time. Is it too much to hope for, that something of the father should reveal itself in the son?'

I hope that day never dawns, Mr Hobbes, Mrs Tyll thought, but did not say. She was thrilled at the master's return, and saw now how very wise her instincts had been, to attire the new girls in the most sombre apparel and keep them at the far end of the line where Carradine would be too impatient even to step over and meet them face to face. That Joan girl was quite comely, seen close to and given half a chance, so it was as well to have positioned her at the end of the portico. Now all that remained was to see if he had the same demands as of old.

'Where the hell's Tyll?' Carradine's bellow rose from the kitchen.

'Coming, sir!'

Hobbes watched Mrs Tyll rush off, her skirts drawing sibilances from the marble flooring. He harboured all manner of suspicions about the household at Carradine Manor, but never voiced them even to himself. He went towards the library, shaking his head.

The tour of Carradine Manor was accomplished at lightning speed. Carradine enjoyed this part of his return, feeling a stranger, even an interloper, until he had touched every wall, tapped the heavy gilt frames of the oil paintings along the staircases, even disturbing the curtains as he hurried past. The servants rushed along in his wake.

He kept up a commentary, admonishing and observing. 'This curtain's different, Tyll – where's Tyll got to? – and that colour's new, isn't it? And who's shifted the hall stand? Wasn't there a great walnut-wood thing here once?'

The housekeeper and steward were hard put to keep pace. 'Yes, sir, but the walnut tends to fade in sunlight. I removed it to regain its colour, the shade being rather delicate . . .' But answers went unheeded, for he instantly was off on some other tangent, into another room.

'Those books weren't there last time I was home, were they, Hobbes? Where the hell's Hobbes got to? Hobbes?' in a great yell, faintly answered by the old man, breathless in the rear. 'Coming, sir.'

'Paused for a quick prayer, has he?' Carradine said, grinning and charging on as the maids gasped at this outrageously sacrilegious jest. 'And where's the dogs? Who's said Lennon could keep the dogs out of the house? I want Ringer and Bell. Send for Lennon. I'll have it out with the bloody man . . .'

Every room, every wall, every hanging. The people who served and waited and cleaned and cooked were incidentals. Mrs Tyll welcomed the return for this very reason. Without the master's hard judgements, her own life would be the less. She hurried with him, reassuring, soothing, answering as best she could.

'I've to be in Sealandings in an hour. Send to Lennon, get the grooms busy.'

'Yes, sir.'

Mrs Tyll nodded for a maid to run out to find Hobbes and pass the word. In the whirlwind of Carradine's presence she was at peace, replete before the repast, as it were. She smiled at the master. Carradine was home. That was all she asked.

Hunterfield took his breakfast sombrely, without much relish. This was out of character, for when returning from Thalia De Foe's bed he was usually hungry and calm, emptied of those toxins which had accumulated in the enforced absence from her closet ministrations.

Lydia had provided the usual excellent breakfast for him. This morning he could not do it justice, though it was universally agreed to be the most important meal of the day.

He took a small quantity of the veal and ham pie, and some cold game to toy with. Cold tongue had long been his favourite, and to complete the cold buffet Lydia had produced a long game and rumpsteak pie which was beautifully garnished in her own manner. Yes, Lydia was almost wasted in the absence of her husband. She certainly exercised her talents admirably at Lorne House in the meanwhile.

The hot dishes were more plentiful, as befitted breakfast, but for some reason – not far to seek considering the events of the dawn – failed to appeal. She had had composed a broiled fish dish, whiting and mackerel, with broiled sheep kidneys in the hot plate, its small wicks heating the metal beneath. He managed to finish a hot rump steak, and two or three muffins, with some slices of her usual breakfast cake, but the dried haddock he declined. He had simply no real appetite. The bacon dishes could go hang.

Such a wretched business, all in all. That Mehala girl had undoubtedly saved the day, for Tom, if he had actually drowned, would have been missed. Then there would have been the ugly business of his corpse being washed ashore, and still further explanations needed as to where he had been, what he had been doing, how came he drowned when it was known he never left Squire Hunterfield's side. No, ugly, ugly.

Then for the doctor to come strolling along, at that ungodly hour. Ye gods! It was worse than London's Strand, or Convent Garden! What on earth was the man doing, coming at that hour? But that too had been a stroke of luck, since he had found Tom's mount and taken it in hand. His mare Betsy had been no such problem, for, probably worried by the incoming tide while Tom had slept on the sands for forty winks, she had wisely moved to shore and returned to the place she had last seen her master, which was the wooden valley in which Milton Hall stood. Sensible to have always arranged to meet Tom there. Good old Betsy. He admitted to being more than a little startled when the mare had whinnied alone at his muted call, and he had found Tom missing.

The question was this Mehala creature. Carmichael would be able to keep silent, though the man doubtless guessed what was in the wind. Very well, let him guess, but let him also keep silent. Hunterfield had

144

no illusions. He was sure that Carmichael too understood where his duty lay. A lone country doctor in a small place like Sealandings was in no position to reveal what ought not to be revealed, especially about one so highly placed as the largest landowner, the head of the most esteemed family in the entire district, the Eastern Hundreds' senior-most magistrate. No, Carmichael was safe. He knew his duty.

Tom was returned home an hour since, so he too was well. Now, apart from some servant gossip about a chance misadventure on the sands, explained by Tom in the kitchens at meal times with the aid of his waving hands and expressive sign language, all was a storm in a teacup.

Except for that damned Mehala.

Who was presently at, where did she say, the tavern? Donkey and Buskin, John Weaver's place. He would make a point of visiting, maybe take notice of her, see how she could be given post in some house. A ragamuffin if ever there was one, daubed with mud and in the most bedraggled clothes he had seen for many a day. Pity she wasn't more presentable. But something would have to be done, for sanity's sake. And for Thalia De Foe's confidence. And, most of all, for his own reputation.

Pity the girl couldn't be got rid of. If only she could be returned home, wherever her home was, all would be solved. He made a resolution to see her placed securely, where her tongue could do no damage. Second, then, to find where she came from and hand her over to her people. She would be so grateful she would never disclose his confidence after that.

That decided, he served himself a dish of hot bacon rashers and a couple of poultry breasts from the cold buffet, with a layer of potted meat, plus a few slices of breakfast cake. He would have to eat something, for God's sake, or he would never get strength to start the day.

145

19

Mrs Tyll was sent for as soon as Carradine had finished his bedroom
bath. The maids were still carrying out the buckets of waste water, so as
to empty the bath sufficiently for it to be carried downstairs, when he
started bellowing, 'Tyll, Tyll! Time to do those household accounts,
Tyll!' and demanding of the maids, 'Where the hell is that woman?
Can't you keep her in tow, for Christ's sake?' Which set them giggling
at the thought of themselves even trying to boss their stern housekeeper
about. For, at thirty-one, and a married woman at that, she was
unquestionably their superior in every way. Authority was all in life.

Mrs Tyll was listlessly supervising the settings for the master's
conference in the library with Hobbes when the shouts came and a
maid flew in to repeat the summons.

'And please to bring the household accounts, ma'am.'

'I am coming forthwith, Becky, say.'

'Yes, m'm.'

Mrs Tyll tried to walk with serenity but her feet almost danced her
up the stairs and along the great landing. The maids were removing the
bath, struggling with it and setting the remaining water sloshing wetly
over the side.

'Tch-tch, you girls!' she scolded, making way for them in the
doorway of the master's bedroom. 'Haven't you had the sense to
deplete the bath water enough in eshets, first? Surely you know that by
now!'

'Yes, m'm, but the master said – '

Carradine called, 'Get out, you, and in here with you, Tyll. Time you
got down to earning your crust.'

The maids went, giggling and scandalized at Carradine's
irreverence. Mrs Tyll entered and shut the door on them. The master
was sitting on the edge of the bed, wrapped in a towelling robe which
trailed on the carpet. He smiled as she approached.

'So, Tyll. Those your accounts for the last few weeks, are they?' He
eyed the books which she carried.

'Yes, sir. They are all up to date.'

'Come and show me, Tyll.'

She crossed to stand before him, with the books. Her heart was pounding, and her breath laboured at his proximity. For one fleeting moment the thoughts she had harboured over the long weeks of his absence recurred, of outrage, of distress, of the sordid nature of all this. There was, too, the sense of being used, of wretchedness, of sin and self-disgust, but those were moral feelings imposed by others. From within came far more treacherous feelings, of hopeless weakness, and even of love. She suppressed them all in her eagerness to answer as he wished.

'Here, sir.' She held out the first of the small ledgers, opened at the morning's date. All the details of expenditure were there in her careful hand.

'Here, Tyll.' He pulled her roughly to a sitting position on the bed beside him. She tried to take her weight on her feet, not to sit, almost stifled by their closeness, but he only grinned and nudged her. He ignored the ledger.

'How's your man, Tyll?'

'He's very well, thank you, sir.'

'He still holding the toll gate at the Norwich road turning out of Sealandings?'

'Yes, sir.'

'Makes a pretty penny, does he?'

'No, sir. We are quite poor still, but holding our own. The costs of victuals and the price of corn, as you will see from Carradine Manor's accounts, is a sore vexation. It troubles all households increasingly – '

'How often do you see him, Tyll?'

'My husband, sir? I try to return home each day for a short time, sir, as long as my duties here permit. I cannot always manage to visit home, though it's but a short step.'

'Do you do him your wifely duty, Tyll?'

'Sir! That is unseemly for a man to ask! And for a wife to reply!'

'Come back, Tyll.' He spoke without humour now, his eyes fixed on her. She had risen, and stepped away a pace in upset.

'Sir. My purpose here is the checking of the accounts of Carradine – '

'No, Tyll,' he said, suddenly seeming cold and angry. 'Your purpose here is something different. You understand that fully.' He waited, gauging the distance between them. 'You women choose to pretend that everything is other than it really is. We never *do* check the accounts, Tyll, do we? I never have. You know it well. You come here to be lain. I call you in to lay. You crave to be pleasured, and will hide the bruises with all the feminine expertise that four thousand years of learning and skill have taught you. I want to pleasure you. We don't need your books.'

'Sir! I prepare and keep – '

'Stop that, woman.' He spoke with soft certainty. 'I have no doubt that, were I to seize on each one of those pages, they would be meticulous and trustworthy down to the last farthing. For you are an honest woman, Tyll. Honest with the materials and the coinage of others.'

Tears were starting to stream down her face at the humiliation. 'This is not what should be spoken of, between master and servant. I must request with respect, sir, that you – '

'But dishonest with your bodies, you women are, Tyll.' He beckoned her. 'Nearer, Tyll. You have work to perform. Nothing to do with ledgers, nor book-keeping, nor balancing fivepence here and elevenpence-halfpenny there.'

She stepped closer, trying to maintain a semblance of dignity, her voice shaking. 'Sir. Please, I ask, do not speak in such terms – '

'Even in the absence of the servants, Tyll?' He laughed, mocking her. She had uttered those very words the last time, in the same circumstances. It was the same degradation. He grabbed her wrist, spun her so the books went flying and caught her round the waist, tumbling them both back on to the bed.

'Sir. The door, the door!'

'You locked it, Tyll, on your arrival. Have you forgotten?'

He started to tear at her garments with such savagery that she cried for him to let her, and then she too was frantically unclothing herself and hurrying as fast as he.

Mehala's return to the tavern caused a riot of laughter. All in all, she thought she got off lightly as she arrived back at the Donkey and Buskin, considering the state she was in. Not only that, but the amount of mussels she had purchased was problematical. Thirty quarts was not a great deal, but that was all she had managed to find by the time she had arrived on the hard at Whitehanger.

The return journey, with the mussels sacked in the bottom of the boat, was easy. The sea was tranquil, the visibility a clear two hundred yards, and a pale sun feebly washing the remnants of the mist from the gentling surface. The shoreline was easily seen, the tide mill at Watermillock standing in etched view, the lanthorn light from its upper corner barely detectable now in broad daylight.

'Where were you, lanthorn, when I needed you during the journey out?' she mocked, pressing homeward. 'And why didn't you come to my assistance, William Maderley?' She laughed to herself, as much from relief as a sense of fun. 'You're only good for following a girl about a market place like a moonstruck calf! Is that the case of it?'

She laughed and bent to her rowing. For speed, hoping to make up time, she rowed double-bladed, facing the stern in proper fashion. With the tide inshore, it was simple to cut across the bay and round the headland, keeping within a few cables of the shore. Several times she stood in the thwarts, casting a series of sharp glances towards the nearing mole of Sealandings to judge the positions of sandbanks, for even in a shallow-draught boat like the little pram there was no safe-chancing the East Anglian estuaries.

The reception in the harbour was to be expected. The men on the schooner called and jeered, laughing at her muddy appearance.

'Is that *HMS Mehala* of Sealandings?' they yelled, pointing. 'We feared a ship-of-the-line at least, from the fuss you made on the outward voyage earlier!'

'Why such powder and paint, lassie?'

'Beautiful is as beautiful does!'

Mehala laughed and pulled a face, giving as good as she received. 'Go back to sleep, Navy,' she jibed. 'I was out guarding the shores while you loafed and snored!'

'Then you lost the battle, Mehala!' they called, talking among themselves until their bos'n set about lashing them back to work.

She told the kitchen staff at the tavern she had fallen into the mud, having grounded upon a mud flat during the inrushing tide. Mrs Nelson scolded, and blamed her for the meagre quantity of the mussels in view of the need, but Mehala recognized the cook's anger as pure relief at seeing the boat and herself safe after all.

Only Little Jane, who had seen the expert way Mehala had embarked, said nothing about the mishap. Though young, she had a head on her shoulders, Mehala realized. The rest were all about her, telling her fresh warnings about the estuary and gruesome tales of drownings, capsizings and wrecks. Mehala was glad to hear them, now she had made her trust with the sea and would for ever remain safe on the North Sea. Even Old Alice and Bone put in their ounce, speaking of great storms of the past and narrating tales they only half remembered.

Eventually Mrs Nelson cut them short, pointing out that next time she might as well go and buy herself, seeing that even an apparently sensible girl like Mehala could not be trusted to make a simple purchase. The mussels were not of the best quality, and she had been charged a farthing too much per three quarts, which was an outrage and an utter scandal. A penny a quart for prime fat mussels was everything from unpatriotic to a foul sinful theft, and for charging that murderous price the wicked fisher folk of Whitehanger would surely burn in hellfire for all eternity. Which was no more than they deserved.

Mehala was glad to be back at work, exhausted though she was. She desperately wanted to tell her story to Little Jane, and possibly Nellie, if only to give herself the pleasure of using Doctor Carmichael's name. But your word is your word, and she had given it. To break her bond would injure Squire Hunterfield, and more importantly bring damage upon Doctor Carmichael.

She kept silent.

20

Thalia De Foe awoke in a foul mood. She was furious, mostly at the differences between men and women and the lives they led.

Blame was everywhere, and she hated the hideous grotesquery of the countryside. She hated Milton Hall and its enormous distance from London. She hated Henry Hunterfield. She loathed the fact that she was chained, hopeless in this great house without help of any kind whatsoever. She detested every single one of her disloyal and oafish servants. She was utterly repelled by the few paltry rags which she had to wear – the new lace gloves still hadn't come from Jermyn Street near St James's in London, would you believe. She despised the drab sky, the weather, the plight she was in.

And the absence of Carradine.

That was her third assignation with Henry Hunterfield. It seemed like the three thousandth, each as boring and repellent as the last. But what was a woman to do?

She yelled for Meg and started up, complaining about the delays as the maids fetched the hot bath water into the bedroom and started filling the bath.

'You've brought the wrong bath again, you hideous sluts!'

She struck the leading maid, lashing at the idiot's face and kicking her as she stumbled.

'Yesterday you said the short bath, m'lady!' the girl wailed, trying to shield her head from the assault.

'That was yesterday, you stupid ignorant baggage!'

Meg shooed the girls out and the long bath was fetched in place, the maids hurrying in silence, desperate not to spill a drop and giving apprehensive glances along the bedroom carpet as they poured. Mrs De Foe paced, tutting and glaring when one seemed particularly slow.

Meg stayed to provide the lotions and the soaps, keeping the towels warm on a towel-warmer beside the bath. Her presence was usual, but the mistress wanted her there in any event. She had a bone or two to pick with the wretched slut.

'Why do you give me white soap?' Thalia demanded.

'It is what you wanted yesterday, ma'am.'

'Don't answer me back, bitch! Why am I allowed no choice in

my own house, but for your say-so? I only give you board, provision, pay!'

'Which is it you want, ma'am?'

'What soaps have you?'

'The white, the yellow turpentine soap which you like – '

'Don't you try to fob me off with that cheap imitation!' Thalia screamed at the hapless Meg. 'I know what you are up to, buying from soap-makers who add rosin to their tallow soap, so as to ease the cost of manufacture to their miserable wallets! I'll not *have* turpentine soap in this house, d'you hear?'

'Yes, m'm,' Meg stammered. 'And various perfumed soaps. Mottled soap is here today, from the new soap-maker in St Edmundsbury, who has just paid his four-pound licence. Does ma'am wish. . . ?'

'Give it here, and stop prattling, girl! I have a vital task to do today.'

'Yes, m'm.'

'And while you're standing there doing nothing, tell me why you told me that the Honourable Howard Carradine would be returned to Sealandings by yesterday.'

'I was told so, ma'am.' Meg was wailing now. 'The drovers in the market were full of his coming.'

'Were they, now! Yet no word has been heard in the whole of Sealandings other than by your shell-like ears, trollop! Why is this?'

'I don't know, ma'am. They were very sure, telling as he was already at Chelmsford and likely to be here by – '

'Likely?' Mrs De Foe screamed. '*Likely?* I don't pay you for likelys and probablys, dolt! I pay you good King's coinage for news, proper reliable trustworthy news, you ignorant mare!'

'I'm sorry, ma'am! But they were saying the gentleman had very pressing reasons to be here at his soonest ability. They said he was like a mad thing, craving to be at Sealandings for a most important meeting. In fact, word is that several gentlemen are already lodged at a tavern there, against his coming.'

Thalia's temper subsided. She resumed soaping her arms, and gestured for Meg to soap her back and shoulders. 'They did? They said that?'

'Most certainly, ma'am. And I know that they speak the truth, for one of the waggoners, who drove to market from the Tendring Hundred, is a . . . a cousin of mine. And I had it from his very own mouth, ma'am.'

Yes, and I'll bet that's not all you had from him, either, Thalia thought wryly, judging the girl. The waggoner in question was no cousin of Meg's, nor ever likely to be so. She felt slightly mollified. The girl had after all spoken her variety of truth. And it was pleasing to hear, even from this dubious source, that Rad Carradine was eager to return to Sealandings. There could be no doubt about the particular 'meeting' in question. Nor of his urgent reason for a galloping return along the old Roman road into East Anglia. She knew all about that.

For it was she herself. He was as desperate to be here as she was for his return. That much was plain.

Her body began to glow, as much from the news as from the hot bath. He would be over the moon with her. She had a real plum to offer him, when finally he came, rapacious and greedy as ever, to reclaim her. Charles Golding, her true first cousin, had agreed to stand for Parliament in the forthcoming elections. That had been her instruction from Carradine, to see that Charles would propose himself at the hustings. Not only that, she remembered with delight, she had pulled off a marvellous feat of deceit on her part. She had persuaded Henry Hunterfield to support Charles's candidature. That would please Carradine immensely, for he was experiencing some difficulties in his financial affairs – only temporary, but temporary financial difficulties had an irritating knack of longevity. That would save her Carradine and Cousin Charles the enormous expense of bribing as many as several hundred voters to obtain a majority. And she had more: she had manoeuvred the Church itself to support Cousin Charles.

'Meg?' she said suddenly, making the girl start at the sudden breaking of her mistress's silence.

'Yes, m'm? I have the towels ready.'

'Not yet, fool. That woman who serves Mr Golding, my cousin at Bures House. His housekeeper. Who is she?'

'By name, ma'am? She be Mistress Blaker, Judith her given name.'

'That's the one. How long has she been at Bures House, Meg?' Thalia was almost purring now, for she had found a good, sensible and truly enjoyable task today.

Meg was apprehensive. 'Not very long by all accounts, ma'am. No more than a few weeks.'

'And before then?' Thalia asked silkily. 'From where does she hail? One of the local Hundreds?'

'Please, ma'am, she came of a sudden. 'Tis said that . . .'

'Go on, girl! I've asked the question. Answer!'

' 'Tis said . . . she was met of Master Golding at a place by London.'

A place 'by London', Thalia thought. Odd expression. But in the circumstances it was probably as fitting a reply as the girl could bring herself to make. Well, she thought, letting herself soak luxuriously in the hot water, it *would* be a pleasure to call upon Cousin Charles today! And inspect the accounts of this new paragon of virtue and housekeeping skills at Bures House. It would be quite refreshing. Properly considered, it was her cousinly and familial duty to correct any aberration in the Golding household, especially if Charles were to become a grand parliamentarian. There would have to be no taint of impropriety. Everything should be done properly, in the manner of his forebears.

'Meg,' she said sweetly. 'As soon as I am bathed, send to Ennis. Say I shall need the coach. I am going to take the air when the mist clears.'

'Very well, ma'am,' Meg said, thinking: God help Bures House this morning. And especially may God in his mercy spare Judith Blaker from the forthcoming visitation.

Mehala was able that morning to see Sealandings as she had never yet.

The place in its full daylight managed to seem sprawling, for all its small size. This was the result of its many different roofs, chimneys, a veritable mixture of styles and shapes which had simply grown as each building thought fitting at the time.

She stood at a roof window in the loft, having been sent to bring more pallets for yet more travellers, and stared out across the roofs. Thatch vied with tiles, treble tiles vied with Roman slat tiles, flintstone walling vied with wattle and daub, and Tudor external beams competed with frank brick. It was a mess, but a fetching mess, with women coming out to beat carpets and shake linen, and men rattling carts and calling along the waterfront.

A large warship – large for these parts anyway – was standing offshore. It was still, hove to, and lowering a small boat. She could just make out the sailors like tiny ants. The sea was calm, though the recollection of its recent threats to her safety made her shiver. Sealandings. The name had quite a ring to it, as did Whitehanger with its long slanting brooding woods. The schooner she had passed on the south mole was about to leave the harbour. Smaller fishing vessels were leaning away from their moorings, taking both wind and tide to make distance offshore by midday. Pretty, really, in a way of looking.

A figure below caught her eye. It was that artist man, William Maderley of the tide mill family, the one who had made calf's eyes at her in the market. Little Jane had told her he was slightly touched in the head from his painting and staring at things instead of doing a proper man's job.

Maderley could not see her, of course. He was standing by the kitchen yard, staring at the kitchen doorway. There was something appealing about that intensity in a man. It was sad, as well as rather forbidding, even frightening. Women were given more to obliquity, rather than the direct head-on approaches.

What on earth could he be waiting for? Mehala was worried, never having met an artist before. It was generally admitted that they were consummately strange people, capable of madness at an instant's notice. Perhaps they were afflicted only at certain phases of the moon, like the mad folk in London's lunatic asylum of Bedlam? Yet for all his barminess he seemed at peace, quiet in spite of his passion, and mild. That might be the calm before the storm, though. She couldn't risk being sought after by a lunatic, for her position here in the Donkey and Buskin was in very delicate balance. Each day that passed she was more vulnerable. She would have to make a move soon. Which reminded her she had to move to her duties, or risk a scolding.

She took hold of the first pallet, dropped it down the ladder on to the landing, and dragged the other four across the loft flooring towards the aperture.

The sea made her think of Doctor Carmichael. He had been so kind after Squire Hunterfield had ridden away. It was his suggestion that they should sit with Simple Tom until he recovered sufficiently to remount and start his way back to Lorne. She had been relieved, needing the rest at least as much as Tom. The doctor offered Mehala a restorative, mere brandy thinned with water, but she had declined. He seemed indrawn and spoke softly, while they waited beside Tom, telling her of the sorrows people suffered, as he expressed it, 'all in the cause of life'.

'Are those not sent by the Almighty to test us, sir?' she had said in reply. It was how she had been taught.

'I simply wonder, Mehala.' He was so downcast, so earnest. 'I think it might – just might – be within our own capabilities to effect changes in suffering. Somehow, as people, make suffering less.'

'How, sir?'

'I don't know yet. I wish I did, Mehala. Think, though: less in number, and less in kind. Imagine how it would be, Mehala! A world wherein a doctor could actually ease pain!'

She was shocked. 'But it says in the Good Book that we should feel pain, Doctor!'

'Which might mean something different from what we read into Holy Scripture, Mehala! Don't you see?' He grew excited, talking with increasing animation. 'It could be that we really have . . .' He quietened, looked at his hands as if seeing them for the first time. 'Maybe we have powers we do not even imagine. You know, Mehala, this disease of the croup. You have heard of it. It kills hundreds of children each year in this country, and we are powerless. We give a few emetics, a purgative, a few powders of this or that. It is in the lap of the gods if the children die or live.'

'That is the way of life, Doctor. If diseases are of divine coming and are sent to try our faith . . .'

'But are they?' He looked out sombrely at the tide, which was still coming in on the sands below. 'It afflicts me more than I can say, Mehala, this terrible thought. I should try something new each time, instead of old remedies which do so little good.' He gathered himself up then, as if in apology. 'I am wasting your time as well as my own. I must let you go instead of prattling here like a Whitehanger fishwife. You'll get into trouble with the redoubtable Mrs Weaver and her servants at the tavern!'

She rose with regret, dismayed as the lightening day increasingly revealed the state of her dishevelment.

'My only regret, Mehala,' he told her, coming down to the water's edge to see her push the boat off, 'is that Squire Hunterfield's request means that you cannot receive credit for your saving of Simple Tom. He will be grateful, I know, could he express it properly to you. As I also. And as Hunterfield has good cause to be.'

'Only my duty, Doctor.' This man's praise embarrassed her. She busied herself readying the boat, which was mudded stem to stern from her attempts to pull Tom inboard. She would receive a scolding for this. She started to invent stories to explain the boat's condition to Mrs Weaver.

'Duty excellently done, Mehala.'

'Thank you, Doctor Carmichael.'

And that, Mehala thought, throwing the pallets down to the landing, had been that. A conversation with a poor tormented man was nothing on which to build hopes of any kind, naturally. But if things changed, was she in a position to approach him – of course through inter-mediaries of proper status – and somehow gain his support in achieving a post? Perhaps in one of the private houses nearby Sealandings? Though a country doctor was of such inferior status it was unlikely that his word would carry any weight with anyone.

She sighed, adjusted the ladder, and started down it to resume her duties.

Mary Prothero was speaking with Mrs Weaver downstairs during the latter's supervision of the kitchen preparations for the day, while Mehala was seeing to the pallets and helping old Alice to place them ready for the day's influx.

'I need a new maid-of-all, Mrs Weaver,' Mary Prothero announced, trying to seem firm and in control of the meeting. 'And I warn you, Sarah Ann. Even though we shared places at the local school together, I shall not be fobbed off!'

Mrs Weaver smiled and offered her visitor coffee. They sat beside the long table, with the kitchen active all around.

She was filled with nothing but pity for Mary Prothero. As the youthful Mary Calling, not all that long ago, she was so full of promise, so alluring and captivating that rumours abounded of handsome swains seeking her company at social engagements all over the Three Counties. Then, so sudden and wicked was fate, her parents were gone and, without a brother to fend for her, she was in the grip of that odious husband of hers, and doing his bidding at every turn. As now.

'Shared places, Mrs Prothero? Not us! For my sister was older than your good self, and I older still than she! But you are kindly condescending to say so, and I thank you.'

'Well, we are all folk of Sealandings and must help each other against all, Sarah Ann!'

'That is true, Mrs Prothero.' There was an implicit appeal there. The publican's wife felt an instinctive warmth towards the small recessive creature. If only she had not taken up that Jason Prothero, what position might she have reached by now?

'So I ask if you would see your way to sending me this Mehala who has come to you. I trust she is a good and loyal worker?'

'Yes. She is all of those. Though,' Mrs Weaver remembered with a laugh, 'she had an unfortunate mishap this morning.'

'Nothing damaging or injurious, I trust?'

'No. Heaven forbid! While out bringing the mussels from the beds at Whitehanger, she mistook the road in the incoming tide – it was until an hour or so ago a very thick low-lying mist, you will recall. The poor silly took a spill from the boat upon a sandbank.'

'Oh, my goodness!'

'No harm befell, Mrs Prothero. Thanks be to God. She dragged herself back into the pram and made her way onwards, but sadly missed most of the good mussels. She bought thirty quarts at *very* exorbitant prices. I was only too glad to see her return, though, in view of her ordeal. And, she brought the boat safely back, as duty bade. Its replacement would have been an unwonted expense.'

'How true. Still, she preserved your property, which speaks well for her.'

'Indeed. It is all that needs be, in any servant these days.' Mrs Weaver paused to glance along the length of the long trestle oak. Little Jane had just finished scrubbing it white. Satisfied, she nodded to dismiss the girl, and resumed. 'But there is a problem with Mehala. She has not yet recovered her memory. And Doctor Carmichael has taken responsibility for her, as has Miss Euterpe, of Reverend Baring at St Edmund's rectory. I promised to see that Mehala stays here the week, working for her costs. After that, I'm afraid it is open to question where she goes and what they find for her disposal. I know that Mr Weaver has been approached through others, whom I cannot say.'

She left the conversation in a pause there, making busy with hams being brought in for Mrs Nelson's inspection. The real purpose was to give Mary Prothero time to reflect on exactly whose approaches those might have been. Did the poor deluded creature not know that in fact one of them was from her own husband, by way of Ben Fowler of the Goat and Compass?

'Then I may expect this Mehala by the week's end, Sarah Ann?' Mary Prothero said anxiously.

You poor thing, Mary Calling, Mrs Weaver said to herself in pity. You dear, poor thing. I've as good as told you that your husband is playing a wretch's game coming after Mehala so, and still you are so subdued that you are only the more desperate to please! She sighed, nodding a partial nod.

'Well, Mary, I shall tell my husband that you have made the offer, and that you want Mehala to come to Calling Farm after the seventh day. Against the usual wages and circumstances?'

'Most certainly. She will come, then?'

'Probably, Mary. It is the very best that the poor girl might expect. Of course, if she regains her mind and her folks come for her, then there can be no bargain. Is that agreeable to you?'

'That is excellent!' the poor innocent said, gathering up her reticule and smoothing her dress down as she rose. 'I'm so pleased that you can comply, Sarah Ann.'

'As far as I am able, Mrs Prothero,' Mrs Weaver said, following her through the corridor to the main entrance where her barouche waited.

In the kitchen Little Jane was sternly rebuked for a slight spillage of the stock pot. Nellie swore at the girl angrily for not having the salmagundi ready for the serving girls, who were all famished.

'Once they get started, Little Jane,' Nellie said loudly, 'my girls don't get the chance to relieve themselves, let alone sit here in the warm kitchen niddling on whatever takes their fancy. Just you remember that!'

'Sorry, sorry, sorry,' Little Jane panted, scurrying for the salad to make the dish up. She was desperate to find Mehala and tell her what she had heard, and what was in store for her, mere days from now.

21

Thalia De Foe approached Bures House with a faint stirring of excitement. It was the same frisson of delight one experienced when forced into a contest. And it was as thrilling, no matter how lowly or highly placed the adversary. But Judith Blaker, house mistress of Charles Golding, was about to discover that her sinecure was something of a shifting sand.

When the carriage scuffed gracefully along the drive towards the façade of Bures House, Charles, of course, was a-slumbering somewhere upstairs, the sloven. Thalia sat for a moment studying the attractive building as the coach drew slowly in. It was as much hers, by family feeling and tradition, as Charles's. It was built with porticos in the grand style, after one of her own ancestors had achieved some signal defeat of the Dutch fleets in the olden days. He had received the reward of a grateful nation. And now Bures House, with its great imperial history, lay in the hands of a drunkard wastrel who doubtless spent himself nightly upon some tipsy sluttish stray who was allowed to hold the purse strings.

She called to the coachman not to descend from the driving seat. He stayed there uneasily, having drawn up before the wide steps and clucked his team to a stand. The grounds all around were silent. A few gardeners worked nearby on the ornamental rose garden, semi-enclosed by red brick walls in the new fashion, and did not pause in their work of replanting. Thalia De Foe laconically took in the changes. Charles had never shown interest in gardening in his entire life, and it was unlikely that he had started now of his own volition. No, those were alterations ordered by the new housekeeper. She smouldered with indignation. That dear Mistress Blaker was already changing Bures House, outside as in, to suit her own precious wishes! Perhaps she even saw herself as the wife-to-be of the Honourable Charles Golding, mistress and possessor of the man, house and estate alike. Very well, Thalia De Foe thought, sitting motionless in the carriage, very well. We shall in a moment see how far *that* particular ambition throws the grasping bitch.

Women and men. Men, it was her experience and belief, could find their ecstasy in, on, through any woman who presented herself to them.

The poor things were simple followers of their urges, lust their natural bowsprit which gave direction according to available circumstance. Women were different. All was pretence, that great instrument of prowess and skill which enabled a woman to keep her head above water. And herself in control.

Yes, she had indeed pretended with Henry Hunterfield. The man had been interesting the first time, a sheer bore the second, and excruciatingly dull the third. Enough to set any woman screaming from sheer ennui. And each time he had appeared replete, doubtless thinking himself a devil of a chap, while she had all but nodded off beneath his lurchings and groanings. Poor creatures. Yet they deserved little mercy, for their stupidity was an infringement of a woman's natural ambitions. They make the ground, define the game, she told herself, but it is we women who play it. And who win it, when all's said and done. We are the champions, and men merely the chessmen on the board.

Poor Henry, suppressed by his three sisters – all as different as chalk, cheese and cherry – and finding simple amusement in the local agriculture and peasant voices. Not a shred of ambition. He would eventually shrink his family within his compass of meek endeavour. Three generations from now they would be peasants to a man. No amount of dexterity from the odious Lydia and that emerging young cat Tabitha, and no amount of dreaming over her Byron by the utterly boring Letitia would rescue their fortune. And very satisfying it was to contemplate. Thalia hoped that she was still here to see the Hunterfields damned for the yawnsome burden they were to Sealandings.

And here came La Blaker, dashing and bustling, red-faced with pleasure at so august a visitor, swinging her chatelaine to show who stood in authority at Bures House.

'Welcome, ma'am,' Judith Blaker said, showing delight and summoning a footman – the effrontery! – to see to the folding step to assist Mrs De Foe's alighting. 'Welcome again to Bures House again, so soon!'

'It is rather becoming a habit, is it not, Blaker!'

'One which I hope will become all the more frequent still, ma'am!'

Thalia swept slowly up the steps, pausing to take in the scene then continuing until she stood on the top. She turned and glanced down, taking in the garden and the men busy at the angle by the summer-house.

'I see Mr Golding has ordered some work on the summerhouse.'

161

'Yes, ma'am. He has found it somewhat lacking in taste, he thinks, and has required that it be exchanged entirely for one which has a turning base. Sunshine will become more plentiful to its interior. There is a new design which has been favoured by the Royal Family, it is said, and I expect – '

'Lacking in taste?' Mrs De Foe considered the phrase. 'It was built by my grandfather, if I remember correctly. He was a lovely gentleman. A considerable hero, you know.'

'Ah, quite so, ma'am,' the housekeeper said, flustered. 'Mr Golding has taken into account – '

' – Everyone else's wishes except my own, it seems!'

'I'm sure Mr Golding fully intends to discuss the matter with you as soon as circumstances present, Mrs De Foe.'

'Once it is built, I suppose.'

She moved distantly inside to the hallway, standing as if slightly bored. Two maids there curtseyed and stood immobile, scenting trouble.

'Is there anything which. . . ?' Mrs Blaker was discomfited and worrying now as to the outcome of the visit.

Thalia De Foe raised her eyebrows slowly, appraising the housekeeper from head to foot, as if discovering her there for the first time.

'I am naturally waiting for someone of the household to appear and express some sort of a welcome. Indolence seems to be his newly acquired habit.' She waited, swept a finger along a table for dust and announced casually, 'The attendance of Mr Golding upon his cousin might not be inappropriate, madam.'

'I'm afraid Mr Golding is somewhat . . . indisposed, Mrs De Foe.'

'Madam.' Mrs De Foe fixed the housekeeper with a gaze like sleet. 'By what authority do you serve as intermediary between members of my family and myself?'

'I apologize, Mrs De Foe. I did not wish to seem – '

'But you do seem most impertinent, Blaker. And furthermore you have *not* received my permission to use my name in so familiar a manner!'

'Ma'am! I am indeed sorry to have given offence – '

'You are not, Blaker, or you would not have presumed in the first place.' Thalia's wintry gaze slowly swept the hall. 'Now kindly get about whatever business you seem to regard as yours, for the time being. I shall seek my cousin and ascertain what duties have fallen to my unhappy lot at Bures House.'

She beckoned the two maids and swept off imperiously, leaving Judith Blaker stranded and gasping with outrage.

Twenty minutes later Thalia De Foe descended the stairs. Charles was still snoring in a drunken stupor, despite her attempts with the maids' assistance to rouse him. The chief manservant, Clark, an elderly man Thalia had known since she was a little girl, revealed under interrogation that Charles had drunk the best part of two bottles of Portugal and a third of a bottle of brandy. Lately, the master had taken to eating very little.

It was clearly time for action. She summoned the Blaker woman, along with the senior maid, plus old Clark, to the study. The account books were to be brought, and all supporting documents necessary for a complete and immediate audit.

This was her stage, and her theatrical moment. She entered, calm and decisive. She was pleased at the way things were going. Had Charles been sober he might have put up some resistance, however weak and ineffectual. As it was, she had a clear field for whatever punishment she chose to inflict. This upstart woman had dared to intervene, set her cap at her wayward cousin, and furthermore was trying to take over an entire section of a noble family without the slightest pretence to any right other than innate greed. The impudence of the commoner slut!

'Give me purchase lists for this week,' she demanded, sitting at the accounting table and propping her reticule against the small crescentic brass railing thereon. The book was opened for her. She looked, holding her spectacles, which she did not really need but which she had seen once used to great effect in a London art salon, and ran her finger down the items listed.

'Fuller's earth, I see. Hampshire, Blaker? *Hampshire?*'

'Yes, m'm. The best fuller's earth comes from Hampshire. So I purchase – '

' – So you purchased enough to occupy an entire team of fullers at their manufacture, Blaker. Why so much?'

'To take precaution against a future need of further buys, ma'am.'

Thalia held the silence, loving every delicious moment. 'You appear to be equally cautious in the instance of tea purchases.'

The maids shifted in the silence. Old Clark shuffled his feet, peering from one lady to the other. He desperately wished for the master to waken and resume authority.

'Let me enlighten you, Blaker,' Thalia went on. 'You were so kindly disposed as to serve tea to Mr Golding and myself recently. The tea purported to be Chinese Ball tea. I happened to observe that there was also Souchong tea, in a separate caddy, and a further sort of Bohea tea known to commerce as the Campoi. Do you have anything to say, Blaker?'

'No, m'm.' The housekeeper was white, her anxiety showing. 'But the caddies are always kept locked, as is proper, against loss of the tea, ma'am. That I'm sure is what you would require in any household conducted by your good self. I accordingly – '

'You accordingly missed a few obvious points of recognition in a lady who is properly educated, and of a class to which you cannot aspire, Blaker!' Mrs De Foe's voice ripped through the study. One of the maids swayed slightly, faint at being present in such a scene. Old Clark stepped close to lend his support should she fall. Thalia De Foe blistered on, ignoring the girl.

'Souchong tea, brought in half pounds across Russia, is *invariably* purchased in that original quantity by all the households of my family. Including this! It has never been simply left for a loose commodity – except when and unless it is being filched from its caddy in small amounts for resale to the undeserving by someone apparently in firm control of its distribution, Blaker!'

'But, ma'am . . .' the housekeeper said faintly.

'Furthermore,' Thalia stormed on, 'the Chinese Ball is composed with a gumaceous substance, of Chinese manufactury in Canton. That binding material is entirely devoid of taste, Blaker! Unless it is adulterated by a tea merchant who is in clandestine arrangement with a housekeeper, who shall be nameless. Shall I expound on that arrangement, Blaker? Shall I reveal here and now what I think?'

'But, if you please, ma'am, I have honestly had no intention of – '

'Honesty? You speak of that esteemed exemplar, Blaker?' Mrs De Foe's voice was becoming shriller as she found yet more self-righteousness with which to fuel her feelings. 'And were you honest in a like manner when you adulterated the Campoi tea? In its caddy, any lady knows that it should have a definite violet scent, amounting even to a perfume – unless it too has been diluted with hedgerow leaves heated in a dry copper in an oven, so that the same high price may be paid to the tea merchant, and a proportion of that price fed back to the wicked housekeeper who perpetrates such a ghastly crime!'

'Please. ma'am, I assure you that I – '

'I see you are shaking now, Blaker! Not at all the great lady you were pretending to be! I suggest, Blaker, that you have deliberately adulterated the Chinese Ball tea, diluted the Campoi variety and apportioned off to your own purposes large quantities of the Souchong! Now, Blaker! You will reveal this to me: how many of those imported labourers out there, so unnecessarily active in the rose garden, are related to you and your foul schemes to strip this house of its valuables, to dupe the Honourable Charles Golding of his possessions, and to remove the purchased goods from this estate?'

The housekeeper was reduced to tears. 'Please, ma'am. I beg you. It is but a small thing, this accidental loss of some of the commodities here. And my friends there are – '

Mrs De Foe rose grandly into a silence as the blubbering woman sank to her knees. One of the maids made to step forward and aid her rising, but Clark shook his head to stay her.

'Clark. You will send for the shire reeve, and hand this wretch into custody. You shall further take with you several of the men, including the head footman. You will then lay in charge all of those men working in the rose garden, until such time as you have distinguished between the interlopers who are bound in criminal conspiracy with this creature. You will then have them charged.'

'I beg of you, ma'am, in mercy – '

Thalia De Foe smiled down at the grovelling woman. It truly was a delightful experience, to feel such satisfaction at the restoration of proper order in society. It was a trust properly observed, a duty nobly done, and a loyalty to class and order which, regrettably, could not be supported without giving pain. That the pain was profound testified to its perfection. Pain was love executed, love to country and class structure, and those, as was well known by all, were bestowed by God. Set for all eternity.

'I have no further need of investigation here, Clark,' she said sweetly, smiling at the servants, utterly at peace as if she had undergone some catharsis. 'I shall make notes in these books presently, for the master's next housekeeper to peruse. Meanwhile, to you, ma'am, I have to inform you that it is best for you to reveal to the magistrate the fullest extent of your perfidy. The bavins of small coal, the canal coal, the purchases for this household of poultry and meats, flour and fish, the adulteration of coffee by roasted substitutes, all I am certain are similar faults to be laid at your door. I should recommend that you change to a policy of truth, Blaker, for your tea merchant accomplice alone is liable to a fine of no less than one hundred pounds – ' A maid fainted, slumping with a muted cry at the mention of so vast a sum.

'I need say no more, Blaker! Tend to your own defence, for my

165

cousin, Sir Philip Banks, will be the superintending magistrate in your case when you are brought to trial. I shall see to it. Now, I shall retire to my other duties in my own household. See to things here, Clark!'

'Yes, ma'am.'

'And let me know by messenger when Master Charles rouses.'

'Certainly, m'lady.'

She swept out, taking her time and deliberately not looking at the surrounds. A maid rushed in fright, flinging open doors ahead of her and not staying to close them after but skittering on to the next as the lady progressed serenely outside to the steps.

As she arrived at the portico a footman, cloaked for message running, was hurrying by along the grass verge. She heard him calling to her coachman, distantly, a few words, and laughing. She glided slowly down the steps, and thanked Clark, who had made his way to attend her departure. She even smiled sweetly to thank the maid, who was now standing in frozen apprehension.

'What did that man say, Clark?'

'Man, ma'am?'

'That man. I distinctly heard him call.' Her heart was banging unaccountably loudly. She felt almost giddy with a sudden sense of being stifled, wondering if she had heard correctly. 'I do hope that he was not being impertinent, Clark, if he is one of our own servants here? Or, if he was being impertinent, that he is not any longer permitted to remain so!'

'No, ma'am. He is of Bures House. But I did not hear him call.'

'Please, ma'am,' the maid intervened, frighted at her own temerity. 'Please, ma'am. He only called to the coachman that a prize fight is to be arranged by the master of Carradine Manor, lately arrived in Sealandings this morn.'

'Oh, is that all!' She entered the carriage, smiling her thanks to the old man and the maid servant. 'More trouble, I expect, from those goings-on.'

She tapped the panel behind her coachman, and the carriage moved slowly off.

'Faster, if you please!' she commanded, leaning back, replete. Her heart was singing.

Carradine was home. At last. He was at Sealandings, and in Carradine Manor. She should never have doubted. He had been hurrying on his way back to her all the time, exactly as he had promised.

22

Breakfast was never easy to face. This morning, Doctor Carmichael could not bring himself to look at what the old lady offered. Mrs Trenchard moved herself slowly about the kitchen at Shalamar doing lethargic battle with its vast range. The scene was one of despondency. He stood, seeing the hopelessness of the starting day, so like many others. Yet it was the world's first day without little Harry Darling's life in it. It was the world's first spin through the Firmament bearing the deceased body of the little boy. Once a marvellous planetary orb, the world was now a bier bowling through space.

Returning from Whitehanger, he had slumped in his study at Shalamar, seeing only the wall. A damp patch of old fungus showed where the plaster corroded somehow against the corner of the window. Paint flaked. Books had to be placed on old newspapers against the rising damp. His sheets were more simple; up in his bedroom he hung them from the top window on a fine day, but on a wet hung them inside the bedroom on a string passed over the wardrobe door. Old Mrs Trenchard was a treasure, of course, but though good of heart was unable to defeat her years. She was crippled with rheumatism, aged before her time. He was only too glad to see her arrive each day from her cottage. He paid her nearly six shillings a week, which was good money, though he was hard put to find that sum. She was friendly and happy, painfully aware of her slowness, but charitably concerned for his welfare.

All the same, it was chill, dispiriting. The old lady had left some cold porridge by the hob for him, and a dish of cold tea from last night. The fire was burning in the grate, with some small coals beside it in an old oaken eshet. The house felt empty, adding to his feeling of redundancy.

He had resolved to burn the letter. Times were past. Harriet was past. There was no reason to read, no sustenance to be found in her words. But after hesitation he pulled the paper from his pocket. It was so worn as to be parting along its creases. He was careful unfolding it lest it tore, as if it were something precious and not a source of pain.

The letter was cross-written across the bottom half, the terrible half he knew by heart. That too was unfair, as if she meant her rejection to seem hardly worth the bother of finding a new page to finish. But bitterness was ungentlemanly, as was keeping a lady's letter. He read, foolishly hoping to discover hope where there was none. The worst began after her 'reflection of the most serious kind . . .'

. . . serious kind has at last guided me to an apprehension of duty as conceived by others, close and dear to my heart, and not merely by myself.

It has not escaped you, sir, I am sure, that for a lady to escape from *her truest self* is an exceeding difficulty; there will be many of her acquaintanceship, with so little understanding of the deepest of human motivations, eager to lay against her that most dread accusation whereby sordid, material, practical ambition receives an award of precedence within her breast.

It is, in addressing myself directly to your last serious proposal, my foremost desire to assure you, sir, that I have given every attention to the consequences which an acceptance would signify, and to demonstrate by this frankness my willingness to face the possible disapprobation of friends. I accordingly bring to your notice the expressed wishes of my dear parents, who have lately indicated a preference for another, as being one who would be appropriate to my own and my family station. The individual, whom I shall not name herein, is known to you, sir. He is far from being the 'arbitrary gentleman' of cruel Reputation; his is an honourable position of some eminence here in London, and accords appositely with the prospects which my dear parents have ever held for me. Furthermore, he has approached Father with an avowal of having for many months been my secret homager, with nought but achieving my favour his sole purpose.

Were Fortune to have reconsidered your circumstances, which you regarded in your proposal as those of a beneficence rather than sadly meagre, I should have been able to give an immediate dismissive; but Charity is ever the investment of manners, and I was reluctant to deal you such a severe smart; hence this lengthier, yet I trust more charitable, reply. Your wish was, sir, from first dash regrettably bound to evoke a rejection, for the clear distinguishment in our respective situations has, since my nonage, made evident to all except yourself that your destiny lies outwith your wishes.

Permit me, sir, to close this letter with the intimation that by regarding your proposal fully and satisfactorily answered you will most sincerely oblige

H. Ferlane

The letter had chilled the room still further. Her truest self? A fraudulent attempt to put herself in a favourable light, he now saw. A creature to whom her own self-esteem was all. Three condemnations in one proved it.

That *arbitrary gentleman* was a reminder. He had once stupidly called Rodney Treggan that, after Harriet had shown Rodney some trivial mark of favour. Yet Rodney was a toad. But – second condemnation – a wealthy one. Quite fair of the Ferlanes to counsel affluence over affection for Harriet's betrothal. He couldn't blame Harriet's elderly father, of whom he'd been fond, or her agitated mother. The last condemnation was the worst: if his prospects were good instead of 'sadly meagre' Harriet would have been able to reject him out of hand. As it was, he was clearly so far beneath her notice that from charity she had written her scorn instead of laughing at him out loud.

He was baffled. Women were uncertain creatures, he knew, in affairs of the heart. It was admitted by all as by themselves. But where had Harriet's friendship gone? Had he imagined her smiles, her seemingly obvious wish for his company? Hadn't she in fact encouraged him, even hinted that one day perhaps they could mean more to each other than their then youth could permit? She wrote of 'nonage', her young years, possibly meaning that youth speaks silliness in words that one must later forget. So he was being instructed to forget how close they had been. His face felt scarlet.

The tone of her letter was so carefully chosen. The beginning was friendly. Then it became a searing dismissal, at once final and aloof. Failure in career was somehow bearable, likewise defeat in battle could be borne. But to be rejected in love, and with such utter disregard, left an unhealed wound. How could he ever trust his judgement in the future? What if some lady cast the same hints of approval, favour even, responded to him with a seeming warmth? Could he ever risk making an advance? Or brave a start in, say, corresponding somehow? No. He now had no criterion for gauging a woman's response.

He had been so sure of Harriet's liking for him. God, he'd *known* her parents favoured him, had expected his proposal to their daughter. And Harriet herself had spoken outright enough to make him breathless, saying how it would be when they attended the salons of London together. It hadn't been the fancy of a passionate imagination.

Yet it was all a quicksand. Failure, more personal than any. Why then – indeed how – were some men successful with women? Perhaps failure with the fair sex was his destiny.

He folded and replaced the letter. He told himself that he only kept it as a warning to the harm that false assumption could do. Harriet Ferlane was probably now the lady wife to Treggan, and beyond the ken of an impoverished provincial doctor.

He still had medical notes to make up from three days past. He had started, in medicine's modern fashion nowadays, to make notes on the patients he saw. It was a most admirable inventive way to recapitulate events to do with people as actual instances of disease. Not only that, but there was a new sense abroad in medicine, that statistics – the collection of data – was itself somehow beneficial. The enterprise of medicine and surgery would be helped, even if the doctor's understanding of how to use the information was sorely lacking. He had a battered old copy, much treasured, of John Graunt's *Observations on the Bills of Mortality*, which, it was said, had founded an entire new scientific discipline concerning medicine and that new and suspicious branch the Epidemic Fevers. He had read and re-read the treatise. Indeed, he had, at various congregations of doctors during his apprenticeship days, suffered heavily at the hands of opponents when he had lauded Graunt's *Observations*. Why, opponents cried, the man was a mere captain of militia in the Strand; the man was a humble haberdasher, not even a doctor; the man was a charlatan, or worse, and so on. But it seemed to Ven Carmichael that, if he had struck upon a great inherent truth, what did his qualifications matter? It was not long since that you could walk down the Fleet in London and buy a Doctor of Medicine degree of practically anywhere you liked. Especially cheap were those of the Continent, without the hindrance of any study whatsoever. A public scandal.

Worse still, Doctor Carmichael could remember being disciplined by an elder of the Royal College of Physicians when he had asked to speak on the analysis of the Bills of Mortality, on the grounds of associating with an unqualified man's findings. The interview had been painful, as he had been forced to listen to the old doctor's stern admonitions. Graunt the haberdasher had employed, during the Great Plague in London, a cluster of prostitutes and old parish hags to go round and simply count, as best they could, all the corpses in the various wards of the City. The old physician's voice had quavered at the man's outrageous effrontery. He had then simply written them down, listed the dates and the numbers, and was pleased to foist the wretched pages on the public as some new kind of medical perusal. Insolence, which ought to be punishable by hanging or, at best, a public flogging and a massive fine. Unpardonable.

Yet . . .

Here was he, defeated after a night and more of loss, mourning the departure of a small boy who had struggled for life, unaided by whatever medicine, doctors, drugs, could do.

It ought not to be so.

He tried to eat the cold porridge, hearing Mrs Trenchard slowly plodding from room to room in the gaunt old house, busying herself as best she could about the cleaning and airing. He gagged on the thick stuff and laid it aside. The cold tea he managed to drink, placing some sugar in the dish to render it sweet in the new fashion. He gnawed a piece of bread, wondering if he should try to get something hot to eat from somewhere, but the kitchen seemed bare and unpromising so he sat and thought, and finally dozed.

He dreamed. The whistling, of that terrible disease as it had throttled little Harry and slowly strangled his life away. He slept, nodding, often coming to with a start, bleary-eyed, then nodding again with the child's laboured gasps and that ghastly stridor and his despairing little face, his pleading eyes, his restlessness and the terrible, truly terrible understanding of the horror that was asphyxiating him. And the final dull whistling, *distantly shrill yet dull*. Once heard, no doctor was ever likely to forget it, no matter how much he wished to . . .

He woke in a sweat, despair deep within him. He looked around the bleak room.

That whistling. Why did it stay in his head? It was not new. He had heard it before, several times, in his youth. He had heard it recently, listening yet turning away, in a place not far from here. Nothing to do with little Harry Darling's illness. Nothing to do with medicine. He had heard it, and commonly. He could remember, if he tried hard enough. He had been walking, somewhere in Sealandings, and had gone a different way, turned along a different street, among houses, thinking nothing of it. Yet the whistling of little Harry as he had died, struggling for breath as his throat had narrowed and the sickly thick membrane had closed off his life . . .

He grabbed his hat.

'Mrs Trenchard!' he called up the vast wide stairs.

'Yes, Doctor?'

'I shall go out now, for an hour or so. I have to visit the church vicinity for a short while.'

'Very good, sir. Will you be back, then?'

'Yes, presently.'

'Did you have your breakfast?'

171

'Yes, Mrs Trenchard. And thank you.'

He left the house, walking briskly down the drive, among the overgrown verges and having to duck his head where the vegetation had encroached on the pathway. The gate had long since fallen from its hinges. He smiled wryly at the sign: Shalamar, in wrought iron, fallen into the grass from its lofty perch on a side turret, absurdly fanciful, which had once stood to ornament the gate. A grand house it must have been in the past, too, with music and orchestras and balls and parties and suppers. Now, the only reason he was able to afford the poor derelict place was that it came at a peppercorn rent from agents at Maidborough. They had been only too pleased to let him have the place. And why not? That way, they were rid of the obligation to look after it and spend money on its upkeep to no gain. Also, there was the relief of somebody resident there to prevent roaming bands of gypsies from burning the manor house down, and gutting the premises and making off with what furniture was left therein. A bargain, Carmichael thought, stepping out with a bitter laugh on to the South Toll road which headed into the township of Sealandings. He found himself whistling abstractedly as he went, trying to copy the sound of the little lad, and failing even at that.

At Milton Hall there was no message. Thalia De Foe was not unduly alarmed, though disappointed. She hurried upstairs, calling for Meg and sending for Ennis to tell off a messenger to stand by to carry an urgent letter into Sealandings.

Carradine was probably exhausted after what must have been a rapid journey. After all, from St Edmundsbury into Sealandings was not a mere stone's throw. It would need changes of horses. By all previous experience he may well have felt obliged to call in at Cambridge before hastening on towards the coast. No, his silence was fully accountable and quite understandable. She would chide him, though, about his reticence, and joke with him about having other women to whom he was a great deal more attentive.

But that thought was no joke. It had better not be so.

Entering her bedroom, she changed quickly into a half dress, sparing her ankles. It was in a lime green, which of course was something of an unlucky colour among the stupidly superstitious country girls, but that was only for a woman dressing for a first encounter with a man. Green then was naturally to be avoided at all costs. Afterwards, for a second and all subsequent trysts, green was a suitable colour – for those few who could wear it with gain in appearance, she thought smugly, examining the effect in the cheval half glass. It possessed, with scarlet and the harder colours such as yellow, an immediacy which other colours – blue, violet, indigo, greys – could not give.

She bent to the business of preparing the list of guests for her forthcoming ball while she composed herself and Meg prepared her cosmetics. It would not do to present Carradine with half a plan. He was an immediate man, given to expletives and sharp rebukes when thwarted. Leave his expectations unmet, and you would receive his cruellest chastisement. Please him with a ready response, do something to his instant advantage, and you could bask in the sun of his approval for days at a time. She smiled secretly, thinking of Carradine's anger and his rewards. In her case, both were equally desired if she cared to face the truth. They had shared some experiences which even her modern mind could scarcely believe as she sat savouring them. But his approval gave her that which she wanted. It made her position that bit more permanent in his life, whereas his anger ran the risk of possible severance. Losing Carradine was unthinkable. Thoughts of keeping him, though, gave her as much relish as . . . as, well, thinking of that punishment currently meted out to that horrid slut now being carried away in fetters from Bures House, thanks be to God.

No. Carradine's loss would be the end of the world. It would leave her with Henry Hunterfield, dull and adoring. And with Charles Golding, a drunken sloven, last of a noble male line, at every passing tart's beck and call. It would leave her with an absent husband, busy in the City and doubtless wenching the nights away instead of coming to please his wife in this backwater of a swampish estuary. No. Carradine was hers. He had said so often enough, and she knew he meant it. As she was his, body and soul.

The list. It had to include old Sir Philip Banks, of course, her cousin. Carradine himself. Charles Golding, the cousin in question, naturally. Hunterfield? For certain. His utterly repellent and scheming odious sisters? Pity that they would have to be given licence to adorn themselves and press their way through her supper and her entertainment, but a ball was a ball, and she had been forced by that pushy bitch Lydia Vallance to ask Letitia as well. Ugh! Then there were the Prothero folk, Jason and Mary. An unknown quantity, in a way. He seemed a brute of a man, but was undeniably wealthy and influential, since his recent marriage with Mary Calling had placed him in possession of such a fortune, so large an estate. She considered, decided against Prothero. Not Quality. Carradine would have for her a list of at least a dozen more, for his unfathomable political reasons. And

Hunterfield would have a half dozen. There were perhaps two dozen other families of prominence, all of which she would include as possibles. She could discuss the ones who mattered with Carradine – in proper seclusion, of course. The ones who scarcely mattered at all she would talk over with Henry Hunterfield. It was important for Carradine's plans to give Henry the illusion of deciding everything while in fact he was allowed to choose nothing at all.

She rose and stretched luxuriously, already feeling Carradine's lust, sensing his hands clawing at her body, his mouth sucking and teeth biting . . . yes. This was a return to very life, instead of a mouldering existence in the countryside.

All prayers were answered, now Carradine was home.

The rectory at St Edmund the Martyr was a great deal better maintained than his own Shalamar, Carmichael saw as he walked towards the door. That is it was maintained somehow, whereas his own place was dilapidated. But with so excellent a housekeeper as the bonny Miss Euterpe Baring to administer the residence, it was only to be expected that her qualities would show in its external appearances as well as, doubtless, in its interior organization. A woman made a house into a home, he thought wistfully.

He knocked on the door and was surprised to be greeted almost instantly by Reverend Baring himself. The rector must have just been passing in the hall, or seen him coming up the drive.

'Good day, Rector. Might I have a word with you, please?'

'You may, Doctor.' Baring made no move to step aside and allow him admission.

Doctor Carmichael hesitated. This was most unnatural. He cleared his throat and said apologetically, 'I wonder if I might trespass on your good nature and beg a few moments' confidential discussion? It is not a matter for the open air, if you will forgive my presumption.'

'Forgiveness is my industry, Carmichael,' Baring said coldly. 'But being taken advantage of is certainly not. Nor, I might add, is allowing those under my protection to become vulnerable to one who appears determined to take an advantage.'

Doctor Carmichael almost recoiled, disbelieving his own ears. 'Sir, I cannot understand what you mean to say. Surely you do not mean that you suspect – '

'I mean what my words mean, Carmichael.' Reverend Baring stood tall and ascetic, hands behind his back and peering down at his visitor, inspecting him through his spectacles. 'I mean to say that I have very little to say to you on any subject which might concern you. Please be informed that I do not wish you to call here in any capacity whatsoever, neither to converse with me nor with my sister. And I shall expect you henceforth to address your worship from another church than St Edmund's. Naturally, I shall forbear refusing you entry directly, but I wish you to know that your attendance at St Edmund's sacraments is entirely without my approval, should you so far presume to attend, on Sundays or at any other time.'

Ven Carmichael felt the blood drain from his face. 'Rector. I do not know what has given you occasion to speak so. I assure you – '

'Assure all you want, Carmichael. Please vacate the step, and the garden. And do not return.'

Carmichael turned, paused. 'Then to whom can I go, Rector?'

'To whomsoever you wish, Carmichael. Not here. Good day.'

The door closed. Carmichael stood, stunned by the swiftness and firmness of the rebuke. He could not believe what he had just heard. What had happened? He'd foolishly assumed he was on the very best of terms with the Barings. They had shown him extreme kindness on first meeting. Then only two or so days ago Miss Euterpe had exerted every endeavour to assist with that girl brought in by *The Jaunty*. And then there had been his uncomfortable call at which he had passed on the message to Miss Euterpe via the Reverend Baring – but surely that unease had been the result of some tiredness, or misunderstanding? This was impossible, beyond anything in his experience. It was shaming. His face burned.

He walked down the path towards the open market square. A few waggons were turning there, preparing to move out of Sealandings after taking up the fish loads. The little school was chanting its multiplication tables, as if some inner engine powered its very being. He would have smiled as usual at the sound, but now he replaced his hat and made his way along the side wall of the churchyard. There he paused, nodding a greeting to the watch-and-clockmaker's apprentice Richard Bettany. The lad would have spent some time with him, if he had shown willing, but Carmichael was too distressed to be conversational, and told Richard he had better be running back to Veriker's shop on the Norwich road before the clockmaker came in search. Veriker was famous for his temper.

Carmichael made to cross the road, then paused. The church was open, of course, as always. No service was being held there. It was free to all. If he could not speak with Reverend Baring about his problem of permitted evil and the diseases God seemed willing to inflict upon little children, then surely he could not be barred from speaking directly to the Almighty?

He walked through the lychgate and into the church porch. Nobody was in, and the church seemed vacant. He entered, doffing his hat, and went soft-footed into the first aisle.

Kneeling on the right, he bent more in thought than prayer. Sealandings was all around here. Even the silence of Sealandings was thick with the sense of the place, its past worshippers, its wall plaques showing relics in words and scant carvings of the legions of folk who once had knelt and breathed and lived here. The schoolchildren were coming to the end of the tabulations, their little voices rising and falling in unison, as he himself had once been taught so far away in time and distance.

And how many of them would succumb to the diseases, sicknesses which he was impotent to cure? He prayed then that there would come a day when some means of prevention was available.

'Doctor?'

'Yes?' He roused himself, not looking up. The woman's voice was familiar, young yet firm. He was ashamed of his moist eyes, and stayed in his position of prayer to avoid her face.

Mehala was standing in the aisle beside him. 'Are you ailing, sir?'

'Doctors do not ail, Mehala.' He tried to make a wry joke of the remark, but failed as miserably as with everything else lately.

'Have you suffered some injury?'

'No, Mehala. I am very well, thank you.'

They were whispering, so as not to offend the grace of the building. She did not move, but remained standing by him. Then she shifted, into the pew immediately next.

'I heard what Rector said to you, Doctor. It was cruel, and not fair. He had no right to say that.'

'You had no right to eavesdrop, Mehala. Surely you know that?'

'I didn't do it of my will, Doctor,' she whispered towards his bent back. 'I was coming from the garden, sent on a proper errand. I was to give Rector a message from Mrs Weaver, for his sister.'

'And?'

'And I heard you knock, so waited until you had done, thinking you were to go inside. Then I should have knocked at an interval, as would have been proper.'

'That's all right, Mehala.' The girl's behaviour had in fact been correct. 'I hope I may trust to your discretion?'

'Yes, Doctor.'

'It seems,' he whispered, turning his head slightly for the first time, 'that everybody in Sealandings relies on your assurance that you will observe their confidences, Mehala! And you barely ashore!'

'You should have given that old rector a piece of your mind, Doctor . . . begging your pardon.'

'For what?' He was puzzled at the vehemence in her voice.

'For daring to assume you were being less than honest with him! And him the parson!'

'Less than honest?' He did turn now, then, conscious that he was presenting his back towards the altar. He rose, bowed in the aisle, and made his way quietly from the church. She followed, with more perfunctory ritual.

In the porch he faced her, then started back a little in surprise. It was the first time he had seen her clearly in daylight. She was beautiful, the black hair lit with deep russet strands, her brown eyes alert. She was young, lovely, captivating. And she looked full of wisdom, alert beyond her years. He tried to speak, found his words had evaporated.

'Yes, Doctor?'

'My apologies, Mehala.' He found himself stammering slightly, then had difficulty restoring his train of thought. 'This is the first time I have seen you not covered in mud, you realize!'

She smiled, the force of the beauty almost moving him physically. 'And you clearly prefer the seaweeded version, Doctor!' Her smile faded as he continued staring. 'I did not mean to give offence, Doctor, speaking about Reverend Baring as I did. But you should not take on so. Some people are too gentle in their natures to bear what folk say. You should not mind so deeply. Forgive my impertinence, Doctor, but you have been most kind to me. I mislike seeing you treated shabbily.'

'You spoke of honesty, Mehala. What did you mean?'

It was her turn to stare. 'Why, Doctor Carmichael. Don't you see what he thinks? It's plain as a pikestaff to anyone that you had come to speak with him doctor to rector, but all he can see is his own good.'

'I'm at a loss, Mehala.'

'He thinks you're come to take Miss Euterpe from his household, have her go to Shalamar and housekeep for you there, leaving him short on his commons and comforts.'

'He *what*?' Carmichael was speechless. Mehala was impatient with his inability to realize the obvious.

'It's plain as this church porch, Doctor.'

'You mean Reverend Baring honestly imagined that I had come to

177

invite Miss Euterpe to become my housekeeper? But I was calling to . . . to . . .'

'I know, Doctor. It shows, to anyone as will cast half an eye. But there's none so blind as them as will not see. Isn't that what it says?'

'More or less, Mehala.' He tried to smile. 'Well, it seems I was victim of a misapprehension. And you are quite right to have spoken to me as you did. I failed to make proper reply. It serves me right.' He stepped outside the porch, glancing towards the rectory. 'I think I have an obligation to call again, and try to put right that error, explain my failing and misunderstanding to the man.'

She shook her lovely hair. 'No, Doctor, saving your presence. Rector will not listen. He turned a deaf ear when you wished to speak of God. How will he ease his attitude when you wish to speak of yourself? No, sir. Please leave it a day or so. Let him learn from others the error was his and not yours.'

He paused, judging her and seeing her anew again. 'I swear, Mehala, that if I didn't know better I'd think you a new creature every time I gazed upon you. In any case, I have to thank you for your wisdom and your advice. As well as your help with the drowning man this dawn.'

'I am glad you have not taken offence, Doctor Carmichael.'

'Offence? Impossible!' Clumsily he tried to make a joke out of his mock gallantry, and of course failed. 'Good day, Mehala. And if there is any way I can help you, I shall.'

'Good day to you, sir.'

She went, not being able to find any reason to remain longer, and conscious of his eyes following her along the path to the lychgate. She risked a glance as she turned in at the rectory gate a few moments later, and was annoyed with herself for having done so, for he was still standing there, looking after. At that she was glad, but she vowed that she would manage any further encounter better than she just had.

23

Carradine felt he looked truly excellent in his jemmy coat. The multiple pockets suited him very well and showed his carefree attitude towards fashion while keeping abreast of the prevailing London modes. It was a short shooting coat, frocked in style. He wore the fashionably new purple material, the big flap pockets 'all the better for my winnings', as he informed Sir Jeremy Pacton when they met for midday dinner at the Donkey and Buskin.

'Winnings, hey?' Pacton laughed, shaking his head. 'There've been precious few of those these last five weeks for yours truly, Rad.'

'For me likewise, Jeremy. But it's a sore day when you can't have a flutter on the races, eh?'

'True, Rad, true. Or into something far softer and more welcoming than a heavy landing on the racecourse!'

'Your lust will get you into trouble one of these days, Pacton,' Carradine cautioned mock soberly, and they laughed as the meal was brought. Nellie herself served them, in one of the ground-floor alcoves outside the common press of the taproom.

'What's this, your ladyship?' Pacton demanded, eyeing the girl and her two assistants.

'Please sir, it is dormers, being a cold meat cookery Mrs Nelson much favours, roast ducks, fillet soles, a salmon, salmagundi of course, hessian soup made with a whole ox's head – that being Mrs Nelson's way, here at the tavern. There's battered oysters, I think, to come, with a light set of oyster darioles somewhere, and pullet marengos, with several puddings including quaking pudding, and stone cream and various afters of sweet kinds, sir. Is there anything that the gentlemen would prefer in addition? I think Mrs Nelson could have the list written out in the new French fashion, but cannot write herself so it would have to come from the tavern master . . .'

'Looks as if we shall have to manage on that, Carradine,' Pacton said. 'That do all right for you?'

'It better had, Jeremy!'

They waited until the meat dishes were laid before they resumed their conversation. Carradine shook his head when Sir Jeremy made to speak, tapping the side of his nose in warning. It would have been safer if Alex Waite had been first to arrive to meet him today, but Carradine felt almost desperate. He had to accept what Lady Chance offered, and she had come up with this seasoned gambler instead of the relatively innocent and ignorant Scotchman.

'There's an opportunity looming, Jeremy.' They made a start, sorting the fowl while a maid flew up with bread of both rice and flour sorts.

'For the winner or loser?' Pacton joked, laughing.

'For me, certainly, and possibly for one other.'

'One only? Not for *all* one's friends?'

'Alas, no. That's against the law of Nature, Jeremy.' Carradine said his carefully prepared words as if making casual conversation, knowing that one slight show of eagerness would tip his friend off. 'Would that it were possible for all birds to feather their nests.'

'You mean the local races, Rad? I'm somewhat out of mood with those, after that event at Hyde Park last autumn. God, but I almost had to sell the family silver!'

Carradine chuckled, shaking his head, inwardly raging. The infuriating thing was that Sir Jeremy had lost almost exactly the same sum as he on that occasion, when an enfeebled mare out-galloped every piece of horseflesh on the course in two separate races. It was unbelievable. He had been almost unnerved at the extent of his losses, while having to maintain an air of unconcern as a gentleman should. Yet this man opposite, who had seemed so worried and dejected at the time, recovered the very next day – when his father had picked up the IOUs and restored him to solvency. Such were the vagaries of Fate.

In London, until this week past, there had been the welcome charms – and purses – of the Honourable Mrs Isabella Worthington. Until she had come across some past indiscretion – well, not even an indiscretion, not the sort a man could think of twice in the same year. But women are contrary and unfriendly souls, and she had flown off the handle. Now she was in a dreadful sulk, having twice refused to cover his debts. It was degrading, and a confounded nuisance. Women were never the same two seconds together.

Money was urgent. He had to clear this betting caper before Peter Quilter arrived to queer the pitch, or to set some different hare running.

'Races, Jeremy, you can keep. And with my compliments.'

'I'm glad to hear it, Rad, as long as you give them to me with a likely purchaser who has plenty of scrip and coin!'

Carradine shouted for more rice bread and cursed the little girl who scurried up with the baskets. He eyed his friend while they set to again.

There was a slight hiatus, since Pacton wanted some soup to make a partial start, but they were quickly back to trenchering as Flemish soup was hot and to hand, though Carradine to show willing insisted on a soup Crécy, as if concerned that the right balance of victuals was being maintained.

'Then what, Rad?' Pacton asked. 'What was it you hinted – a good risk – but not on races?'

'Prize fights, Jeremy.'

'That's more to a man's taste, now, even in these parts! But have we any knowledge of a prize fighter worth his salt? There can't be many in Sealandings, can there?'

'Heavens, man! Sealandings has all it can do to make ends meet with its fishing and farming and its little shooting parties and its waggoners and drovers. It is, as you've already seen, a place of minimal commerce and no pleasure. No, I refer to relatively more serious places further inland.'

Sir Jeremy was intrigued. 'But a particular fight, Rad? I insist on a particular mulling. I won't have anything to do with these rough and tumbles in every field you pass betwixt here and Bristol docks. They don't know what they are doing, other than hating each other for a few pence.'

'I think you're right, Jeremy,' Carradine soothed. 'I too have wasted more hours than God sent over such rural maulings. Waste of time and money. It's a guess, a lottery. No. I talk of something much, much better.'

Pacton glanced about, almost furtive, and breathed, 'Fixed?'

Carradine smiled. The man was on the hook now. He noted how Pacton's voice had instinctively lowered, to the pitch where greed spoke its truths.

'What a word to bring into a gentlemen's conversation, Jeremy! No, nothing so sordid or unfair as that. But I need to do you a favour, so here it is. For your ears only, I'm afraid.'

Pacton was taken aback 'Favour? You owe me a favour?'

'Certainly. You recall that introduction which I sorely needed, for reasons of the . . . well, shall we say for reasons of personal desire? You introduced me to Mrs Worthington, my fair Isabella. You recall, surely?'

'Ye . . .es,' Pacton said doubtfully. He had been to that party, and made that introduction, true. 'But I had no idea that you were so smitten, Rad, or I would have made sure you were introduced months earlier.'

'Be that as it may, Jeremy, you did me a great favour. And I am not one to forget. This is the occasion of my favour's return to you. It shall be the last, mark you, in full and final settlement!' They laughed at the pretended sternness in Carradine's voice, since they were extremely good friends.

'It's a good risk, Rad?'

'Excellent. I too shall partake of it, but only after you've had your fill.'

'Why is this, Rad?' Pacton was hard at the Portugal wine, but his innate caution had still not deserted him.

'I felt it too, that day at Hyde Park when that damned moth-eaten mare wrecked our purses for days after, Jeremy. I saw your face, and grieved for you. I was lucky, just having brought in a partial cargo with a cousin from the eastern trade, silver and opium moved across the three Eastern ports. It was dashed fortunate. Without that assistance, I'd have been in Queer Street, that's for sure. I just didn't have the nerve to offer you the assistance you needed at the actual races. But I can tell you I was plainly relieved when you said how your father had made you solvent the following day.'

'That's kind of you, Rad.'

The man was still wary, Carradine saw. 'Too kind, Jeremy. It shan't happen again, I can tell you!'

They laughed, setting on the fowl and the salmon. 'When is this?'

'Shortly. Tom Spring is ill, as you have doubtless heard?'

Spring was the famous Hereford pugilist, Champion of all England. Pacton pulled a face. 'Yes, worse luck! I was thinking of betting at short odds on this Battler Goring to run over sixty rounds with Tom Spring, even if Spring is the champion.'

'Goring is still to appear. But there is a local man, Rendell, who will beat him.'

'Beat Goring?' Jeremy Pacton was astonished. 'But Goring went seventy-five rounds in the north and won, with – '

'Shhhh, Jeremy. I know.' Carradine leaned forward, smiling. 'Goring will lose to Rendell after sixty rounds. After all, Tom Spring is the greatest, and Champion. So with him out of the way lately, it's more than likely that there will be an enormous attendance of the Fancy at this fight.'

'But the odds, man, the odds!'

'Ah, there you have me, Jeremy. All I know is the detailed certainty of the arrangement, not the way the bets and odds will fall before the off!'

Pacton ate on, a slow smile spreading across his face as light dawned. 'You sly old dog, Rad Carradine! You're going to let the dice fall, as it were, then start in with some pretended argument as if on the spur of the moment, and then – '

'Then lash out and bet wantonly – against the run of the mill, Jeremy.'

'How much, Rad?'

'It'll have to be thousands rather than hundreds, to make it worthwhile.' Carradine's mouth was dry as his friend moved on to the hook.

'But letting me know this will be sure to foul your scheme, will it not?'

'Partially, Jeremey – I'm not *that* generous! It's the price you pay for friendship. At least, it would be friendship, if . . .' He paused as if grave at some recollection.

'If what?' Pacton halted, his eyes suddenly shrewd and observant.

'If that damned Mrs Worthington hadn't utterly worn me out in bed and damned near killed me, Pacton, thanks to your introduction! I ought to challenge you to a duel, instead of obliging you with foreknowledge this way!'

Pacton's eyes showed relief and they laughed along. Pacton knew it was a sound scheme, and one not to be spoken of even with friends.

'I shall want your word, Jeremy, to remain mute about it all. Until it's over, of course.'

'You have it!'

'And that you won't lay wagers in a part of the ring where our mutual friends are placing their bets? Is that all right?'

Pacton's brow cleared. That was the honourable thing he had been waiting for. Carradine was giving him a true bill. He felt his spirits soar. His father, damn him, had bailed him out so often that the old man was now proving a stickler. This scheme of Carradine's would set him up for months, put him on his feet and let him return from these godforsaken coastal marshes to the lights and gaming tables and ladies of London.

'Of course, Rad. I promise.'

'Look, Jeremy.' Carradine felt almost cheerful now the plan was set in motion. 'Isn't it time these girls started feeding us? I'm half-starved here.'

They called for more food. Carradine could not remember ever feeling quite such relief.

24

Early on, the horses were too frisky to allow proper judging. The cattle field set back from the winding Norwich road lay a mere three furlongs from the schoolhouse corner of the market square, and was crowded today with people come to see the horses offered for sale.

'I like them docile,' Alex Waite told Quilter.

'Horses and women, opposite to the life?' Peter Quilter laughed, shaking his head.

'You dislike gaming, Peter,' Waite said, critically appraising a mare with a forehead blaze. Its coat was smooth and kempt, its legs in good order. Its haunches suggested a lack of staying power, however, which meant that it would be only useful around the manor, or possibly between shafts. 'But not gamesters, eh?'

'Gamesters are my game, Alex. You fancy that filly?'

'She's brisk enough, I wonder if they have given her some sort of simple, though.' Waite appraised the man leading the young animal round the field. He had the appearance of being akin to a gypsy. You could never tell. 'These romanies have lore the rest of us do not know, what with their herbs and potions. I heard that races at Newmarket are more decided by grooms' galenicals than by breeding!'

Or by other means still, Quilter thought sardonically. He could tell a tale or two about jockeys receiving hidden benefits – aye, some as would turn your hair, for titled ladies would brook no defeat – and trainers and gamblers paying heavily to win, and sometimes even to lose. Fantastic, the ambitions of Man! He had nothing but contempt for the high gamesters, Alex Waite and Sir Jeremy included. Carradine, however, was a different kettle of fish.

They watched the horses parade, frisk and trot. Farm women and estate servants, gypsies and wandering horse jobbers were well represented. A pretty dark-haired girl arrived on a tavern cart, and with a little girl helper started to sell ale to the menfolk. Alex Waite saw her, and stared idly. He knew he had seen her somewhere before, but where?

As the animals were led about the field and bids were shouted where small impromptu auctions began, he watched her with increasing interest. She was striking, young and beautiful . . . no, not at all beautiful. Yet she carried something in herself, so convincing of her inner loveliness that he could not take his eyes from her. She was everything anyone could wish to have, see, share, converse with even. Yet she was only a girl dispensing small beer and ale from a mundane tavern cart in an open field by a small sea town. It was weird. He shivered.

'What's with you, Alex? Angel walking your grave?'

'No, Peter. Something in my Scotch blood, I suppose. I had the strangest feeling that yonder girl's one I have seen before, only in different circumstances.'

'Which one?' Quilter scanned the field, followed the direction of his friend's gaze. 'The black-haired one, I take it? Why, isn't she the lass from the Donkey and Buskin?'

'That's her! I remember now. Who failed to return when we wanted her last night.'

'And sent a substitute, if I remember aright!'

'No. I have an idea I know her from somewhere. She's not a face or soul you can easily forget.'

Quilter did not like this talk, leading as it did away from the true point of coming to Sealandings, which was to find a play for gaming, and so lead the gentry into incautious bets. An opportunist could make a fortune at these local fairs if the circumstances were right. Without them, he was without income. He laughed, nudging Waite as a neat and compact animal was led past, blowing and sweating. A young stallion, it was angered by the presence of so many other horses in its vicinity, and roused by its proximity to such a herd of mares.

'She's simply probably one of the servants who served you particularly well on the road to somewhere or other, Alex. Your memory is acting up, that is all.'

'I think not, Peter. The . . . situation was different.' Waite continued to scrutinize the far side of the field, wondering if he should walk over that way and purchase a tankard merely to get a glimpse.

Quilter led the talk away from the girl back to the horseflesh. He said more than once that it would be interesting to match this against that, hinting heavily all the while that boredom could be allayed by arranging a contest between animals, of course for a side purse.

'Carradine would be very attracted to the notion, I am sure,' he suggested.

'Mmmmh?' Waite was not altogether drawn away from the black-haired girl, 'Yes, I suppose so. But he shows little interest in gaming this week.'

185

'That is on account of his return home, being here with his people distracting him night and day.' Quilter thought sourly of the chits and papers which bore Carradine's signature, and which he held. A promissory note was only as good as the promisor, as promisees the country over knew only too well. But to refuse Carradine the grace of a delayed payment for a wager was to risk giving him a fearsome insult, one he would insist on settling by any means, sordid, sinister or duel. 'I swear that in another couple of days Rad will be champing at the bit, wanting a small flutter here and there.' Against proper payment this time, Quilter told himself. Carradine would not dare risk defaulting on payment here in Sealandings. What London allowed and thought the norm, here would be astonishing. Word would spread throughout the Eastern Hundreds like wildfire, and then London would hear – for London heard everything. Then it would be a matter of pay or dismay, even for Carradine.

'Look at your wench now, Alex!' he said maliciously.

'Some sort of row, is there?'

'Looks like the other tavern's arrived to dispute the pitch.'

'Perhaps you should make a book on the outcome, Peter!'

Though he laughed at his friend's sally, Quilter felt rage rise in him. He smiled, and suggested they stroll that way. People such as Waite, Pacton, and Carradine depended upon such as he, to underwrite their pleasures, their gambling, their activities in the great London clubs. Yet they invariably spoke down to him. He counted himself the more honest man, who never adopted airs to which he was not entitled. Without me, Quilter thought, the bastards would have to pay on the nail for everything. Only with my compliance can they act the lord and roar about the countryside doing as they will. If they are useful to me, I am utterly essential to the likes of them. To me they may be a source of income, but I am the means of everything to them, including their grand style of life.

'Perhaps, Alex,' he responded calmly, as they idled across the grass among the horses on show. 'If there is revenue enough!'

The contumely by the waggons was more of an uproar by the time they had made their way over. A crowd had gathered. Some of the grooms were placidly ignoring the dispute between the two women, but most of the people stood around in a small crescent, joking and goading.

'You've no right to be here, you bitch!' one was screaming. Her cart was not yet parked. She was the newcomer, her helper girl sitting glowering at the reins of her dray. It was loaded with four beer casks set ready for selling.

186

'I have every right.' The girl already there stood her ground. She did not raise her voice, yet it carried, Melliflous, Alex Waite thought. 'This field is set aside for the public use, and the grooms and people are thirsty. They were thirsty an hour ago, too, until I came.'

'You're an incomer, you whore!' the other screamed, appealing dramatically to the surrounding crowd. 'She isn't even from Sealandings! She's but lately taken from the sea! She's a pauper, a fraud! Her ale's waste water from the drains!'

'It's the ale sold at the Donkey and Buskin, Agatha, and you know it. And I sell it cheaper. *And* it's better. *And* it's longer known in this township than any from the Goat and Compass!'

The dark-haired girl was composed, standing beside her waggon and speaking with calm assurance. That more than anything seemed to infuriate the other.

'Don't you use my name, you bitch! Why, you haven't even got a name of your own, save some made-up name you use to put on airs. Mehala!' Agatha screeched shrill laughter. 'It's something you invented! She might even be a thief, a runaway!'

'Very well, Agatha.' The girl spoke with regret. 'It is with remorse that I make an offer, as a means of settling the argument. Since you are clearly not going to be satisfied without some redress for your imagined wrong, let us proceed with the business. If we do not, all these good men will go thirsty to an early grave, and we shall never get to our duties.'

Mehala stood waiting, resigned. Agatha stared about the throng, wondering.

'What the hell does she mean? Settle how?' A grin spread slowly across her face. 'A scrap, is that it?'

'A fight of fisticuffs would be wasteful, Agatha. You know it. It might give tremendous satisfaction to you, and possibly to me. But it would be a prodigal expenditure of time for all concerned – these gentlemen, their business of selling and buying horses. And it would detract from our usefulness to our employers. We would render ourselves unfit for service, and that is against the Eternal Law.'

'Trying to get out of it now, are you, cow?'

'Not at all, Agatha. I am suggesting we settle our dispute simply and effectively, and in the space of a few seconds only.'

'How? Draw lots, you mean?'

The crowd roared with laughter, Agatha leading them, howling and pointing. Mehala did not smile, waited patiently for the ribaldry to subside.

'No. Let us do it properly.' Mehala's eyes wandered among the crowd, evenly appraising the individuals represented. 'There must be some gentlemen here willing to loan firearms for the purpose, I am sure?' A mild amusement lit her countenance as her gaze passed Waite and Quilter, returned to settle there. 'Are there?'

'A . . . a. . . ?' Agatha was speechless.

The word was first spoken in a mutter, then ran round the crowd. 'A duel? A duel? Between *women*?'

'By God,' Quilter said to Waite, astonished. 'She actually means it!'

Waite could not look away from Mehala's eyes. She was striking, something within her compelling attention. She had seen everything, her eyes said, and she had survived to understand all the follies of the human race. She was almost queenly, possessed of an inner silence which made ridiculous the hurly-burly all around. Serene, he thought. That was it. She was tranquil, with the serenity of a nursing mother while preparing for the violence of the horse fair all around.

'Get flintlocks, somebody!' The cry rose. 'Flinters, flinters!'

Waite pushed his way through, the excited crowd making way for him as a recognizable aristocrat. He reached Mehala, just as Agatha's expression was changing, the boisterous grin changing to a half-uncomprehending worried smile.

'Mehala,' Waite said. 'You cannot mean this. The crowd will urge you to any folly. It is unprecedented.'

'It is necessary, sir.' Her face was calm. Only the pulse which beat quickly at her throat revealed the height of her emotions. 'I cannot withdraw without some sort of contest. That is plain for all to see. It is, after all, only what they desire. My position here is tenuous. I must defend it, however little and lowly it is. That is Nature, sir.'

'But . . .' He paused helplessly. 'Do you not know of the Proclamation? It is in force since 1679, and its consequences are grave in the extreme for any person, win or lose.'

'That any person winning a duel shall forfeit his life? Yes, sir. I know of the Proclamation.'

'For God's sake, Mehala! It has been forbidden even in the Army this half century gone!'

'Yet gentlemen follow the duelling code, sir, do they not? Even the Duke of Wellington approved it.'

Quilter took his arm to move him from the area. 'Step aside, Alex. The girl means to go through with it.'

Agatha was talking furiously with her supporters, gesticulating and shaking her head. Mehala was speaking quietly with the small girl who accompanied her. Waite pulled his arm free and returned to the Donkey and Buskin waggon.

Mehala was talking quietly to her friend. 'Do not be afraid, Little Jane, whatever happens. You understand what you must do? After the first shot you must drive our cart from the field, and do not pause. Return to the tavern, taking the route across the market square. If it comes to it, simply my name is to accompany me. You follow my meaning, Little Jane?'

'But Mehala . . .' The small girl's eyes were filled with tears.

Waite saw that a space had opened around the waggon. Sealandings was declaring its allegiance with its own, and retreating from any show of loyalty to a mere incomer. Agatha was drinking from a tankard, waggling the emptied vessel to show her prowess.

'Please, Mehala,' Waite interrupted, clearing his throat and conscious of his anomalous positon. 'I shall speak with the taverner for you, if you do not go through with this. I shall see that no harm comes to you, and that you are well taken care of. There shall be no injury done you here, upon your withdrawal. I can send for men to assist and get you from the field – '

Mehala looked at the gentleman. He was her age, perhaps a year older or so. And educated, doubtless, as befitted his station. Yet he had no comprehension of the various positions in life, not the slightest. You were what you made yourself to be, not what you seemed to others, nor what you showed in outward appearances. You were, or you were not, and there was an end to it. She had come through so much, and was here by Providence's grace. To hold what little position she had, it was necessary to fight and defend it. It was the way of empires, countries, peasants. That was all. There was no explaining to this gentleman. He had simply not learned these truths yet.

'I thank you, sir. But this is nothing to do with selling a few quarts of ale. Nor is it to do with the Weaver waggon being here before Agatha's. It is to do with what I am, and the way life is. That is all.'

The shouts arose that flintlocks had been procured, to cheering. A groom from one of the local farms pushed his way through and showed them. There was a great deal of pushing and shoving about the waggons. Some men were laughing, calling for seconds to be appointed. Somebody was pacing out a line and casting straws up to test the wind, laughing.

Waite withdrew to where Quilter was busy engaging a small group of gentlemen in conversation, doubtless preparing to make a book on the outcome.

'Would some gentlemen inspect these firearms, please?' people were calling, pushing back to give space round the two waggons.

Several weapons were being produced now, an astonishing number. There were all sorts, from ancient Spanish miquelet-locked pistols to decrepit doglocks right up to elegant Nocks and Mantons, and even a pair of hatched-grip Eggs with shining new Suffolk flints from Grime's Graves.

'Would it please you to do so, sir?'

A groom was presenting a pair of flintlocks. Waite pulled his gaze from Mehala and examined them. Mantons, about sixteen bore. They were badly scarred but doubtless serviceable. He hesitated, and inspected the others proffered to him, rejecting many and finally coming to a sombre pair of weapons which were very similar to each other. It was difficult to get an exactly matching pair. He saw Quilter laughing and pointing, the gentlemen with him nodding and striking palms. He felt sickened, suddenly aware of the stupidity of the process. He had always felt thus. War was useless, but somehow necessary. This was a travesty, where one person was forced into battle simply to defend some small circumstance of life which should be merely incidental and peaceable.

'These.' He decided on a matched pair of Wogdens, long in the barrel and sombre, their barrels browned. They were unadorned, and bore no escutcheon on the simple silver plate set in the stock. 'They seem sound in lock, stock and barrel.'

'I believe, sir, that I am permitted the choice of weapons? Then I choose these, as this gentleman has indicated.' Mehala stepped closer, looking at the pistols in the groom's hands. 'I wish to see them loaded, and to check that they are sound. I shall want there to be no hanging fire.'

Waite gave Mehala a glance. The crowd were sobering slightly. There was no laughter now, and Agatha was looking around at the faces of her supporters, still wearing that half-comprehending grin but seeming less sure and certainly less jovial. For a girl to understand weaponry was unusual. In contrast Mehala was behaving with utter calm, in spite of the telltale pulse in her lovely throat, but she was keeping her eyes on the handarms, not wanting them out of her sight now they had been decided upon.

The danger of flintlocks was the risk of a hung fire, when the flint struck its spark into the priming pan. Then, it should burn swiftly through the vent hole and ignite the mass of powder tamped down into the barrel. The explosion of the black powder would shoot the leaden ball up the barrel and out of the muzzle in a great spurt of smoke. But if the spark merely fizzled in the priming pan and failed to ignite the main powder mass, the protagonist was left merely holding the hung-fire weapon, and would probably die as his opponent shot him dead.

'You want them loaded again?'

'Please, sir.'

'Then do so,' he ordered the groom.

The weapons were unloaded, and fresh black powder poured from flasks into the barrels, tamped down and the spherical lead bullets wadded down in place. The priming pans were emptied and cleaned. Waite raised a forbidding finger as the groom made to bend his head and blow the old priming away, and the groom obeyed with a nod. The breath's moisture could so dampen the powder in the priming pan that a hung fire was inevitable.

'Ready, an you please, sir.'

The crowd was silent now. None present, save possibly himself and a few of the gentlemen with Quilter, had probably seen a duel, though they were well known. Agatha's grin had long since faded, and she was anxiously staring from face to face as if hoping now that somebody would prevent this stupidity. Mehala was calm, standing with her hands folded at her waist.

'Ready, then.' Waite lowered his voice. 'Is there anything I can say, Mehala?'

'No, sir. But I thank you.' She gazed into his eyes with a sad smile.

'Then . . .' He shrugged and stepped away. She was going through with it.

Mehala took a pace to the groom and examined the weapons. The groom was holding them by the barrels. They were on half cock, the flints glinting along their sharp edge and the priming pan cover down to guard the outside power.

'Sir?' Mehala said directly to Waite, who had retreated to stand among the now-silent crowd. 'I am allowed to test the weapons first, am I not?'

'To your satisfaction, Mehala, yes. As is your antagonist.'

'Then may I do so?'

Without waiting for a reply Mehala stepped forward, took the pistol from the groom's right hand, and glanced about. The crowd shuffled away, widening the area around her. She took three paces from her waggon, and glanced towards the hedge which rimmed the cattle field.

'The stake marker,' she called clearly, and presented the weapon. It stood fifty feet off, a simple broad stave left to indicate a furlong for the horses to pace when on show. Nothing stood in its line. The area beyond was empty.

She stepped a yard closer to it. Raising the handgun, she held it directly horizontal, then rotated her wrist so the pistol's priming pan was nearly uppermost.

'Hold your horses!' she called in the traditional cry at the discharge of a firearm, and the gun clicked, spurted smoke and gave a crack-boom. She stood steady, her arm holding the position of slight flexure, the wrist in direct line.

The stake was not broken, but a piece chipped from its side about two feet from its tip. It was not a perfect shot, but very creditable. A murmur rose from the crowd. Waite could hardly believe it. There were officers in line regiments who were less capable with handguns than this. And her twist of the hand, making sure that the flint's spark was accelerated by a downward progress rather than a horizontal one, showed that she was familiar with the use of flintlocks.

'Very well. I accept the weapons.' She handed the spent gun to the groom. 'Could you please do the honours of reloading, sir?'

The crowd was muttering. Agatha was staring at Mehala, occasionally darting desperate glances round the crowd.

'Very well.' The groom made no move in spite of his words, but stood with the flintlocks in his hands, looking at Waite, at the cluster of gentlemen, at Agatha and her group of friends, at Mehala and back again.

There was silence. Agatha gave a short moan, climbed on to her waggon and snatched the reins from her assistant. The man holding her horse's head jumped aside with an angry shout as she flicked the horse's rump. She dragged savagely on the reins to pull the startled animal into a narrow circle, and drove from the field in silence. Ale spilled from the barrel spigots, and one cask was rolling freely for lack of a frame, but Agatha paid the clumsiness no mind in her shame.

Mehala returned calmly to her station by the cart, and nodded to Little Jane, who resumed her stance at the tailboard ready to resume selling the ale. Mehala went to her horse's head and stroked it softly, talking and reassuring. Conversations began, people exclaiming and chattering. The horses were paraded again, but nobody approached Mehala or Little Jane, not even the more cordial of the grooms.

Waite stepped up and asked Little Jane for a vessel of ale, paying her solemnly and standing aside to drink the beverage. It was quite good. In fact, Waite harboured a suspicion that they had brought out the very best ale for the occasion. He stood there, ordered a refill. Gradually, the grooms and farmers began to approach and follow his example. A few made laborious jokes to Mehala, who repaid them with a smile. Within a few minutes more, a crowd had gathered about the Donkey and Buskin waggon, and all was normal again as the horse parading resumed.

'Thank you,' Waite said, returning his tankard to Little Jane and walking towards Quilter's group. They too were laughing and talking again.

'Thank you, sir.' It was Mehala's voice which spoke the words after him. He did not turn, knowing she would be too busy for any further converse.

25

Her opportunity came when, after his meeting with the church-wardens, her brother was free until his next breviary reading.

She was less prepared than she should have been. Safer, wiser perhaps to have waited until he was less heated. And until she herself was cooler, able to pretend more skilfully. That was the woman's way. Except.

Except? Except what, when?

Except – she made herself attend to herself closely – except when Ven Carmichael was upon her mind. Not merely in her mind, note. Upon. Occupying. Fully predominant. Unyielding and implacably there, her spirit half-blinded by his presence, and no longer able to use its normal skills. She felt maimed, yet determined as she had never before been. Perhaps it was time to confront her brother with this new Euterpe, a sister who would now no longer be fobbed off with his private decisions, be allowed to hear only half his reasons for decisions about their joint fate.

She knocked on the study door.

'Come in.' She could tell he was quite pleased with himself. She knew that voice so well. He would begin by rising, standing affably before his study fire and say, raising his coat to feel the warmth, 'Ah, Euterpe! So glad you came, because something quite capital has occurred and I wish to share it with you.'

As he did. The something this time was to do with a repair to the chancel, a structural fault showing up in some weathering feature which funds had been found for of a sudden.

Politely nodding, she heard him out and showed interest as befitted a dutiful sister. Mrs Thalia De Foe had every good purpose of the church at heart, and had somehow managed to allocate funds sufficient for the purpose.

'How marvellously Christian of the good lady!' she said.

'Indeed, Euterpe, indeed! And,' her brother emphasized gravely but with joy, 'she made a visit here express for the purpose of conveying to me her good intentions about the support I could expect should her assistance ever be invoked.'

Here would come some light joke, as it inevitably did: 'Of course,

Euterpe, you know as well as I' – with a twinkle – 'there is no such thing as a bottomless well!'

'Indeed not, Josiah.'

Followed by a statement of his own feat in the matter, indicating fairly modestly that he wanted his expertise to be admired by any listener who happened to be handy: 'It has not been a simple matter, Euterpe. I can tell you that. And I should be the first to admit that my gifts were found wanting in *some* aspects of the transactions. Yet I have to concede that my innate skill was matched by a kindly dose of good fortune – or perhaps kindly acts of Providence – which proved successful in the long run!'

And now a sigh to conclude the issue, but with a few words to leave his success indelibly in the memory: 'Yes, Euterpe. I can now face the future with a little more equanimity than before, but remain mindful of the responsibilities of this parish. It seems that everywhere in Sealandings there stands some difficulty towards which I shall have to pay close attention sooner or later. Efforts have to be sustained to be of any benefit, sister. I think I can rightly say that our dear father would have been overjoyed to see the progress I – I mean we, my dear, of course – are making here at Sealandings.'

For a single instant Euterpe experienced a complex of impulses. Her mind took on a floating, quite startling power all its own, thinking its own thoughts and uncaring about propriety. She felt in a shifting cloud land of images and patterns and emotions quite frightening. The experience was always brief, yet terrifying when it came to her as she lay alone at night. This flash was revelation: Older generations would not use that term of endearment quite so easily. Older generations spoke sir and madam and m'lady and mister and mistress, even between husband and wife and father and daughter and son and mother. Now, the world was dwindling its reserves in human, personal terms as well as in its material expenditures. What next? Darling and m'dear and sweetheart and love to every passer-by? Or, God forbid, first names uttered by strangers who simply overheard the designation given at any mere gathering? Personal names used at a party after a single introduction? Perish the thought! Clearly such a world could never exist, for it would fall inward upon itself as all society vanished in such looseness. Yet here was her brother, that soul of propriety, who had made decisions for her and about her, speaking with a term of endearment which pronounced her his responsibility. No more. Her time had come.

'This is very promising, sir,' she said. 'It bodes well for St Edmund's. You are to be congratulated.'

Euterpe wanted to burst out that every servant in Sealandings joked at Prothero's visits to Two Cotts on the Norwich road, and even the fishermen wondered at the landowner's curious appetite for that company. Impatiently, she waited for propriety to make its limits clear through the person of her pedantic brother.

'While pondering my reply to Mrs Weaver, I had occasion to upbraid the girl for a delay in coming,' she invented at last, losing all patience with him. 'She was quite delayed.'

'This paragon of virtue? A sloth?'

'It seems I was unfair to judge her so, brother,' Euterpe said meekly, thanking God that she had found a way through to accuse him now. 'For she had run all the way, across the square and past the boys making ready for the gaming meet. She was only anxious to do her duty and carry the message that she risked their catcalling and rowdishness.'

He was puzzled. 'Then how came she so tardily?'

She thought grimly: Puzzle no longer, brother; and went straight ahead with what she had been told by Mehala.

'It was that she was approaching the door when Doctor Carmichael called. Mehala did not see him, but came accidentally upon your conversation with him.' She saw his face change, and thought triumphantly: Mehala spoke the truth.

'Ah, yes. That was an unfortunate incident, Euterpe. I did not think it sufficient to your interest to require giving you an account. A sorry business, Euterpe. One best forgot.'

'Is it?' Euterpe continued remorselessly. 'I demanded to know why she had not disclosed herself, brother. I made her reveal what she had heard, in case it was something to your detriment. She narrated the discussion word for word. A most nimble memory. Though of course, with a fine sense of what is proper, she was sorely ashamed at having knowledge which should not have been hers in the first place, but which was forced to her attention by a combination of unfortunate circumstances which she could not avoid.'

'The discussion,' Reverend Baring said. No paper shuffling now.

'The discussion, brother. How Doctor Carmichael came to ask your guidance about the will of God concerning the persistence of evil and disease in the world. How you chose to upbraid him for impertinence in calling here. How Doctor Carmichael tried to interpose, to express his anxieties about the Holy Word's admonitions. To ask guidance, when there is a seeming incongruity between Divine Will and the agonizing deaths of little innocents. And how you continued to refuse to speak, saying that the issue did not concern you in the slightest, but that

197

imbalances, for the issue to become completely resolved in even the most dubious mind! I shall make it my firm duty to – '

'Forgive me, Josiah. That is no longer the problem before us.'

'It isn't?'

'Not as I see it, Josiah, no. For did you not forbid him access to your very own services?' She waited, but he was badly shaken as he realized how he had misunderstood the doctor's intentions. 'It seems that Doctor Carmichael has been deflected from a proper path of inquiry. He has been rebuffed, when he sought consolation from the rectory. Where he will go to, now that the church has alienated itself from him, I do not know. The Puritans, the Methodists, those Nonconformists, heaven knows.'

'And forbid!' he cried.

'If heaven so pleases, Josiah. But there is the other far more pressing and immediate matter.'

'Which is that, Euterpe?' For a moment he tried to recover his position. 'I do think you are making too much out of what seems to be second-hand prattle from a serving girl we know hardly anything about – '

'Her word can be trusted, Josiah. As I think you will agree, when you have occasion to allow her to pay you her respects. No, she is with the Weavers, in a tavern, at the very hub of life in Sealandings. Yet she is not one for loose talk. In fact, I swore her to observe the strictest confidence in this, not to divulge to anyone her opinions or knowledge. To keep secret, brother, your error in making a wrong assumption about the intentions of the doctor who is becoming so well favoured in Sealandings and its locality.'

'Euterpe,' her brother said weakly. 'I do think that perhaps you should pause, take stock . . .'

She allowed him to sink into his chair and watched him attempt to grasp the extent of his mistake. It was strange to feel so little sympathy. The twinge of pity she did feel was easily suppressed to enable her to go on.

'It seems there is only one way which can ease the situation, Josiah. After all,' she added, 'Mehala is reliable and trustworthy. Even in the few days since her marvellous rescue from the North Sea it has become apparent that she has many admirable attributes of character. She is able to give advice on domesticities, on all manners of household organization, even as they exist in a tavern setting. She has skills beyond her years. And a wondrous facility for proving the most useful person in any, even unusual, circumstances.' Euterpe had heard bizarre accounts of the scene at the horse fair in the cattle fields, and of the retreat of the Goat and Compass dray from serving the grooms and the horse traders. To have made some dry comment about it to Josiah would set him wondering what sort of wild creature this Mehala was, which would not suit her purpose at all. Let him discover what he could later.

'The way I mean is possibly to find this girl a place where she might be less exposed to aberrances of memory.'

'I see.' His brow cleared. He was beginning to understand, yet was watching his sister narrowly. It was unthinkable that she was bargaining with him, surely? Yet . . .

'Yes, brother. This girl might prove useful in one situation, while being saved from any chance recurrence of memory which might lead her to blurting out details of . . . more recent events. After all, let us keep in mind that the poor creature is only lately starting to recover her identity, and faint glims of consciousness about herself.' She added piously, 'We ought to have her best interests in mind at all times, Josiah, don't you think?'

'I do, Euterpe, I do!'

'Then we shall have to ponder the matter. And produce a solution. We must think of the places where she could serve a useful term, while endeavouring to discover as much about her origins as we can. Under close supervision. For,' she concluded with charming innocence. 'her own good. Wouldn't you think that the best plan?'

'Indeed, Euterpe. Excellent!'

Euterpe paused to let the barb sink in. 'I have been thinking that, since I was instrumental in giving this girl assistance when she was brought ashore, I might consider having her in the house as an assistant. And so expose her to the influence of your personality, Josiah, in a minor way, to help her to adjust her outlook. There would then be no possible chance of her misunderstanding anything she might have concluded when so unfortunately – through no fault of her own – overhearing your discussion with Doctor Carmichael.'

'I see.'

And he did. She was now sure that he fully understood her ploy. That was her aim. She hoped that her motive was still concealed somewhere in the interstices of the argument. He was so unused to emotion that he still could not see the direction in which they were heading.

'Within, say, a week or so, Mehala might well have recovered her memory, Josiah. We should then be in a proper position to correspond with the family of this poor unfortunate, and so give her the assistance

200

she will need at that time. For there is no question as to who should be responsible for her, it seems to me, when that happens.'

'Correct, Euterpe!' He had risen again, and was pacing the study, hands behind his back. 'She must come through here, at least administratively. It will become necessary for our Church to play the most important role in restoring her to her family. For, Euterpe, there is something here which is instantly clear to me, as it might not have yet occurred to you. And it is this.'

Thank heavens, she thought, hearing him out. At last he has a road on which to travel. All is well.

'Yes, Josiah?' she said innocently.

'This Mehala. I perused her while she walked through the market the other day. Do you know, I truly believe that she is no mere common servant girl? I truly think that she is somebody of family, of even distinction, perhaps. I might be wrong, but I do not think so. I believe this young lady might even be able to exert some sort of influence beneficial to the Church, and even to this living more directly, once she is restored to her own.'

'Of course, Josiah! I see what you mean!'

'It would be wrong of me, Euterpe, to avoid accepting this duty. For the sake of our Church I ought to make the offer. And, incidentally, save her from the possible importunings of . . . well, let us say, unchurchly folk who might feel tempted to take advantage of a poor unconnected serving girl.'

'How wise, Josiah.'

They made pleasant conversation about her preparations for supper then, making comparisons with tonight's meal and their likes and dislikes of various dishes provided at their home when children. It was very enjoyable, and left Euterpe wondering why it was that Josiah proved so obtuse and difficult in some ways, yet could be exasperatingly good company in another. Men were a mystery in some guises to women, as much as women were, she hoped on this occasion, to men.

For, with a capable housekeeper like Mehala in the rectory, the way would be open for the resident housekeeper to escape, even if that person were the rector's sister.

And escape meant only one thing and one direction: along the South Toll road from Sealandings, towards the great old gabled semi-derelict house called Shalamar, home of Doctor Ven Carmichael.

She went to supervise preparations for the meal with a light heart.

*

'When a man sees a horse for the first time, Alex, something happens which determines, all of an instant, their life: good, bad, marked by cruelty, with love or without.' Carradine had to speak louder than usual, in the noisy confines of the crowd assembled for the cockfight.

'Are you serious, Rad? Is all so grave? Horses are simple creatures!' Waite was amused.

'It's not the same as with womankind, Alex,' Carradine continued. 'It's much more personal, yet there is a similar basis.'

'That's your gospel, Rad,' Waite said, laughing at the impossible arguments. They always bantered over issues like this, even in the London clubs. 'But does practice bear it out?'

'Certainly I do. Doesn't every man?'

'I doubt it, though I bow to your experience!'

Waite cast a glance round the cockfighting pit where the main was already well in progress. Faces were heated by sweat, greed, despair and something far more terrible and cruel. The pandemonium was enough to deafen a man. The stench of stale sweat-encrusted bodies, the perennial risk of fleas, the sheer moist energy of mankind at his baying, predatory worst, were enough to make a man want to leave and vomit to rid himself of the encounter. Yet he stayed, fascinated by the murderous contest in the sand and sawdust. To depart, while the two protagonists clawed and leapt and stabbed their spurs into each other's breasts, would have seemed unmanly, and he had no excuse.

'Look about you, Rad,' he said dryly. 'You see here a mixture. Those of us who want the excitement of a bet. Those of us who want money to line their pockets from the proceedings. And those who are at the game of engendering lust by proxy, in the time-honoured way. We are here because of this ghastly occasion. It is nothing like the horse fair of which you speak.'

Carradine laughed. 'I swear, Alex, you amaze me sometimes! This is a country cockfight, set up by farmers' lads with nought else better to do. We are here from boredom. Quilter, over yonder with that crowd of countryside loafers, is merely here to take bets, as is his wont and his occupation. It is how he lives – and don't we all know it! A horse, that noble beast, is incomparable to this.'

'Admittedly, a horse has a spirit like that poor cock. Yet it can do no more than obey mankind, Rad. There's the core of it.' Alex seemed to be thinking as the crowd all about roared one of the cocks on. It was leaping now, the opponent fluttering in disarrayed retreat with a wing dragging, trailing blood on the floor of the great barn. 'A woman has spirit, but there is a sense of love, a possibility of her becoming something more than a mere fancy of the moment.'

'Impossibly romantic, Waite!' Carradine laughed. The losing cock gave an audible gasp and was covered in a stabbing frenzy by the victor. 'Good main, good main!' he shouted with the rest. It had been a splendid scrap, and the blood-smeared arena, improvised from slats of wood and empty casks, resounded with the crowing of the victorious cock as the defeated enemy died on the sand. 'We won, my friend, I think!'

'Three guineas, and from Peter, too! He'll not be very happy.'

'True, Alex. He counts every small bet as if it were something handed from the Prince Regent's coffers. I swear he thinks as highly of a single Spanish gold as he does of twenty thousand English guineas.'

'It is his religion, Rad. You mustn't mind him.'

'I wish there was a bet we could place on the outcome of our argument, Alex. Think up a way, and I swear I shall take it.'

'Bet? On an argument which is a mere difference of unprovable opinion?'

'Yes. I know that, if you place a woman beside a horse, all things being unconsidered except herself as she stands, without inheritances or skills showing, and a noble beast which promises everything that a horse is and can be, it's a brave man who would say the woman would always win!'

'I saw something here, Rad, which would have convinced you otherwise!'

'Here? We've hardly arrived, man!'

'Here,' Waite affirmed. 'Sealandings. This very town.'

'Tell me.'

Carradine was intrigued. Quilter, across the far side of the ring, was accepting payments from the punters with alacrity, not even smiling. Carradine watched without revealing his animosity for the man. To owe a veritable fortune to another gentleman was a heavy responsibility, a debt of honour which the creditor took, an incurred imbalance of funds which, in God's good time, would of course be readjusted. To owe to a man like Quilter was odious. That his debt to the bookmaker stood so high was perilous. And Quilter's implied threat the other night that he might sooner or later be tempted to put the promissory notes into the hands of debt-slashers, the Strand jews who would hound a man – aye, even a gentleman – once they had paid a fraction of the debt's face value, had not gone unnoticed. He hated Quilter.

But soon the balance would be restored. Then it would be

mortification for Peter Quilter the bookmaker, hobnobber with princes and lords and gentlemen, as he was pressed down, back into the street mire from whence the grovelling snivelling bastard came. Vengeance, as the Romans said, is best taken cold. It would be an enormous delight and relief to be present at the scene when Quilter knelt and begged for respite. And an even greater delight to be the instrument of his condemnation. With any luck he would get Quilter barred and gaoled, even maybe exiled or transported.

'What you say is impossible, Alex. Sealandings is no maker of convictions. It is not even a maker of gentry. I know, for I live here. It produces fish, and that is all. Except for a few useful variations in the local people, some of whom might be useful in time, it offers nought.'

'It offered me a sight which I've never before seen, Rad. It gave me a glimpse of two women, and a duel.'

'A duel?' Carradine's attention was turned from Quilter. 'Two women? Isn't that a trifle unusual, Alex? It is, as I have heard tell of these affairs, more typically a concern of two gentlemen and *one* lady.'

'Not in Sealandings.' Briefly Waite narrated the alarming events at the horse fair. 'I swear to you, Rad, it happened exactly as I tell it. This girl, Mehala her name, stood proud as a peacock – peahen, then – and insisted on all proper procedure. Then she took hold with a sailor's slant, checked the groom's loading of her selected piece, and shot a stave at some seventy feet.'

He thought his exaggeration of the distance pardonable in the circumstances. Carradine stared at him, almost disbelieving.

'And the woman was prepared to *duel*. . . ? To duel, you say, with another servant, over a pitch in a horse traders' gathering?'

'As I stand here, Rad! It was so. I tell you that any man, however well fitted he was with firearms, would have had his work cut out to make a decent fist of flintlock matters, with an opponent like that Mehala.'

'Mehala,' Carradine mused. 'Where the devil have I heard that name before?'

'At the tavern, Rad. The Donkey and Buskin, where we stay. She served the three of us as we arrived. Me, Jeremy Pacton, Quilter.'

'Pretty, eh?' Carradine's eyes narrowed. He still suspected his friend of telling a tall tale, perhaps to land him into some amusing joke compromise with a so-say lady in a tavern. London clubs fed on such stories, and he was wary.

'No,' Waite answered, surprising himself as much as his friend. 'She's rather . . . well, alluring, attracting and even compelling. Beautiful, yet something more. I swear that there's no man can walk past her without wishing thoughts his wife would cheerfully kill for.'

'How stood she?' Carradine was intrigued in spite of himself. 'Calm? Frightened? Determined?'

'I swear that if the other wench had not backed down she would have gone through with it. Aye, and fired her flintlock to kill. She told me as much, and in her voice not a quiver.'

'And then?'

'The enemy dray was driven meekly from the field, leaving this Amazonian to serve her ale as if nothing unusual had transpired.'

'Then the woman's mad!'

'Then the woman is not, Carradine.' Waite was not smiling. 'Ask around. Quilter's there. He was making book on the outcome of that same duel. And that great oaf next him.'

Carradine glanced across, recognizing Prothero from Calling Farm. 'But it was a set-up stand, Alex?'

'As I live and breathe, no, Rad. Ask throughout the grooms. They'll tell you.'

'Perhaps I shall ask this Mehala herself, for further confirmation!' Carradine said the words as a challenge to Waite's veracity, but was unprepared for the reaction of his friend, whose eyes narrowed.

'I do not think we should set out to offend this girl, Rad,' Alex Waite said evenly. 'She is no mere servant. She was pulled from the sea a few days since, and has quite forgot her origins.'

'Then she definitely *is* mad. All are who have suffered rescue.'

'Not so. She is better minded than most people I have seen today.' He smiled to make a joke out of his words, but added for good measure in view of Carradine's known inflammatory temper, 'Present company excepted – who has won me a share in three guineas from Peter Quilter!'

'And all for a dead cock!' Carradine exulted. They crossed the ring, which was being readied for another fight to the death with fresh sand. The birds were being prepared, the single stabbing spurs being strapped to the birds' heels.

Carradine wished each of those gold pieces had been ten thousand. Solvency stood ever by ruin's door.

They collected their winnings, and stood watching the two new cocks be brought out for the face-off. The owners crouched, holding their birds in the cockfighter's clutch, at arm's length.

'There's a whole art to this, Alex, they say,' Carradine observed as the crowd gathered, leaning over into the small arena. 'Watch how the more experienced man makes his approach slowly, never a sharp rapid thrust, but only a gradual extension of the arms so his animal has time to size up the opponent. It imbues his creature with awareness of the inherent weakness of the enemy. I shall bet on the fat man's cock. It'll win, without a doubt.'

'I'm unsure, Rad. I shall sit this one out.'

'I'll lay a hundred, my friend!'

Waite was startled. A hundred guineas was a deal to expend on a mere cock main like this local match, but he knew better than cross opinions with Carradine when he was in this mood. He was becoming disturbed by the faces all around. They often joked in London that to lay a woman with consummate ease you merely had to take her to the nearest cockfight – many lewd similes and metaphors were in the common street rhymes and vulgar chapbooks sold around Convent Garden market. The promise was that, once a woman's blood lust was roused by the sight of death and creatures in mortal combat, that excitement translated itself naturally and swiftly into a rapacious and crude sexual craving unequalled by any other tactic. A look at these faces, the slavering rapacity and the howling frenzy of the spectator in at a death, was almost too much. Suddenly he was sickened by their expressions. There was something terrible about life at these meets. He was on the point of turning away when Carradine rejoined him and leaned across the barrier to observe the spectacle as the birds were released to fly at each other. The crowd was roaring, the stench of animal passion almost stifling.

'It makes me think, Alex,' Carradine said, leaning close to be heard, 'that there is a possibility of an excellent wager to be made on a local prize fight.'

'How much is excellent, Rad?' Waite was not interested.

'Oh, quite a pinch, Alex. I thought, in view of your friendship, we might share a wager or two. Quilter's likely to remain here all the week, is he not? And the prize fight is due very soon.'

'I heard Tom Spring, the Champion, is ill. Is that not the case?'

'On the nail, Alex. But there is a local man called Rendell who fancies his chances against Battling Goring.'

'In Tom Spring's place?'

Waite was startled at the news. The names of the leading barefisters were as well known to most as the names of the country's greatest generals and admirals, and even Royalty. For a new contender to emerge into that exalted few was so rare that the event was usually trumpeted abroad as soon as the first wagers were laid.

'I know what you're thinking, Alex.' Carradine smiled at his friend's astonishment. 'But people hereabouts are most secretive. This man can stand against Goring. I haven't disclosed this news to any other person. I swear to you that I have good reasons to place quite a wager or two on the outcome of this fight.'

'Which way?' Waite was intrigued now. The cockfight was continuing, blood spattering in thin drops as the animals shrieked and raked their spurs at the eyes and breast of the other.

'Promise that you will not disclose to anyone what I am about to impart?'

'I promise, Rad.'

'Not even to Peter or Sir Jeremy?' Carradine smiled, and nodded reassuringly at Waite's slight withdrawal at the request. 'I understand your reluctance, Alex. But I owe you a favour. Remember the night you covered my bet at the cribbage wager, with that crowd in from Brighton all after my blood? You stood up and offered to back my hand against theirs when I was a little, shall we say, short for the moment?'

'I remember.' Waite spoke wonderingly. 'It was only a matter of seventy sovereigns or so, wasn't it?'

'Seventy or seventy thousand, Alex, I honour you for it. And I do not forget.'

'Rad, this is truly kind of you. I don't really deserve . . .'

'Listen.' Carradine drew Waite closer by the sleeve of his coat and spoke into his ear as the crowd bawled and jostled and sweated in their stupid rut-by-proxy. 'This is the event: Rendell will be challenging tomorrow. Goring shall have to accept, for his backers are already on their way from the capital. The wagers will go heavily against Rendell, and Goring will be heavy odds-on. Now, Alex, if anyone were to place, very early, bets for Tom Spring – as if he were actually about to fight, acting as if the news had not yet reached here that the Champion was not able to toe his line – what then?'

He waited, but the young man was nodding, listening to get it clear. Carradine sighed. He had understood implications of this sort at his father's very knee, and here was this grown man as thick as a ship's timbers unable to grasp the opportunity without a full explanation.

'Why, Alex! Then the Fancy will take up any and every bet laid for and upon Battler Goring's opponent, right? Now, you know and I know that that opponent is not Tom Spring the Champion of All England. *We know* it is Rendell, our local man! The Fancy will fall over themselves to take our wagers, at practically any odds we suggest. You see?'

'And when Rendell stands in place of Tom Spring we make a play to suggest the bets be declared null and void, eh?'

'Which they will refuse, with laughter, doubtless thinking themselves the cleverest gamesters of all time, Alex!'

'But what if Rendell loses?'

'He is reputed to be a splendid fighter, Alex. Formidable, capable, and a lion in the ring. He has worked at the new iron foundries in the north, and can withstand any man on earth. Also, certain shall we say *arrangements* have been made for Rendell to win after the sixtieth round. But we needn't disclose that little gem of information, need we?'

'True, Rad, true.'

'Promise you'll keep this privy, Alex, and use it only for your own bets on Rendell? You should use the agent called Sumner.'

'I promise. And thank you.'

'What are friends for, if not to please?' Carradine said, smiling. They turned their attention to the main in the arena, but it had ended and all they saw was the final leap of the triumphant cock upon the fallen. Very symbolic, Carradine thought it. He smiled to himself, and decided he would seek out this Mehala girl and celebrate the coming of solvency, wealth, and freedom from creditors like that obnoxious Quilter who, beaming and waving from across the ring, was indicating with delight that Carradine now owed him a further one hundred golden guineas.

He smiled and waved back, pleased at the certainty of Quilter's coming doom.

Long overdue, long overdue.

26

Sunday service was so well attended that latecomers had to stand for lack of room. Those who were faithful to the tenets of Reverend Baring's Church exceeded the nonconformers in number and wealth. They were the central flow of population in Sealandings, though lately inroads had been made by Quakers and Methodists and Congregationalists and the Scotch Glasites and the English Sandemanians. Reverend Baring was convinced that all of these, and their various iniquitous offshoots, were all political subversives and traitors to truth, honesty and justice, and relentlessly unpatriotic; he frequently sermoned so when in the right temper. He expounded at least once a month on the core facts as he saw them, arguing that the wheedling claims of the Independents to be considered loyal subjects and honest labourers were demonstrably false. He tried out his sermons each time beforehand on Euterpe, and she made constructive comments which he heeded, though her continual advice that brevity should be observed at all costs he thought a needless encroachment on his fluency.

This Sunday they were all there, he was delighted to see. He spoke at length on the foul iniquities of the Independents and their aberrant reasonings regarding Sacred Writ. Their hymns he abhorred, their leaders should be imprisoned and their persuasions banned. The congregation paid heed, but were less than animated. The organ, lately purchased from a Bristol importer, hardly carried its sound beyond the first few pews, so small was it in proportion to the church interior, but Reverend Baring was proud of it and Euterpe did the best she could. The two children pumping the bellows for her worked assiduously, but since one child fell asleep at its post the melody was always slow to start. She had not the heart to waken the poor little lad, and deliberately reduced the number of stops she should have used so as to minimize the organ's needs for air. Mercifully, the children were out of sight of the congregation and of Reverend Baring, except at the consecration and the final blessing.

'And so it is, brethren,' he thundered in conclusion, 'that we who live in the Lord must show eternal vigilance, bewaring of the company of those who do not. And they are many and growing, brethren. They hold in their hands bribery, and all manner of enticements, yet they are instruments of Satan and must be shunned. Not only that, but their places and blandishments must be abhorred . . .'

Euterpe knew where Doctor Carmichael usually placed himself. Third pew, no nearer the altar than that, and left of the central aisle. It was only by a supreme effort of will that she forebore to look in that direction. Everyone in the congregation would have seen. In her position at the organ she was clearly visible from almost any pew in the church, and Reverend Baring of course had his priest's pew positioned directly across. Worse still was the new device which every church worth its salt was installing, an ingeniously placed mirror, angled so as to provide a view of the officiating clergyman without an organist having to suffer the temptation of actually turning to ogle, and so facing the congregation. A commendable improvement to morality, her brother had called this marvellous invention. A nuisance, Euterpe called it to herself. The wretched mirror gave her a view of her brother's back, and that was all. Its surface was somehow curved, so that with very little movement . . . She stared, moving her body slightly in a slow sway. The congregation came into view, at least in part. But which part?

She inched her weight on to her feet, carefully placing her soles away from the pedals. Gently, so as not to cause distraction from the rector's vital words, she reached out, frowning slightly, as if to turn a page of the music, easing herself forward then successfully moving a fraction to her right. She inhaled, straightening, and was delighted to see that faces were now in view. Mrs Lydia Vallance, from Lorne House, in the grandest feathered hat ever. Squire Hunterfield, too. So she must now be looking at the end of the pew, aisle side. That meant the first pews, three of them. Doctor Carmichael was nowhere to be seen; she must be somehow seeing the wrong side. Miss Letitia Hunterfield, in a dark green shawl, was seated next her sister, Miss Tabitha. The latter – no respecter of places or persons, it was said – showed little interest in the sermon and was moving her head about quite carelessly, giving scandal to all who noticed. Which, in Sealandings, meant everyone there.

A similar slow tactic, and she was moving inchwise in the other direction along the organ seat. The first face she saw, contorted in that wonderful ingenious article of reflection, was Doctor Carmichael's. So he had come, after all! He was unhappy. Her heart melted. The poor man had come to church knowing he was disfavoured by her brother. He was staring at his hands, or something on his lap – prayerbook perhaps? – and did not look round. And, with a faint motion as if

210

checking the music again, the looking glass contained the compelling face of Mehala. A bonnet, probably borrowed for the occasion, latched under her chin with grey ribbon, very decently capping an expression at once intelligent and perceptive. This girl was bright, as well as knowledgeable.

A movement behind Mehala caught Euterpe's eye. Mrs De Foe's gloved hands had shifted, to place her canezou-pelerine more comfortably about her. The slight stirring she made was not so noticeable as to give occasion for criticism or to indicate inattention, but Euterpe saw it gave Mrs De Foe the chance of a swift glance round. The lady's face tightened as she stilled. Somebody was not here, Euterpe guessed. Somebody who should have come, perhaps? But who on earth was there left? Most of the gentry were in, and only those who were away or legitimately unable to attend . . .

Yet Thalia De Foe was not the most convinced churchgoer. And her attendances were marked by a singularly bored appearance throughout the sermons. She seemed impatient with the prayers, irritated by the hymns, and was least inclined of all to stay and converse with the rector. Who on earth could she have expected to meet at church that she could not have met to greater benefit elsewhere? It had to be someone she could not communicate with more directly, for fear of scandal.

'So it is, brethren, that we who walk in the way of the Lord . . .'

Euterpe dragged her attention back from the brink. Her thoughts were definitely unchaste, wholly wrong for this place of worship, and surely would not go unnoticed in the Final Reckoning with the Almighty. But Doctor Carmichael seemed so downcast. If Mehala could be somehow brought to assume the housekeeper's role at the rectory, it would be wholly proper to encourage Doctor Carmichael to offer the position of housekeeper at Shalamar to the rector's sister. Surely. . . ?

'Maddie,' she whispered, making a faint tutting noise to rouse the two dozy children. The poor lambs were so tired. She extended her right foot, tapping it softly against the organ's side. A small hand crept round the wooden fascia, gave two silent touches, and withdrew. They were both awake, thank heavens. Euterpe pulled out a number of stops, risking the vox humana in her pleasure that the service was moving to a close, and waited for her brother's sign. She now thought the mirror a most useful device, having glimpsed Doctor Carmichael.

The last hymn was The Old Hundredth, which was easy enough despite its four flats in the Bourgeois version, though hard on the four

211

little arms ploughing the limbs of the bellows up and down. She played with vigour.

The voluntaries, which she normally played as the congregation retired, she completed in almost indecent haste. She made sure that she was out of the church with respectable alacrity, and waited modestly for her brother to finish his chore of bidding the worshippers his good mornings.

She caught sight of Doctor Carmichael's hesitation as he made to emerge from the church door, and guessed his intentions. With becoming slowness she went to stand meekly out of sight of the main concourse, by the side door. An old Lady Chapel had been a feature of the church in the past days, but of course such was considered idolatrous and papist in these modern times. The side entrance was little used, and nobody nowadays would think of being so disloyal as to pray at that inner chapel to the exclusion of the main body of the church.

He came, adjusting his old coat against the wind. She affected to be surprised to see him, stepping back slightly to show how unexpected his sudden appearing was.

'Doctor Carmichael!' she said. 'Good morning to you. I trust you are not in such a hurry that you seek to avoid the Barings?'

He reddened with embarrassment. 'I am sorry, Miss Baring, but I think it inexpedient to meet your brother today. Nor for a considerable while, I fancy.'

'So you steal from the church unseen, Doctor!' She then allowed her concern to show. 'I trust that no member of my family has given you offence?'

'Not your family to me, Miss Baring. But me to a member of your family.'

'Are you certain of this, Doctor?'

'I regret it is true. I have been so informed. Naturally, I would seek to learn why, how, whatever . . . But I am disallowed the privilege of inquiry.' He scanned the churchyard anxiously. Only a few children, and those playing noisily about the gravestones, were in view. The rest of the people were making their way down the church path towards the market square, conversing. 'In fact, Miss Baring, I fear that even by speaking with you here I am in some way contributing to the grievance I have caused the rector.'

'Then I shall explain to him that I insisted on your company, while waiting for his long-winded fare-thee-wells and chats with the laity!' She tried to make light of it all, but felt fury at her brother's interference. 'Doctor Carmichael, I am so sorry that this has happened. I am certain it is based entirely on a misunderstanding. In fact, I shall have a great need of your company, now that an important matter has arisen in which you and I have a joint obligation.'

'Oh, dear.'

He looked forlorn. She walked a pace, to encourage him to accompany her away from the church door. He followed, anxiously looking back as if judging the distance to escape.

'It is the matter of Mehala, Doctor Carmichael.'

'Yes.' His face brightened, to her slight irritation. But if a mention of Mehala brought her own goal that bit nearer, then she had to be discussed.

'My brother thinks Mehala would be the better placed in somewhere decent and god-fearing, a natural home, as it were. And that in Sealandings, until such time she recovers sufficiently to bring back her mind.'

'That is a splendid idea, Miss Baring.' Carmichael spoke guardedly, as if expecting a trap. Euterpe felt anger, but swiftly suppressed it. She could kill her stupid brother, jumping to his ridiculous conclusions.

Anger made her bold enough to skate close to the edge of truth. 'In fact, Doctor, my brother has hit upon the notion of having Mehala move into the rectory, and there assist me in performing the duties of a housekeeper. That befits her proper station, he feels, somewhat more truly than her present stay at the Donkey and Buskin.'

'He does?' Ven Carmichael asked in surprise.

'Yes, Doctor. What is your opinion?

'It seems a good and sensible move, Miss Baring. Yet . . .'

'Yes?'

'Has Mehala been approached?'

'Not with this particular proposal in mind, no. But I thought that, after speaking with you and drawing my brother's suggestion to your attention, it would then be correct to send word to John Weaver at the tavern and let Mrs Weaver speak with Mehala herself.'

He thought a moment. 'Very well, Miss Baring. Though I feel that it is a situation better resolved by the ladies of Sealandings than the gentlemen.'

'You do not object, then?'

'No, Miss Baring. I shall be guided by you in this.'

'Thank you, Doctor. I am very relieved.'

The natural thing would have been now to broach the subject of his own need of a housekeeper's skills at Shalamar, but that might have

213

caused his mind to leap from Mehala's need for placement to his own need of a housekeeper, which would never do. The last thing in the world Euterpe wanted was for Mehala to be seen – or even thought of – as Doctor Carmichael's housekeeper.

He donned his hat, much crumpled as it was in testimony to his lack of a hat brace. Another chore needing attention, she observed with satisfaction. He made to move away with that sideways apologetic smile he had, but the smile and a desire to extend the conversation made her speak.

'Doctor. May I say that I overheard, from within the rectory hall, quite accidentally, some of the words which passed between yourself and my brother . . .'

'Oh. I hope I gave you no cause to . . .'

'No, Doctor Carmichael.' He looked so stricken her heart went out to him. Doubtless worrying himself into sickness, when he had enough to grieve him without her idiot brother's sillinesses. 'It is all due to my brother's error, in supposing that you wished to lay upon me the task of finding more assistance for Mehala. Naturally, he was concerned that I should be not unduly troubled. He jumped to wrong conclusions, in short.'

'Miss Baring. I would not have so presumed . . .'

'I am aware of that. I am also certain that, in better moments, so would my brother be. I shall do my utmost to ease his attitude towards you, Doctor Carmichael.'

She expected him to be pleased, or a little relieved. To her alarm he seemed hesitant. He even seemed to withdraw a little.

'Miss Baring. I regret that your efforts will do little to help, however well intentioned. My attendance at Morning Service was by way of a farewell.'

'A. . . ?' She could not speak the word.

'Not a farewell to Sealandings, of course.' He did not notice her drained face. He stared after the departing throng, their bright gig coats and cardinal cloaks fluttering in the rising sea wind. 'But a farewell to the Established Church. You see, Miss Baring, it is this way with me.'

'But . . .'

'No, please.' He spoke on over her interruption. 'Your brother spoke the truth, in his own way. It is I who am deficient. Reverend Baring is right. Faults do lie in my behaviour, in my assumptions about my position here, the work I do. The achievements I try for, the few lives I manage to save.' He smiled that lopsided smile, adding wryly, 'Even

214

sometimes managing to rescue them from my own treatments, when heaven is with me.'

She was in despair. 'Then what is wrong?'

'My arrogance, Miss Baring. I have always believed that, with thought and concern, I have held somehow quite legitimate and proper hope for medical successes. I see from what your brother has said – as much from the pulpit as from the unhappy conversation we had at the rectory – that I have been guilty of an erroneous conscience. I *believed* in my own attributes. And I was wrong. I do not think I deserve the Church's benign influence.'

'But it is for all, Doctor Carmichael!'

'Not for me, Miss Baring.' He nodded a further apology. 'I shall miss the church, and your playing, and the services, and the opportunities it has afforded of meeting the folk of Sealandings.'

She was aghast. This was the only place she could reasonably expect to meet him, and now he was moving further out of reach.

'But, Doctor, where shall you go?'

'I shall have to find a place to worship, Miss Baring. They say there are others.' It was his wry joke, at her brother's hectoring on the subject of religious menaces mushrooming everywhere.

'In the parish, Doctor Carmichael?'

'Of course it will need to be near to Shalamar. That goes without saying, for I could never afford another place half so well appointed.'

She heard his goodbye and saw him leave the churchyard the back way. Having no chaise he would walk the half mile to Shalamar along the South toll road.

For a few moments she simply stood there, her mind in turmoil. What had seemed a good sensible tactic had become a matter of supreme urgency. She would have to move fast as lightning to accomplish the changes she wished for. Mehala to the rectory, and herself to Shalamar. There was no time to waste. She would have to be resolute and decisive. And nobody had better stand in her road, brother or other.

She almost ran into the vestry for her cloak.

27

If she had had a whip to hand, she would have used it to flog her way out of the church and into her barouche. And then done the same to put her coachman to greater action and so to home at Milton Hall all the faster. Thalia De Foe was fuming.

Carradine had not come to church. Not that prayer was his practice, but they had always agreed that the first Sunday after his arrival home in Sealandings, they would meet at church. And so regularize their accidental recognition of each other, for the sake of all local gossips. That was the ideal way, she had told Carradine, who had concurred.

And the result? Here she was left like an idiot, going to listen to that canonical ignoramus mouth stupidities in his pulpit, while Carradine probably snored his head off at Carradine Manor. And she had taken special pains this day in expectation of his arrival. His presence at the church always caused a stir. She had her first speeches all ready for him. She had practised the faint start of astonishment when, oh so accidentally, she left the church and paused in the aisle to admire the flowers at the baptismal font and found herself coming up against him saying his good mornings to the vicar. And, eventually, the conversations which, so guardedly, would lead up to the inevitable passion later today. That had always been reserved for the afternoons, when he would come to pay his compliments at Milton Hall, by an open and perfectly respectable arrangement established that same Sunday morning, in the plain hearing of all. At church, the one place where no breath of scandal could taint their encounter, or its courteous extension.

Inevitable? Not so inevitable as all that, it seemed!

Thalia blistered her way into the reception hall at Milton, cursed Meg, and blamed Ennis for tardiness in coming to welcome her return.

The next hours were pandemonium, in which she found release in shrieking abuse at the elderly housekeeper, Mrs Randon, and succeeded in reducing her to tears. She then sought out Mrs Thornton, the cook, and in front of that lady's three assistants in her own kitchen reduced her to a babbling wreck while lecturing her on her deficiences and lack of foresight, on her inept management of the victuals and provisions of the entire house, and her hopelessness when it came to planning the banquet which was to accompany the ball she planned for the coming fortnight.

'It seems to me, Mrs Thornton,' Mrs De Foe shouted, sweeping a row of skillets from the long kitchen table to the floor, 'that I am the only one round this house who is expected to work her fingers to the bone while everyone else sits back, idle as you please, bleeding me dry of coinage and goods and food and protection! It is not good enough, d'you hear?'

She smashed a Lowestoft jug in the fireplace, an unlucky sign in any household, but Thalia felt that ill luck had already come a-plenty and deserved recognition.

'But, ma'am, you have not yet delivered to me the list of required dishes for the – '

'Shut up while I am speaking, you harlot!' Thalia shrieked like a mad thing. 'You have the effrontery to criticize me before my face when I bring your atrocious defects to your attention? When I have spent hours on my *knees* in a draughty church praying for the good of your worthless souls? How dare you. . . !'

The turbulence lasted a quarter of an hour. The house was silent as the mistress of Milton Hall retired with a terrible headache to her bedroom, forbidding the slightest noise anywhere in the house, the estate, the grounds.

The outcome was unavoidable, as always after Mrs De Foe's tantrums. A bird calling to its mate in the landscaped garden, a groom unable to stifle the whinnying of a horse while stabling the beast, the distant shout of a traveller on the South Toll road as he hove in sight of Scalandings and knew that his journey was almost at an end – anything was construed by Mrs De Foe as the darkest expression of malice on the part of the household, and punishment would fly fast and personal. The staff would be fortunate to keep their positions for the rest of the day. They had all seen sackings happen for this and lesser causes before now, when one of these fits of rage lay upon their mistress's brow.

In her bedroom, lying on her bed, Thalia De Foe went over the possible reasons for Carradine's absence at church today. He was sick – no; she would have heard. He was busy – but too busy to come and love his woman, when that had always been his first priority? He was gone from Sealandings back to London – no; she again would have heard. He was unable to come . . . probably yes, for she knew he wanted her as feverishly as she craved him. And he was never slow in claiming what he desired, not Rad Carradine.

The reasoning logic calmed her. She rose, blotted her face with a corner of her sleeve, and wondered how she should dress for his coming this afternoon, for come he surely must. He had been especially delighted by the new half-dress fashion she had worn when seeing him off at their last meeting, and there was a faint possibility that the pink shade was something he had not seen even in London. Well, *almost* a faint possibility.

That was the answer: Carradine was delayed. His very absence from church was his signal that he would be arriving here at Milton Hall shortly, as soon as the early afternoon came, to apologize and pretend some business or some messages from her husband Fellows in London. She would hear him announcing his fictitious message to Ennis or Mrs Randon in the hallway down below. She would descend, casually, clearly on her way to the garden. She would make a pretty and youthful picture, coming shining down the staircase, her hand charmingly placed on the dark banister and her lace glove showing an ivory white against the solid carved wood . . . Yes, that was it. He was coming soon, and she would captivate him as ever by her glamorous entrance.

She pulled the bell to bring Meg, and was humming to herself before the cheval looking glass when the girl made her breathless arrival. Thalia was using rose-water admixed with glycerine – Doctor Scheele's famed 'sweet principle of fats' – to smooth her countenance into the youthful and lovely complexion which Carradine adored.

'Yes, ma'am?'

'I shall bathe now, Meg,' the mistress said brightly. 'Could you send for the hot water, when you will?'

'Yes, ma'am.'

Thalia smiled to herself at the relief in her maid's voice.

Mehala walked out from the Donkey and Buskin, by permission of Mrs Weaver, to share the air.

'Stay well wrapped up in that shawl, Mehala,' the taverner's wife warned, 'and never with your back to the sea wind should the tide change, d'y'hear?'

'Yes, ma'am. And I thank you. I shall be back within the hour.'

'Don't you dare, Mehala! You take your time, and don't go too far.'

'Yes, ma'am.'

'Not as far as Whitehanger, and stay this side of the roadways.'

'Yes, ma'am.' Mehala was smiling openly now at Mrs Weaver's concern. That lady insisted on her servants taking the air once a week, a great and daring innovation in the wellbeing of her workers about the tavern, which not all appreciated. Little Jane was especially downcast whenever she was sent out on promenade, and Nellie had openly rebelled against this excercise, invoking the natural Law of God as being contrary to Mrs Weaver's scheme. Sarah Ann had had to invoke John Weaver's authority to win *that* battle, Nellie being a harridan in her righteous mood. Even Old Alice was prised free of her inglenook and made to accomplish three progresses from the tavern along the hard to the far side of the wharf and back, with the head cellarman Bone and his dozy dog Ranter for reluctant company.

'And take good breaths, to expand your lights, Mehala! They need fresh air to rid them of the last taint of sea water, d'y'hear?'

'Yes, ma'am.'

Mehala set out with the sea and harbour to her left. A few houses, thatched and squat, formed a narrow street down which she passed. All were mere cottages, with smoke ascending and the Sunday composures being observed, with windows half-shrouded and doors left open that neighbours might call and compare progress made with the weekend's cooking. Ahead, where the narrow wynd ended, she could see the few cobbles peter out and the wooden bridge over the River Affon showing among willows.

Distantly beyond there was the shoreline, that same shore where she had so nearly foundered in finding Simple Tom and effecting his rescue. That way too lay Watermillock and its great tide mill where the sea came a-visiting to somehow provide the power to work the great grinding wheels for the corn, and the few local weavers' cottages which had come to cluster the sides of the estate.

That would be her direction. Unless the wind made a sudden veer, she would avoid its iniquitous cold on her kidneys, as sternly directed by Mrs Weaver, during her return walk. She consciously took a few deep inhalations, but soon lost her enthusiasm for that in the pleasure of the walk.

The countryside hereabouts was not as flat as Mersea Island. There, low salt marshes and flat sea lands had been the only view. The long Ray Channel, with the sea glinting in vast expanse beyond Ray Island, had been her home. The Colne water, snaking inland between Wivenhoe and ugly Rowhedge village, the Blackwater, the hugh brown sails of the boats moving at a slow glide between fields and ever startling the visitor by their unexpectedness. And the birds, the unusual and the rare, pleasing with their odd behaviours.

And her mother. Less of a mother than an imposition, eventually, at her drunken schemes to aid her further drunkenness. No caring chiding there, to avoid the chills and take a walk to share the fresh air and look to your health. How unfortunate it was to remember, and then wish that you hadn't done anything of the kind.

To the right, as she walked out from Sealandings and left the cottages behind, the rise of the ground obscured the great houses of the district. Bures House, with Mr Golding resident. Before and right stood the Hunterfields' Lorne House, soon to come into view, while behind and right you would come upon Shalamar, that exotically named shambles of a dwelling currently rented by Doctor Carmichael.

Odd how the grand houses and hall stood in a crescent around the town, as if the gentry properly wanted to be near yet not to share. Her previous suitor, in the days so long ago, when she had been different and lived to the south in Mersea's fastness, would have said that they were nearby to bring the lower classes into subjection. Mehala would have laughed, and plagued him, taunting his reasons, and mocking his logic with coined examples to have him floundering then laughing among the sedge and sands while gathering the samphire plant for food. Now, with him elsewhere and lost to her, she could turn her new mind to Sealandings.

She reached the small domed wooden bridge over the Affon and stood for a few minutes, looking at the small flow. Quickening, though, the river seemed to scent its destination and the very edge of the township. Townsfolk drew their clean water from it before it disgorged at the start of the hard. She wondered, casting a glance behind towards the cottages she had just left. It would have been comparatively simple for John Weaver to have made some contrivance, would it not, to fetch water from the River Affon and channel it somehow into his yard? Instead, an exactly similar set of drains brought water from the wells and dewponds and reservoirs on the Charles Golding estate of Bures House.

Strange. Probably some ancient concession had applied, and thus been present when John Weaver had taken over the tavern? Or perhaps it was something the Weavers had inherited, and John Weaver had come to see the arrangement as given by God since Time began. That was the way of country people and fisher folk: all should stay as it was. They remembered the good times – as if any had ever existed.

Mehala now had direct evidence to prove that memory was a cruel master, and a worse deceiver. Its absence could be freedom from a gaoler.

The fact was, she had learned a sort of happiness here at Sealandings. The anxious business with that Agatha woman from the Goat and Compass at the horse meet had been frightening, yes. But it had exhilarated, as few things could. The sheer giddy exaltation with which she had faced the decision! The awesome expressions on the faces of all, the disbelief of the grooms, the astonishment of the gentlemen whose talk had gradually silenced as they came to see her resolve. And the final sense of glorious abandon when Agatha had taken up the reins of her dray and driven from the place, vacating the field to her. It had been power, power of the kind surely that had seemed men's preserve until that moment. She had felt a goddess. And no wonder! For once she had directed the course of her life, and that of others.

Yes, she was happy in Sealandings. And free, in a way that she had never experienced before.

Her own mistress, even if she was lowly in status and no more than a serving maid-of-all at a humble tavern in a fishing village-cum-town in East Anglia. She was powerful within herself, *for* herself. She felt unique, gloriously individual. And she had seen recognition in the eyes of Doctor Carmichael as he and she had spoken together, caring for Simple Tom.

Happiness was her new discovery. It had to be said in words, brought by herself to her own attention. And, a most curious thing, it was definite, a thing defined not merely by the absence of its opposites, misery and gloom and oppression. It was alive, a consciousness and brilliance and lightness of the heart and mind. It was sheer power, and enemy of Time. Happiness was hers.

The difficulty was that it was here somehow in Sealandings. To return to Mersea, to the startling rise of Colchester Town from that river plain, to the Blackwater and the Colne River and their slow swirling rush into the sea marshes, would spell its loss to her. Surely she had the right to persevere in pursuit of it, to the furtherance of her own interests? Happiness was hers for the taking, the keeping – but only here in Sealandings.

It was a new discovery. It was something undreamed of before.

Before, happiness was a fluke, a chance, a gift from a benevolent but capricious and even wayward God. It was the result of prayer, diligence, obedience and compliance. It stemmed from doing one's duty, as defined and seen by others. It came as reward from doing the tasks set by others. Always, *others* were around, involved, in authority, stern and unyielding in their insistence.

One serious problem seemed more to her than the risk of its ending, however. Fine for the people of Sealandings, with their ways as set surely as those of the Ray Channel villages and the Stour and the

Blackwater and Mersea. There was the terrible gauntlet she ran of her 'disposal', which Mrs Weaver now mentioned increasingly. For she was, however one saw matters, supernumary to the tavern's need. Even with the improved trade for the grooms at the horse field, she was more than was required. Little Jane could easily cope, now Agatha's dray was away and no longer in competition. She was not needed in the kitchen, where Mrs Nelson could more than manage. She was not really needed to serve, for Nellie ruled her team rigorously and had them going like a Tompion clock, to fine time and order.

No, Mehala knew she was not long now for the Donkey and Buskin. But where could she go? Mrs Weaver had hinted, in her admonitions as Mehala had set out on her compulsory walk, that the last of the sea water was finally from her chest. She was in health now. Implicit was Mrs Weaver's intent, to see her off the premises. Kindly, though, for she had looked after her and seen her well received on shore, when many a girl would have found herself worked nigh to death by a welcoming land family, and even sold as a wife to some drunkard. That misery happened too often to bear the re-telling on these very same shores.

With a sigh she made to step along the small bridge and continue on, but a voice arrested her movement.

'No, stay if you please, miss.'

'I beg your pardon, sir?' she called, startled.

The voice came from her left, down the slope which led to the mole by the Sealandings harbour. Willows made the faint sun's sheen glint badly, its reflection almost blinding her. She was unable to see the figure seated among the vegetation there for a moment, until her eyes accommodated to the light.

The voice called, 'A few moments only, miss. The light hereabouts is treacherous.'

'The light, sir?' She was amused, but baffled.

'My pigments are trying hard not to impede you further, Miss Mehala.'

She relaxed. He knew her name, whoever he was, so he could not be a perfect stranger. From Sealandings in any case.

'Pigments, sir?' Painter. He must be that Mr Maderley, William Maderley, whose lanthorn light she had eventually – but too late – seen at Watermillock's corner window. 'You are painting?'

'Indeed, Miss Mehala. It is all I do!'

'Are you sure I do not spoil your view?' She felt a smile coming.

'Do not taunt, Miss Mehala. I have little time.'

'May I not be in haste also, sir?'

'Please. I apologize, but I need silence.'

'Yours as well as mine, I trust, sir!'

'Thank you, Miss Mehala. A few minutes more.'

Very well. She would humour him a little while. She held her pose, looking down at the flowing water. William Maderley. Widow Maderley's son. And, depending on which opinions you overheard at the tavern, either a profligate who, wastrel to his bones, was shirking his duties by idling about the contryside, or a simpleton who was mentally unstable and incapable of working the fine wide tide mill.

From her position on the rise of the wooden structure, she could see a small piece of the road – no more than a narrowing unmetalled trackway, in fact – which followed the line of the shore and ran towards Whitehanger. A movement along it caught her eye. A man, striding purposefully, carrying a small bag in his off hand, his caped Cambridge flapped unbuttoned as he strode.

Even at this distance she recognized Doctor Carmichael.

'Sir,' she called quickly without moving. 'I am afeared of delaying in my walk beyond the time I am allowed by Mistress Weaver. Will you be long at your paints?'

'A few moments only, Miss Mehala. Then I shall effect a proper introduction, I promise.'

'That you shall not, sir!' she gave back sharply, still keeping her place on the bridge. 'Without one to introduce, there simply cannot be such! I thank you to remember that!'

'I shall bring my sister, Miss Mehala. I promise!'

'And risk causing embarrassment to two ladies instead of one?'

'Please, I beg . . .'

She heard him swear angrily under his breath at some unfortunate occurrence, and smiled to herself. From kindness, she stayed as still as possible. The man was probably doing no more than sketching the distance, catching the light across the trees on the brow of the slope, and using her own person as a feature of position. But Doctor Carmichael was dwindling along the road, and even as she checked his movement among the trees lining the track, was lost to view. This was irritating, a loss where a double gain had been possible.

'Thank you, Miss Mehala. I am done.'

'Not a moment too soon, sir.' Mehala caught at her shawl, felt her bonnet latchets to ensure the bonnet was in place, and turned to continue her walk.

William Maderley was waiting as she left the bridge, and doffed his hat to her.

'Please, Miss Mehala, we did actually meet in the market square when you were with Mrs Weaver on market day. I raised my hat in greeting to her and she responded. You were in her company. Do you not recall?'

That was all to the good, then. She paused. Doctor Carmichael was probably on his way to the Darling family, to assess the chances of the other Darling child. Little Harry was burying at the church tomorrow. The doctor would probably return to Shalamar along the same road in any eventuality. She had time therefore to give to William Maderley, which would also prove her obedience to Mrs Weaver's admonition to take her time.

He stood, dishevelled and stained with his pigments. His hands were blotched, his spencer jacket smeared with grey pigment down one side. He wore a small brat apron about his waist, and looked so comical that she laughed openly.

'Not very well, sir. For I lately lost my mind in the sea. I was fetched ashore – '

'I am aware, Miss Mehala. I know your past, in so far as it is to be known. I must first thank you for pausing to speak, and for your keeping the position on the bridge that I might paint you into the scene. Might I in these circumstances introduce myself afresh? Mr William Maderley of Watermillock.'

'How do you do, sir.'

'How do you do, Miss Mehala. I am pleased to renew your acquaintance, and count myself most fortunate that I am able to do so.'

'Did you say it was your intention to paint me, Mr Maderley?'

'Indeed! I have already done so, saving your permission,'

'So might I see the masterpiece?'

'With pleasure.' He was almost pathetically eager to show her to his easel.

It was lodged among the low reeds on the river bank, with a small stool set beside it. The painting was no distant landscape. Startlingly, it was of Mehala's face, seen in close view.

'Sir?' Mehala asked the question, not knowing quite what the question was.

She stared at the painting. It was no watercolour sketch, as exterior painters did in such fashionable numbers these days. It was in the heavier oils, and on thick canvas laid upon a wooden frame. The easel was of crude construction only, no more than a lean of four struts upon each other. The canvas was nailed against the stretcher edges, frayed ends projecting roughly from the back.

But the painting.

The woman's head was tilted, showing wit and an alert life in her features. Her eyes held amusement as well as a strange gravity which brought complexity into the simple design. Black lustrous hair, smooth skin and a depth to her.

'Sir?' Mehala repeated, staring from the portrait to the artist and again to the canvas.

'Yes, Miss Mehala. It is yourself. I cannot explain to myself why I have gone to great lengths to see your hair as slightly darker even than it almost could possibly be. You will observe that I have made your hair longer than you wear it presently.'

'It is myself, sir,' she said faintly.

'Yes, Mehala.' He became less formal when he realized her response was favourable. 'I have been painting you ever since I caught sight of you in the market.'

She did not take issue with him over his interpretation of the encounter. 'I wore my hair longer, back in the days when . . . when . . .'

'I *knew* it!' He was triumphant, almost hugging himself with delight. 'I see you with long, almost straight hair, your face even younger than I have depicted! For the greater contrast with your features, you see.'

'But you did not know me then, sir?' She was disturbed.

'No, Mehala. Of course not.'

'Then how did you suppose my hair in that manner?'

'I see it through you, Mehala. If an artist's eye is true to the subject, he can surmise all the woman's ages. If he surmises her inner truth, why, he may state any aspect of it in whatever terms he chooses! But all depends upon that rightness of vision within.'

'I feel quite overcome by this, Mr Maderley.' She had never heard anyone speak this way before.

'Is it a shock, Mehala?' He was even more pleased instead of being sympathetic, losing his concern for her in delight at seeing her respond to his painting.

'Indeed it is, Mr Maderley. It is me to the life, some two years or so ago.'

'You remember, then, Mehala?'

'No, not at all.' She forgave herself the lie in her fright at seeing the painting. The old looking glass in the family cottage had shown her this exactness of herself, the one which had stood on the mantel before the cottage had been so cruelly burned down . . .

225

'What alarms you, then?' He was as puzzled as she was shocked.

'I . . . I suppose that is how I should have looked, is what I meant, Mr Maderley. You have worked with great assiduity on this painting.'

'I tried to capture some spirit, and hope it is coming, Mehala.'

'It is not finished, Mr Maderley?'

He seemed surprised. 'Of course not. A deal of labour is yet called for.'

'I cannot imagine anything else being required for its completion.'

'The background, Mehala. You see the brown, dark against the canvas?' His eagerness caused him to push her rudely out of the way so he could reach past and point. 'That's where the background must be painted in; only I am somewhat at a loss.'

'Background?' Her throat dried. She had difficulty in speaking for a moment. 'Background? Does a portrait have background?'

'Since the new fashion, Mehala. We have learned how the setting of a portraiture can enhance the sitter's appearance. It shows the context of an individual, bringing her into focus with greater facility for the viewer. That increases the power of a painting, y'see?'

Power again. Only this time the power of external vision, not interior sight. She felt desperate to stop him adding to the portrait.

'Will it not spoil it, Mr Maderley? Detract from the viewer's experience?'

'Very astute, Mehala.' He nodded soberly. 'It is a serious contrary opinion, true, and one with many adherents these modern days. But it is a risk we artists take. If once I only get a vision of the right setting, of your background, I know I shall create here a masterpiece.' He smiled apologetically. 'That I do not know – and you yourself remain in ignorance – of your true origins matters little. But if I could somehow activate my understanding of the place from which you took your last sight of land, say, before you started your terrible journey to the sea's depths, then I should be able to place the background all about your lovely shining locks, about your most comely face, to the glory of the art and the person depicted!'

She gazed at him. He was transformed, almost in a fit of exaltation. He was no gibbering idiot who was throwing his life away, as if with the phthisis or some wasting disease taken upon himself like those ancient saints who called down blights and sores upon themselves, making deranged claim to heavenly glories. No; this man was a poet, but in paint.

'Mehala,' he asked, shyly coming to himself again. 'Might I ask a great boon?'

'What is it, Mr Maderley? You already seem to possess more of me than I would have allowed. A favour too?'

'If you would be so kind, might I ask my sister to make your acquaintance? I confess frankly that it would be a device, a means of becoming acquainted for the purposes of persuading you to sit for me as a subject for my painting. I have several canvases in mind, each concerning you as the principal sitter. It is essential, Mehala.'

'To what end would this be, Mr Maderley?'

'Towards discovery in myself, Mehala. It is an artist's duty. I need the subject in order to make the advance my painting now calls for. Without the subject I am like a person frozen in ice.'

She shivered suddenly, and drew her shawl tighter around her. Frozen in ice? This was all too much for an innocent walk. She had chanced upon a simpleton, and discovered him to be a fiery mystic who could sway her powers of reason. 'A truly terrible vision, sir,' she said.

'I trust I have not discommoded you, Mehala, I realize it is a grim assertion. But it would be true, and distressing to me in an unbearable degree. Please say you will permit my sister to send her address?'

'My permission is hardly needed, Mr Maderley. You know I am but a serving girl at the tavern.'

'Oh, yes it is, Mehala.' He was smiling, not at her but at her portrait. 'Yes it is. Most definitely.'

'Then, as you ask my portrait and not myself, Mr Maderley, I suppose it can only comply with your wishes – in this instance only, mind.'

'I am grateful, Mehala.'

'I bid you good day, Mr Maderley.'

'Good day, Mehala, and a thousand thanks.'

It was with serious misgiving that she set out along the narrow path which ran parallel to the shore. She aimed for a point between Watermillock and Lorne House, not wishing to risk encountering Miss Olivia Maderley so soon after meeting her brother. She hoped she had done the right thing in agreeing to further acquaintanceship with the artist. If he did actually possess some inner vision that could reveal truths about herself, it was essential that she learn as soon as possible what he discovered. And as she could not approach him directly, perhaps his sister's agency would provide a means which suited her purpose.

An hour later she was sitting by the stile which stood at the juncture of the two tracks which skirted the coast line from the direction of

Whitehanger. She had given Artist Maderley considerable thought, and decided after all that she had been too hasty. Suddenly to confront your own visage, startlingly young at that, and with every appearance of having been taken from life no less than two years before, when she could have been only eighteen or so, was surprising enough. But to see that picture, as the result of a mere chance meeting with a gentleman when out walking, when one fully expected in any case to see a water sketch, or a landscape distanced among trees, with perhaps a grand house set among the woods of a fine garden, was a serious upset. Was he in fact more of a threat than a mere dauber? She shivered. It was almost occult, this vision of his, and spiritual things had always frightened her.

No. The truth must be that she had been so alarmed that she had conceded Mr Maderley's demand. When the time came, if her concession was acted upon, she could easily laugh it off as the result of unguarded surprise, and leave it at that. The Maderleys, the tide mill and their family problems of coming to terms with the artist son's endeavours were none of her affair.

She heard him first attempting a whistling sound, even before his footfalls caught her attention. In fact, she was wondering if the faint shrilling were perhaps some swan caught in an angler's twine, or some other living creature in distress, before she heard the sound of the steps on the rough track, and then knew it for Doctor Carmichael at last.

He approached, seeing her in the bend of the track at the stile, and raised his hat.

'Good day, Mehala. Well met, miss.'

'Good day, sir. Are you sharing the air also?'

'Not really, Mehala.' He approached and sat on the wooden step, as she sat on the stile's higher crosspiece. He was more downcast than she had seen him.

'You are about your duties?'

'I'm afraid I am lately to the Darlings. The child Harry, you know, was taken with the croup and passed away. I have feared for his sister Clare. They have one of the waggoners' cottages in Whitehanger.'

'And?'

He sighed, looking abstractedly across at the Whitehanger woods. 'It is looking very bad, Mehala. The parents have done all I said, but the child is now taken sick, with a delirium on her, and a dry cough. In short, I fear for her life. That means they will lose their only remaining child to the disease.'

'How truly terrible! Is there no treatment, Doctor Carmichael?'

'There is, but it never stems the onset or even retards the pace of the thing. When that membrane takes hold on the throat it seems so thick, almost like leather in some cases I have seen.'

'Does nobody recover, then?' She was as stricken as he appeared. She too had seen children die of the dreaded croup.

'Some. But why they do, we know not.'

'That noise you were making, Doctor.' She searched for some means of lifting his spirits. 'Was it a whistle you were attempting? A swan? A goat at a distance?'

'No, Mehala.' He smiled his lopsided smile, a little shamefaced. 'It is a horrid sound. It is the sound children make as they die of this disease. In their agonies, the poor mites make a sound within their chest, audible to the applied ear, which has that kind of a whistle to it.'

'Exactly so, Doctor?'

He shrugged. 'Not quite, Mehala. But I am sure that I have heard it, and while out walking in the open air. From somewhere locally. It stays in my mind, and wakes me when asleep. I feel perhaps it might give me some clue, a suggestion as to a mode of treatment we perhaps might try.'

'You hear this whistling, in the dying of a child?'

'When applying an ear to the chest, in a certain manner. Auscultation, we call it, from the Latin. It occurs when the child is in extremis.'

'The sound you were making, sir,' Mehala said. 'It is familiar. I too have heard it. From the sheep pens and the cattle paddock, the common field along the Norwich road, you might hear that sound, at any time they will take the beasts on the hoof for slaughter.'

He stared at her, for so long a period that she became nervous under the intensity of his gaze. She was red-faced and uncomfortable by the time he spoke.

'The cattle field, Mehala?'

'Why, yes, sir.' She hesitated. 'I trust I have not given offence, Doctor Carmichael. But that sound is not from children. Almost exactly as you made it, it is from beasts.'

'What sound, Mehala?' His voice was almost a whisper, so low that she had to bend to hear his words.

'When they kill the cattle, Doctor. And sheep.'

'How? The country method?'

'Yes, Doctor. I saw it but one day since.'

'How do they, then?'

'With a knife, Doctor. Across the throat. The poor beasts are then troughed, by some, for to catch the blood in containers for the purpose.

Blood is used in cooking, by some north country folk. You see, the drovers from those parts are more used to a rough fare made of – '

'Can you do it, Mehala?'

She stared. 'No, Doctor! It requires great strength to hold an animal.'

'How do they hold it, then?'

She grew flustered. His eyes were almost burning into her. She felt exhausted of a sudden, wanting away and back to the tavern where at least she could perform simple repetitive tasks and hide from all this severity. Two obsessed men in one morning was too much.

'Sir, I do not recall. Forgive me, Doctor, but I must home to Mrs Weaver. She expects my return.'

He stayed her, actually gripping her arm with a cruel strength. 'Mehala. Please. What makes the sound?'

'I forget, sir. Good day to you.'

If he made reply she did not hear it. As he let her go she rose, dropped from the stile and quickly made off across the footpath towards the River Affon's wooden bridge. Once the other side of that, she felt she would be secure. It had been a sorry mistake coming out to take the air. She should have remained at the tavern.

Mistake, to have conceded Mr Maderley's request. Mistake, to wait – brazenly, that was what she had actually done, with considered deliberation, and she admitted it to herself – to lie in wait, almost, for Doctor Carmichael.

She fled towards what had passed for safety, almost running, as if to recapture the past few days of sanctuary that she had enjoyed, and which now were quite in the past.

Her peace had come to an end.

28

'All right. I admit the woman was not bad.'

The whore mistress glared at Carradine in anger. 'Sir, I want more than that! I provide only the very best and tutored girls, all of whom are capable and dexterous!'

'Aye,' Carradine growled, still dressing, 'and able to filch from a man's pocket with the best!'

'That is untrue, sir, and well you know it!'

'Not with me, I grant you. But word is – '

'Word is foolish, sir, if you please, and the dafter when listened to!'

'Mistress Wren. I am pleased by your services, believe you me.' Carradine realized he was openly trying to make amends for his previous grumpiness when he had complained, but he was right to have done so. The bitch of a girl had expected to be entertained, even pleased, when chosen by the infamous Carradine, and had turned sulky when simply used and then told to get out. Naturally, any gentleman would complain of poor service. 'The girl should have shown more grace, that's all I am saying.'

'I shall correct her attitude, sir. But I will not have my good name bandied about in an unfair manner, sir. And I desire you should know it!'

'Very well, Mistress Wren. A truce. I on my part will forgive your girl's misery. And you on yours will accept that in future I shall require an occasional smile or two, and a show of some endeavour.'

'Very well, sir.' Wren sniffed. It was the best that she could expect in the circumstances, the Honourable Howard Carradine being Lord of the Manor locally and everything. And she had gained in the past from some remarkable favours. Yet she had been right to stand out against his complaints, for if word shot round that Carradine had been ill pleased at Two Cotts, no amount of reputation among the local gentry would save her business.

She sent along a half bottle of port for his thirst, and a fricasy of eggs which was well known for reviving the spirits and strengths of gentlemen too livered to enjoy the favours in which Two Cotts specialized. Mistress Wren was proud of the dish, which she had brought in some secrecy from her mother in the village of Islington. So special was this dish that she always fried the artichoke bottoms herself, and before now had given an overly inquisitive girl a thrashing when that impertinent female had noticed the fact that veal gravy was always used as a sauce, and never merely chicken or beef gravy. As folk rightly said, where there were too many women there were too many eyes.

'Your visitor shall be here as you requested, sir,' she informed him as she withdrew.

The upstairs section of the twinned establishment was reserved for privacy. Certain clandestine transactions required concealment, and Two Cotts catered especially for these. Carradine always had a small suite of two rooms when he called, with a fireplace set with a warming fire of sea-coals placed upon wood for fragrance, and deep land coal for heat in the iron grate.

He sat, still smarting over the dispute with the whore mistress. That bitch Wren hadn't sent him a full bottle, he noted with sour grace. She was reminding him of his debts, accumulated over several sessions earlier this year. He was sorely tempted to tell the cow where she could apply for custom, and get to hell away from this sordid little whorehouse. But what then? He needed her evil reputation, as she needed his more respectable one. He had the breaking of her in his hands, and she the breaking of him too, if she but knew it.

The girl hadn't really been too bad, not really. But certainly not too good, either. She had lain still and spreadeagled while he used her – hardly the most inventive woman with whom he had lain, not even this week for heaven's sake. Why, even Mrs Tyll, that more staid woman, was better at serving him. Plus there was the added spice of the illicit, the treacherous abandonment with which dear Barbara Tyll flung herself into his bed, that same bed the making of which she had supervised with such assiduity, while her husband laboured out in the tollgate so nearby.

The wine tasted fresh, though, and sex always brightened him. He felt restored by the dissipation of his energies into the hired bird, and bent to demolish the fricasy with fair appetite. He was pouring a second glass when a movement outside the window caught his eye. He rose and went to see. A figure was walking in the fields opposite Two Cotts. A man in a rather shabby overcoat, long and unfashionable, and high-collared against the sea wind which was blowing in as the tide changed.

'Doctor Carmichael,' he murmured to himself. 'What the hell is he doing?'

The figure walked a few paces, stopped as if listening, looked around quite openly, trudged to the opposite end of the field, stood again and stared about.

'Looking for birds' eggs, perhaps,' Carradine smiled. A naturalist, like doctors often are? Or did he pace the field because it was the common whereon horse fairs were held and the cattle were brought for the selling? Perhaps the doctor had news of an excellent piece of horseflesh coming into some race royal, and was secretly judging where he might best place himself for some wager. . . ? No, the man was being as unsecretive as possible. He seemed oblivious to anything except his own meanderings.

Still, the man ought to be allowed whatever small pleasures he could garner in this godforsaken hole of Sealandings. To serve a place like this and prevent injury to the folk from the workings of their own stupidities was surely enough to entitle the oaf to a little respite. Some wild flowers, perhaps? That was it. Searching for autumn blossoms, for want of a more enthralling pursuit. Yet he had no collecting jar, or pressing book . . . Probably couldn't afford them, poor sod.

Carradine returned to his table, shaking his head at such simple-mindedness. And him supposedly an educated man! But the remoteness of Sealandings was enough to send any man out of his mind. Look at what young Waite had told him, a woman challenging another to a duel, and shooting pieces of staves at a distance!

A knock on the door sounded. 'Come in,' he called. In London it was his game to address the unseen visitor by name, as if he really did have spies everywhere or was able to see through the door. But that trick was for London, where mouths could be shut by a little discreet silver. This was a town, where words carried further than the Lord gave ears to hear. It would be Prothero, he guessed, and was right.

'Glad you came, Prothero. Sit down.' He did not offer the burly man a glass.

'Mr Carradine.'

'I gather you enjoyed the main?'

'Yes. I saw you at the cockfight. A sorry loss, that fourth fighter.'

So he saw me lose a hundred, and possibly more, Carradine thought. Just how close is he to Peter Quilter? Alex Waite had mentioned that they were together at the horse fair, and now he had noticed them thick as thieves at the main. Were they as close at other places? He would have to stay his utterances from caution, until he found out the depth of their friendship.

'So it was, Prothero. But a trifle, in the grand design of the globe, eh?'

'To some, sir.' The landowner sat, observing his host's slight flush, his steady hands, his springy step. A rutting man, but one risking all, and for what? A reputation among freaks and fancy walkers of the Strand? To be admired by ephemerals? It was all he could do to stop his lips curling in scorn.

'But not to a careful gentleman like your good self, Prothero, eh?'

'Indeed not, Mr Carradine! I have had to take the greatest care on my road, and the habit dies hard.'

'Pleased to hear it, Prothero.' Carradine nodded at the window. 'What do you think that man out there is doing? I'm beginning to wonder if some strange distemper afflicts him.'

'I do not know, sir. The doctor, isn't it? Perhaps looking for herbs, as a cheap basis for some of his simples, I shouldn't wonder. He is a poorish man.'

'Perhaps. Or seeking the spent bullets from the display of shooting that took place there?'

'So you heard, sir!'

Prothero smiled. Carradine found the experience displeasing. A smile should be good-natured at the very least. On this big man a smile, such as it was, sat incongruously. It was an animal's smile, in process of becoming a snarl. The intention wasn't there. A grimace, as at some private discomfiture known only to the smiler. That made the smile come at the witness's expense.

'Yes, Prothero. I heard. Some woman who shot a pistol, eh? Merry transactions in Sealandings! I'd always thought it a tranquil place.'

'Two women, yes. Only serving maids from the two taverns. One has the right to sell ale to the drovers, grooms, any folk, as you know. Squire Hunterfield donated the land for the common purpose. The Goat and Compass folk have the right by custom. This time they suffered an encroachment from the Donkey and Buskin. Word is that John Weaver was astonished when he heard what his wenches had been up to, and gave them a sore chastisement – though I've yet to see that taverner roused to such a degree. Especially when it improved his pocket.'

'I'll believe it of his goodwife, though,' Carradine joked. Prothero did his travesty of a smile, making Carradine want to turn away in disgust at the sight.

'So must I, Mr Carradine. The Goat's girl drove off her dray in shame. The Donkey's girl stayed and won the day. Everyone is talking of what might occur next cattle meeting, five days from now.'

'And a few wagers on the outcome, eh?'

'Already several fisher folk are being drawn in with accounts of the duel. The grooms are talking of setting up a shooting contest. Others are saying Mehala is a natural markswoman who once campaigned with the Army as a follower.'

'High talk for hereabouts, Prothero,' Carradine said. There were such women around, who had for love or nature followed the Army and stood with their men against cavalry in the thickest of battles.

'Nearly as high as the current chat about prize fights, eh, sir?'

'Nearly, Prothero, but not quite.' Carradine was pleased they had at last got down to the problem. His problem, so far, and not yet Prothero's.

It was a pity that he was obliged by circumstance to use such a man as this, but needs must when the Devil drives. He could vaguely recall Prothero as a big burly man working in the harvest fields and calling on his team for greater exertions when there was a shilling – a single shilling! – to be won by a turn of speed at bringing in sheaves. And he could recall, too, the man standing beside the roadway when, as a boy, Carradine had followed his father's chaise on the Norwich road, riding on a tit. Then, this very man opposite had bowed, pulled his hairlock at the chaise, and fawned to help hold the tit's head while Carradine had dismounted.

And from that sinister smile it seemed that Prothero also remembered those days, not long off. Now, with Mary Calling transmuted by a willing church into Mrs Prothero, the servant was now the master, and the mistress the humble servant by all accounts. Every jack now a lord, as people said sarcastically behind Prothero's back. Hated, yes, but that is always the fate of the fattest fox, as Jonson the playwright suggested.

'A match will be arranged, I have heard, between Battler Goring and a local hero called Rendell. Is that so, Prothero?'

'I believe so, but I have been unable to discover much about the locality and the time.'

'Supposing I were to hear of the details, and wanted to borrow a sum to bet on the outcome?'

'Yes, sir?' Prothero was surprised. He had paid quite a price to learn of Carradine's money problems, but scarcely believed them. The gentry were the gentry, there in great mansions like the stars in their heavenly courses, never to be dislodged from their allotted places. Set there, indeed, by the hand of the Almighty for the instruction and guidance of the lower classes. The Church itself taught so, and society reinforced that belief. 'How could I be of assistance, Mr Carradine?'

'By providing such a sum, Prothero.'

'Providing. . . ?' Prothero's strange smile faded. 'To *loan*?'

'Yes.' Carradine noticed that his wine had dwindled to nothing, and that Doctor Carmichael had now stopped walking the field opposite and was now standing motionless, his head bent and tilted as if listening to some distant sound. He made himself stay calm while his visitor deliberated.

'Sir, this is a very unusual request.'

'Indeed it is, Prothero. I am aware of that.'

'Might I ask the reason for it, sir?'

'Money, Prothero, needs no explanation. In all things it is its own motive and reason.'

'Might I inquire how much, sir?'

'Ten thousand guineas, Prothero.' Carradine felt his heartbeat accelerate as he uttered the words. It was a vast sum. That much gold no man in England could carry, and scarce one man in a million had ever seen such treasure in one amount.

'Sir, I don't know quite what . . .'

Prothero had gone white. It was a quantity he could barely manage to raise even if he were to pledge his own Calling Farm, his private estate adjoining, all Mary's personal wealth which had come with her in the form of jewellery and heirlooms, buildings and dwelling houses attached to the lands, and the share in two small coastal vessels which plied from the mouth of the Humber in the north to London in the south. He was admittedly a wealthy man, but this was borrowing to the hilt.

'You *do* know what, Prothero.' Carradine lit a small cigar, of the sort which was now becoming so fashionable in Brighton and London. 'You know that you, alone of the gentry locally, could provide me with that sum.'

'This is indeed an honour, sir,' Prothero managed to say. With a glow of pleasure he observed Carradine's use of the word 'gentry', and looked at the aristocrat with something approaching warmth.

Carradine, for his part, looked back with disarming simplicity. The man was about the level of Quilter, and could be handled easily, he was sure. All he wanted was Prothero's agreement, on practically any terms in fact. In reality, hard bargaining was necessary for the terms of the loan, as a means of convincing Prothero that he was desperate for the loan from him alone, and from nobody else. Untrue, of course.

'It is more than that, Prothero. It is a risk, and well you know it.'

'But I confess myself surprised, sir. That you did not apply in the first instance to your known friends in the vicinity.'

'Charles Golding? Squire Hunterfield? The De Foes? My cousins

236

over at Whitehanger? Come, man. If you were about to win the greatest wager of your life, to whom would you apply, eh?' He waited, sure from the man's response that he had him now. 'To your county set and talkative relatives? To your friends, each of whom might cast a wager higher than your own, and so bring the odds – the amount you stand to win – tumbling about your ears? No. Not Rad Carradine, my friend. So I come to you, a known and respected landowner, a man of the gentry without too many affiliations. A man who can give his word as his bond, and accept a small risk, for a reasonable return.'

'Reasonable return, sir?'

'Reasonable, Prothero.' Carradine glanced with regret at the empty wine bottle. 'I cannot invite you to join my enterprise, I regret to say, for that too might signal that I was in the know – not that you are the sort who would unwittingly divulge the information in my possession. But all the details are not yet known for certain.'

'Ten thousand?' Prothero's mind raced. There were possibilities here, for himself as well as Peter Quilter. There was wealth – not mere coins, small pieces of money here and there – but wealth, real genuine fortune to be made. He stared at Carradine, now affecting interest again at the window. 'Well, Mr Carradine, I should have to consider . . .'

'No, sir. No considerations. Here and now. Yes or no.'

'But that is impossible . . .'

'Not with sufficient surety, Prothero. Impossibilities are simply not.'

'Surety, sir?' It was the word he had dared not utter, suggesting as it did a hint of unreliability in the borrower. Suggestions like that might get oneself shot to death in a morning duel, Carradine being venomous where his honour was concerned.

'You didn't think I was asking for such an enormous sum of money without surety, did you, Prothero?' Carradine turned back from the window as if amused. 'I offer Carradine Manor, its first estate and the far lodges.'

'But is there . . . is there time for the drawing up of the necessary documents, sir?' Prothero hurriedly added, 'I only mean that I need to give you adequate assurance that I will honour my pledge to deliver that sum. I must have time to provide you with enough proof, should you need to use that assurance in a note-of-hand when making a wager, or for some other purpose.'

'Nicely put, Prothero,' Carradine said easily. 'Yes, the documents will be drawn up in good time. I have a pair of lawyers at Lincoln's Inn Fields doing nothing but drink away fortunes and spending my moneys on their victuals while they draw up the necessary papers.' He sighed theatrically. 'Spongers, filchers, nothing but light-fingered robbers, they. But necessary in such an instance as this.'

'Then I shall provide the money, sir. Three days' notice?'

'Three days, Prothero. And I assure you that, at the odds I shall obtain in that fight, I shall have more than enough to reimburse you. Shall we say at a small consideration? Three per cent?'

Prothero hesitated. 'That is less than I had hoped, sir.'

Carradine asked easily, 'Surely not four?'

This was less than usual for a risky enterprise like funding a wager, and both men knew it. Prothero waited until Carradine realized he had something in mind. Then he spoke.

'There is something, sir, in which you could aid me,' he said slowly, turning his hat in his hands. 'A slight matter, but one I am sure which you could be instrumental in solving.'

'Something personal, Prothero?' Carradine tried to look casually disinterested, but was thinking, here comes the core of the man's ambition.

'As a tribute to my wife I had promised her a new maid, and I know she is set on having a particular girl. Some friend of the family, I believe, though not a local girl. Mrs Prothero is anxious for her welfare, and the girl unfortunately is at risk of bad company in a tavern . . .'

'Yes?' Carradine watched him. This was a new development. The man was showing a twitchiness he had never previously revealed. It was almost as if he were besotted, or worse. Curious, and a revelation that could be used against him, with luck.

'My dear wife has invoked my assistance, but the girl seems not to have been told, or not to respond, for reasons of her own.' Prothero licked his lips. He was sweating, unconvincingly trying to appear cool and unconcerned as if at a trivial matter.

'So?'

'The Weavers have her as a serving maid.'

'Mehala,' Carradine said wonderingly, the motive becoming instantly clear.

Prothero said quickly, 'Only on account of my wife's absurd notion of duty to the girl, you understand, sir. I wondered if you could use your influence with Charles Golding, your friend.'

'Golding?' Carradine said blankly. 'But how? What on earth does he have to do with the Weaver tavern?'

'Their water comes from his land, sir.'

Carradine thought. Bures House stood on higher land, back from the edge of the township and on an eminence that reached round towards Whitehanger, backing even as far as the Lorne House estate of the Hunterfields. It was true. The Donkey and Buskin was served by rivulets which drained from the Bures House estates. The tavern was truly vulnerable.

'This Mehala. You know her, then?'

'No, sir. I have seen her only. A rough and ready girl, as willing to brawl as to do decent work about a home, but you see it is my wife who feels this ridiculous sense of obligation. Silly and weak, I know, but I try to please her.'

'Very well, Prothero. In so trifling a matter, how could I not offer to help? I shall use my best endeavours to persuade Mr Golding to exert himself on John Weaver the taverner, and bring this Mehala creature to you . . . I mean, to your good lady wife.'

'And, say, the consideration to be . . . ten per cent?'

'Ten, sir? I suggested four per cent at most!'

'Then nine, sir?'

'And all the efforts I promised over your slight difficulty in pleasing Mrs Prothero? No, Prothero. Four's my limit.'

'Perhaps a compromise at five, sir? In view of *all* the factors involved?'

Prothero was becoming sullen, Carradine saw. He couldn't be pushed much further.

'Then, five, Prothero. As a double favour.'

Prothero swallowed. 'Very well, sir,' he managed eventually. 'Five per cent, then.'

They shook hands on the agreement, settled the details of the documentation, and Prothero left. Carradine waited until he heard Prothero's cob clopping away down the Norwich road, then rang for Mistress Wren to bring up another bottle of her very finest port. He could afford to indulge in dreaming a little now, for all was settled, and the road to his fortune's restoration was made safe. It was a wonderful life.

This Mehala, meanwhile, seemed to be everywhere in Sealandings, it seemed. And she was worth five per cent of ten thousand guineas, *which made her worth five hundred guineas*! Ye Gods! And to a man like Prothero! A maid-of-all, worth that vast sum? He could not recall having laid eyes on the woman. Who on earth was she?

He watched the girl bring the bottle, and a clean glass. She was one he had had before, he vaguely recalled. From the west country, if his memory served.

'Stay,' he said, indicating that she should open the bottle and pour. 'It is time to celebrate.'

29

The day wore on at Milton Hall.

Thalia was now at her most beautiful. She had decided after all to risk the new half dress, which was so fetching when viewed from the slightly higher angle of a taller person. Carradine's height. Then she changed her mind of a sudden on account of worry about the material – taffeta was not so bright as satin, and in pink could be something of a disaster in certain lights.

Carradine might not arrive in broad daylight, when she would be able to use the curtains to cast more subtle glows across the long parlour where, changing her mind, she now decided to be discovered on his arrival.

. No, the pelisse-robe finally won the day. It was the more acceptable day dress still, fastened as it was with ribbon bows all the way down her front. Its outrageously modern hem stood just short of the carpet. The new fashion was to conceal cunning hooks and eyes for fastenings, but they were thought somewhat easy-virtue tricks by the more staid elements of society, and she did not wish to give any hint of wantonness, not even to Carradine. Not openly.

By mid-afternoon she was fidgeting, wondering if she still had time to rush back upstairs and change again. The ribbon bows might in fact be just that bit too much for a man. Yet Carradine had often confessed to her – in most intimate surroundings – that like all men he was something of a magpie. 'The gaudier, the more conviction,' had been his way of putting it, shocking her to the core.

No, this dress was right. The newest fashion, to call the pelisse-robe a redingote, was something she abhorred. Traditional dress was proven, though it was wonderful to move with the fashions. And she knew that Carradine was hers, always was and always would be, for as long as she desired. Dress was incidental to love, though important.

By six she was fretting. By seven distraught.

By eight she sat, cold and as beautiful but now on fire with hatred. Someone had come between Carradine and herself. She had known it, right from the very first moment of the Sunday service, when he did not appear.

The ball was the next move, unless he called in the morning.

By nine o'clock she rang for the servant, and had a long supper in silence.

Afterwards, white hot with fury, she silently penned a message to give to Ennis, with instructions to deliver it to Carradine Manor.

'It is of vital importance, Ennis,' she informed him. 'On no account must you deliver it to anyone else, saving the hand of Mr Carradine himself. You understand?'

'I understand perfectly, ma'am.'

'And do it immediately.'

'If Mr Carradine is not at home, ma'am?'

'Then bring it straight back here undelivered, Ennis. It is a most important communication concerning my husband's affairs.'

'As you instruct, ma'am.'

From the conservatory windows she watched his departure. He took a hack from the stables, and a lanthorn against the dark, though there was little risk as the road lay directly through Sealandings itself.

The answer to Carradine's neglect would lie in her cousin Charles Golding, for suddenly he had assumed a pivotal importance for her.

She needed a housekeeper for him, and it could well be this Mehala. The girl would naturally be thrilled, and so overcome with gratitude to be suddenly so well placed that she would be an effective instrument at Bures House. At one stroke, Thalia would have her own agent watching over Cousin Charles, able to respond instantly to whatever instructions she sent her, at any time. And she would warn her benefactress at Milton Hall immediately were Carradine to make any direct approaches to Charles about his parliamentary aspirations. Mehala had no connections with anyone among society families in Sealandings – how could she, drawn from the sea and virtually anonymous? So she would be proof against all importunings and bribes, and practically a perfect slave. Yes, Charles must only be reachable through herself at Milton Hall, which would force Carradine to come back to her in supplication.

That way, killing two birds with one stone, she would put Charles into a position of security, proof against the imprecations of that stupid bitch Lydia Vallance, of the Hunterfields, and preserve him from Letitia's forthcoming arrival at her ball. And would thus deliver Charles into Carradine's hands only when she herself permitted, for political development of the kind which, while pleasing to Carradine, would do herself no harm at all, for she had always had the ear of Charles Golding and always would have. She controlled the dolt, even if she was powerless against the savage Carradine. It all worked out perfectly in her mind.

The only casualty in all this would be this girl Mehala. But she should in any case be able to take care of herself. And if she was seriously wounded by the events which would now take place, the more fool she.

Thalia could see that she had left matters in the lap of the gods for too long. Gods were notoriously tardy. They needed speeding about their work. She should have done it all herself in the first place.

She drew out the list of invitations for the ball, and set to work.

Old Mrs Trenchard had done her best, but was unable to lay the fire on account of her rheumatik. She had left soup, but it was badly over-salted, with a batch of Sally Lunns, but they too were faulty: he had vague recollections of his mother leaving the big flat rounds for some time beside a warm stove to grow to twice the size before oven baking. These were heavy and almost indigestible.

Had there been hot embers, he would have placed his house door key, as the biggest handiest piece of iron, therein and used the red-hot metal to mull his small beer in the time-honoured fashion, but he simply sat and struck the flint lighter, blowing tiredly on the cotton wads to gain fire to ignite a candle.

His mood was almost one of despair. He felt almost as sick as the Darling child, little Clare with her racking cough and those terrible signs of worse to come, her face flushed and her breathing stertorous. He was lost, sickened.

The books he possessed were too few, even for a country practice. Of course there were always tales, of miracles, of observations and interpretations which promised all manner of cures. But in the end the children died. They all died. Always. Wounds festered. Coughs turned croupish, lungs inflamed and people wasted away, lingering and sometimes perhaps rallying to give false hope, then confirming the forebodings as death took hold.

Alexander Wood's book was one of his hopefuls, with its criticisms and its flagrant title, 'Homoeopathy Unmasked; Being An Exposure Of Its Principal Absurdities And Contradictions. Yet could it be worse than all the established doctors' bleedings and simples and unguents, the inhalations and the cuppings and the terrible deaths that seemed to him more and more the influence of luck? Medicine was hopeless.

At his last visit, the fever was making little Clare slightly giddy. She was not yet delirious, but had asked him, recognizing his face as he bent over to examine her throat, 'Will I die too, Doctor, like our Harry?'

'Let us try to stop that, shall we, Clare?' he had replied with a smile of

243

confidence. Walking home, he had realized with quick agony that that had been the very expression he had uttered when little Harry had asked the same thing.

Walking home. Meeting Mehala. That striking, fascinating girl with the most direct of looks, with her swift understanding and perception. How odd that she had still not recovered her memory.

What had she said? Cattle, sheep, animals when their throats were cut? That faint shrill, incomplete whistle? He had gone to walk the cattle fields, to no avail.

He thought, and laid aside Doctor Wood's venomous attack upon homoeopathy – which was probably as useless as the more orthodox versions of medical practice anyway – and went to his meagre store of medical instruments. He brought three more candles, lit them and stood them with all his instruments on the kitchen table. He examined what he had.

The house was never silent. Its old beams creaked faintly and readjusted themselves to the vagaries of the weather. He liked the place. Shalamar was not its original name, but was conferred by some former owner charmed by the exoticisms of the East. Its gardens were a tanglement, its lawns overgrown. The place was nigh to derelict, and he did not know how much longer he would be able to withstand its terrible draughtiness. Water leaked into every one of its sixteen great echoing bedrooms, and rats scurried through all twelve cellars. The great parlour and the enormous withdrawing room were almost unprotected now from the weather, for the windows had long since decided never again to shut. The doors left as much space as they filled, it seemed to him. Last winter, snow had left its stains as drifts had formed inside the house. Now, with autumn fast ending, he was beginning to dread the effects the old house would have on him should it be a severe winter.

In the short time since his arrival in Sealandings, he had come to love Shalamar. It was however his sad experience that a beloved object – house, woman, town – only wreaked vengeance as return for the gift of love. Maybe Shalamar would respond with malice in like manner? He prayed it wouldn't be so, but had lost the art of hope.

The house seemed kindly, though, as it seemed to watch his efforts to go over in detail the uses of his few instruments. He thought of the worsening signs in Clare Darling. Maybe the disease could not be stayed by these instruments? Maybe some clever unction, or an infusion perhaps, might prove a more sovereign remedy? Whatever might come to be in later years, the truth *now* was that his efforts and knowledge would prove the death of the little girl, however much he grieved.

That whistling noise. Mehala had said cattle, sheep.

He glanced out at the sky. Darkening, approaching rain, possibly within an hour. There was time to visit that field again.

And perhaps the butcher's shop in the market square?

The instruments which attracted his attention were two, and they were not even considered instruments. The first was simply a curved metal tube. It should have been made of fashionable silver, of course, but his was a crude thing once manufactured by an elderly blacksmith in expiation of his doctor's fee. It was a sick syphon, a small scroll-shaped tube used to feed convalescent patients. Its broader end, which ended in a thin perforated metal plate, was placed in a cup, sieving the food as it was sucked up by the patient. A hook on the tube's side enabled it to be fixed firmly on to the cup's rim. Simple, yet effective.

The second instrument which drew his attention was a pap shield, a metal nipple cover. He had three of these, for they were still common in spite of their growing disuse in the countryside and cities. Once, all women fed their children at the breast until long after the babes' incisor teeth were cut. These shields were simply tiny coned discs, less than two inches in diameter, with small perforations for the babe to apply suck. He favoured glass ones, for it seemed that these could be cleaned simply, as when washing dishes. They were commonly found of lead, for ease of working, as it was a very malleable metal, but he knew only too well that lead when eaten produced madness and even death. Though, medicine being a disputatious art, many physicians opposed this opinion.

He took wax from the candles, rolled it into a soft pliable ball, and began to fashion a tube from it, copying the sick syphon but omitting the fenestrated end plate. There would be need of wings, in the form of projections extending from the tube's sides. Perhaps a combination of the nipple shield, with the tube projecting from the central point, as a boss from a shield?

He worked on, guessing, experimenting.

The cattle field had produced no clues, though he had stood and looked, wandered and thought. The belief that terrain itself produced illness was strong in many people still. Undoubtedly it was fashionable for rich folk to go to better places when advised, to protect themselves against illnesses prevalent in an area. But he had been looking for some instrument, perhaps, something the butchers and fletchers might use, and of which he might be completely oblivious. Nothing.

245

To go and ask about, himself, would be a terrible mistake. The folk of Sealandings would shun him for the rest of their mortal lives, irrespective of whether they needed to call on him for help or not.

No. He would have to do this himself.

The question was, what did he know of cutting into a trachea, into a bronchus? And, if it was attempted, could a child survive that procedure? On the face of it, it seemed a dire extremity, an almost impossible course of action. He racked his memory for information. What had that elderly doctor always taught, in those few history of medicine lectures which all the students hated so? Ven Carmichael was ashamed to say that he had attended only a few, for they had cost almost as much in entry fee, payable on the door to the lecturer, as the more vital ones on physic and surgery and anatomy. He had been too poor to attend more than an occasional lecture as a luxury now and again, such as medical theory and historic physic. Perhaps there would come a time when all aspiring doctors would be able to attend all subjects, freely, from some charitable donations of money? He abandoned such foolish fantasies and bent himself to complete his task.

The Arabs, those superb physicians of ancient days, had done an operation to make a breathing hole into the throat. He could remember that much. And, because he had found solace in reading around the discipline when unable to afford the entry fee for particular lectures, he could well recall that Hippocrates had urged doctors to introduce a long cannula into the throat when a patient was about to suffocate. But as far as he could remember no details were given. He cursed his poverty, for he had had to sell his books as soon as he qualified and received his imprimatur, so he had no means of checking now. He vaguely remembered that the Arabs had written of using a golden cannula for the purpose.

Rumours abounded about the croup, he recalled, and the French doctors' current methods of treating it. He had met, quite by chance, a fellow student – now a very fashionable doctor held in high esteem in the houses about Tottenham Court in London – who had visited France. He had spoken with enthusiasm of a Doctor Bretonneau, who had reintroduced the old notion of making a stoma in the trachea, to cure croup. The Frenchman had used the term diphtheritis for the disease, and this was becoming the name among doctors everywhere. But an evil illness by any other name . . .

Yet, how on earth did one do a tracheotomy? And what with?

Worse still, it was unknown land. Did a child endure the operation that the French physician had revived? *And survive?* How long did the

246

child need to be so treated? An hour, perhaps? A day? A week, month? For life? And what if the child in delirium struggled, tore out the contraption? Or did the child lose consciousness anyway under the influence of the diphtheritis, and lie moribund for hours, days? And, most frightening of all, was the child sane after such a terrible procedure, if she survived at all? It was a horrendous responsibility, and grew worse with every second that he gave it thought. To risk killing, in attempting cure.

The only thing was to try, quickly, upon some carcass. He could not go himself, so would need assistance. Euterpe Baring? She came instantly to mind, for she was a woman of respect and position. But her brother, with his fearsome antagonism towards him, daunted the sudden hope.

Mehala? She was next to mind. Trustworthy, intelligent, bright and helpful. Yet that encounter with her down by the Whitehanger track had seemed a little unsettling. She had almost fled from him, refusing help, as if his very presence, or perhaps his words asking for her assistance, had been an unwarranted intrusion into her very being.

No. He would have to find someone else.

An hour later, he had completed his small model of a crude tube which seemed to give most advantage, though it would probably need modification after he had tried it on some animal cadaver.

Then he thought of Mrs Mary Prothero, the lady of Calling Farm. That was the place where Mrs Trenchard obtained most of her supplies, such as they were, for Shalamar. It would be quite in order for him to call, perhaps pretend that, from kindness, he intended to save Mrs Trenchard the bother of finding the shopping this week, and while conversing make a point of meeting Mrs Prothero. He would have to take care not to give offence. He could ill afford antagonizing yet another important family in the district. Yet she was kindly, and was helpful and good-spirited. And had been a childhood friend, however fleeting.

Yes. There first. Then, in the light of the knowledge gained, to the blacksmith, and see if the man could engineer a device, copying the model in metal.

He almost ran from Shalamar.

30

Hunterfield was not unduly concerned when he failed to receive the acknowledgement of his note to Thalia. Simple Tom had ridden across to Milton Hall with the note, only to convey by mime on return that his master's letter had been accepted at the side entrance by Meg, Mrs De Foe's personal maid, and that he had then waited for more than two hours in want of answer. Finally, he had gone round to the kitchen entrance, and had there seen Meg helping Mrs Thornton and the scullion girls. No, there was no sign of any answer being forthcoming.

The squire had experienced this before, however, when Mrs De Foe was receiving guests or otherwise busy in some social enterprise. It was well to be guarded at all times, naturally, for a lady's reputation was like fine Canton china; once fractured in the slightest, it was marred for all time and irreparable.

Not only that, but Fellows De Foe was notoriously short in the fuse, perhaps like Carradine in a similar way. Henry Hunterfield had altogether too much to risk by flaunting convention where Thalia De Foe was concerned.

When he was called for tea, he was greeted by Lydia. Tabitha and Letitia were already there. Lydia seemed in high spirits, very chatty, and his hopes rose. He might easily be able to introduce Mrs De Foe into the conversation, and so learn if she was available for an invitation to supper, or perhaps tea at some near date. He was certain Lydia was unaware of his assignations with their neighbour, for which heaven be thanked. As long as this remained so, it would be safe to talk of neighbourhood matters without arousing suspicion.

She had the large-leaved Congou tea, which she knew he liked for its highly coloured infusion.

'Very apt, Mrs Vallance,' he approved, sitting in the chair beside the tea table. 'Though I must confess that your eagerness for economy in Lorne House is distressing. I see that you have decided upon the use of the tea table, with that dashed irritating fret rail. It prevents me getting all the Congou I may require!'

She smiled playfully. 'So you have sounded my scheme out, Henry. You will also have noticed that I have placed the teapoy out of your reach, and locked it well, that you might not steal extra from it!'

'Damned three-legged monstrosity,' Hunterfield growled. 'I don't mind those of Irish bog yew, for they are indigenous and natural. But this new fashion for the papier-mâché construction is wholly weird. It is anomalous to me.'

'But ours is rosewood, brother,' Letitia said. 'And very pleasing.'

'May it remain so. I hate the modern fashion of altering furniture to seem like that of former ages. God knows what our descendants will think of our execrable taste!' He chuckled at his two young sisters. 'You are looking uncommonly well, Letitia. As you, Tabitha, and of course my dear household mistress, who rules us all!'

'Please leave praise until you have tried my chestnut tart, Henry.' Lydia poured, passing cups, careful to avoid catching her trailing sleeves on the low railing, always a hazard for the hostess.

'Capital! I shall do my very best, Lydia.'

'I have done it as a pudding,' Lydia smiled at Letitia, signalling this was the day and the time to strike at her brother's kindness. 'Two quarters of cream, and eighteen eggs in the original recipe, with the rose-water and orange-water, is I fear too much for us. I have lowered the scale somewhat, and only used half of the amounts.'

'You see what I mean, you two?' Hunterfield laughed at his younger sisters. 'Promise that you will never become so abstemious.'

'Oh, Henry!' Letitia was of heightened colour, knowing what was coming and wondering how her clever sister would attack. 'Lydia is nothing if not kindly and considerate!'

Lydia flashed a warning glance at Letitia, while Tabitha glanced from one to the other, wondering what was afoot.

'Thank you, Letitia. Praiseworthy indeed for a sister to defend her own, against all mankind, according to old custom. And,' Lydia twinkled, 'hath not old custom made life more sweet?'

They laughed at the sally, recognizing the quotation as one from Shakespeare which their governess had often quoted.

'That is why, Henry, I shall see to it! We must refuse the invitation — if one arrives, that is.'

'Invitation, Lydia? To what? From whom?'

'Why, from our recent guest, Mrs De Foe.' Lydia concerned herself with pretended worry at serving tea and setting plates for the tart.

'Invitation?' Tabitha squealed, excited. 'A party? A dance, Lydia?'

'Tush-tush, Tabitha,' Lydia reproved severely. 'Compose yourself, please!'

'Fellows De Foe's return, doubtless?' Hunterfield supposed casually.

He was immediately melancholy at the notion. It would ruin any opportunity for seeing Thalia in intimate circumstances.

'Regrettably, no, Henry,' Lydia said smoothly, to his relief. 'Mrs De Foe is moved to entertain. She will furnish a ball for the neighbourhood gentry. I hear that we are to be included in the list of those invited.'

'From Mrs De Foe herself?'

'Indeed. It is a very wise move for a lady to send out preliminary inquiries as to whether those expecting a possible invitation are to be available. Refusal can give injury where none is intended.'

'Very wise, Lydia.' He was pleased. That explained Thalia's lack of more personal communication.

'I shall expect the invitations to arrive shortly. The ball is to take place very soon.'

'And we shall refuse, you say?' he added jovially, over Tabitha's mounting anxiety and excitement.

'Of course, Henry! Why would we want to go traipsing over to Milton Hall in the wettest autumn we've had in years? After all, it is simply an immoral waste of time, with dancing and music and a banquet – '

'Oh, how could you, Lydia!' Tabitha shrieked, almost dancing where she sat.

'I could quite easily, Tabitha,' Lydia answered with mock severity. 'Mrs De Foe begged from me the recipe for the Prince Regent's sauce for supremes of pheasant, and insists on using it for sweetbreads, which goes contrary to my own usage. I shall not be pleased if her concoctions prove a success, and do not wish to be there to witness it!'

Letitia joined in the laughter at Lydia's teasing, shaking a correcting finger at Tabitha while Henry roared.

'But there is one concession from you two sisters which, if given me, will make me weaken.' Lydia gave a knowing glance at Henry, who nodded to signal his complicity in the amusement as he dealt with his chestnut tart.

'Granted!' Tabitha squealed.

'It is this,' Lydia said. 'That you employ your gift of persuasion on your brother, for I need assistance in that direction.'

'Anything you ask, Lyd!' Tabitha cried, shocking her oldest sister into a gasp at the familiarity.

'Goodness, Tabitha!' Letitia interjected, hoping her anxiety was concealed. It was too exhausting, to think that Lydia would bring out her request for intervention with Henry here, in the very open, at parlour tea. But Lydia was far cleverer than herself, and surely should be trusted in these matters.

'Less of that childhood endearment, if you please, miss!' Lydia corrected. 'This is no place for it!'

'Oh, Lydia, I am sorry and apologize. But how on earth can we help you?'

'Letitia cries *goodness*, Tabitha *on earth*!' Henry chuckled.

'In the matter of our features, the pair of you.' Lydia saw their puzzled frowns and smiled gently. 'It has long been in my mind to wonder at the very unusual gap which shows in the likenesses of our family, here at Lorne House. Every great family hereabouts, after all, has employed notable portraiturists to create the splendid likenesses for their halls and staircases.'

Henry frowned. Suddenly this was all too serious for his liking. 'You mean, have some London madman in from the Royal Academy? Have you seen the prices charged by those crazed colourists from New Somerset House? A fortune, ma'am, a veritable fortune!'

'You now perceive my grave difficulties, sisters,' Lydia said smoothly. 'We must find a solution which satisfies everyone and no one, yet which pleases the head of our household. How do you suppose we might do that?'

'But what is that to do with the De Foe ball?' Tabitha asked, appalled.

'Nothing, save that I choose to see them conjoined. Both, or neither!'

Lydia shot a covert glance at Letitia to warn her to say nothing, then converted it into a sweet smile of complicity for her brother's benefit.

'But there are artists, colourists, living not very far. Surely in Norwich, Ipswich even, there must be whole clusters of them!' Tabitha was almost despairing.

'Possibly Tabitha is correct, Lydia,' Letitia put in meekly.

'Oh, tush, you, Letitia,' Lydia chided. 'Agreeing with your sister, and always to the detriment of my argument! Ever since you were little, the two of you have – '

'But Tabitha has a case there,' Hunterfield put in suddenly. 'Is there not that Maderley man, at Watermillock? They say he can achieve a remarkable likeness, when he has a mind. Though I doubt if he is up to the task of a family set.'

'That is exactly my point, Henry,' Lydia said implacably. 'I shall not have the family exposed to ridicule by suggesting that you engage an inept artist for what is a great purpose. *Other* families might do as they please.'

'Has anyone seen his work, anyone we know and trust?' Hunterfield wondered.

251

'Mr Maderley? Mrs De Foe has, I know, Henry,' Lydia mused, as if thinking seriously of the proposition for the first time. 'I wonder if she might be approached? I saw her admiring his painting in the churchyard only last market day.'

'Well, then!' Tabitha exclaimed. 'The problem is solved! So discerning a lady, and a family friend, would be sure to exercise only the very best and most capable judgement on Fine Art!'

'Not so fast,' Lydia said severely, dampening Letitia's hopes just when her cause seemed won. 'I insist, before we take this serious matter an inch further, that his work be most strictly examined, and that a proper and detailed appraisal be made of his completed pieces. No!' She held up an imperious hand as Letitia and Tabitha made to speak together. '*No!* Please do not argue. I insist. And I am sure that your brother will concur, for it is in the whole family's interests.'

'Your sister is right, ladies,' Hunterfield agreed. 'Let it be so, then. See his paintings – but only the fully finished ones, mind. Then advise me as to their degree of excellence. Only then shall we commission him.'

'And so save his living expenses, for he lives locally,' Lydia said thoughtfully. 'If we hired from London we should have had to maintain the man, and provide travel expenses. And incur heaven-knows-what costs during his sojourn.'

'Very well,' Henry said. 'But who is to do the judging, Lydia?'

'Why, Letitia of course!' Lydia said sweetly.

'Me?' Letitia said, astonished that all had suddenly come her way after her doubting. 'But . . .'

'Now, Letitia! You are not to be tiresome and try to wriggle out of this important family task simply so you can stick your nose into your books again. Please obey your brother's wishes without further ado. You know full well that Henry has the whole estate to worry about, as well as family matters.'

'Yes, Letitia,' Tabitha scolded. 'It is your duty to assist Henry and Lydia in all parts of daily life. Expedite the inspection of Mr Maderley's canvases, and make report at your speediest!'

'We all insist, it seems,' Lydia said flatly. 'So, Letitia, your solemn duty lies before you. Please correspond with Mr William Maderley at Watermillock, care of course of his sister and mother there. Compel him to call upon you here at his earliest convenience. Inform him that it is at your brother Squire Hunterfield's insistence. Please brook no delay. I suggest tomorrow in the forenoon.'

'Yes, Lydia,' Letitia said in a small voice. She did not understand

252

how it had come about, but merely that of a sudden here she was actually being instructed, if you please, to do that which under normal circumstances would have been forbidden at any cost.

'And hurry, Letty,' Tabitha whispered, nudging her sister.

'I heard that, miss!' Lydia rebuked sharply. 'Who gave you right to whisper at tea?'

'I apologize, Lydia,' Tabitha said immediately, desperate now not to lose the gains made. 'And to you Henry, sir.'

'I suppose this means now that we are to go to Mrs De Foe's ball, does it?' Hunterfield gravelled out in simulated annoyance.

'I suppose it does, Henry, unfortunately,' Lydia said, smiling. 'Now we may have tea in peace.' Victory, but inwardly she wished it had been the one she had wanted. Exchanging Charles Golding for William Maderley was something of a Pyrrhic triumph. So far, she had gone along with Letitia's madness for the sake of peace with the girl. But soon she would be forced to find some way of expelling the artist in favour of the aristocrat.

31

Galling to be savaged by a puppy, but that was how Rad Carradine felt. For he had lost at the races, out here among the country bumpkins, and quite badly.

It was not much of a meet, as race meetings went these new modern days. He would have expected more of the Fancy to attend had the meet taken place nearer London, but there was still a fair crowd. No shrewder judge of a sporting gathering existed than himself, he believed. Wealth seemed to be everywhere, what with barouches, giant coaches, personal traps, the neat calabashes which, driven as they were by the traveller himself, lent themselves to use by ladies. Carradine approved of this new fashion, where bolder society ladies wished to travel alone and in style, to show their finery in the open-topped slender vehicle. Such determination, to endure the discomfort for the sake of flair and ostentation! It pointed to a tempestuous nature, a challenge and an affront to such as he. As always, Carradine thought wryly. Appearances first, comfort second. Or should it be, achievement first, *then* grandeur's display and comfort? The correcting thought made him even more downcast. He kept remembering the letter in his pocket, the one which had come from the hand of Thalia De Foe's manservant late the previous night.

Carradine laughed, joking with a few acquaintances up from Cambridge and Newmarket, where the horse race meets were becoming so fashionable and where royal patronage had spelled out their permanence. Sir Jeremy Pacton waved to him several times, and Alex Waite also showed great friendliness towards him. Quilter was even more demonstrative, and had sent across a hamper of fruits and hot savouries, including a pair of Portugals to cool his thirst. Carradine so far had been openly gracious, waving to Peter Quilter, simulating rage at having lost yet again when the big grey had failed badly at the last stretch. The stupid bastard of a jockey had let his whip lie too idle for Carradine's liking, and he had already seen to it that the man would suffer by not receiving any riding commissions for the next race meeting, through the agency of friends. Punishment, or the threat of it, was the one golden corrective.

He went behind a bush less to relieve himself than to exclude himself from the company. There, he walked on, finally setting himself down on a blanket next to the horse lines, where for a sixpence a gentleman could leave his mount part-tethered under the supervision of a groom appointed by the meeting's arrangers. It was the cheapest way to travel, but was ominously revealing about states of wealth. A gentleman who changed his habits significantly and for no apparent reason was immediately suspect, highly vulnerable to rumours. Carradine had had to invent a plausible story to satisfy Quilter – that odious upstart who, never a gentleman or with chance of becoming one – was only interested in the likelihood of recovering his dues from Carradine's IOUs.

'I have an affair, Quilter,' Carradine had told him in sworn confidence. 'I must be less than obvious here, after a certain hour. You understand?'

'Ah. I see.' Peter Quilter's brow had cleared. 'You wanted to come solo?'

'As ever was, Quilter.' Carradine gave him the wink. 'Grooms tattle more than cottagers in these parts. If I'd brought my man along, why, there's no telling what tall tales he would carry forth – to the detriment of myself.'

'And of a lady, perhaps?'

'Please, Peter.' Carradine pretended to be pained. 'A lady's honour is not to be impugned lightly. I can afford a sixpence for a rope in the common horse lines, so dearly do I value a certain lady's honour!'

That had done it. Quilter had laughed, shaking his head at his friend's boldness, and gone on to the stands of staves where the established wager-makers waited for bold spirits to come and lay bets on favoured beasts.

Carradine had wagered only lightly at first. And had won on the very opening race. A triumph, too. At odds of six to one, he had drawn a yield of three hundred guineas. It had of course seemed an omen. He went giddy with the thought that, here at last, at this ridiculously unfashionable race meeting at Horseheath, he was about to recoup all his fortune. Restoration come early! He had gambled, lost, doubled up, gambled, lost, doubled up, gambled, lost . . .

More laughs, more smiles, as he nodded to a passing acquaintance. He made as if to stretch out on the blanket to doze, then took out the letter, making sure he was unobserved.

Thalia. That bloody, persistent, aggressive woman he had almost forgotten in the hurly-burly of returning home. Mrs De Foe, pestering him again. Were all women like that, for God's sake? Clingers, intruders, forever making demands on a man?

Did the woman not have a husband to keep her stilled? What on earth was the matter with the creature? Surely she was not so silly-minded that she had taken a few minor trysts as serious commitments on his part? God Almighty, if that was the result of every chance lay men and women had these hectic days, there wouldn't be a bed in England ever stopped creaking. Had she no sense?

He read it, following the graceful court hand to its harsh conclusion:

... the outcome of the attempt of my cousin, the Hon. Charles Golding, upon the elections for the Parliament at the hustings next to be arranged. It would be vital, were he to be so persuaded to your advantage, for some encounter to be arranged most expeditiously between your good self and my cousin. I cannot emphasize this enough in mere words, Mr Carradine, for I fear his lack of resolve will cause an outcome contrary to your interests were this problem not discussed immediately. My purpose is to produce a result which will be beneficial to all concerned.

I cannot, I regret to say, allow this situation to continue much longer, and shall have to regard myself free of this obligation towards you if you find yourself unable to join discussion no later than eight o'clock of the evening after receipt of this letter. I am, as you are aware, still as eager as always to further my cousin's career in the manner you decreed.

'I have the honour to remain, sir, yours faithfully,

Mrs Thalia De Foe

He crushed the letter finally, placed it in his pocket, and rose. The common groom hurried forward, received his consideration with a bow and a grin, and unleashed Carradine's mount from the lines.

The woman would have to be acted upon, as much as her damned letter, Carradine thought angrily. The bitch had the gall to think that, because she was set to do him some trivial favour, she now owned him, to be her plaything. Or companion. Or friend. Or permanent lover. Good God Almighty, what pests women were! Why on earth could she not be practical about things, like Mrs Tyll was? Pleased at a brief attention, sharing in the physical pleasure, then getting about her business as a woman should? Isn't it the fairer sex that's supposed to be the more practical? So what on earth afflicted the ignorant cow? Yet he needed a creature in Parliament, to serve as a source of income got from influence, bribery being the tallest wage in London. And the inept Charles Golding was just the man.

He rode off to his next meeting. This one at least would be profitable.

32

The blacksmith was baffled by the two pieces of metal.

'They are simple items,' Doctor Carmichael wearily explained for the fifth time. 'As you see, they comprise one nipple shield in metal. And one sick syphon, in metal likewise.'

'They be mortal small, Doctor.'

Ven Carmichael was becoming agitated. 'That is the very idea, Temple! The instrument I need has to be *made* small. I want the breast shield perforated, by any means which may suffice, and then the sick syphon's narrower end thrust through, the two parts thus fixed to be annealed as one. Here is a wax copy, very rough. Don't you see?'

'Immovable, you say, Doctor?'

'Immovable, Temple,' Carmichael said, almost distracted. 'One part must not move relative to the other. That is an essential, for no air can be permitted to flow through the join. You follow the idea?

'Yes, sir. But it's a mite small task, Doctor. And it will take time.'

Temple scratched his head. His smithy wheezed and grumbled like a veritable Midland foundry. The heat was inordinate. Remarkably, the two great dray horses in for shoeing remained calm, occasionally shifting their great bulk and waiting to be shod with giant patience. Carmichael recognized them as those of the Goat and Compass, which Ben Fowler slyly lent out on occasions which the Revenue coast watchers never could trace.

'How long, Temple? There is not long.'

'Oh, a week, Doctor?'

'A whole *week*?'

'Well, by next market day, perhaps. Will that serve?'

'No, Temple. I fear I shall need it tonight.'

'How if you send to Ipswich, Doctor? One of the wherries goes through. It calls in regular at the north wharf here in Sealandings, from Norfolk. It could be persuaded to stop in after Oulton Broad, and – '

'Tonight, Temple,' Carmichael said brokenly. 'Tonight. There is so little time, you see.'

'For why, Doctor?' Temple thought it something to do with a philosophic trial of some glassware, as Doctor Carmichael had told him, and could see no urgency.

'I am impatient, I fear, Temple. That is all.'

Carmichael forced a smile, took back his model and instruments and bade the man a good day. He set out quickly to walk the distance to Calling Farm. He never should have paused at Temple's smithy in the first place. A week! When the poor Darling child was worsening by the hour, and likely to enter relapse some time during the night hours.

It was getting on for the late afternoon. He took the most direct route, due west through the town and along the narrow street folk called Blakeney Road. Thence it would be fairly short, passing the Corn Market building to his left, across the market square and up the long straight trackway between the churchyard of St Edmund the Martyr and the schoolhouse, and so directly to Calling Farm.

The child Clare showed every sign now, as he had seen to his horror. There could be no doubt. It was acute croup. All the terrible signs of diphtheritis were there. Little Clare had not yet the horrible sense of coming suffocation, but her voice had become shriller and harsher in the intervening period, and her persistent cough was now of that dangerous ringing quality which heralded the final outburst of the disease. The inflammatory fever, as it seemed to him, was somehow lurking in the child's throat in a way that he could hardly imagine. It was building, coalescing, growing, biding its time. Then it would grip the child and fling her into delirium and panic, throttling the poor innocent to extinction. She would soon die, in the most frightful distress.

And the Darlings' meagre cottage still decorated with heather and moss for respect to the passing of Little Harry, a mere handful of days gone.

Her hoarseness had been remarked by Clare's mother only on the previous day. The recurrent sneezing, then the curious shrillness and singing quality of the child's voice, as if the words were coming down deep in the chest from a hollow brazen tube. The pain in the throat, somewhere in the vicinity of the larynx, had come on early today. Plus the difficulty of inhalation. Onset had already started . . .

He hurried on.

He saw Miss Euterpe Baring coming round the side of the church, saw her hesitation, as if she would speak if invited to do so. But he could no longer bear the thought of the poor child's impending doom. He had no time for talk, however serious the matter. Little Clare would soon experience that sense of foreboding as horror and death stole upon her. Well, true that he could do nothing to stay the disease. But the child would not stand alone. No longer. Not this time. Too long he had supposed that God was working out some great plan to His glory and the benefit of all mankind. From now on, Carmichael resolved to take a hand and try something, anything. He would stay with the child, and do whatever human ingenuity and resource would devise. And if the smithy could not help, and if Mehala ran from his plea, why, he'd manage without.

He raised his hat absently to Miss Euterpe, and hurried along the track until he came to the gate of Calling Farm. He was practically running as he reached the door of the main part of the house.

33

The tavern where Carradine had arranged to meet the bookmaker was some miles inland from Sealandings. The man would wait. Carradine was not worried that he himself was riding a little late. The roads nowadays were intolerable, even the great trunk arteries proving sometimes impassable.

The Leather Bottle stood not far from one of the creeks which was mud and salt sea marshes at low tide, but flowed thick and dark at high, so adding to the problems for travellers. And many strangers were unaware of the dangers a sudden marooning could cause. What seemed so shallow and mild on a summer's day, with an ebbed tide letting all the underlying mud be baked almost to the hardness of firm brick, was within an hour a life-threatening swirl of encroaching sea as the trackways vanished and pleasant vistas submerged.

These features were a benefit, however, to the people along East Anglian shores. Estuaries ramified everywhere, providing inroads for smuggling and night traders. The Revenue cutters which lay off most of the ports waged constant war against the sea runners who fetched from the Continent, but were usually the loser. Penalties were heavy, and growing heavier whenever Parliament sat on the matter, yet smuggling continued unabated.

The Leather Bottle was a gathering place for the night boats, being at a crossroads upon the heath not far from the busy port of Maldon, and it was able to run with hare and hound, turning whatever way suited best.

Able Sumner had already arrived. He was a small dwarfish man, forever seeming as if about to run to cold. His clothes were made by the most fashionable tailors in London, yet looked handed down from some bulky older brother. He conveyed an impression of wanting to speak, but those who waited in expectation for his next witticism waited forever, since he seemed to have little to say, even in the most erudite and heady conversation.

He was however the richest bookmaker in the capital. Fairly well connected, he used relatives to build up his large clientele among the gentry. Even Royalty could sometimes be seen discussing with Able Sumner bets and wagers and discounts, and time to pay, when the more obvious commission agents who haunted race courses were shunned at all costs.

Sumner was in an alcove in the main taproom. The tavern was quite noisy, even at so early an hour, though the customers were lowly merchants or farm people. There were plenty enough about for him to pass unnoticed in the press. Carradine entered half an hour later than arranged, by which time Sumner had consumed half of his pint of small beer, and a third of the piece of lardy cake he had purchased.

He saw Carradine arrive, and stand looking. Oh, that handsome face and aquiline profile! Sumner made no sign. He would be noticed in the man's own time. That was the arrangement. So grand a gentleman, and so plain a fool! For a moment Sumner felt like smiling, though his face remained impassive. His illusions had gone early in life, when he realized with astonishment that all people were deceivers, firstly of themselves, and secondly anyone else they could con into their deceptions. The purpose of all this trickery was baffling, almost ridiculous. Women were deceivers of age, of features, of hair. They sought beauty at any cost to dignity and common sense, whereas, if they were to let Nature take her course, they would seem wholesome and naturally pretty as they descended the sweet valley of years. Men too were at similar fraudulent games. They had to be strong, resolute, powerful and rich – when their stupidities of behaviour proved otherwise with the monotonous regularity of a Liverpool clock.

Wryly the bookmaker observed the grand gentleman's imperious arrival across the crowded tavern room. Just look at this Carradine, posing so silently in the tavern doorway! Young, aggressive, strong, a dueller of fearsome reputation, a horseman of considerable fame, inheritor of a large estate bringing in a reliable and useful revenue, all legitimate. And, if rumour blessed truth for once, receiver of quite a proportion of the income from supplies shipped ashore north of Sealandings while Revenue luggers patrolled in the sea lanes between Whitehanger and the lighthouses to the south.

How insane it all was! With all these attributes of health, personability and wealth, he was still hell-bent on driving himself to ruin. Able Sumner himself had heard of two duels, with Carradine the victor and escaping the magistracy's anger by somehow managing to prove himself several leagues distant at the time of the deeds' perpetration. Gambling his downfall, though of course such a volatile spirit could not choose only one road to perdition. Oh dear no! Wenching was as natural to a man of this stamp as breathing, and the Devil drives always at speed. Carradine could be forgiven his lusts, which naturally had to be satisfied. Yet he did still more. Carradine was infamous for taking risks where none need be. If there was a complaisant clean pleasant girl in some wholesome tavern, willing to supplement her wages of a few shillings a week by offering her charms to such a splendidly desirous gentleman, why not use her, for a crown or perhaps as little as three shillings – the usual grace fee in these parts for that service? It was little enough, for much enough.

But Carradine? Not he! A naturally blameless course was too dull, too ordinary for him. No; he had to seek out the great ladies, the courtesans, the rutters of the salons, the destroyers of empires, the women who were parasites on wealth. The greater the risk, the greater the pleasure for him, it seemed. Able Sumner was hardly much older than Carradine, but for all the world he was unable to understand what drove the man. Now here he came, probably complete with some scheme for netting solvency. Yet again. And it would be a total failure, yet again. This would be the fifth, or happen the sixth, occasion when Mistress Ease was to be bought by some mad plot. Carradine the schemer of perfect schemes. God's gift to a greedy bookmaker.

'Ah, sir!' Sumner rose on cue, calling to accost Carradine as the man casually strode past. 'Would you join me, sir? You recall me! We met last at – '

'Ah, sir! I am pleased to.' Carradine maintained the appearance of one surprised as he came and sat, doffing his hat and shedding his cloak on to the bench. 'Well met.'

He glanced around the tavern, smiling and returning his gaze to Sumner. 'All linsey-woolseys, eh, Sumner? No broadcloths here, I see!'

'True, sir. No gentry, saving your good self. All aritsans, of the best and most honest sort.'

'No racegoers, then?'

They chuckled at the sally. 'I have ordered a mutton pie, sir,' Sumner informed Carradine, to explain why he was signalling to the far end of the taproom. 'This tavern is mostly unknown to me, and I mistrust the victuals of such places.'

'Good old Cotswold lion, eh?' Carradine seemed in great good humour, thank God. 'But why not the veal squab pie, sir?'

Sumner shook his head. 'Their veal I would not think genuine, sir. And their squabs should be honest small chicks, when instead they all too often are the old wild pigeons they buy from boys who go bird-scaring. Mutton pie is honest mutton pie, done with apples in the west country fashion, so any faults can easily be detected by the diner.' He shook his head at the sad state of morality these days.

'Sumner, I swear you are a marvel. You consider details of life which no other man would even begin to contemplate!'

'It is a regrettable trend, sir, that all men tend to crookery and corruption these days. I blame modern society. It imposes demands upon the country for everything. All must change, or it is not good. Newness is everything nowadays. I think we should return to the old times – not so long ago! – when ladies who wore chintz, that horrible printed calico, to the detriment of our honest country linens and woollens, were apprehended by the courts and fined heavily for their transgression. It is unpatriotic, and damned sacrilegious, to appear in foreign apparel! As is the demand for more wages, more returns on investments – '

'Speaking of which, Sumner,' Carradine put in, smiling with real amusement at the man's dour observations, 'I think we should arrange the business of the percentages due to me.'

'To each, sir. Due to *each*.' Sumner reflected on the man opposite as the mutton pie came and the aroma rose from the platters as they set to.

'But mostly, sir, due to me.' Carradine served himself a thick slice and dipped the ladle after, knocking with the handle on the table to summon bread.

'Why so, sir? I shall join your scheme, whatever it is. So I'll take the risks, as you will. The fifty per cent we arranged at the previous meet was very much in your favour.'

'A badger baiting, Sumner?' Carradine made a small gesture of dismissal. 'To my favour? It sure as hell was *not* to my advantage, Sumner.'

So Carradine still blamed him for the outcome of that fiasco, Sumner thought. How very tiresome. These firebrands of the nobility were nothing but spoiled children when their schemes went wrong. 'What happens is not my fault, sir. All I can do is give a guarantee then stick to the original agreement made between us. I cannot order the universe. Would that I could!'

'This time, I have already accomplished that miracle, Sumner.'

The agent listened intently as Carradine explained, nodding at crucial points to indicate his understanding. He thought a moment as Carradine concluded.

'I had actually heard that Tom Spring, the Champion, is in difficulties with his health. After all, an ageing Champion is a dead one, is that not so?'

'Inevitably, Sumner. Trust my word. Tom Spring will default.'

264

'As always, sir,' Able Sumner interjected politely. 'And this . . . this Rendell man will stand in his place?'

'Yes.'

Sumner digested the information in silence. Battler Goring was a legend of staying power and brute strength. Admittedly he lacked Tom Spring's precision, and was nothing to equal the great Mendoza, but still he was solid as any ox and twice had gone more than sixty rounds before Sumner's own eyes. And against men of reputation and physical prowess, too. This Rendell man must be some newcomer.

'How is it, sir, if I might ask, that so formidable a talent has not already been discovered? And, if his abilities are so worthy, why are they not already famous throughout the land?'

'Because I have paid for the news to be suppressed, Sumner. I've bought him a poor reputation, to keep the odds down. It has not been easy. Nor has it come cheap, for he is an impatient man and wants fame and fortune instantly.'

'Has he sparred?'

'Yes. With Tom Spring himself.' Carradine caught up three more mutton chops from the pie and scooped the apple flesh after. 'It will not have escaped your notice, Sumner, that Tom Spring's absence coincides with Rendell's readiness.'

Able Sumner froze, and gazed at his guest. 'You mean. . . ?'

'I mean nothing, Sumner. But if you had seen Rendell sparring with the Champion, and realized exactly how hard put Tom Spring was to defend himself from Rendell's onslaughts, you would understand why it is that the Champion is not quite well enough to toe the line next week!'

Sumner almost whistled with astonishment. 'This Rendell is so good that he injured the Champion in training?'

'Exactly, sir. His performance will convince all – until the sixtieth round when he will suffer defeat.'

Carradine shared the jug of small beer, eyeing the agent.

'But this information is worth . . .' Able Sumner quickly caught himself and tackled his food in silence.

All around passengers were being called for the coach, to general upheaval. The mail coach was due very soon, and a groom was yelling abuse at the landlord for not having the coach yard cleared for its reception.

'Honest to God!' Sumner growled. 'Just look at the pandemonium! I don't know why the penny post cannot be set up as beneficial for the entire kingdom. London had it in 1683, from that upholsterer Mr

265

Murray, and Dublin less than a hundred years later. Here in the very centre of the world we still struggle with the worst system imaginable, on the most hopeless roads, all to least effect! It is a disgrace, sir.'

'You weep for lost profit, Sumner,' Carradine said candidly. 'Not for lost opportunities of advancement.'

'Advancement is profit, and vice versa, sir,' Sumner rejoined with equal candour. 'Which brings me to the scheme you propose.'

Carradine leant forward, confident he had hooked the man. 'You accept wagers that Rendell wins. I have a list here of friends who will bet heavily on him.' Carradine tapped his chest. 'It is yours, once we concur.'

'A list?' Sumner could not take his eyes from Carradine's breast. Such a list meant profit, money in rather than money out. 'How came you by that, sir?'

'By skill, my friend. And a great deal of expenditure.' Carradine gave a short laugh. 'Why, I have even had to engineer the transfer of a serving girl from a tavern to the household of one who has promised to underwrite the scheme! Would you believe it? Thousands of sovereigns, solid gold, for the mere chance of a particular woman? Beyond belief!'

'Indeed I would believe it, sir.' Sumner nodded, half-incredulous in spite of his words yet knowing that such madness could afflict all humanity. With the single exception of himself. 'Who is this ardent lover?'

'No one you would know, sir,' Carradine said easily. The less Able Sumner knew of the background to the scheme the better. And safer. But he would have to remind himself sooner or later to do something about that Mehala woman, and get her transferred to Jason Prothero's farm. As if he didn't have enough to do, he now had to serve as go-between for a rustic boor and a slut. 'But if you yourself wish to have a share, I could arrange it for a fee.'

'That, sir, is *my* function!' Sumner caught the joke and laughed along. The passengers were moving out as the four horses were being changed outside, amid much shouting and hurrying. 'Fifty to fifty per cents, sir?'

'Forty to sixty, in my favour, Sumner. That is it.'

'But sir!' Sumner protested. 'I'm the one who will have to accept the risk of the entire book of wagers!'

'I can endeavour to make life easier for you, Sumner,' Carradine said coldly, 'but I am unable to provide you with total sinecure.'

Sumner swallowed at the sharpness of Carradine's tone. 'I did not mean to impugn . . .'

'Then kindly do not, by acceding to your own wishes, sir.'

'Indeed. If I have given offence, then let me apologize immediately. I shall fall in with your suggestion, sir. Sixty to forty of the profits of all the wagers laid on the match, then.'

'No, sir,' Carradine countered sharply. 'Of the gross laid, not on the profits alone. And *not* of all laid on the match, sir. Only of those laid from the friends I have on this list. For they will lay only in one direction, and all extremely heavily. They will all lay for Rendell. And that will *all* be profit, will it not?'

'But, sir,' Sumner protested weakly. 'I have my own expenses. I shall have to accept wagers on Goring, and against, some of which I shall know are certain to lose!'

'I can see that goes against the grain, Sumner,' Carradine said cruelly. 'But there have been times you have profited exceedingly at my expense. Let this be some redress – for me! And let your usual behaviour not waver from its set path. I shall be observant as never before on that day. Mark well.'

'Indeed I shall, sir.' Sumner wiped his brow. He felt smothered in the pace of it all. Risk was one thing, but this level of deceit was wholly another. One word of this transaction out in London, and he would be floating face down from Wapping Stairs within an hour of the next nightfall. 'I agree. But one thing, sir. What if . . . what if Rendell wins?'

'He will not. You have my word on it.'

'Then I am under no obligation to lay off the bets against that eventuality?'

'No. You are not.' Carradine was ice now. Sumner felt danger in the gentleman's manner. 'That would expose the plan as nothing else would. You might as well shout the scheme from the rooftops.'

'The risk is considerable, however you view it, sir.'

'For you it is no risk at all, man.' Carradine was disgusted with the wretched agent. Sumner was rumoured to be from a noble family, yet here he was making his fortune by grubbing around meetings and matches for coppers on grubby little pieces of paper. Like a common merchant or shopkeeper. It was utterly loathsome. Some people were born with the souls of aristocracy, and some without. God knows what the explanation might be. But here was a by-blow, an aristocrat in origin, with the soul of a Strand jew. He felt repelled by the creature, and suddenly wanted to get away from the sordid business with all possible speed.

'No, sir. I realize that, owing to your kindness and consideration, I am in an excellent position. I only am concerned lest – '

Carradine lost patience with the man's reticence. 'I shall bear half of any related debt you suffer, sir.'

'You will?' Sumner beamed at the promise. 'That is very gracious, sir. I thank you. Shall we draw up the notes-of-hand now? Or shall I send them over to you?'

'Do it now, Sumner.' Carradine gazed coldly at the agent. 'I may not have time to meet you again privately before the meeting.'

'Very well, sir.'

Sumner quickly took out his travelling case and opened the mahogany lid, carefully concealing the lock as he did so. He had come prepared to register the transaction. Whatever happened now at the fight he stood to make a fortune.

Carradine observed him with contempt. How low could a man sink? Able Sumner was adequate answer to that question.

'The papers, sir.'

'Such a lot, in so brief a scrawl,' Carradine said, mollified by the knowledge that his fortune was now made. It was only a matter of time before gold sovereigns would come in like a North Sea shoal.

'I trust this will all come out to our great benefit, sir.'

Carradine gave a wintry smile. Sumner felt as if he had encountered a sudden squall, and shivered in spite of himself.

'It better had, Sumner,' Carradine said, and appended his signature. 'It better had.'

34

The summons from Mrs Weaver unaccountably came during the rush for the evening meal. Mehala was immediately worried, since she had already approached Mrs Weaver earlier during the day, when that good lady had seemed placid and untroubled by the problem of Mehala's forthcoming departure.

Now Mehala had of a sudden to rush from the kitchen, smoothing herself down and wondering if she should try to borrow a clean mobcap from Little Jane or wait to see if Nellie had any more orders. Mrs Nelson put paid to any hesitation and shooed her along with a warning to tarry neither on the way to Mrs Weaver nor on the return.

'Mrs Weaver, ma'am.'

Mehala curtseyed at the door after knocking. The taverner's wife was making accounts for travellers, and motioned her inside. It was on the second floor, and overlooked the harbour's fading day. Offshore the Revenue lugger was standing, her lights early set. She was clearly expecting night runners very soon.

'Come, Mehala. I have spoken with Mr Weaver, and he thinks you should be sent to a position, should we be able to find one to suit.'

'Ma'am. I am conscious of your kindnesses and generosity. I am fortunate to have been received here, and will ever remain – '

'Tush, tush, child. Stop that this instant. I did what any soul would have done in the circumstances, and everyone knows it. I was merely to hand, that is all.' Mrs Weaver laid aside her accounts. 'The problem now is that you have several opportunities available to your acceptance, Mehala.' Mrs Weaver was judging her reaction as she spoke. Mehala stood before the small rent table, waiting her fate.

'Several, ma'am? Can this be?'

'Indeed it can! You already are aware of the offer to place you at the rectory with Miss Baring as your supervisor and you as a maid-of-all? There are possibilities in due time of your rising to the position of under-housekeeper there after a few years, pending your satisfactory work. It is not to be sneezed at, and promises security.'

'Yes, Mrs Weaver. I remember taking the message.'

'That still stands, Mehala. And I have had converse with Mrs Mary Prothero, a lady with whom I might even claim friendship from childhood. She is the mistress at Calling Farm. Mrs Prothero is very anxious for you to go there as maid-of-all.'

'Then you recommend that I go to Calling Farm, Mrs Weaver?' Mehala said innocently. She had learned more than enough of this Prothero. The evasiveness of Mrs Weaver's eyes was sufficient confirmation that Calling Farm should be avoided. But if that was the implication, why did Mrs Weaver not frankly advise her against it?

'I urge you to think of it, Mehala,' Sarah Ann Weaver managed, the best she could under the circumstances. 'Mrs Prothero is very fair-minded and honest and everyone always speaks well of her.'

But not of Prothero himself, thought Mehala.

'There is another just arrived,' Mrs Weaver continued. 'Hence my haste in wanting to bring this to your atttention. It is from Mrs De Foe.'

'Milton Hall?' Mehala asked, astonished.

'Not there, you understand,' the taverner's wife said hastily. 'But the house of her cousin, the Honourable Charles Golding. He owns a great estate, Bures House. He wishes to have a new under-housekeeper. I believe there has lately been some trouble there – I speak in total confidence, Mehala, on this – involving the previous housekeeper, a Judith Blaker. Mrs De Foe says nothing of this in her note, of course, but merely that on receipt of this you are to repair immediately to Bures House and take up your post. She will send detailed instructions as to your duties by a personal maid, who will see to your induction.'

Mehala waited. 'Yes, Mrs Weaver?'

'Why, that is the sum of the opportunities, Mehala.'

'But which am I to accept?'

'Whichever you wish, girl!'

'Do you advise me to Bures House, then, ma'am?'

'If it accords with your wishes, Mehala.' Again Mrs Weaver seemed evasive. 'Naturally, I have to explain that Mrs De Foe is a most influential lady in these parts, with great rights in Sealandings. Her husband is a notable gentleman in the City of London, with great powers and influence there, as here. And of her cousin at Bures House I need not speak, for he is a gentleman with political aspirations, it is said. The opportunities are great.'

'I have to thank you, Mrs Weaver. You are kindness itself.'

'Then, Mehala?'

'I shall attempt to please a prospective master at the rectory, ma'am, if by doing so I do not return offence as payment for your thoughtfulness, ma'am.'

'The rectory?'

270

'Yes, ma'am. I do not know of the Prothero household at Calling Farm. And, with deference to your high opinions of Mrs De Foe, I also do not know of that lady – '

'She was the lady who alighted from her carriage as we stood near the market, Mehala. Do you not remember?'

'I do indeed, ma'am. But I feel obligated to the Miss Baring, in view of her kindness to me. I shall therefore apply in the first instance there, if you agree.'

'Very well, Mehala.' Mrs Weaver seemed doubtful about something more than the mere allocation of a serving girl to another post. Mehala could detect no clue to explain what caused her worry.

She made her thanks, and promised to be away by the last hour before midnight. It felt strange to be leaving the Donkey and Buskin, which was the only home she knew in her new life, but she was bright with expectation, as at a fresh beginning to something greater.

35

There was a sensation of strangeness in him as he knocked on the door. Several problems seemed to come together, as always when he had to face emotions coming out of his past, but the fear for the little girl drove him on past thinking of himself. Ridiculously, his mind focused on which door he should approach at Calling Farm. He settled for the most direct method, and braved the front entrance. And no chaise, nor even a calabash, but only himself arriving incongruously on foot.

He recognized the chief housemaid who opened the door.

'Why, sir!' she exclaimed, reddening as she recognized him. 'It's you, Doctor Carmichael, excuse me!'

'Indeed, Libby. Could you please ask permission for me to see the master, Mr Prothero? It is an urgent matter, and cannot brook delay.'

'I fear the master is away, Doctor. The mistress is in.'

'I have no personal calling card with me, Libby. Please extend my sincerest apologies to your mistress for the fault, and beg that I may see her. Very urgent.'

'Very well, sir.' She bobbed, dithered an instant as if uncertain whether to leave him there or not, then shut the door.

Three minutes later, by his reckoning, the Calling Farm housekeeper opened the door and bade him enter.

'How do you do, Mrs Perrigo?' he greeted her, conscious of the unusual occurrence of his unannounced arrival. It would be a talking point around Calling Farm for quite some time, as well as around Sealandings itself.

'How do you do, sir?'

He had never quite got on well with Mrs Perrigo. She was dark-haired, dour and somewhat forbidding, though he suspected that was on account of her ferociously protective attitude towards Mary Calling, rather than towards him in particular. He wondered briefly if her savage loyalty had stood in Mary's way. She certainly believed she knew what was best for her mistress. Perhaps things would have turned out a deal different for Miss Mary Calling – and perhaps even for himself . . . But that was useless speculation, and he dismissed the thought as it tried to surface.

'I apologize for disturbing the household at this hour, Mrs Perrigo, but I am in sore need of assistance. A case of an illness, you understand. I have taken the liberty of visiting unannounced in the hope of procuring Mr Prothero's assistance.'

Mrs Perrigo's manner was defensive as she allowed him to enter. She eyed him forbiddingly. 'The master is in town and will not be home for some time. I have sent to the mistress who is willing to receive you, if you will wait in the withdrawing room a moment.'

'Thank you, Mrs Perrigo.' He was ushered along the brick-tiled hallway.

It was a handsome house, very well appointed, and was more of a manor house than a lowly farmhouse. Part of the foundations lay on the ruins of some ancient convent. The medieval structure was discernible at several points when walking the grounds. The gardens were beautifully landscaped in the modern fashion, and the upkeep was as serviceable and diligent as he remembered. Mary Calling had done very well to maintain her ancestral home with all its old elegance. Fresh, that was the word for Mary's attitude towards her gardens. Her parents would have been proud of her.

'Please make yourself comfortable, sir,' Mrs Perrigo said, pausing in the doorway to allow him to pass.

'Thank you, Mrs Perrigo. Is Mr Perrigo well, if I might ask?'

'Very well indeed, sir, thank you. He has taken up a bid for the toll at the Norwich road from Sealandings, sir.'

'Has he, indeed? I am pleased to hear it, Mrs Perrigo. Please wish him very well from myself, and say that I trust he will be successful. It is Mr Tyll, husband of the housekeeper at Carradine House, who presently has the concession, is it not?'

'It is, sir. Mr Tyll has renewed his own bid, so there will be a contested allocation of the toll.'

'Let us hope that you receive the success due to you, Mrs Perrigo.'

'Thank you, sir.'

He sat, nodding his thanks. The housekeeper remained a moment as if unwilling to leave. He raised his eyebrows inquiringly.

'I fear I have very little influence with those who allocate the tollgate concessions, Mrs Perrigo,' he said. 'Though I hope that you know that, were its disposal in my hands, I should ensure that Mr Perrigo received the toll concession for the maximum possible time.'

'Thank you for saying so, sir.' She still did not leave, and he wondered worriedly if she had strict orders never to allow him to visit without strict supervision. Not another house where he was to be barred?

273

'Is anything the matter, Mrs Perrigo?'

'No, sir.' She glanced over her shoulder, afraid of being overheard. 'Doctor. I am concerned for Miss Mary. She is so overborne by the master now that I am fearful. She has changed out of all recognition, and I wonder sometimes if I should even stay, or if I should call on some friend of the family to come visiting in spite of what Mr Prothero says. He forbids her happy family visits, which I am sure you well remember from the times you yourself came here, sir. But she is . . .'

A sound outside made her start suddenly. She gave a brief curtsey and said in a controlled voice, 'Thank you for your kind wishes about the toll bid, sir. I shall tell my man about your felicitations. I shall inform the mistress that you are – '

'Thank you, Mrs Perrigo.' Mary Prothero entered from the opposite direction, where a small conservatory doorway led into the garden.

Doctor Carmichael rose, feeling colour warm his face. This was the first time he had seen Mary Prothero face to face since she had emerged from the church at her wedding. He was shocked at the change in her appearance.

'Doctor Carmichael,' she greeted him, warmly advancing and extending her hand. 'How very kind of you to call!'

'It is my pleasure, ma'am, but also my sad concern for a sick child which has brought me here . . .'

'A sick child?' She paused, motioning him to be seated.

He faced her. She sank into the sofa beside the fireplace, a wise choice in view of her pallor. The light from the garden window fell from over her shoulder and into his eyes. He could be seen clearly in the sombre room, but she was almost in silhouette. He paused for the correct length of time, then seated himself on a narrow squab immediately across from her.

'I regret so, ma'am. I have a most unusual request to ask of you. I hope that it will be within your unbounded kindness to grant the help I require.'

'For a sick child, Doctor? I have no knowledge of any child seriously ill in Sealandings – '

'Whitehanger, ma'am.'

'Oh. Whitehanger.' Her tone expressed a faint regret. There was little love lost between the two places, and great competition in the area of sea produce, sales of materials and the rights of cattle grazing and arable farming.

'Yes, ma'am. As you are no doubt aware, they have no doctor there. Any assistance they can obtain from the pharmacies to the south is very meagre. They called upon me recently for help in the matter of a small boy with the croup, who sadly passed away. He has a sister, who is now grievously afflicted.'

'And you want money to recompense the family for the children's lost labour, Doctor?'

'No, ma'am. I wish to have the assistance of one of your stockmen, and an animal, for a little while.'

'A stockman? Animal?' She fingered the pendant at her throat. It was one he recognized, a gift from her father the year before he himself had been introduced to Mary Calling. This had been the first house he had called upon to leave his card when arriving as a qualified doctor in Sealandings.

'Yes, ma'am. I need to investigate to see what the structure of the animal's throat is, and what amount of strength the breathing organs have for a surgical procedure.'

'My goodness!' she exclaimed faintly.

'I regret the possible impropriety of bringing so indelicate a matter to your attention, ma'am,' he said apologetically. 'But I would have brought my request to the attention of Mr Prothero instead had he been at home, or time afforded delay.'

'What is it you wish to do?' She clipped the words. He realized she had almost used his name from habit, and hurried on to cover embarrassment.

'I wish to see if there is some animal your stockmen have lately killed, ma'am. To measure part of the throat. That is all. I shall not touch it otherwise, nor shall I remove any part of the animal.'

Mrs Prothero was silent. She had no illusions, or so she told herself. This man was quite possibly the one she would have allowed to come as a friend, once. A personal friend, one whose company would be gratifying and pleasing. He had laughed in those days, so short a time ago. Why, they had once even been out riding together, with of course the responsibility of staying in view of her parents at the main house, but still a step overly bold and full of unstated meaning. But that was before both her parents passed away so suddenly, and before she married Jason Prothero.

Ven Carmichael's visit shocked and alarmed her. For one brief instant, hearing the identity of the caller, she had believed somehow that he had come to seek her company for the most personal of reasons. Horrendous to relate, she had felt a burst of gladness within that had stunned her by its force and intensity. She was badly shaken, so had sent Mrs Perrigo to admit him while delaying her own arrival.

It was dismaying that he came only to assist some sick child. He had not come for her, nor to suggest a renewal of their past brief friendship. Foolish and stupid it had been, too, to imagine that that would have been the case. And it would have been a hopeless attempt on his part. For she was a married lady, mistress of her family home, and bound by all custom, laws and social practice to remain faithful to her husband in thought, word, deed and expectation. No. To think as she had been in danger of thinking was treachery and wantonness of the worst kind. She should be ashamed, instead of glad.

'Then you have permission, Doctor.'

'Thank you, ma'am. I am deeply in your debt.'

He rose, and she with him. Together they stood in the room, facing each other across the carpet. Neither spoke, each wanting to say more than they had risked so far. Carmichael wanted somehow to express regret at his dilatory offers of company to her in the past, but did not dare risk saying so. She knew there was no possibility of extending his presence here without giving rise to scandal. That the majority of servants at Calling Farm remained steadfast in their loyalty to her was no proof against tittle-tattle, for already the length of the doctor's stay would be giving rise to speculation below stairs.

'Might I ask . . . will you be pleased to send a stockman, or some messenger to convey your permission, ma'am?'

'Of course.'

She pulled the bell rope, and together they waited in uncomfortable silence. He cleared his throat. She smiled vaguely. He shuffled his feet and twice made as if to examine the small painting which hung over the fireplace, a countryscape by Wilson showing the Italian skies over Tuscany, but in the nick of time remembered that once, while riding a perambulation of the grounds at Calling Farm, he had made some joke about inviting her in due time to a tour of that wonderful region. It had been almost frighteningly risky to make even that amusing sally, but fortunately she had taken no offence. Still, it was not the sort of memory he should thrust upon her.

Times were new. Everything nowadays was changing. The young vivacious Mary Calling, she of the laughter and gently amusing humour, was gone. In her place stood the withdrawn and almost reclusive mistress of Calling.

Mary kept back her distress at his appearance, his gaunt features. She ought to offer something, perhaps send a courtesy gift of the farm produce, but would he be offended? And her husband would be outraged at such largesse. She wanted to ask after Harriet Ferlane, whose family now resided in London, for rumour had convinced the Eastern Hundreds not long ago that the two were betrothed. They had not mentioned the past, each afraid of what their eyes were witnessing.

Mrs Perrigo came instead of Libby, and was told to send for one of the stockmen to assist Doctor Carmichael.

In silence Mrs Perrigo stood while the doctor made his farewells of the mistress, then ushered him through the house towards the back door. There she summoned an ostler and passed on the instruction. Within minutes, Carmichael was in the cattle yard, where a bullock had been slaughtered only that day.

He was shown the animal by Perrigo himself, a taciturn man with some humour, who often ran with the hare coursing. They had known each other for some time. Perrigo was pleased to see the doctor again and greeted him warmly.

'It's the throat I want to see, Mr Perrigo. May I be shown the ventral surface?'

It was an obscene shape, in death, and already flies were settling on the flesh. Most of the offal would be left for feeding the dogs or burning, so little attention had been paid to it.

The throat was skinned, of course. The skin was sent for tanning at the earliest opportunity after the death of the animal. The beast had been flayed roughly but effectively. Finally he was able to identify the various tissues. The trachea was huge in comparison with a child's, but roughly in the same position relative to the oesophagus and the nerves and carotid arteries. He made a brief sketch in his notebook while Perrigo watched with curiosity.

'Is it for a philosophic trial, Doctor?'

'Yes, in a manner of speaking, Perrigo. I am interested to compare the shapes of animals with the structures we are sometimes able to discern in Man. Though of course,' he added piously, not wanting to give offence, 'only as a means of illustrating how far removed from the brute animal form the great Architect of All has been pleased to make us, and not for any of these new blasphemous reasons one hears so much of these days.'

'I am pleased to hear that, sir.'

'Indeed, I hope to bring these studies to the aid of the Established Church by making that very point,' Carmichael ended vaguely, hoping that Perrigo was not really listening and that the man had not become more religiously inclined than previously. One could not be too careful. Any scientific investigation, or any new practice in manufacturing or

277

farming, was likely to be interpreted as a malicious threat to subvert anything or anyone, political or religious.

'Might I make a trial with a measuring instrument, Perrigo?'

'Ma'am has said so, sir.'

'Thank you.'

Carmichael held the windpipe firmly between finger and thumb, trying to brush away the thick cloud of dark flies which swarmed and buzzed everywhere about the carcass, and placed the tip of the sick syphon's narrow end against one of the recesses between the tracheal rings. With a firm shove he tried to penetrate the tissue with the syphon but it would not enter. He exerted all his force, and the tissue gave with a sudden lack of resistance which almost sent him sprawling on to the remains of the animal.

'Good grief, Perrigo!' he exclaimed, trying to be jovial and raising himself. 'I had no idea you needed to be such strong men to cope with these fleshed animals!'

'Well, sir, we have to be pretty strong, y'see, sir.' Perrigo was grinning. 'It isn't like children and babes and humans, not at all!'

'Thank you, Perrigo. That is all. I wish you well. I shall convey my appreciation to the mistress and Mr Prothero by letter, and mention your kindly assistance.'

They made their goodbyes. Carmichael left immediately without returning to the main house, walking cock-apace down towards the market square, wiping the sick syphon on his frock coat as he went.

36

The situation was impossible.

By late afternoon Hunterfield was almost beside himself. He decided to accost his sister, and try to find out if she had taken any action at all. At least he would be doing something instead of simply waiting and hoping, moping about Lorne House.

He found Lydia in the conservatory, where Crane had sent a maid-of-all to lay a fire. It was exceedingly comfortable, providing the day was not too cold outside. One had to take care, for with the glass walls being all that intervened between interior and the weather, draughts could easily set in and chill the body. Also, it was not good for reading, unless many lamps were set. The family had therefore evolved the custom of having exterior lanthorns hung to augment the illumination of the dying day. It made for a picturesque scene, his sister a pretty sight at her chair, using the pole screen's beads to reflect the available light on to her embroidery.

He knew exactly what he wanted to say, having already made up his mind on the way.

Thalia De Foe was either being cruel by forgetfulness or deliberately so. He remembered having intimated most pointedly that he would desperately need her company within days. Now it was an unconscionable time since he had last lain with her. It was insufferable. Was ever a man used so?

Out of the question that she had decided to spurn him. No, he was certain. He knew his women better than that. She was infatuated with his company – not too strong a word, for she had practically begged him to be sure to send her a love-note, and come back to her as soon as he could without arousing the suspicions of the neighbourhood.

Yet the days were dragging past, since that day when Sir Trev Bunyan had come to supper and the events had begun, with Trev doting on that mad artist's sister Olivia, and he himself had decided to risk visiting Milton Hall to bite the cherry again after so short an interval.

He had written to Thalia as she'd asked, without reply. Simple Tom had gone at his orders three times, no fewer, within a week. And not a word. No intimation that she was ready to receive him, that all was well. Twice, he had ridden out with Simple Tom in attendance, and had stared from the darkness of the trackway towards the southern aspect of Milton Hall, only to suffer disappointment by the absence of Thalia's lanthorn signals. Did women have no inkling of the pain and sheer distress they caused their lovers?

Thalia De Foe must of course be suffering equally with him, thank goodness. He was certain of that. She had pleaded with him, to be sure to keep her in his mind at all times. She had sent him to the door with a posy of pressed flowers which she had made with her own fair hands. Forget-me-nots were prominent, which in the language of flowers spelt all that mattered.

No. It was clearly time to act. She would have to be sought more vigorously. Knowing women as well as he did, he was convinced that Mrs De Foe was perhaps merely suffering a few qualms of conscience. That was it. The delicious thing was wracking herself in torment for having transgressed the bonds of matrimony. He smiled as he reached the logical conclusion. Was not true love the main spur to all existence? Did it not transcend the shackles of mere morality? It did, of course. He knew it. Thalia De Foe knew it.

'Good afternoon, Lydia,' he said as he entered.

'Good afternoon, Henry. Not a fine day, but one we might exchange for many worse, don't you agree?'

'I do.'

He paced a little, his invariable habit when wanting to broach a subject. She, wise in anticipating his moods, said nothing, but held up the embroidery she was completing, a table screen decorated with symbols of woodland and river antiquities. The design had been drawn for her by Letitia, and was greatly pleasing. It was to be a present for Aunt Faith in Gloucester, if she managed to finish it in time for Christmas. She explained all this, quite casually. Her brother admired her work briefly before coming down to it.

'Lydia,' Henry said after clearing his throat several times. 'The orangery is coming on well. It seems not quite the correct design, I fear. How do you. . . ?'

'The orangery, Henry?' This was mere diversion, for he himself had approved the design of the building. It stood immediately adjacent to the conservatory, and was a splendid small extension to the facilities at Lorne House. Lydia was quite proud of the erection, and hoped to see its completion in time to have the orange plants brought in some time well before Easter.

'I think it wholly admirable. No, sir. I am well pleased, and am sincerely proud of it as a venture. We shall be the only great house with that benefit in Sealandings. The Hunterfields have the right to a modicum of pride.'

'I'm not sure, Lydia.' He gazed through the conservatory windows. The men were just stopping work for the day, and the stonemasons were telling off their banker-hands one by one, notching their tally sticks in the time-honoured way to show half days of complete work.

'Please be reassured, Henry. I have every confidence in the execution and design of it.'

'Very well, then. If you're sure. Oh, Lydia. There is one other small thing.' He turned, as if struck of a sudden by a recollection.

'Yes, Henry?' she murmured, ready for the meat of the matter.

'You remember that day, when we had Sir Trev Bunyan and Mrs De Foe to supper? Some incident occurred which required your temporary absence from the table. What was it, please? It has been on my mind for a little while, and worries me for reasons I cannot recall.'

Now she was honestly surprised, and it showed in her face as she laid aside her embroidery to look up at him. He was quite a handsome man, and her own dearly loved brother, yet he was not the most nimble thinker. Only rarely was she ever taken aback by his pronouncements.

'Why, Henry, I gave you a full account once our guests had retired for the night. And I intimated sufficient for your immediate purposes while we dined and our guests were still present.'

'Remind me, please, ma'am.'

'The woman taken from the sea. The lugger *The Jaunty*, of Master Jervin's. Doctor Carmichael called to report the knowledge to you. She – the female, I mean – was taken to the Donkey and Buskin in Sealandings, and Miss Baring was in attendance. That was all.'

'And what did I undertake to do?'

'Nothing that I recollect, Henry.'

'Nothing.' He stood, musing at the window. The stonemason's men were already moving away, lighting their pipes as they walked. Some were from Whitehanger, no fewer than nine men all told, six of them skilled men of the guilds. A large expense.

'What concerns you, Henry? Is there some action you wish me to undertake?'

'Regarding this woman? I'm not sure, Lydia. Only, it seems remiss of me to hear of this rescue, and then do nothing. The woman might be ailing, be suffering. As the squire of Sealandings, I perhaps should be seen to act. And from Christian charity alone, I ought to take some interest.'

'Perhaps send a few shillings for the creature's comfort?'

Lydia was quite composed. Was that all that troubled him? A woman taken from the sea was no uncommon thing in these parts, where the sea ruled and people lived as its subjects.

'I don't think so, Lydia. It will not be enough. Perhaps I shall ride out this evening and cross past John Weaver's inn. I should send Simple Tom in there and perhaps inquire after her wellbeing, make some gesture of sympathy. I have not heard anything about her family, her background, which surely I should have by now, don't you think?'

'Oh, you great soft kind man!' Lydia scolded. 'It is only a serving woman, for heaven's sake! And, if her family have not already set up a hue and cry along these coasts, or sent for all the coastal wherries to bring flying notes of her loss, then, why, she is merely a lost servant, without notable connections. So she can be comfortably forgotten! She is comfortable, or we should have heard otherwise. She is happy and providing the Donkey and Buskin's establishment with adequate help for her board and expenses, or we again should have heard to the contrary. No, Henry, ease your mind about the creature.'

'No, Lydia,' he said in a brooding voice. 'I think I should call on the rector, perhaps, and investigate through John Weaver. I shall take Tom as soon as I have had supper. Please bring it forward to an hour's time.'

'Certainly, Henry.'

Hunterfield nodded, smiling at his sister and walked out of the room into the hall, hands behind his back. He would cast an eye over the orangery in the last of the daylight, and estimate progress. One thing, these stonemasons knew their labour and were getting along famously well. Though, as even the stonemason's labourers were paid at the currently inflated sum of eight shillings and elevenpence a week, it would be a damned high cost for the benefits eventually received.

He rode out that evening on Betsy, following the straightest line to the River Affon, and then in the darkness turning left along its left bank. There was an ancient trackway there, cutting inland, away from Watermillock and the margins of Sealandings.

The wise move was first to ride into town, openly, along the roadway, and leave the route at its nearest point to the Donkey and Buskin. That was the thing. Then, after a proper call there, during which he would send Simple Tom in with the message, already written, to inquire of Mistress Weaver how the girl was coming along, he would then deal with whatever problems she had - a shilling or two might suffice, as

Lydia said – and it would be off as if home. However, on reaching the River Affon, he would cut inland along the nether bank, skirting the estate of his nearest neighbour Charles Golding, and then pass Doctor Carmichael's derelict old pile of ramshackle stones and windy gables, and so reach the south aspect of Milton Hall.

Of course, he thought as he rode, it was Thalia De Foe's passion which he was satisfying, not his own lust. Anyone could see that. This night, he would be more resolute than at his last two abortive visits to the woods overlooking Milton Hall. Whatever the lanthorn signals indicated, he would send Simple Tom with a message to the side door to find Meg. That would bring the summons, probably by the combination of lights from the windows as before. A passionate woman like Thalia De Foe would not be baulked when she knew her lover was waiting nearby. And he had enjoyed sufficient evidence of her undoubted passion recently to understand exactly how carried away she was by her love for him. One could even say she was besotted. It was mightily pleasing, and very promising.

There were dangers, of course. But they only added spice to the pudding. When Fellows De Foe came riding home, restoration of his conjugal rights would prove a difficulty to the lovers. But that bridge could be crossed when they came to it. Thalia would have some scheme to hand. Women always did, especially when in love.

He rode into Sealandings, and headed Besty down the narrow lanes, coming eventually to the Donkey and Buskin. The tavern lamps were set out in fine order. It must be doing very well as an enterprise, Hunterfield registered. He was pleased, for it had been a source of concern to him that the rumours of Revenue-skulking were all joined somehow to the tavern belonging to Ben Fowler, over on the north side of the harbour, and never to John Weaver's establishment. Thus, the rumours were probably true. As senior magistrate for the locality, allegations of smuggling complicity were always near to the tips of the gossips' tongues when he was within earshot. The propriety with which Weaver ran his tavern would provide evidence, were any needed, that smuggling and similar improprieties lay away from the side of Sealandings which the squire inhabited.

He motioned to Simple Tom to dismount and enter the tavern. Two great waggons stood in the yard, and a dozy dog snored and twitched nearby. Waggons themselves were a comparatively new thing on the roads of the kingdom. They had been very unusual at the end of the eighteenth century. Only during the first few years of the 1800s had waggons come into their own, even though they had been taxed ever since 1783. The waggoners were probably drunk by now, singing to the arm-pipes indoors. All in all it made a happy and contented scene, with the sea shushing and sucking under the faint moonlight and the scudding silvered cloud.

'Squire, sir!' Weaver emerged, smiling and rubbing his hands with embarrassment. He wore the brat apron, probably from cellar work. 'A pleasure to see you here, sir! Can I do anything to serve?'

'No, thank you, John. Tell me if that girl you pulled from the seas is well or no, and I shall be on my way.'

'She is well, sir. I was about to send word later this night that she is about to leave us, if you please. Taking a station at the rector's house, if that accords with your wishes, sir?'

'Well enough, John, well enough.' Hunterfield looked about the tavern yard. 'All well with you, is it?'

A cloud seemed to flit across Weaver's features, but he answered that all was well, and courteously expressed thanks.

'Bures House and Calling Farm also were so kind as to make offers to take the girl, sir. I am grateful, for here she was a virtual supernumary.'

'Did they, indeed!' Hunterfield said. 'I shall take a look at her, John, and wish her well.'

'As you please, sir.'

The taverner called indoors to a servant. A drink of Portugal wine in a glass was brought out by a tiny girl, who was overcome when Weaver beckoned her forward to offer the drink directly to the squire. She almost stumbled from confusion, and Weaver gave her a mock buffet to send her scampering back to the safety of the kitchen.

'A glass is a rarity in a tavern, John,' Hunterfield said. 'Am I entitled to this honour?'

'As ever, Squire, as ever!'

'Yet it seems not so long since you were calling me all the names under the sun, and every sort of blackguard!'

Weaver laughed shamefacedly. He remembered the squire as a mischievous boy forever stealing pigeon eggs from the cotes at the rear of the tavern.

'I hope your honour will forgive that, sir,' he said. They were both still laughing when a figure emerged.

Against the indoor light, she was in silhouette, and stood there waiting to be summoned forward.

'Is this she?' Hunterfield asked. He could hardly recognize the same creature. Was this the one he had come across on the mud flats by Whitehanger? Who had struggled ashore, dragging Simple Tom and clinging on to the half-drowned man like a desperate terrier, smothered in mud and dishevelled beyond description? He nodded and John Weaver beckoned to her.

She stepped forward into the lanthorn light. Hunterfield almost gasped at her appearance.

The girl was radiant. Her face could never be described as pretty, nor indeed was she prettified. Beautiful, lovely, yes without doubt, for her features were classic and stark. Her black hair was long, she had not been given time to arrange it before responding to the taverner's summons, so it hung loose and was unpinned. Even in the subdued light it fired russets and dark umbers in its raven silkiness, and set off her pale face with its strong lines. Lovely, he thought. Such perfection of form and face was enough to set a man smiling for life at the recollection of a single glimpse years before.

'Mehala,' he said after a pause.

'Sir,' she said, with a curtsey.

She did not speak to him as if he were a superior, but rather faced him as if dealing with a visitor to her own premises. She was a lady of quality within, if not of status in position.

'You are well, I trust?'

'Indeed I am, sir. And thank you.'

'You have received many offers of employment here in Sealandings, I believe?'

'Thanks to the generosity of all who have made them, sir. I am undeserving, but grateful.'

He cleared his throat. Betsy shifted lazily beneath him, wanting to go.

'I believe too that you are to the rectory, to serve Reverend Baring?'

'If it please you, sir. I am to report to Miss Baring soon after eleven, sir, this night.'

'Very well. Let it be so. Have you . . . have you any recollections regarding your origin, Mehala?'

'No, sir,' she said evenly.

He waited, but she did not go on. He thought: *She lies*. She has some reason for pretence, and she knows I have seen through the deception. And, worse, also she knows that I shall not reveal that I understand. She knows of my own deceit, from the events of the night on the Whitehanger coast when she came from the sea with Tom . . .

'Not an idea, eh? Only your first name?'

'If it is my first name, sir. It does feel apposite to me, sir. I am contented that it is mine.'

'Then let it be so, Mehala. I bid you a good evening, John.'

For one instant as he pulled the mare round he saw a dark brown flash in her eyes. Amusement and appreciation together, and a deep wisdom. He felt her image stay in his mind even as he rode away, with Simple Tom running to mount his own nag and follow on as fast as he was able.

The picture of her, standing in the lanthorn light, obliquely lit by the gold of the flame on one aspect and the silver of the early racing moon on her other, stayed with him. It was a vision made for the admiration of all men.

He smiled at the thought of the houses in which she had been offered positions. Bures House, rectory, Calling Farm estate. He almost laughed aloud, in spite of his longing to return to the tavern and somehow find excuses to prolong the conversation with her. Only three? Had he looked at her properly that morning on the sealands, it might well have been four!

An hour later he reached the trackway crossing, pleased at having followed the circuitous route so successfully.

The house was active, he could see from his position in the thicket. Two lights burned in the side windows, second storey. That was in order. He had almost turned to signal to Simple Tom to take the letter down to the door when he saw a movement down against the side of the house.

A horseman was riding round on the gravel. Even at this distance the sounds of the hooves were audible. The man was making little effort to conceal his approach, so it must be Fellows De Foe returning home. Hunterfield almost gasped with relief. A narrow escape from trouble there!

Yet . . .

The horseman halted, reined in from his casual walk, and slid to the ground. A man emerged, to hold the beast's head. The lanthorn was lit outside the door, so no concealment was possible in any event, or even seemed attempted.

'Ennis?' Hunterfield said, having held out his extended arm so Tom would realize he was asking a question. Tom nudged his mount nearer, stood in the stirrups to see, and nodded, walking his gloved fingers along the back of his left hand. A servant of the house. Ennis, the head footman down at Milton. No deception there, none at all. Yet the rider did not resemble Fellows De Foe.

Hunterfield sat on the mare, observing. The light caught the figure as

286

the gentleman entered the house, giving a swipe to the maid – Meg, as always recognizable – as he did so. The glow lit his face, and Hunterfield knew that he was watching Carradine.

The door closed. The footman walked the horse round to the stables. It would stay there, doubtless, for the period of Carradine's sojourn, but would not be unsaddled.

Hunterfield sat thunderstruck. Carradine had entered the house as if it were his own! He was a man going in, with the full and certain knowledge that he was master of the place. And its women.

And the mistress in residence was Thalia De Foe. Hating his own desperate need to know the purpose of Carradine's visit, Hunterfield remained still, staring down the vale at Milton Hall, disgusted with himself. The inevitable happened within a few minutes. The two lights were dowsed. The exterior lanthorn also was extinguished, this one by Ennis on his return from the stables. No mere grooms to attend Carradine, oh no. This was an established procedure, a ritual observed often.

It was the norm. And he, Hunterfield, had been the dupe. He had assumed that he was the one true love of Thalia De Foe. He almost laughed at his own idiocy, though with bitterness. He was only fit for Bedlam, to sit and giggle among London's mad, and be shown as comic exhibits to visiting London artisans who tormented the lunatics with bits of bread through their bars, like captured animals.

Despondent, feeling more wretched than he had ever done in his life, he pulled Betsy round and rode homeward. Oddly, he found the image of Mehala consoling, which was strange in the circumstances. Especially as he had been used so badly by La De Foe.

He had almost reached home when he realized what course of action Thalia had persuaded him to, when they had lain and loved. The furtherance of Charles Golding, as a parliamentary candidate, to be elected for the Shire. Had that possibly been her scheme all along? Was he even more of a dupe than he supposed?

His spirits slowly rose as Betsy clopped along the dark lanes. The night was not all loss. Nobody knew of his cuckoldry – except of course the loyal Simple Tom. And he was forewarned now. He had met a woman of prodigious beauty, lost a mistress, but gained immeasurably in knowledge as to what ambitions were abroad. The Honourable Charles Golding, cousin to Thalia De Foe, who was mistress to Carradine. The same Carradine, who was by all whispered accounts desperately close to ruin.

Carradine, who wanted – *needed* – power to buffer himself from his accumulating debts.

Carradine, who probably instigated Thalia's acceptance of Hunterfield's advances. Hunterfield began to smart. Were they already laughing at her tales of his simple-mindedness? Was she already pleasing Carradine by telling him that he was twice the lover that the inept and stupid Hunterfield had ever proved himself to be?

Arriving at the Lorne House stables he gave a rueful smile to Simple Tom. The groom made no sign that he had seen anything at all, nor did he vary an inch from the usual ritualized goodnights, merely taking his master's reins and touching his hat in salutation. Hunterfield was moved by the man, the loyal friend who had years ago taught him so much, and who had helped him through his first paces on a horse. He stayed Tom by taking his arm, and smiled.

'Good night, Tom,' he said, patting Tom's shoulder.

The mute groom smiled a wide smile, merry and consolingly bright, and led the horses away.

Hunterfield went indoors almost feeling surprised by life. How extraordinary everything was these modern days! Life seemed filled with the most astonishing events. There was Tom, smiling so cheerfully, full of sympathy and understanding, and almost restoring his master's spirits with a change of expression. And there was that girl, lovely beyond accounting, transformed by a simple candle glow into a goddess of wisdom and perfection, where before he had stupidly only seen a muddy harridan on a seashore. And Thalia De Foe, from being a wonderment of beauty and excitement, was now no more than a scheming trollop, up to heaven-knows-what games of ambition, all for her lover, a sordid gambler in desperate need of profit.

He went and called for a hot brandy posset. He had three, and read one of Letitia's books, by that madman Byron, lately deceased in the Greek wars, until it was midnight.

Then he retired in a mellow mood, wishing he felt wiser at the vagaries of life.

37

'Darling!'

Thalia De Foe was radiant. Before all her best features, nothing could stand in her way. She saw him come through the doors and waved Meg away. The serving woman withdrew from the bedroom, smiling with pleasure for her mistress.

Carradine stood, making Thalia come to him. She advanced confidently, eyes brilliant with gratification, the open-robe she wore in a colourful pink, with a satin petticoat showing in the frontal split. It had no fewer than eleven hemmed frills on the ornamental underskirts and was the height of fashion for both evening and day duty. The result of hours of careful planning. Gathered at her narrow waist, it flared below and parted above at the bodice to show the marginal decorative stitching to its best advantage.

'You came with two whole hours to spare!' she said mischievously, eyes shining up at him. She came against him, moving her body in close for her perfume to tell and excite.

He stood there, motionless, looking down at her. For the first time she felt a faint thrill of unease.

'What is it, Rad?'

The blow spun her round, the room whirling in one mad savage spin as she was knocked part way across the room, tumbling gracelessly to the carpet, her head reeling.

'Bitch,' Carradine said coldly, his voice scarcely audible.

He crossed to the dormant, which Thalia had had built since last he had been in the bedroom suite, and lifted the bottle. He turned to her.

'Sack? What the hell use is that to a man?'

'Rad, darling . . .'

She came to, holding her face, quickly seeing if blood showed as she took her hand away. She sprawled in an ungainly fashion. Her head cleared a little. She gazed at him, unable to believe that this was happening to her. It simply could not be. Carradine was hers. He loved her. She was his adored woman. He had sworn it on innumerable occasions.

'Where's the brandy, woman?'

'It's . . . it's on the loo tables, downstairs, I think.'

'Fine use it's put to there! Ready for a game of lanterloo which will never be played?' He gave a bark of a laugh and poured sherry instead, sank the glassful with a quick lift and poured a second.

'And get up, you bitch. You look ridiculous like that.'

She rose unsteadily, still disbelieving.

'Why did you call me that? And why did you. . . ?'

Her eyes filled with tears. She stood in disarray. He glanced aside, completely losing patience.

'Listen to me, you manipulating cow. I'll tell you this once, and that's all. You understand?'

'Yes, darling.'

'I'll be told what, by no woman on earth. Do you hear what I am saying? *No woman on earth!*'

'Darling, I wasn't trying to do anything except advise you!' She was wailing, pleading with him. 'I've done all the things you asked! I have obtained – '

'Shut up, you stupid bitch.' He went to refill his glass, paused and looked about. 'Where's the table cupboard?'

'I had it removed, darling,' she said anxiously. 'I thought you would be pleased if I had the window space more arranged for opening the curtains to show the morning sun. You know you always like that. The table cupboard used to impede the curtains when they were cast, you see? You yourself remarked on it when last . . . last time you called. Don't you remember?'

'No I don't.' He spoke rudely and shoved past her to where the small side table had been. 'Bring it back. The space looks ridiculous without it.'

'Yes, darling. I shall have it brought back directly. I shall send for the brandy. I have a meal waiting for later, when . . . when you have had time to adjust to coming home.'

'Home!' He gave a sharp laugh, sitting on the wide bed and pushing his feet up on to the head bedstock. 'Home. If only you knew the half!' He rolled his head round to look at the room. 'Can't you get rid of those bloody awful better lamps? I hate those things. They always make my eyes sting.'

'But you liked the betty lamps, darling! I had them brought down from the crusie makers in Edinburgh because you – '

'Get rid of them,' he growled.

'Yes, dear. I shall have candles and lamps instead.'

'About time.'

'And, darling, please.' She sat by the foot of the bed and smoothed his

290

hair. 'I wasn't trying to stir you up, make you come here all the faster, against your wishes. Truly I wasn't. It was that I have so much to tell you. I was hoping against hope you would be in St Edmund's on Sunday. I'm sure I have pleased you, Rad. You know how much I want to do that, darling. It's my purpose. You know it is.'

'Tell me.'

Stroking his hair was always enough to calm him, set him drowsing even. She attended to it, carefully making her gestures repetitive, slow and gentle. His rages weren't his fault, though they always frightened her and she could nearly faint with relief when they were past. He was a child, really, no more than a great child. Like all men, perhaps, but this one more than most. It was simply in his nature to be impetuous, angry, a rebel, his childhood irrascibility and suddennesses still there in spite of his manhood and his great responsibilities. And he was hers. He did not yet know it totally, of course, but that scarcely mattered. She was the repository of his desires, and she knew that was her destiny. She wanted no other. He was all.

'I have gained my cousin Charles's agreement to stand for Parliament.'

'At the next hustings?' He half rose, swivelled to look her in the eye. She smiled, pleased at the effect her news had on him.

'Yes, darling. He is not as keen as he might be, but I have made him determined to come along.'

He sank back with a grunt. 'That's a good girl,' he said as if speaking to a child. 'That is really good news at last, thank God. About time I received some, too.'

She cooed, 'Has my darling had a bad time, in that wicked old city? Has London not appreciated my darling as it should have?'

'Stop that,' he commanded, but he was gentler now, mollified by her ministrations. 'I'm no infant that you talk to me that way.'

'No, darling. You're my great strong man, aren't you, darling?'

'Mmmmh.'

'And I have done what you said about Hunterfield.' This was a shifting sand, and she altered her voice persuasively, hoping he would not pick her up on the subject too closely.

'Hunterfield?' He was awake again, with that startling Hereward-the-Wake immediacy which always alarmed her and made her wonder how long he had been alert. 'What about Hunterfield?'

'Henry Hunterfield will obey your instructions, darling.'

'Which were. . . ?' he prompted, dangerously quiet.

'To support Charles Golding in the hustings, provide necessary funding for briberies and backhanders, so the polls will favour the Golding stand.'

'Hunterfield actually promised that?'

'Offered it to me, darling.'

'Very, very good girl!' Carradine murmured. 'You are clever beyond my expectations. Marvellous news.'

She glowed, stroking his forehead and placing her mouth on the skin, gnawing the brow gently with her teeth.

'Stop that. You're like an animal, a puppy.'

'No.' She was in command now, as she ought to be, until that moment when he imposed his will on hers and she was forced into that surrender which was the sweetest conquest of all.

'You have done superbly, Thalia. I'm more than pleased.'

'And you know I would never, never want to make insistences upon you, don't you, darling?'

'Yes.' He stirred a little. 'Obtained?'

'What, darling?'

'You said you had obtained. . . ?'

'Obtained?' She remembered, in the moment before he had struck her to the floor. 'Obtained, yes. There was a housekeeper which my cousin Charles had procured from somewhere or other. A Mrs Judith Blaker. She had imported a gang of cousins. The estate was rife with them. I had her removed, and have arranged to have another put in her place. One who seems sensible and most capable, and who though only a brief moment in Sealandings is well spoken of. She's reputed to be capable beyond her years.' It did not occur to Thalia to doubt for one moment that matters had not gone absolutely as she had wished, in the matter of a mere servant girl's disposal.

'To what purpose of mine?'

'Respectability, darling! You didn't want your candidate offering himself to the public at a general election with scandal tainting his name, did you?'

'No. That is well thought out.'

She almost purred at his praise. 'And I could see that, what with so many itinerants and hangers-on round the estate, people would begin to resent that Blaker woman's presence. Which would soon set tongues wagging. Which would reduce the effect of Hunterfield's assistance with the polls. Which would lower Charles's chances on the hustings. Which would act against your interests.' She kissed his brow. 'Darling.'

'Clever girl. One thing. The same criticisms could not possibly be levelled at the new housekeeper, then?'

'No. She is some young woman, but without connections. That mad artist seems enamoured of her, since he dashed to paint her face – far too plain, and somewhat coarse, but not without a certain country-bumpkin charm, I grant you – without a by-your-leave.'

'And her name?' *Mehala*, Carradine said inwardly.

'Mehala,' Thalia De Foe said. 'She was fetched from the sea.'

Mehala, Carradine mused. Impresses Alex Waite when simply waiting-on with ale at a tavern. Conquers Sir Jeremy Pacton by doing no more than placing a tankard for him at supper. Has Peter Quilter eating out of her hand when refusing – *refusing!* – to be bedded for what must seem to her a vast sum of money. Torments the odious Prothero into forking out an extra profit of several hundred sovereigns, when the man can have done no more than clap eyes on her once or twice in passing. And setting that demented artist Maderley scrabbling for his colours when merely walking through Sealandings to buy carrots or whatever. And now, practically sight unseen, here she was being thought highly recommendable to a position as housekeeper to a great house, because she was reliable and trustworthy and . . .

This was becoming ominous with portent. He smiled at Thalia.

'This woman. Could she have got another post, I mean other than at Bures House?'

'Indeed. The rector and Miss Euterpe were supposed to be offering one at St Edmund's rectory. And word is that Prothero has offered, by sending Mrs Mary down from Calling Farm. I heard this through Meg yesterday.'

'In spite of competition, you won, eh?'

'Yes, darling.' She was smiling. 'Wasn't that what you wished?'

'It's the way it always must be, darling,' he said, thrilling her.

He swung his legs from the bedstock and stood erect. Quickly she rose, anxiously wondering if he was moving into yet another swift mood. He stood to observe her for a moment.

'Get that stupid dress off,' he said, grabbing her to him and ripping it into its twinned parts down the front.

'What will you do, darling?' she asked, breathlessly complying.

'Anything I damned well want,' he said. 'Come here.'

An hour later he lay back, gazing at the four-poster's ceiling where the red velvet hung in splendour.

Prothero would be a difficulty now, though indeed the woman Mehala was handily placed for a transfer. And that would be simply achieved, with a word from Thalia here. She would see to it that this Mehala was shifted to Prothero's Calling Farm.

The rest of Thalia's news showed a marvellous industry on her part. Excellent. With Golding compliantly doing as he was told in Parliament, the bounds were unconfined for the Carradine ambitions. It looked roses all the way. At last. And not a damned moment too soon. He had had it too hard for too long. Yes, Thalia De Foe had proved a wise investment of time and energy. She repaid effort, like a good and willing mare. As long as she expected no more than she was receiving. He could not afford a breath of scandal attached to his own name, either. And Fellows De Foe was an irritable man who could fly off his calm in short order.

No. Thalia had done well.

But this Mehala. She seemed to be everywhere, yet nowhere. A girl pulled from an ocean was not usually such a mystery. Her memory was faulted, Waite had said the other day at the cock main. Most unusual, but not unknown.

'Here.' He elbowed Thalia awake.

She was sleeping naked. Weals showed on her fair skin where he had raked her with hands and teeth, and a bruise was mousing up under her left eye where he had struck her. She would need to be busy with her powders and unguents to conceal that before she went out in her barouche next morning.

'Yes, darling?'

'Are you all right?' he asked roughly.

She moved experimentally. 'Yes, darling. A bit sore.'

'This Mehala. Why did you pick on her for Golding?'

'She'll be a fine ally, darling. A woman can tell.'

'A fine ally?'

'Yes. I am certain of it. My dear Cousin Charles is easily controlled, but others are not. I thought it wise to install this woman as a means of knowing which politicians were seeking Charles's support. And for what.'

'Good.' Fine ally, bitter foe. Wasn't that the saying? Carradine pondered for a few moments more, then pulled Thalia over and roughly began.

'Gently, darling, if you please,' she murmured.

'Save your breath, woman,' he told her crudely. 'Get about. You have a deal of work to do before the morning.'

38

The child worsened by the hour.

Mrs Darling sat by the fire, occasionally rising to go outside and attend to the wash boiler she operated for other wives in Whitehanger, but for the most part sat observing the child's struggle.

Carmichael sat holding the child's hand.

Twice he had tried to persuade her to drink some fluid, but the closing throat so frightened her that she refused and became only more agitated when he persisted. He ceased the attempts, nodding reassuringly to the little girl.

She was beginning to sweat profusely. The hoarse cough had worsened. Her agitation increased almost by the minute towards midnight.

On three occasions he called for a light to be brought. With the aid of a small lens he managed to see a piece of membrane which Clare had coughed up. It seemed to be ripped away by her exertions, her struggle to breathe. It was a definite membrane in form, but yet came apart quite easily in its wet stickiness on the blood-smeared patch when he pushed it with his fingers.

He had never before been this close or this questing, in contact with a dying child. Sometimes she flailed about, restless and occasionally keening in fright, babbling incoherent snatches of speech in that high resonant shrill voice, as if . . . as if shouting down some tube, perhaps? He remembered as a child, calling sonorous noises of a similar kind down a hollow pipe, a simple draining hollow beneath an earth bridge which joined two fields. It was almost as if the sound was trying to make an echo, somehow a tiny echo of itself.

The distress of the little girl was almost too affecting to watch. When consciousness returned she was terrified throughout each fitful episode of clarity. Increasingly, she entered a stage of delirium whenever the disease carried her mind away from reality.

That membrane which wasn't quite a membrane . . .

Early on, soon after his arrival, he had managed to get the child to drink a little fluid. Only water, but he was mindful of the fact that it would be a long struggle, successful or otherwise, and no child could survive several days without drinking. Food, yes, for the girl was well nourished. But fluid, no. She would die of simple thirst. Yet, terribly, theories came and went in his brain, swirling in great patches of half-remembered notions. Sydenham's ideas of the total lack of value in medical theories came to him in his desperation, that great doctor's convictions that the final causes of diseases must remain outside our knowledge forever, since our human mind is a fallible thing.

And Sydenham, the 'English Hippocrates', dead over a century ago, seemed now, here at the bedside of a child fast entering the terrifying stage of impending death, simply foolish with his notions. That physician was known to practise the art of venesection on everybody, for everything, practically for nothing. Sydenham's Liquid Opiate was a famous therapy, of course, and it did not become a humble country doctor to contradict so learned a man. Yet . . .

Carmichael mopped the child's brow. She was twisting, her chest creaking almost with exertion as she tried to draw in air. Her cheeks were now pale, now almost blue. Asphyxiation was setting in. This came episodically, a burst of breathing in that strange thick sound, then a struggle, with the limbs flailing in the spasm, as if the action might assist the indrawing of breath.

He looked at his sick syphon. He had cleaned it with boiled water and straws, and drawn through candle-wicks to ensure its patency. The nipple shield was useless now, for he would never have time to pierce the metal and affix the syphon through its centre into an immovable position.

And in any case it was hopeless. The child was dying. That could no longer be in doubt.

'The lanthorn, please, Mrs Darling.'

'Yes, Doctor.'

He crossed to the fire with the lanthorn. He carried a watch glass in his pocket for the purpose, and slipped the membrane from its bloodstained slither of purulent saliva – it wasn't even mucus, for God's sake. What the hell was it?

He tried to shove the membranous piece along the surface of the watch glass. It fragmented into small flakes. It was definitely *not* a true membrane. Definitely not a tissue in its own right. So it was not, of itself, the impediment to breathing. It alone was not the obstruction. It simply couldn't be. It was a layer of something, but something which could be broken and divided. In fact, which almost dissolved itself once handled.

It alone could not stop a tube being shoved through the throat. *Nor could it block a metal tube.*

His hand was shaking as he returned to the child. The little girl was almost convulsing now. Her face showed that awful lividity which had preceded death in her little brother's case.

Was the membrane really a secretion which, by its presence, thickened into this patchy lining and so suffocated a sufferer?

He stood over the bed, looking down. He was afraid of trying to reason, for all his thoughts were now urging him to act, to try, to risk. His innate caution and training cried him back. But that sound . . .

Little Clare's breath whistled, gagged, choked.

And whistled.

Her back arched in a convulsion. She was livid, her face almost puce with distress. Her small frame was drenched in sweat. She had soiled the sheet. Her struggle to breathe was terrifying. Mrs Darling was silently weeping, trying to hold the child and console, calm, still her. And he was standing there.

That whistle. *It was the same sound,* as Mehala had said. The very same. Now the child was gurgling, breathing with that shrill whistle but gurgling. And suddenly he remembered. 'Crying cockle'! That was it! The slang which meant death by hanging, from the strangulated noise the poor condemned souls made as they struggled for a last breath on the public scaffold. The last inhalation. It was the sound of cattle as they died when their throats were cut. It was the sound of breath through a narrowed windpipe. It had to be.

'Mrs Darling,' he said, shakily taking out all the instruments from his bag and laying them on the parlour table. 'I am to tell you that Clare is passing away. I want to try a surgery which might assist her breathing. I do not know if it will manage to, but I hope so.'

'Oh, Doctor! What will happen?'

The poor woman was beside herself.

'I must try,' he said. He was disgusted with his voice, his lack of resolve. It was as if he were asking the suffering woman for permission, asking for her approval even, to take the reponsibility he himself would not shoulder. He despised himself.

'Mrs Darling. With what I am about to attempt, Clare may still die. But she is passing away, and we will lose her within the half hour. That is true, as God's my judge. I have to do this, madam. Please assist me.'

'What must you do, Doctor?'

She was holding the child in her arms as the little girl flailed and struggled. Astonishing that there was no external sign of inflammation or lesion, that the throat was the same now in appearance as it was in normal healthy states. But the lesion was in the moist warm interior, the throat was somehow definitely closing.

'Take away those pillows,' he said. 'Uncover her. I need all light, and any spare cloths you possess.'

'Yes. But . . .'

'Hurry, Mrs Darling. I fear delay will mean there will be no need of haste.'

He tried to conceal the trembling of his hands. He realized – absurd, at this juncture – that he had not eaten for some time. Ridiculous to prepare instruments, thought, theories, and to put the man in default. A sense of hopelessness enveloped him, but he laid the little girl flat, pulling her down the bed so he had room to move. He dragged the bed away from the wall, and threw off his spencer, hurrying now.

The child's pulse was thready, feeble yet faster than he had ever felt one throb. The whistling was now episodic, a distant piping. He reached and felt for the throat. It was smooth, drenched with sweat. Too slippery. He dried the skin with part of the bedsheet, having to be rough as the child convulsed. It seemed nothing more than a desperate effort on the little girl's part to draw breath. Well, he would at least see she did not die of asphyxiation.

Lancet. The sick syphon, inverted, to thrust down the trachea – if he could find it in the tissues of the throat. God knows what struggles he would have to keep the child still if she regained consciousness to find a doctor piercing her throat with metal.

'Mrs Darling. Keep Clare still at all costs. You hear me?'

'Still,' the mother repeated, eyes glassy at the horror of it all.

'I am attempting to give Clare a new way of breathing, to stay her passing. *You must help*. You need not look. Just keep her head still, and her arms and hands from my work. That must be done at all costs, or we shall lose the child instantly. You understand? Head, arms, hands.'

'Yes. I shall try.'

The woman was resolute, and came quickly round the other side of the bed to stand where he indicated with a nod. She took position, kissing the sick child instinctively as she crooned and talked softly to her. Wisely she passed the child's right arm beneath her body, that the weight of the girl's frame might hold that limb, and leaned over the bed, her own breast against the child's face as if about to breast-feed.

Marvellous what women know by instinct, Carmichael thought wearily. If I had only a tenth of their natural understanding, all my theories and teaching could go hang.

He stared for a second, returned to the table where he had placed his instruments. The sick syphon, the nipple shield, a phlebotome, two lancets, a long suture needle, and a few small saws for amputations. And himself. Not much.

Temptation struck: should he even now leave her, let her take her own chance? He was so tired, so ashamed of his ignorance.

He had never even seen a human throat cut at the low point of the larynx. He had witnessed the dissection of one cadaver, and that was all. It had been a gruesome display of crude expertise in the hospital teaching theatre, with the doctor lecturing from a high stool and the students, including himself, crowding round to catch glimpses of the abdomen's internal structures and organs.

'Doctor!' It was a quiet wail from the mother.

He turned. The child was now moribund. The whistling was fading, the body arcing in convulsions which were becoming more feeble. How long had he remained standing here? He took up the lancet, a small dish, four cloths, and stepped to the bed. He knelt, his shirt sleeves rolled back. He too was drenched with sweat, as bad as little Clare.

May God help me, he thought. He felt the prominence of the thyroid cartilage, the slender thinner ring of the cricoid circle below. Two arteries ran there, asplay the median line, so any incision would have to be exactly in the midline, or . . .

'Turn away, Mother,' he said gently, and placed the lancet between the two fingers of his left hand, its blade touching the skin. Midline. He cut down, astonished at the ease with which the blade parted the tissues. Not much bleeding. But he laid the knife aside and swept a linen piece over the wound.

He was astonished to see the dark blue vein on one side. For a second his heart leapt in anguish – had he cut the vein which drained from there into the greater ones beneath? But it did not seem so. It was intact. He tasted salt on his tongue, his sweat running down his lip into his mouth. A white sliver of some tissue ran down obliquely from the exposed area, but from his meagre anatomy studies he could not recall what the thing was. Nerve? Tendon? The origin of some small muscle?

The fascia below parted with another cut. He was having difficulty keeping the lips of the slit apart, using the fingers of his left hand thus, but he could think of no other way. He really needed some assistance, but the mother was doing well to keep the child still enough for him to continue.

He decided to keep the point and cutting edge of the lancet pointing up, turning it away from the areas below. God knows what complexities of structure lay down there. The substance seemed pinkish now, overlain by a fascia layer, thin and faintly sheening with an opalescence he had never seen before. Was this the honest appearance of the inner areas of the neck? Or was this the result of the croup, spreading interiorly and changing the organs and tissues as it extended its malign influence?

Cut, again upwards. And another incision. To his astonishment he saw the trachea appear between his fingers. He was so amazed he almost let go, and consciously had to force the two fingers of his left hand to stay in position. They were almost stiff from cramp and effort, but they had to remain there, splaying the margins of the wound apart. He had to get on. No way to turn back now. He would have to enter the trachea. But where? And how?

Walking along the trackway to Whitehanger, he had never stopped fingering his own throat, measuring distances against the lengths of his fingers like an obstetrician, judging the depths and the lengths of the trachea. Of course the sick child's was that much smaller. And he was unsure of the distances of the great vessels from where he was working. The blood was seeping faster now. Thank God he had not cut across some artery, though he could see one clearly, flicking its sharp pulse along its shining length beneath his left forefinger.

No time to wonder vaguely where it ran, from where, what areas it served.

He looked round for the sick syphon. For one awful moment he though the had mislaid it, but there it was, on the table which he had dragged close. He took it, almost puzzling at its weight. He flipped open the cover of the stouter end and measured the length against the child's trachea. It would go. No doubt about that. Yet what was the size of the lumen inside the trachea of a girl this size? Was it sufficiently wide to. . .? He didn't even know a child's normal anatomy.

Damn it, he thought. His hand was quivering as it lifted the lancet. One ring of the trachea would not suffice. Two? Or, if he made a slit through three rings of the trachea, was the tissue strong enough to remain intact? Or would it split along its length, as some woods and grasses did once the stem was cut into?

He placed the tip of the lancet, cutting blade uppermost, against the upper ring of the trachea, and cut. It was hard. *Hard!* Whoever would have thought it? As hard in its formed state as the throat rings of the bullock he had examined.

He felt the child heave in a terrible spasm, the convulsion nearly knocking the lancet from his hand. He gripped the handle and cut through the second ring, again an upward cut. And the third.

The blood was starting in earnest now, and he had to wipe the wound twice with the linens to see where he was. The syphon was to hand. He shoved it firmly into the wound, through the vertical slit in the trachea, and let the curve of the syphon follow the line of the windpipe. A gust of appalling stench blew into his face.

And the whistling stopped.

Instantly.

The fetor rushed from the wound. He gagged, almost retching at the stink, but kept his grip on the wound, watching. The air was rushing into the syphon. It halted, and he felt a moment's panic. But then the chest moved, and the stench came rushing out.

The child was merely breathing. In and out.

He knelt there, holding the metal tube in the throat wound he had created. The convulsions were lessening, stopping even as he watched. She lay still, flaccid in her mother's arms.

'Doctor? Has she gone?'

'Mmmmh?' He collected his thoughts at Mrs Darling's fearful question. 'No. Not yet.'

What was he to do now? He knew nothing about the disease from this point on. Or of his treatment, either. The child's colour was returning. That terrible bluish tinge was fading, leaving her lips. The dreadful ghastliness of her frantic efforts to breathe had gone.

She seemed to be slipping into a vale of peace, here on the shambled bed. Or was this the death which she had so long struggled to avoid? Was this merely a different sort of death, one which he himself had engendered? He felt an utter loathing at his own ignorance.

He was terrified of letting go of the instrument. He stayed kneeling as the child's agitation lessened and dwindled into sleep. The air whistled in and out of the tube he was holding.

'Doctor?'

The mother's mouth was moving. He saw the lips move, even heard the gentle tone. He felt his head shake in a negative. Do not hope. Not yet.

She was still, clutching her child as he had instructed. She would stay thus until Doomsday, with that natural ease women possessed somehow, proof against all bodily ailments as long as the child was being helped.

Aches began, however, in him. His knees hurt, his back was stiffening. His hands were almost in tetany, spasm paining his fingers where they still held the wound open. What had that French doctor done at this stage? Simply gone home? Or was there some second stage

301

to the proceeding which he had not revealed? He felt hopelessness return with leg cramps. He was becoming giddy.

The fourth and last linen was to hand. This open wound was a risk, almost as much as the diphtheritis itself. Honey? He had heard that sworn by, during his studies, but that was also a danger. Treatment killed as much as cured.

He felt sickened himself at the misery of the entire art. Learning was a waste.

The pulse. At least he could take the pulse without injuring the sick child more than he already had. He moved his right hand, found the child's arm beneath her, and fumbled along the wrist. The pulse was there still, and possibly . . . stronger? It definitely was slower. He hardly dared hope. Definitely still there. And was it truly slower?

How marvellous it would be to afford a watch! But that expense was out of the question. He dreamt sometimes of owning one, a genuine timepiece which gave unfailing time, like the ones for which the Admiralty had offered vast rewards.

And now for absolute certain it was slower. Faster than that of a healthy child, but steadying. No extra beats. Increased in strength? He tried to stop thinking.

He stirred, shifted his position.

'Mother,' he whispered.

'Yes, Doctor?'

'Have you any form of timepiece? Or an hour glass?'

'Yes. Hour glass. There.' She indicated a position on the mantel.

'No. Do not move, please.' He straightened his back, settled again. 'Have you help among the neighbours?'

'Yes. A cousin should be along presently, to help with the . . . with . . .' With the laying-out of the child, once she was dead. By prior arrangement, he thought bitterly. So sure were they of his doctoral skill.

'How long have I been here?'

'It is two hours or more gone since you took the knife to Clare, Doctor.'

'Two hours?' It was impossible. Time did not fly so fast.

It could not be. The child should have died ninety minutes since if the woman was right.

But the sweat was drying on Clare's face. It was pale, and had not taken on that terrible waxen glow which he had seen all too often as a child's body had cooled in death.

She was still alive.

302

It was at least another full hour before a knock sounded and a woman slipped into the room.

Carmichael pursed his lips, shushing her.

'Please bring the hour glass within reach.'

The woman did so, placing it on the table properly with a candle behind. It was a handsome piece, mahogany, with an original Turks-head collar on the blown glass for proper function. Of course, Carmichael remembered, Darling was a waggoner who worked mostly for Squire Hunterfield at Lorne House's estate. Perhaps this grand piece was some token of esteem for loyal service.

'Now,' he said. The woman inverted the hour glass and the sand began to run.

Frankly, Ven Carmichael felt at a loss. He was practically turned to stone in this kneeling position. What if he let go of the child, let go of the syphon? Would it stay there? What if the child convulsed again? What if the delirium returned? Yet the child seemed simply sleeping. It was almost like a genuine catapausis, a respite from the resolution of uneasy tumours.

'Mrs Darling,' he said quietly. 'This lady. . . ?'

'My cousin, from here in Whitehanger, Doctor.' Emiline Darling whispered the words, holding her position cradling the sick child. 'Mrs Overton.'

'Could you ask her to do several things?' he whispered. 'First, to get my hat over here.'

'You won't leave us, Doctor?' The mother was frightened at the thought.

He shook his head impatiently. 'I'll not leave you, Mrs Darling. I have already promised. Only I must stay and hold this tube, to give the child a chance to rally. It may not come, but we must pray so. The hat, please.'

'Winifred,' Mrs Darling said in compliance.

Mrs Overton brought the hat to the bedside and laid it down.

'Now some water, please. Warmed. That from the kettle on the hob will suffice. Have you a small jug?'

'No, Doctor. But a large one I keep for the milk.'

'That will not do. Mrs Overton?'

'I can get one from a neighbour, if you please.'

'Try, and soon.'

He could get some fluid into the child, he was almost certain. His confidence stemmed from his only period of practice after qualification in London. The old doctor had been a reprobate, a fraud if ever there

303

was one. Drunk twice a day on any alcoholic liquid available, yet he had taught his young assistant one valuable procedure.

'It's the doctor's one use, boy,' the old man had wheezed, mopping food from his cravat. 'And God alone knows we're hard pushed to find even one purpose that does any good to poor suffering humanity! Catheterismus is our one golden function, for as God makes cheeses we have no other!'

He had demonstrated the procedure, intruding the catheter into an old gentleman who was suffering from stoppage of the urine. Old Doctor Arbuthnot had the most amazing dexterity at the art, and slipped the catheter in with astonishing facility.

'It is simply the passage of a tube into an orifice, boy, and it pays handsomely. The gentleman is able to pee again, and I go away a sovereign the richer. And I am thus highly recommended by this old soak to the rest of his fraternity.'

The young Doctor Carmichael had paid no less than three whole sovereigns and contributed a whole month's extra unpaid work to be shown the trick of catheterismus. The gum elastic catheter, was always on his person and had never yet been used.

Fat old Dr Arbuthnot had wheezed one last bit of advice, chuckling weightily as he had uttered the pronouncement. 'And always remember this, my boy. Keep your catheter with you, for those old buzzards who obstruct in their natural passages can pop off this earth quick as you please. Always have it with you, and you'll get yourself paid on the nail, so relieved are they.'

He had interrupted himself to take a swill of brandy and coughed himself bleary-eyed before continuing the lesson.

'You know how to tell the only difference between a doctor and an apothecary, boy? The doctor's got a catheter coiled inside his hat!' And had laughed himself almost into apoplexy.

Well, Ven Carmichael reasoned, the throat swallowed food in quantities. Where solid matter could go, so could a gum elastic instrument, passed gently through the mouth, or maybe the nose. It would be worth a try, though he had never seen it done.

Winifred Overton returned in breathless silence, carrying the small jug.

She made up the fire, re-set new candles and positioned the lanthorn to best effect. All Whitehanger's cottages must have been raided, judging by the weight of candles she had fetched.

The child hardly stirred. Carmichael removed the catheter one-handed from the hat, flicked it to straighten its length, then asked for some butter to make it slippy. He was so apprehensive of letting go of the breathing tube that he became clumsy, and had to ask Mrs Overton to smooth a little butter on a piece of linen and hold it just so while he trailed the gum elastic across the cloth.

He had the two women take position and hold the child's limbs. 'Stay still, and turn away both, please.'

They might shriek alarm, or refuse to help if they saw the nature of his interference. That would be the end. He passed the catheter inside the nostril gently, using only one hand, his other still gripping the precious syphon.

The child stirred, stayed, was crooned to and murmured at, and stayed motionless. It was as if the intrusion had never taken place. Yet there she lay, still in her mother's arms, with the catheter projecting five, maybe six, inches above her lips.

'Pour in some warm water, Mrs Overton.'

It entered a little only, much being spilled on their arms. During the administration, the sick child gave a single convulsion and he feared that he had misdirected the point into the bronchus, but she as quickly stilled. They managed to get perhaps two fluid ounces into her stomach.

He stayed, kneeling by the bedside in that incongruous position, head bowed and no longer looking at the recumbent child. She was sleeping, and to all appearances it was a simple unhindered sleep. Now he had no spare hand wherewith to feel the pulse, for he could not leave go of syphon or catheter, not knowing what would transpire if either became dislodged.

'You may rest now,' he said to Mrs Darling. 'Let Mrs Overton take your place.'

'No, thank you, Doctor. I shall stay. Winifred can brew a little tea, if you please.'

'Thank you.'

'Shall you stay on, Doctor?' Mrs Darling asked.

'I'm here, Mother,' he said. 'Don't keep asking that. It vexes me.' Then added, clumsily attempting humour, 'In fact I think I shall be here for life. I cannot move, having lost the facility.' Neither woman smiled. Both nodded a quick acknowledgement.

He kept grip on the instruments in the child's throat, and stayed still. At all costs do nothing, he told himself. Do not sleep. Do not move. Above all do not relax the fingers for an instant. There must be no rest.

He remembered to ask how many inversions of the hour glass there had been since Mrs Overton's arrival. He was told four. Four hours? It seemed impossible. Why was time not slowing, to help the child?

39

Some hours into the night Mrs Overton whispered Carmichael awake. He shot into consciousness, his hands all but immovable now on the instruments at the child's throat.

'Doctor. Clare. See?'

Clare's eyes were open. He could see the glint in the firelight.

'Clare?' he said. 'Don't try to speak, pretty. Just stay still.'

The child moved her lips soundlessly. He was bemused, not knowing if his caution was necessary or not. Could a person speak at all, with a tube through their trachea as a separate airway? Which way did the voice-breath go? What happened anyway, to the perforated larynx? He needed a few moments to recover, to relieve himself, recover the skill of movement in his frozen limbs.

'Am I dead?'

He recognized the words from the shapes made by her lips.

'No, sweet,' he said, smiling. He heard the women weeping and exclaiming quietly. 'You're here, with your mother, Auntie Winifred, and me.'

'Hello, love.' Mrs Darling came round the bedside, holding the child again. 'You're still with us.'

'Mrs Darling. I need to make . . . certain adjustments to the tubes in a short while, I fear. This requires assistance. I shall need help to be brought.'

He had made up his mind during the vigil. He would send for somebody more at the soonest opportunity. This seemed to be the moment.

'Who, Doctor?'

'I want a message taken to the rectory. Someone is to ask Miss Euterpe there, and say would she please be so kind as to make her way here, if at all possible, to assist me for a short time. Please impress upon her the serious nature of my request, and urge her no delay.'

'I shall have one of the tavern boys away in an instant, Doctor.'

He heard movement, a man's voice outside, and guessed that the father Jake Darling had returned and was waiting outside the cottage with his friends. Horse's hooves beat, and someone ran calling out which road to take.

'Can we clear up the bed, Doctor?' Mrs Darling asked.

'Not yet, Mrs Darling. I will say when that can be done shortly.'

Carmichael knew what she was thinking. Emiline Darling was naturally apprehensive, even in these circumstances, of receiving a strange woman into her home with the child's bed messed and stinking, and the fetor of the child's breath adding to the miasma.

More than ever he was conscious of his own failings. The child had a right to guidance, some instructions, but was likely to receive none from him in his abysmal state of bewilderment. For he remained in ignorance of exactly what he had done. How he had done it, yes. He could repeat the same procedure on another child, he hoped. But why, what mechanisms had operated, he was at a loss to explain.

The tragedy was that he did not know now what to do, any more than he had at the beginning. Then, his desperation and grief at the child's plight had driven him to act. Now, he was baffled, exhausted to the point of dementia himself, almost. Twice he had imagined himself back in his home, talking with his mother and laughing at some antic of his brother. Several times he had caught himself muttering explanations to his father, and once had actually seen his own father, long since passed away, in his rocking chair before the fire singing a country song.

And had actually caught himself joining in with the alto part, singing along gently while his father nodded and smiled, and the shadow of the rocking chair on the cottage wall had swung to and fro, to and fro . . .

'Doctor.'

'Yes, Mrs Darling?'

'I'm sorry, sir. They are returned.'

'Returned?' Who? He bethought himself, and pronounced carefully, 'Ah, yes. Very well. Miss Euterpe is brought, then?'

'No, Doctor. She is not with them. But the girl is come, who stayed at the inn when brought from the sea.'

He roused himself wearily. He should have known it. Now that she had come, it seemed inevitable. He should have recognized there was no means of evading what will be.

'Mehala?' he said.

'Yes, Doctor. It's she. May she come?'

'If you please,' he said. 'I need her now.'

Mehala stepped over the threshold. Her expression was bright and alert, and betrayed none of her inner revulsion as she met the stench of the dark interior. 'Doctor Carmichael?' she said quietly.

'Yes, Mehala. Here, if you please.'

He was kneeling, half-hunched in a strange posture, over the form of a dozing child. His hands were fixed around two tubes. One, a sick syphon, she recognized, but it led from his fingers into the child's neck. It made a soft shushing noise as the little girl on the bed breathed, the air seeming to enter and leave through its opening with a muted hiss. The other was worm-shaped, and came from the child's nostril. The bed stank. Ordure and urine smeared the sheet. The sick child was a mess, her legs and waist smeared and fouled. Her neck was bloody, the doctor's hands encrusted with darkened dried blood.

'What must I do?'

'First of all, I want you to help Mrs Darling and her cousin to clean the bed, please. With great care. I am sorry. Then I shall want you to take a hold of these two instruments for me, in exactly the same position as I. Take your time.'

The women set to, manoeuvring the sheet away and washing Clare slowly. A clean sheet was brought, and blankets. A pallet was fetched downstairs to replace the soiled one.

'Can we open the windows, Doctor?'

Weary, he bent his head. He simply did not know. Could fresh air do damage to a child in Clare's condition? Was there some dreadful miasma out there which should be prevented from gaining access? Should a separate entrance into her windpipe this way be exposed to new air? Or was only used air safe?

'I am unsure,' he confessed. 'As long as she is kept from chill this way, let her stay so.'

Clare's pulse was steady now. She opened her eyes as often as she slept, and twice had asked for a drink in silent speech. He had allowed trickles down the catheter, and told them to moisten her lips with drops from the fingers.

Mehala came round behind him. He tried to edge away to give room, and almost screeched as his limbs shot agony through him. He groaned involuntarily with each attempt, finally settled for explaining to Mehala what he wanted her to do, and letting her take over his grips on the tubes, before rolling aside to the floor in a slow helpless tumble.

She was talking softly to Clare as he finally managed to stand erect, ashamed of needing the aid of the two other women.

'I apologize, Mrs Darling,' he said. 'Mrs Overton. I fear I cannot move very far for the moment. If I might sit, please . . .'

They found a chair for him, and brought him tea and some caudle. His hands seemed sclerosed, swollen to twice their normal size, blotched and reddened with immobility. His elbows and knees felt the same.

'How long is this now, Mrs Overton?'

'Eighteen hours, Doctor.'

'That long, is it,' he said, nodding gravely as if that was only to be expected, and that his measurements of the child's condition had somehow come out right. 'Is this accurate?' He indicated the hour glass.

'Yes, Doctor. It is very fine for time.'

'I'm sure it is,' he said courteously, managing slowly to stand up with the aid of Mrs Overton, and stretching his arms.

The timepiece stood on the table. The greened leather base which supported the bulb of the glass was etched with a monogram. It caught the light in a sudden flare from the grate. HH, he saw in the leather beneath the bulb. The glass had just been inverted, so little sand covered the base. And . . . UT CERVUS showed in the surround. Some family motto perhaps? The Darlings might once have been well connected, or the thing was a gift from some eminent personage.

He checked that Mehala was positioned correctly and had the right grip of the instruments at Clare's throat, then slowly lumbered from the cottage, feeling a hundred years old. He was astonished to see that it was day. A fine rain was falling. The small garden plot was well cultivated, vegetables and two fruit trees showing neat industry on Jake Darling's part.

With difficulty he walked down the garden path to the petty, and used it with occasional groans as his limbs complained. He was able to inspect his joints. They were bulbous, as of an old man's ruined by arthritis. His hands simply refused to obey him. He took almost half an hour doing up the latches of his trousers.

Outside, he was able to breathe the clean air, and wash his hands in the rain cask there. He saw a small group of neighbours from Whitehanger gathered about the cottage door, eyeing him in silence. He knew only too well of the distrust which existed between the folk of Whitehanger and Sealandings, so he did no more than nod ageeably to them, and walked about the garden a little to regain the use of his aching body.

None of them responded, though Jake Darling was absent, which might have accounted for their suspicious stares.

He entered the cottage, pausing by the door to adjust his sight.

Mehala was kneeling there as he had left her. Her hair fell in lustrous waves down her back. It glistened in small lights from the rain still, and russet glows streaked through its dark waves. She was truly lovely. Her hands, strong and brown, were in contrast to the hands of a lady, for those should be kept white and unsullied by work. But her pose was one almost of repose, and as he looked he saw Mrs Darling, on the opposite side of the bed, look at Mehala and smile, mouthing some comment about her sick child.

'Doctor will know, Mrs Darling,' Mehala was answering softly. 'We must ask him, but not yet. Only presently.'

He cleared his throat and stepped forward. 'I shall need your assistance, Mehala. Please stay thus while I impose stitches through the long tube.'

'Very well, Doctor.'

He had spoken more brusquely than he had intended. He recognized Mehala's tactics, to be kind in allowing him a little longer to recover before returning to his obligations. For some reason he was irritated by her immediate understanding.

The sutures were simple twine. He fixed the round-bodied needle into a small blob of wax, and inexpertly threaded it. Standing to the bedside, he passed a suture through the free end of the catheter and tied it round Clare's head firmly.

'That should keep it from slipping in, or from coming free,' he said, straightening. 'Which gives us one more hand free among us all. You can give Clare a little broth, very clear, Mrs Darling. As before, down the smaller tube, but taking care of the throat syphon.'

He sat and watched them feed Clare, seeing with satisfaction the way the child responded. He felt he should express gratitude to Mehala for coming in place of Miss Euterpe, but was too stubborn to unbend and speak out. He was still in ignorance of what to do. He needed rest, food, some time to think alone, even if only for a few moments.

Someone was shaking his shoulder.

'Doctor, if you please.'

A small bowl of caudle was placed into his hands. Mechanically he started to sup from it.

'White wine, water, and almonds ground to paste, with cinnamon and a little nutmeg.' Mrs Darling stood back. 'It is made with best, Doctor.'

'Thank you, Mrs Darling.'

'Doctor?' Mehala said. 'What was it, if I may, that you wished from the blacksmith's? I apologize for asking so, but I was told by one of the servants at the Donkey and Buskin that you came almost a-running from there, and that Mr Temple called after you but you did not heed.'

'Temple?' Carmichael racked his brains, 'Oh. Yes. I recall, I wanted an instrument made.'

'And he was not able to furnish it for you?'

'Not in time.'

'For this?' she persisted. He looked up in sudden irritation, but she was still there, fixed in her position, holding the throat syphon and not taking her eyes from it.

'Yes. I had no time.'

'Would . . . Could I oblige, Doctor?'

'Oblige? How?'

'Could I obtain an instrument for you, in a fashion you could devise? I think that perhaps I could persuade someone to make one.'

'I have no . . .' He coughed, cleared this throat, finished the caudle and placed the bowl down on the table. He could not speak of money, not here in this suffering family's cottage. '. . . No need of it now, not really.'

'May I try, Doctor?'

He thought for a while. If she could obtain an instrument, made as he had wished, he would have two hands free for the moment when, if Clare continued to improve, he would be somehow needed to close the throat wound, try to return her breathing to normal.

'Could you?'

'I might be able to, Doctor.'

He decided suddenly. 'Give me a few moments, Mehala. I shall exercise, and then resume charge. I shall draw the instrument, and give you a wax model. Take them with you, please.'

An hour later he was kneeling by Clare's bedside in his old position, holding the throat tube steady as the child slept and her pulse grew stronger and the day started to lengthen.

Three hours afterwards Mehala returned, and took over from him at the bedside without a word. Carmichael sat in a chair by the bedside and slept fitfully.

At eight o'clock that evening Richard Bettany, apprentice to the clockmaker Veriker, arrived at the Darling cottage, to deliver a silver tube, flanged with a fenestrated extension both sides of its wider aperture. The doctor received it in silence and took it to the table to examine by candlelight. It was beautifully made, and almost as well finished. He dismissed the young apprentice with a word of thanks, observing in silence the radiant smile which Mehala gave the lad.

Carmichael was too frightened of the unknown consequences of replacing the syphon, so he laid aside the new instrument and instead passed a twine suture through the syphon's perforated cover, leaving

312

that in the open position still. That meant he was able to tie the twine loosely to a ribbon passed round the child's neck, as a collar to hold it in place. She no longer was delirious, and slept almost continuously.

He stood, and the three women with him. Clare was looking up, almost wide awake now. How long was it since the start of the disease? He no longer knew, or cared. He shook his head when Mrs Overton made to invert the splendid hour glass as it reached its pause.

'No need now, I think,' he said.

They seemed to be waiting. He shrugged, with yet more ache, and gazed round at them all.

'I think she may live,' he said. The words were an astonishment to him. He smiled, nodded. 'I honestly think she may.'

40

The letter from Letitia Hunterfield to William Maderley came as a surprise to the family. It was especially pleasing to Olivia, who was becoming conscious of time's swift passing without any signs of activity from her mother on her behalf.

With great excitement, she demanded to see the letter and was furious when her brother demurred and showed signs of shyness.

'But you will go, William?' Olivia cried, in horror at the very idea of refusal.

'It's so strange a request, Olivia, I'm not at all sure.'

'Mother!' Olivia appealed in anguish. 'You will surely make him?'

'Now, Olivia,' Mrs Maderely said, trying to keep the peace. 'This is not a usual approach, as from one family to another in this neighbourhood. This is Squire Hunterfield's family, making a specific request – '

'So?' Olivia shrieked, almost beside herself. 'So? Isn't this what William has always dreamed of? A genuine invitation – nay, *request!* – to attend on the squire's own sister! With a view to commissions in the best and . . . What does it say?' She seized the letter, to her mother's indignation, and perused it eagerly. 'You see, Mother? With a view to presenting the artist with commissions for portraiture executed in the very best and most artistic manner appropriate to the modern times!'

She was in awe, and stood transfixed, glowing at the imagery flitting through her mind.

'That my brother should be so summoned! And to Lorne House! *Personally!* Squire himself has clearly given approval! It's . . . it's marvellous, William! Why, Squire Hunterfield could have asked anyone in London, from the Royal Academy! And instead he chooses you!'

Her brother frowned, uncomfortable and undecided. 'It's not that simple, Olivia. Paintings are personal and peculiar things, each with a life of its own – '

'Oh, tosh!' Olivia said, pacing and sweeping her trailing gown aside in her agitation. This was so demonstrative an act that Mrs Maderley was finally forced to act.

'Don't you dare show your temper in that fashion, miss!' she scolded. 'And especially not in front of your brother, if you please!'

'Oh, Mother – !'

'Oh Mother nothing, miss!' Mrs Maderley cried in anger. 'And do not answer back! You have already shown yourself in serious breach of good manners by snatching – not too strong a term, miss! – *snatching* I say your brother's letter from his hand without so much as a by-your-leave! And then to read it out in open family without permission! It is an unthinkable transgression. What your sainted father would say I cannot imagine! And now you use abusive words in the parlour, to no gain except liberation of your temper's silliness. I want an apology, and so will your brother.'

'I am sorry, Mother. And I do so apologize, William.' Olivia fidgeted in despair. 'Please accept my regret. I promise to adhere to proper address.'

'Very well, Olivia,' her mother said coldly.

She suspected Olivia's interest in Lorne House was more than the furtherance of her brother's ambition as an artist. News was that Sir Trev Bunyan was about to arrive soon, in the cause of the great ball soon to take place at Milton Hall. Which doubtless meant several more innocent rides past the tide mill of a morning, with Sir Trev casting glances at Watermillock during his tardy passage, and more of Olivia's eager attention to her embroidery, prominent by the bay window with the curtaining pulled shamelessly wide for all the world to peer in.

'William,' Olivia pleaded. 'You won't decline this invitation?'

'The trouble is, I don't know what is expected of me,' he confessed. 'I have never before undertaken a commission.'

'You have, William!' Olivia urged. 'Don't you remember? You painted that horse picture, of the canal on the Stour, by the undershot mill. And then two more, of Wivenhoe House, and one of Bergholt. It was a splendid achievement!'

'Don't please force him against his will, Olivia.'

'I do not think I am doing so, Mother,' Olivia answered carefully. 'But he has so often spoken about his dreams in this direction. To gain a huge commission! From a county family, at that! One which might make his name among many more famous painters! I suggest that our William could do worse than attend on Miss Letitia and inquire as to the purpose and extent of the commission.'

'What if it is beyond my feelings, Olivia?' William asked.

Olivia pretended to consider, though she felt like screaming out in frustration. His course of action was all so obvious! 'Why, William! Then you express regret and offer suggestions as to where they could possibly procure the services of another artist. Is that not fair? And surely it is in the interests of the whole art of portraiture to just consider the proposal?'

'Do you think so?' William's doubts were not allayed.

'Of course I do!' Olivia could have wrung his neck for obstinacy, though in cooler moments she worried for his timidity and gentleness. 'How often have we deplored the way people take artists for granted, Will? How many times have you complained that artistic societies are in the doldrums, here in East Anglia, and do so little to further the progress of the pictorial arts?'

'What will this small commission do, though?' He took the letter to the window and read it again, turning it over as if hoping to find some information he had missed. 'I am an unknown. I have as yet done nothing. I am a local dauber, as far as they know at Lorne House.'

'But they obviously act on advice taken! They surely have not simply picked your name from a hat, William! They must have seen one or two of your pictures somewhere. You have done several. So many, in fact. Please do remember that the Hunterfields have connections inland. Why they have probably written to ask for opinion! And remember that Squire Hunterfield is a magistrate, with connections among many other families of the nobility. Who knows what they have said to each other in one of the squire's visits? He is possibly an ardent admirer of your works!'

'That's quite impossible, Olivia. I have done so little.'

'Then how came this here?' Olivia pointed to the letter.

Her brother remained silent. He worried that it was a simple device to somehow bring himself in closer proximity to Miss Letitia. The affinity between himself and that lady was undoubtedly strong. It was more painful than endearing, for he had begun to despair of having the chance to establish contact with her in proper surroundings, where they could talk and learn about each other. Now, though, for some reason he could not quite fathom, his intensity for Letitia had suddenly lessened somewhat. Naturally he was still ardent, and was convinced that, should opportunity present, he would even make a proposition to her that would be the firmest any man ever could. Yet lately he had weakened towards her.

The reason, he believed, was that he lacked opportunity. Absence does not make the heart grow fonder. It dilutes, makes indolent, causes a loss of ardour where before there had been nothing but yearning. How many times had he blamed the separation of the classes, that gulf which caused him to live on one planet and Miss Letitia on another? It was beginning to seem that he would never have the opportunity of meeting

316

her. Even Sunday excursions were a loss, for he seemed always to be outmanoeuvred, either by his own mother or by Miss Letitia's two sisters when leaving St Edmund's after evensong.

But did he not perhaps owe it to his art? He would go, he decided. But without much hope that his affairs would progress anything as a result.

'Very well, Olivia,' he said, while she squealed her delight. 'I'll attend on Miss Letitia.'

'Oh, splendid, splendid!' She danced around the parlour, while Mrs Maderley nodded at the decision. Money in rather than money out made for fewer creditors knocking at the door. At last here was some good from his painting. It was a godsend, quite unexpected. And Olivia was right in one regard: who knew where it might not lead?

'How do I do it, though?' William asked. He felt baffled. 'What do I say?'

'Your paintings, William,' Olivia said sweetly. 'They will speak for you. And they will emerge triumphant, of that I am certain!'

'If you say so, Olivia,' he said doubtfully.

He had already made up his mind to take the painting of Mehala. It was virtually finished, though the use of copal varnish on it might be premature, and could well prove dangerous at this stage. Yet patrons were often rumoured among artists to have a preference for the darker gleams that such varnishes provided. It was without question his very best work. He had high hopes for the impression it would make on Letitia's sensibilities.

'You see, Mother?' Olivia crowed delightedly. 'Already he is smiling at the thought of visiting Lorne House!'

She had long known of his obsession with Miss Letitia. The matter had never been in doubt. He was as desirous of visiting there as she was, almost. Why, with any good fortune at all, she herself might be invited to Mrs De Foe's ball, with Sir Trev somehow managing to effect a proper introduction through the agency of William. For William would have to be there many hours a day, several days a week, to carry out the commission. It was probably to paint several members of the Hunterfield family, or possibly scapes of the gardens and estate as well. Yes, she might soon be seeking a new gown to wear. Altogether a very, very new and special kind of gown!

'I shall go into the studio this very minute,' William said, 'and pick out the works most likely to please.'

'Shall I help you, Will?'

'No, thank you. I do faster and better alone.'

'Very well, William,' Olivia said meekly, thinking: Your isolation won't save you from my best efforts, William Maderley! For you will be primed as never before to glean news of the doings at Lorne House, and especially of the impending arrival of Sir Trev Bunyan, and his eventual movements once there.

The note was in the vestibule, and was found by Mrs Goslett when she was checking the activities of the maid-of-all, Bridget.

Miss Baring was listening to her brother expound the contents of his next sermon. Characteristically, he wrote standing at a reading table of walnut wood, beautifully carved and darkened by use and polishing. He was displeased at the interruption, and stood in stony displeasure while his sister read the note from Mehala.

'Dear Miss Baring,' Euterpe read. 'I regret that I must request a delay in attending on your service, if you will allow. I have received an urgent call for assistance which in all charity I may not refuse. I shall join your service at the earliest opportunity, and crave your indulgence in this excercise in compassion.' Euterpe frowned at her brother. 'She closes with the usual courtesies, Josiah.'

'What does this mean, Euterpe?' he said irritably. 'First, the girl does not come. Then she delivers this cock-and-bull story, to our neglect. Then she craves our indulgence. What on earth is the creature playing at? Has she no sense of duty?'

'How can we know, Josiah?' Euterpe asked helplessly. 'She makes it sound a sincere request for her help.'

'Given by whom, might I ask?' he demanded. He interrupted his own sermon now, and crossed grumpily to the decanter to pour a glass of sherry for himself. 'It is really too much. Who on earth deserves the charity of this Lady Bountiful, that I cannot possibly know about? There is no one in sore need or distress in Sealandings but what I know. I am the first to be apprized of those in need of the Poor Law's ministrations, and quite properly too!'

'Perhaps Whitehanger?'

'That, my dear sister, is a suggestion which indicates the limits of your understanding of the ways parishes are administered. St Edmund's is unto itself. Whitehanger is also.'

'She says nothing of where, nor who, nor what the reason is in particular, Josiah.'

'So she has clearly decided to act independently of us, and may now go and find for herself, Euterpe. That much is plain.'

'Yet she gives every indication of returning here to our service as soon as she is able . . .' Euterpe scanned the note. It was on a piece torn from

318

a small reticule note case, as if the girl had run to borrow a piece of paper and the means of writing from some acquaintance, and made haste away after delivering the note. Her brother was not mollified.

'Then she will find, to her sore dismay I trust, that she has missed the boat, and that we may not be so profligate with our time as she has been.' He sipped at the comforting drink. 'Mehala has been kindly disposed to give away *our* time – and *our* money – to anyone who invokes her assistance, while neglecting her duties here. She can reap the rewards of her laziness. Wanton, with *our* assets! She must learn that she is not the mistress of Sealandings, not in this rectory's book!'

'There might be some genuine and legitimate explanation, Josiah.'

'Might? Might is not good enough, Euterpe!' He returned to his reading table and adjusted the height of the top plane.

Euterpe placed the letter into her small pouch table, thinking hard. Mehala was not the sort of woman who would undertake this kind of postponement lightly. Yet her brother, for all his faults, was constrained by the problems of being – and seeming to be – a rector of a town like Sealandings. Weakness on his part might well be taken as an affront to the proper values of his calling, even weakness towards immorality among servants. He had to behave so, for society and the Church compelled him to.

She was well into her needlework, a difficult piece of under-couching, and Josiah almost through his sermon, before she remembered the Darling child who died at Whitehanger. Doctor Carmichael had attended that little boy, who had a sister. And the croup was known to afflict the children of a family in swift succession.

Instinctively she knew that Mehala had gone there. To help Doctor Carmichael? Or to help that Darling family in its distress, while only incidentally assisting the doctor? She felt almost sick with distress at the notion. How had Mehala learned of the need for help? Had Doctor Carmichael sent for her by name? Or had he sent to the rectory for herself, only for Mehala to intercept the call and go, in her stead?

She hardly heard the rest of the sermon, but praised it judiciously in any case.

41

Word came to Milton Hall by posthaste that Fellows De Foe was about to return to Sealandings for the occasion of the ball, and would be bringing with him some seven or eight gentlemen to stay for a few days. Two would be accompanied by their ladies. Since they included some Guards and cavalry officers, Thalia surmised with much pleasure that the majority were as yet unmarried, which always offered opportunities at gatherings.

It was a slight difficulty, however, since the news left her intentions somewhat disarrayed. The plans she had formulated needed urgent revision. She had arranged several nights more of seeing Carradine. To invite him to her bedroom for what was now becoming an orgy of addiction, was out of the question.

'Not for long, darling,' she told him earnestly. 'Not for long. Fellows stays only a few days at any one time before his duties recall him to London. A fortnight at most. He cannot be deprived of the capital city.'

'I shall expect him to be gone long before that,' Carradine said bluntly. 'It is I who suffer the deprivation, not him.'

'Darling,' she exclaimed, in pleasure at his admission of reliance upon her. 'Fear not. I shall see to it.'

Not as convincingly as I, Carradine thought, for I have already ensured that Fellows De Foe will be only too glad to gallop back to his rooms in Bloomsbury. He will have lost considerably during his stay at Sealandings, if the prize fight goes to plan. And it was no accident that his return to his loving wife's arms at Milton Hall coincided with the pugilism contest arranged locally between Goring and Rendell. He had primed Thalia well – with the falsehood that Rendell was an arranged winner.

De Foe's name was one of the ten on the list he had given to the repellent Able Sumner. Carradine *wanted* De Foe to suffer. Gullible fools, most of them. Who all richly deserved to be stripped of their wealth. Pity that Thalia would probably suffer along with her dear husband, but that was the harshness of the modern world, was it not? And if she had chosen to marry so dedicated a fool, she deserved to go down alongside him.

'Promise me one thing, dearest,' Thalia asked.

They lay together on the bed, fondling a little in the lethargy of after-love. Thalia felt almost beside herself when thinking of Carradine left to his own devices, without her to supply his wants. What he said was true. A man could only take so much deprivation. After that he lay prey to any chance strumpet who set her cap at him. Carradine was worse than most, she knew.

'Only if you reward me, Thalia.'

She smiled at this, still further evidence of his craving for her, and only her.

'I shall, darling. Promise that you will not dally with anyone else while my husband is home?'

'How could I?'

'Promise!' She raised herself on an elbow. Her breasts dandled invitingly. It was a pose she knew tantalized him almost to madness, and smiled as she saw his eyes open, focus, and his breath quicken.

'I promise.'

'No visits to Two Cotts. No visits to those places inland. Nor to the Ipswich houses, nor to Great Yarmouth, or Lowestoft? Hasten, for we have not long.'

'I promise. By all that is holy, Thalia.'

'Then your reward,' she said softly, shoving him gently over on to his back and raising herself above his body. 'It shall come in instalments, dearest. For your pleasure, to remember me by. Are you ready?'

He reached up and cuffed her gently. 'Get on with it, woman, and stop your chatter.'

Three hours later Carradine lay in a different bed, thinking.

The name Mrs Wren had told him was very, very pleasing, and augured well for his scheme.

Soon he would have money enough to burn. Soon he would be able to set himself up as the Lord of the Manor of Sealandings, possibly, with liveried servants by the score, as befitted a gentleman of his standing. For far too long Squire Hunterfield and that miserable gaggle of pale women at Lorne House had ruled these Eastern Hundreds. And he ruled in that hideously effective but seemingly gentle way, by merely indicating his preferences – in the most gentlemanly fashion, of course. Well, that would all have to change when Carradine of Carradine Manor became senior magistrate, Squire of Sealandings. No longer would it be enough for people to oblige him simply by touching forelocks. They'd have to do better. Or receive a great deal worse. It was high time for a change.

He kicked the girl beside him into arousal.

'Get awake, girl. Bring some brandy. And none of that admixed wine stuff you purloin for the sake of customers.'

'Yes, sir.'

She rolled off the mattress and drew on a shift. 'Am I to clothe, sir?'

Carradine pondered the question seriously for a moment. He liked the girls to wear their garments, as much for the pleasure of seeing them undress as for grace about the rooms here at Two Cotts. But that would take time, and he wanted the roughness of the raw brandy in his throat at the earliest. He had already consumed the Portugal sent up with the girl by Mrs Wren as a makepeace.

'Yes.' Some sacrifices were worth the delay, and what was delay but heightened pleasure banked for later?

The girl smiled anxiously, and quickly dressed in her piedmont robe. She seemed proud of it, for it was only lately that she had been promoted to wearing the highly priced garments Mrs Wren reserved for her best girls. The piedmont was a form of the old-fashioned sack-back gown, and swung alluringly with the right manner of walk, yet was low-cut in the bodice so the breasts showed very fetchingly. Such a garment could be used to great advantage.

'Do I please you, sir?' the girl asked.

'Saucy bitch,' Carradine rolled over on an elbow, eyeing the creature. 'Have I had you before?'

'Please, sir, yes.' She was slightly put out by his question. 'You asked for me deliberate this time.'

'So I did,' he said without conviction. Trust Mrs Wren to remember when he had been satisfied by a girl's inventiveness. That woman didn't miss a trick, as people were beginning to say nowadays since the Prince Regent popularized the slang of the card table. 'Go, then.'

'Yes, sir.'

He lay on his back, glad of time to think.

The odious Sumner would have the day of the match set by now. He would send word to all the places frequented by the Fancy, him and his promoters who laid guarantees on the pugilists. Then all that was needed was for Carradine to come and partake of the rich pickings to be had there. In fact, there was now nothing to do except collect his winnings. Simple. The scheme was so ingeniously elementary, that he wondered why he had not thought of it before.

The pity of it was that so many of his neighbours and friends would lose their wagers, and indeed their whole fortunes. But if they lost to benefit Carradine, all would be well. He smiled at the image.

Hunterfield might not gamble as much as he ought, not even on a certainty. The man was no more than a mental serf anyway, an upstart whose family had too long lived on the supposition that, since they were of noble blood back along their ancestral stem, they could high-hand it around the county irrespective of true inherent noble qualities.

And of the rest? Why, they would wager beyond their means, of course! The Honourable Charles Golding was one. Fellows De Foe, another. Prothero too, possibly, would have been another, but he was a part contributor to the scheme, through the arrangement to fund the venture, by providing a third of the moneys necessary to make a large killing larger still. But caution was needed. Sir Philip Banks the magistrate was an elder cousin of Thalia De Foe. Odd, come to think of it, how many of the neighbours near or distant proved to be vaguely related to the De Foes! The forthcoming bout would drain the De Foe coffers very badly, if Fellows took the bait. Well, they deserved it. And the bitch Thalia along with them. He had suffered that tiresome mare for far too long, with her importunings and whinings for company and bedding to the exclusion of all others. The woman was obsessed, like a madwoman ofttimes. She was too troublesome, and far too confining. Time that family was taken down a step or two. Then she would be beholden to Carradine, and so would Fellows, Charles Golding, Alex Waite. The lot of them.

And he would make them all pipe his tune.

The girl returned carrying the brandy.

'Who is the girl who wears the merkin?' Carradine demanded, watching her place the flask.

'That is Phoebe, sir.' The girl looked askance. 'You don't want her, sir?'

'Not in your stead,' Carradine said. 'Is she free?'

'Yes, sir. Always is, sir, for our gentlemen customers do not want a girl who has to wear a merkin wig, not ever. None of the gentry wants a girl without a bellybush, sir, as you will be aware. Too often it is a sign that a girl has lost her waist hair from the smallpox, hence the need for such a wig. She does not do proper work, save in the kitchen. Occasionally she serves the porters and fishers and grooms, to bed such as arrive with their masters for a few pence, but that is all.'

'That's enough for my purposes.' He took the glass the girl poured for him. 'Send word to Mrs Wren that I shall want Phoebe brought here to me in another hour.'

The girl pouted. 'But I shall stay, sir?'

'Yes,' he snapped irritably. 'I've already said. You stay here.'

The girl went smugly to deliver her message then returned, pleased.

'Sir? Can I be your regular girl here in Two Cotts?'

'If I say,' he said coldly. 'I shall think on it. Strip, girl, and shut your prattle.'

He lay on his side. She knew what to do, placing the candles to either side of the bed and slowly starting to unclothe. She liked watching his eyes change as she performed, feeling her confidence gather and grow as his gaze traced her movements.

'You tell Lucy you like her, sir?'

'Shut your mouth, bitch.'

Her hands stilled at her breast, toyed with the latching ribbons there.

'You tell Lucy, sir.'

'You bitch!' he spat, fury and desire melding in his eyes.

She smiled and resumed her disrobing, watching him. They were like children spoiled of a sweetmeat, the lot of them. But this gentleman was hotter than most, more impatient, greedier, easily driven to a fury by baulking. Cruder, even, truth to tell. In a way, he craved the anger of being thwarted. He seemed to thrive on impediment, refusal, partly concealed denials. How strange it all was, she thought in wonderment as his rage and sexual desire grew with every passing minute. How weird and wonderful and terrible, that she too craved the anguish of this usage as much as he. But that was a special quality in him, this man they called Rad, who had almost beaten a girl to extremis over in the loose houses at Norwich, so they said, for his own sheer pleasure. A man who was going to be great one day, in London and other great cities of the land. Maybe even a lord! A *lord*! As her very own private possession. And possessor.

What could a girl not aspire to, with such a man as her secret own?

'You must behave, sir,' she said, as he weakened at last and beckoned her to hurry. 'Lucy has an inclination to take her time.'

'Hurry, you cow.'

'Patience, sir. What may I call you, sir?'

His voice was hoarse. 'You'll address me respectfully, you cheap whore. Or I'll have something to say about the matter.'

But his voice was thickening. He could hardly speak for the desire taking hold of him. She laughed, slipping her dress down.

'Rad, dearest, you really must learn patience, or I shall be very, very cross.'

'You call me that, you slut?' He was amazed at the whore's effrontery. Bawdy houses had been broken and razed for less, and here was this country mare having the unmitigated gall to . . . His eyes fixed on her hands, which were beginning to stroke her flanks. They seemed to leave phosphor traces, as does night in the wake of a ship in the warmer climes. He reached for her. 'Come here.'

'Lucy, Rad. You call me by my name.'

'Come here, Lucy.'

'Mistress Lucy. And say your pleases.'

'Come here, Mistress Lucy, if you please.'

'That's my little Rad.' She stepped towards the bed, her eyes shining with power in the candlelight. 'Now to work. Lucy for her Rad. A fine handsome catch for his little Lucy.'

An hour later, Phoebe knocked on the door, and was admitted. She was a plain simple girl, who brought an aroma of the kitchen with her.

She stared, to see one of the house girls, Lucy, sitting up in bed with the gentleman, and sharing his brandy glass bold as you please, breasts bare and hair awry. For all the world like man and wife!

'Please, sir,' she said nervously. 'I'm Phoebe. I was sent for.'

Carradine eyed her. 'Phoebe. You know why I sent for you?'

'Yes, sir. The news of the other gentlemen coming to the pugilistic contests, sir.'

'You have heard who they might be?'

'Some, sir.'

She began to recount the names she had learned from the grooms and ostlers and footmen and menservants. Carradine listened intently, occasionally staying her summary and demanding more details, wanting the names of the grooms and the menservants who accompanied their masters, and once wanting a description of the horse kept stabled at Two Cotts for a particular titled gentleman.

He paid her a sovereign, in gold, and told her she had done well. She left, blushing at the praise, and darting an envious glance at Lucy.

'Was that the news you wished for, Rad darling?' Lucy asked as the door closed behind the kitchenmaid. 'You've made a mistake. Your little Lucy's a deal more observant than poor old rotten Phoebe.'

'Watch your tongue, bitch,' Carradine said icily.

'Oh, I do, darling!' She laughed as he cuffed her, the brandy spilling. 'You wish to know who else is arriving for the prize fight?' She added two names to those given by Phoebe, and saw in his eyes a gleam of gratification. 'You see, Raddy dearest? Lucy's the whore for you. No one else.'

'Don't trust too much to that belief, bitch,' he said gruffly.

'Yes, sir,' Lucy said, but she smiled inwardly.

Next time he would ask for her by name, and mean it. There would be the occasional vagary, of course, for a man was a man and always they had the minds of little boys, especially when in their cups. But he was hers from desire from now on, as much as she was his for a few shillings. That was certain.

And she was going to be beside him for a great deal of life's journey. In fact, perhaps all the way.

42

He was appalled at how weak Clare was. She only had to move a hand and her pulse leapt to a thin gallop. It frightened him, that she might be so close to failing heart.

That worry made him give instructions that she was to be permitted no action, but was to have everything done for her until he changed the order. She was fed the same, cared for the same, and was rested by every means at his disposal.

The cottage was kept at its quietest. Outside, as was the custom for grand houses and an invaried precaution in London, straw was strewn thickly in the roadways, so as to muffle the sounds of horse hooves and the rattle of carts. Relatives of the Darling and Overton families stationed children outside to warn carters and passers-by of the need for quiet. Inside, it was a haven. Only the occasional crackling of the fire and the stirring of the women disturbed the silence, and those few sounds added to the tranquillity rather than disturbed it.

Clare slept most of the time. Occasionally she tried to speak, but only infrequently. Now and again she opened her eyes, drowsing off again almost immediately when she saw the familiar faces there in the semi-dark. He felt that each hour was an hour gained. Mehala was as constant in her work for the sick child as the other two, and helped with the washing and cleaning of the bed, and stood in place of the doctor when he drooped. She seemed indefatigable.

The second night after her arrival Mrs Darling was asleep in the chair by the fireplace. The pretty Mrs Overton had returned to her own cottage, which stood nearer the wharf of Whitehanger, since her husband was due to return, but was promised back for the morning. Jake Darling was out on a driving task overnight, hauling along the wet inland roads with his massive team of shire horses to the bustling Suffolk town of Hadleigh.

Mehala was holding the syphon steady. Carmichael was inspecting the new instrument she had ordered from the clockmaker.

'I should be able to replace that syphon with this,' he mused in whisper. 'It should be quite simple. And it would hold with sutures alone, without our hands.'

'Will you do it, Doctor?'

'I am reluctant, Mehala. Afeared, I should say. The child is not strong. I have rarely seen one so weakened. But it might be two weeks, more, before she is able to start coming upright again. That is why I insist on her being recumbent all the time.'

'If it is to be so long, then should we not do it?'

He sighed. It all seemed so clear cut when Mehala was around. But the risk . . . 'I should,' he agreed, 'but not yet. Perhaps tomorrow. You see, Mehala, it is exactly as you guess, for all your kind silence. I simply do not know.' He was sitting at the table to make notes of the case. They might prove a most useful means of affording comparisons between cases of disease. He was exhausted, but determined to stick to this new medical fashion of note-taking.

The candle's light caught at her hair as he wrote. It was difficult not to watch her. She sat with that innate grace a woman has, even though she was on the flagged floor and held the position of reaching over the sick child. There could be no doubt, he was drawn to her. But this he put down to the closeness, the warmth of two people who briefly became as one in intention and effort. It often happened, even with the street sluts and prostitutes who served as nurses in the London hospitals and who slept on the bare landings outside the wards. Sometimes a bond was established between those who strove during the owl hours for the good of others. Even when their crude attempts failed, the sense of understanding and affinity remained.

That was all it was, probably.

'Your place, Mehala,' he said. 'I heard you were about to be offered a secure position in Sealandings. Will you lose it now?'

'I am not sure, Doctor,' she answered immediately. They spoke in whispers, neither able to see the other's face. 'If it is to be, let it be so.'

'Which was it, then?'

She hesitated, 'I had written through Mrs Weaver to the rectory, to accept the offer at Reverend Baring's.'

Carmichael thought of Euterpe with a pang. 'You did the right thing, Mehala. I hope that this has not caused your replacement?'

'Who knows?' She sounded quite calm about it. And, before he could ask how her presence at the cottage had come about, she told him. 'I was on my way, when I encountered the Whitehanger boy you sent. He was almost entering the rectory gates. I asked him what was the matter for his haste. He told me. I took the message from him, and returned to the inn. There I wrote an apology for Reverend and the Miss Baring, and placed it inside their vestibule for discovery.'

'Why, Mehala?'

'I felt I had to.' She judged the child's recumbency, then turned her head and glanced at him. His face was illumined by the candles, hers in shadow. He felt disadvantaged by this somehow. 'You asked my help about where the sound could be heard. I declined to help. I had to come, whether Miss Baring did or no. You understand that, Doctor. I know you do.'

Her direct speech made him uncomfortable. 'But it might serve you ill, Mehala. And will be talked of as an indication of your unreliability among the great houses here.'

'That is for them to decide,' she said. 'Also, I wanted to repay, Doctor.'

'Repay? The town?'

'I do not know. Repay something, somebody, for being alive. The country, perhaps.'

The fervour in her voice made him say, 'You love the sealands, Mehala.'

'Oh, who could not!' He caught the sound of a smile in her voice.

He warmed to the fondness which emanated from her as she began to speak softly of the lands of the east coast.

'You see, Doctor, others coming here might only see the wet low-lying flats, the salt marshes, feel the winds and the sleet of winter coming across the chill expanses, yet perceive nothing else. Oh, I know that people such as Reverend Baring talk of the people of the Eastern Hundreds being muddy in body, muddy in mind, only slightly advanced in the scale of beings above dumb beasts and more helpless than the brute.'

'And your thoughts, Mehala?' he prompted, interested at her passion.

'This desolation has *beauty*, Doctor. And the people can be angels. Folk are sometimes blind to loveliness, as you well know. In summer, the thrift grows and mantles the sea marshes with shot satins of every hue from a baby's blush to lily white. After comes the purple, a true inner-lit purple glowing all across the waste lands as the sea lavender bursts into flower. It is exquisite, nothing less! And every pool and creek is royally fringed with sea asters. Only a little later, the glasswort comes, that same plant which shoots up a transparent emerald in early spring and soon after turns every shade of carmine!'

'You make even me want to live here, Mehala! Why have I never noticed this beauty?'

She turned her lovely gaze on him. 'Because you are too worried by the sorrow of the sickness all around, if you please,' she whispered

329

frankly. 'Were you ever able to rest a moment from your anxiety, you too would see.'

'No, Mehala,' he whispered back. 'I should have to be a poet.'

'You already are,' she countered, smiling again. 'My own favourites are the birds, though. They come best in winter, when the wild duck and grey geese join the roysten crows and sea mews.' Moisture glistened in her eyes as he listened in fascination. 'The whooper swan sounding his trumpet and showing his reflection as a white flash on the blue fleets, the heron like a prince stately in the pools, the curlew pipes, the brent geese in great flocks barking, just like flying pups might sound!'

'You have always loved these sealands, Mehala.'

'Yes.' In the answer she was admitting the return of her memory, knowing he understood. 'It is my countryside. My land. That the sea intrudes is only part of its nature. It must not be criticized for it.'

'Seeing your love for the marshes, Mehala, I shall not blame any part of it.'

She smiled at him for his joke. 'I only ask that others do not blame us for our faults. For our smuggling ways. For condoning the parson who leaves his nag and his cart to be taken from his stable, left unbolted at night for the purpose. Or for the vagabonds among us, who deal door to door in silks and tobacco and liquors taken from night boats on the salting creeks. The situation is only the same as the rest of the Kingdom, perilous and barbarous with highways unsafe from footpads and marauders who want money. We have those risks, as well as our own here by the low seas.'

'Will you stay, Mehala?'

'Stay I shall, Doctor, if Sealandings will have me.'

'Not Whitehanger? After the assistance you have given here, I am sure somebody in the place would be delighted to offer you a position, for there are some great houses and gentry hereabouts. And your reputation has spread even in the short time since . . .'

She was shaking her head. 'No. Sealandings it must be.'

'Might I ask why?'

'Why, Doctor, is the only word we women never know how to answer. How, when, whither . . . all of these and more we have explanations for. But your whys are lost on me, sir.'

He had to smile at the levity of her tone. 'Come, Mehala, let's change over. You rest while I take post. Seeing that I have talked my way through my rest time, it will be a sorry watch, so keep me from slumber somehow.'

He reached across and took hold of the child's throat and instrument. Mehala relinquished her position and slowly rose. He watched her in the candlelight. She stood tall, lithe, steady, her bearing erect, her skin firm and her eyes fire-bright and dark set. Her hair she had done up simply in a knot, yet lustre still showed in its blackness.

'Yes, Doctor?' she asked, waiting.

'Nothing,' he said, feeling suddenly foolish. 'Nothing. You rest now, Mehala.'

43

Lorne House impressed William Maderley more than he could even feel. He entered like an automaton, smiling diffidently at every wall, piece of furniture, window, person, servant, chandelier. With the aid of one of his mill men, who hauled them on a tax cart, he carried his canvases in from the side entrance.

He was graciously received, Letitia herself being the first to be informed by Crane that her visitor had arrived. She was joined, after a few minutes' stilted yet breathless conversation, by Lydia, and then a Tabitha filled with curiosity at so strange a creature as an artist entering her home.

'And is the art of landscape painting so very different from portraiture, Mr Maderley?' Letitia was asking methodically as her sisters settled on the knole sofa opposite the artist.

'Indeed, Miss Hunterfield,' William replied earnestly. 'I use only the very best techniques to achieve the effects in the exterior, whereas inside, in a natural household setting, there is only restricted use to be made of technical advances.'

'To what advances do you refer, pray?' Lydia asked pleasantly. She had ordered tea for a quarter of an hour from now, which would neatly curtail Mr Maderley's visit at the correct point.

'I use the Claude glass, as recommended by the very best authorities on the subject, Mrs Vallance.'

'May I be allowed to see it, sir?'

'Certainly.' William fumbled, dropped the small book-like object as he brought it from his pocket, recovered it and stood to show its working. 'The observer opens the pocket book, and inside finds a dark glass lens, plano-convex. He stands with his back to the view he desires to behold to its best advantage, and gazes at the reflection thereon. Is it not ingenious?'

There was a brief silence. Lydia ahemmed gently to end the pause. 'But what is its purpose, Mr Maderley?'

'Why, ma'am! It brings into contrast the viewed land scaped into bands of receding degrees of shade, all in monochrome! The *colours* of the view vanish. Don't you see?'

Tabitha stared. The man was nearly beside himself with enthusiasm. There was no doubt about the madness in these artists.

'And, ah, that is a benefit, Mr Maderley?'

'Undoubtedly! To the artist's eye, it shows the land scaped as Claude the French painter would view it, as an ancient Italian stratum of vision. It enables the artist to introduce the backgrounds of, for example, a beautiful series of gardens such as is seen here at Lorne House *exactly* as they would be perceived in ancient form! That of course means to best effect.'

'For portraiture?' Letitia was eager to promote his cause. She thought it was all going exceedingly well. Tabitha had not yet spoken. She herself was only just perceiving that this was not as simple a transaction as she had imagined.

'Exactly, Miss Hunterfield! The portrait is placed thus in the most marvellously antique landscape, by means of the use of this device.'

'Excellent!' Letitia exclaimed eagerly. 'Is that not marvellous, Lydia?'

'It is indeed, Letitia.' Lydia added, as William made to bring out still more delights for their instruction, 'I suppose that there are so many of these that you have not adequate time to demonstrate them all, Mr Maderley. So we must take them on trust.'

'What are you presently working on, if I might ask, Mr Maderley?' Tabitha had received Letitia's urgent signals begging assistance in the limping conversation.

'I have recently completed a portrait which I think might well be considered my very best work to the present date. Though this is unusual for me, since I am sorely addicted to landscapes of the region.'

'Which, I suppose, might well be combined with portraits, to show a person in context?' Letitia prompted.

'Indeed, Miss Hunterfield. You are so perceptive! There is a school of artists abroad in Italy, who are of the mind that no portrait can exist but what it relies utterly upon the background for its very artistic life.'

'How interesting!' Lydia said, bored out of her senses by this tame lunatic and wondering where the tea had got to. 'You are a very dedicated man, Mr Maderley.'

'Thank you, Mrs Vallance,' William said, enwrapt. 'I find the subjects truly compelling. I believe there may come a time in the future when the people of this country – and, who knows, possibly others – will come to realize the true inherent value of canvases currently being painted. For history, for the ideas of art, for social comparisons, for the proper understanding of ancestry.'

'Let us pray that time comes soon, for the sake of all artists!' Tabitha said brightly, then wished she had not spoken as Letitia's brow furrowed slightly. Tabitha wondered for the first time if her sister was truly serious about this dishevelled man, who seemed so poor and preoccupied yet who owned the region's only tide mill. So wealthy an establishment, to serve two towns! She glanced swiftly at Lydia in hopes of receiving guidance, but was not heeded.

'Have you received commissions, Mr Maderley?' Letitia asked, to prompt.

'Why, yes, Miss Hunterfield. I have painted the landscapes of Sir Philip Banks, inland. And several of my canvases have found favour at certain salons in Suffolk and Norfolk towns, and been especially commended.'

'Landscape,' Lydia mused. 'That appears to be your forte, then?'

'Yes. But I am capable of creating excellent likenesses, Mrs Vallance. I have been informed so on many occasions.'

'Have you examples with you?'

'I have only one, I regret to say. It has rather preoccupied me for quite some time, and I fear is not finished even yet. I am having difficulty with the hair. I paint the tresses longer than appears in reality. And the background I have only recently come to see as none other than that in which the people of Sealandings dwell!'

'Is your subject one of the Hunterfield sisters, Mr Maderley?' Tabitha demanded mischievously.

'Oh, no, Miss Hunterfield. I would not so presume, not without permission of your good selves and of the squire. No. It is of a servant, that is all.'

'May we see it, Mr Maderley?'

'Mrs Vallance, I am loth to put it on display, since it will only show imperfectly what I am capable of. And it is not yet completed. The varnish is always a problem, and dammar is a – '

'I think we should be pleased to inspect it, Mr Maderley,' Lydia said. This was going quite well. After he had taken his leave, her options to refuse or accept him as the family's portraiture artist would remain open, and she would have plenty of time to discuss the implications with Henry while having done her duty in support of Letitia with seeming fairness and lack of bias. All was plain sailing.

'Very well, ma'am.'

William crossed to where the canvases had been placed by Crane, and selected one with great care. It was guarded on its painted surface by a thin screen of wood. The stretchers were formed of old slats of oak crudely nailed together, the canvas margins fraying and projecting.

'This is the one, ma'am. I think it will show . . .'

Lydia did not hear anything else. She stared. The painting was magnificent, of a young woman, seen only from the shoulder up, as if in the act of turning to glance back over her shoulder. The wind seemed to be rising. Her black hair shone with tinges of amber light. Her gaze was at once questing and mild, yet from within there seemed to shine a vigilant and demanding soul. Soul. That was the word. It was a depiction of a girl's inner being, and gave a lustre to the parlour in which they were seated.

The background was of a sea marsh, with hidden hues guessed rather than shown, and a sky of scudding clouds low hanging over a sea that was becoming choppy. A lugger leaned against the gusting wind, starting to make for harbour. The long north mole of Sealandings was glimpsed somewhere in the distant ground. Stunted hawthorns struggled at a lean in a receding row.

Her garments consisted of a strange cloak, hooded in Italianate fashion. It was velvet, a brilliant royal blue, and hung in folds about her shoulders as she spun round. She was looking past the viewer, out into the room as though searching for something concealed, or perhaps some time lost from her memory but which was yet near and half remembered.

'It's a man's cloak!' Tabitha exclaimed. 'How very shocking, Mr Maderley!'

'It was the only thing which came to mind, Miss Hunterfield,' William stammered. 'It was painted from memory of some cloak once seen when I was a child, on a gentleman and lady out riding when I was a-visiting a relative elsewhere.'

'It is a hooded genoa cloak, sir,' Lydia said quietly. 'Of a gentleman.'

'So it is!' Letitia put in courageously. 'And it sets off the form very well indeed. A most wonderful imagination you have, Mr Maderley! Don't you agree, sisters?'

'It was actually partly taken from life, Miss Hunterfield,' William owned. 'But only at a distance, with the subject at first imperfectly envisaged.'

'Oh?' Lydia said, raising her brows. 'Is this creature then some person who exists locally? A servant, I think you said?'

'She is, Mrs Vallance. She is presently a servant-of-all at the Donkey and Buskin, where she is paying her time to the Weavers.'

'She has no wages or funds to pay of her own, then?' Letitia said. 'Poor thing!'

'She is doubtless the girl fetched from the sea, Mr Maderley. Am I right in supposing so?'

'Indeed, Mrs Vallance. It is she.'

'You make the person very . . . noticeable.'

'Thank you.'

'Doesn't he, though!' Letitia took the remarks as complimentary to his talent, innocently supposing that he had proved his case. 'It is most wondrously executed, is it not?'

'Indeed it is, Letitia,' Squire Hunterfield's voice said soberly from behind them.

'Henry!' Lydia greeted smoothly. 'How good of you to join us! Mr Maderley has shown us this painting, to convince us of his worth as artist for our family. You find it a pleasing portrait?'

'Wholly admirable, ma'am.' Hunterfield stared for a long time at the painting, nodding occasionally and moving a pace here, a pace there, to judge the effect. 'You are very . . . affected by the subject, sir?'

'The lady is the one recently brought ashore by *The Jaunty*, sir. I have attempted to see what lies behind the act of drowning, saving, rescue, loss of mind.'

'And achieved yet more, sir,' Squire Hunterfield said. 'The background adds most imaginatively to the construction of the scheme. I commend it.'

'Thank you for the compliment, sir.'

'Oh, I'm so thrilled you admired the painting, Henry!' Letitia exclaimed, pink with pleasure.

Lydia was not quite so delighted. She glanced from William Maderley's face to the painting he was still studying, and was seriously disturbed by what she saw there. It was a painting with imagination, yes, but also with something deeper and more lasting than mere appreciation of beauty.

She instantly detested the woman in the painting.

Just then tea mercifully arrived, Evie the chief maid bringing it in and setting riband-backed chairs about the table for their use. To Lydia's annoyance, her brother urged the artist to place the portrait on her tambour table, the better to inspect it as they seated themselves.

Letitia was thrilled that the visit seemed to have gone so splendidly, falling right in with her designs. Lydia was secretly irritated at having suddenly lost ground somehow, and all on account of some wretched girl servant dragged from the muddy estuary. Tabitha was quite bemused, suspicious that something was going on of which she was being kept in ignorance.

Henry saw the painting as he had seen Mehala in the doorway of the tavern when leaving it the other night, and thought Maderley had captured the truth. If the artist was so capable as this, was he indeed the one he wanted to paint the truth of all the Hunterfields? Now, he sincerely doubted it. Truth has its limits, especially with imperfections.

William was pleased. He had fulfilled the best expectations of his mother and Olivia back at Watermillock. He would have a wondrous tale to tell on his return. Olivia would be delighted. His mother would be thrilled, almost overcome at the honour of his selection, but her pride would be tinged with regret that his success took him another step further from the responsibilities at the tide mill. He did not care. His painting skill was admired.

They placed themselves for tea and Lydia poured, making small talk about the pictures she had seen on a varnishing day, executed by a Mr Turner at the Royal Academy in London, once, with her father the late squire.

'The paintings were quite incomprehensible, of course,' she commented. 'Swirls and streaks. La! One could hardly discern a figure anywhere in any of his pictures!'

William drew breath as if to challenge her, but to her disappointment and Letitia's vast relief he kept silent and merely smiled, and mercifully the tea proceeded according to plan.

'Tomorrow, then, Prothero.'

No title, no sir, no mister, not the courtesy any true gentleman would give to a roadside beggar. Spoken to as if he were still the farm hand, or merely an estate man at Calling Farm.

Prothero looked up as the arguments started around the inn doorway. The King's Head at Stowmarket was always popular, being an 'end', the tavern where the coaches found terminus. And as always the rows – buffets, and the journey not yet started! – were about the prices charged. Threepence a mile for the outside passengers was a veritable fortune, of course, but some stagecoaches only charged tuppence-halfpenny a mile like years ago, which was better. People were always complaining at the cost, Prothero thought wryly. Before they had gone ten miles they would be paying in other ways. The rude coachmen would see to that.

'I have one pre-condition, sir,' he said placatingly.

Sir! He almost choked on the politeness. He had to call Carradine sir, who treated him like dirt. The gentleman was smiling, enjoying the squabbles and near-riots as the crowd of intending passengers surged out into the inn yard.

'You have. . . ?' Carradine's cool gaze turned and transfixed him. 'You have . . . *what*, sir?'

The man could show naked aggression with a single glance. Prothero felt it. He was no dueller, no pugilist. He was a, well, a thinking man. A gentleman, at least one who should be. He was a pillar of the local community, a true loyal subject who owned land, a large estate indeed, and the most prolific farmer in the area of Sealandings. Not great on a national scale, true, but locally considerable nonetheless.

He swallowed, felt himself disciplined. But a gentleman like Carradine should remember his promises. 'It's about the girl Mehala.'

Carradine was irritated. 'I'm becoming sick to death of that bloody name, Prothero.' That servant's name seemed to follow him wherever he went. It was becoming intolerable. 'It is everywhere. What on earth has she to do with me?'

'Your promise, sir. I only wish to remind you of it, that you will exert influence to procure her services to my dear wife.'

'Ah yes,' Carradine mused absently. Prothero breathed relief into his small beer. Carradine could so easily have taken offence at the implication of deliberately forgetting an undertaking, especially as it was part of the standing arrangement in their contract.

'It is just that . . . well, Mrs Prothero is becoming somewhat, well, sir – '

'Impatient?'

'In need of her assistance, sir. You see how it is.'

'I do indeed, Prothero.'

Carradine was becoming sick of the fellow. He was squirming on his bench, a big sweaty man, oaf with aspirations to grandeur. Thinks himself a gentleman, simply because he has shoved the mistress of a goodhearted farm into bed, shagged her into marriage and the subservience which all that entailed.

He eyed Prothero, wondering whether to make an issue of the jack-jumped-up's reminder, then deciding he could not be bothered. This Mehala creature had earned enough attention for herself without his joining in the absurd hullabaloo about her. Strange, but there really were some women who, despite all their apparent shynesses and evasiveness, attracted attention without seeming to make any such invitation. The attention of course was of the usual specific kinds – the eyes and hot cravings of men, and the enmity of all women, who quickly sensed a rival in such a paragon. Perhaps Mehala was one such? It was becoming rather interesting, as well as annoying.

'Of course, Prothero. I shall be taking active steps to that end within the day. Ease yourself, man.'

Man! 'I thank you, sir,' Prothero replied as if grateful.

Inside, he burned. One day he would make this arrogant bastard beg to be acknowledged in the street. One day he, Jason Prothero, would ride in his festooned barouche down the South Toll road into the market square of Sealandings, and be bowed to, scraped to, saluted on all sides by gentlemen and their ladies. His servants would be in livery, and he would have procured coats of arms for the sides of his conveyances. And he would see this grand Carradine firebrand grovel. Strangely, in his daydream, now becoming so frequent, it was always Mehala, discovered to be secretly a grand lady of a noble family, who was seated beside him as the carriage was drawn through the saluting throng . . .

'There is actually considerable need for haste, Prothero,' Carradine was saying indolently. 'I shall want the money sooner than I thought. And as hard cash, not as stiffs.' Carradine wanted nothing to do with stiffs, as IOUs were now called. He'd written enough of those to last a lifetime. 'The fight has been brought forward, you see.'

'Brought forward? But I thought you implied that . . .'

'Ah.' Carradine smiled, shaking his head with regret. 'Circumstances change, Prothero. It's a sad fact of life. You see, the magistrates of the counties and boroughs are now so antagonistic towards the exercise of a Briton's natural right to batter any willing opponent into extinction, that they have established special watch patrols along the borders of each district, God damn them.'

'But this they always do, sir!'

Prothero was thinking of the difficulty of obtaining the vast sum so quickly. He would need to ride to Norwich, and establish promissory notes drawn on several provincial branches of the banks, for so much coin. And he would have actually to raise the amount, since sovereigns were needed for on-the-nail wagers, against Calling Farm's assets.

Carradine watched a shapely young serving girl passing tankards of small beer along a bench by the door. She was laughing, wagging her finger at two joking grooms in mock admonition. Idly he wondered if he had the time . . . He dragged his attention back to this preposterous villein seated opposite. 'Indeed they do, Prothero, bad cess to them. But more than a dozen patrols have been hired, for a fortnight hence. Word is out. That old sod Banks is talking of London charleys being fetched in convoy, to snare offenders.'

Prothero grimaced. This enterprise was seeming less attractive by the hour. Charleys were London watchmen. All were street-sour bullies of evil reputation.

'Netting a crowd of the Fancy would more than recompense the expense,' Prothero nodded.

'So it is to be brought nearer.'

Carradine smiled at the sudden tension in the man's face. That was the hallmark of the serf, apprehension at the thought of some slight disturbance involving moneys. A gentleman naturally took it lightly, for he had breeding, that inner core of excellence which was given by God. Everyone knew it, from servants to lords. It was just an irritation, and an amusement, that every now and then you encountered one such as this lout Prothero, who thought himself entitled by the simple act of breathing to the prestige which only birth rank could convey. A ridiculous notion, though one becoming more widespread than should be allowed. Wait until he himself achieved a high position. Then he'd change a few minds, by God!

'Nearer by how much, sir?'

'The sixth day from now, Prothero. That will offer many additional advantages, with good fortune. There is to be a ball, thrown by the good lady at Milton Hall. A considerable number of the gentry . . .' he let the word hang '. . . are to come, from all the counties of East Anglia, even from London. The ball will take place the following evening.'

'That implies the barefisters will meet close by to Sealandings, I surmise, sir?'

'You can surmise what you like, Prothero.' Carradine nodded to the tavern servant who was hovering nearby. 'I simply inform you of the arrangements. Pay the man, will you?'

He rose and took his leave with scant courtesy. The oaf was becoming a victim of his own silly ambitions. Well, a fool's arrow is soon shot, and flies not far. Ridiculous to be the slave of fantasy, to that degree. Why on earth could the man not be thankful with what he had already got? It was more than most, at least for those born outside the sparver. For gentry born within the bed curtain, however, all followed on course, like night followed day. He strolled towards the stairs, signalling to the taverner at his counter, and indicated the comely laughing girl with a faint nod. He'd make time, and rid himself of the unease of doing business with the peasantry.

44

The signs were becoming favourable, Carmichael was astonished to realize. The air of confidence in the Darling cottage was almost visible, brightening every passing hour.

As the day changed again into night and then day wore down once more, he began to think dazedly that she might really last, and live out the illness. It was a miracle.

Several times she had threatened relapse, but that was apparently caused by the attempts to shift her on the bed, to clean her and, to mistakenly, encourage her cooperation in moving. That, he had learned with great alarm, was utterly the wrong thing. Now, Clare lay in a position of absolute recumbency. She did nothing but lie there, and occasionally come to, doze, awaken long enough to recognize those about her, and slip under again. Once she became agitated, and he risked a trace of laudanum, though it tended to make shallow the breathing. But she settled again at last, and he almost sank with relief.

Towards that next new night, he was sufficiently in control to observe himself, and had the grace to apologize to the ladies about him for his condition. He was ashamed. Mrs Darling only smiled and tutted, that he should find it necessary to express regret so. Mrs Overton almost laughed aloud, thinking that only a man could be so simple-minded as to think that women, who did all the laundering and counted garments almost hourly, would think the worse of anyone grubby from work that was so essential.

'I shall go, Doctor,' Mehala said at these signs of returning normality.

They were all free of the need to sit holding the sick syphon. With great trepidation, Carmichael had replaced the tube with the one Mehala had gained from Veriker. It was successful, though it gave a fraction less of an aperture. Yet the sick child's breath came through it easily enough, which made him wonder if there was some natural law of air motion governing the tube's width and the lungs' requirement.

Two stitches held the tube's wings in place, and they were all free to stand. He examined the old removed sick syphon with interest, seeing how far down it had reached, and wondered how further modifications could be achieved.

'Go, Mehala?' The words struck home finally and he looked her way.

'Yes. Allow me to enter Shalamar for you, and bring your new linens. I shall of course address my request to your housekeeper.'

'Mrs Trenchard?' he mused. 'Yes. She may still be there at this hour . . .'

He gauged Clare's condition, and nodded assent. 'Please however take one of the Whitehanger boys with you, Mehala. I do not want you missing your way in the evening. It gathers so fast at this time of year.'

'This young lady knows her way across the sea marshes like a curlew, Doctor,' Mrs Overton smiled. 'I seed her bringing her row pram in the other day. Better than many a fisherman on these coasts. You need have no fear on Mehala's behalf.'

He swallowed his retort. He was not afraid for her. Why should he be? Mrs Overton was exceeding her licence in speaking in that fashion. His expression was naturally the polite way of wishing someone well on a short journey, not because he felt anything special about Mehala in any way. It was ridiculous to assume so. It was also far out of the question, for he was here as the doctor, in a house where sickness ruled, and he was solely occupied with the task of promoting Clare's wellbeing.

'Then you will go, Mehala, if you please,' he said stiffly, and returned to sit with the child and hold her hand.

Mehala indicated her concurrence and got ready for the long walk round the bay. She had a shawl, and Mrs Overton loaned her the scarlet woven cap of a Whitehanger boatman against the coming night's chill.

Doctor Carmichael did not turn as she left the cottage and started northwards along the shore round the wooded slopes of Whitehanger.

She walked at a steady speed in spite of the gloaming. The lights of Lorne House could be seen inland a way, to her left, and gradually the upstairs corner window light of Watermillock's house came into view as the silent woods erased the lanthorn lights of Lorne.

This was the trackway where, at the stile leading into the sea fields, she had waited in hope of encountering Doctor Carmichael on his return to Sealandings . . . how many days ago now? They were all so fleeting, even though the static somnolence of little Clare's parlour-cum-sickroom needed only silent vigilance from the helpers; at the best, no events happened to quicken time's passing. Too fast, Mehala recorded, knowing full well why she thought so.

Carmichael was a lonely man, she thought as she walked. He even

342

seemed unable to realize his loneliness, as if resigned to its permanence. And lost, within himself as well as without. He was like a child in many ways. As, for example, that show of irritation when Winifred Overton made that unnecessary hint about Mehala's skill and his concern for her. A child, found out in something it thought unrecognized.

Of course, she told herself, seeing for the first time the distant light of the marker lanthorn which was left burning across on the far side of Sealandings harbour's northern mole, that was not to guess that Doctor Carmichael thought anything more about her than, say, the natural transient bond which occurred in any close encounter. He had spoken innocently enough about that. Quite legitimate, in the circumstances, and easily explained away. And just as easily dissolved in the mists of morning when, please God, little Clare finally recovered and all rode home and resumed their normal lives. No. He was simply annoyed a little that he too was capable of feeling that bond. For heaven's sake, he probably felt exactly the same towards Mrs Darling, though she was of course somewhat older than Mehala, and towards Mrs Overton – and here, though she too was married, there was the slightly added complication that Winifred Overton was younger, pretty and viva- cious, as well as having proved herself a devoted and diligent helper. And her gaze irritatingly tended to linger on the tired man kneeling by her niece's sickbed a little longer than was seemly.

The sheen of the reflection from Watermillock's tide mill showed enough of the way to let Mehala trust the left fork as Sealandings came into view, its lights showing in small golden crystalline patterns. Lorne House was brightly lit, she saw as she passed the gates. The gate man called her a good evening, and she returned the salutation. He was an estate man also, receiving his gatehouse free of rent for the service he did about the Lorne properties.

'Is it true about the Darling child?' the man called. 'That she has bettered the croup?'

'She is holding, sir,' Mehala called back, but not pausing. 'Doctor Carmichael is treating her still.'

'Will she live, then?' The man sounded incredulous.

'Please that God wills it, sir.'

'Amen!' he rejoined. 'Let the miracle happen.'

She walked on, covering the shorter distance to the River Affon well as the road took on a proper form, and descending the slope from the river bridge towards the first rows of fisher cottages with the bright lights of Bures House to her left.

She could hear the clatter of the hand-weaving going on as she passed the doors. That was one of the means by which the people brought added income to a family, though the expense of the handlooms was inordinate and the labour long and intensive.

Then it was along the first of the side alleys between the cottages, leftwards, and on to the South Toll road, and so towards Doctor Carmichael's house, with Milton Hall showing brilliant illumination of its fountain displays, away and uphill to her right.

Shalamar was in total darkness when she finally reached it. There was no sign of Mrs Trenchard, and no lights showed at the gatehouse. She herself carried no light, nor tinder, and the evening chill caused her to shiver as she made her way through the ramshackle gates and up the drive. It was overgrown, patches of long couch grass underfoot alternating with the occasional solid stone. Brambles caught at her as she went.

The house was vast, and stood high and broad, simply a thick solidity of darkness in the night sky. A moon emerged as she stood hesitating, revealing great gables and the tall chimneys, the speckling reflected moonlight of the leaded windows. Creepers shuffled in the quiet breeze – the tide must be changing – about the house's walls.

Braving the silence, she walked to the great wide steps and found herself on the expanse of verandah. She had never encountered a house as large as this, and as seemingly derelict, with the exception of her own distant Red Hall. She put the memory of that accursed place from her mind, wishing she had never even remembered its name, and pulled the bell.

No sound. An owl screeched nearby, probably thinking itself intruded upon by this night visitor and outraged because of her. Nobody inside, to judge from the feeling. It was almost as if Shalamar too was taken aback by the sudden appearance of a caller, and was withdrawing to take a better look. Mehala smiled at her silliness and began to walk cautiously round the walls, feeling her way when she encountered plants which in parts had made the path their own, and recovering her direction whenever the moon showed its reflection in the windows.

And *he* lived here? It was gaunt, the loneliest dwelling in Sealandings, surely. Even the little cottages she had passed in town were more comfortable than this great empty barn of a place. And where on earth was this famous housekeeper, Mrs Trenchard? She should have the maids-of-all busying themselves by now towards the evening meal, getting the fires banked up for morning, perhaps getting the laundry organized and the grooms fed ready for the master's

344

return . . . Unless there were no maids, unthinkable for so grand a hall, and no grooms. She had never seen Doctor Carmichael ride, and he was spoken of as merely the doctor locally, without respect for any status . . .

A window stood ajar in the kitchen. The two doors which formed the vestibule entrance nearby also allowed access. She went in and stood uncertainly in the cold air of Shalamar.

'Good evening, Mrs Trenchard!' she called nervously. 'Good evening!'

No answer. It was as if there were no one resident at all. The house *felt* empty. She had always had an absurd belief that houses feel, and somehow have a right to examine an intruder, or even a legitimate new arrival, equal to the newcomer's right to make her own appraisal of the house. It felt smiling with interest at seeing her. Foolishly she called again.

'I am sent by Doctor Carmichael, Mrs Trenchard!'

This was ridiculous. There were no embers in the kitchen grate, no sense of warmth anywhere.

For another moment she stood, waiting for the moonlight to reappear, and with its aid went through into the hallway, speculating that one flight upstairs would take her to the main entrance. It was old, musty, deserving better than all this neglect, she thought. The house seemed to agree, to her amusement, and she made the entrance safely, her feet echoing on the marble floor.

Here it was not so dark, as the moonlight was reflected from the floor and the central chandelier. Several doors seemed to lead off. She opened each in turn, finally coming upon one which led into a place dustier than the rest, even though it seemed slightly warmer.

There had been no fire in here, either, but its relative smallness and a fragment of carpet made her guess that this was Doctor Carmichael's study. She hoped for kindling, and entered. There was only half a curtain at the window, and that moved slightly in the draughts from the broken diamond-shaped panes. A desk, and mercifully a tinder lighter to her exploring hand. Tinder too, and the Suffolk flint was cut sharp. She snapped it against the steel. Several tries before she caught the spark exactly right on the tinder. She breathed slowly on it, keeping it as a source of illumination, and by its red glow found half a candle. She worked the spark across the tinder wadge, blowing with increasing vigour, until it burst into flame and she was able to light the candle from it.

She laid it aside and held the candle aloft, and almost died of fright.

There was an old woman staring at her from the doorway.

'Who are you?' she demanded.

'Oh, ma'am!' Mehala almost dropped the candlestick in her terror. 'I am so startled. I called. I did not know . . .'

'My husband's dog roused him, and he called me. Don't you try any of your gypsy tricks, my girl. My husband is along of me, and has weapons.'

'Are you Mrs Trenchard, ma'am?' Mehala managed the words, but weakly. Her heart was pounding. She had almost fainted, and was still dizzy at the shock. 'Only, Doctor Carmichael sent me to Shalamar. He said to come.'

'For why, if your tale's true?'

'For new linen, ma'am. He attends the child at Whitehanger, and I have assisted, with Mrs Darling and her cousin there. The cottage of Jake Darling, the waggoner.'

'I heard.' Mrs Trenchard sniffed, trudging towards Mehala to take hold of the candle. 'Very well. You can come. Though where I'm to find new linen for the poor gentleman God alone knows. He has only the two sets. One's barely from the wash. And other one's on his back!'

Mehala followed, recovering herself. The study was almost bare, very little furniture, and signs of dereliction and neglect everywhere. The grand carpet she had felt beneath her feet on inspection proved to be a fragment of old drape laid near the desk. Outside, the hall seemed ashamed of being revealed as barren. Mould and damp smudged the walls as high as the candle glim could carry. The grand balustrade of the staircase was almost falling out of position, with one huge stretch tumbled noticeably from its stairs and leaning dangerously over the hall concourse.

The old lady took her along a corridor and into what seemed to have been a parlour, once grand with shutters and wall hangings no doubt, but now a place where rats scurried from sight at the approach of light and the breeze blew through so severely that Mehala drew her shawl round her all the tighter.

'You shouldn't be wearing a boatman's woven cap, miss,' Mrs Trenchard groused as she went through the double doorway. 'You were taken for a rascal by my husband. He could easily have shot you. Mind that left-hand door. It's fallen from its hinges and crushes down on you without warning.'

'Thank you. I am sorry about my attire, Mrs Trenchard. It was lent me for haste.'

'You'll be the girl from the inn, then?'

'Yes, ma'am. I am she. Do you live here, Mrs Trenchard?'

'No, bless you, girl. I live with Trenchard, at the old gamekeeper's cott at the rear of this great place. Terrible small, but easier on old bones than this. They gave it to the doctor for hardly a pepper, so that it's left occupied. The poor man couldn't afford even a cottage, you see, when he came. He's not much more now, truth to tell. This was the cheapest, though it's more than a mite ridiculous. He lives a seeming lord but a real-life beggar.'

The old lady conducted Mehala along a further corridor, which led from the parlour into a small accessory room. There the embers of a fire glowed feebly. Three pieces of linen were draped over a rickety chair which lacked its seat.

'Under-waistcoat's almost dry,' Mrs Trenchard said, and caught Mehala's eye. 'Well, m'dear, it's just that it's been such a hard day or two, looking after this old place. The wind whistles right through my old bones, y'see.'

'Has Doctor Carmichael a shirt?'

'Yes, here!' Mrs Trenchard was suddenly pathetically eager to please, smiling and nodding as she took the shirt from the floor where it had fallen. 'And under-drawers, y'see? Of course, I once worked in a high position, for the gentry. I'm used to having several under-maids, even two or three maids-of-all, to help. Here, well, you can see, Miss Mehala.' She gestured, indicating the house.

'They are not yet dry, Mrs Trenchard.'

'It's the damp, y'see, Miss Mehala.' The old lady looked about hopelessly for somewhere to sit, found nowhere and set to convincing the visitor. 'I'm used to gentlemen who had four, maybe six shams each, good soft linen half-shirts, and shawl waistcoats most beautiful to feel, and lovely to wash and take care of. You can turn your gentleman out like a king, so you can, if only he has the right attire. Why, no gentleman of mine ever thought but to wear his Hetherington, even out to ordinary walking round the estate!'

'You were here in this place earlier, Mrs Trenchard?' Mehala asked. It was not the old dear's fault. She was defeated by life, the fantastic changes which were occurring all round, spinning the world faster than she wanted. Or deserved.

'I was *born* here, Miss Mehala.' The old housekeeper smiled, getting courage back. 'But I never worked in the house itself. I was sent out to service at the old sir's great house. I was happy there. I met Trenchard, who gained no position. We came here because we lost our home. It was by the toll road to the south. We took this place to guard Shalamar against vagabonds and such. It was the only place, y'see.'

347

'I understand.' Mehala had once been in the same position, and really did appreciate the difficulties.

'I see you do, Miss Mehala. Are you . . . are you coming to serve here, then?' It was hopeful speculation rather than a serious question.

'Who knows what God wills, Mrs Trenchard?' Mehala replied, taking up the garments and folding them over her arm. Damp. Wretchedly washed, and already hardly fit to wear. No wonder Doctor Carmichael had been reluctant for her to come and collect his clothes from Shalamar.

'Who knows?' the old lady echoed.

'Please lend me a light, Mrs Trenchard, wherewith to return by the sea road. Have you a lanthorn? Or has Mr Trenchard?'

'Bless you, Mehala! Old Trenchard snores yet on his truckle. He'll not rouse before cockshout. I lied about his vigilance from fear, may heaven forgive me! I'll find you something to light your road, though.'

She shuffled away, Mehala taking a second candle lit from the candlestick and coming after. Mrs Trenchard wore a shawl made of Western Dozens, the coarse off-white kersey woollen. It was an indication of the poverty at Shalamar. A housekeeper should have better, even here. And be able to offer a messenger from her own master a drink of something, tea or warmed milk or caudle, before sending her out into the night for the return journey. Not that Mehala felt scorned by the old lady's attentions, but rather that somehow she herself was intruding unfairly upon the personal life of Doctor Carmichael. He deserved better. As did this great old house, Shalamar.

Mrs Trenchard found a lantern and lit it for her with shaking hands.

'Give my best services and obligations to the doctor, please, Mehala,' she begged. 'Tell him I shall have everything prepared by his return.'

'I shall. Thank you, Mrs Trenchard.'

Mehala took her leave and went out into the night by the front door, through the great hall and down the fine weed-covered steps to the drive. It would be easier walking with the lantern now, and she struck out along the drive at a fair pace, wondering at the endurance of Doctor Carmichael in that old mansion house, living virtually alone save for Mrs Trenchard's inept and forgetful ministrations. How on earth did the man eat? And what food did they manage to procure between them? Or did Trenchard shoot something, or go fishing from some small craft in the estuary, and so maintain the three?

She paused, not far from the gates, to inspect a pair of stone circles set low in the encroaching grass and weeds. She smiled, recognizing the pattern.

'A Flora's dial,' a man's voice cut in on her reverie.

She cried out, startled, and whirled, trying to see into the gloom from her pool of lantern light.

A mounted man, his horse's eyes gleaming small lanthorns back at her, was laughing at her fright.

'Did you get much in the way of pickings, girl? I watched you approach, knowing you would be stupid enough to return the way you entered! A foolish thing to do. Did you learn nothing when your folk taught you to thieve?'

'I left the house by a different route, sir, from the old saying.' She felt herself in danger somehow, though he was a gentleman and mounted and no mere highwayman or footpad.

'Never leave by the door you enter, eh?' He laughed. 'More peasant foolery. Give those things here, girl. I shall have you taken in charge.'

'That you shall not, sir,' she gave back heatedly. 'And I have instructions from the gentleman resident at Shalamar to bring him his things. Mrs Trenchard herself has passed them to me.'

'That old bitch still bellowing God's good air, is she? Much good she'll ever do anyone again.' He seemed indecisive for a second. 'You answer as if you own the place, girl.'

'I am here under order, sir. I have more right to trespass than your good self, it seems!'

'God, but the bitch speaks as if she's asaddle and I afoot!' The man burst out laughing, shaking his head. 'Come nearer. I can't see you well in that glow-worm of a lanthorn you carry.'

'No, sir. I have my master's duty to perform, and must be on my way.'

She was safer among the stones and brambles of the weed-covered garden than on the path, for the horse too would have to watch its footing.

'You're a troubling wench, bitch,' he said thoughtfully. 'I really do believe you aren't a common thief after all.' He nudged his beast nearer a pace or two, coming within a few feet of her, and inspected her soberly.

'Mehala?' he said suddenly. 'You're Mehala, I'll bet my life!'

'Yes, sir.'

'By God, so we meet, and all out here in this derelict rat hole!'

'Good night, sir,' she gave him and made to move away, but watching the movements of the horse warily.

'Here,' the horseman called. 'Why do you not serve at Mr Charles Golding's residence, up at Bures House? You were promised there. Or at Mr Prothero's residence at Calling Farm on the estate?'

'I was promised to nobody, sir. I was *asked* by some, and very kindly.'

'And took to none save that cheap tradesman, eh?'

'I am helping at the house of a poorly child, sir. The Darling household in Whitehanger, where they have the croup and a child near death.'

He held his horse at that. 'You tell Whitehanger to keep their agues and distempers among their own bastards, then,' he said, angry that the fear of illness made him stay his hand and not come too close. 'And hear this from the Honourable Howard Carradine, Mehala: you'll be begging me to tell you into service at the Protheros' place within the week. You hear me?'

'I hear you, sir,' she said, her voice floating back to him from the darkness. She had taken a path among the trees, to reach the road. He glimpsed the lanthorn occasionally as she receded. 'And I thank you too for the kindly offer . . .'

He was furious, then began smiling and finally laughed aloud. The bitch was as beguiling as he had guessed. Too far to see more than a mere glimpse of her in the shadowy darkness – a lanthorn's gold and the moon's silver never added light, but always stole each from the other on the coastal lands, it was rightly said.

But what he had seen had shown him that lustrous hair, that smooth reflecting skin, that picturesque face, that carriage and that long slender figure. Yes, she was woman enough to be what was promised, right enough. Perhaps she was too much for that peasant Prothero. Maybe she was enough to replace Thalia?

He turned and rode off in the direction of Carradine Manor. One thing, she would be a deal more interesting than that boring Mrs De Foe. Time that bitch with all her querulous importuning was returned to her husband, bag and baggage. It was time he was free of hangers-on and whining women. That Mehala, though, had possibilities. Maybe. Just maybe . . .

45

Little Flossie Jervin it was who first saw the grand carriage. She was even spoken to by the irate and tired coachman. 'He leaned right down, Miss Gould!' she cried with all the vigour of her six years, excitedly demonstrating a leaning position for her awed schoolfriends.

'Keep control, miss!' Matilda Gould reprimanded sternly. 'I hope you were seemly and gave proper reply, for if you weren't . . .'

'No, Miss Gould. I mean yes, Miss Gould!'

Flossie Jervin had so much to tell, and stumbled her words into incoherence as she babbled the account.

'He wanted to know Squire Hunterfield's place, so I told him! There was a coat of arms on the side door, Miss Gould!'

'Ooooooh!' the children gave out, thrilled at Flossie's meeting with such grandeur.

'Silence!' Miss Gould closed her eyes, hitherto a certain way of gaining attention. 'For the exercise class, Flossie, you will describe the coat of arms accurately, and say what conversation passed between yourself and the coachman.'

She was herself avid to hear, and for the first half hour of the day rejoiced in having so superb a witness as the fisherman's grand-daughter. Had it been anyone else in the class the child's verbal embellishments would have been so effusive that no trace of the truth would have been discernible. As it was, Flossie seized her moment with pride, and gave enough factual detail for Matilda Gould to be certain that a definite titled personage, accompanied by at least one other companion, or possible spouse, had arrived in Sealandings in a grand carriage, having travelled some distance.

It was to be the first of many arrivals.

During that day, the evening and the whole of the next they came. Several were directed to Milton Hall itself. A couple arrived and were sent as they requested to Carradine Manor, several more to Lorne House, and three, more rowdy than the rest, to Bures House where Charles Golding was already carousing and throwing parties late into the night.

An air of festivity grew in Sealandings. Veriker the clockmaker sold two good timepieces, and obtained requests for his services in the repair of no fewer than six London watches, of which three belonged to ladies. The gunsmith, a solemn unyielding man called Bartholomew Hast, and cousin of the famous Colchester firm of gunsmiths of that name, was soberly gratified to have a pair of belt pistols purchased from his stocks. Not only that, but a titled lady's manservant had called and shown interest in a percussion muff pistol for his mistress's use when travelling in the streets of terrible London.

The stables were becoming filled. Already arguments occurred where incoming grooms and coachmen had taken issue with the common stable in the Norwich road. One serious fight had taken place, to the amusement of all, about the composition of the food fed to the newcomers' horses. Squire Hunterfield, as the greatest local authority, was invoked as judge, and gave a ruling in favour of the 'foreign' groom, much to the satisfaction of the grooms and coachmen wanting stabling.

'It's only fair reason,' the aggrieved groom preached to anyone who would listen in the Donkey and Buskin. 'That man Parker might own them common stables, but he has no right to ruin our horses. No beast can work a full day on what he was supplying. I ask you! Twenty-eight pounds of steamed turnip per horse, which costs threepence-ha'penny only, and a penny for the seven pounds of coals to steam them, with only sixteen pounds weight of straw! Ridiculous! He feeds my master's horses for sixpence ha'penny apiece a day, and charges the earth! The man should be well and truly prosecuted, I say!'

'True,' he was told by the others who drank with him. 'These sea-coast folk are a thick clan, not natural folk like us from inland. Impossible to keep a sound working horse on less than a shilling-ha'penny a day.'

The groom thumped the table for emphasis. 'Ninepence a day per horse, in good oats alone, from three-shilling bushels new bought, I saw . . .'

And Sealandings grew. And grew.

A pugilistic contest about to be fought, word was, though the incoming coachmen and footmen, who strayed occasionally into the local taverns when certain they would not be required, were too wise to risk severance from their jobs by broaching confidentiality, and said nothing.

An impromptu race took place on the estate of Squire Hunterfield, between three speedy mounts of the officers who had arrived at Milton Hall. A party was thrown afterwards to celebrate the victory of one, but that was an incidental. All talk was of the ball and the arrangements for it. Seamstresses brought for the purpose worked into the night, and maids – less reticent than their male counterparts – prattled of materials and textures and colours and dyes and fashions and decorations and styles. The incoming personal maids discovered new enmities among new acquaintances and roused hatred among the residents at the grand houses of hostesses by ostentatiously showing themselves less than awed by local fashions.

The return of Fellows De Foe to Milton Hall was attended with much ceremony. His wife was on her sweetest behaviour throughout the day, showing her servants how very kind and condescending she could be.

The problems with Mrs Thornton, the cook, had long been solved. Mrs Randon was especially in favour, and her dispositions throughout the entire hall found warm praise. The floral arrangements and the new gleam that the housekeeper had managed to impart to the display furniture in the reception hall and the withdrawing rooms were highly regarded by all. Mrs De Foe had gone to great pains to boast of her housekeeper's excellence in Mrs Randon's hearing.

Ennis, the head footman, was less in focus since he was in no position to take umbrage, and in any case was not responsible for anything very essential.

Mrs Thornton was as capable as any cook in East Anglia, and was well known to have a secret receipt book which had come down to her from her mother and her mother in turn before her. It was sacrosanct, and she had refused several written invitations to sell or swap certain of the recipes. Now, with the heavy responsibility of the ball and banquet looming, she was nervous but proud that she would be able to produce an impressive and worthy feast. Not only that, her own desirability as a cook would soar after a notable triumph, such as this occasion would represent. She was ambitious enough to crave advancement. With several titled people attending, she might well become highly sought after, should all go as planned.

She told herself that she owed Mrs De Foe very little. Secretly she would be pleased to depart. She was determined to choose a time to leave, when the chance presented itself, which would cause her foul-tempered mistress the maximum embarrassment and inconvenience.

On the day, Mrs De Foe welcomed her husband with delight. This was always her greatest marital pleasure, to dress in her most fetching day attire, with colours as brilliant as respectability would allow, and stand meekly in the best position at the top of the grand sweep of steps. Her favourite accessory was the fashionable pagoda-shaped parasol, no matter what the weather, for she knew that it showed her colouring and face off to the best advantage. Her redingote was of a subtle pastel blue. She had toyed with the idea of having her hair done in serpents, the dragons being long enough to cope with her naturally long hair, but this mode was long since displaced in London fashion. She thought it too risky now. What with Fellows coming back from that fashionable capital, it would not do to seem too provincial to his other guests.

The recent modification of the Spanish hat, which was returning to favour, she finally selected with some confidence. Her muff was an adornment of crested grebe feathers, which were so frequent in these parts that they were among the commonest forms of decoration for a lady. She had rejected as too obvious the frisette which she had once bought while in Cambridge. If she wanted a crimped fringe for her forehead, she would have one of her own hair, thank you!

The coach was signalled as being in Sealandings while she was still having her afternoon tea, but that was all to the good. He would see how meekly and clandestinely she lived, and how frugally, while he was away. She saw to it that a small book of devotions lay open beside the sofa table, for his eye to catch as he entered and sat with her.

Fellows alighted briskly, pleased at the line of servants and the way Ennis leapt forward to open the door.

He was a smart man with a moustache, hair dressed to a nicety and clothes of the most sumptuous. Thalia heard Meg, behind her on the verandah, give a muted murmur of appreciation, which would require a certain amount of correction when the minx could be got alone, the little whore. She had no right to be heard on such occasions as this.

'My dearest!' Thalia greeted her husband and ushered him into the house, giving him no time to address the servants awaiting him. 'Welcome, my dear, to your own Milton Hall, and to your wife.'

'Greetings, sweet,' Fellows said, offering his arm. 'I shall have three visitors for you to entertain before nightfall, and a half dozen more tomorrow. I trust you'll appear as entrancing then as now!'

'For you, anything,' she said endearingly. He was a sentimental fool, the victim of his age, his male gender, and a doting set of parents for whom he could do no wrong. A man like this was to be despised more than followed or obeyed. Easy, simple, almost utterly facile, as long as you left him playing with his London toys – politics, gaming, merchant banking, probably wenching as well and carousing the nights away. Though she seriously doubted the latter.

'And this grand ball, my dear! Everything is prepared?'

'Musicians, of recommended excellence, who have played before Royalty and given delight, dearest. The food will be memorable, I

354

promise! The lights have been a special problem, but one which I do not want you to be bothered with, so soon on your arrival. Trust that I have decided upon fireworks, should it be fine outside, for the evening. Marquees will be provided, and fairy grottoes are to be set among the landscaped portions of the gardens.'

'Excellent, as always.'

He was smiling, looking about. Thalia always had been capable, so superb in her organizing, that a man had to be justifiably proud of such a creature for his wife.

A whore, of course. And transparent as water. But that went without saying. He beamed affection on his own dear Thalia.

'And now, dearest,' he said, his eyes twinkling. 'What of the extra special surprise?'

'Surprise, dearest?' She feigned a little-girl innocence. 'What on earth can you mean, sir? I have no surprises!'

'Nonsense.' He reached across, simpering, and took her hand. 'I know you through and through, my dear. I know that my darling Thalia has never – but *never!* –given a ball, or indeed any other entertainment, but what she has provided a marvellous astonishment for the delight of all who come to enjoy her features.'

For a fleeting second Thalia wondered worriedly if there was some hint of a double meaning in those words, but her husband, dolt of a man, was fawning most assiduously on her hand, almost at a grovel, the fool. No, this subservience proved yet again that he was devoid of subterfuge. And what on earth could he have heard in London anyway? Nothing. Nor in Sealandings, either. The only source of betrayal was Meg, and she had Meg cowed to a degree unmatched in anyone's experience. And, possibly, Ennis, but there again he was sufficiently wise to understand the implications of letting go any loose word that might reach the ears of Mr De Foe.

'Sir! You accuse me of sinister motives, keeping my plans from you?'

He observed her mimicry with a knowing smile. 'Ah, lady! Yes, I do. I know you only too well. Tell me the secret of your surprise, and I shall forgive all!'

'Alas, sir. You have caught me out.' She allowed him to take her hand and kiss it lingeringly, feeling actively repulsed by the man. Why on earth could he not stay in the capital and leave well alone here in Sealandings? It would be two, possibly three or even more, days before she would be able to see Carradine now, unless she took inordinate risks. And that was unthinkable.

'Tell, lady. *All* your secrets! This instant!'

That fleeting worry returned. A hint of emphasis on the word 'all'? Surely it was her imagination. Or his London wit, more like.

'I succumb, sir. Yes, I have arranged a scheme of entertainment which includes a surprise for the guests. A waterfall, with limelights set therein, and white doves to fly from it, unveiled in the grounds near where I had the willows removed. It will be as spectacular as anything you might have seen in your great cities, sir!'

'How excellent, Thalia! It sounds to out-Purcell Henry Purcell himself!'

'Yes, sir. Nothing will have been seen like it since Purcell's great oratorios, I warrant.'

'Thalia, my dear, I am so . . . taken by the awesome constancy you always reveal!' He kissed her hand. She smiled, certain now that glint of shrewd understanding she had seen in his eyes for half a second was only the result of her imagination.

'You shall always have my devotion, so far as I am able to give it, my dear. You know that, and I hope shall always know it.'

'My darling,' he murmured. 'Come. Let us retire for conversation to the bedroom.'

'But your tea, sir! I have wined strawberries here for you. And French pancakes, Devonshire junket to come, and dry gooseberry chips! Oh, dear, sir . . .'

'I insist,' the troublesome cretin said, with a degree of firmness which surprised her, and stood, drawing her with him. She had no choice but to accompany him towards the staircase.

'Oh, Fellows,' she sighed. 'You are *so thrilling* when you are like this! I wish it could be every day that you come home.'

'Well, now I have a surprise for *you*, Thalia,' he said, eyes twinkling, and pausing in the doorway. Servants scurried away in the hallway so as not to overhear the master making his love to the lady.

'For me, sir?' Now the anxiety was suddenly real as she gazed soulfully up at her husband. There was an adult, knowing look about him she had never seen before.

'For you, ma'am, and one which will give you all the delight your constancy has given me over our few married years. I am returning to live for good in Milton Hall!'

'Oh, Fellows!' she cried, aghast but striving to beam with delight. 'How truly marvellous! That is such a gift, a real delight!'

'I knew you would be thrilled, my dear.'

Fellows smiled inwardly. He had no intention of staying on this mouldy, windswept sea coast any longer than he had to for the sake of appearances, but was inwardly enjoying himself at the ingenious responses his dear Thalia was making. So valiant, so clever, so utterly hopeless at concealing her own inner longings. He wondered vaguely who it was this time that had caught her fancy. Time enough to make that particular discovery.

'Oh, I *am*!' Thalia said fervently, adding lovingly, 'My mind is in an utter whirl, dearest.'

'I knew it would be,' Fellows De Foe said with great fondness, and drew her up the stairs towards the bedroom.

In the early evening, Fellows decided that he should ride over and pay his respects to Squire Hunterfield, whom he had always considered a friend. Thalia pleaded that, since Mrs Randon had begun to encounter certain difficulties in raising the number of experienced maids for the banquet and ball to be serviced to the necessary superlative degree, she herself would have to take matters into her own hands. To do this, it was urgent that she take the carriage and ride to visit her acquaintances among the local ladies, and seek their advice. Fellows said he was proud to have a wife so devoted to excellence that she was willing to postpone her religious readings even further. She smiled meekly, and dressed in a sober and matronly fasion, enduring the hideously sombre Manchester velvet gown of dark green for the purpose. The Memphis cashmere wool which she had obtained for an outdoor visiting dress – Carradine had loved her in the Macabre silk wool, and had adored the rep imperial's rich silk only the night before – would have to wait until Fellows had found his niche back at Milton Hall. The news of his permanent stay was too urgent to brook delay. Carradine would have to be told. It would affect all of his plans, especially since word had reached Sealandings only that afternoon that the hustings for the new parliamentary elections were to be held within the month. This, she knew, was a deal earlier than Carradine had supposed. Also, Cousin Charles would have to be alerted, that he could start his bribes and the necessary secret deals immediately.

Fellows came to the steps, showing his best paces on his mare, doffing his hat with great bravado and calling her his lady love. She applauded, vastly impressed, and waved until the idiot had trotted out of sight into the gloaming, then hurried inside immediately, the smile dying on her face as if a light were extinguished within.

Twenty minutes later she was in her barouche and being driven towards Sealandings, having given directions for Bures House. From there she would be able to control at least part of the evening, send a message to Carradine and arrange a clandestine meeting. As long as that dolt Fellows didn't return too soon, or take it into his empty head to visit his neighbour Charles Golding on the spur of the moment. Still, she could always say she had called to solicit the help of the new housekeeper she had arranged – what was her name. . . ? Mehala.

Fellows De Foe returned to Milton Hall within a few minutes of seeing his wife ride out on to the South Toll road. He stood in the stirrups to see where the carriage turned, and was not surprised to see its lanthorn light swing slowly to the right into the drive at Bures House.

'Nothing between cousin and cousin; at least not there,' he murmured conclusively, turning his mare homeward. 'She scorns the man.' The question was, whom did Charles Golding have as close friends, or as acquaintances who might serve Thalia's white-hot ambitions?

He entered the hall through the grooms' entrance, and sent a maid-of-all for Ennis. The head footman came immediately, having been waiting for the summons as soon as he had seen the master and mistress leave separately. Fellows received him in the library.

'Ennis, man. Good to be home . . . I think.'

'If it please you, sir.'

Ennis knew the pattern, knew his job. He had no illusions about his position, nor about the sums of money being laid aside in his name in a London vault for the extra services he rendered the master of Milton Hall.

'You no doubt have a great deal to tell me, Ennis?'

'Sir. It is not all pleasing information.'

'Tell now, Ennis.'

Fellows lit his pipe with a taper from the fire, flicking it out and placing the taper with the others in the jar. He listened as the footman narrated the visits Mrs De Foe had made, the errands he had been sent on, the letters delivered and the origins of the replies brought back to the Hall for her.

'When does the mistress ride out from Milton Hall, Ennis?' Fellows asked. 'And I do not mean on local visits to friends, nor to places where other ladies congregate.'

'Sir, very little. In the past few weeks she has been only to visit relatives, such as Sir Philip Banks.'

'Very well, Ennis. You have done well. Tell me one thing more, though. Have you ever heard talk of anyone of Mrs De Foe's acquaintanceship seeking news of the coming elections?'

'Not of coming elections, sir.' Ennis pondered a while. 'But I heard the grooms talking, of the Commission of Inquiry at Norwich, sir, with the masters all a-being mortal heated about the affairs there.'

'Excellent, Ennis.' Fellows fixed the man with a level gaze, not wanting to daunt him or frighten him into inventions, but showing the extent of his concern. 'Now, try to remember this, if you can. Did anyone mention any names? If so, give me them.'

'I know of two, sir. They seemed . . . to stay in my mind. A Mr Wilde was often spoken about, and the grooms laughed at what he told to the Commissioners, sir.'

'And what was that?'

'Alas, sir, I did not hear. But it gave amusement, something about buying shopkeepers, about bribery and cooping and dealing, sir. But it was beyond me.'

'Good, Ennis. You've done well. The other?'

'Angell, sir. Alderman Angell.' Ennis shuffled apologetically. 'But of him I know nothing, sir. It was the names, being easily remembered, sir. Or I should not have recalled either.'

'I am very pleased, Ennis. You shall have your reward, do not fear. And see to it that I am spoken of as having ridden for quite some time, will you? To the mistress, I mean, and to the essential staff. I shall leave again fairly soon. See that my mare is not unsaddled. And make the usual appointment upstairs. Ten minutes.'

'Very well, sir.' Ennis withdrew and closed the huge double doors silently.

Fellows thought for a few moments, shaking his head. Surely Carradine and Golding couldn't be thinking of standing for Parliament? Because neither would have an earthly chance without massive support from some wealthy individuals tied to their cause. The expense of bribery and cooping at General Election time, the complexities of deals to be arranged, were so enormous that a single individual had no hope of success. A candidate, in these days of corruption and political fraud, must be the tip of the iceberg, the flag on the unseen fleet, to succeed.

Wilde was the political agent who had made Norwich a byword of parliamentary electoral intrigue and political double-dealing. And Angell was the alderman whose faction had been the principal beneficiary of Wilde's undoubted skills. That the grooms of gentry newly arrived at Sealandings for the grand ball and the pugilism contest knew of the doings of the Norwich Commission of Inquiry was really so strange as to be disturbing – for one such as he, who was

359

politically inclined. For the grooms of Sealandings itself to be so well versed in the goings-on of the political gentry in East Anglia was weird in the extreme. It meant there was a faction brewing.

Somebody was making a bid for grandeur and power in Sealandings. It would not be Henry Hunterfield. Golding? Carradine? Prothero?

He made his way into the servants' quarters and, in the end room of the east wing, opened the door without knocking and stepped inside.

'Good evening, Meg.'

'Good evening, sir.'

Meg was breathless, having run as soon as she had received the word from Ennis. Her small room was cramped, and she had been so hard worked ever since the mistress had announced the master's return that she had had little time to tidy it. However, she had done the best she could. Her clothes were bundled out of the way into the small press she was allowed as Mrs De Foe's personal maid, and her own tiny chest, brought with her from her father's when she was first hired, was crammed with washing not yet done. The single truckle bed was of course made, as Mrs Randon inspected every day and bated the servants' wages for untidiness.

She rose from her seated position on the bed. There was no chair. Even though this house and all its dispositions were in the direct ownership and gift of the master, she felt embarrassed when he visited here.

'The servants all at supper, I take it, Meg?'

'Yes, sir.'

'That is all to the good. May I sit here?'

'Indeed, sir.' She stepped aside, but he sat on the edge of the bed and pulled her down gently. She made an involuntary grimace, and he gazed quizzically up at her.

'Meg? Are you hurt?'

'A little, sir.'

'Where? And from what?'

'Nothing, sir.' She could not meet his eyes.

He nodded knowingly. 'Is it the usual cause, Meg?'

'Please, sir, I did nothing wrong. I was chastised by the mistress earlier for speaking out of turn, and for showing my feelings, sir.'

'When?'

'Just now, sir. In the lady's chamber when dressing her for the visit.'

'Let me see, Meg.' In spite of her reluctance he insisted, and she drew down her bodice. It was once an elegant fine woollen striped cloth of toilonette, but Meg had cut it down from a dress to make a work shift to wear under her linen apron.

Her back was badly marked, her shoulders showing weals between some of which the skin was broken. Fellows sighed.

'This is becoming more than you should be allowed to bear, Meg.'

'Yes, sir. It was just that the mistress blamed me for exclaiming when you arrived, sir.'

'Exclaiming?' He looked blankly up at her.

'I saw your clothes, sir. The sirsaka, sir. The maids talk of nothing else, we never having seen a spencer of that new material. And the cravat, sir. Is it cccclidc? Mrs Randon says it bc mortal costly, sir, silk and cashmere in the one textile. It's enough to amaze, sir.'

'The mistress punished you this severely for that?'

'It is right, sir. I behaved outside my station.'

'Well you too shall be paid, Meg. Clothe, and tell me all you know.'

'Yes, sir. I'm afraid to tell all exactly, sir, but the gist is that . . .'

She spoke at length, Fellows nodding and listening intently. He put to her the same questions he had previously given Ennis, but without success this time. He pressed her about the messages, then the nocturnal visits of Carradine. She became easier, sitting beside him diffidently but finally adding observations of her own as they occurred to her.

The mention of Squire Hunterfield, though, was an utter astonishment, and he questioned her repeatedly about Henry Hunterfield's night calls, the lanthorn signals, the way that gentleman was admitted, and the duration of his stay.

'Sir. I fear I shall be missed, sir. The supper will be over presently, and I shall be blamed if I do not return soon.'

'Very well, Meg. You shall away. But know that I shall not forget this. In taking that unreasonable punishment, yet in staying here at Milton Hall in the mistress's service, you do me a great service, better than all the other tasks you fulfil. I have made arrangements for sums to be paid for you, in due course. I promise also that you shall have any gifts of dress you require. Watch at the ball, and pick out from among the gowns you see. I shall see you rewarded.'

'Thank you, sir.'

Meg rose, as did he.

'And Meg? Your friendship with Ennis . . .'

'That is not yet announced, sir,' she answered, colouring immediately. 'I think I did wrong making mention of it when the master was here last, sir.'

'Not so, Meg. But as that is the case, then I would want to see you for conversation at the earliest opportunity.'

'You will, sir?' Conversation was the usual polite code word for serious physical dalliance of the most passionate kind.

'Of course, Meg. Did you doubt it? I find solace with you that I do not find with anyone else. And that is the truth. I want you to know it.'

'Thank you, sir. I shall be ready.'

He sighed as the door closed quietly behind the maid. She was pretty, serviceable, and willing, and secure – insofar as any woman could be thought secure. So he had at least two sound allies here in Milton Hall, his family home.

She would be gone by now, down the back staircase into the kitchen level. He stood, looking around.

The first time he had taken Meg, it had been in this room, with her muffling her own cries and his mouth while they had loved on this very truckle. Now, the poor wench was thrashed for her very innocence. What a mad world servants lived in!

But the world of master and mistress was madder still.

He would do nothing, he decided. Hunterfield was being duped by Thalia into supporting Carradine's political ambitions, it seemed, from what he had learned tonight. Or some puppet of Carradine's? Charles Golding would fit exactly for that role in the pantomime. He would wait up late tonight, and pen a few letters to London.

In the meantime, he had a courtesy call to make on Squire Hunterfield. His friend.

46

Mrs Darling had made a small tea, with nelson cakes, to speed Mehala on her way.

'How will Sealandings seem now, Mehala?' Doctor Carmichael asked, smiling as Mehala gently kissed Clare and went towards the door. 'After all, it has been some days since you ran away to join us in looking after the child!'

'As well as can be expected, Doctor.' Mehala tried to seem a deal more convinced than she felt, aware that Winifred Overton and Mrs Darling were taking in every detail of her behaviour. 'The place has been very kind to me. I only hope that kindness will continue, for at least a little while.'

'They are strange folk at Sealandings, Mehala,' Mrs Overton said, 'saving the doctor's company. But it's mortal true.'

'What'll you do, Mehala?' Mrs Darling asked, anxious for her. It was quite a severance, after the closeness of the cottage.

'Go to the rectory and offer my service. I shall not be too readily welcomed, I surmise. I think the rector and Miss Baring will be wounded at the suddenness with which I escaped them! But I shall attempt to fulfil my former promise at last. Better late than never.'

'They will be gaining the very best housekeeper possible, Mehala,' Carmichael said. He made as if about to say more, but instead silence fell.

The four of them stood by the door. It was an evening. Several women with children were across from the cottage. One or two waved as they emerged, and Mehala acknowledged them. She even did that as if entitled to their salutations, Carmichael thought, watching. He felt something disturbing, as if he too should be leaving, but with the child still too sick to raise from her recumbency he knew that was out of the question.

Mehala paused before him. He thought how absurd he must seem to her, as if he were tongue-tied and she someone grand and senior, when she was merely a young dispossessed woman with very few prospects.

'Goodbye, Mehala. Fortune attend you.'

'Goodbye, Doctor. God bless your work.' She smiled. 'One day, if Providence permits, I shall render your Flora dial as good as new again for you, that you might enjoy the blossoms in your garden.'

'My. . . ?' He looked blankly at her.

She smiled. 'Flora's dial. You have – had – one at Shalamar. Two rings of flowers are arranged in a circle, giving flowers which bloom in turn throughout each of the two clock cycles, through twelve hours of opening, and twelve closing. I shall establish them again one day for you, all four.'

'Four?' He thought a moment. '*Two* cycles of flowers, and you'll establish *four?*'

'A clever gentleman should be able to reason why,' she said impishly, and said her goodbyes as she turned and walked off.

'Mehala,' one of the watching men called. 'Mind them folk in Sealandings. Come back here to Whitehanger if you be sore treated!'

'I promise!' she called with good humour.

Doctor Carmichael watched her go. She carried nothing, walking straight and firm with an ease and style that caught the eye.

'Doctor,' Mrs Darling said slowly. 'Forgive the intrusion. But . . . would it not be a grand thing if Mehala became your housekeeper, saving Mrs Trenchard's excellent service to you?'

'What a good idea, Emiline!' Winifred Overton exclaimed pleasantly. 'The old lady would have Mehala's most reliable help, and find her a place to suit. And your service would be improved thereby, Doctor! Why on earth did we not think of it before!'

'I wish there was permission, promise, coin and opportunity, ladies,' Carmichael said sadly, still following Mehala's dwindling figure with his eyes.

'Should I not call her back, Doctor?' Mrs Overton urged. 'She wants to . . .'

Mrs Darling caught her cousin's glance and shook her head warningly. There was danger in saying too much.

'I am in the best circumstances I shall know for quite some time, I fear,' he said heavily. 'It is either leave Sealandings or stay and improve my situation but slowly.'

'Yes, Doctor. Forgive my thoughts, always running ahead of my sense.'

'It was kindly meant, Mrs Overton,' he said. He was the last to turn and re-enter the cottage, and then only when Mehala had finally disappeared from view.

It was over.

All over, Mehala thought as she started along the sea dykes from Whitehanger.

The strange but vitally needed episode of recovery from the sea was ended. Her new life was about to begin.

For the first step into it, she would repay the debts outstanding: her duty to report at Reverend Baring's home, to see if they would still accept her for service there; somehow recompense the Weavers at the Donkey and Buskin for their kindnesses. Then, with whatever she could legitimately obtain by way of money for the journey, she would leave Sealandings. She had to. There was no other way.

Return to her origins? She doubted that would be a realistic choice. No, stay away from the sea marshes of Mersea Island where those evil memories lay.

Her sense of belonging was the treachery in all this logic, though. The doctor's lone struggle against his ignorance – and against everyone else's – cried out for help. Not only that; it was help of the kind she could give. But a cry of silence goes unheard; until it is uttered outright nothing responds, no one comes.

The tide was in. Distantly across the bay, the brilliant gleam of the North Sea had spread up to the land completely, flooding the mud flats and spreading from the fleets so the channels were now as one. A Yorkshire lugger, the leading vessel of three, beat slowly out into the onshore wind. She recognized *The Jaunty*, and stood for a moment, exhilarated at the spectacle.

Though they were quite two miles offshore, she hoped they would be scanning the shorelines and the estuary banks, the best way to detect where the sands might have shifted. She imagined Jervin, hard at prayer for success of the fishing, sour Old Lack grumbling at the nets, and young Hal Baines busying himself at the sheets. She waved hopefully, but they were too far into the faint mists for her to see if they made any reply.

She walked on, keeping the slopes of Whitehanger to her left, deliberately not in haste. It was as if she were playing the child's trick all over again, of pretending she was not going to school, that she was out walking to somewhere pleasant, on holiday even, and by that evasion hoping eventually that it might actually become true.

Ahead, the track became a more solid roadway, metalled though still badly pitted. She saw a long waggon halted there, and recognized the coloured vehicle of Jake Darling. He sat atop, smoking his pipe, and waved as she left the sea wall to greet him. As she approached, she saw him raise a palm aloft in dismissal, and, turning, recognized a group of three small boys from Whitehanger on the far margin of the woods.

'Have you been having me followed by young highwaymen, Jake Darling?' she reproved.

'Yes, Mehala.' He was grinning sheepishly. 'I feared for you. Sealandings has grown mortally these few days past. You'll see when you get there.'

'But gentry, by all accounts, Jake? She climbed up, placing her feet on the dashboard where he indicated.

'That's so, Mehala,' he said soberly. 'But these riotous modern days you don't know what the carriage company will do, any more than you can guess what footpads lurk about.'

'Even here at Sealandings?' She was amused.

'Sealandings, Whitehanger, it's all the same.'

'Doctor Carmichael sits with Clare,' she informed him. 'Your daughter seems bettering still. She cannot sit up without the doctor becoming agitated about her heart, but she seems more alert.'

'Thanks be to God,' he replied piously, unbraking the waggon and geeing the four horses expertly into motion. 'Do you think she will survive, Mehala?' He looked away in embarrassment. 'I should not ask so, I know. But you have a sense of fitness in things, and I trust what you say.'

She was distressed. 'How can I answer, Jake?' If I say I am confident and Clare passes away, what then? And if I say I am still afeared for her, I make things worse without immediate reason!'

'I know, Mehala. But you know the doctor as most others don't. My Emiline says to ask you, for you'll tell best, see?'

For a while she rode the waggon, holding on to the side board against the rocking, and spoke at last.

'Doctor Carmichael hopes now, Jake. He didn't, early on. Now, he feels that maybe Clare will live, and live normally. But he is still uncertain of the operation he must do to close her throat when she is recovered. That is all I can say.'

'That'll do for me, Mehala.' He glanced at her as the gateway of Lorne House came into view. 'Do you intend to stay in Sealandings, Mehala?'

Jake Darling saw more than he pretended, she observed. 'I go to repay my debts. First to the rectory, offering my service as I promised. After that all is in the lap of the Lord.'

'There's your artist, Mehala.'

Jake did not need to point. William Maderley was walking a small tit across the pasture from the direction of Watermillock. He stopped as the waggon passed nearby and stared intently, keeping himself and his horse motionless for as long as they were in clear view. Then, when the hedges started to intervene, he moved on, pulling the reins.

'Why *my* artist, sir?' Mehala demanded.

Darling smiled. 'He's said to paint nothing but that picture of you, with the sealands and the ocean all distressed in the background. I trust he paints something more pleasing than that for the grand folks at Lorne House, or Squire Hunterfield's sister Mrs Vallance will be sore vexed. They have made him Hunterfield family painter of likenesses.'

'Perhaps he is mad. They say all are . . .' Her smile made a joke of her words.

A group of riders came at a walk from the gateway of Lorne. Darling slowed the waggon, hauling and clicking gently to his team to allow the horsemen passage.

They were a bright cluster, mantles and cloaks and uniforms and dashing attire, and were talking loudly as they came. Mehala recognized Squire Hunterfield, third of the six, as they came abreast. Darling pulled his horses to a halt and raised the margin of his ancient nivernois hat in salutation.

'Odds gods, Henry!' one rider exclaimed. 'Yonder's the pick of Sealandings, eh? D'you grow them all like her hereabouts?'

The rider was a youngish well-mounted gentleman, wearing a Royal George stock at his throat, of black genoa velvet tied with its satin bow at an extravagant slope.

'We are famed for the beauty of our . . . characters, Cav,' Squire Hunterfield gave back with good humour.

Some of the party stopped as others rode on ahead, laughing.

'The girl in the boatman's red wool bonnet, Henry. Who is she?'

'Coming to the ball, I trust, m'lady?'

Squire Hunterfield was obliged to remain with the two riders who had decided to loiter, though Mehala could sense his displeasure at the interlude.

'Shall we take her along, Sir Cavan?' a uniformed rider asked. He wore the attire of a regimental captain, but with hussar points to his waistjacket as if from cavalry. 'Captain Bussell, at your service, ma'am.'

Mehala did not rise to the banter, keeping herself composed and staring straight ahead. She felt Jake Darling stiffen as the riders approached closer. Most of his work was for the squire's estate, she knew, so they were in no danger from the rowdiness of his party, but a waggoner in charge of a team of giant shire horses was right to be apprehensive.

'And I Sir Cavan Webb, mistress!'

They were making mock of her, but Mehala felt quite at ease.

'Good day to you, Darling.' The squire spoke easily, smiling at the waggoner. 'What's that load, then? Something of mine, I take it?'

He wore a hunting necktie and a long riding cloak, and seemed willing to pass the time of day in spite of the underlying tension Mehala was sure they all felt.

'Barley, Squire,' Jake Darling said evenly. 'I have several loads for the Donkey and Buskin. John Weaver there'll be brewing beer as soon as . . . as soon as the town settles and gives him more time.'

'Wise John Weaver,' Hunterfield said with a smile. 'And Mehala. Whitehanger's loss, Sealandings gets the gain?'

'Thank you kindly, Squire.'

'She talks as well as she looks, Henry,' Sir Cavan said. 'Are you sure she's a waggoner's mate?'

'That boatman's woollen should be replaced by a straw cottage bonnet, miss,' Captain Bussell said. He was an older man showing signs of dissipation and already leaning heavily in his saddle. 'Well? You'll not answer me?'

He flicked his riding whip suddenly. The woollen hat flew from Mehala's head. She felt strands of hair torn, and she gave an involuntary yelp at the pain.

Captain Bussell was laughing, waving his whip in celebration. The other riders were turning, looking back at the commotion. Jake Darling was having difficulty suddenly, trying to control his team which sensed the disturbance and were suddenly skittish and shifting worriedly. In sudden fury Mehala seized Jake Darling's whip and stood, clutching the side board with her left hand, the whip in her right. It cracked, and the captain's riding hat flew into the lowly hedgerow which rimmed the field.

The loud laughter of the returning riders made Darling's four shires back and pound. Captain Bussell also had difficulty controlling his mount, which had been startled by the snap of Mehala's whip.

'Of all the damned. . . !'

'Retrieve my hat, sir,' Mehala called, 'and I shall retrieve yours!'

'The damned bitch!' Bussell cursed.

'This damned bitch would call you out for that insult, sir,' Mehala shot back as the captain gained control of his horse. 'Except I doubt you would have less control over your Mantons than you do over your other accoutrements!'

'I'll flog that bloody waggoner of yours for letting his woman go mad on me, Hunterfield! Be damned if I don't!'

368

Mehala sat and gazed at Squire Hunterfield. She was quite calm. The obligation was his. She was unprepared for the firmness with which he accepted it.

'Not just yet, Neville,' Hunterfield said with easy humour. 'Remember that I shall be blamed if there's less beer in Sealandings than the townsfolk expect by All Hallows!'

'And that would never do, eh?' Sir Cavan took his cue, nodding to help his host defuse the situation. 'As long as I receive adequate sustenance for the fight contest tomorrow, Henry, I shall be satisfied!'

The returned riders were laughing, their mounts swirling on the narrow roadway and into the adjoining field. One of them laughingly retrieved the captain's hat by getting it on the point of his sword, and nudged his horse towards Bussell's.

'Here, Nev,' he said, laughingly trying to replace it on the captain's head. Captain Bussell snatched it in fury, now not knowing what line to take. 'I shall stand you a bottle of Portugal at the fight tomorrow, in appreciation of some fine entertainment. And that even before we have started out! It's quite remarkable . . .' He paused, staring at Mehala.

She felt something cold grow within. The gaze of men was something she had become used to. But this was something far more disturbing than admiration, lust, hunger, pleasure . . . It was recognition.

'Miss. Have I not seen you somewhere? Were you not. . . ?'

'Come, gentlemen,' Squire Hunterfield interposed. 'I have promised you all a ride to Maidborough heath, and the hours go faster than we!'

'Let Neville ride first,' some wag called. 'We shall follow his hat!'

To loud laughter the group rode off along the road. Squire Hunterfield was last, from courtesy. He seemed thoughtful though and hung back.

'All right with you, Jake?' he asked quietly.

'Yes, thank you,' Darling replied in the same quiet manner. No courtesy title, Mehala observed, wondering.

'The child?'

'Stays yet. She is no worse, thank God.'

'Amen, Jake. My prayers are with her.'

'Thank you.'

They stayed in silence, watching the horsemen ride towards the town. Only when they had descended from sight did the waggoner click his quietened team into motion.

'Squire Hunterfield is a gentleman, Mehala, is he not?' Jake said at last.

'Indeed he is.'

369

'I am sorry I took no action to save your embarrassment from that Captain Bussell, Mehala.'

'I only hope I haven't caused you any trouble. Captain Bussell looks an ill friend to anyone, and a worse foe.'

'No, Mehala.' Darling sounded confident. 'I shall fear nothing from him.'

Mehala said nothing. She had noticed, over the endless hours of watching little Clare and turning the hour glass for Doctor Carmichael, the monogrammed leather base inside the instrument. Heaven knows, offspring were unplanned when passion rode its most urgent journey. It would be nothing uncommon for the Darlings – either Emiline or Jake – to harbour an illegitimate by-blow of the Hunterfields. Or little Harry, rest him in peace? Or Clare, even? She too had noticed the letters HH on that costly hour glass. And when the party of riders moved on its way, Jake Darling had not given Henry Hunterfield his sir and squire and your honour. But it was all none of her business, and the uncomfortable encounter was now over.

The waggon came in sight of the first houses of Sealandings.

'I do not know if I love the place or not,' Mehala said involuntarily. 'It has things terrible, yet lovely.'

'That is the lot of all life, Mehala,' Jake said, grinning now he had recovered his composure. 'None of us knows what we love.'

'Doctor Carmichael should have discovered the answer to *his* riddle by now,' she said as the waggon approached the market square. 'He should restore his garden, if ever circumstances allowed. I posed him a question about a Flora's clock, of flowers in Shalamar. There used to be – '

'It was a splendid thing, Mehala.' Darling sang and whistled gently to his team, negotiating the corner of a narrow thoroughfare and coming in sight of the schoolhouse across the square. 'Four half days, hour by hour, opening and closing. Beautiful!'

'Wiser than Doctor Carmichael, Jake!' she smiled. 'You already know the answer!'

'Only from having seen it many times, Mehala, when young.'

That must have been when Shalamar was a grand house, before its dereliction. And before its family moved out. She avoided glancing at the waggoner.

'Promise you will not disclose the answer to Doctor Carmichael,' she said.

'Let him find out by his own reason,' Darling agreed, smiling.

He deposited her before the rectory gate, and waved his goodbye.

She stood for a moment, then entered and walked up the path, Jake watching her.

A tongue always returns to the aching tooth, he reminded himself with an inward sigh. An old but true proverb, too often forgot.

He clicked to his horses and the waggon rolled on, with Jake Darling singing the ancient ballad 'Chevy Chase' as he went.

47

The study in which Reverend Baring received Mehala was certainly not sparse, to her eyes. It was however book-lined and seemed ponderous, but then to her eye masculine rooms always did. Nothing feminine, no flowers, no ornamentation except a few small keepsakes from his many journeys abroad.

Mehala could see immediately that he was displeased. She was kept standing, as was quite proper, while he deliberated. Miss Baring remained seated on a wheelback after having admitted her.

'I think your conduct reprehensible, Mehala.' They were his first words to her after Euterpe brought her in. 'To make a promise, then to break that most solemn undertaking, is deceit. It cannot be justified under any circumstances.'

'But, Josiah,' his sister tried to intervene, 'I truly do believe that in this case – '

'If you please, Euterpe.' The rector closed his eyes and waited painfully for silence to reassert itself. 'There might be extenuating circumstances, I know. Those I am perfectly prepared to consider should they be brought to my notice, as a simple Christian gesture of goodwill. But they will have to be firm and truthful. You understand me, Mehala?'

'I do, Reverend.'

'Very well. Let me continue by saying that I will expect your accuracy and brevity in this. Explain why you transgressed.'

'I learned of a need to help Doctor Carmichael in caring for a sick child, Reverend. I left a note, and directly made my way to assist.' She decided to hide the fact that Doctor Carmichael had sent for Miss Euterpe and not herself.

'And was your aid necessary, Mehala? Wholly and completely?'

Mehala recognized the trick. Affirmative, and she was arrogantly accusing Doctor Carmichael of incompetence. A reply in the negative meant she had deliberately and frivolously rejected her duty, in order to seek a diversion.

'My assistance was of some value, Reverend, for Doctor Carmichael himself expressed his appreciation, I think too kindly. But it would be presumptuous of me to claim more. I simply felt burdened by my Christian duty.'

'Burdened?' Reverend Baring was horrified. '*Burdened?* You use that word? That "burden", as you imply, is no mere load! It is an expression of the responsibility, the true holy impulse which indicates the road we should tread. Let me never, never hear you use that expression again!'

'I apologize, Reverend.' She made as if to hesitate, conquered the apparent reticence, and spoke on. 'It is just that in the past I have heard the word used of our religious duty, and thought it proper.' She was so downcast at her mistake.

'Where, Mehala?'

'Alas, Reverend, I do not recollect. I know . . .' She passed her hand across her forehead as if in puzzlement. 'I do know that I have heard at a service those words used, Reverend. But the other Sunday, in the church, I felt so much more at peace than in that other place I cannot quite remember. It was more to my . . . preference, Reverend, if that term does not abuse the holiness of the Church.'

'Another unfortunate expression, Mehala!' His eyes were glowing, however. He leaned forward. 'But one which in the circumstances I am prepared to overlook. Tell me, Mehala. You think it possible that you were once enticed into some, ah . . . nonconformist form of worship?'

'Please, Reverend. I do not know what that is.'

'Very well. But you definitely sensed that the church services I performed more to your . . . ah, your. . . ?'

'More to my calling, Reverend,' she completed gently for him. 'It was fitting, somehow. It seemed proper, in a way I am unable to express. You must forgive me, Reverend, for I am unlettered in the significations of the churches.'

'Church, Mehala,' he corrected mechanically. 'One Church. Singular.' He turned to his sister, almost smiling. 'It seems that the Lord has returned Mehala to the fold, Euterpe! Perhaps this fault which she committed, defaulting on her agreed arrangement, was the Saviour's means of redirecting Mehala to our flock.'

Was it indeed, Euterpe thought dryly, but only said obediently. 'As you say, Josiah.'

'Very well, Mehala.' He gazed sternly at her. She was too meek to meet his eyes. 'Very well. You will be taken on here as housekeeper, but at maid-of-all wages, until such time as you prove satisfactory in the judgement of Miss Baring, when I shall reconsider.

'Thank you, Reverend.'

'You may go. Wait outside the door, if you please.'

'Thank you, Reverend. Miss Baring.' Mehala curtseyed and left to await instructions.

It had been a narrow thing, but here she was at last, with a roof over her head and the rectory to serve as protection. Mehala breathed a sigh of relief. The reverend had picked up his cue and given his little lecture, as she had hoped.

She heard the door go, and saw Miss Baring emerge. The two women stood eyeing each other for a moment. Euterpe made certain the door behind her was firmly shut.

'Well, Mehala. You coped with that very well. I am pleased you managed it.'

'Thank you, Miss Baring.'

'Between you and I there is to be no religious philosophizing, however. You understand?'

'Yes, Miss Baring.' Trust another woman to catch the unspoken evasions, Mehala thought with an inward grimace.

'Now, Mehala. Come.' Euterpe beckoned her towards the parlour. 'I have some tea fresh made. Let it be your induction into life at the rectory of Sealandings. And you can tell me all that has transpired at Whitehanger with Doctor Carmichael's charge there!'

Mehala followed dutifully. There was a radiance in Miss Baring's manner when she spoke of Doctor Carmichael which she found disturbing, even unpleasant. She could see that she would need all her circumspection in describing the events at the Darlings' cottage.

'You get the idea, Goring?' Carradine said, consciously gentling the man as he would a horse.

The prize fighter nodded. He had trained all afternoon and was sweating heavily. His seconds were rubbing him down as the gentleman addressed him.

'I understand, sir. I must fight him slow, like, right from the first. Then I must start attacking him, weakening him down.'

'But only after a large number of rounds, you understand, Goring.' Carradine wanted there to be no mistake. Everything depended on Rendell seeming a capable challenger.

'How will I know the number of rounds, sir?'

'I shall signal you. It will be soon after twenty rounds or so. No,' Carradine corrected himself. 'Let it be that you will start on him properly after, say, easing him along up to twenty-five rounds. After that, you can start buffeting him as you will.'

'What round do you wish him knocked out, sir?'

'About the sixtieth, Goring. That should be convincing enough.'

'The trouble is, though, sir,' Able Sumner put in, listening, 'that Goring here will be somewhat the loser in all this.'

'Loser?' Goring asked. His seconds paused in their work at the ominous tone of the giant fighter.

'Mr Goring cannot lose to Rendell, Sumner,' Carradine told the agent impatiently. He had not liked the agent being present, in fact had not wanted him along in the first place, but Goring's backers and handlers had insisted.

'I do not mean lose financially, sir, for you are paying him handsomely for his work tomorrow. Nor in the ring. But by reputation, sir, alas . . .' Sumner shook his head with regret.

'What do you mean, sir?' Goring demanded.

'You see, there's such a thing as reputation.' Sumner addressed his remarks to Carradine. 'And we know, the whole Kingdom knows, that Goring here could defeat this unknown Rendell in any number of rounds he desired. For a contender to Tom Spring's throne to require no fewer than sixty rounds to knock out a country bumpkin is a most notable lapse in repute, sir, for which Goring should be handsomely rewarded.'

'How much more, then, Sumner?' Carradine asked, feeling loathing for the contemptible commission crawler. This scheme was proving an inordinate expense. Every meeting meant money out, never money in. Yet.

'Another two thousand sovereigns would be appropriate, sir. That is the kind of sum I was contemplating.'

'Two thousand. . . ?' Carradine nodded. He was in chancery, with the fight now less than twenty-four hours away. 'Very well. Done. I shall pay you the extra after the fight's successful conclusion.'

'Alas, sir,' Sumner said smoothly. 'It will have to be now. All wagers and payments relating to a fight are payable at the time of making the agreement. That's the gentleman's code, sir.'

Carradine swallowed. One day he would run this wheedler through, and take delight in doing so.

'I shall have it for you as I leave. Two thousand.'

He left the barn, shouldering his way past the two guards on the door, and made his way along the narrow street opposite.

Jason Prothero was seated in a small English hooded gig borrowed for the occasion. Carradine clambered inside, smiling, making sure that confidence radiated from him.

'Is all arranged, sir?' Prothero asked.

Carradine gazed contemptuously at the man. The bumpkin was actually sweating with apprehension, fear even.

'Yes, Prothero,' he drawled, not bothering to conceal his dislike. 'All is arranged. An extra two thousand to Goring has been agreed. You can pay over the money now.'

'I'm pleased to hear it.' Prothero hesitated.

'Yes? What is it? I've just told you that – '

'The woman, sir. Mehala. You had said that she would be at Calling Farm by . . .' Prothero let his sentence hang, not wanting to push the gentleman even at this late stage.

'Ah, yes.' Carradine smiled easily, cursing himself for a forgetful fool and for letting this odious oaf rile him so. The upstart, a meacock jack-on-horseback, was as haunty as a colt at its first outing. But things were too far gone to jeopardize this golden hour which, tomorrow on the heath at Maidborough, would bring him his ultimate independence, unbelievable wealth, and mastery of all Sealandings. Plus power in Parliament a certain guarantee in the future. 'I have made arrangements for Mehala to be at your place tomorrow evening,' he lied smoothly. 'I have seen to it that she will be eager to enter your service for two consecutive periods of three years apiece. And I have already paid her her earnest-money for the hiring.' He embellished the fable. 'Once she attends on Mrs Prothero, she is yours. She will not retreat under fire, Prothero. Take my word on that.'

Prothero looked put out of countenance, so Carradine added easily to keep the man drawn in, 'There is one thing. Prothero. I think that it would be better if you were to start meeting some of the gentry in Sealandings. On a social plane, I mean. An excellent opportunity for this presents itself. It takes place the day after tomorrow, at Milton Hall. I shall see to it that, now the notion has occurred to me, you and your good lady wife shall receive invitations to Mrs De Foe's great ball which is to be held then. I trust you will be able to come. . . ?'

'Oh, yes, sir!' Prothero exclaimed, pleased at the recognition he was finally receiving, even though it came through this swaggering swine. 'Thank you. I can say that Mrs Prothero will be quite overcome!'

'Good, good,' Carradine said, thinking that Mrs Prothero would probably be overcome simply by the relief of meeting other company than that of her repellent husband. 'I shall enjoy your company at Milton Hall, especially after our forthcoming triumph. Something to celebrate, eh? And I shall be pleased to meet Mrs Prothero, at last.'

'Very well, sir.' Prothero wondered if he should urge Carradine to expedite Mehala's arrival, but decided from the steely glint in his companion's eyes that he had better remain silent. 'The main sum shall be in your hands tonight, sir. My men will bring it to Carradine Manor, if that is your pleasure.'

'It is, Prothero,' Carradine said briskly, descending from the carriage. 'Make sure they are not late.'

'Yes, sir.' Prothero said obediently.

He hated Carradine's arrogance with a fervour that was making him steam with sweat and silent rage. One day he would make that man kneel. He did not watch Carradine saunter off along the narrow pavement, just sat there with the reins in his hands, hating and hating and hating.

The kitchen was not the easiest to find her way about in, Mehala was just realizing, when she heard a frantic tapping from outside.

Little Jane's face was at the window. Mehala looked round carefully, not wanting to give offence to Miss Baring, but she could hear the rector's sister going upstairs. It would be safe to open to Little Jane. She went to the garden door and unlatched it for the girl to slip inside. She seemed out of breath and distressed.

'What on earth is it, Jane? Here, sit down and get your breath! But keep as silent as possible!'

'I have no time, Mehala.' Little Jane was gasping, desperate to get her story out and be away. 'She's coming! She will be here directly!'

'Who will? Here to the rectory?'

'Yes. Mrs De Foe. Oh, Mehala! It's such a terrible thing, her temper! She's threatened all sorts to Mr Weaver. And Mrs Weaver was nigh to fainting, so terrible was the lady!'

'But what about, Jane? And why come here to tell me?'

'Oh, Mehala. It's all on account of you.' Little Jane was almost in tears, babbling the news.

'But . . . What's the reason, Little Jane?'

'She's angered that things haven't gone as she instructed, Mehala.'

'Instructed? But to whom? When? And wherefore?'

'I don't know, Mehala. Only I heard the mistress tell Mr Weaver terrible news after Mrs De Foe had left, which was why I come a-flying to say. Mrs Weaver was saying, all tearful like, "Oh, John, what'll us do? For Mrs De Foe swears her cousin Mr Golding will cut off our water stream from his lands, and without fresh water and with the brewing season upon us we shall all be set to starving." Her was mortal distressed of it, Mehala, something terrible!'

'But why am I brought into it?' Mehala cried softly.

'Don't you see, Mehala? You should be in the housekeeper's post, in Bures House. Not here at all!'

'I what?' Mehala sank on to the kitchen bench, aghast.

377

'In the service of Mr Charles Golding. Mrs De Foe has ordered it so. When she learned that you were left from Whitehanger and had come to offer yourself here, she flew into the most terrifying rage you ever did see.'

'But this is disaster. How can I resist her?'

'Everything's awry, Mehala! Why, today I overheard John Weaver turn away night riders wanting to lodge a conveyance from Norwich to Maidborough. Turn away! And them giving Prothero and Carradine for bond names!'

A doorbell rang in the house, and the kitchen bell clonked in sympathy. Little Jane gave a frightened squeal.

'That's her! It's her!' She made the gesture of a buss and fled, thumping the door emphatically to behind her.

Mehala smoothed her apron and went to answer the front door.

A coachman stood there, one she had seen before. From Milton Hall, in the dark olive-green jacket and black coacher's hat.

'Please to inform the rector that Mrs De Foe will receive him at her carriage immediately, miss.'

'Very well,' Mehala said awkwardly, and closed the door as the man turned on his heel.

Reverend Baring was smiling with pleasure at the theological considerations in the small error Mehala had perpetrated during the discussion he had led her through. *Burden*, indeed! So typical of those terrible nonconformist sectarians and their loose shoddy thinking! As if the laws of reason could not be applied equally to science, logic and theology! It was worth a sermon, two possibly. Supposing he blended the approach of Doctor John Donne the Divine by melding a comparison with the . . .

He heard Mehala's message and quickly dropped his notes and books, and almost ran down the rectory path to greet Mrs De Foe in the coach.

'Please, Reverend,' Mrs De Foe cut through his effusive gallantries. 'I am not here to bandy words.'

'I trust I have not occasioned any displeasure, ma'am?' he stuttered anxiously, casting a glance about to see how few of his parishioners were overhearing this.

'I shall be brief, Reverend. That Mehala female. I gave explicit instructions to Mrs Weaver that on no account was she to leave her service to anywhere else except Bures House. And I find that you have purloined her services behind my back, and without so much as – '

'Ma'am!' he cried. 'Nothing was further from my mind when the girl appealed to my sister for shelter and a post!' He wrung his hands. 'I had nothing in mind except the highest precepts of Christian charity when the girl appeared, without appointment, to seek my benevolence. And I can say without fear of contradiction that she gave not the slightest hint that she was already assigned to the service of another.'

'I see. So the female can be evasive when it suits her fancy, it seems.'

'Indeed, ma'am. I should have suspected it. I see that now! Naturally, I would never have countenanced my sister's employing her, were it not for the fact that Mehala begged – actually *begged!* – to be taken in. And she did not intimate for a moment that she had any other opportunities in Sealandings. I hope and trust that, ma'am, in the circumstances, you will forgive any apparent transgression on my part . . .'

'It is quite a clear-cut issue, Reverend Baring,' Thalia De Foe curtly cut through his protestations. 'This creature thinks she can play ducks and drakes with the gentry of this locality, and so far has managed to succeed.'

'Indeed so, ma'am!'

'I have to say that I simply do not care one way or another whether she attends on Bures House for employment or not. But it does seem to me that we are in considerable danger of allowing this slut to use us exactly as she pleases! Think of the atrociously bad example that would be, if word got around among the servants!'

'Terrible, ma'am! Atrocious!'

'Therefore, simply in the interests of domestic economy she shall *have* to be compelled to work a period at Bures House, in however low a capacity. Which should reassert the rights of the gentry, and prove to this oh-so-haughty a nicebecetur that she is not such a fine, pretty lady after all!'

'Of course, ma'am! A most excellent solution to the problem! And, ma'am, I trust that you will overlook any indiscretion on my part as simply one of accidental non-compliance with your wishes, for nothing would ever induce me to act in a manner contrary to your – '

'Drive on,' Mrs De Foe called imperiously, and the carriage moved off, leaving the rector wringing his hands by the rectory gate.

48

Mehala reached Bures House still smarting at her abrupt dismissal from the rectory. She felt abused, under a cloud.

Walking across Sealandings from the rectory, her most direct route lay past the market's Celtic cross, past the junction with the South Toll road – along which Shalamar stood so near – then eastward, towards the harbour a little way, to reach the road which led eventually to Whitehanger, from where she had ridden on Jake Darling's waggon earlier. As she walked, she thought of Little Jane's account of the night riders and their need of safe overnighting for a valuable conveyance. Surely that was the practice of bankers shipping gold coin?

She regretted her choice of route, for as she emerged from the rectory gates into the market square she was surprised by the concourse of vehicles and horses now milling through the open space. She had never seen such a melee in her life. The carriage company was here in force, to be sure, with worse folk still among them, if such there could possibly be.

Dancers already made up in costume, jugglers and musicians seated on the ground drinking hard for the long walk towards the fighting field, individuals merely setting out to march the distance to Maidborough, leagues away, all mingled among the barouches and carriages and tax carts and horse omnibus vehicles, with converted farm carts equipped marvellously with benches and small ladders – it was a veritable army preparing to move. There was even a high-flyer phaeton, with rear wheels a huge eight feet in diameter and the near-side leader of the six horses ridden by a postillion in gorgeous livery. Mounted gentry were moving through the square, too, and it was seeing these that she was tempted to withdraw, for Carradine was riding by in the company of several others. A small fly was with them, driven by an elderly gentleman with a young lady in the passenger seat.

'Hey, Mehala!' Carradine called, in a fine extravagant mood. 'I had best raise my hat to you, mistress, for surely you'll raise it for me if I don't, eh?'

A loud roar of laughter greeted this sally, the gentlemen pointedly glancing towards the far corner of the square, where she recognized Sir Cavan Webb and Captain Bussell just preparing to mount their horses.

Her heart leapt with anxiety, for there too was that Royal Navy lieutenant, the one who had seemed to remember her from before, the one they had called Percy Carmady. She quickly glanced away and turned aside, keeping desperately to the churchyard wall and moving swiftly through the press, her face flaming.

It was unfortunate to pass by when all were there, and to be noticed by the rake Carradine, for talk only ever breeds more. She was certain that those gentry who had not already heard of her encounter with Captain Bussell were now being told, no doubt in extravagantly embellished detail, how she had bested him. Her dexterous use of the whip too was already probably entering legend, in the same way as her skills with the flintlock pistol.

But Lieutenant Carmady was a more serious problem. The more talk there was about her, the more likely he was to recall exactly where he had seen her . . . if indeed he had. Though she was only too keenly aware of her indelible effect on men, it was still a possibility that a widely travelled seaman such as he would confuse appearances and women from the world over. As long as he remained unsure and reluctant to speak, she was safe.

She proceeded briskly, not wanting to annoy Mrs De Foe anew by her lateness. There was a lady she herself could recognize, indeed. Opinionated, determined, ambitious to an obsessed degree, anger and passion combined and blended into her womanhood. Unscrupulous, too. A loose friend, but a lifelong enemy, and no hesitation about which category you might fall into. With Thalia De Foe, everything would be on the spur of the moment. She was a woman to be wary of, even feared.

It had been kind of Squire Hunterfield to detect her distress so speedily when the Navy officer had come forward to eye her. She was convinced that her expression had not changed, so perhaps the squire had simply sensed her concern. He had moved the party on, to leave her be. Perhaps because, since she was clearly accompanying Jake Darling as more than a chance girl given a ride into Sealandings by a friendly waggoner, he felt obliged to extend his own protection to include her also? Or perhaps because there really was some connection with the Darlings from the wrong side of the blanket which was simply better concealed than usual. . . ?

She approached the turning and made the gate. Bures House stood back less than a furlong from the road, a path leading from that metalled surface towards the rear of the house through the large estate's ornamental gardens. It would have been nearer to her heart to walk the longer route, along the South Toll road and make her way up the grand drive. But that would nave taken more time, and been regarded as very forward of her. Yet it would have taken her a happy distance towards Shalamar. Her reward would have been a glimpse of the ancient derelict mansion house, even though Doctor Carmichael must be still at the Darling's cottage.

There was a small arbor by the side gate, trellis covered with climbing country roses. She went to thc gatc, hcsitated, and entered, hearing the clatter of pans nearby. A young maid-of-all, her mobcap askew and breathless from work, opened the door to her knock, and passed her to a second maid who hurried her along corridors to an alcove off the scullery. An elderly man there rose and asked her to follow, informing her that he was Clark, the butler.

'You are to be received by Mrs De Foe immediately,' Clark announced, showing her to the library. She waited while he obtained permission for her to be sent in, then withdrew.

It was an arranged scene, an episode from a masque, Mehala thought. With grudging admiration she knew it was done well, for all its formality.

Mrs De Foe was seated in the smaller of two writing chairs, this one situated with its back to the window light. The fan-shaped seat allowed the lady's exquisite dress coat to be shown off to the best advantage. It was made of gourgourans, the ivory satin stripes catching a gleam of light and drawing eyes to her youthful form. The one front leg of the writing chair enabled her to lessen her figure by gathering her ample dress skirts nearer than otherwise. She had not removed her gloves, which quite properly were a pastel colour for day wear. At evening Mrs De Foe would change them for the most brilliant white to accord with custom.

Clever woman, Mehala thought, and curtseyed.

'Mehala, is it?' Mrs De Foe asked, nodding to herself.

'Yes, ma'am. At your service.'

'No, miss. At the service of Bures House, and of my cousin the Honourable Charles Golding, and do not forget it.'

'As you will, ma'am.'

'You were . . . inclined to go to the rectory, instead of coming here, I believe. Why? And no lies, please.'

Mehala cast her eyes down meekly. 'I was afeared of so grand a house, my lady. And with the Honourable Charles Golding being a great personage I'd never seen before, and a bachelor and all, and me having no real experience, I went to Miss Baring at the rectory, whom I knew as a kindly lady . . .'

Mrs De Foe eyed the girl during her explanation. Plain dress, borrowed or begged, ill-fitting but sewn to appear properly made. That striking form, her youthfulness, and those memorable features. Yes, she seemed everything she had been led to believe from her sources around Sealandings. A disturbing thought crossed her mind, that here was an alert and even deep intelligence, someone capable and strong, even though her words were exactly in accordance with propriety and as unassuming as one might expect from a humble unconnected serving girl. Very well, she decided, let us see.

'You are here because I need someone to trust. The previous housekeeper was nothing more than a harlot, one Judith Blaker. She made a series of mistakes.' She paused, inviting questions, but Mehala remained silent. Thalia continued, 'She tried to fill up the estate at Bures House with a throng of her idle relatives, to milk the finances. She succeeded, and would have gone further still if I had not arrived to maintain eternal vigilance over my cousin's affairs.'

Mrs De Foe eyed Mehala. The two women waited, Mehala a picture of meekness, the lady determined and austere.

'Hence she is being punished in the gaols of Norwich, for her wicked presumption. Now, Mehala. It might seem unusual – though I am sure a great blessing to you – for a sea waif to be picked for this grand position.'

Mehala said nothing yet into the silence.

'But I have had some reports of you, ever since you were brought ashore, which made me wonder if you are not the right woman for the post here. I have not yet decided fully, but I am tempted to appoint you, even though you have had no commensurate employment on which I might base an opinion. I hear you are determined. Your honesty at the Weavers' place is already spoken of – a very unusual trait, I assure you, in tavern circles, where every coach stop is a temptation to defraud the Exchequer and the proprietors.

'Your conduct in defending your master's property at the cattle field when the horse fair was in town is also a commendation, Mehala. And you adhered to your promise to assist one who served you well, namely Doctor Carmichael. Then, when you could have stolen from the Darlings and made off, you returned to Sealandings to take up service at the Barings' place, without knowing what post you would be given or wages you would receive. That too, seemingly, because Miss Euterpe gave you assistance when you were first brought ashore. So far so credible, and creditable.'

Mehala stood listening attentively, her head bowed.

'For all of these reasons, and because I have heard that you are discreet and do not chatter the affairs of your betters at any and every opportunity, I am prepared to take you in here, and see that you are given the post of acting housekeeper, for a limited period. Note that any transgression will be met with the full power of the law. You understand?'

'Yes, ma'am.'

'Have you anything to say?'

'Please, ma'am, if I may.' Mehala hesitated diffidently, still not raising her eyes. 'If I could ask what system of book-keeping of the household accounts the master wishes to keep?'

'I prefer the journal and cash book system,' Mrs De Foe stated. 'Should you wish instruction in – '

'Begging the lady's pardon, ma'am, but *with* a double entry, debt-and-payments book besides the ledger, or no?'

Mrs De Foe gazed at Mehala for a moment. 'Yes. Keep a central ledger. The cash book may be kept as the chief auxiliary, however, in that case.'

'Thank you, ma'am. Are there books to be continued, or shall I start anew?'

'You shall start anew immediately,' Mrs De Foe decided. She had not thought ahead quite this far.

'Very well, ma'am. If it is your pleasure to set me in post, I shall see they are maintained as is proper, and available for your inspection at all times. Please, ma'am, if you will also give me any instructions for my improvement, I shall make my best endeavours to execute them.'

'That is only as I expect, Mehala.' Thalia De Foe inspected the girl, now a little puzzled at the servant's attitude. The creature seemed quite undaunted by the prospect and the heavy responsiblity. It really made one wonder what strange aptitudes some of these servant classes actually might possess.

'And, ma'am, might I be permitted to meet the other servants at Bures House?'

'You may. And in my presence.'

'Thank you, ma'am.'

'Ring for Clark. He is the butler, trusted because of his lengthy service here. You will do well to seek his opinions, but not be entirely ruled by them. You understand?'

'I think so, ma'am.'

'There is a cellar, in Clark's charge. You will assist him in keeping the records for it. In *all* possible detail, I warn you! That is a requirement about which I am most particular.'

'Yes, ma'am.'

While Clark was sent to assemble the servants, Mehala kept up her subdued manner, but her mind was racing. The master was clearly too addicted to the bottle for his cousin's liking, or why the mention of the cellar? The house was also obviously a shambles as far as its records were concerned, or Mrs De Foe would have been anxious to see the old accounts continued as exemplar to the newcomer. Further, Mrs De Foe did not trust her, in spite of the good reputations she had received from her informants. And a woman without trust was to be sent none, as the proverb had it.

'The servants are ready, ma'am.'

Mrs De Foe nodded imperiously, and Clark admitted the house servants one by one.

There were six besides Mehala and Clark. The footmen seemed no more than average, one Hugh and a lad called Walt, and the maids an apprehensive scatter of persons trying to appraise Mehala while wanting to escape at the earliest chance. They made their salutations to Mrs De Foe and retreated. There were two Mehala noticed particularly. Mrs Glasse the cook naturally demanded attention by virtue of her position. A buxom and unyielding woman, she stood her ground and gave Mehala a direct stare, finally nodding and bobbing quickly to Mrs De Foe before leaving. And the chief maid, last in the quick succession. Mehala caught a hint of a special glance exchanged between the mistress of Milton Hall and this Faye Sandwell. She was definitely trouble.

'Excuse me, if I may, ma'am,' Mehala said diffidently, causing the chief maid to pause. 'Might I be permitted to ask. . . ?'

'Yes, as long as it does not detain the girl from her work.'

'Could I be permitted to inquire if the maids receive batement ever?'

'Not without just cause, Mehala, and then only rarely.'

'Thank you, ma'am.'

Batement was the hated procedure at work and households whereby a servant or worker was marked for wage deductions because of minor transgressions. It was a chief abuse in the factory systems of the north, and was copied in the houses of the gentry and on their estates. All too often it was used as an excuse to restrict the servants' few freedoms and to reduce their costs. It was an abuse, too, which favoured the unscrupulous housekeeper, who could retain a proportion of the sum withheld.

Mehala saw the sardonic look on Faye's face as she made to curtsey and leave.

'Thank you for your kindness, ma'am,' Mehala said meekly, making certain Faye Sandwell heard the humility in her voice.

The door closed. Mrs De Foe rose to make her departure. 'The chatelaine is in the keeping of Clark, and you will find all the keys restored and the locks on all caddies and doors and containers properly secure. I have myself recently ensured that this will be so.' She paused. 'Note that I shall be informed of your progress from more sources than my own observations, Mehala. You do understand?'

Englished properly, Mehala thought sardonically, that meant Faye Sandwell was her spy in Bures House.

'Yes, ma'am. And I thank you. Only . . .'

'Come on, girl. Out with it. I can't be kept here all day long while servants dither.'

'Only, I can prove more reliable than Sandwell, ma'am, is all I wanted to say.'

Mrs De Foe froze in position. It took a while before she spoke. '*What* did you say?'

'Begging your pardon, ma'am. I can prove more reliable than Sandwell. In reporting to you all that transpires here at Bures House, ma'am.'

Mrs De Foe glanced at the door as if caught out momentarily. 'What exactly do you mean?'

Mehala took her time replying, choosing her words. 'I surmise that Sandwell is appointed to keep vigilance upon me and my performance, and that she attempts to curry favour on her own behalf by conveying to you reports of those events at Bures House which relate to the master's wellbeing.'

'And?' Mrs De Foe demanded quietly.

Mehala's gaze lifted. For the first time her eyes met Mrs De Foe's directly.

'And, ma'am, it would be of benefit to the master and your good self, ma'am, if you accepted such reports from one who is personally disinterested, rather than one like Sandwell who is interested in her own advancement.'

'And you are not?' Mrs De Foe was taken aback by the directness of the creature's look and the deep intelligence in her eyes. Not to mention the alacrity with which she had picked up the fact that Sandwell was her privy informant here at Bures.

'How can I be, ma'am? For I am lately brought from the sea, without connections or memory. Therefore I can have no cause to advance in any way.'

386

'That is true,' Mrs De Foe said guardedly. This had been one of her reasons for bringing the girl here in the first instance.

'And I am grateful to you, as I ought to be, for this opportunity you have kindly given me. I owe a debt, ma'am, if it is not presumptuous of me to express it so, to you personally for the trust you repose in me. For, having nothing, every benefice incurs an obligation which I feel obliged to attempt to repay.'

'I see. Go on.'

'Ma'am, if you doubt my honesty in the matter, or if you are reluctant to entrust the making of these observtions to one so untried in your service, then I shall offer reports which you will be able to compare with those provided by Sandwell. She need not be told.'

Mrs De Foe was silent in turn. This was a remarkable creature. In observing so astutely the relationship between Faye Sandwell and herself – a commercial one, it is true, but there nonetheless – she showed herself observant to a degree. And to risk her new position by broaching the matter in confidence this way . . . A spy upon a spy? It had a certain piquancy.

'Very well. Make any report you see fit, Mehala. But ensure that the substance is such as to be in the master's interests. And mine.'

'As you please, ma'am.'

Mehala curtseyed and followed Mrs De Foe through the reception hall, where Clark was already waiting by the entrance door.

There, she said a meek goodbye and watched the carriage depart. She turned immediately it was out of view and spoke to the elderly butler.

'Mr Clark, the chatelaine, if you please. I shall see all the keys fit straight away.'

'Yes, miss,' the old man said. He smiled and ushered her through towards the stairs. 'I'll show you round. May I say how pleased I am to see you here at last?'

'At last, Mr Clark?' She smiled. 'Was I expected, then?'

'By myself, miss, not in person as such. But by Bures House itself, miss, I think so. And long overdue.'

49

Every step of the way, as she was shown around the great house, Mehala could not help comparing it with poor ramshackle Shalamar.

For all the foreboding Mrs De Foe had spoken of, and the terrible time the house had experienced under the housekeeping of the infamous Judith Blaker, it now appeared fairly well kept. The floors were clean, the rooms aired, and the furniture was polished.

The kitchen itself, heart of any mansion's household, shone, and Mrs Glasse, prepared for a fight and disinclined to give her no more than a threatening glance when Clark ushered her through, took Mehala's effusive compliments without reply.

The bedrooms were more or less orderly, and the servants' quarters no more than could be expected. Her own room was that vacated by her predecessor. It had not been recently cleaned. Mehala made a mental note to see Faye Sandwell about it very shortly.

'Now,' Mehala said after thanking the old butler, 'where, pray, is the master?'

'Ah, the master,' Clark said evasively. 'Well, Miss Mehala, he is still abed, I'm afraid. He has taken to rising late these days, ever since . . .'

'Ever since Judith Blaker and her . . . team of assistants left Bures House?'

'Quite so, Miss Mehala,' Clark said tactfully. 'Before that, why, there was no telling what time of day or night the master would rouse, nor what time he and Mrs Blaker would . . . engage in conversation, so to speak.'

'I understand, Mr Clark.'

And she did, conversation in this context meaning nothing less than sexual abandonment. The master was a bachelor and the consequences almost inevitable, when living alone with so many females under his authority. She looked out of the landing window. The gardens of Bures House were splendid. She was pleasantly surprised to see how much of the locality was in view. The sea was visible through a small valley to the east, and to the south a gaunt house's roofs could be seen. With a jolt she recognized the outline of Shalamar among the distant trees. She would be able to glimpse the lights at night time, should Doctor Carmichael return there. If lights were affordable at that dwelling.

'Yes, Miss Mehala?' The old butler had perceived her start.

'Mr Clark. That house over there, the one you can see along the willows and the oaks.'

'Shalamar? Yes, a faded property, in decline I am sad to say. It once was a grand dwelling. You could see the glow in the sky when the house was occupied, so brightly was it illumined in the old days.'

'What happened to the family?'

He smiled, wistful. 'Ah, they eventually moved away, Miss Mehala. It fell into disuse, nothing but the occasional vagabond passing through and taking what scraps were left. A sorrowful business. The doctor lives there now, though the poor man has not two coppers to rub together.'

'Will they ever return, Mr Clark?'

'Not at all likely in my lifetime, miss. They have scattered like chaff before the wind.'

He would say no more, not even who had owned the place. It was seemingly given to Doctor Carmichael by an agent. She could not quite understand why the secrecy, remembering how little Mrs Trenchard had been willing to disclose about the old manor. The only person who had spoken of it without undue reticence was Jake Darling.

There was time to start the inventories, seeing Mr Golding was yet abed. She began checking them with the old man, and found enough books to start going over the necessary book-keeping. She was in the study when Clark finally came to summon her to see the master, who had risen at last and breakfasted.

The Honourable Charles Golding looked worn. Dissipation does not come alone, Mehala thought, inspecting him. The man was young, but could hardly raise his eyes to the light. The curtains he had ordered partly drawn, to provide a gloaming instead of direct daylight. He wore an old dressing gown of elaborately patterned silk, with a waist sash. It was horribly crumpled.

'You are the girl of whom I've been apprized, eh?' he asked, wincing at having to look up.

'Yes, sir. Mehala.'

'I heard, yes. No name, then?' He frowned. 'Time you learned your first duties, Mehala. The main ones are to keep me supplied with an adequate amount of brandy. And to try to stir the stumps of these idle backs here so that I am turned out looking at least properly attired.'

'Yes, sir.' She paused a moment, then added candidly, 'Perhaps the first duty, then, would be for me to have that gown cleaned and pressed, sir. Who is your man-servant?'

'Manservant?' he echoed vaguely. 'Oh, one of the louts Judith had in. He went with the others I'd had working on the grounds somewhere.'

'Then I suggest that I take over that position, sir, for the whilst. Until your garments are all to order and cleaned. Then I shall ask about employing another servant proper to your needs.'

'Can you do it?' he asked, surprised but not really interested.

'Yes, sir,' she said flatly. 'It is urgent to check your wardrobe, sir, in view of your needs very soon.'

'What?' He glanced at Clark. 'I haven't forgotten anything, have I, Clark?'

'If I may, sir,' Mehala quickly put in before the hesitant butler could form a reply, 'there is the pugilistic competition, which all the visiting gentlemen seem to be embarking for. Sealandings is in quite an uproar over it.'

'Good God!' he said. 'I'd quite forgotten that. It's . . . When is it?'

'There is ample time, sir, but you might wish to stay overnight at Maidborough. I have heard it will take place there. Then the evening of your return next day there will be the great ball at Milton Hall, sir. It would be proper for Mr Golding to make certain of reaching there early, if anything, so as to lend support to his cousin, the mistress of Milton Hall.'

'You're damned right, Mehala.' He held his head, poor man. Mehala moved the brandy decanter out of reach.

'With your permission, sir, might I suggest that instead of more of this for the moment you bathe and dress for the journey? In the meantime I shall look out your attire.'

'That's the way, Mehala,' he agreed, relieved she seemed to be taking charge.

While his bath was prepared in his bedroom by Dora and May, the two junior maids-of-all-work, the two of them scurrying up and down stairs fetching buckets from the hot copper in the kitchen, Mehala inspected his clothes.

She found them soiled, for the most part, and certainly not the result of endless labour by the maids. Mrs De Foe would be unlikely to examine every inch of her cousin's clothing, so the maids had got away with murder here.

The problem was finding him enough to wear respectably to this pugilistic contest. She found one plain shirt, which he could use for riding out, and one with fancy chitterlings, plus a half-shirt which would also do. She kept the plain shirt out for him, and carefully packed the others. Linen drawers were lacking, save for one pair. These she kept out. A riding stock for his neck, of palmyrienne, might do well for his journey, though its mixture of silk and wool felt uncomfortable to her face when she tested it.

A spencer jacket, of a dull blue, was all she could find clean enough for him to wear. He seemed to have plenty of outdoor wearing clothes, but many were stained with food or worse. She came across a good shawl waistcoat, however, which seemed never to have been worn, and swanskins for under his breeches of Bedford cord.

A tunic suit was available, still in its wrapping from the retailers, but it was of a hideous bottle green. She hated it, thrust it back, for all that it was labelled as having cost two pounds, six shillings and eightpence, a heady sum.

He could fight with the footman Hugh over his boots and shoes, and in any case they were young Walt's problem, so he could earn his money, and high time he went about it, too.

'Your garments are ready, sir,' she finally called through to his outer bedroom where he was finishing his ablutions, attended by Sandwell. She carried down the bag of his overnight clothes, taking a razor and brushes and fitting a small dress mirror into the leather pouches.

In the hall she waited, knowing he had ordered his mount for departure within an hour. He came down the stairs looking years younger and almost clear-eyed.

'God, Mehala,' he chided her ruefully, 'I trust you will not be rousing me this vigorously every day?'

'Only when there is cause, sir,' she replied, listing for him the contents of his case. 'I have also put inside two towels. Please *not* to use those provided, should Mr Golding decide to stay overnight in Maidborough or at Saltworth or some inbetween place. They may not be clean. That is very important, sir. Do take care.'

'Very well, Mehala.' He eyed her, as Hugh took the bag. 'My razor?'

'Included, sir, and in the leather pouch to guard its edge, sir. And, sir, please observe that I have placed in a separate wrapper a tablet of hard white, sir.'

'Yes?' he said blankly, taken aback. 'Soap, Mehala? So?'

'Hard white is very expensive, sir, compared with the yellow turpentine, sir. I have undertaken to provide Mrs De Foe with complete pennywise accounts. Might I request that the master remembers to retain the tablet, should any remain unused?'

'Soap,' he agreed, smiling, shaking his head. 'My friends will never believe this.'

'The master's acquaintances may waste their provinder, sir,' she said with a smile, making him laugh.

She accompanied him to the front entrance as Hugh ran down the steps to help the groom strap the case on to the rear of the saddle. It was then that she decided to take the risk, and drew breath.

'One last thing, sir, if I may. What must I do about the water supply, should questions arise in the master's absence?'

'Which water supply, Mehala?'

'The water supply which Bures House is about to curtail, sir. For the Donkey and Buskin, sir.'

'Ah, yes.' His brow cleared. 'I do remember Thalia saying something about that. I think there's orders been given for the flow to be soon discontinued.'

'Yes, sir. I understand that Mr Weaver from the tavern might be about to make an appeal to your clemency some time later today, sir.'

'He is? Well he can wait, Mehala. I've too much to do without waiting on every Tom, Dick – '

'There's just the matter of the man's worth, sir.' She let her silence be her prompt. 'He has a vote for the next hustings, sir. And he is so admired hereabouts for a loyal subject, sir, having very many connections among locals and travellers, that I wonder if his difficulties might prove disadvantageous in some way, sir.'

'Disadvantageous?' Golding paused. 'To whom, Mehala?'

'To Mr Golding, begging your pardon, sir.'

'How?' He was looking hard at her now.

'In the countryside, sir, and along the shores of East Anglia, many might make that association. Even though the man's discomfiture is clearly brought upon himself, sir, there are still those who might be deluded sufficient to think themselves likewise aggrieved.'

'So you are suggesting that I let the man's water continue unabated?'

'To make suggestions is not my place, sir. But these simple people might be distressed by the lack of common-brewed beer, since he will require the water for the brewing season. It is upon Sealandings soon. Also, Mr Weaver qualifies for the vote by reason of his poundage rents paid, sir.'

'Does he indeed,' Golding mused. He pondered a moment. 'It *would* save the need for yet another bribe, eh? Very well, then, Mehala. Send word to the estate men, will you?'

'If it please you, sir,' she said obediently, and stood while he mounted. 'May I ask a boon, sir? Only for your care, sir.'

'*You* ask a favour, for *my* benefit?'

'Yes, sir. I have had a premonition, sir, or a dream. I know not which. It relates to the prize fight, sir.' She hesitated, inventing quickly as he grinned his scepticism. Prothero in league with Carradine meant evil was out riding. 'Only, I dreamt that you won a wager today, sir – when you bet one hundred guineas.'

He laughed outright. 'Then perhaps I should wager a thousand, Mehala!'

'No, sir,' she begged quickly. 'I dreamt you then waged a hundred guineas plus a farthing, and lost all you possessed, from the advice of a friend.'

'Oh, did you indeed!' He examined her upturned face, only half-amused. 'Is it some warning, Mehala?'

'Yes, sir. I'm sure of it!'

Charles Golding stared down at the figure standing with such stillness on the entrance porch, and thought to say something. Finally, he pressed his soles into the stirrups as a check and moved off. Oddly, he found he had raised his hat – to his own housekeeper, for God's sake!

He laughed, ruefully shaking his head, and rode out of the gate to the fight contest. It would be a good ride. He would be there in good time, and in the best shape he had been for many a day. Better to wager only a hundred, in any event, come what may.

50

The day even felt enormous, as he woke. Today was it, his time of coming power, and wealth beyond wealth.

He nudged the woman next to him.

'Wake, Tyll.'

'Yes, sir.' Her hand reached out under the bedclothes to fondle him. He laughed and stayed her a moment.

This was the hallmark of a woman who had proved herself. Not in the fierce possessiveness of Thalia De Foe, nor in the flat mercenary styles of the women at Two Cotts. And neither in the crude attempts to own him which Lucy made, for all her attractions and sexual inventiveness –and that inevitable fee, payable to Mistress Wren on departure. Admittedly he liked and even craved Lucy oftener than he should. But the old true sayings stood the test of time: A whore once, a whore for always. More ominously, a whore for one, a whore for all. And he could afford to take no risks. Secrecy was everything today, and whores blabbed. Tyll, though, never would.

'Today is the greatest of all days for me, Tyll.'

'It is, sir?'

'Indeed it is. By tonight I shall have money to burn. And I promise that you shall be the first to benefit.'

'You are not going away again, sir?' She raised her head from the pillow.

'Not immediately, Tyll. Nor even permanently. But your man shall have his concession along the Norwich road at the tollgate, I promise.'

'You will not throw me, sir?'

'Cast you, Tyll? No. A man tires always of exotic spices and fine wine. Then he comes back to bread. And you are my staple, Tyll. You are my bread.'

'Sir.' Barbara Tyll hesitated. 'Will you take me, if you leave? Or must I stay?'

'Carradine Manor is yours, Tyll, as it is mine. It will stay so. I think of coming home like coming to you, almost as my wife. I would not change that for the world.'

'Thank you, sir.' She let her hand lie on his chest, emboldened by his promises. 'This great day, sir. Is it to do with anything I should know? Nothing for which you need my help?'

He laughed, his chest shaking at the very idea. 'Your help is not needed for me to deal with pugilists, Tyll, though I have no doubt that you would win hands down!'

Her face smiled along the pillow at him. 'I shall have everything ready for your return, sir, tonight. What will you want?'

'I shall decide later, Tyll. I aim at the day's celebrations first. And before that, Tyll, you have bed work to do. Come on. Earn your keep, lady.'

She smiled, free now to resume her slow urging. Nothing set this man up for the day like country matters, as sexual love was always called, and from the sound of it this truly would be the greatest day in his life. For one terrible moment she had feared he was going to announce his engagement to one of the fine ladies who lived locally. For the whilst all was normal at Carradine Manor, exactly as she wanted it. Today's glory, whatever it was, could look after itself. For now, she possessed Carradine as he possessed her, and that was all that mattered.

It was a simple delight to her that the master had come into such enormous fortune. No wonder he was confident, almost ecstatic. His successes he found outside his family home. She found hers within it. She gasped audibly as his mouth and teeth seized on her breast, and pulled him close in a fierce embrace to confirm her triumph.

The morning roads inland from Sealandings were dense with traffic.

The day mercifully proved fine, allowing good starts to be made by most of the tavern travellers. Others were already on the road.

Coaches started off in groups out of Sealandings. Barouches, flies, traps, one-passenger sulkies, Stanhope phaetons, crowded French-style banquette-seated diligences pulled by unicorn teams, carriages of all sorts and shapes, with coats of arms and plain, set out along the Norwich road. Parker's common stables worked frantically to see their horses delivered in fine condition, providing sufficient meal for the horses' return journeys.

Riders travelled in small cavalcades, sixes and sevens, against the dangers of footpads, and every person in each entourage was armed in some fashion.

Further inland, the traffic became denser at the junction with the main coast road from the south. There, the stream of horses and people turned directly inland to join yet more elegant carriages and longer columns of travellers. Recognizable coaches, with their side panels hung over with discreet decorative plaids to conceal coats of arms, moved smoothly on springs; their coachmen's livery was also hidden, by the use of the great wrap-rascals. Curtains at each coach window tended to be closed rather than open to show the grand personages.

Eight miles inland from the road junctions, the old Roman Road was reached, now made according to the famous Mr M'Adam's system, containing no stone cubes above a six-inch side, and the entire carriageway topped for smoothing the carriages' progress. Travelling became easier there and the traffic picked up speed, coachmen shouting abuse and showing bravado in their eagerness to reach the fighting ground first. Ladies were few, though some joined the great procession hoping to seize the opportunity of diversion among so many eligibles, or to realize the chance of an assignation. One or two were already infamous by reason of their extravagant relationships, and these travelled with ostentatious disregard for the rules of incognito.

However, politeness ruled, and nobody noticed what was requisitely not to be noticed.

Fellows De Foe had joined the group from Lorne House, with his contingent.

He was riding a strange horse, for his mare seemed a little knee-sprung from the previous day's work, possibly due to the weather along the coast, he thought. He explained his beliefs to Sir Trev Bunyan, with whom he had fallen in.

'Very wise, Sir Trev,' he said, 'of Henry Hunterfield to remain at Lorne today. Him being the senior magistrate and all, I mean.'

'I think so too, Fellows.' Sir Trev was peeved that the company had objected the night before to a ride along the sea dykes towards Whitehanger, and he had had to take a lone canter along the shores past Watermillock, very obviously seeking some reaon for calling at the tide mill and seeing Olivia. He had not succeeded, and he had merely pretended interest in watching the tide mill's great gates closed. Now here he was travelling even further away for the whole day, and the chances of encountering the girl at this jaunt were infinitesimally small. She was not the kind to pass her time with giddy courtesans. 'But I do not blame him. Henry is so attached to this part of the country that he actually enjoys his residence.'

'Do I detect a longing for a sea-coast dwelling, Bunyan?' Fellows was smiling as he chided the baronet, who shrugged and adjusted the barrel-snaps on his cloak.

'Quite possibly, Fellows. I suppose that will depend on the outcome of today's ventures!'

'You are going to try a wager, Trev?'

'I think I may. This new fighter Rendell seems to be everybody's darling, as underdogs always are in this Kingdom. But when it comes to laying a wager, I like all others trust form, as you know. The odds always win in the end. I go with the short odds, every time.'

'Take care. Rumours are of heavy wagers this day, Trev,' Fellows warned. 'I fear for some of my younger companions.'

Ahead, laughing and joking round a blue coach, they could see Sir Jeremy Pacton and Alex Waite, in company with several other young bloods.

'Meaning those, Fellows?'

'Well, let us say that I wish them every good fortune for the day. I pray for their sakes that it will be as joyous a journey homeward, that's all.'

'I have never before seen such confidence abroad, on any morning,' Sir Trev mused. 'Or such a press of the Fancy. What on earth accounts for it?'

'A certainty, mark my words. Nothing cheers like a sure bet, Trev.' Fellows nodded sagely to himself as another group of riders overtook the long column of carriages and horsemen, whooping and cheering. 'There's another group of a like mind.'

'Morning, Captain Bussell! Sir Cavan!'

Shouts answered Bunyan's greeting, but they rode on ahead without a pause. Another wager being tested against fact, Fellows thought. Pray all could afford today's losses and malfortunes, though there never was a match where that came out so.

'The entire world is here,' Fellows observed, seeing Carradine among a cluster of admirers. 'You see the brave Carradine, Trev?'

He was especially dashing today, overtaking at a gallop and shouting his way past the slower traffic. Dust rose as the dew dried underfoot, but did not obscure Carradine's superlative dress. His riding coat was of a brilliant blue, cut away to expose his waistcoat beautifully shawled and made of finest Pekin. Fellows smiled and acknowledged the cheer Carradine made as he roared past.

'Hey, Carradine!' Bunyan called. 'Save some of that vigour for afterwards, man!'

Carradine doffed and waved his hat. 'After the fight I shall have vigour enough for the nation itself, Trev!'

Fellows watched Carradine's crowd plunge on ahead. 'This new man,' he mused. 'Rendell, isn't it? He must be more of a dolt than we assume.'

'I've thought the same thing, Fellows,' Bunyan remarked, having to rein hard to return his excited mount to a steady walk. 'Or, perhaps, less?'

'Mmmmh. If he is so stupid as to risk himself in the ring against the great man – and Goring would be Champion were it not for ill luck in Worcester that time a year since – why, then he must be almost an imbecile.'

'Or he is stronger and fitter than we have heard?' Bunyan finished for him.

Fellows De Foe laughed, shaking his head. 'You see, Trev? Already we are talking ourselves into believing that mere logic will lift us into a position of certainty! Well, I for one will not let myself be swayed. I shall bet a small amount on the man with the greater reputation, and that is all. After all, I have debts in London to pay off still. And a house and wife to keep.'

'True, true. Very wise, Fellows,' Bunyan said. But he registered: Aye, poor old Fellows De Foe, and keeping the both for the use of another, by all accounts. He thought, but did not say.

The mob clattered and plodded and galloped and walked and rolled on, past the Saltworth crossroads and skirting Wentleham, and finally coming within sight of the church spire of Forreston.

Towards noon they had formed one long stream, with the pugilists' agents riding along now and swearing boastfully that they had enough bullies from the streets of London with them to prevent any magistracy men from interrupting the proceedings.

Touts and commission agents rode along the length of the crowds, reassuring everyone in loud voices that all would be well, that the coming fight would be superb, indeed the greatest ever witnessed, and urging all to prepare for an enjoyable day.

Noon came and passed as the great concourse wound through the countryside. The Suffolk border was called by the leaders about one o'clock from up ahead.

There the columns were joined by vagabonds and beggars, all in their campaign rags, all chorusing poverty, some holding up babies and infants in supplication. Gypsy vardos and caravans with ragged horses tethered beneath the trees clustered about campfires in groups by the roadside, tinkers trudging alongside the travellers selling their wares.

Two o'clock, and the fighting heath was only one mile away. The throngs were almost at a standstill between the lanes' hedgerows from the press of vehicles and horses and people.

Carradine was already at the ground by then, his mount left at the common lines formed around the great heath above Maidborough.

He was joking with the bloods who today would pour money into his pockets through the agents, backing heavily on Rendell and clearly delighted with life. This was even more exhilarating than he had imagined. The massive turnout meant an even greater fortune would be his. Would that all life was this simple! He had already seen a good dozen of Abel Sumner's men, taking and dispensing notes, each with his two guards in their bully-cock hats.

It was heaven, and promised better heaven still.

Sumner on the other hand was a trifle worried, for the limits he had agreed with Carradine were coming close, and very fast at that.

All round the great heath colourful parties were picnicking and talking. Coach gatherings were already on the go, blankets everywhere spread on the grass and hampers of food being opened. Ladies were now more in evidence than on the journey, as carriages arrived and were found space to rest. At the far side of the great expanse, a double row of beeches and elms gave protection from too much common view. The places there were highly sought by the coachmen eager to prove their worth.

The common groom lines were set up at the end of the trees. Already no fewer than three hundred mounts were given over in charge, the gentlemen riders milling and arguing about the forthcoming contest.

Sumner tried to reach Carradine, but the gentleman seemed reluctant to greet him for some reason, turning away and making certain he was laughing at some sally when the agent next made the attempt. But the problem was a serious one. The odds on Goring were coming shorter than even he had envisaged.

Poor Rendell was eight to one against. It was an enormous difference in odds, far too great a discrepancy for a commission agent's inner calm.

'Totalling another five hundred sovereigns, on the local lad.' One of his roamers came up, pushing past a cluster of people to hand him the chits. 'Still take, then?'

'Hang on a while,' Sumner ordered, making up his mind. He hurried towards the group where Carradine formed the central attraction.

One hundred was all very fine. And five hundred sovereigns was also all to the good, since risk was a wager agent's lifeblood. It was necessary for survival. But a thousand was a worry. And seven thousand eight hundred in gold was almost beyond belief. It was all fast becoming a nightmare. For the underdog to lose – as lose he must – would mean a golden harvest. The risk was, that a *win* for the underdog at such odds would mean total ruination for himself, never mind Carradine. And a risk was still a risk, however small that risk was.

He stood on the outskirts of Carradine's group, seemingly in thought but trying to catch Carradine's eye.

Eventually he heard Carradine exclaim, 'Hey! I must lay a bet of my own, without giving all this advice to the benefit of others!'

The admirers laughed as he pushed his way through them and came upon Sumner.

'You'll do!' Carradine exclaimed loudly. 'Sumner, isn't it? Here, sir! More wallpaper for your excellent Chelsea residence!'

Carradine took Sumner's arm and led him away, pretending deep converse while his friends looked after and speculated on what wager he would decide on.

'What the hell do you mean, Sumner, ogling me while I am with friends?' Carradine demanded quietly, keeping the appearance of enjoining a friendly transaction. 'I'll not have it, d'you hear?'

'The amount is growing apace, sir,' Sumner said with grave intensity. 'It now moves on to Rendell by the hundred.'

'So?' Carradine had never felt such contempt for any man. Not even that noisome Prothero was so lily-livered as this apology for a gentleman. 'It's all profit, is it not? The more you take, the more we make. It is exactly equal to the profit gained. Take more.'

'Can I shorten Rendell's odds, sir? The risk is greater if I take more as they stand presently.'

Sumner could see from the corner of his eye no fewer than six of his touts hovering, waiting orders. There was a new rush on Rendell. He would have to shorten the odds still further.

'There is no risk, man. Goring it is, and Goring it shall be.'

'A risk is a risk, sir. However small, my motto is, why take any risk?'

'Because it is non-existent, Sumner. That's why.' Carradine could hardly bear to look at the man. This is what makes the difference between a gentleman and a serf. Sumner, for all that he was reputedly a by-blown member of one of the highest families in the Kingdom, was a peasant and always would remain so. No wonder that he found his natural niche among the scavengers of the world! He was like a puppydog, who would run alongside any grand carriage barking and thinking himself a fine fearless fellow.

'So I continue?'

'You take every penny piece on Rendell, for me. Take nothing on Goring. Do it. And keep on doing it. Understood?'

'Sir. I beg you. Bring the odds lower, at which I take wagers on Rendell. For your safety.'

Carradine stared Sumner down. 'Do no such thing, Sumner. Or you shall rue the day.'

Characteristically the man began to cringe and whine. 'Look, Carradine,' he tried, skirting dangerously close to giving offence. 'I *cannot* afford to lose today. I have plenty of stiffs, notes and IOUs from people. But paper buys no bread. And I must somehow keep my own head above water.'

'I have several thousand for this eventuality, Sumner.' Carradine took delight in seeing the man's eyes light up. 'Knowing your limitations, I have brought along my own bailiff with three men. They guard the Norwich chaise on the far side by the trees. You see it? There are sovereigns enough there, as you will see from the way it leans over from the gold's weight. Satisfied now?'

'I did not mean to impugn your position,' Sumner began thankfully, but already Carradine was walking away in disgust.

Uproar began along the Maidborough side of the heath. Cheering spread as the spectators recognized the pugilists and their seconds.

Great crowds of commoners followed, walking alongside their heroes and cheering, waving blue billies to make a forest of the white-spotted blue neckerchiefs. It had been the fashionable emblem of the old Regency barefister William Pace, and seemingly had become the symbol of Goring's followers. On the road behind, another contingent raised more uproar, booing and jeering. They were at least as noisy, and consisted of the local people, tradesmen and apprentices and farm labourers predominating. Their favour had a superficial resemblance, being a blue neck cloth with large white spots, but each spot having an inner spot of dense blue, in copy of the great champion Belcher's favour.

The two factions came, shoving noisily through the press and unceremoniously dragging an unfortunate carriage out of the way of the centre.

'A ring! A ring!'

The cry went up for the contest to be set up.

'How much more?' one of Sumner's men came up to ask. 'That lot's from Cambridge, around Rendell. They'll put on every farthing they have, and walk the way home gladdened should they win or lose.'

'Take nothing less than ten sovereigns,' Sumner ordered. 'I can't be doing with tiddlers.'

'Right.' The man scurried off to spread the word.

The odds were being signalled around the heath at three to two on for Goring, eight to one against Rendell. Sumner remembered Carradine's confidence, and the great sum in gold for support should anything go awry, and took heart. But he went to some pains to listen and kept check on the other commission agents round the heath.

It was becoming more difficult now. The picnic parties had virtually all finished, and the ladies were ensconced in their carriages around the perimeter of the heath. No fewer than three thousand were crammed around the ring, which was being formed of the seconds' friends, standing to form a square with arms linked and a rope passed through crooks of their elbows.

The sun had gone in. A grey sky extended gradually, making the proceedings slightly less merry. On the outskirts of the press, stalls had been set up to purvey foods and drinks. Waggons from Maidborough's taverns had done heavy business. Tinkers and actors and buskers worked frantically on. Lookouts were signalling their all-is-wells, the runners flying in from the distant high points of tracks and roads leading to the heath to tell that no magistracy men were coming, and begging could they now stay to see the fight.

The hubbub grew as the two fighters stripped off and their seconds boasted loudly of their heroes' records.

Carradine was pleased by Goring's appearance. The man was in fine fettle, steady as a rock and looking quite ferocious. He was doing his impressive display, glowering and strutting, glaring across the human ring at his opponent.

For the first time Carradine saw Rendell. He was shorter than Goring, but solid. His muscles were compact rather than bulky, and he too seemed steady and resolute. In fact he seemed calm, even, Carradine saw with surprise. This was commendable for an untried newcomer who was shortly going to suffer extinction at the fists of one of the great fighters of the age.

Rendell shook his head at the offered drink, another surprise. Onlookers murmured with astonishment. Instead, he flexed and drew breaths, looking about, anywhere except at his opponent.

But there could be no real concern, for Rendell was inexpert. Prize fighting was as much an art as a feat of strength, as Rendell would soon discover. And expertise won every time. Carradine felt almost fond of the giant Goring, and began to estimate how much he would give the man as gratuity when he had won the contest. Two hundred sovereigns? Another fifty, say, for effort? Maybe three hundred, in gold, to show appreciation of how accurately he had followed his instructions?

The introductions to the crowd were made perfunctorily, everyone now roaring for the fight to begin.

Carradine glanced round. Fellows De Foe was across at the far side of the ring, standing with others on a trestle near to Rendell's corner. He saw Carradine's glance and saluted, raising his high-crowned beaver. Carradine responded by smiling and touching his constable to his own Cumberland hat. He wondered if De Foe had placed a wager. He had been included on the list of confidants fed the falsehood that Rendell would win. Waite, Sir Jeremy, the Hunterfield group, including Sir Cavan Webb and Lieutenant Carmady, were nearby – how much of their precious possessions would be his by nightfall, he wondered. They might even include part of their estates! He knew that it was unwise to cash in immediately. Then, whole estates might come his way!

He saw the two pugilists advance, saw the chief second drag the toe of his boot in a line diagonally at the ring's centre.

As the two fighters stood facing, Carradine almost laughed aloud. Rendell was so much the shorter man, almost three inches. That in itself was not great, but the actual size difference was considerable. In contrast with Goring, Rendell seemed almost lightweight. Goring appeared immense, three feet thick and barrel-chested.

What had Sumner said at his last report? So many thousands on Rendell that it no longer mattered. He had merely nodded, thinking only with regret of the proportion to be given to Sumner as his share. He should have argued, stuck out for less. It was his scheme, not the money-grubbing agent's. All an agent did was cadge from what the gentleman deserved.

He waved to Peter Quilter, of a sudden clambering up from the press of people to stand beside Fellows De Foe on the trestle table. Alex Waite was waving, pointing and applauding, with Sir Jeremy also cheering and the crowd roaring, and Carradine realized that the fight had actually begun during his reverie.

Goring began with a rush, trying to topple his opponent and, failing, making a bear grab at the smaller man. He succeeded finally, and threw Rendell down to the ground to howls and cheers from the excited throng.

The minute's rest was counted by the chief second, whose calls of time were greeted with applause and shouts of encouragement.

A pack of Cambridgeshire supporters was already threatening abuse, trying to shout down Goring's fanatics. A bottle was thrown, to general cries deploring the ominous sign. Carradine watched the crowd more than the fighters as they rose to toe the scratched line and so indicate their fitness to continue the next round. Several things could produce disruption, not least a melee among the crowd, causing the fight to be called off for another day. It would not be a tragedy, but it would seriously delay his acquisition of the money for Sumner. The fight would have to be fought over again, though the bets would stand until it had. He did not want that.

Or the magistracy could come over the hill to arrest the pugilists and their seconds, and even the backers. Happily though the lookouts were at their posts and their runners were still up in the trees in the distant vantage points, and all seemed well.

Or there might ensue such uproar, as one fighter failed to come forward to toe the scratched line, that the commission agents could take off the wagers and so avoid paying out. That was unlikely, with Sumner's men there in force and his arrangements being so firmly contracted in advance.

No. It was all set. And in his favour. Carradine saw with some surprise Prothero's face among the standing crowd. Prothero was watching him, in return. It seemed a day for surprises. So the oaf himself had come to the scene of his triumph. Well, well. Prothero made a salutation, which Carradine did not return.

He gave his attention to the fight, and saw Rendell take a heavy blow to the ribs. Already three blotches showed there, where Goring must have given him a few hefty buffets.

'What round, sir?' Carradine asked the gentleman next to him as Rendell sank to one knee and the round was called.

'This is the fifth coming up, sir,' the man replied in mild surprise, turning to pass comment to his neighbour with some laughter.

Carrdine had looked but not seen. He hoped Goring was not overdoing it. The plan called for a relatively slow approach, to entice further wagers on to Rendell. If Goring stopped Rendell too soon wagers galore, as yet unmade, would escape Sumner's net.

But it was all going to plan, as far as one could judge. Goring was in the ascendant, the crowd was in good humour, the pickpockets were busy at their trade – causing diversions aplenty when one of their number was caught in the act and impromptu fights started on the outskirts of the press. It was a typical prize fight, the alleged purse of four hundred sovereigns being held by four prominent men of renown, with their manservants standing guard beside them.

Carradine pushed his way from the crowd and walked over for an ale to one of the brewers' drays. A girl served him. He paid her well, leaving a penny for her trouble.

The crowd was roaring still, though Goring should have taken it a deal slower, he fancied. Still, the man knew his business. Fifty rounds would take well over an hour, probably. He was not so interested in the fight game as many others, who observed every nuance – real or imaginary – and kept notes in their studies at home and wrote texts about the fights. No, the battle was incidental.

Another roar. He smiled at the girl and asked if her dray carried brandy.

'Oh, no sir. I am not allowed. The brewmaster's from Bury St Edmunds, sir, and he is mortal taken against liquors, sir. He is all for natural British brews, sir.'

'So I go a-thirsting, eh?' But it was in good humour and he made her smile. He leaned against the dray's great stern wheel, happy beyond measure.

The first thing would be to celebrate, perhaps with Lucy. Strange how a man's desires caught up with himself, in the race against peace. For so life was, and no mistake about it. Peace, calm, tranquillity, were the three perversions of existence.

Look for instance at the women available to him, in the narrow constraints of Sealandings. There was Thalia De Foe, with her insistences and her infuriating dependence upon him at every turn. The woman was sometimes a pest. Not without her interesting foibles, though, for she had a streak of savagery which was nothing if not diverting.

That Lucy, now. For all that she was a whore, and on sale to anyone who happened by with silver enough in his pocket, she was inventive and clever. Skill comes to some women with very little practice or thought, but to other women is denied a lifetime. Curious, that. Lucy was a natural temptress, as capable of assuming the superior position of mistress to his master, as of lying meekly doing his bidding as the most submissive servant eager to abase herself. It was a profound skill, neither teachable nor yet taught. And she was pretty, a fetching girl who should by rights be restricted to his use alone. Yes, he might do that afterwards, take her from Mistress Wren, shake the dust of Two Cotts from her feet and set her up in some small outlying dwelling in London's Bloomsbury. About time he had some incidental blessings, some few rewards for all the anxieties he had suffered. That would be one in the eye for Mrs Isabella Worthington, damn her, who had the insolence to cast him over, and all because he had been seen with that hussar's woman from the cavalry barrack.

Then there was Tyll, what was her name, Barbara. There now was a curious thing, but he felt almost warm inside when he thought of her. You see how strange and affecting women can be? He smiled to himself, shaking his head ruefully. It was a most damnable thing, that women were of a consequence even in their own absence, whereas men were simply not. Prothero, De Foe, Sumner, the rest, were simply out of consideration for the moment, in spite of their proximity among that crowd howling and baying for more gore over there. Yet the women he knew and needed were here with him in spirit far more than the people actually within reach.

Yes, Tyll had somehow come under his skin. She had crept there by inches, by days and nights when he had taken her. And that too was remarkable. Using her was something far from mechanical. He had noticed lately that, when all was going well, he took over women instead. But when things were proving worrisome, or when he had suffered too much to London's gaming tables or the races, or when he was sickly from having caroused the previous nights, it was Tyll he called for and who brought him a kind of sanity. It was as if there were something healing in her touch, her ministrations, and him a small child again. Most odd.

However, thinking of Barbara Tyll in comparison with the others, it was not that she was any the less able to give him the relief he craved. No. She was as able, and even as capable, as Thalia De Foe any day – or night. And while she was not as inventive, and never as dominating, as Lucy at Two Cotts, Tyll never proved disappointing. Her love-making was convinced – dedicated, you might say – and fervent. Was Thalia's? Yes, and perhaps to the same degree, but while there was a thrilling exciting quality to Thalia's sexual exertions, they lacked the totality Tyll brought. Gave? Whatever, Tyll was immersed in the act, and somehow managed to convince by her offerings that she would always be thus, there, and would never change. Less intoxicating, maybe, but somehow a cause for rejoicing.

Yes, it was truly odd how women could express their presence by their very absence.

'Begging the master's pardon?'

'What?'

The girl on the brewer's dray was staring down at him. 'What you said, sir. About ladies.'

'I spoke aloud? Then promise not to repeat my words, girl.' He left, laughing. This brewmaster's girl was one more illustration. And Mehala was still another.

See how she had taken over Sealandings. He had heard on the road this morning that the slut had somehow talked herself into Bures House. Thalia's doing, of course. And the girl barely into petticoats, for God's sake! Not only that, without a stitch to bless her back with, and brought from the sea. Mistress of land, if not of seas, he thought sardonically.

The girl seemed to have the knack of making impressions of the strangest sort. On the ride out he had glimpsed Charles Golding, a dissolute degenerate if ever there was one, coming along in the press of riders at the Saltworth crossroads, and seeming better than he had for many a day. Clean, sober – apparently, though who could tell with an habitual drunkard? – and turned out neater than for weeks. Thalia De Foe was resolute on her cousin's need to mend his ways, that was for sure. So it was probably her doing. Or was it Mehala's?

Mehala. Who had the effrontery to shun him. The whore doubtless was simply enticing him on, proving herself one of these teasing bitches who deserved only the worst, for they brought out the worst in others by showing their own feebleness.

No. The bitch deserved a good hiding. He relished the thought of making her suffer. Perhaps Charles Golding, always too pathetically weak to resist a promising wager, had placed a small fortune on Rendell! That would be delightful, for he could make the man grovel and surrender Mehala without a fight. As well as showing what a meacock he was begging – Golding would beg, wheedle, promise, even show tears like any woman, if his toys were taken from him. Carradine made a fervent prayer that Golding had placed heavily on the underdog Rendell.

She would be worth the trouble of imposing his will on Golding. Of course, Thalia would scent a rival. She could at any distance, and in any circumstance. She was that way, jealous and spiteful where other women were concerned. Let her be. For quite honestly he was tired of Thalia De Foe. And if her husband was, as Thalia sent word, thinking of settling permanently in Sealandings at the family home, why, was it Carradine's fault? It would save bother if Fellows stayed forever at Milton Hall. He would be forced to look elsewhere for a companionable lady. What one table could not supply, another would have to. Not that Mehala was a lady. For no lady of his acquaintance could shoot, would duel – God's sake, *duel!* – use a whip, if the story of Captain Bussell's doffing was true. Word was it had been seen by enough gentlemen to bear witness.

It was in the girl, this strangeness. She was more of a woman, yet less of a woman somehow. Lovely to see, and her movements enticing yet forbidding. Strong, even tough, but there was a frailty which gave those qualities the lie. She had been something in her former life, perhaps? Yes, that much was plain. But for all the world he could not –

'Rendell! Rendell!'

A shout came to his ears. Pandemonium was spreading through the crowd. Fights were breaking out among the Cambridgeshires. He could see the blues and whites waving everywhere.

'Rendell! Rendell!'

He found himself walking towards the crowd, his throat drying slightly with excitement. This sounded as if something significant was taking place. But Rendell's name? Why Rendell's name? The game newcomer must be putting up a great-hearted fight in defeat. That was often the case, with a crowd switching its allegiance by the minute as first one then the other contestant showed his mettle. He decided to move in, watch the final battering of the upstart.

The crowd was delirious, excitement making each man almost buffet his neighbour.

Many were despondent, shrugging and throwing their arms up in disgust. The losers? Surely it could not be over yet, not so soon? Carradine was becoming slightly angry as he forced his way with difficulty through the press, finally having to shove himself between people and leave off his expressions of apology.

His mouth was dry. The fight was over. And he glimpsed a scene that etched itself instantly into his mind. Goring, the great battler, was being dragged towards his corner, blooded and battered. The time-keepers were yelling out the seconds. People were casting in nobbins, the coins which showed approval for an excellent showing.

But it was Rendell who stood there, bruised and red-blotched in his face, across his shoulders, his left upper arm a mass of scarlet where Goring's fists had pounded. His eyes were cut and bleeding down his face. His left ear stood proud, thickened from swelling from blows which had fallen there. An eye was blackened. His ribs showed daubs of red, and his left rib margin showed a great wheal of red and white. But he was the victor.

He had won. Rendell had won. *Rendell* the underdog had defeated Battler Goring.

Even as Carradine watched, a howl of victory went up from the Cambridgeshire faction, and Rendell was walking round, holding his hand aloft, blood streaming down his arm from his raw knuckles.

'Time. Goring fails to toe the line.'

'Rendell! Rendell!'

Lost. For one strange moment Carradine felt a gibbering laughter rise within him. He strangled the impulse. That would really be madness. Lost? It couldn't be. But it was fact, a riotous tumultuous scene all around the great concourse to prove it. He, Carradine, had lost.

So what if he had lost? It was not the end of the world. Not really.

He walked away. Sumner broke away from the crowd, five of his touts trailing, and slowly followed, trailing after Carradine in ominous silence.

51

Deep into the lanthorn hours, Mehala awoke with a start, wondering where she was. For a horrid moment she was back in the sea. She dozed again, woke again, frightened into dreaming. She understood that her mind was in a spiritual limbo, knew that she was dreaming but unable to make herself stop the torment.

A clock struck three. She rose, wrapped an old gown about herself, and descended to the kitchen with a Norfolk cup lantern candled up to cast light before her.

Nobody was about. Mrs Glasse slept in a small room on the ground floor of the west wing, and the two scullion maids were given cubicle rooms adjoining it. A dog was posted outside the scullery door in a kennel. The stables where the grooms slept began immediately across the rear courtyard, so she was quite safe.

The house felt warm. It also felt magnificent, and welcoming to her. She sat, staring into the embers of the great fire, wondering how she was in herself. There was no simple way of knowing the answer. But it was surely good fortune that had brought her here, from nothing, was it not? *Was it not?*

At Red Hall, down in the marshes to the south, there would be few people to minister to its wants. The house would stand gaunt and, probably, empty, now that she was gone and her madman husband was drowned. It was piteous, for an empty house always was. Yet even if one was inhabited it did not mean the house was a home, nor that the house was happy.

This one, for example.

Unhappy, rueful, as if it had tried somehow to put on its best face and been scorned in spite of its willing welcome. It was the fault of the woman, always, when that sorrowful thing happened. For a man was by nature a roamer, a thinker beyond his own self. A woman was the vehicle on which civilization rode, from generation to generation and down the lengths of years. Houses knew that, for they were the vehicles' motive power. They had a way of meeting the woman as either a rival or friend.

Poor Bures House had been alone too long, in a state of limbo. Clark the old butler knew that. He had told her, in so many words.

And so, Mehala? What now?

Shalamar, she thought in answer. The real question is, what about Shalamar? That friendly house across the small vale of the River Affon, where Doctor Carmichael would soon return and sleep in lonely discomfort.

Shalamar. With its faded circles of Flora's dials, its overgrown drives, its statues and stonework covered in creeper, owls hooting in the rafters. Shalamar, with its solitary inhabitant.

Nothing to steal, Mehala. Not at Shalamar.

She took up her Norfolk and walked upstairs. The master wing was not locked off. She went quietly along the carpeted corridor, and tried the door of the second largest she came to on the right. It opened into a large bedroom, a woman's, with the tall four-poster and the velvet curtains showing muted colours in the sparse light from her cup lantern.

A dress caught her eye, as it had when Clark had shown her round. It stood on a stand in the corner of a dressing alcove by a sideboard table.

It was of silver satin, with lilac buttons, many small ones covered by embroidery of intricate decorative style. Hooks and eyes formed the latchings at the bodice's back. The seams were piped, the skirt long and quite full, pleated. Its long sleeves were almost of beret style, short and widely distended, with a restraining band. It was a shimmering mass of silver satin, lilac its dominant accessory colour.

The bodice was of a close-fitting dipping form. A paisley shawl was loosely cast over one shoulder of the stand, a lovely mushroom and ivory colour.

She stood there inspecting it, letting the light fall along the length of the dress. At Red Hall there had been no time for fripperies. No occasion, for her obsessed husband had seen to that. It was tempting.

In the alcove, she lit a candle here and there, four in all, and disrobed to her shift. The dress seemed to have no petticoat. That would not matter, for who was to see?

A few minutes more, and she stood gazing at her reflection in the long mirror. The light was shed along one side, since she dared not light the central ceiling lamps – they always squeaked as the pulleys returned the chandelier upwards.

The dress was lovely, and fitted almost. She moved slowly so the dress skirt swung. Would this be the one to wear, if ever she had the choice?

'What. . . ?'

She turned quickly, hand flying to her throat.

411

Charles Golding was standing there in the doorway of the bedroom. For a second she was too alarmed to speak, then she took breath and recovered slightly.

'I am sorry, sir, I . . . I could not sleep – here in so large a house, sir. I came up here. I saw the dress and thought to try it on, sir.' She babbled on, trying to calm herself. 'It requires cleaning and some mending, sir, but that I can easily do when daylight is sufficient. Or if there is a needlewoman's flash globe, with some spirits of sulphur . . .'

He entered slowly, and sat on the covered bed watching her. From his garb and the splashes of mud and dust on his outer clothes, which he was still wearing, he had ridden long and hard to reach Bures House.

'Who *are* you, Mehala?'

'I am Mehala, sir. That is all. I know . . . I know really nothing beyond that.'

He inspected her form. 'You wear that like a queen. You show no fear, beyond what is a gesture. You harbour within you such a fund of feeling that all Sealandings talks of you.'

'Sir. I think you are mistaken, begging your – '

'No, Mehala. All the folk at the prize fighting – the carriage company, grooms, people of Sealandings, everyone – talk of you. I feel I am looking at more than the eye can catch.'

'Then that is for others to decide, sir, not for myself to explain, since I cannot.'

'Very well. So be it.' He hesitated after rising. 'You said something to me as I left. A warning. From where did you learn the information on which to base it?'

'Warning, sir?'

'You said to beware the wagers recommended by a friend.'

'My dream, sir? Just my silly fancy, sir. It was simply that I was suddenly solicitous for your welfare, sir, these prize fights being a notorious venue for – '

He made a dismissive gesture, plainly disbelieving. 'All right, Mehala. All right. Let it be so. I shall not ask, and you will not tell. That suffices.' He walked to the door and paused to look back at her. 'I suppose it must be a source of great tribulation for a woman such as you, to be so much what all men want?'

'I do not know how to reply, sir.'

'You reply very effectively, for all your ignorance, Mehala,' he said dryly. 'Your warning saved me from folly earlier. I am indebted to you. I will require your company at an event locally in Sealandings. You will accompany me somewhere. I shall give instructions in the morning.'

'Very well, sir.'

'Good night, Mehala.'

She bobbed a curtsey, and murmured her goodnights. He closed the door. She realized with surprise that he was quite and utterly sober.

52

Nothing could go wrong, Thalia De Foe thought, smiling. Radiance shone from the eye of a woman whose beauty could, exactly as her own, extinguish all other mere prettiness within radius of its lustre.

She spun before the great half-cheval glass, excited and adoringly.

'Tilt, you stupid bitch!' she cried, but without malevolence, to Meg, who obediently leapt to angle the mirror exactly right to catch her mistress's form.

'There!' Thalia waited, adjusting the *en coeur* slightly herself, then calling Meg to attend to it. 'I believe it's high time the English practice must soon follow the French, of former times, with carriages, where sumptuary laws proved most effective! And the Italians, in Venice. The restriction of wearing attire proper to the raised class is utterly essential, I believe, Meg. Do you not?'

'Yes, ma'am.' Meg had heard all this before, and knew she was permitted a limited number of options for reply, all of them in agreement.

'See to these pleats, girl!'

'Yes, ma'am.' Meg thought privately that Mrs De Foe was no longer slender enough to carry the heart-shaped front, since the *en coeur* always terminated to a point which could draw attention to the wrong figure. She fussed over the narrow pleats along the low neckline. 'Permit me, but the mistress looks absolutely gorgeous!'

'Ye-e-es,' Thalia mused, turning, eyeing the mirror. 'The seeming glass, girl!'

Meg darted to the half-cheval, rotating it as Mrs De Foe moved a genteel pace or two and returned.

'You know, Meg, I seriously did think of the newer bodice, the à la Roxalane, but I heard that Mrs Prothero, the poor hopeless lady, is trying to wear that. May she survive its central bone line!' She looked at Meg, for the first time directly. 'Do you think Mary Prothero has the figure of one who could wear it, Meg?'

'It is presumptuous for me to express an opinion, ma'am. But even to my eye it seems there are ladies who can wear such, and ladies who cannot.'

Thalia De Foe laughed, showing off her waist. 'A diplomat, Meg!'

she crooned, very pleased with the answer. 'I shall be interested to see what the Hunterfield ladies are wearing. I heard Mrs Vallance say that she has brought in some new material, and that her sister Miss Tabitha has evinced great eagerness to try it out.'

'That lady has had put about the tale of being enrheumed this last week, ma'am.'

'She has?' Thalia demanded in alarm. 'That means the scheming little . . . that the lady in question is up to something, does it not.'

Meg knew better than reply at all, merely finished adjusting the neck pleatings.

'The chimes are gone for the hour, ma'am.'

'I can hear, you stupid girl! The lip rouge, then the hair powder perfume – no wait, Meg! Who made that hair powder?'

'From a licensed man, ma'am,' Meg said anxiously. 'It was procured by Mrs Randon most particular. From Norwich.'

'Bring it to me.' Thalia took the bottle and removed the ground-glass stopper, sniffing experimentally. 'Did Mrs Randon see that the pulvil powder was made from apple-tree moss?'

'Indeed, ma'am! Mrs Randon checks everything like that most carefully!'

'Nothing retains a scent half so long as that moss lichen.' Mrs De Foe continued to doubt it, though. 'Ambergris? Civet? Musk?'

'Yes, ma'am. And I asked Mrs Randon did they use the very best loaf sugar for pounding in the mortar, and she said yes. And lavender oil and rhodium – that's why Mrs Randon sent to Norwich, ma'am, they being the best for lavenders.'

'Very well, Meg.' The lady returned the bottle of powder, still half mistrusting the girl's reassurances. 'I do not want the perfume fading with the night's dancing. If it does amenuse, I shall have a few things to say!'

'Yes, ma'am,' Meg took the bottle and placed it with the rose cerate for the final making-up before the dressing-table mirror, just as a maid-of-all came knocking, crying that the first coaches were seen from the Hall steps.

'Hair powder, then, Meg!'

Thalia De Foe was unaccountably in a fluster now the last few moments had arrived. She let Meg perform the dusting of her hair, which was nothing if not glamorous tonight.

She attended to her lip salve herself, not trusting even a girl as reliable as Meg for that vital toilet. She always liked a little otto of roses added to the rose cerate before it was placed along her lips for that final enlivening. It was her mother's method, and had served her well. This had exactly the right proportions of oil of almonds and alkanet root, thank goodness, for she had seen it made her very self. The colour was rich, a deep rose. Carradine would be in heaven at the first glimpse.

Tonight was more her night than anyone's. She hummed secretly to herself as she carefully applied the lip colouring. Tonight would be the ultimate declaration of her intent, all the signs there for Carradine to read. Others would see and admire – and the more fools they. And that included her husband, that unperceiving idler Felows. Strange how, for one so well versed in the elegance of London fashions, he was so strangely without sight, devoid of imagination.

Well, since he was so easy to deceive, let him be hoodwinked as long as it pleased her.

She smiled at her reflection.

'Well, Meg? Will I do?'

'Do, ma'am? They will fall at your feet, ma'am!'

For a fleeting second Thalia caught something in Meg's admiring gaze. It was surely a trick of the light, but in that instant there seemed a flash of . . . of triumph, perhaps even malice, in the girl's eyes before she bent her head and stood back to concentrate on her mistress's hair with a frown. No. Surely it could have been nothing more than the innocent pleasure, and even pride, with which a loyal maid always completed her mistress's preparations for a grand ball. That was it. Meg was simply thrilled to be allowed to be present, to praise her own handiwork, and admire her lady.

'Dress at the back, Meg?' Mrs De Foe stood, posing one last time for the looking glass.

'A moment, please, ma'am.' Meg knelt, adjusted the skirt slightly, then rose smiling with innocent delight. 'Beautiful, ma'am. Truly a picture!'

'Door, Meg.'

'Yes, ma'am. Good evening, ma'am.'

Thalia De Foe did not reply. She swept slowly out, measuring her steps for the best effect, and proceeded grandly along the great landing towards the staircase.

Meg watched her go, then withdrew back into the master bedroom. As she started to tidy up, her own set face caught her eye in the tilted mirror. She sat back on her heels, stared at her reflection for a long moment. A slow smile crept into her expression. The image in the mirror smiled knowingly back.

*

The carriages arrived in such numbers of a sudden that they were in a long queue along the great drive.

Footmen stood there, torches in hand on the lee side of the curved roadway. Other torchbearers stood in statuesque isolation among the ornamental gardens, setting off the fountains which played and gushed. They were borrowed for the occasion from the household of Sir Philip Banks, cousin to Mrs De Foe, who was already a resident guest at Milton Hall, and were more an indication of the De Foe connections than of necessity, for the De Foes' own grooms were coping well with the carriages.

Berlins, landaus, great coaches, barouches with the half-head raised in pretence that they too were of significant status and of appropriate class, edged in column towards the stone staircase leading up to the brilliantly lit porch of Milton Hall.

An orchestra of music played, and the hubbub grew with each arrival. Sundry gentlemen came on horseback, but they were relatively few, and latecomers whose carriages had suffered mishaps on the dismal roads of East Anglia. Their manservants rode behind, carrying trunks or leading horses bearing carrypacks of their masters' apparel. Occasional fireworks exploded in the sky, in promise of the entertainments to come when the night had deepened still further.

The Hunterfields were given right of passage as their coaches arrived, since Squire Hunterfield was to be the guest of honour.

Tabitha was in the first coach, with her brother. She could hardly restrain her excitement as the carriage drew close to the step for them to disembark.

'Oh, Henry! Isn't this the most splendid occasion of all time?'

'Almost, my dear,' Hunterfield said with mild amusement. 'I am sure that Thalia De Foe has excelled herself in preparations for tonight. But she always did provide an excellent table. As long as that infernal music doesn't drown out all chance of a good converstion, I shall be fairly satisfied.'

'Oh, Henry!' his sister pouted. 'You must dance, no matter what happens. I shall demand it!'

'Please allow me some privileges in that direction, Miss Hunterfield,' Lieutenant Carmady said. 'I am far from excellent, but can caper a little.'

'He can caper a great deal, Tabitha,' Hunterfield put in, smiling. 'Take my word for it. I have heard in considerable detail how your gallant escort capered and yelled, at the most recent of these highly illegal prize fights he attends.'

417

'Oh, now!' Tabitha protested. 'You gentlemen surely aren't going to talk only about that wretched barefist affair again, I trust! I am heartily sick of the same stories, over and over!'

'It was very exciting, Miss Hunterfield,' Carmady assured her. 'I would have given almost anything to have been present at that other great fight, when Tom Spring defeated Langan for a thousand pounds – '

'Stop it this instant!' Tabitha cried in mock rage, striking the lieutenant with her fan. He laughed and promised never to speak of it for a twelvemonth.

'I shall claim the privilege of waiting for your sisters, Tabitha,' Hunterfield said as they descended and the carriage drew away. Simple Tom was serving tonight as personal footman of the Hunterfields' larger coach, so stood at the bottom of the steps as Lieutenant Carmady accompanied Tabitha into Milton Hall.

The second Hunterfield coach came.

Letitia was accompanied by Sir Cavan Webb. She felt that this obligation was something of an imposition, since she had hinted more than once to Lydia that she would have received with attention any request from William Maderley to be her escort for the evening. Lydia ignored Letitia's hints, and gave her instructions to concede to the naval gentleman when, as naturally happened, he made his request.

Still, her spirits were high, because Mr Maderley too would be here at Milton Hall, in the company of his sister Olivia. It would be an excellent opportunity to make the further acquaintance of Miss Maderley, which was all to the good.

The gentlemen in the second Hunterfield coach had proved more than a little tiresome this evening, for they had talked of nothing but the fight they had attended. Both seemed to have made excellent wagers, and had spent much time discussing what they would do with the money. Sir Cavan Webb was thankful that he would no longer have to beg his bread in Cheapside when next he got to London, so he said with an attempt at humour. Captain Bussell entered heavy handedly into the spirit of the evening by telling his lady for the evening, Mrs Vallance, that he would no longer have to eat horsemeat like the French when next he was on manoeuvres with his regiment.

The carriage halted, and they descended on to the boarding placed there for the guests. As they joined Squire Hunterfield and slowly made their way up the stone steps towards the entrance, a great explosion of fireworks cracked overhead and blossomed in the sky, lighting up the night.

418

'An omen to augur well!' Carmady greeted them, smiling, as they prepared to enter the reception hall. 'On the ocean a rocket is a distress signal!'

'Now, gentlemen,' Lydia chided. 'This promises to be a lovely evening which we shall *all* enjoy. So no talk of distress if you please!'

'Quite right, Mrs Vallance!' Sir Cavan agreed. 'What is distress for one is another's rejoicing!'

Squire Hunterfield noticed the three gentlemen exchange significant glances at the remark as the group entered the reception hall and the gust of music and chatter engulfed them. He knew that heavy gains had been made at the Goring-Rendell fight the previous day, but was in darkness about who had sustained the serious losses. Somebody had to pay winnings. In polite deference to his position as senior magistrate and Squire of Sealandings his guests forebore to mention the details of the wagers made.

The customary fiction that the De Foes had not yet noticed the new arrivals was correctly maintained throughout the disrobing, the cloaks and mantles and coats and shawls being shed into the hands of maids and footmen. In accordance with custom, Fellows De Foe and Thalia kept up the converse with other guests until Squire Hunterfield signified that his party had in fact arrived, by advancing and clearing his throat and exclaiming loudly on the glittering spectacle Milton Hall provided. Then the feast marshal made his announcement and the De Foes gave the obligatory start of recognition and exclamations of delight, coming forward to take hands and rhapsodize at the lovely gowns worn by the ladies.

'I think this is the most delightful occasion Sealandings has ever experienced,' Lydia Vallance said, in congratulation to Thalia. 'Don't you, Henry?'

'I certainly do.' Hunterfield greeted his hostess and host in turn and formally introduced the three gentlemen to the De Foes.

'Oh, come now!' Thalia gave back, smiling. 'The ball you gave less than two months ago shall never be exceeded. I simply hope that the music is to your liking, Lydia!'

'I'm sure I shall adore it!' Lydia said brightly. 'They sound so . . . carefree and expert at their instruments!'

'Perhaps they will oblige by prolonging their rest for supper, eventually!' Hunterfield put in, sensing the presence of barbs beneath the chatter.

The company laughed as they made their pairs and entered the ballroom.

Normally little use was made of the music room at Milton Hall. Tonight however it had been enlarged by the removal of the end partitions which normally reserved parts of the large space for storage of unwanted furniture, carpets between changes and accessory items such as chests and extra clothes presses. Lydia Vallance, entering on Captain Bussell's arm, noted how cleverly Thalia had managed the extension. New paint, its offensive odour scented to extinction, adorned the far walls, and so cleverly were the decorations and paintings hung and the ornaments and vases placed that nobody could detect that it was not one long hall.

'I beg the Captain's pardon,' Henry Hunterfield said, 'but if I may have a single word with my sister. . . ?'

'My pleasure, sir.' Captain Bussell withdrew a few paces and stood admiring the congress. No couples were dancing as yet, but the musicians, finely placed in a small gallery above the opposite wall, were already showing their enthusiasm.

'Fine music, Lydia,' Henry said to his sister. He deliberately kept his voice low, so as not to be overheard.

'Very fine, Henry.' Lydia was subdued. She had not imagined Henry would have detected the animosity between herself and Mrs De Foe in so few words of greeting. He was angry.

'Explain, madam.'

She knew that voice, and tried to maintain a cheery smile while obeying. 'I advised Thalia on an orchestra, Henry.'

'Go on, madam.'

'I . . . I think I may have advised her wrongly, Henry. Through no fault of my own.'

'Of course not,' he said coldly. 'Otherwise it would be sheer malice, would it not?'

'Yes, Henry.'

Hunterfield smiled and bowed to William Maderley and his sister Olivia as they passed, heading for chairs arranged along one side of the interior ornamental garden which Thalia's servants had arranged for display facing the orchestra gallery. He ignored the eager smile which Letitia gave to Maderley, and the uncertain attempts to pause which the artist made as he gave his bow. Olivia, his wise sister, quickly checked the gaffe and made certain they walked on. Henry felt that he had enough to concern him, with the evening not two minutes old.

'What was wrong with the orchestra you recommended, Lydia? A full account, madam.'

'It had once played for Queen Caroline, Henry.'

420

Hunterfield drew a long slow breath, smiling still to show acute observers that he and his sister were merely debating arrangements for later in the evening. Sisters were clearly made by God for the plaguing of brothers before their marriage and whole families after.

Queen Caroline's name still sent shudders down the spine. Many years before, she had married George, Prince of Wales. Her behaviour had been so gross that the infamous Delicate Investigation had taken place. Allegations of her lewdness had not been proven when her trial had taken place in the summer of 1820, but even so she had been locked out of the Coronation of King George IV. The huge public outcries and disturbances had resulted in deaths after the sad lady died at Hammersmith in the August following. For Thalia De Foe to have contracted an orchestra which had entertained at some pro-Caroline function would have spelled social disaster for Milton Hall.

'Permit me to make but one observation, Lydia,' Hunterfield said to his sister with a sigh. 'In all my years as your brother, and responsible for you during your husband's absence, I have felt let down many times. But I can honestly say, Lydia, that you have *never* disappointed me.'

Lydia swallowed the bitter barb. He was really furious, but concealing it well for the sake of others. 'Sir, if I am a disappointment, I beg your apologies – '

To rebuke her further Henry cut her off by turning smoothly to where Captain Bussell still hovered, and called, smiling, 'Thank you, Captain. May I return my sister to you now?'

'It is my pleasure, sir.'

Hunterfield made a good-humoured withdrawal and crossed the ballroom to talk with Sir Trev Bunyan, who was in earnest converse with a rather plain young lady. Hunterfield knew her from her having stayed at Lorne House once previously.

'Don't tell me, Brillianta,' he guessed. 'Sir Trev is discussing with you the relative merits of red-heart or white-heart ash timbers for the construction of support in sprung carriages. Am I correct?'

'Henry!' Brillianta received his buss courteously, smiling at the jibe. 'How very pleasant to see you here. I had been hoping to see you at my sister's gatherings, but you pretend affairs of estate every single time!'

'Henry's pet aversion is music, Brillianta.' Sir Trev's eyes were elsewhere, Hunterfield observed, and guessed that Olivia Maderley must be somewhere to hand.

'Not at all, Trev!' Hunterfield laughed. He enjoyed the girl's company. She was bright, friendly without losing composure or her place, yet had the knack of saying things in a way that could quite disarm. 'I simply like it muted – the less the better.' He rather liked her company. His sisters however did not, which was strange as she was most companionable.

'Then I promise I shall reform you!'

'How will you manage that, Brillianta? Not some scheme to make me caper and gambol about like you people are all about to do, I hope?'

'No, Henry. Nothing like that. But I shall compose a group of ladies – from among these present, if you like – and shall throw an entertainment for you and yours! It will prove light-hearted, and I swear you will love it.'

'What sort of entertainment?' He pretended a sourness he did not feel towards her invitation.

'A musical one, with no dancing, but strolling in the gardens of Arminell. There, you will be able to talk about your precious East Anglia to your heart's content.'

'Do you mean without interruption, Brillianta? Answer yes or not!'

'Cruel man, Henry!' Trev Bunyan laughed mechanically, eyes still roaming in quest of Olivia Maderley.

'No, Henry. You shall be interrupted every half hour. But I shall make certain it is not Lorela who worries you!'

'There's a promise, now!' Henry scanned the ballroom as the musicians took up the ballad 'The Mallard'. 'Is your sister here, then?'

'I regret to say, Henry, that Lorela . . .' She hung her reply mischievously, though annoyed at his show of preference ' . . . . *is* here!'

'How delightful! I hope to run into her.'

'She is with a lumpish gentleman who's done nothing but talk about horses, their weights, the chances of having them all replaced by these iron mechanicals they are using on curtain railings in the north. Did you ever hear such?'

'Very pleased to see you here, Brillianta,' Hunterfield said, and moved away with a murmured apology.

It was hard work, very definitely difficult going. He was already sweating.

The ballroom was now becoming thick with strolling gentry and their ladies. He had never seen such a show of colours, dresses, accessories, feathers and jewels. The chandeliers were sparkling, the music – for all he felt it an intrusion into his enjoyment of an evening – quite accommodating, the ladies pretty, the gentlemen all in good humour after the excitements of the recent days. But these undercurrents among the ladies were feelings he could never understand.

Quite simply, there seemed to be no earthly need for them. Why could it not be a casual get-together, with friends talking and laughing and dining and then going out to observe Thalia De Foe's entertainments in the evening air? Instead, it was war instantly between Thalia and Lydia, and now Brillianta was upset because he was more inclined to think of Lorela, her older sister, than of her herself. He sighed. It was all too wearing.

It was definitely time that James Vallance, his brother-in-law, returned from India. Lydia would soon be more of a problem than he, as her brother, should be expected to handle.

'Ah. Squire Hunterfield!'

'Prothero. Good evening.' Hunterfield gave a slight and distant bow, and a deeper one to Mrs Prothero, who walked in her husband's shade for all the world like some Mussulman's spouse in the East. 'Mrs Prothero. How very pleasant to see you here. How are matters at Calling Farm?'

'Very – '

'Very well, thank you, Squire!' Prothero cut in. His wife seemed to shrink an inch further.

Hunterfield gazed at the man. He seemed to have swelled, become even larger than his form somehow. It was as if the fellow had come into, what, a knighthood? Hunterfield felt a twinge of unease. Was there some event in Sealandings he didn't yet know about? Prothero had been at the prize fight at Maidborough, for some casual remark dropped by Sir Cavan Webb on the ride over from Lorne had suggested so. But this new ebullient Prothero was extraordinary, a transformation.

'I have something with which to reproach your good lady, Prothero,' Hunterfield said, keeping his manner friendly so Mary Prothero would not be alarmed.

She knew him well, from their similar ages and background. She smiled, shyly, suspecting one of Hunterfield's mild attempts at humour. Prothero however drew himself up and barked out, 'Reproach, sir?' so loudly that people nearby turned and halted conversations.

'Why, sadly, yes, sir.' Hunterfield wagged a finger at Mary, showing the ballroom that all was innocent in this corner. 'I am given to understand that Mrs Prothero has designs on joining Miss Brillianta Astell soon, at Arminell Hall, and that together they will form up a musical evening for all concerned. Their purpose, sir, is to make yet more infernal din about my poor ears, justifying the racket by terming it music.'

423

'Oh, Squire!' Mary blushed and gestured at him playfully with her fan.

'See, Prothero? She doesn't deny it. I swear the whole district is determined to make me like the wretched stuff. Me! When I can't tell a Handel from a Purcell, nor a madrigal from a lute!'

Prothero joined uncertainly in the laughter. Hunterfield could tell that the man was gratified at the thought of his wife associating with the inland gentry. And the Astells of Maidborough occupied the same status at Arminell Hall as he himself did at Lorne.

'I shall be pleased if Mrs Prothero does visit Arminell Hall,' Prothero said stiffly. 'How does Sir Edward, may I ask? I have heard excellent accounts of his horse farms, and of the breeds he maintains.'

'Alas, I have no further information than that, Prothero. But you were at Maidborough recently, I believe, were you not? Perhaps I should be inquiring after Sir Edward from your good self. . . ?'

'I regret to say I did not have time to call and leave my card, Squire,' Prothero replied ponderously. 'I was there on other business.'

'Yes, Squire,' Mary Prothero said excitedly. 'Such amazing good fortune – '

'Mary!' Prothero said as softly as he could.

His wife blushed and nodded compliantly. Hunterfield passed a few more moments with them, then moved away to claim a drink from the punch bowls.

This was becoming more fraught still. Here was Prothero, behaving among the gentry like a dog with two tails, and that terrible implication of what poor Mary Prothero had said. Had Prothero won a fortune on the prize fight? It was unthinkable that he, meanest and most carping of the landowners in the locality, should now be posturing so.

'Penny for your thoughts, Henry Hunterfield?'

'Thalia, my dear!' He made an extravagant show of being overcome by her approach. 'What a splendid evening yours is, to be sure! What surprises do you have arranged for our delectation?'

'You will discover that in *my* time, Henry!' she teased. 'But you have not replied. Your thoughts. . . ?'

'I was wondering how much longer it would be before the truly important guest arrives,' he said, amused.

'The . . . the who?' She caught at her baroque pearl pendant, twisting it as if suddenly distraught.

'Why, Mr Bettany!'

Thalia laughed with relief. 'Silly man, Hunterfield! I of course sent an invitation to Bettany, since he is so important in Sealandings, having the only windmill hereabouts and us all obliging to him. But of course I received a reply couched in strongest terms, deploring my depravity in throwing a ball for the enjoyment of everyone, and informing me that he will pray most ardently for my soul and those of all attenders, that I might be released from further temptation.'

'A Puritan is a most devout creature, I agree, Thalia,' Hunterfield sighed. 'I just wish they did not wish *us* quite so much of *their* own good.'

Thalia laughed. 'Why am I so certain that was not truly your meaning, Henry Hunterfield? Come, now.'

'I was admiring your beauty, Thalia.' He smiled. 'But while as delighted as you at the return of your husband, I must secretly own regretting that Fellows is now in residence. It has spelt the ruin of many of my intentions lately.'

'Now, now,' she said sotto voce, her eyes peeping beguilingly over her spread fan. 'You must *not* give cause for scandal! At least, not with so many astute observers present, and all doubtless trying to read your lips!'

hesa 'It is an art I wish I had, Thalia,' he said. 'Lip-reading. It must be a profound advantage. Sadly it seems it is a skill only possessed by ladies.'

Thalia smiled, but was slightly discomfited by this chatter. There was again that faint thrill of unease, the one she had experienced when catching sight of Meg's glance in the mirror. Yet nothing could go amiss, not on this superb evening, with her arrangements having gone swimmingly and the evening balmy for love and romance and excitement. And her husband Fellows now safely talking to her elderly cousin Sir Philip Banks, doubtless swilling himself into a stupor as they bored each other to somnolence.

'My, you are obtuse these days, Henry Hunterfield!' Sparklingly she glanced around as if pointing out the decor and speaking of the decisions she had had to make. 'I had rather expected you to come calling on me before now, Henry. Not a note, nor a word. And you failed to appear, sir. Have I been cast, then?'

'Never,' he said easily. 'Thalia De Foe? Cast off, like some woman who did not know how to love? Who is always the most beautiful lady present in any company? Never!' He chuckled, raised her hand to his lips and took his leave as Lorela Astell entered from the gardens on the arm of a stolid gentleman wearing an Anglo-Greek front to his coat of superfine merino.

Thalia now was certain there was something seriously amiss. In a state of agitation she crossed to where Fellows was talking with company.

'And I actually saw with my own eyes,' a thin-faced gentleman was saying earnestly, 'the entire contents of the carriage being carried into the barouche! There must have been sums, in gold, in excess of . . .'

He caught sight of Thalia and exclaimed pleasantly, 'Ah, Mrs De Foe! Might I say how much I am enjoying myself?'

'Thank you, sir.' Thalia tried to place him, but only knew him as one who usually rode with the Hunterfields at sport. Something to do with the merchants or bankers, Saxmundham way.

'In fact,' the man joked, 'it promises the best evening I have had since my wedding!'

The gentlemen laughed dutifully. Thalia made a moue of pretended affront and drew her husband aside.

'I think that the dancing may commence any time, dear,' she said to him. 'And the supper brought out within the hour? There will be ample time after that for the entertainments out on the lawns.'

'Very well, my dear.' Fellows was at his most maddeningly affable, and made to move off again until she restrained him.

'Fellows. I am a little puzzled.'

'Yes, my dear?' Fellows looked about. 'Everything seems to be in order.'

'My cousin Charles is not here yet.'

'Charles? Are you sure?' Her husband glanced about, then shrugged. 'I shouldn't worry, dearest. As you know, Charles is very much a law unto himself. I have no doubt that he is well. He is quite able to look after himself.'

'Was there word of him yesterday, at the prize fighting?'

'I think I saw him there. Yes, I am almost certain I did. He seemed in fine fettle, better than I had seen him for many a long day.' He eyed her candidly. 'And sober, for once.'

'Did he say anything to you?'

'To me? No. No message, nothing. I rather think he did quite well out of it, though. He wasn't . . . the worse for wear, if you understand me. He seemed remarkably in good heart.'

'He did not get into any trouble?'

'Not that I know of, Thalia,' he said. His smiling eyes raked the ballroom as the pairs started on to the floor and took up positions for dance. 'Look, my dear. If you are seriously worried about Charles, why do you not ask Squire Hunterfield? He is after all the senior magistracy in these parts. If anything untoward had taken place, the petty constables would be sure to have reported to him. Or shall I ask for you?'

426

Sickened, Thalia shook her head. Fellows rejoined his group and the converse began anew. Thalia went to talk with Brillianta Astell and her seemingly new paramour Sir Trev Bunyan. Thalia detested the Astell woman, not only on account of her plain features and scalding wit, but also because she had often suspected the bitch of setting her cap at Henry Hunterfield.

But Henry was badly dated now, for her whole world was Rad Carradine. Everything, everything was Carradine. She would fly with him, if he asked. If only she did not have that terrible nagging suspicion growing within that something had happened involving Charles. And possibly Carradine. And Hunterfield?

'I love your dress, Brillianta!' Thalia greeted her, extending her hand for Sir Trev to salute. 'What is it, remodelled silk, is it?'

'Yes, Thalia. It is my mother's material, from her family. I love silk, and have always liked this.'

Thalia had to admit it was beautifully remodelled, as was all the fashion among those ladies who could obtain older silks. This was an embroidered pink, the skirt full and eased on to the bodice with cartridge pleats. The piped waistline was enviously precise. She could not help wondering if the bodice was boned at the centre, but of course could not ask with Sir Trev in such close attendance. It would have to be strengthened, though, or the silk would wrinkle at every step.

The one good point, Thalia thought sweetly, was that the girl was plain as a pikestaff.

'It is most charming, Brillianta,' she said, artfully placing her hand as if consolingly on Brillianta's forearm. 'And Sir Trev! I believe you were at the prize fighting again. Ah, you wretched gentlemen! Always at wars, or their poorer imitations!'

'I shall renounce them instantly, Mrs De Foe, if those activities fail to please you!'

'Most gallant!' Thalia said. 'Do you notice, Brillianta, that these gentlemen never actually tell us what transpired? We are always to be kept in ignorance, it seems!'

'Why, it is general knowledge!' Bunyan said, smiling. 'Your local Cambridgeshire man defeated the great Goring. Somewhere near the fiftieth round, I think, though by then most of the spectators were beside themselves with excitement and unable to keep their feet.'

'He means there is argument,' Brillianta translated. 'I have heard the gentlemen actually wagering whether it was the fiftieth or the fifty-first round. Would you believe it?'

'Scarcely,' Thalia said, smiling in spite of seeing Henry Hunterfield introducing himself to the gentleman accompanying Lorela Astell. 'But the ways of gentlemen are never to be understood, are they?'

'Hardly,' Brillianta replied. 'Look at the absentees, for instance.'

'Absentees?' Thalia almost allowed herself to whirl round and stare at the entrance, but caught herself just in time as Brillianta smiled wickedly.

Thalia realized she had been hooked by this plain bitch in the dazzling dress. The simpering girl's jewellery was exquisite too. Another cause for hatred.

'I meant the ones missing,' Brillianta said innocently, 'not those arriving. I should have thought Mr Carradine at least could have managed to make the journey from across the road. In honour of the occasion, so to speak. And I should also have expected your cousin Charles to be here, Thalia. He always was such a marvellous dancer, and see, the dancing is already begun and the Honourable Charles still not here! I suppose it is the consequence of his lady. Well, it often happens that a lady can exert, almost without seeming to try, the most extraordinary power upon a gentleman's intentions.'

'Lady?' Thalia laughed nervously. Now she was sure other things had gone badly wrong. She could do no more than stand and listen to this overdressed bitch in hopes of discovering what was awry. 'Cousin Charles? Courting a lady? Without even telling me, his dearest cousin?'

'Why, Thalia! How you pretend to ignorance! I am almost sure that I saw him escorting a lady in his carriage. She stopped off at the South Toll road for some reason, as we were riding past. Was that not so, Sir Trev?'

'Why, yes, I could almost swear so. But I do not have a lady's eye for instantaneous assessment of situations.' Bunyan laughed anxiously, aware that some fencing was going on but unsure exactly as to what.

'Then I must keep an eagle eye out for his arrival, Brillianta.'

'And Mr Carradine's,' the impertinent cow had the effrontery to say, right to her face. Thalia made herself smile.

'Yes? Mr Carradine? What of him?'

'I should have thought, as I said, he could have managed to come, even in such awful circumstances.'

Thalia felt dread seize her. The glint in Meg's eye. The double meaning in Henry's manner. This ugly slut's impudence. The . . .

The Honourable Charles Golding was announced from the doorway, to her relief. An ally! At last! Ennis was there, making the announcement directly across to where her husband was standing. Thalia started

428

towards her husband's cluster of friends to make the reception, then halted as if stunned.

On Charles's arm was Mehala.

Letitia was just congratulating herself that she had finally managed to manoeuvre William Maderley into her group when she saw his face change.

She was bringing out his most favourable attributes in discussion, extolling his abilities to the ladies and having him enlarge on his own skills as a painter of marvellous artifice, when his words dried and his gaze became fixed.

For a moment Letitia was unable to see exactly what had caught his attention. She only obtained direction by looking elsewhere round the crowded ballroom. She saw others turning and heads bowing in sudden talk, glances cast to show where the subject of all attention stood.

It was the girl from the painting. Mehala. The girl who accompanied Mr Golding. She stood there, stunning in her simplicity of dress and hair.

The dress was older than any present. It was from fashions of quite ten, fifteen years previously, an entire age, as fashions speeded through their ranges nowadays, Letitia thought. Yet she carried the anachronism beautifully, almost regally.

It was a simple evening dress, in white silk with a woven stripe of stylized flowers in various shades of light pale lilac. The sleeves were trimmed with net, blonde lace and piping. Most remarkably, the hem carried a padded rouleau mount. A diminutive lilac velvet beret, fashionable a dozen years ago, was on her head, its flat halo crown surmounted with feathers in a yesterday's style.

She looked breathtaking.

Charles Golding walked slowly across the ballroom, the dancing petering slightly as the dancers paused to stare. The musicians battled gamely on, the leader desperately striving to maintain the tempo and sound. In spite of their efforts, almost everyone present heard Golding effect his introductions.

'Mrs De Foe, may I present Mehala? Mehala, my cousin, Mrs De Foe. Mehala, may I present to you Mr Fellows De Foe of Milton Hall? Mr De Foe, Mehala.'

'How do you do,' Fellows De Foe said.

The perfect countenace opposite him smiled and said she was very well, and asked after his wellbeing.

Thalia felt giddy at the strain of it. Hunterfield, no less, was walking across and asking to be introduced, smiling at her and her husband and

429

saying that he had almost once had the honour of meeting Mehala, but had narrowly been cheated of that benefit.

'Ah, quite so,' Fellows De Foe was replying. 'Yes, Mehala, I have the honour to present Squire Henry Hunterfield of Lorne House . . .'

'Introduce me too, Fellows!'

Carradine came close behind Ennis, roughly shoving the footman aside as he attempted to announce Carradine's arrival to the company.

'Very well, Mr Carradine. Do come in.' Fellows signalled gently to Ennis, who withdrew swiftly to make signs to the musicians. They accelerated into their piece with gusto, the music deafening the introductions by the entrance.

Carradine was almost drunk, but not quite. He stood grinning at Charles Golding and Mehala, who was now the centrepiece of the tableau.

'How do you do, sir?' Mehala replied to Carradine's greeting. She did not extend her hand in response to his bow.

Thalia made an attempt to move towards Carradine but he kept his eyes fixed on Golding.

'Dearest Cousin Charles, is it, who's got the bird in his hand? I never dreamt you had it in you, Golding! Too besotted with your own bottled company, I'd heard. Or those tarts you plucked from the hedgerows when your highborn cousins weren't looking!'

Mehala squeezed Golding's arm, who concurred by moving her sedately away into the ballroom, where now the dancing was resuming and the orchestra dementedly crashing out the next melody.

Fellows and Hunterfield blocked Carradine's further penetration into the ballroom, pleasantly chatting as they did so. Carmady and Sir Cavan also intervened, and together the gentlemen made a show of talking good-humouredly while shepherding the tipsy Carradine towards the entrance hall.

In the ballroom, Sir Trev made the most of his opportunity by approaching Maderley and Letitia, and at last starting up an impromptu conversation with the artist's sister.

'Sir,' Olivia managed after his rather frantic introduction. 'Is that she? The redoubtable Mehala?'

'I believe so, Miss Maderley.'

'I have seen her portrait painting, of my brother's. In fact, I helped him with it, but only to admix his pigments and in similar small ways. But I had no idea she was so . . . so . . .'

'Beautiful,' William Maderley said quietly.

Letitia turned to look at him, finally understanding what effect Mehala had had on the artist.

'Not beautiful,' Olivia Maderley said, worrying the word until her brow cleared. 'Attractive. Alluring? Compelling? I would believe anything of that girl. She cannot be older than twenty-one, you think, Miss Letitia?' Letitia made no reply.

'How came she with Mr Golding?' Maderley said. He seemed to have forgotten everyone else.

'Mrs De Foe made her housekeeper for Bures House after the problems there, I understand,' Sir Trev said blithely. 'She's the girl who took the whip to Captain Bussell's pate.'

'I understand,' Letitia said quietly, so quietly that only Olivia heard. In anguish for Letitia she desperately strove to think of something to say which would return her brother's attention to Letitia.

'Beautiful,' William Maderley said a second time.

Olivia could have hit him, but he was mentally across the room gazing at Mehala. Only the strange circumstances of the music, the grandeur all around, the press of dancers and the bright spectacle of the ball kept him from running over to stare and admire from a closer range.

The night sky was set afire with sky rockets and exploding stars. Bonfires burned in the grounds, where decorative walls had been built to form grottoes. Arcadians danced in gauze dresses, and country shepherds stood in tableaux. Lanthorns hung among the trees.

A waterfall cascaded down before lights set in a false mount erected as a centre for a lawn, artificial flowers of coloured silks opening and closing magically in the exotic setting. Two knights jousted on a sward laid out especially for the purpose. Musicians played soft music. Several small summerhouses had been constructed about the grounds, with miniature fountains playing before each. Two dwarfs worked a miniature watermill at a false stream.

Everyone agreed that Arcadia itself could not be more beautiful than Thalia De Foe's representation of it.

As the fireworks shrilled aloft and exploded, and the fires burned brigher and the servants plied the guests with yet more drinks and food, Thalia finally found Carradine.

He was sitting in silence by the start of the false rivulet. Two men were directing the course of the water from the raised reservoir which had been formed and filled days before.

'Do you see that, Thalia?' Carradine said, sensing it was she who had come upon him. He did not turn to look. 'That work these men are doing?'

431

'Yes.'

'To Henry Hunterfield that would be beautiful,' Carradine mocked. 'Labour. Hand work. The bloody fool sees worthiness in it, as if there's some merit in grubbing with your hands. For peasants, yes. For others, how could it be so?'

'Rad.' She sat on the wall of the artificial reservoir. The two men were strangers anyway, fetched over from Sir Philip's, and were going about their business in dutiful silence. 'You suffered a grave loss? At the prize fight?'

Carradine nodded. 'I didn't show it, Thalia. Not for a single instant. Not even with a blink of my eye. I could have won. In fact,' he said with morose pride, 'there are scores of people here who still think that I won every damned penny I wagered on the fight.'

'You lost seriously? Irreparably?'

He laughed as if unable to believe her words. 'You mean, can it be mended by a stitch or two? No, Thalia. It's pretty bad.'

'What of Carradine Manor?'

'Carradine Manor? Someone else's house now, I should think. No. That too, probably.'

'It can't be, Rad.' Thalia found her nails digging into her palms. She felt faint. 'What will you do?' She almost asked, what shall *we* do?

'It will smooth over. Nothing can happen.'

'It's as if . . .' In the gardens beyond the small summerhouse, she saw her cousin walking with that pauper woman on his arm still. An idiot with a whore, at her ball, enjoying her entertainments, swilling her banquet.

A star shell exploded above. Charles saw them in its glare, and started across the grass towards the ornamental lake where she and Carradine were seated. The two artificers were still engaged directing the water courses.

'A splendid evening, Carradine!' Charles Golding called, approaching. 'And good evening, Thalia. You have excelled.'

Thalia observed her cousin in the half light from the tree lanterns. There was something new about him, as if he were suddenly capable, in control. The girl with him said nothing, but surely her composure was either madness or sickness, or both? In any event Thalia found herself maddened.

'Charles. I do not recall having extended an invitation to your servants. I shall speak with you presently.'

'About what, Thalia?' her cousin gave back just as sharply. 'Fresh instructions? Messages which I must follow, obedient to your whims, in default of which I will incur your displeasure? No, madam, if that is the content of your speech, then pray keep your words to yourself.'

'Charles! Of all the – !'

'I merely came by to acquaint you with a message in my turn, Carradine,' Golding said equably. 'Prothero said to find him at your soonest convenience. He sounded as if he would brook no delay.'

Carradine stirred in unease. Thalia stared at him in astonishment.

'No man speaks to Carradine in such a fashion!' she burst out, now quite distraught. 'He will . . . he shall . . .'

'Duel with the man?' her cousin asked. He seemed filled with genuine sorrow. 'I think not. Mark that I have passed on his . . . instructions to you, Rad.'

'What *is* this, Rad, darling?' Thalia watched her cousin and his companion stroll into the darkness under the trees, conversing. 'The world is falling apart. Sealandings has changed. Topsy-turvy! In every way. It is not . . . not really like this. Is it?'

'It seems so, Thalia,' Carradine said, morosely staring after the pair. 'You know, the world was sensible, stable, all in its place and all orderly. Sealandings and the Eastern Hundreds were tidy. All conformed. Then that cow was filched from the sea by the lugger's people. And Sealandings turned upside down. That Mehala bitch is everywhere, yet nowhere. She is a servant without a farthing, not even with a name, and she is here taking charge in your grand ball.' He laughed, incredulous of the sheer effrontery of it all. 'She is mistress of your Milton Hall, madam! And of Bures House. She has sway over the commoners in one tavern, and subdues another. She is the talk of the place. She has the folk at Whitehanger speaking her praises. She knows all. She has Henry Hunterfield ogling her, people in the great houses competing for her. She turns the pathetic worm Golding into a man at last. It's as if the bitch is immortal, with strength beyond – '

'Carradine?' a man shouted from the path below.

'It's . . . It's Prothero.' Thalia glanced wildly from Carradine to the man climbing the artificial mound where they sat. 'What will you do to him, Rad? Please do not create a disturbance here, or take him out before the end of the entertainments – '

Carradine stood, swaying slightly, as the landowner approached and stood before him, arms akimbo and staring balefully.

'Carradine,' Prothero said coldly. 'I told you to be at the release of the doves on the hour, sir. I observe that you were not.'

'Yes. I . . . I had something to discuss with the lady.' Carradine sounded defeated, subdued into shiftiness. Thalia listened, astonished.

Prothero in contrast seemed authoritative. 'Ma'am. Might I ask if I can accompany you down to the main party? This gentleman and I have business to transact.'

Thalia waited indignantly for Carradine to speak at the upstart's outrageous presumption, but her lover was silent. She drew breath and turned away.

'I can make my own way through my own gardens, thank you.'

She gathered her skirts and moved down towards the path, leaving the two men. The landowner waited until she made the torchlit path, where she was safely out of earshot.

'I gave you until ten o'clock, Carradine,' Prothero said icily. 'Your time's up. Well?'

'I'm not sure, Prothero. It's just that – '

'If you please, Carradine.' Prothero gave a curt sign to the other, and they began to walk from the mound to the path. 'Come along of me.'

'Sir,' Carradine began, but Prothero impatiently cut him short.

'The fact is, Carradine, that you are in over your head to the tune of several thousands more than your estate is worth. I require immediate settlement, seeing that I alone hold your promissories for more than half that amount.'

'I have other debts to consider, Proth . . . sir. London holds some twelve thousand sovereigns, the Strand jews the most. They shall have to be taken into account.'

'No, Carradine.' Prothero stopped by the path. Several couples were strolling by, admiring the glowing waters and fountains. He modulated his voice. 'I am not responsible for the debts you have incurred with *others*. That is between you and them. It's all no concern of mine. The notes I hold of yours are very much *my* worry. And mine alone. I require settlement.'

Carradine swallowed. 'How long will you give me?'

'You defaulted on other things than money, Carradine. I want the woman Mehala, now on Golding's arm and in his house. You defaulted on that. You couldn't even deliver me a nine-shilling servant.' Prothero was openly scornful. 'That disallows you charity from me, for in my book you have welched on the wager!'

'Welched?' Carradine stared. The man dared to speak to him like that. . . ! Then he sagged as realization came on him. It was unthinkable for a debtor to challenge a creditor to a duel. The implication might be that he was using the code of honour as a dishonourable means of avoiding payment. No. He would be shunned for a lifetime for that trick, and Prothero knew it. It would be exile, or worse.

434

'Welched, Carradine.' Prothero gazed at his victim, smiling. 'I knew it. You haven't the strength, for all your gay posturing. You are a sham, Carradine! You with your splendid house and great estate and fine horses, and all your grand assumptions. You're a fraud, Carradine. You aren't worth a tenth of any man I know.' Prothero tapped the man on his chest, smiling. 'I'll give you until morning to come up with something. After that I call in the bailiffs and the petty constables, and arraign you for fraud, forgery and whatever else I can think of. Understand?'

'Yes.'

'Yes. . . ?' Prothero prompted, waiting.

'Yes, sir,' Carradine said.

53

The morning at Bures House seemingly had not been the most correct example of the gentilitial houses of Sealandings. For a start, Mehala saw as she came early to make a quick breakfast, Mrs Glasse was astonished to see her enter and hear her express a firm intention to be into the day before ten o'clock. Old Mr Clark was already down, but clearly was accustomed to quite some hours' leisure, though he was more amused than put out to have the lazy routine disrupted.

'You will please to awaken the master, Mister Clark,' Mehala told him.

'Immediately, miss?' This was unprecedented, and now the senior servant did begin to look somewhat worried.

'Now, please, and brook no procrastination,'

Mrs Glasse was about to settle into a peaceful morning cycle of tea and victuals and comfortable, not to say indolent, cleaning of her kitchen. She was put out by all this. She said so.

'We have a routine here at Bures House, Miss Mehala,' she remarked brusquely.

'Indeed you have, Mrs Glasse,' Mehala shot back. 'If I remain it shall be rearranged forthwith!'

Mrs Glasse seemed about to make some retort, but found the girl's direct gaze too daunting. The look in the cook's eyes, however, showed openly what she thought, the speculations which were running around in her brain. Her and the master? Mehala said nothing, and let her think what she pleased.

'Give me only that breakfast cake, and marmalade, Mrs Glasse. Please save yourself the trouble of preparing more.'

The cook was astounded. 'No cold meats? No collared dishes? I have broiled mackerels and lovely dried haddocks, several sausages, rump steaks, and – '

'That for the master? No, thank you. He shall have but fruits, muffins and some toast, please. Give him only that.'

Mrs Glasse halted, arms akimbo. 'He won't like that, Mehala! And that's for certain!'

'He is not to be given preference,' Mehala said back, as strongly.

'But that breakfast cake is stale. I was about to throw it away – '

'Kindly stop your protests. I've already examined it. It is wholesome. Breakfast cake makes better toast than ordinary bread, when left to that degree of staleness. Kindly get *on*, Mrs Glasse.'

The cook obeyed, grumbling the whilst in the manner of her kind. Mehala went over the household accounts in the kitchen as breakfast was made. Clark reappeared, shaking his head, reporting that Mr Golding was bewildered at being roused, but was already washing and about to come down into the dining room. He was prophetic of absolute catastrophe when he saw what the maids would have to serve.

'This house is seeing some changes!' he chuckled, shaking his head. He was really rather pleased at the innovations. 'We've never had fewer than twelve dishes, eight piping hot, for the master's breakfast!'

'And thrown away how much, Mister Clark?' Mehala shot back. 'No. Let these changes stand. If I remain, we shall put into action a longer scheme still, all for the master's benefit!'

Word came from a footman, sent by Ennis from Milton Hall, that Mrs De Foe was on her way over. Her dilly was to be expected shortly. Mr Golding was to be apprized of his cousin's impending arrival. The young footman was given the customary dew-cup of warmed small beer and sent on his way.

'Did you know she would be coming, Miss Mehala?' Clark asked, interested.

'Thank you, Mister Clark,' Mehala answered obliquely. 'I shall see the master the minute he is at breakfast.'

Golding entered the dining room to find Mehala waiting by the door. She had sent a maid-of-all to serve him, and signed to the girl to stay.

He looked somewhat tired, but better than she had yet seen him. He was puzzled by the paucity of the dishes put before him, but started on the meal, glancing at Mehala.

'I have to thank you for bringing me home sober, for once. Waking so early, and without a splitting head, is something of a novelty. I remember this sensation of normality from when I was a boy.'

She smiled at his heavy humour. 'I am glad. There are a few details I should acquaint you with, sir. The first is that Mrs De Foe is on her way. Her diligence should be here within the half hour.'

'I thought as much,' he said ruefully. 'Will you be here, Mehala?'

'Yes, sir. The second item is that Bures House is sorely in need of a young assistant housekeeper. I have a recommendation to make. It is a girl called Little Jane, presently employed at the inn of John Weaver.'

'Will he let her go, though?' Golding asked. 'If you recommend her to me, she is as good as offered the position. But a promising young trainee housekeeper is something of a rarity, who can add, read, work out credits and debits . . .'

'She can do only some of those, sir,' Mehala said frankly. 'But I would be willing to induct her into these arts. I am certain she will prove an excellent learner. As to the Donkey and Buskin being willing to let her go, sir, may I remind you that you are owed a considerable obligation by John Weaver.'

'I am?' Golding halted as the maid served his tea. He signalled for the brandy, but Mehala shook her head slightly when the girl glanced at her.

'Yes, sir. Do you misremember? You were careful to allow John Weaver an uninterrupted water supply from yours. You gave me orders to that effect the day before yesterday, as you left for the prize fighting. His brewery activities are thus assured, sir. Consequently he is indebted to you, and I should think only too glad to express his appreciation by letting Little Jane come to Bures House.'

'Very well, then. Send to that effect, please.'

'Very good, sir. The other item is that the maids here should be allowed some walking-out clothes. Perhaps Berlin gloves, a bibi bonnet, and cazenou cape.'

'Anything else, Mehala?' Golding asked, somewhat put out, 'The suggestion might antagonize the other gentry, as setting servants an undue expectation all around Sealandings. Their place is their place, after all.'

'Indeed, sir,' Mehala said with asperity. 'And you know that I would be most unwilling to alter any social arrangement sent to us from Above. I must say, though, that the cost will be defrayed in better behaviour from some, and prove a most fitting example to the servants of other houses. It will, after all, do no harm to the reputation of Bures House if its servants are seen as examples of decorum and propriety.'

He thought, then smiled. 'Indeed it wouldn't! Especially if political reputation is linked in the popular mind with outward visible appearance. Good, Mehala!'

'I shall make a list, then, sir. The outside men servants I shall try for Anglesea hats, and good thick box coats for the coachmen and grooms. Except I have already found the costs of these in Sealandings far too high – quite two shillings and threepence above what is proper – so I shall have to send away. I want a careless or a wrap-rascal, something of that order, for each.'

'God, Mehala! Don't break my fortune's heart! You'll have me in the spunging house if you keep on like this!'

The spunging house was the dreadful room where debtors were expunged of all their assets before being dispatched into a debtors' prison.

'I think not, sir,' she answered evenly. 'A good housekeeper will effect very sensible economies in Bures House, which will more than compensate for the expenses involved. It is always very necessary to attend to the details of sending out for purchases, sir, in order to carry out proper household budgeting.'

'It's all very tiresome, Mehala.' In spite of his protests he was surprised and pleased; he could actually taste his food this morning.

'It has to be done, sir, in every household, whether cottage or kingdom.'

He was laughing. 'You're very persuasive, young lady. I'd rather be adonising for a night's entertaining.'

Dressing up is all very well, Mehala thought candidly, but you probably look better now than ever you did.

'Good morning, Charles!'

Mrs De Foe swept in unannounced, her outer coat and cape still on. She stood, smiling a brittle and dangerous smile, as Mehala went demurely to stand by the wall. Mrs De Foe shed her cloak, not minding where it alighted. The maid scampered to retrieve it.

'Good morning, Cousin!'

'Please don't rise, Charles! I should continue at that inadequate repast, sir! It will hardly enable you to get very far, though, when you finally realize you should have taken leg bail much earlier to avoid my anger!'

'It is what I want for breakfast, madam,' Golding said gallantly, without a glance at Mehala. 'If I want more, I shall take it.'

'I hope that this scantiness is not an indication that you will now skin a flint by nature, sir!'

'Have I always been mean, madam?' Charles asked gently, smiling at their governess's old saying. 'To you, or to any other member of my family? And I have never asked for an accounting!'

Thalia De Foe sat, slowly appraising him. This was a new Charles, one as ready to respond as to receive her criticisms.

She had come prepared to correct the vagaries of character which he had shown the night before, and to set things to right. Now she felt that terrible sensation of matters even further out of control. She was already in turmoil over Carradine's fantastic loss of assurance, and his tales of impending ruin. She had not slept. She smiled with malice at Mehala, standing composedly against the wall by the serving table.

'No repenter's curls, woman?' she asked. 'I'd have thought they would have been most appropriate for this morning!'

Mehala took the slur calmly. Repenter's curls were once the emblem of the reformed prostitute. 'That hair styling is far above my station, ma'am. It is now fashionable among the royal party at St James's.'

Mrs De Foe's cheeks reddened slightly at the stinging threat implicit there. Criticism of Royalty hinted of political disloyalty. 'It seems you have learned insolence as well as boldness! Mate to your crocus, perhaps!'

'I too have heard Doctor Carmichael called that nickname, ma'am, by uninformed village urchins. Though I am mostly unacquainted with pedlar's French, I have witnessed first-hand his endeavours on behalf of unfortunates and have learned from his example.'

'Doubtless you have, woman, doubtless you have!'

'Will that be all, sir?' Mehala let her have the last word, now certain there would be other condemnations coming, for which she would have to get herself prepared. 'If I may have leave to make the arrangements for Little Jane at Mr Weaver's inn myself . . .'

'Yes, Mehala. Please do not be too long.'

'No, sir. I shall be as quick as may be.'

She made her politenesses and withdrew, leaving the hapless maid-of-all in attendance, and went to get herself ready for the walk out to the Donkey and Buskin. She went to put on her cottage bonnet with strong chin stays, since it was blowing heavily in from the sea this morning and would soon come on to rain.

As she left, her brides fluttering about her cheeks and clutching her cape – cut down the previous evening from some old man's garment she had discovered while turning out a wardrobe – she felt like praying that Charles Golding would be able to withstand Mrs De Foe's assault. Yet there was no way she could protect the poor man for ever. Sooner or later he had to fight his own battles, or lose the struggle for life itself. Her cape was heavier than she liked, being made of durant everlasting, but that would protect her all the more if the weather became even more inclement. She struck out for the town, blazing inwardly at Mrs De Foe's insults.

The sheer cruelty of the woman! she fumed as she hurried along, stooping against the stiff onshore breeze. To insinuate that she had resorted to the cruellest and simplest method of ingratiation with Charles Golding! Or, worst of all, was simply leading him along for her own gain. Whatever had occurred at the prize fight, Mehala had learned sufficient to know that Carradine had suffered grievous losses,

440

maybe faced total ruin, and that consequently, in some way she yet did not know, Thalia De Foe's schemes now were threatened with disaster. Well, the woman had made her own bed, and must lie on it.

At Bures House, Mrs De Foe turned on the maid. 'Are you going to stand there all day, getting out of the work you're paid and fed and clothed to do?' she demanded. 'Get about your business, girl!'

The maid fled, thankful she had only received abuse. Thalia inspected her cousin.

'I see you wear your hunting necktie, Charles. Very handsome. Are we perhaps seeking to impress some new little slut here at Bures House?'

'Thalia. Is there anything at all I can do to please?' Charles sighed. 'I obeyed you in every way. I have entertained your friends. I have danced like a travelling bear, to your hornpipe. I accept, admittedly against my will, an unknown girl drawn from the sea, as my housekeeper, at your bidding. Now it seems I have done wrong in agreeing with you at all times. I must now undo all this, discharge her from the position to which you appointed her?'

'Is it too much to ask, Charles? Your ways – very educated, I know – are not attuned to household matters.' She smiled, attempting to allay his irritation at the turn of events. 'Leave things in my hands, I beg you. The influence of this Mehala woman seems so pernicious, so all-pervading, that it proves quite iniquitous. It has spread throughout Sealandings. She is poison, Charles. She spells trouble and difficulties – ' She caught herself, lowered her voice and tried to continue with more composure. 'In fact, I have seriously entertained the idea that she might well prove to be some kind of spy, sent by political rivals to discommode your entry into political life, which will – '

'Thalia, please.' Her cousin went to serve himself more tea, fumbling with the silver teapot and almost dropping the thing. He swore gently, shrugged an apology to his cousin and returned, carefully balancing the cup. 'None of this fanciful rubbish. Not to me. I have heard your tales all too often. I have seriously begun to question whether I am quite cut out for political life.'

'You will go back on your word, Charles?'

'No, Thalia. I am thinking of withdrawing my nomination, that is all. Circumstances have changed, you see. As you may have heard.'

'What circumstances, sir?'

He deliberated before speaking. 'These past few days, everything

441

went into the melting pot around Sealandings. Some gentlemen, I fear, may be ruined. There are already rumours – signs indeed! – to that effect. I have become aware of the place I should hold, were I to stand for election. Now, I hear that Squire Hunterfield is considering putting himself forward. That would almost be a foregone conclusion, would it not? With his money, influence, his standing among the lowly and the ratepayers, the tradesmen even? And remember that these all qualify under the ten-pound rule for their two votes apiece. No, Thalia. Times have changed of a sudden.'

'It's that Mehala bitch who has put you up to this, Charles!'

'Nonsense, Thalia. She has not said a single word about hustings, politics. Do you know what she was asking this morning when you arrived? She was petitioning me for some walking-outs for the servants.'

'A leveller!' Thalia breathed. 'I knew it! A subversive, undermining the proper God-given social order! I should have seen it from the first!'

'Thalia, that is a ridiculous claim, and well you know it! You are clutching at straws. She has sought the promotion of one of the serving maids from the tavern there, into assistant housekeeper here. That is not the action of a divisive troublemaker.'

Thalia was desperate. His nomination at the political hurstings was the last remnant of her plans. Perhaps it would even save Carradine.

'Charles. I appeal to you. Keep to your intention. Stand for Parliament. Think of the influence you will have! Of the fortunes which will accrue to you, as proper return for your acceptance of national responsibilities! Why, Charles, here on the coast there is so much money to be made from influencing imports – in the proper way, of course!'

'No, Thalia.'

'But everybody of influence does it, Charles! Great families, tradespeople, innkeepers, they are all at the night trade, culling money from dark boats which come into these creeks from the Continent! Why, Carradine has made a small fortune over the past three years simply by leaving certain of his stables unlocked and a pair of haulage carts unshackled!'

'*No*, Thalia! What I do on my estates is my own business. I shall think about the possibility, but I shall no longer simply be a creature of obedience to your intentions. I shall of course accept my responsibilities to the family. That goes without saying. After the discussions I had last night with Fellows about the wisdom of standing for the hustings – '

'Discussion?' Thalia's mind almost reeled under the impact of the news. She'd had no idea that her cousin and husband had talked the matter over. Carradine was now isolated, without a vestige of the help she had promised to give him.

'Yes. We had a long talk. He seems of the view that it would be very unwise for me to – '

'*Talk?* You talked with Fellows? Behind my back?'

'Scarcely that, my dear,' Charles said dryly. 'It was in your house, your ballroom, in your presence, with scores of your guests all within earshot. As I recall, several gentlemen also took part and gave conflicting opinions which entertained your guests mightily. Those,' he added pointedly, 'who were not strolling in your gardens having problems with ladies' dickeys and bosom friends.'

'I am not referring to under-petticoats, nor bust-improvers, Charles. Nor do I want to hear your smutty allegations.'

'No? Yet you come to my breakfast implying in your very first breath that I have pleasured my housekeeper.' He added, 'Would I'd had the good fortune!'

'That will do, Charles!' She rose and rang the bell. 'I shall consult our eldest cousin, Sir Philip. Doubtless he shall have something to say about your defection.'

She made a grand exit, Clark ready to open the door as she reached it.

Charles did not accompany her. Since Sir Philip Banks was his cousin also, and since his quavering old voice had been the one raised the strongest in advising him not to stand in the elections, Thalia was in for a ruder awakening still. He wondered if all the rumours about her and Carradine really were true. A woman could come under mighty influence from a man, that was certain. As most men could from almost any woman, indeed. But the influence was different, sometimes total, and to a different degree of strength.

He sighed. It was all beyond him. Things should always be simple between the sexes. With Judith, now, all had been simple. She had served him, as he had served her. She had filched, doubtless, but was that not all to the good? It kept her in place. Now, all was disorder. Thank God for Mehala, he thought, was astonished to find himself quite well satisfied with that curiously small breakfast, and went to summon the grooms for his mount.

Mehala entertained herself during her walk by thinking of the order of flowers round the Flora's dials which kept coming to mind. Of course, the first priority at Shalamar was really the setting up of a pepinnier, where seeds could be raised and fruit produced that would serve a household for use as the seasons did their slow spinning. A pepinnier was a most important part of a garden, as vital as a herb plot.

She had accounted for the first three opening flowers by the time she approached the yard of the Donkey and Buskin. Yellow goat's beard came to at two of the morning, exactly as the sowthistle closed, so that was the usual start. Then at three o'clock the common ox-tongue opened, followed by the hawkweed – though here there was an important choice, for the wild succory and the late-flowering dandelion were of a time with the hawkweed, and much would depend on the eight o'clock openers, for too much imbalance of daytime appearance could make ruination of a planting scheme . . .

They gave her a heroine's welcome in the kitchen. Little Jane was beside herself, and so proud that a friend of hers had gone about like a real lady for the night ball among the gentry, and had stepped down from a real coach exactly like Cinderella.

'We were so excited, Mehala,' Nellie told her shyly. 'When we heard we just didn't believe it. You and Mr Golding, just like . . . Oh, you know!'

'How did you feel, Mehala?' Little Jane cried, drawing her on to a bench by the fire and helping her off with her covering coat. 'Tell us! Tell us!'

'It was absolutely splendid.' Mehala decided not to give any account of the conversations she had overheard or taken part in. 'The lights quite outdid the thousand lights of Vauxhall Gardens. They could not have been more splendid. There were so many fireworks.'

'We saw them!' Nellie cried. 'We went up to the roof! Mr Weaver said we could. There was such drinking here that we all woke this morning with sore heads!'

'True.' Mrs Nelson was in good humour, laughing and shaking her head ruefully at the lack of sense of her young scullions. 'I think there'll be more to regret than swilling back a gotch of ale!'

'Oh, Mrs Nelson!' Nellie chided, colouring.

Mehala smiled, recognizing that Nellie was the cause of Mrs Nelson's foreboding. Some young man coming through Sealandings, probably, enjoying the evening by carousing more than he should.

Pressed by their questions, she told them of the dresses, the food, the drinks and the music. Little Jane said how one of the men servants had crept close to hear the orchestra and had hummed them their melodies on his return, to everyone's delight. Mehala described the materials of

444

every dress she could remember, and scandalized even Nellie by a description of the low-cut bodices and the caroline corsages and bosom knots. She speculated for them on the probability of under-corsets, and gave good accounts of the jewellery worn by most, and told of the elderly ladies at the ball actually still wearing bosom bottles. This called for detailed descriptions, which Mehala supplemented by drawing outlines of the flat ribbed containers of perfume sewn to ladies' bodices.

'Were there any. . . ?' Nellie had the rest of the servant girls laughing and giggling as she dared the question. 'Were any ladies wearing nipple jewels, Mehala?'

'Yes, Nellie. One, but she was mostly shunned and mortal shameless! A regimental officer had brought her in company. Though she attracted a great deal of attention among the ladies there – and not less among the gentlemen – she was not spoken to with welcome.'

'Does it hurt?' Little Jane speculated. 'I wonder if it would?'

'Having ears pierced is troublesome enough, Jane,' Mrs Nelson scolded. 'Without you trying those sort of stupid tricks. Nipple jewels are worn only by the loose ladies of this country, please! Never mind what these Frenchies do. We know they get up to all sorts of practices. You mind your thoughts as well as your actions, my girl!'

They talked for too long, Mehala realized, but Mrs De Foe would be unwilling to see her back at Bures House too soon. And she had to see Mr Weaver about Little Jane next. That too would take some time, and Mrs Weaver would probably have to be consulted.

The inn was filling up with new travellers as they chatted. The serving girls, in and out of the kitchen with orders, came faster as the tavern's tempo rose.

Reluctantly, Mehala left them to their work and went to seek John Weaver, wondering if he would approve. She had given no hint to Little Jane, nor to any of the others. They talked of her housekeeping with awe, though, and Little Jane had expressed more interest than any. Mehala thought she would be a natural success in the post, and would train excellently.

Also, Little Jane would be there should anything amiss befall herself.

54

It was the most beautiful morning. He stirred in the silent cottage, conscious that his hand was still holding Clare's. She was in profound sleep. Her pulse was strong, firm, her breathing through the silver tube seeming almost melodious, so even and sweet was it.

Outside, a gull called abuse at some malfeasance. A cart creaked by; it wasn't Jake Darling's heavy road waggon, for that was perfectly maintained, and ran as silently as any vehicle could.

For a few moments Ven Carmichael watched Clare. She was there still, a mystery and triumph. 'I treated but God cured,' as the old doctors' wise saw had it. Wherever the truth lay, he had done something new. As a result, he and Clare together had blundered into survival. She was alive, and seemed well. The feeling of health was in the room, slowly filling it. The dawning realization that she had come through moved him. He felt tears well from his eyes, and sat trying to · mend himself. This would never do. Doctors did not weep, neither from relief nor sorrow. Pity was the province of others. Love was to be suppressed, allowed to show only in the work one did for the sick. He remembered the ancient prayer of the Hospitaller Knights: 'To our Lords and Masters, the sick . . .'

That was how it should be.

Gently he slid his hand from the sleeping girl's. Today he felt he could go home to Shalamar. Mrs Darling and pretty Winifred Overton could manage for a day. They had seen the tube become displaced three or four times, when Clare had relapsed into a transitory delirium. He was becoming confident in its management, though the first displacement had almost frightened him to a faint as Clare had stopped breathing until he had managed to slip the tube back in place. And twice now he had shown the two women how to replace it, the last time allowing the mother to do it alone herself. He was sure she could now cope.

He rose, creaking painfully in every joint, slowly stretched and went to the door and lifted the Suffolk latch on Whitehanger.

Outside, the cottage garden in a single patch between the cottage and the road. Across, a scatter of cottages, then the spread of the North Sea beyond the village green and the seafront hard, where small boats were drawn up. A harbour, much smaller than that of Sealandings, and a tavern. A mole to serve as breakwater, a minute stone wharf, a hoy already hoving out with its passengers.

He watched it enviously. He had never had the money to ride on the sea. Hoys, the smaller vessels used always for coastal passenger transport along these shores, were generally faster and safer than riding or walking the treacherous roads, where footpads were many. Every day travellers, even stagecoaches and carriages, were held up. It had been the same ever since the great wars against the tyrant Napoleon had been so triumphantly concluded. Vagabonds and wanderers, some quite legitimately poor and unable to fend for themselves any other way, infested the entire country.

Yes, a vessel at sea was a truly lovely thing. And these people who sailed them were a magic race. They had the gift of water flight, he always thought, like the great ocean birds. He felt soiled, inept, dull. Perhaps if he had a gelding, a mare, to ride about the practice he would feel more justified? He smiled and went in, rueful. There would be no possibility of that. Perhaps a donkey one day, if the Lord smiled kindly on his endeavours.

He took the kettle to the fire, silently placing sea coals on the embers and sitting by it to read. The terrible stories of new dreadful diseases they were experiencing in the Indian Empire were rife. And the Russian saga of the 'cholera morbus', as they were starting to call it, was horrendous. Please God let it not come to this Kingdom.

Clare was settled still. He needed Mrs Darling to rouse, then he could leave Clare and go to the privy at the end of the garden. The problem was that he could not feel justified in leaving the child unattended, and leaving her in the charge of one guardian was to leave her so, for one person alone could not keep sick-watch effectively. A patient needed constant cover, one at all times. Too many mistakes were made, when a mother or nurse decided that all was well and that the suffering child could safely be left 'just for a moment while I . . .' No. Two guardians, and he could go home for a brief rest, perhaps make some plan about the next stage, the removal of the throat tube.

There was no tea, for the Darlings had run out of that valuable commodity. He would make a hot ale for himself. You could not mull beer properly from an early fire, as was well known, since the poker could never reach the necessary degree of redness. There was some cold potato left over for him, Mrs Darling had said. He would heat it. That excellent vegetable, the commonest esculent root now used, was mercifully no longer a rarity. He smiled, watching the fire begin to

447

draw, reflecting on the engraved picture he had seen once, in the 1597
Herbal book by John Gerard, showing that botanical doctor proudly
holding a potato plant in his Holborn garden. Could the expert Gerard
have ever believed that plant would form a staple food for a populous
kingdom?

He found the cold potato and put it on a plate skillet to heat. It was
slightly waxy, so was probably the famous Cardington variety, grown
from the stocks that the famous Mr Howard – that so-called 'patriot of
every clime' – had introduced decades ago in Bedfordshire.

Around him the cottage slowly warmed. Outside, the day began.
Whitehanger started its sounds. A dog barked, a second tax cart rolled
along the wharf. Somebody at the inn on the green called as a heavy pan
tumbled, and women's voices cried out in alarm then dissolved in
laughter. A girl child complained about her pantalettes, her mother
scolding not to give cheek. Some children played and skipped along the
path behind the cottage:

> Golden apple, lemon or pear
> A bunch of roses she shall wear
> Gold and silver by her side . . .'

So many things brought out a smile it was almost impossible not to
feel uplifted here, sometimes by the most mundane things. When had
he last heard that skipping song, now? He remembered finally. It was
one Kissing Friday, when he had interrupted a girls' skipping game –
they had all been chanting that same rhyme, on a long cross-rope – and
he had felt so emboldened by the power given him by that day. His
kissing partner had been none other than little Mary Calling, when he
was on a rare visit with his father to study coastal flowers. A stolen kiss,
and no rebuke possible! How marvellous life was, back then in
childhood.

Little Clare was breathing steadily. She was beautiful in her repose.
It was over, by all measures that he could bring to bear. She was
rescued – God alone knew how, but saved from death.

Sudden weariness enveloped him. How long had it been? Many,
many days. How many other urgent calls had gone unanswered,
though, while he'd stayed here at the side of this child? Impossible to
say. Mrs Trenchard wouldn't quite know for sure. She was the most
unreliable taker of messages he had ever known, but that was not her
fault.

Mehala. She knew the workings of boats, sails. She had hardly been
at her best when she had emerged from that shallow sea mist,
struggling to drag poor Simple Tom from the mud on to shore. Could

she skip too? He had no doubt; she would have been unquestionably the best, most graceful skipster of all girlhood. He almost laughed aloud as the kettle at last began to sing, enlivening the cold cottage.

The children were almost inaudible now, receding:

'Now you're married, I wish you joy
Father and mother you must obey;
Love one another
Like sister and brother . . .'

Yes, Mehala. There could never have been another child like her. He caught himself smiling again. Clare's lips were moving, bless her heart. Reflexly she was responding to the girls' song,

'And now's the time to kiss away . . .'

He gazed at her. She opened her eyes, saw him and stirred, stretching slightly. Her lips moved: Is it time for school, Doctor? He smiled and shook his head, making a mime of tilting his head and blinking as if he too was rousing from slumber.

'Rest, love. Sleep again if you want. Your mother's asleep in her room. Daddy'll be home today with his great cart. Your Aunt Winifred will be along presently. She's making breakfast in her cottage.'

Clare's lips moved: Am I better?

'It seems you are, love,' he said. He had to turn away a moment, his eyes misting. He busied himself with the fire, poking it unnecessarily and finding the small beer to warm. He had forgotten the potato and had to scramble to fetch it away before it charred to black ruin. He stood there, sighing at the problems of life. How could he manage surgery so well, and fail at this?

There was bread anyway, for toast, and a scrape of jam. That would do.

He saw Clare smiling, almost grinning, and made to threaten her with the skillet in mock fury, setting her to grinning all the more. Which was how Mrs Darling found them when she emerged in apologetic hurry, bidding good mornings.

'It wasn't me, Mrs Darling,' he said with a show of aloofness. 'It was Clare. I left her to watch over it and she said she wouldn't.'

Clare's eyebrows rose at this scandal. Mrs Darling took over, making a grand show of disapproval but secretly smiling at her daughter. Clare enjoyed the banter, Carmichael maintaining the false tale for the whole of the next hour. They enjoyed the joke, prolonging it with endless variations, even until Winifred Overton came.

Ven went to sit on the rear step. Strangely, Mehala was in his mind. This was a family. He had been part of it, for day after day. He felt more

449

at home here in the Darlings' cottage than anywhere. That, though, was only because they were a family and he had none. Service for others, yes, so he was now as he had to be. There was no other way, probably. To travel fast was to travel light. Who took a wife and children gave hostages to fortune, the great essayist had written. Yet how marvellous the shape and texture of a man's life could become. How Jake Darling must feel, returning home to his family. How marvellous Mr Overton must feel, coming home to be welcomed by a lovely woman, especially one with the gift of smiles like his happy attractive Winifred.

His duty was done here. He felt it. Clare could be handed over. He could leave now. The two women had other neighbours, and he had been assured there were several more contenders for the duty. Tomorrow he would return, and soon complete the surgery by removing the throat tube to give Clare a trial period as he restored the anatomy to normal. He would stay here, probably, for the covering period of, say, one more night, checking Clare's ability to breathe. Then she could be left, to make a slow return to fitness –along a prescribed gradual path. He would write out detailed instructions carefully, step by step and day by day. Fortunate that so many people could read in Whitehanger. Jake and Emiline Darling were accomplished in the art.

The world felt at distance. He was dizzy, almost uncoordinated, even in the mundane act of walking the garden. In fact, when he had gone the little distance to the petty some time ago he had almost keeled over from weariness. As long as he wasn't becoming enrheumed and taking cold himself he could manage.

Slowly he went indoors to tell Mrs Darling that his work was almost done.

It was three hours later that, feeling light-headed still, he set out quite slowly from Whitehanger along the coast track. In spite of his embarrassment, the people of Whitehanger turned out to wave him off. They had given him provisions, in fact offered enough for an army; declining most proved a difficulty, and he had had to depend on Mrs Darling to make a small sensible selection of bread, cheese, a pippin and some medlars. He had confessed a partiality for these small fruit. From somewhere Mrs Overton had procured several and put them in a cloth, telling him that they had reached the right degree of rottenness to be eaten that very day.

It was unlucky to look back, an uncle had once told him, and he passed that superstition on to the Darlings. They nodded sagely, undeceived. He said his goodbyes to Clare, promising to return the day following, and left. Their calls of goodbye and shouts followed him until the trees slipped down the slope and cut him off from them. Then he eased his walk, and felt himself gradually coming to.

Odd to be tired, yet not realize quite how very tired you were. It gave a vision, a bliss of melancholy, that he did not often experience.

Mehala had walked this road not long since – how many days ago was it? No way of telling. He was following her, in a sense, treading home to Sealandings after her.

What would happen to her? Only that which she wanted to happen, perhaps. Knowing her strength of character, her depth of understanding – maybe by now she was advanced to some high position in Sealandings, for certainly she was no ordinary creature. She was above the mundane in every way he could imagine. She was strikingly fetching, with innocence that was somehow compelling in its power to baffle the brain. And clever, but without the deceit which that word usually implied. She could become almost anything, a woman of her capacity. He thought wistfully that any man who had Mehala would be king within a week. If not on a throne, then in a royal position in commerce, trade, great estates, in control of powerful lineages. Yet she had stayed by him – well, little Clare, really, to help from pure impulses of charity – when she could have been advancing her own life instead.

Perhaps there was news at Sealandings? Maybe claims for her had come from her own people? Was she in fact, as he suspected, of a great family? Though, if that were so, how to explain her skills at serving in the tavern? She knew beers, housekeeping, had domestic skills which required dedicated industry to learn. She seemed all things – aye, and to all men too. He felt invigorated as the day began to move away its morning chill. He felt better, quite recovering himself at the thought that he was returning to Sealandings where Mehala was. He began to stride out as optimism took hold.

During the long candle hours, as they had kept sick-watch together, he had come to know fragments of her background, though he was always conscious that she was keeping back more than she said. She seemed at her most unguarded when speaking of factual things, the price of corn, of building, astonishingly once of the costs of installing a new ornamental mechanical fountain. She seemed to hint at possessing enormous expertise in running a large household. And still she busied herself with the most menial nursing tasks, tenderly coping with the child, washing the fouled bed linen.

The breeze had turned onshore with the tide. Ahead was the stile where he had encountered Mehala. He paused to stare towards it a moment, quite as if expecting her to materialize. She had rested there, just so, as he had approached. She wasn't there today, needless to say. He felt disappointed as he glanced about. Stupid to expect her company, especially when there was simply no way of her knowing that he had decided to leave the Darlings' this bright morning. At a whim he turned into the wood along a footpath. This must be the path to the charcoal burners' place of which they spoke. It emerged somewhere near Shalamar, he had heard vaguely, or if he turned right it would cut off part of the seaward track and let him out of the trees on to the Sealandings road between Lorne and Bures House.

For almost an hour he plodded upwards among the trees following the path. Without landmarks, he soon began to wonder if he had taken the wrong route, but came upon charcoal burners at work in a small clearing. Tired and still in the grip of that feeling of remoteness, he thankfully accepted their invitation to rest and share a meal.

They spoke oddly, using a cadence which sounded unfamiliar. Even the children seemed to join in the work. The burners' families lived in makeshift shelters constructed for the summer months, and returned to their cottages beyond Whitehanger only when winter stopped their work. Carmichael found their presence comforting. He watched them build the stacks of skillets, and was entertained to see the way the hordes of children joined in to drag the mares, the low framework barrows piled with cut wood, to join the roofs of each stack awaiting firing.

Smoke was everywhere. Sitting peaceably for the first time since he had gone to treat Clare, he felt a languor steal over him. These people simply accepted him, a stranger plodding into their work clearing out of the forest, and seemingly without conscious thought made way for him, accepted him quite naturally into their gathering, seated him at a fire and proffered him a meal. It was loveliness, a kind of grace. It was the sort of innate graciousness of attitude that . . . well, Mehala bestowed upon anyone she encountered.

All people were special people, he thought, almost slipping into a doze. How many different trades and livings existed in the land? It was almost infinite. Each with its own language, almost, its own superb folk skills. Only Mehala would know them all, be as easy with these charcoal-burner families as they themselves, and be as rightful in a grand house as in a waggoner's cott. But she was uncanny, above the rest of mankind.

'See, Doctor?' one charcoal burner was saying to him. 'This is how we test our coals once made.'

This direct speech was unusual, Carmichael knew, for nobody was as secretive about their lore as the burner families. They had the reputation of being more clandestine even than miners and stone-masons, who would kill to preserve their trade crafts.

'We take the charcoal on our shool,' he was shown, the grimed man sliding a heap of charcoal on to a long-handled shovel. 'We chose a piece, and cast it down hard upon a solid board which we keep for the purpose. See?'

The man threw the charcoal, which made a curious muffled ringing noise on impact. He grinned, white teeth in a blackened face.

'It's the right sound, so the charcoal's good in heart.'

'Thank you,' Carmichael said. 'I'll not tell of it to others.'

'You're welcome.'

He was given a meal of turbot preserved in sugar. Their bread was heavy brown meal loaf, all tasting slightly of smoke.

'Doctor expected kippered mackerel, then?' the men joked, setting them all laughing. They provided him with small pieces of sugared salmon and buttered drop cake, insisting that he ate well. He was becoming almost sleepy when finally he decided that all this laughing and talking at the branch shelters of these good folk was all very well for the indolent traveller, but not one who was walking home to prepare for yet more work.

He said his thanks, and received directions. A woman approached him shyly as he rose to brush himself down, and gave him a small carving.

'Only wooden, Doctor,' she said. 'But that's our stuff, you see.'

It was heavy, some wood he had never met before. The surface was finished to seem ebony, though faintly grained. Maybe some further evidence of hidden craftsman skill? But the carving itself was the thing. A woman, perhaps some ancient goddess, looking downcast. A simple bust, but beautiful.

'I cannot take this,' he said, startled. 'What on earth could I give in return?'

'Oh, shush!' the woman scolded. 'It's just for that great barn of yours.'

He stammered his thanks. The clearing all around was now active, with men trying to stop fire breaking out from the tops of at least two stacks. They were mixing mud quickly, throwing it hard into the vents where fire was sprouting, to block its open burning. He could see he had kept them from their work, and left quickly, striking away from the clearing along the only upward path. Less that forty paces on, he was interrupted by a call off to his right.

'Good day to you, Doctor.'

'Is that you, Mr Maderley?'

The painter was among the trees, at his easel. He must have been there some time, for his canvas was already set up, his paints spread all around him.

'Will you share a glass with me?' The artist indicated his flask. 'No mixed capsicum and isinglass in *my* brandy, Doctor, I promise! This is the strongest you can get on this shore.'

Carmichael began to laugh. 'This is preposterous, Maderley! I have been travelling homeward some three hours, and have got less than as many miles! Is hospitality always so relentless in these parts?'

'You know it is not, sir.' The artist shrugged at the declined offer. 'But if you must press on . . .'

'I regret I must. But thank you for your kindness.'

The artist stayed him with a raised hand. 'Mehala served as your apprentice down in Whitehanger, I believe?'

'Yes.' Carmichael paused, returned the artist's stare candidly. 'And no physician could ask for one more dedicated.'

'I knew that would be so.' Maderley sounded dejected. 'Mehala could not be otherwise. I am beginning to wonder if she is mortal.'

'Have you heard of her, then?'

'Yes. She is housekeeper now at Bures House. Golding wore her on his arm at the ball – you were aware of the grand entertainment Mrs De Foe threw at Milton Hall? It was a splendid, extravagant occasion.'

'I am pleased Miss Mehala has been successfully advanced,' Carichael said heavily. 'No lady is more deserving, in my opinion.'

'I saw the burners give you a present.' Maderley nodded, as Carmichael replied by taking the carving from his pocket.

'Yes. I was surprised.'

'It's more than just a token, Carmichael,' the artist said with a trace of bitterness. 'They do not confer gifts lightly, nor without purpose. It is a charm, Doctor, against its lack.'

'Its lack? I do not understand.' Carmichael inspected the carving, turning it over in his hands.

'Within the month the carving will become reality for you. Though modern folk of course cannot possibly believe in such pagan superstitions.'

'Become a reality? The carving?'

'Just so. Thus, if the carving had been a stallion, by the month's end you would be riding the highways grand as any peer.'

'But as you see it is of a woman.'

'Who will come into your life by the next moon, Doctor.'

Carmichael laughed with embarrassment, and gave a glance back to the clearing, where all was intense activity now. He might never have visited. The women were busy around their branch-wood improvised homes, the children and the men dragging and stacking billets, others cleaving and sawing. 'Why would they give that to a stranger?'

'Because you are no longer a stranger, Doctor. Not to them. It incurs an obligation, of course, as any gift.'

Ven smiled. He liked the artist, and felt himself warming to him as much from sympathy as from affinity. '*Do* gifts exact a price?'

'Certainly. As a woman does, when she comes to a man. As a gift carved from living wood and given to someone they have never seen before.' Maderley reached for the carving, nodding his thanks when the doctor passed it over for inspection. 'There is this tale that charcoal burners have a wood – only silly superstition, of course – which is known only to them, not to any botanists or scientists. They alone can recognize it. Some say it grows invisibly, only becoming visible to outsiders when it is carved.' He chuckled, but without humour. 'Naturalists have haunted this wood, seeking examples for their bottles and jars to adorn their museums. But they have never been successful.'

'This is that wood?' Carmichael was only half-amused.

'I don't know. I have never seen an example of it before.' Maderley returned it, with evident reluctance. 'I believe it is simply wood imported as ballast in the holds of ships from Far Eastern countries, nothing more.'

'You think they are wishing a wife on me, then?'

'That's the strength of it, Doctor. I think you shall have to be in my painting.'

'Might I look, sir?'

Carmichael stepped round and gazed down at the canvas. It was superb. It depicted the clearing, the trees catching the slanting light of the sun, a hint of distant sea through branches, and women, men, children, moving among the stacks of billets ready for the firing.

'It's marvellous! You are very talented, sir.'

Maderley sighed. 'You wish my innermost secret, Carmichael? I am heartily sick of the portraiture on which I am engaged. Lorne House. There, I feel so chained and confined. Here, at least I am painting what

455

I desire.' The artist smiled. 'Yes, I shall include you. Your embarrass-ment when accepting the carving was most amusing.'

Carmichael coloured. 'It is an unusual experience for me, sir. I am unaccustomed to receiving gifts from strangers.'

'Or fees from your patients, if what I hear is true.' The artist reached out and patted Carmichael's arm to show no offence was intended. 'Be off with you, Doctor! Leave this artistic genius to his morbid meanderings. And my congratulations to you and felicitations to your lady, when finally she appears!'

'Thank you. My compliments to your family, sir.'

Carmichael embarked on his journey. The sun stood almost at midday now. He examined the beautiful carving as he walked, but found the low branches catching him unawares, so he wisely pocketed it and made faster time through the wood. Finally he came out by the River Affon, and saw the town in the near ground across the place where the road began.

He walked down between Lorne House's lands and Bures House, following the permitted line of the hedges and striking the town within the hour.

There was activity at the Donkey and Buskin. He decided to take a rest there before continuing the next leg of the journey. He was practically home now, so there was no haste.

Strange that he felt so unaccountably sad. Was it something William Maderley had said? About having a carving of a woman as portent? Maybe he felt that, with the news he had just heard about Mehala, he possessed the lovely little wooden figurine in vain, and that it was no more now than a mere ornament.

It was as if a whole segment of life had finished, somehow become complete on its own without any chance of his retaking a part in it for himself alone.

He reached the tavern yard as the coach pulled in. Already two great haulage waggons had arrived, bright in their Suffolk blue as the goods vehicles were in these parts. There would be company, and much conviviality. He would not want to join in, of course, but he seemed to want evidence that at least part of life was glad.

55

In the adjacent part of the taproom three gentlemen were arguing about the way traffic was congesting Britain's roads.

'I blame the policing,' one was stating, thumping the table so loudly that he could be heard all through the tavern. 'Watchmen aren't enough! Parishes should go.'

'Ridiculous! Parishes, sir, are the backbone of society! Once they go, all will be perdition!'

'I disagree with both, friends,' an urbane voice chipped in.

Idly listening to the arguments, Carradine hated the smooth tones. He would wager his all that the man was a poisonous lawyer, and therefore evil by nature as well as education. He toyed with his tankard. That had been a noble thought, but was an expression of the impossible. 'Wager his all,' he had said to himself. He had no 'all' to bet on anything. Not now.

'Look at de La Rochefoucauld,' the first gentleman was arguing with fervour. 'He had the right idea!'

'That was two score years ago, that he and his friends came here from France to teach us how to live!'

'And went away repining,' the third said knowingly.

Carradine was sitting alone, though the inn was nigh full. Travellers seemed more on the move than ever these days, so the first speaker was right in one way. He listened desultorily with only half an ear, thinking. De La Rochefoucauld, plus his two friends and three servants, had made quite a splash when they arrived in Bury St Edmunds in the January of 1784. 'To learn of the English', as they had grandly announced. They had used the acquaintanceship of the Duke of Grafton, at Euston Hall, Professor Symonds the Cambridge historian and others, and formed a notorious view of East Anglian life. De La Rochefoucauld had said that four o'clock dinner was the 'most boring of all things English'.

'I remember my father saying he was most critical of the free use which diners made of chamber pots on the sideboard,' one gentleman recalled. 'And the dull Sundays where nothing *ever* transpired.'

'But he liked that everybody was well attired and clean,' another said. 'My uncle heard his views. And that there were no real poor.'

I, sir, Carradine thought bitterly. *I am poor.*

The thought chilled him. He drank for support, and felt none. He had never felt like this before. He saw his house, Carradine Manor, home of his family for generations, becoming the residence of that toad Prothero. The vision of that man eating from his plates, ordering his servants, sleeping in his bed . . . Carradine seized the gotch and poured himself more wine. This bill too he would owe, the landlord's settling.

He had joked with himself in a long night's drinking at Two Cotts – though he had said little to Lucy as he had used her, or to Mrs Wren when signing her chit with a flourish. Her knowing look he had dismissed, in his drinker's hazy bravado, but with the headaches of morning he had not been quite so sure. La Wren surely must have heard of his disaster, and was biding her time. She knew of his grievous losses, all right. But she must be assuming, in her simplicity, that the gentry stuck together and would not let one of their number fall for lack of assistance. Poor deluded thing.

No. The stark truth was that he could see himself with the pedlar folk at Norwich's Pedmarket, humping a scant-filled ped on his back along with the market women who showed eggs and vegetables for sale. Or, worse, touting his knowledge of East Anglia's roads to such newcomers as saved the five-mile journey into King's Lynn from West Lynn. Was he doomed to try to be another Sumner, a gentleman born but living on pickings from all and sundry?

The thought of Sumner made him fume. Sumner's principal picking was now the Carradine estate, as was Prothero's. Already the vultures were gathered, here, at the Goat and Compass, at the creditors' offices in Saltworth, Forreston, Wentleham, and most of all Maidborough where the fight had taken place. They only needed to identify the main loser, and all was elementary to them. He would be gnawed clean, by carrion.

'That's all very well, sir,' the oily man was contending. 'De La Rochefoucauld might have deplored many segments of East Anglian life. But what was the outcome? He claimed to have been transported into another world, as he put it, when landing in England, by the air of contentment. As well he might, for within a handful of years his country bled itself to death and anarchy.'

'That is not the point, sir . . .'

It was *exactly* the point, Carradine thought. He had never before felt desperate. Not in this sense. Oh, desperate for some girl, for success of a wager, for his plans of political advancement to come to fruition. But those had been choices of his own, hungers invented for the delights of satisfaction. This evil hanging over him was something new, a nameless fear. Poverty had been unknown, unknowable even, to him. The problem of having enough money to . . . well, feed a horse, hire a carriage, even buy food. Dear God! The world was a madhouse.

And it was the fault of malice, in others.

Of course he could see it all now. It was transparently clear that he had been betrayed. There was simply no question about it. Prothero had somehow managed to lace Goring's drinks, perhaps using some sinister Venetian travelling poisoner in the old fashion. Or Sumner had dosed the seconds liberally with cash, while secretly hiving off his own bets, hedge against hedge for each wager. And his own 'friends', dupes to a man, had strolled confidently along into the trap he had baited for them – and been delirious with excitement when they unaccountably won fortunes. All of them, who had trusted in his word. Quilter, Sir Jeremy Pacton, young Alexander Waite, Golding even, plus those base wastrels from Hunterfield's party up at Lorne House. Even the dullard Captain Bussell, already a laughing stock on account of losing his tussle with that bitch Mehala, had come out a winner by several hundreds. The boor had even thrown a party on the strength of it.

Thalia reported that Fellows had declined to intervene, when she had approached him about Carradine's plight. He had received her letter to that effect less than an hour since, and thrown it into the fire without returning an answer.

The truth was, he had few friends. He realized that now. A friend was someone who could be relied on to get one out of a scrape. Sir Cavan Webb and that Royal Navy man, they were each other's friends. He had seen Lieutenant Percy Carmady pick up the scrip note written by his friend at the horse racing not long ago, and, tutting regretfully at the amount Sir Cavan had lost, simply fire a Congreve between his finger and thumb and set light to the debt, throwing away the sandpaper striker and match, so signifying he himself would discharge the debt in spite of his friend's protests.

That was friendship. Where were Carradine's friends? He had had many, until he had lost his fortune. Well, he dared not be like that de La Rochefoucauld, a simple observer of the customs of others while his own world burned to ashes about him. Oh, no. He was Carradine. Carradine of a noble line, Carradine of Carradine. He would triumph over this disaster, and regain his wealth and power in order to punish the upstarts who had betrayed him.

His head ached. Children were scampering around the taproom. He snarled at them as they kicked noisily against his bench, and they rushed away. The place was now crowded. The stagecoach was due to leave shortly, and waggoners were already taking up space near the kitchen serving counters. They stood, strong and sure. He stared at the taciturn men. Their status was suddenly new to him. It was as though he had never noticed such mortals before.

They were not in debt. Their standing was that of free men. Was it the conversation he had just overheard which was affecting him so? Probably. Contentment, the Frenchman had written. The waggoners were rough people, aggressive on the roads, capable foes if troubled. Even the highwaymen who haunted the trunk roads into London, especially around the heathlands near Colchester and Huntingdon and Barnet, were reluctant to tackle them. They also went armed, it was said. And they had every appearance of being able to pay their way, however lowly they lived.

For himself, he could not even any longer afford the two-guinea tax upon a single one of his horses should he decide to enter one for a race. Less than hours ago, he would have not even considered the cost had he entered a score.

Morosely, he began thinking what costs he could no longer reach.

The five shillings receipt-duty for payments of debts. Dear God! Could he not even afford the stamp duties on those?

He began to sweat. Ten shillings for a promissory note exceeding a thousand pounds, by the law of the land. Two guineas tax was payable on any male servant in a gentleman's employ. Two pounds for a Class One servant in employ. For eleven male servants and over, six pounds and six shillings tax, plus one pound ten shillings for each of those who had never been married. Christ Almighty! He felt distressed enough to find a piece of paper and start to list his debts, but would have been wasting his time: he did not even know how to compile a correct profit-and-loss account. Carradine Manor must have in its employment more than thirty servants. A fortune in taxes and duties! Why had that idle bastard of an estate agent never told him how much simple *living* cost? He seethed with hatred and rage. Traitors and malice, all around.

And the windows! He cursed under his breath. How many windows did Carradine Manor have, for God's sake? He vaguely remembered one fact – for twenty windows in a gentleman's dwelling house the tax was ten pounds annually – because of its simplicity. He knew that Carradine Manor possessed more than a hundred, for he had once heard his father arguing that an estate manager should be able to keep the house down to that number, however grand the family domain. That bastard Lennon, his chief bailiff, would have some reckoning to do . . . Except that Lennon had sent word this very morning that he was leaving, and could the master please return to Carradine Manor to accept the estate accounts which ought to be signed over . . . *Traitor*.

The swine were leaving. That was only natural for mere low-breeds, hangers-on. He drank deeper. Well, let the idiots go. If they had anything in them they would stay, demonstrate their loyalty.

Dogs too were taxed, he vaguely remembered, at ten shillings a pair. His own two greyhounds had been dutied so when he was a child. Very proud he had been, too, of that certificate of tax duty paid on his pets! Or had it increased? He didn't even know that.

It was all utterly hopeless. The gaming debts from the prize fight fell for payment due at the week's end. Prothero had already sent him an ill-mannered loutish note, virtually commanding him – Prothero, command a Carradine! – to wait upon him forthwith this afternoon.

He signalled for more ale, was fetched some.

And saw Mehala.

The news about the water supply from Bures House estate was greeted rapturously at the Donkey and Buskin. Mehala went to give the news to the taverner himself.

John Weaver characteristically said nothing at first, silence being his response when deeply affected. When she made to leave, however, he cleared his throat a score of times and came after her in the corridor, saying he was eternally grateful. His inn would now continue another year, limping through its costs and taxes, thanks to Mehala. He asked her to keep in touch with them, through Sarah Ann, and not to forget him and his, who owed her such a debt.

She was touched by this show of gratitude. He was a man of few words, and declined to accept any thanks.

'I owe a debt, Mr Weaver,' she told him. 'You and yours saved me from destitution. I know its consequences, and you were kindness itself. I shall never forget. I might indeed come to such advancement that I shall be seeking employ here at the Donkey and Buskin some time soon, and so extend your burden *and* obligation!'

'Do not joke about poverty, Mehala,' he said with gravity. 'You know such jokes lack humour.'

'Yes, sir,' she said so meekly he made a mock swipe at her head and fell to laughing.

'Don't think because you keep house for the gentry that you are above being corrected when you come visiting my establishment, miss. I won't have you turning into a disappointment, not as long as you stay in Sealandings.'

'Oh, sir!' She made him laugh even more with a pretty display of mock alarm. He sent her away with a gentle push, saying he had to get on with his work even if more ambitious folk were now idlers. She took a quick look round the taproom, and sighed. Regrets were of least consequence, her old mother used to say. So she determined to feel none.

She was making her way through the corridor leading into the yard when her arm was taken in a rough grasp.

'It's the bitch, is it not?' a drink-thickened but cultured voice demanded.

It was Carradine who had hold of her arm. She pulled, but could not escape. It was an awkward moment. No one else was passing to whom she could make appeal. She kept her composure, and faced him with a show of calm, seeing how unsteady he was on his feet.

'Please, sir. Leave go. I am not in your company, nor am I in your acquaintance.'

'Shut the fine talk, Mehala.' Carradine thrust her against the wall of the corridor. Behind him, Mehala thankfully saw Little Jane's frightened face peeping at the scene. 'You *bitch*! It's you that's set folk against me. I'd have had Golding, the De Foes, a score of others, acting as I'd wanted – '

'Sir. You are obliged as a gentleman to – '

'Stow the talk, you arrogant cow. I'll have none of it, especially not from you. You're a road woman putting on airs.'

'Sir. You have taken drink too much for this day, and I beg you – '

He struck her. She fell with a small yelp, her head spinning. He stood over her, glowering.

'You're the bitch that brought me to misfortune. I'm going to take you to Calling Farm if it's the last thing I do – '

'Sir. Stand off, if you please.'

Carmichael stood in the doorway. The tavern was falling silent, Little Jane having carried the news of Carradine's importuning Mehala. John Weaver and several people, passengers from the coaches, carters and farm people, fisher folk in for their midday meals, were pouring into the yard doorway in expectation of a fight. They stopped, seeing it was merely trouble between maid and man. The rougher element retired in disappointment. Weaver came closer, asking what was the trouble. Carradine grabbed Mehala's arm and roughly hauled her to her feet.

'Sir,' the doctor said. 'I asked for you please to let the lady go.'

'Carmichael, isn't it?' Carradine stepped aside, moving slowly into the space outside. 'The cheap croaker, who can't afford horse or manservant? Or food, even, if word speaks truth round Sealandings.' Carradine was his old self again, feeling that at last he had a chance to prove he was still Carradine of Carradine, the force in Sealandings.

'Doctor Carmichael at your service, sir. Mehala, please leave.'

Mehala tried to step aside, watching. For once her wit had deserted her. She felt sickened at her stupidity. If only she had gone through the crowded taprooms she might have avoided this. Now Carmichael was confronted by Carradine in all his fury.

'Oh, it's *you* who gives the bitch orders, is it?' Carradine lashed his hand backwards across Carmichael's face. The doctor reeled, recovered his footing. 'Then I owe you something, friend!'

'Mehala, please leave,' Carmichael said, recovering.

'No.' Her voice could hardly be heard. The yard was filled now, but the space where the gentleman stood facing the doctor was left as a circle.

'See, croaker?' Carradine laughed out loud, shaking his head in disbelief. 'Even your tame whore doesn't heed you! How much does she charge? I've heard she gives decent value for service!'

'Mehala,' Carmichael said without taking his eyes off Carradine. 'I ask that you leave the inn, please. This is no scene for you to witness.'

Carradine had out his small sword, showing its blade in the sun's mild gleaming.

'Yes, Mehala,' he mocked. 'I have work to do. Gentleman's work. For if a challenge is ignored, then a gentleman has the right to exact punishment as he sees fit. Isn't that right, croaker? For the offender is nothing more than a vagabond, a cutpurse, a thief, wastrel and whoremonger. Am I right, croaker?'

Carmichael's face was white. He knew what was coming, but stood his ground. His voice quavered as he answered.

'Mehala. Please go. Mr Carradine shall not follow, I assure you.'

'No?' Carradine really laughed at that, roared and slapped his thigh. 'Honestly! Whatever do these leeches learn at medical schools these days?' He glanced joyfully round the silent crowd. 'Ladies and gentlemen! I am about to exact retribution from this quack, who has insulted my person. I shall start by giving him an anatomy lesson he never thought to learn. His teaching was lacking – '

'No.' Mehala stood by Carmichael. 'Then you teach me the same, sir.'

Carmichael tried to push her away, but she shook her head and stayed. Her eyes remained on the drunken aristocrat as she spoke.

'No, Ven. I think that together we might try to make this drunkard slip on the stones. We can evade, not simply stand here and let him do with us as he will. I shall move to his left, as you move to his right.'

'Listen to the bitch!' Carradine roared, laughing and swaying. 'A fighter, no less!'

'This bitch has two cobblestones, drunkard,' Mehala said coolly. 'I shall not miss with both, not at this distance, I promise you.'

'Stones?' Carradine said dully, puzzled.

'These.' Mehala held out a flint cobble. Somebody in the crowd laughed, muttered approval.

'Mehala.' Carmichael's voice was anguished. Men in the crowd were muttering among themselves.

'I am not ashamed to fight, sir,' she told Carmichael coolly, eyes still on Carradine. 'I have done it before. It is necessary even against drunks who count themselves better than the sober ones among us.'

A murmur rose. Carradine glared round, feeling the crowd's animosity. He had better start on the doctor immediately, or they might turn in the wrong direction.

'Ready, croaker?'

'That's enough, sir!'

Jake Darling pushed from the crowd and came alongside Carradine. He had with him three waggoners, who moved behind Mehala and Carmichael.

'*What?*' Carradine was aghast. 'You dare to speak to me?'

'I do.' Darling was pulling on his heavy leather driving gloves as he spoke. 'You'll leave this gentleman and girl, sir. That's all I have to say, and no more. Let them be. And go on your way.'

'This is . . .' Carradine paused.

An ugly muttering began in the crowd. Feet shuffled on the stones, tapping ominously in the common signal for an impromptu fight.

'Landlord!' Carradine bawled. This was ridiculous. He was the gentleman here. All others were peasants.

Weaver and two of his men servants approached from the yard gate.

'They're right, sir,' Weaver said. 'You shall let them go. And you shall put up your sword in this yard.'

His two men came to either side of the gentleman, one deliberately hindering his use of the sword.

Carradine stared round at the sea of faces.

'Are you all mad? I shall have you in chains for this! And this inn razed to the ground. I swear it. I'll bring the militia down on you, Weaver. And you waggoners. The magistrates will take you to Ipswich goal by evening. I swear it on – '

'On what, sir?'

The throng made way for a horseman, who advanced at a slow walk, gentling his mare into the yard.

'Hunterfield!' Carradine's voice sounded his relief as the squire reined Betsy to a stand. 'I have a magistrate's work for you here, by God I do! Here's a fine seditious assembly! Weaver and these waggoners preaching disloyal address against the country and Kingdom! That whore there I accuse of brothelry. That quack I accuse of assaulting a gentleman unprovoked. This herd I accuse of . . .'

'Darling?' Hunterfield said sombrely. 'Is that you?'

'It is, Squire.'

'Tell your account, please.'

'Here, Hunterfield!' Carradine called in anger. 'Are you going to ask the word of a common carter over me? I protest, sir! You'll hear me first, by God!'

'I shall hear as I please, Carradine. Darling?'

'The gentleman abused and struck Miss Mehala, Squire. He was seen to do so from the windows. The doctor stood between to save the girl. The gentleman drew his blade, and promised to injure both of them.'

'And you, Jake Darling?' Hunterfield seemed to be concealing some dry amusement. 'How come you in this, you who never raise a hand to anyone?'

'I saw, and stood with the both.'

'Against so highborn a gentleman?' Again there was that faint suggestion of a hidden smile.

'Yes, Squire,' Darling said evenly. 'Is there necessary wrong in that?'

'I see. And you, John Weaver?'

'It's as Jake Darling says, Squire.'

'It appears I am surrounded by brave men,' Hunterfield said. He beckoned from the saddle. Two of his own men pushed through in response. 'Take this gentleman home to Carradine Manor. Let him be handed to his steward – '

'Hunterfield! You're damned for this!' Carradine struggled ineffectually, but the two men disarmed him with ease and held him fast.

'One of us is, I promise you, sir.' Hunterfield gave a gesture with his riding crop. 'Disperse, if you please, friends. All is well and peace reigns. Home to your loved ones, or back to the ale. Disperse.'

The crowd thinned as the people slowly started to withdraw, looking back.

'I see how it is, Hunterfield!' Carradine thrust his face up at the mounted man. 'Everybody in Sealandings knows whose by-blows are whose! And we all know well why you take the word of common waggoners over that of a gentleman!'

'Thank you, everyone!' Hunterfield called, easing his mount to start a slow perambulation of the yard. 'Thank you. About your business, everybody! All is peace here again.'

He paused and beckoned to Mehala. She hurried over to stand by his stirrup as the crowd dispersed and Carradine was bundled, still bawling protests, towards the yard gates. Hunterfield leant down from the saddle and spoke to Mehala, giving her a small object. She curtseyed as he reined away and guided Betsy from the yard. Mehala rejoined the doctor and waggoner.

Carmichael was still pale. He nodded his thanks to Jake Darling as Carradine was taken away. A carriage with a splendid hammercloth over the box seat drew up to receive the drunken man.

Carmichael did not quite know what to say. 'Jake, I owe you my gratitude.'

Darling too was embarrassed. 'Not so. I was trying to catch you up, Doctor. To give my own thanks.'

'Evens, then, I suppose.' The two men stood awkwardly without further speech. Mehala marvelled inwardly at men's stupidity. They both knew what to say, how they should say it, but, manlike, remained silent. Who could understand these dumb creatures?

'I see you come adorned, Mr Darling,' she put in to relieve them of misery.

'Adorned?' Darling saw the direction of her gaze and laughed sheepishly. 'Yes, Mehala. I took out my father's old Lunardi, and put it on my waggon. To celebrate Clare's recovery, you might say.'

A gaudy red bow, of gigantic size, was on the waggon's driving seat. In country areas the favour still retained the name of the famous balloonist of decades before.

'It will add weight to the three tons of grain you'll carry today, then,' she said gravely, and finally the men eased into smiles.

'Not enough,' Jake Darling told her. 'Even my horses feel glad. The heavier the load the better they'll draw today, Mehala. The day my little Clare was made well.'

He glanced at the sky and nodded to his three companions, who had already begun to edge away.

'I had best be driving, or never get back this week. My goodbyes to you both, then.'

'Travel safely, Mr Darling.'

'And you, Doctor. And you, Mehala.'

She and Carmichael stood to see the waggon unbraked and rumble out from the tavern yard. Neither spoke. Mehala glanced at the doctor's face and drew her shawl round her. The sea breeze was freshening with every passing moment.

'Mehala.' Carmichael coughed, glanced round, tried again. 'Mehala. I . . . I should thank you also.'

'For what?'

'For coming to take my part as you did. I am ashamed, really, that I did no better.'

'You were endangered because you took my part, Doctor.'

'I hardly proved a mighty protector. Instead you were my protect-ress. I must say thanks.'

'Evens, then, I suppose,' she parodied.

Carmichael smiled. She was lovely, her face rimmed by the shawl which she had now drawn over her head and gathered about her throat.

Mehala drew out a small leather pouch and gave it to Carmichael. 'More gratitude, Doctor. Squire Hunterfield passed this to me for you, as an expression of his.'

'Me?' Carmichasel loosened the pursed bag, and drew out a new silver watch. It was a hunter, engraved, *To Doctor Carmichael; Sealandings.*

'What have I done for this?' he said wonderingly.

'Perhaps more than you know, Ven.' She gave him an impish smile.

'I've never owned such a treasure in my life, Mehala.' He turned the timepiece in his hands, admiring the beautiful milky gleam of the silver, then shyly glanced up at her. 'You'll be off to Bures House, then, I take it?'

'How did you hear I was at the Golding household?'

'William Maderley told me. I was with the charcoal burners for a while, breaking the journey from Whitehanger. He was painting them in the woods.'

'Am I a common source of gossip, then?'

He reddened. 'No, Mehala. I mean, I was not gossiping. I was simply walking by. I would not have seen him had he not – '

'I was joking, Doctor,' she said evenly.

'I'm sorry. I feel so . . .'

'Yes?'

He shrugged, shook his head. 'I'm tired, I suppose.' He gazed down at her ruefully. 'Sometimes I'm tongue-tied and can't say what I should. I've always been hopeless like this. It never happens with you, I observe.'

She gazed directly at him. He was conscious of her frank eyes, the clarity of her expression. She seemed beyond his or anyone's reach, though they stood close.

'You mean I too should stay silent when words should be spoken?'

He remembered the small carving in his pocket.

'I don't know,' he said helplessly. He felt ashamed of his stupidity, his lack of social grace, nodded a good day and walked out of the yard.

Mehala watched him go, smiling and not a little exasperated. What did her old mother say, down at Mersea? Brains don't come alone; they come most often with foolishness.

'Doctor,' she called after him. 'I am going towards Shalamar. May I walk with you, please?'

He turned immediately with a glad face, surprised and pleased.

'Of course, Mehala. I shall be delighted.'

She trotted, caught up with him and walked beside him.

They started along the hard, then by unspoken agreement forking the long way round through the town itself rather than directly across the coast road.

'Incidentally, Doctor. I have remembered the order of all the flowers in Flora's dials. Might I call and arrange the plants for you?'

'Would you?' Carmichael hesitated. 'I'm afraid I haven't money enough to buy plants, though.'

'Many grow wild,' she told him. 'In any case, I might be able to charm a few from elsewhere.'

He looked at her, full of doubt. 'I wouldn't want any from . . .'

'Nothing like that,' she said, smiling. 'It will be all my own unaided endeavours.'

'I sometimes think you can do anything, Mehala.' It was his frank opinion.

She thought: Oh dear. His esteem for her was altogether too high. She didn't want him believing she was some kind of superior being.

'I spoke with Mrs Trenchard when I visited Shalamar,' she told him.

'Yes? She does very well for her age, don't you think?'

'Very well indeed, for one so infirm. And she is getting on. I had the distinct impression she was finding it very hard there, without help.'

'I know.' He gave Mehala a sideways appraisal, hesitated.

'It's just that I haven't the money to hire anyone else, you see.'

'What if I called occasionally, to assist? Would that be acceptable?'

'You?' He stopped to stare. '*You*, Mehala? At Shalamar?'

'Why not? I haven't yet taken any earnest money, to seal my

468

appointment at Bures House. I can transfer myself any time I like, until then. Things have changed at Sealandings.'

'How on earth could I pay?' He seemed overcome at the notion.

'We could arrange some form of income first,' she said calmly. Her eyes seemed paler today, almost grey in the daylight. She changed with every moment, like the skies over the sealands. 'Doctor. You must try to exact fees from those who can afford to pay. That will make quite a number of things possible.'

'I'm not much good at that sort of thing, Mehala,' he said uncomfortably. 'Money embarrasses, I find.'

They slowed as a large town coach in the Carradine livery trundled past towards the market square, driven by a liveried coachman perched high on his decorated Salisbury box. Engrossed in their conversation, Carmichael seemed not to notice it. With a shock Mehala however recognized it as Carradine's luxurious Felton-made coach, the grandest at Carradine Manor. The team of four greys was stepping out friskily. It was a most impressive and ostentatious vehicle.

From its windows, Jason Prothero's flushed face stared pompously out at Sealandings, as if at some private domain peopled by subject fiefholders. Beside him, his wife Mary's stricken face showed for an instant as her eyes met Mehala's, took in Ven Carmichael's animated preoccupation, and swiftly withdrew behind the curtains as the splendid vehicle jingled past. Prothero, now master of Carradine Manor?

'I know, Ven.' She put her arm through his. 'I could help. In more ways than you perhaps dream of.'

'Would you? There's little enough future in a draughty old derelict hall, when you could have great families and mansion houses at your beck and call, Mehala.'

'Yet I would come. If I were asked.'

Distantly a landau moved sedately in from the north road, bearing the Hunterfield ladies. Two mounted gentlemen reined in to acknowledge the conveyance, raising their Wellington hats. Mehala saw one rider glance towards her as they resumed their progress, Fellows De Foe doubtless drawing Charles Golding's attention to his housekeeper's keeping public company with an impoverished doctor.

Mehala kept a firm hold on Ven's arm. They walked along the hard. A hoy was coming to mooring. A lad aboard, Hal Baines, bashfully waved towards shore, and Mehala waved back. Carmichael took her arm firmly in his. When she was with him he too felt part of the sealands, completely at home on the dangerous and shifting shore. It

469

was right, for reasons he didn't dare try to fathom, to slip Harriet's letter from his pocket and skim it on to the sea water. It was the casual act of a man forgetting quite why he had carried it for so long in the first place. They walked on.

He cleared his throat, wondering how best to frame the question, slowly working out the most persuasive way to voice his longing for her to help him. Mehala walked contentedly with him step for step, smiling inwardly, knowing the certainty of her coming life, with all its difficulties, in Sealandings, at Shalamar.